100 YEARS OF THE
BEST AMERICAN
SHORT STORIES

★ 100 YEARS ★
OF THE
BEST AMERICAN
SHORT STORIES

EDITED BY

LORRIE MOORE AND
HEIDI PITLOR

Houghton Mifflin Harcourt

BOSTON • NEW YORK

2015

CONTENTS

INTRODUCTION

A STORY IS A noise in the night. You may be lying there quietly resting in the international house of literature and hear something in the walls, the click and burst of heat through pipes, a difficult settling of eaves, ice sliding off the roof, the scurry of animals, the squawk of a floorboard, someone coming up the stairs.

This is life itself, surprising and not entirely invited. And yet we come to short stories seeking it. Or at least some vivid representation of it: a dark corner that is either turned and gone around or fixed with a light in order to discover what is lurking there. In a civilized society there arrives in a person's day a pause long enough to allow for the reading of it — the corner, the pause, the day, the society: the exquisite verbal bonsai of a moment, of another's life and consciousness, presented with concision and purpose — from a certain angle, in a certain voice, fashioned from a frame of mind that is both familiar and strange, recognizable and startling as a pinch.

It is a lovely shock of mercy and democracy to find that we need to spend time in the company of people whose troubles we might ordinarily avoid. Ring Lardner's clueless barber. ("'Shut up,' he explained," as Lardner wrote elsewhere.) Lauren Groff's bewitched eccentrics. Edward Jones's lovelorn convicts. This is why storytelling exists in the first place. To inform us from and of Georgia O'Keeffe's "faraway nearby." It keeps us posted on the colorful swarming muck beneath a log. It both crashes in and lifts us out of the many gated communities of the mind. It animates (rather than answers) a question or two you may have about, say, Jesus. Finish a story and then you can return to healthy living, getting moderate exercise, appreciating unspoiled nature (good luck to you), and swooning at the wondrous universe as viewed in a clear night sky (rather than that narratively familiar dark and stormy one).

Make it interesting and it will be true: this is what story writers live by. In the way of Flaubert, storytelling is investigative and conjectural: we tell stories to find out what we believe. In the way of Joan Didion, we tell them "in order to live." In the way of Scheherazade, we tell them in order not to die. Dreams, it turns out, are physiologically necessary for life. Presumably waking dreams are just as essential. Neurological experiments have shown that animals deprived of dreams die faster than they would by physical starvation. Science has also shown that stories help the mind make order and sense of random events. Furthermore, in a new study reported in the journal *Science,* subjects who read Alice Munro stories — specifically, the collection *Too Much Happiness* — demonstrated sharper social and psychological insight than those who did not.

Hey, we knew that.

But now there is empirical proof for others. In the words of Lorenz Hart, "When you're awake, the things you think / Come from the dreams you dream / Thought has wings and lots of things / are seldom what they seem" ("Where or When"). He also wrote, "The clothes you're wearing are the clothes you wore," a condition familiar to any writer at her desk. There's always room for a little Broadway.

Short stories are about trouble in mind. A bit of the blues. Songs and cries that reveal the range and ways of human character. The secret ordinary and the ordinary secret. The little disturbances of man, to borrow Grace Paley's phrase, though a story may also be having a conversation with many larger disturbances lurking off-page. Still, the focus on the foregrounded action will be sharp and distilled as moonshine and maybe a little tense and witty, like an excellent dinner party. Writers go there to record hearts, minds, manners, and lives, their own and others. Even at a dinner party we all want to see rich and poor, life and death, the past and the present bumping up against each other, moral accomplishment jostling moral failure. Readers desire not to escape but to see and hear and consider. To be surprised and challenged and partially affirmed. In other words, to have an experience.

It is difficult for a short story to create a completely new world or a social milieu in its entirety or present an entirely unfamiliar one or one unknown to the author — so little time and space — so stories are often leaning on a world that is already there, one that has already entered the writer's mind and can be assembled metonymically in a quick sketch and referred to without having to be completely created from scratch. To some degree the setting is already understood and shared with the reader, although the writer is giving it his own twist or opinion or observations or voice. To someone unfamiliar with such a thing, for instance, the zombie apocalypse might have trouble fitting into this genre, despite the short story's great range of subjects, lengths, voices, and techniques. The short story's hallmark is compression — even if the story sometimes extends to near-novella length. The short story needs to get to the point or the question of the point or the question of its several points and then flip things upside down. It makes skepticism into an art form. It has a deeper but narrower mission than longer narratives, one that requires drilling down rather than lighting out. Like poetry, it takes care with every line. Like a play, it moves in a deliberate fashion, scene by scene. Although a story may want to be pungent and real and sizzling, still there should be as little fat as possible. In its abilities to stretch, move through time, present unexpected twists and shapes, the short story is as limber as Lycra but equally unforgiving. (It is interested in the human heart, of course, an artificial version of which was first made in the 1970s from the fabric of a woman's girdle — a fun fact and a metaphor for inventiveness, which will become clearer if one walks around the block and thinks about it a little.)

The abundant, crazily disparate imagery that comes to mind when considering and generalizing about the genre demonstrates what story writers all know: the short story is pretty much theory-proof. One pronounces upon it with spluttering difficulty. An energetic effort may send one into a teeming theme park of argument, mixed metaphor, tendentious assertion. It has been said that the short story is the only genre of literature that has remained premodern. Here I suppose the speaker is thinking of the campfire tale, and the telling of something in a single sitting: in this paradigm a story retains some of its primitive delights. The size remains organic to the occasion.

But the short story has also been declared the very first modernist literature (with which I am more inclined to agree). As a record of rebellious human consciousness, of interiority and intersecting intents, it is second to none in power and efficiency. And perhaps the original writer of this modern short story would be Chekhov, with his casting out of moral lessons and his substitution of sharp psychological observations (without express judgment) of the human world. He was a doctor and believed in medicine's experimental side. He was a doubter who stayed interested in his encounters.

On the occasions I have been asked to pronounce on and define short stories, which are my main mode of literary expression, I have looked at the story's objectness and the act of its creation and grabbed at rather repellent analogies of a medical, romantic, or pediatric bent. Stories, in this vein, though abstractly, become human biopsies, or love affairs, or children left on the doorstep to be quickly fed and then left on someone else's doorstep. Sometimes I have referred to short stories as puppets or pets or visitors violating the three-day fish rule, and a general derangement of mind and metaphor has set in in the pronouncing. I have likened them to clones, unvaccinated dogs, and poison bonbons. The scattershot defining of such a familiar, miraculous, homely, and elusive thing always has some frantic desperation in it.

One of the many interesting things about the twentieth-century journey of the short story is how, when owing to the replacement of magazine entertainment by television it lost much of its commercial luster, the short story reacquired or resumed or just plain continued its artistic one. It reached back to (or kept going with) the great Russian stories as well as those of James Joyce's *Dubliners* and Sherwood Anderson's *Winesburg, Ohio*. A bold and complex story — such as a J. D. Salinger one included in this series sixty-five years ago and which was originally published in *Good Housekeeping* in pre-TV 1948 and would have trouble finding a home in a housekeeping magazine now. Are there even housekeeping magazines now? In 1957, with television in full swing, Tillie Olsen's "I Stand Here Ironing," proudly reprinted here, was published in the *Pacific Spectator*. The short story was pretty much freed from sitting side by side with ads for soup and spaghetti and has been securely reattached to its project as art. It can be argued — and has been — that novelists as great as Updike and Hemingway have often done their best work in the short form. One can feel in their short works that these writers become simultaneously laser-eyed and loose-limbed, concentrated and unburdened; one can feel them emotionally *intent* and also a little bit on fire in the confines within which they must tell their tale. The ordinary citizens and the fresh vernacular of Hemingway and Anderson continue straight through the decades and help fashion literary heirs in Grace Paley and Raymond Carver.

All this great art, however, does not keep the American short story from being occasionally a popular form again; "a renaissance" cycles through every two decades or so. And anthologies that have been canon-making, archeological, and preserving — especially the ones in this series — become even more culturally important. A short story writer is not a rock star. Yet sometimes nonetheless story writers have been put on tours by their publishers, with the hope that a story collection might sell as well as a literary novel — that is, not all that well. A short story writer is sent out on the road to see who her readers actually are in order to console them.

Now, a short story writer on a book tour is a reassuring cultural idea, even if the writer is pretty much dragging herself around from town to town, like an old showman with a wizened mummy and a counting dog. She is out catching flu and greeting her audiences and answering their questions, and she will find herself bombarded with queries regarding the defining characteristics of the short story "form," questions regarding the difference between novels and short stories, and questions about the mysteries and power of the short form. Such a writer should come prepared — why has she not been given talking points to read from? — but too often the whole matter is not given much rehearsed thought at all but instead prompts fresh (that is, improvised on the spot) and contradictory utterances. Such a writer may while considering these questions begin to scratch her temple, her sleeve, her chin and eyebrow, as if she has caught fleas from the counting dog. Here are the differences, she might say, ticking (ticking!) off things that have just popped into her head. Or she might say, completely guessing, perhaps there are relatively few differences between novels and stories. Perhaps the differences are exaggerated, like the differences between men and women often are, just to make things sexier. The short story writer on tour may find herself stalled and pulling cat hair off her latest recently purchased black outfit even though she will remember as she is doing this that the cat died over a year ago.

On a tour the short story writer becomes a character in a short story (and so the inner workings of the thing are occasionally, glancingly exposed). Though it is her own story, she sometimes feels like a minor character within it. She contemplates possible answers to the audience questions she knows are coming, questions about the writing life. It is hard to feel still like a real writer, traveling through so many airports — including one with a scanner that indicates she has explosives in her head. She is taking so much Dramamine it is difficult to recall what life at the desk was once like. Ah, yes — it was and remains a mysterious process. That is what she remembers best. She has no time for research or contemplation, and so every evening when the Q and A begins, it seems she is assembling her responses from scratch.

What makes and defines a short story? She clears her sore throat: "A story is an intimate narrative composition thoughtfully assembled with illustrations but no argument." The short story writer on tour clearly has no confident idea.

She blunders ahead. "A quick incisive collision with the unexpected," she says, fumbling for Kleenex.

The Somali driver awaiting her at one of the airports is holding up a sign that says MARIANNE MOORE. There is only her, or rather she, the author of a story collection.

"I will have to do," the writer says.

What *is* the difference between a short story and a novel?

The Somali driver puts away his MARIANNE MOORE sign, smiles and says, "I am the captain now!" The short story writer guffaws.

How does a writer know when she has a short story or a novel? This is what readers, or more likely struggling writers, seem to want to know, though she herself has seldom asked that question. She feels it is rather self-evident, and if not self-evident, well then, lucky you. You may have both.

Fibrous asparagus from lunch is stuck in her one remaining wisdom tooth and the person she is about to read with has excellent teeth and has written a book narrated from the point of view of a dentist.

What is the difference at the sentence level between a novel and a short story?

Somewhere, in some bookstore, while she is thinking of answers to this question, a fly lands smack on her forehead, as if to express its opinion about the nature and substance of her thoughts. Perhaps it too has detected explosives.

In Seattle she cannot take her eyes off the amethyst-encrusted manhole covers. Taking the world in in its entirety: did not Chekhov say that is a requirement, even of short stories? Observe, observe: love can be deceiving. This is the theme not only of sad true pop songs but also of the work of one of the great Russian masters of the short story, as well as the Canadian master, Alice Munro. A short story is about love. It is always about love. And yet it is not a love story.

When does a story turn into a novel, or vice versa?

Never, the writer thinks. At least never for her, though that would be a wonderful surprise for her agent if it did.

Another writer waiting in a radio station green room where the short story writer is also waiting is carrying a plastic 3D replica of a female pelvis, though the program they are participating in is a radio program. The woman with the plastic pelvis is going on first to speak of female incontinence. She has written a book on it. The story writer feels bereft not to have such an interesting and practical topic for discussion; she feels deprived not to be holding a multicolored, anatomically correct plastic pelvis herself. One can never look too hard for metaphors; perhaps a replica of a human pelvis is precisely what a story is — something that listeners will not be able to see but that she could describe and that perhaps would give the story writer some jocularity, protection, weaponry. Chekhov was a doctor, she could say repeatedly. He believed in the exploration, the experiment, the questioning of received wisdom that is both medical science and fiction!

Once more: *What is the inspiration for a short story versus the inspiration for anything else, say, a novel?*

A short story is about love. Yet it is not a love story.

She barely makes her connection in Houston. Dehydration. Where is her Gatorade? In some airport or other she falls down the escalator, the wheels of her suitcase having got stuck and pulled her backward. When someone some evening in some city somewhere asks her whether being "an author" is what she had expected it would be, she starts laughing and cannot stop. She places her head down on the lectern, attempting to collect herself but keeping her eyes open to look for a glass of water.

How does one know when one's idea is suited for a story rather than a novel?

She has no plastic pelvis to show or tell. She is thinking up titles to her next story: "Dicey in the Dark!" "I Don't Remember You Already." "Two Meats for Dinner." "Intelligence on the Ground." And "The Fish Rule Does Not Apply to You."

Is the story form harder to write than a novel?

The lectern at a West Coast library — what city is she in today? She has crisscrossed North America in a demented way — has a sign facing the speaker that says PLEASE REPEAT QUESTION. Probably it's acoustically good advice, but it makes the Q and A sound as if the writer is in a bad romantic relationship, acting preemptively evasive and on the defensive, as when one person asks, "Where were you last night?" and gets the answer "Where was I last night?" How appropriate for a short story writer on tour! She is doing the dialogue of a love affair on the rocks, where one person asks, "What is going on?" and the other replies, "What is going on? That is your question?"

"Do you ever Google yourself?" someone asks.

"Do I ever Google myself?"

"Yes, that is the question."

"That is the question?"

"Would you like another?"

"Would I like another question?"

Why is she changing the subject? Why is she sounding defensive? Why can't she answer a simple question? Why does she keep repeating the question?

"When you write, do you ever have particular people in mind?"

"Actual people?"

"Or hypothetical people."

"Am I thinking of someone else?"

"Yes, is there someone else that you are thinking of?"

"Is there someone else?" There is always someone else. "Do you mean generally or specifically?"

"So there is someone else? I mean, where were you last night?"

"Do you mean generally or specifically?"

A short story is about love. But it is not a love story.

In Philly the short story writer on tour wakes up not knowing where she is — *she has no idea where she was last night* — and, unable to interpret the room, she literally gets out on the wrong side of the bed and bashes her foot against a chest of drawers (oh, a metaphor for a story collection), permanently loosening then losing her large toenail. Later, in another city, she will put the toenail under her pillow, hoping for a new pair of shoes from the Cobbler Fairy. Perhaps she has gone mad.

When you're writing, how do you know when you've come to the end?

How does one know when one's come to the end? One loses a scarf, sunglasses, two umbrellas, three cotton nightgowns across a large geographical area; perhaps one will be thrown into the federal slammer for interstate littering.

What would you say is the role of the short story in today's world?

What would I say? Or what should I say?

The short story is the human mind at its most adventurous. It must be shared.

Everyone remains so nice. How can she not help but speak in facile, dimwitted remarks inflected with the faux-faded memory of continental philosophy: if the individual is a fiction, then what better place for him to reside than *in* fiction? Et cetera. But she believes in the human mind part.

• • •

What practitioner ever had a good working theory of the short story? Only the great Irish writer Frank O'Connor and his admirable and intriguing positing of the story as the life and voice of one individual within a societally submerged population. "The lonely voice" is as original and astute and as good as it gets yet still doesn't cover everything (not Hawthorne, Coover, nor T. C. Boyle), though it gets very close. And if one were to take it as a prescription and write only stories that are the quasi-exiled voice of that marginalized individual, a writer would do very well.

The short story, of course, is a genre, not a form — it comes in so many different forms — even though its distinctiveness from the novel, say, is primarily one of length, and so a formal one. Shape and structure are naturally essential. When one looks out at the problems of life, and of the world, the problems, as well as the solutions, tend to be structural. When one looks at the success of a sentence, a joke, or an anecdote, it hinges upon structural decisions. Changing the structure changes the story. A short story writer is building a smaller house so fewer troublesome people can get inside. Perhaps the short story allows for fewer things to go wrong in this manner, because of its structural constraints but also because of its demands. Perhaps this is why some have remarked that the story has to be "perfect," and novels are necessarily not, because that is not the novel's aim. "Conciseness is the sister of talent," said Chekhov himself. And perhaps it is also genius's kissing cousin — in strappy shoes so elegantly thin it's as if they were drawn on by a pen.

Yet there are so many different sorts of stories: look at the tremendous variety in subject, shape, and tone. When one assembles a hundred years of them, one is looking thrillingly not just at literary history but at actual history — the cries and chatterings, silences and descriptions of a nation in flux, since short story writers have from the beginning been interested in the world they live in, its cultural changes, societal energies, the spiritual injuries to its citizenry and what those injuries may or may not mean. And North America — a collection of provinces, states, and conditions — has done a first-rate job of claiming and owning and sponsoring the short story, with all due respect to Ireland and nineteenth-century Russia. It may be the apprentice narrative form of choice, but that is only sensible. Student writers are encouraged to practice it, take a stab at it, rather than accumulate drawersful (yearsful) of novels. But the short narrative also remains a true master's art. It is a string quartet, which is often preferred to a composer's longer works. A short story is not minimalist, suggested Angela Carter. It is rococo, with trills and grace notes and esprit.

A novel puts many things in the air at once, a complicated machine that its author then tries to land safely—though more than one novel has had an author parachute out of it, leaving it to circle in the sky on its own: space junk that may or may not have some immortality to it. There are many places with such ghostly items flying around in the atmosphere. Most countries, it should be said, are nations of novelists. At one literary festival I attended recently in England, a couple were consulting their program. "Who is reading next?" asked the husband.

"I believe it's a new American short story writer," said the wife.

"Really," the husband said, then, after perusing the program further, closed it abruptly. "I need a new American short story writer like I need a hole in the head."

Well, we all know what he means.

And yet why not a hole in the head? A new little garden space for planting, a well-ventilated, freshly lit room in the mind? Do we not want to feel the tops of our heads come off, as Emily Dickinson said a poem did for her? A story does not intoxicate or narcotize or descend and smother. It opens up a little window or a door. And the world gets in it in an intimate way. Art is when one becomes "aware of an unfolding," said Matisse. And stories unfold. That is pretty much one thing they can be counted on to do, if they are any good.

The American world we see reflected historically in the short story, as captured in the heroic century-long endeavor that is *The Best American Short Stories,* is one of predictably astonishing and thrilling variety. From 1915 to 2015: in this volume we see America in all its wildnesses of character and voice. James Baldwin's sorrowful valentine to brotherhood and jazz in "Sonny's Blues"; a child's desperate religious questioning in Philip Roth's "The Conversion of the Jews" and John Updike's "Pigeon Feathers"; the adult defiance of an unreasonable God in Stanley Elkin's "The Conventional Wisdom." We see the psychological aftermath of war in stories by Robert Stone and Benjamin Percy. Lives of crime are given all sorts of unexpected angles in Eudora Welty, Mary Gaitskill, and Edward P. Jones. And sometimes the landscape is not only American but those places on the globe that have fed the American experience. Included here are Hemingway's France, Fitzgerald's France, Sharma's India, Lahiri's India, Ireland conjured by Katherine Anne Porter's aging, heartbroken immigrants. Israel sticks its head in the door in the work of Nathan Englander; the Dominican Republic lives everywhere in Junot Díaz's New Jersey. China is both sharply and hazily recalled by David Wong Louie's resilient refugees. Uncontainability rounded up and contained in a small container. The short story captures and cages, though first it seeks, just as the reader seeks. Within these pages are Flannery O'Connor's Georgia and ZZ Packer's Georgia. We go to them all to see how other people make sense of things in their own individual voices and ways, to see what has hounded their hearts and caught their eye. Jamaica Kincaid's loveless Caribbean child-narrators who speak their quiet rage and loneliness in formal, contractionless speech; Joyce Carol Oates's uncertain families whose estrangement is enacted in neogothic violence: in the work of both of these authors, time-swept cultures allow youth and their parents to hate each other as easily as to love. Or sometimes children are betrayed in the ordinary ways, as in Fitzgerald's famous story "Babylon Revisited." There is the hilariously weary existentialism of Donald Barthelme's teacher in "The School," trying to spin his lesson so as to keep the children more childlike. There is the Holocaust seen and spoken of from the margins and from the hypothetical future, by Nancy Hale and Nathan Englander. There is war in the Mideast viewed and absorbed from slightly closer in by the characters in the Tobias Wolff and Benjamin Percy stories. And there is the oddly cheerful and degraded language uttered by the denizens of George Saunders's capitalist dystopias.

We read short stories to see—quickly—how other people manage, what they know, what they are saying, what, privately, they are thinking and doing. According to Saunders, short stories are "the deep, encoded crystallizations of all human knowledge. They are rarefied, dense meaning machines." The meaning is seldom pretty, sometimes hard to believe, and not always precisely factual. But it is the truth of dreams: when, working in an inspired way, the imagination merges a moment of action with a moment of interiority and a moment of truth is born; with luck and skill, there is the perfect voice to speak it, the perfect gesture to perform it. Put together over time, these stories cause an entire world to be glimpsed through the hearing of it. This is where the story owes its powers to poetry and plays: it is (perhaps) an aural art made from visual observation. Hence its origins around the spiky wattage of a campfire.

How do you know when you've come to the end?
An anthology is a small gathering of flowers from a large field. That is the word's etymology from the ancient Greek as well as its action.

It is not a contest, and this anthology especially is not one. Many favorite American short stories will be found here, and some will not. As with any cultural institution, this will be for various reasons. Perhaps the stories were not in this grand but fallible series to begin with. Perhaps John Updike put them into his *Best of the Century* book (we decided on no overlaps, but picking over his gemlike crumbs, I still found F. Scott Fitzgerald's best story, Flannery O'Connor's best story, James Baldwin's best story). Perhaps a story just plain could not fit into the very limited space Heidi Pitlor and I had available—only a handful of stories per decade. Perhaps the lovely Heidi mischievously hid some from me. Perhaps some were being held hostage by the Salinger estate and guarded like national security secrets. (Could we publish a Salinger story even in completely redacted form, like a Jenny Holzer exhibit? We would have had better luck with the Defense Department.) Often if the story was very long—the *Best American* series can proudly claim to have awarded Carson McCullers's "The Ballad of the Sad Café" a place within its pages—the adhesive weaknesses of the bookbinding glue for this anniversary volume prevented us from including it. (Nor did the problematic bookbinding glue help us readhere the wads of hair we had torn from our heads in editorial anguish.)

Although a mechanism of literary canonization, a short story anthology, like the beautiful game of soccer, contains some of the unfortunate facts, restrictions, and hauntings of life: the score does not always reflect the playing. For it to be any good, its intentions must be quixotic, as the very word *best* implies, and one takes one's hat off to it with gratitude and awe. Some favorite stories of mine—by Annie Proulx, Denis Johnson, Deborah Eisenberg, Rick Bass, T. C. Boyle, Thomas McGuane, Susan Minot, Tony Earley, Amy Hempel, Amy Tan, Michael Cunningham, Michael Chabon, Mary Gordon, Ethan Canin, Stuart Dybek, to name but a few—are not here, for one of the several aforementioned reasons. Missing as well are Toni Cade Bambara's exuberant child noticers, whose encounters with the adult world express the worried questions we all should ask ourselves regarding its injustices. Also missing are Karen Russell's roaming vampires in the lemon grove, whose float, drift, and deathless hunger express the artist at society's peripheries, thinly disguised as an ordinary citizen (a timeless literary illustration but one there is no room for except in this sentence). Absent too are the stories of Don DeLillo, whose great work as a novelist has too often eclipsed his brilliant shorter work.

But we could wring our hands forever. The powerful stories that are here — owing to the steady presence of a diligent and questing hundred-year-old enterprise — are full of heat and song and argument, depictions of life and its traps, its home fires and circling passions. This volume is also a celebration not just of authors but of the editors and readers who experienced the stories here in the way they were intended: as serious art. What has been gathered reveals a scrutiny of the editorial eye as well as a devotion to talent, diversity, originality, and our deep history as storytellers. A bouquet of beautiful, piercing, lonely voices. Perhaps a chorus. Along with a purposefully stray measure of "O Canada," these pages comprise our own literary version of a national anthem.

L.M.

100 YEARS OF THE
BEST AMERICAN
SHORT STORIES

1915-1920

AT THE TURN OF THE TWENTIETH CENTURY, SHORT
stories were a preferred form of entertainment in the United States. This
was a boom time for magazine publishing, owing in part to develop-
ments in offset printing technology as well as to the Postal Act of 1879,
which had granted magazines discounted mailing rates. Publications
such as *Ladies' Home Journal, The Saturday Evening Post,* and *The De-
lineator,* all of which published short stories, sold more than a half million copies per issue. The authors of these stories were well known at the
time and often well paid.

A certain formula became evident: a predictable plot tied up neatly
with a happy ending. Most short stories were folksy in tone and told
in a breezy third-person narration of homespun heroes, lovable detec-
tives, or quirky salesmen, the literary equivalent of the Norman Rock-
well paintings beside which they sometimes appeared.

In 1906 the poet and critic William Stanley Braithwaite published the
first of his annual surveys of American poetry in the *Boston Evening
Transcript.* Over the following years he became a mentor to a young
poet and playwright, Edward J. O'Brien. Braithwaite's editor at the *Transcript* suggested that the newspaper publish a companion to the poetry
surveys, an annual survey of American short stories, and Braithwaite,
overextended at the time, enlisted the help of his protégé.

O'Brien had grown up in Boston and since childhood had been a devout reader. He suffered from a heart condition, and during long periods of illness, he'd surrounded himself with books by Poe, Thackeray,
Dickens, Dumas, and Balzac, among others. Because of his condition,
which he kept largely secret throughout his life, he was unusually pale.
Cecil Roberts, a poet and editor, said, "He had such a pathetic air, with

his ill-dress, attenuated body, his wistful blue eyes, and unkempt appearance." O'Brien did, however, benefit from all his reading. He graduated from high school at the age of sixteen, attended Boston College, and transferred to Harvard, but he soon dropped out. He wrote, "I decided not to entrust my education to professors any longer, but to educate myself as long as life lasted."

When he began his new venture with Braithwaite, O'Brien was well aware — and wary — of the reign of commercial short fiction. Authors and readers had also begun to object to the formulaic writing that was flooding newsstands. Even some fiction editors had grown concerned. For example, Burton Kline wrote, "As an editor I have a feeling that some of the writers who should be railroad presidents or bank directors are getting in the way of real writers that I ought to be discovering." O'Brien decided that this new survey would be a chance to showcase literary fiction. He wrote to hundreds of magazines of all sizes, informing editors of the project and asking for free copies of the year's issues. He was surprised by the many responses, and near the end of the year he wrote, "We underestimated the number of stories. There are about 800 in all." Months later, he guessed that he had read 2,500 stories that year.

Eventually O'Brien submitted a proposal for an annual anthology of American short stories, edited by him, to a Boston book publisher, who loved the idea. He laid out his criteria in his first foreword and reprinted it nearly verbatim each year. He vowed impartiality and defined his views of substance and form: "A fact or group of facts in a story only obtain substantial embodiment when the artist's power of compelling imaginative persuasion transforms them into a living truth . . . The first test of a story . . . is to report upon how vitally compelling the writer makes his selected facts or incidents . . . The true artist, however, will seek to shape this living substance into the most beautiful and satisfying form, by skillful selection and arrangement of his material, and by the most direct and appealing presentation of it in portrayal and characterization."

Authors like Fannie Hurst, Maxwell Struthers Burt, Benjamin Rosenblatt, and Wilbur Daniel Steele appeared several times in the early years of *The Best American Short Stories*. These and other contributors — Theodore Dreiser, Sinclair Lewis, and Edna Ferber — ushered in a new and unflinching realism in American short fiction, as well as humor and more subtle characterization. Burt wrote, "I do prefer the 'I' narrator greatly. It does away with the 'Smart Alec' omniscient narrator of the third person, which seems to me the bane of most American short-stories."

O'Brien was almost pathologically organized, a trait likely necessary for the amount of work on his desk. He created an extensive tracking system and in the book featured indexes of every American and British story, story collection, and relevant article published each year, among seemingly endless other lists and summaries. He even included a necrology of writers.

Despite his work, commercial short fiction continued its reign on newsstands through the decade. In fact, O'Brien felt that the quality of literary short fiction lessened during the First World War. In 1918 he wrote, "If we are to make our war experience the beginning of a usable past, we must not sentimentalize it on the one hand, nor denaturalize it on the other." He guessed that it would be many years before writers could write about the war with any objectivity. (He was called before a draft board but was exempted on physical grounds.)

★   ★   ★

1917

EDNA FERBER

THE GAY OLD DOG

From *Metropolitan Magazine*

EDNA FERBER (1885–1968) was born in Kalamazoo, Michigan, and began her career at seventeen as a newspaper reporter. She wrote her first fiction while recovering from anemia and gained fame from a series of short stories — later novels — about Emma McChesney, a traveling saleswoman.

A regular at the Algonquin Round Table, Ferber was well known for her sarcasm. She never married. In her novel *Dawn O'Hara*, a character commented, "Being an old maid was a great deal like death by drowning — a really delightful sensation when you ceased struggling."

Ferber's best-known books include *Show Boat;* the Pulitzer Prize–winning *So Big; Cimarron,* a story of the Oklahoma land rush; and *Giant.* Her fiction often featured powerful female protagonists and characters struggling against prejudice. In her foreword to *Buttered Side Down,* the collection that included "The Gay Old Dog," Ferber wrote, "'And so,' the story writers used to say. 'They lived Happily Ever After.' Um-m-m — maybe."

★

THOSE OF YOU who have dwelt — or even lingered — in Chicago, Illinois (this is not a humorous story), are familiar with the region known as the Loop. For those others of you to whom Chicago is a transfer point between New York and San Francisco there is presented this brief explanation:

The Loop is a clamorous, smoke-infested district embraced by the iron arms of the elevated tracks. In a city boasting fewer millions, it would be known familiarly as downtown. From Congress to Lake Street, from Wabash almost to the river, those thunderous tracks make a complete circle, or loop. Within it lie the retail shops, the commercial hotels, the theaters, the restaurants. It is the Fifth Avenue (diluted) and the Broadway (deleted) of Chicago. And he who frequents it by night in search of amusement and cheer is known, vulgarly, as a loop-hound.

Jo Hertz was a loop-hound. On the occasion of those sparse first nights granted the metropolis of the Middle West he was always present, third row, aisle, left. When a new loop café was opened, Jo's table always commanded an unobstructed view of anything worth viewing. On entering he was wont to say, "Hello, Gus," with careless cordiality to the head-waiter, the while his eye roved expertly from table to table as he removed his gloves. He ordered things under glass, so that his table, at midnight or thereabouts, resembled a hot-bed that favors the bell system. The waiters fought for him. He was the kind of man who mixes his own salad dressing. He liked to call for a bowl, some cracked ice, lemon, garlic, paprika, salt, pepper, vinegar and oil, and make a rite of it. People at near-by tables would lay down their knives and forks to watch, fascinated. The secret of it seemed to lie in using all the oil in sight and calling for more.

That was Jo — a plump and lonely bachelor of fifty. A plethoric, roving-eyed and kindly man, clutching vainly at the garments of a youth that had long slipped past him. Jo Hertz, in one of those pinch-waist belted suits and a trench coat and a little green hat, walking up Michigan Avenue of a bright winter's afternoon, trying to take the curb with a jaunty youthfulness against which every one of his fat-encased muscles rebelled, was a sight for mirth or pity, depending on one's vision.

The gay-dog business was a late phase in the life of Jo Hertz. He had been a quite different sort of canine. The staid and harassed brother of three unwed and selfish sisters is an under dog. The tale of how Jo Hertz came to be a loop-hound should not be compressed within the limits of a short story. It should be told as are the photoplays, with frequent throw-backs and many cut-ins. To condense twenty-three years of a man's life into some five or six thousand words requires a verbal economy amounting to parsimony.

At twenty-seven Jo had been the dutiful, hard-working son (in the wholesale harness business) of a widowed and gummidging mother, who called him Joey. If you had looked close you would have seen that now and then a double wrinkle would appear between Jo's eyes — a wrinkle that had no business there at twenty-seven. Then Jo's mother died, leaving him handicapped by a death-bed promise, the three sisters and a three-story-and-basement house on Calumet Avenue. Jo's wrinkle became a fixture.

Death-bed promises should be broken as lightly as they are seriously made. The dead have no right to lay their clammy fingers upon the living.

"Joey," she had said, in her high, thin voice, "take care of the girls."

"I will, ma," Jo had choked.

"Joey," and the voice was weaker, "promise me you won't marry till the girls are all provided for." Then as Jo had hesitated, appalled: "Joey, it's my dying wish. Promise!"

"I promise, ma," he had said.

Whereupon his mother had died, comfortably, leaving him with a completely ruined life.

They were not bad-looking girls, and they had a certain style, too. That is, Stell and Eva had. Carrie, the middle one, taught school over on the West Side. In those days it took her almost two hours each way. She said the kind of costume she required should have been corrugated steel. But all three knew what was being worn, and they wore it — or fairly faithful copies of it. Eva, the housekeeping sister, had a needle knack. She could skim the State Street windows and come away with a mental photograph of every separate tuck, hem, yoke, and ribbon. Heads of departments showed her the things they kept in drawers, and she went home and reproduced them with the aid of a two-dollar-a-day seamstress. Stell, the youngest, was the beauty. They called her Babe. She wasn't really a beauty, but some one had once told her that she looked like Janice Meredith (it was when that work of fiction was at the height of its popularity). For years afterward, whenever she went to parties, she affected a single, fat curl over her right shoulder, with a rose stuck through it.

Twenty-three years ago one's sisters did not strain at the household leash, nor crave a career. Carrie taught school, and hated it. Eva kept house expertly and complainingly. Babe's profession was being the family beauty, and it took all her spare time. Eva always let her sleep until ten.

This was Jo's household, and he was the nominal head of it. But it was an empty title. The three women dominated his life. They weren't consciously selfish. If you had called them cruel they would have put you down as mad. When you are the lone brother of three sisters, it means that you must constantly be calling for, escorting, or dropping one of them somewhere. Most men of Jo's age were standing before their mirror of a Saturday night, whistling blithely and abstractedly while they discarded a blue polka-dot for a maroon tie, whipped off the maroon for a shot-silk, and at the last moment decided against the shot-silk in favor of a plain black-and-white, because she had once said she preferred

quiet ties. Jo, when he should have been preening his feathers for con-
quest, was saying:

"Well, my God, I *am* hurrying! Give a man time, can't you? I just got
home. You girls have been laying around the house all day. No wonder
you're ready."

He took a certain pride in seeing his sisters well dressed, at a time
when he should have been reveling in fancy waistcoats and brilliant-
hued socks, according to the style of that day, and the inalienable right
of any unwed male under thirty, in any day. On those rare occasions
when his business necessitated an out-of-town trip, he would spend half
a day floundering about the shops selecting handkerchiefs, or stockings,
or feathers, or fans, or gloves for the girls. They always turned out to be
the wrong kind, judging by their reception.

From Carrie, "What in the world do I want of a fan!"

"I thought you didn't have one," Jo would say.

"I haven't. I never go to dances."

Jo would pass a futile hand over the top of his head, as was his way
when disturbed. "I just thought you'd like one. I thought every girl liked
a fan. Just," feebly, "just to — to have."

"Oh, for pity's sake!"

And from Eva or Babe, "I've *got* silk stockings, Jo." Or, "You brought
me handkerchiefs the last time."

There was something selfish in his giving, as there always is in any gift
freely and joyfully made. They never suspected the exquisite pleasure it
gave him to select these things; these fine, soft, silken things. There were
many things about this slow-going, amiable brother of theirs that they
never suspected. If you had told them he was a dreamer of dreams, for
example, they would have been amused. Sometimes, dead-tired by nine
o'clock, after a hard day downtown, he would doze over the evening paper. At intervals he would wake, red-eyed, to a snatch of conversation
such as, "Yes, but if you get a blue you can wear it anywhere. It's dressy,
and at the same time it's quiet, too." Eva, the expert, wrestling with Carrie over the problem of the new spring dress. They never guessed that
the commonplace man in the frayed old smoking-jacket had banished
them all from the room long ago; had banished himself, for that matter.
In his place was a tall, debonair, and rather dangerously handsome man
to whom six o'clock spelled evening clothes. The kind of a man who
can lean up against a mantel, or propose a toast, or give an order to a
man-servant, or whisper a gallant speech in a lady's ear with equal ease.

The shabby old house on Calumet Avenue was transformed into a brocaded and chandeliered rendezvous for the brilliance of the city. Beauty was there, and wit. But none so beautiful and witty as She. Mrs. — er — Jo Hertz. There was wine, of course; but no vulgar display. There was music; the soft sheen of satin; laughter. And he the gracious, tactful host, king of his own domain —

"Jo, for heaven's sake, if you're going to snore go to bed!"

"Why — did I fall asleep?"

"You haven't been doing anything else all evening. A person would think you were fifty instead of thirty."

And Jo Hertz was again just the dull, gray, commonplace brother of three well-meaning sisters.

Babe used to say petulantly, "Jo, why don't you ever bring home any of your men friends? A girl might as well not have any brother, all the good you do."

Jo, conscience-stricken, did his best to make amends. But a man who has been petticoat-ridden for years loses the knack, somehow, of comradeship with men. He acquires, too, a knowledge of women, and a distaste for them, equaled only, perhaps, by that of an elevator-starter in a department store.

Which brings us to one Sunday in May. Jo came home from a late Sunday afternoon walk to find company for supper. Carrie often had in one of her school-teacher friends, or Babe one of her frivolous intimates, or even Eva a staid guest of the old-girl type. There was always a Sunday night supper of potato salad, and cold meat, and coffee, and perhaps a fresh cake. Jo rather enjoyed it, being a hospitable soul. But he regarded the guests with the undazzled eyes of a man to whom they were just so many petticoats, timid of the night streets and requiring escort home. If you had suggested to him that some of his sisters' popularity was due to his own presence, or if you had hinted that the more kittenish of these visitors were palpably making eyes at him, he would have stared in amazement and unbelief.

This Sunday night it turned out to be one of Carrie's friends.

"Emily," said Carrie, "this is my brother, Jo." Jo had learned what to expect in Carrie's friends.

Drab-looking women in the late thirties, whose facial lines all slanted downward.

"Happy to meet you," said Jo, and looked down at a different sort altogether. A most surprisingly different sort, for one of Carrie's friends. This Emily person was very small, and fluffy, and blue-eyed, and sort of

— well, crinkly looking. You know. The corners of her mouth when she smiled, and her eyes when she looked up at you, and her hair, which was brown, but had the miraculous effect, somehow, of being golden.

Jo shook hands with her. Her hand was incredibly small, and soft, so that you were afraid of crushing it, until you discovered she had a firm little grip all her own. It surprised and amused you, that grip, as does a baby's unexpected clutch on your patronizing forefinger. As Jo felt it in his own big clasp, the strangest thing happened to him. Something inside Jo Hertz stopped working for a moment, then lurched sickeningly, then thumped like mad. It was his heart. He stood staring down at her, and she up at him, until the others laughed. Then their hands fell apart, lingeringly.

"Are you a school-teacher, Emily?" he said.

"Kindergarten. It's my first year. And don't call me Emily, please."

"Why not? It's your name. I think it's the prettiest name in the world." Which he hadn't meant to say at all. In fact, he was perfectly aghast to find himself saying it. But he meant it.

At supper he passed her things, and stared, until everybody laughed again, and Eva said acidly, "Why don't you feed her?"

It wasn't that Emily had an air of helplessness. She just made you feel you wanted her to be helpless, so that you could help her.

Jo took her home, and from that Sunday night he began to strain at the leash. He took his sisters out, dutifully, but he would suggest, with a carelessness that deceived no one, "Don't you want one of your girl friends to come along? That little What's-her-name — Emily, or something. So long's I've got three of you, I might as well have a full squad."

For a long time he didn't know what was the matter with him. He only knew he was miserable, and yet happy. Sometimes his heart seemed to ache with an actual physical ache. He realized that he wanted to do things for Emily. He wanted to buy things for Emily — useless, pretty, expensive things that he couldn't afford. He wanted to buy everything that Emily needed, and everything that Emily desired. He wanted to marry Emily. That was it. He discovered that one day, with a shock, in the midst of a transaction in the harness business. He stared at the man with whom he was dealing until that startled person grew uncomfortable.

"What's the matter, Hertz?"

"Matter?"

"You look as if you'd seen a ghost or found a gold mine. I don't know which."

"Gold mine," said Jo. And then, "No. Ghost."

For he remembered that high, thin voice, and his promise. And the harness business was slithering downhill with dreadful rapidity, as the automobile business began its amazing climb. Jo tried to stop it. But he was not that kind of business man. It never occurred to him to jump out of the down-going vehicle and catch the up-going one. He stayed on, vainly applying brakes that refused to work.

"You know, Emily, I couldn't support two households now. Not the way things are. But if you'll wait. If you'll only wait. The girls might — that is, Babe and Carrie —"

She was a sensible little thing, Emily. "Of course I'll wait. But we mustn't just sit back and let the years go by. We've got to help."

She went about it as if she were already a little matchmaking matron. She corralled all the men she had ever known and introduced them to Babe, Carrie, and Eva separately, in pairs, and en masse. She arranged parties at which Babe could display the curl. She got up picnics. She stayed home while Jo took the three about. When she was present she tried to look as plain and obscure as possible, so that the sisters should show up to advantage. She schemed, and planned, and contrived, and hoped; and smiled into Jo's despairing eyes.

And three years went by. Three precious years. Carrie still taught school, and hated it. Eva kept house, more and more complainingly as prices advanced and allowance retreated. Stell was still Babe, the family beauty; but even she knew that the time was past for curls. Emily's hair, somehow, lost its glint and began to look just plain brown. Her crinkliness began to iron out.

"Now, look here!" Jo argued, desperately, one night. "We could be happy, anyway. There's plenty of room at the house. Lots of people begin that way. Of course, I couldn't give you all I'd like to at first. But maybe, after a while —"

No dreams of salons, and brocade, and velvet-footed servitors, and satin damask now. Just two rooms, all their own, all alone, and Emily to work for. That was his dream. But it seemed less possible than that other absurd one had been.

You know that Emily was as practical a little thing as she looked fluffy. She knew women. Especially did she know Eva, and Carrie, and Babe. She tried to imagine herself taking the household affairs and the housekeeping pocketbook out of Eva's expert hands. Eva had once displayed to her a sheaf of aigrettes she had bought with what she saved out of the housekeeping money. So then she tried to picture herself allowing the reins of Jo's house to remain in Eva's hands. And everything feminine and normal in her rebelled. Emily knew she'd want to put away her own freshly laundered linen, and smooth it, and pat it. She was that kind of woman. She knew she'd want to do her own delightful haggling with butcher and vegetable peddler. She knew she'd want to muss Jo's hair, and sit on his knee, and even quarrel with him, if necessary, without the awareness of three ever-present pairs of maiden eyes and ears.

"No! No! We'd only be miserable. I know. Even if they didn't object. And they would, Jo. Wouldn't they?"

His silence was miserable assent. Then, "But you do love me, don't you, Emily?"

"I do, Jo. I love you — and love you — and love you. But, Jo, I — can't."

"I know it, dear. I knew it all the time, really. I just thought, maybe, somehow —"

The two sat staring for a moment into space, their hands clasped. Then they both shut their eyes, with a little shudder, as though what they saw was terrible to look upon. Emily's hand, the tiny hand that was so unexpectedly firm, tightened its hold on his, and his crushed the absurd fingers until she winced with pain.

That was the beginning of the end, and they knew it.

Emily wasn't the kind of girl who would be left to pine. There are too many Jo's in the world whose hearts are prone to lurch and then thump at the feel of a soft, fluttering, incredibly small hand in their grip. One year later Emily was married to a young man whose father owned a large, pie-shaped slice of the prosperous state of Michigan.

That being safely accomplished, there was something grimly humorous in the trend taken by affairs in the old house on Calumet. For Eva married. Of all people, Eva! Married well, too, though he was a great deal older than she. She went off in a hat she had copied from a French model at Fields's, and a suit she had contrived with a home dressmaker, aided by pressing on the part of the little tailor in the basement over on Thirty-first Street. It was the last of that, though. The next time they saw her, she had on a hat that even she would have despaired of copying, and a suit that sort of melted into your gaze. She moved to the North Side (trust Eva for that), and Babe assumed the management of the household on Calumet Avenue. It was rather a pinched little household now, for the harness business shrank and shrank.

"I don't see how you can expect me to keep house decently on this!" Babe would say contemptuously. Babe's nose, always a little inclined to sharpness, had whittled down to a point of late. "If you knew what Ben gives Eva."

"It's the best I can do, Sis. Business is something rotten."

"Ben says if you had the least bit of—" Ben was Eva's husband, and quotable, as are all successful men.

"I don't care what Ben says," shouted Jo, goaded into rage. "I'm sick of your everlasting Ben. Go and get a Ben of your own, why don't you, if you're so stuck on the way he does things."

And Babe did. She made a last desperate drive, aided by Eva, and she captured a rather surprised young man in the brokerage way, who had made up his mind not to marry for years and years. Eva wanted to give her her wedding things, but at that Jo broke into sudden rebellion.

"No, sir! No Ben is going to buy my sister's wedding clothes, understand? I guess I'm not broke—yet. I'll furnish the money for her things, and there'll be enough of them, too."

Babe had as useless a trousseau, and as filled with extravagant pink-and-blue and lacy and frilly things as any daughter of doting parents. Jo seemed to find a grim pleasure in providing them. But it left him pretty well pinched. After Babe's marriage (she insisted that they call her Estelle now) Jo sold the house on Calumet. He and Carrie took one of those little flats that were springing up, seemingly over night, all through Chicago's South Side.

There was nothing domestic about Carrie. She had given up teaching two years before, and had gone into Social Service work on the West Side. She had what is known as a legal mind, hard, clear, orderly, and she made a great success of it. Her dream was to live at the Settlement House and give all her time to the work. Upon the little household she bestowed a certain amount of grim, capable attention. It was the same kind of attention she would have given a piece of machinery whose oiling and running had been entrusted to her care. She hated it, and didn't hesitate to say so.

Jo took to prowling about department store basements, and household goods sections. He was always sending home a bargain in a ham, or a sack of potatoes, or fifty pounds of sugar, or a window clamp, or a new kind of paring knife. He was forever doing odd little jobs that the janitor should have done. It was the domestic in him claiming its own.

Then, one night, Carrie came home with a dull glow in her leathery cheeks, and her eyes alight with resolve. They had what she called a plain talk.

"Listen, Jo. They've offered me the job of first assistant resident worker. And I'm going to take it. Take it! I know fifty other girls who'd give their ears for it. I go in next month."

They were at dinner. Jo looked up from his plate, dully. Then he glanced around the little dining-room, with its ugly tan walls and its heavy dark furniture (the Calumet Street pieces fitted cumbersomely into the five-room flat).

"Away? Away from here, you mean — to live?"

Carrie laid down her fork. "Well, really, Jo! After all that explanation."

"But to go over there to live! Why, that neighborhood's full of dirt, and disease, and crime, and the Lord knows what all. I can't let you do that, Carrie."

Carrie's chin came up. She laughed a short little laugh. "Let me! That's eighteenth-century talk, Jo. My life's my own to live. I'm going."

And she went. Jo stayed on in the apartment until the lease was up. Then he sold what furniture he could, stored or gave away the rest, and took a room on Michigan Avenue in one of the old stone mansions whose decayed splendor was being put to such purpose.

Jo Hertz was his own master. Free to marry. Free to come and go. And he found he didn't even think of marrying. He didn't even want to come or go, particularly. A rather frumpy old bachelor, with thinning hair and a thickening neck. Much has been written about the unwed, middle-aged woman; her fussiness, her primness, her angularity of mind and body. In the male that same fussiness develops, and a certain primness, too. But he grows flabby where she grows lean.

Every Thursday evening he took dinner at Eva's, and on Sunday noon at Stell's. He tucked his napkin under his chin and openly enjoyed the home-made soup and the well-cooked meats. After dinner he tried to talk business with Eva's husband, or Stell's. His business talks were the old-fashioned kind, beginning:

"Well, now, looka here. Take, f'rinstance your raw hides and leathers."

But Ben and George didn't want to take f'rinstance your raw hides and leathers. They wanted, when they took anything at all, to take golf, or politics, or stocks. They were the modern type of business man who prefers to leave his work out of his play. Business, with them, was a profession — a finely graded and balanced thing, differing from Jo's clumsy, downhill style as completely as does the method of a great criminal detective differ from that of a village constable. They would listen, restively, and say, "Uh-uh," at intervals, and at the first chance they would sort of fade out of the room, with a meaning glance at their wives. Eva had two children now. Girls. They treated Uncle Jo with good-natured tolerance. Stell had no children. Uncle Jo degenerated, by almost imperceptible degrees, from the position of honored guest, who is served with white meat, to that of one who is content with a leg and one of those obscure and bony sections which, after much turning with a bewildered and investigating knife and fork, leave one baffled and unsatisfied.

Eva and Stell got together and decided that Jo ought to marry.

"It isn't natural," Eva told him. "I never saw a man who took so little interest in women."

"Me!" protested Jo, almost shyly. "Women!"

"Yes. Of course. You act like a frightened schoolboy."

So they had in for dinner certain friends and acquaintances of fitting age. They spoke of them as "splendid girls." Between thirty-six and forty. They talked awfully well, in a firm, clear way, about civics, and classes, and politics, and economics, and boards. They rather terrified Jo. He didn't understand much that they talked about, and he felt humbly inferior, and yet a little resentful, as if something had passed him by. He escorted them home, dutifully, though they told him not to bother, and they evidently meant it. They seemed capable, not only of going home quite unattended, but of delivering a pointed lecture to any highwayman or brawler who might molest them.

The following Thursday Eva would say, "How did you like her, Jo?"

"Like who?" Jo would spar feebly.

"Miss Matthews."

"Who's she?"

"Now, don't be funny, Jo. You know very well I mean the girl who was here for dinner. The one who talked so well on the emigration question."

"Oh, her! Why, I liked her, all right. Seems to be a smart woman."

"Smart! She's a perfectly splendid girl."

"Sure," Jo would agree cheerfully.

"But didn't you like her?"

"I can't say I did, Eve. And I can't say I didn't. She made me think a lot of a teacher I had in the fifth reader. Name of Himes. As I recall her, she must have been a fine woman. But I never thought of her as a woman at all. She was just Teacher."

"You make me tired," snapped Eva impatiently. "A man of your age. You don't expect to marry a girl, do you? A child!"

"I don't expect to marry anybody," Jo had answered.

And that was the truth, lonely though he often was.

The following year Eva moved to Winnetka. Any one who got the meaning of the Loop knows the significance of a move to a north shore suburb, and a house. Eva's daughter, Ethel, was growing up, and her mother had an eye on society.

That did away with Jo's Thursday dinner. Then Stell's husband bought a car. They went out into the country every Sunday. Stell said it was getting so that maids objected to Sunday dinners, anyway. Besides, they were unhealthy, old-fashioned things. They always meant to ask Jo to come along, but by the time their friends were placed, and the lunch, and the boxes, and sweaters, and George's camera, and everything, there seemed to be no room for a man of Jo's bulk. So that eliminated the Sunday dinners.

"Just drop in any time during the week," Stell said, "for dinner. Except Wednesday—that's our bridge night—and Saturday. And, of course, Thursday. Cook is out that night. Don't wait for me to 'phone."

And so Jo drifted into that sad-eyed, dyspeptic family made up of those you see dining in second-rate restaurants, their paper propped up against the bowl of oyster crackers, munching solemnly and with indifference to the stare of the passer-by surveying them through the brazen plate-glass window.

And then came the War. The war that spelled death and destruction to millions. The war that brought a fortune to Jo Hertz, and transformed him, over night, from a baggy-kneed old bachelor whose business was a failure to a prosperous manufacturer whose only trouble was the shortage in hides for the making of his product—leather! The armies of Europe called for it. Harnesses! More harnesses! Straps! Millions of straps! More! More!

The musty old harness business over on Lake Street was magically changed from a dust-covered, dead-alive concern to an orderly hive that hummed and glittered with success. Orders poured in. Jo Hertz had inside information on the War. He knew about troops and horses. He talked with French and English and Italian buyers—noblemen, many of them—commissioned by their countries to get American-made supplies. And now, when he said to Ben or George, "Take f'rinstance your raw hides and leathers," they listened with respectful attention.

And then began the gaydog business in the life of Jo Hertz. He developed into a loop-hound, ever keen on the scent of fresh pleasure. That side of Jo Hertz which had been repressed and crushed and ignored began to bloom, unhealthily. At first he spent money on his rather contemptuous nieces. He sent them gorgeous fans, and watch bracelets, and velvet bags. He took two expensive rooms at a downtown hotel, and there was something more tear-compelling than grotesque about the way he gloated over the luxury of a separate ice-water tap in the bathroom. He explained it.

"Just turn it on. Ice-water! Any hour of the day or night."

He bought a car. Naturally. A glittering affair; in color a bright blue, with pale-blue leather straps and a great deal of gold fittings and wire wheels. Eva said it was the kind of a thing a soubrette would use, rather than an elderly business man. You saw him driving about in it, red-faced and rather awkward at the wheel. You saw him, too, in the Pompeiian room at the Congress Hotel of a Saturday afternoon when doubtful and roving-eyed matrons in kolinsky capes are wont to congregate to sip pale amber drinks. Actors grew to recognize the semi-bald head and the shining, round, good-natured face looming out at them from the dim well of the parquet, and sometimes, in a musical show, they directed a quip at him, and he liked it. He could pick out the critics as they came down the aisle, and even had a nodding acquaintance with two of them.

"Kelly, of the *Herald*," he would say carelessly. "Bean, of the *Trib*. They're all afraid of him."

So he frolicked, ponderously. In New York he might have been called a Man About Town.

And he was lonesome. He was very lonesome. So he searched about in his mind and brought from the dim past the memory of the luxuriously furnished establishment of which he used to dream in the evenings when he dozed over his paper in the old house on Calumet. So he rented an apartment, many-roomed and expensive, with a man-servant in charge, and furnished it in styles and periods ranging through all the Louis. The living room was mostly rose color. It was like an unhealthy and bloated boudoir. And yet there was nothing sybaritic or uncleanly in the sight of this paunchy, middle-aged man sinking into the rosy-cushioned luxury of his ridiculous home. It was a frank and naïve indulgence of long-starved senses, and there was in it a great resemblance to the rolling-eyed ecstasy of a schoolboy smacking his lips over an all-day sucker.

The War went on, and on, and on. And the money continued to roll in — a flood of it. Then, one afternoon, Eva, in town on shopping bent, entered a small, exclusive, and expensive shop on Michigan Avenue. Exclusive, that is, in price. Eva's weakness, you may remember, was hats. She was seeking a hat now. She described what she sought with a languid conciseness, and stood looking about her after the saleswoman had vanished in quest of it. The room was becomingly rose-illumined

and somewhat dim, so that some minutes had passed before she realized that a man seated on a raspberry brocade settee not five feet away
— a man with a walking stick, and yellow gloves, and tan spats, and a
check suit — was her brother Jo. From him Eva's wild-eyed glance leaped
to the woman who was trying on hats before one of the many long mirrors. She was seated, and a saleswoman was exclaiming discreetly at her
elbow.

Eva turned sharply and encountered her own saleswoman returning,
hat-laden. "Not to-day," she gasped. "I'm feeling ill. Suddenly." And almost ran from the room.

That evening she told Stell, relating her news in that telephone pid-
gin-English devised by every family of married sisters as protection
against the neighbors and Central. Translated, it ran thus:

"He looked straight at me. My dear, I thought I'd die! But at least he
had sense enough not to speak. She was one of those limp, willowy creatures with the greediest eyes that she tried to keep softened to a baby
stare, and couldn't, she was so crazy to get her hands on those hats. I
saw it all in one awful minute. You know the way I do. I suppose some
people would call her pretty. I don't. And her color! Well! And the most
expensive-looking hats. Aigrettes, and paradise, and feathers. Not one
of them under seventy-five. Isn't it disgusting! At his age! Suppose Ethel
had been with me!"

The next time it was Stell who saw them. In a restaurant. She said
it spoiled her evening. And the third time it was Ethel. She was one of
the guests at a theater party given by Nicky Overton II. You know. The
North Shore Overtons. Lake Forest. They came in late, and occupied the
entire third row at the opening performance of "Believe Me!" And Ethel
was Nicky's partner. She was glowing like a rose. When the lights went
up after the first act Ethel saw that her uncle Jo was seated just ahead
of her with what she afterward described as a Blonde. Then her uncle had turned around, and seeing her, had been surprised into a smile
that spread genially all over his plump and rubicund face. Then he had
turned to face forward again, quickly.

"Who's the old bird?" Nicky had asked. Ethel had pretended not to
hear, so he had asked again.

"My uncle," Ethel answered, and flushed all over her delicate face,
and down to her throat. Nicky had looked at the Blonde, and his eyebrows had gone up ever so slightly.

It spoiled Ethel's evening. More than that, as she told her mother of it
later, weeping, she declared it had spoiled her life.

Ethel talked it over with her husband in that intimate, kimonoed hour that precedes bedtime. She gesticulated heatedly with her hair brush.

"It's disgusting, that's what it is. Perfectly disgusting. There's no fool like an old fool. Imagine! A creature like that. At his time of life."

There exists a strange and loyal kinship among men. "Well, I don't know," Ben said now, and even grinned a little. "I suppose a boy's got to sow his wild oats some time."

"Don't be any more vulgar than you can help," Eva retorted. "And I think you know, as well as I, what it means to have that Overton boy interested in Ethel."

"If he's interested in her," Ben blundered, "I guess the fact that Ethel's uncle went to the theater with some one who wasn't Ethel's aunt won't cause a shudder to run up and down his frail young frame, will it?"

"All right," Eva had retorted. "If you're not man enough to stop it, I'll have to, that's all. I'm going up there with Stell this week."

They did not notify Jo of their coming. Eva telephoned his apartment when she knew he would be out, and asked his man if he expected his master home to dinner that evening. The man had said yes. Eva arranged to meet Stell in town. They would drive to Jo's apartment together, and wait for him there.

When she reached the city Eva found turmoil there. The first of the American troops to be sent to France were leaving. Michigan Boulevard was a billowing, surging mass: flags, pennants, bands, crowds. All the elements that make for demonstration. And over the whole — quiet. No holiday crowd, this. A solid, determined mass of people waiting patient hours to see the khaki-clads go by. Three years of indefatigable reading had brought them to a clear knowledge of what these boys were going to.

"Isn't it dreadful!" Stell gasped.

"Nicky Overton's only nineteen, thank goodness."

Their car was caught in the jam. When they moved at all it was by inches. When at last they reached Jo's apartment they were flushed, nervous, apprehensive. But he had not yet come in. So they waited.

No, they were not staying to dinner with their brother, they told the relieved houseman. Jo's home has already been described to you. Stell and Eva, sunk in rose-colored cushions, viewed it with disgust, and some mirth. They rather avoided each other's eyes.

"Carrie ought to be here," Eva said. They both smiled at the thought of the austere Carrie in the midst of those rosy cushions, and hangings, and lamps. Stell rose and began to walk about, restlessly. She picked up a vase and laid it down; straightened a picture. Eva got up, too, and wandered into the hall. She stood there a moment, listening. Then she turned and passed into Jo's bedroom. And there you knew Jo for what he was.

This room was as bare as the other had been ornate. It was Jo, the clean-minded and simple-hearted, in revolt against the cloying luxury with which he had surrounded himself. The bedroom, of all rooms in any house, reflects the personality of its occupant. True, the actual furniture was paneled, cupid-surmounted, and ridiculous. It had been the fruit of Jo's first orgy of the senses. But now it stood out in that stark little room with an air as incongruous and ashamed as that of a pink tarleton danseuse who finds herself in a monk's cell. None of those wall-pictures with which bachelor bedrooms are reputed to be hung. No satin slippers. No scented notes. Two plain-backed military brushes on the chiffonier (and he so nearly hairless!). A little orderly stack of books on the table near the bed. Eva fingered their titles and gave a little gasp. One of them was on gardening. "Well, of all things!" exclaimed Stell. A book on the War, by an Englishman. A detective story of the lurid type that lulls us to sleep. His shoes ranged in a careful row in the closet, with shoe-trees in every one of them. There was something speaking about them. They looked so human. Eva shut the door on them, quickly. Some bottles on the dresser. A jar of pomade. An ointment such as a man uses who is growing bald and is panic-stricken too late. An insurance calendar on the wall. Some rhubarb-and-soda mixture on the shelf in the bathroom, and a little box of pepsin tablets.

"Eats all kinds of things at all hours of the night," Eva said, and wandered out into the rose-colored front room again with the air of one who is chagrined at her failure to find what she has sought. Stell followed her, furtively.

"Where do you suppose he can be?" she demanded. "It's—" she glanced at her wrist, "why, it's after six!"

And then there was a little click. The two women sat up, tense. The door opened. Jo came in. He blinked a little. The two women in the rosy room stood up.

"Why—Eve! Why, Babe! Well! Why didn't you let me know?"

"We were just about to leave. We thought you weren't coming home."

• • •

Jo came in, slowly. "I was in the jam on Michigan, watching the boys go by." He sat down, heavily. The light from the window fell on him. And you saw that his eyes were red.

And you'll have to learn why. He had found himself one of the thousands in the jam on Michigan Avenue, as he said. He had a place near the curb, where his big frame shut off the view of the unfortunates behind him. He waited with the placid interest of one who has subscribed to all the funds and societies to which a prosperous, middle-aged business man is called upon to subscribe in war time. Then, just as he was about to leave, impatient at the delay, the crowd had cried, with a queer dramatic, exultant note in its voice, "Here they come! here come the boys!"

Just at that moment two little, futile, frenzied fists began to beat a mad tattoo on Jo Hertz's broad back. Jo tried to turn in the crowd, all indignant resentment. "Say, looka here!"

The little fists kept up their frantic beating and pushing. And a voice —a choked, high little voice—cried, "Let me by! I can't see! You man, you! You big fat man! My boy's going by—to war—and I can't see! Let me by!"

Jo scrooged around, still keeping his place. He looked down. And upturned to him in agonized appeal was the face of little Emily. They stared at each other for what seemed a long, long time. It was really only the fraction of a second. Then Jo put one great arm firmly around Emily's waist and swung her around in front of him. His great bulk protected her. Emily was clinging to his hand. She was breathing rapidly, as if she had been running. Her eyes were straining up the street.

"Why, Emily, how in the world!—"

"I ran away. Fred didn't want me to come. He said it would excite me too much."

"Fred?"

"My husband. He made me promise to say good-by to Jo at home.

"Jo's my boy. And he's going to war. So I ran away. I had to see him. I had to see him go."

She was dry-eyed. Her gaze was straining up the street.

"Why, sure," said Jo. "Of course you want to see him." And then the crowd gave a great roar. There came over Jo a feeling of weakness. He was trembling. The boys went marching by.

"There he is," Emily shrilled, above the din. "There he is! There he is! There he—" And waved a futile little hand. It wasn't so much a wave as a clutching. A clutching after something beyond her reach.

"Which one? Which one, Emily?"

"The handsome one. The handsome one. There!" Her voice quavered and died.

Jo put a steady hand on her shoulder. "Point him out," he commanded. "Show me." And the next instant. "Never mind. I see him."

Somehow, miraculously, he had picked him from among the hundreds. Had picked him as surely as his own father might have. It was Emily's boy. He was marching by, rather stiffly. He was nineteen, and fun-loving, and he had a girl, and he didn't particularly want to go to France and—to go to France. But more than he had hated going, he had hated not to go. So he marched by, looking straight ahead, his jaw set so that his chin stuck out just a little. Emily's boy.

Jo looked at him, and his face flushed purple. His eyes, the hard-boiled eyes of a loop-hound, took on the look of a sad old man. And suddenly he was no longer Jo, the sport; old J. Hertz, the gay dog. He was Jo Hertz, thirty, in love with life, in love with Emily, and with the stinging blood of young manhood coursing through his veins.

Another minute and the boy had passed on up the broad street—the fine, flag-bedecked street—just one of a hundred service-hats bobbing in rhythmic motion like sandy waves lapping a shore and flowing on.

Then he disappeared altogether.

Emily was clinging to Jo. She was mumbling something over and over. "I can't. I can't. Don't ask me to. I can't let him go. Like that. I can't."

Jo said a queer thing.

"Why, Emily! We wouldn't have him stay home, would we? We wouldn't want him to do anything different, would we? Not our boy. I'm glad he volunteered. I'm proud of him. So are you, glad."

Little by little he quieted her. He took her to the car that was waiting, a worried chauffeur in charge. They said good-by, awkwardly. Emily's face was a red, swollen mass.

So it was that when Jo entered his own hallway half an hour later he blinked, dazedly, and when the light from the window fell on him you saw that his eyes were red.

Eva was not one to beat about the bush. She sat forward in her chair, clutching her bag rather nervously.

"Now, look here, Jo. Stell and I are here for a reason. We're here to tell you that this thing's got to stop."

"Thing? Stop?"

"You know very well what I mean. You saw me at the milliner's that day. And night before last, Ethel. We're all disgusted. If you must go about with people like that, please have some sense of decency."

Something gathering in Jo's face should have warned her. But he was slumped down in his chair in such a huddle, and he looked so old and fat that she did not heed it. She went on. "You've got us to consider. Your sisters. And your nieces. Not to speak of your own—"

But he got to his feet then, shaking, and at what she saw in his face even Eva faltered and stopped. It wasn't at all the face of a fat, middle-aged sport. It was a face Jovian, terrible.

"You!" he began, low-voiced, ominous. "You!" He raised a great fist high. "You two murderers! You didn't consider me, twenty years ago. You come to me with talk like that. Where's my boy! You killed him, you two, twenty years ago. And now he belongs to somebody else. Where's my son that should have gone marching by to-day?" He flung his arms out in a great gesture of longing. The red veins stood out on his forehead. "Where's my son! Answer me that, you two selfish, miserable women. Where's my son!" Then as they huddled together, frightened, wild-eyed. "Out of my house! Out of my house! Before I hurt you!"

They fled, terrified. The door banged behind them.

Jo stood, shaking, in the center of the room. Then he reached for a chair, gropingly, and sat down. He passed one moist, flabby hand over his forehead and it came away wet. The telephone rang. He sat still, it sounded far away and unimportant, like something forgotten. I think he did not even hear it with his conscious ear. But it rang and rang insistently. Jo liked to answer his telephone when at home.

"Hello!" He knew instantly the voice at the other end.

"That you, Jo?" it said.

"Yes."

"How's my boy?"

"I'm—all right."

"Listen, Jo. The crowd's coming over to-night. I've fixed up a little poker game for you. Just eight of us."

"I can't come to-night, Gert."

"Can't! Why not?"

"I'm not feeling so good."

"You just said you were all right."

"I *am* all right. Just kind of tired."

The voice took on a cooing note. "Is my Joey tired? Then he shall be all comfy on the sofa, and he doesn't need to play if he don't want to. No, sir."

Jo stood staring at the black mouth-piece of the telephone. He was seeing a procession go marching by. Boys, hundreds of boys, in khaki.

"Hello! Hello!" The voice took on an anxious note. "Are you there?"

"Yes," wearily.

"Jo, there's something the matter. You're sick. I'm coming right over."

"No!"

"Why not? You sound as if you'd been sleeping. Look here —"

"Leave me alone!" cried Jo, suddenly, and the receiver clacked onto the hook. "Leave me alone. Leave me alone." Long after the connection had been broken.

He stood staring at the instrument with unseeing eyes. Then he turned and walked into the front room. All the light had gone out of it. Dusk had come on. All the light had gone out of everything. The zest had gone out of life. The game was over — the game he had been playing against loneliness and disappointment. And he was just a tired old man. A lonely, tired old man in a ridiculous, rose-colored room that had grown, all of a sudden, drab.

1920-1930

SERIES EDITOR EDWARD O'BRIEN WROTE, "IN BOSTON, I am below the salt with the Beacon Hill Yankees and above the salt with the South Boston Irish. There's no place for me." In 1919, after traveling in France and Rome, he settled in Oxford, England. But he continued to travel — in Italy, where he befriended Ezra Pound; in Paris, where he met James Joyce. O'Brien soon met the woman who would become his wife, Romer Wilson, a British writer known primarily for her biography of Emily Brontë.

He continued to balance a large number of projects with *The Best American Short Stories:* books of poetry and religious prose poems, biographies of Gauguin and Nietzsche. In 1922 he began coediting *The Best British Short Stories.*

In 1923 O'Brien met Ernest Hemingway, a twenty-four-year-old reporter for the *Toronto Star.* Hemingway lamented that his wife, Hadley Richardson, had lost a suitcase of his manuscripts. He was despondent and wanted to quit writing. O'Brien asked to see Hemingway's only two remaining stories and elected to publish one, "My Old Man," in that year's *Best American Short Stories.* It was the first and last time that O'Brien broke his own rule of selecting only published stories. And it was Hemingway's first major publication.

The 1920s were a fertile time for literary American short fiction. As O'Brien wrote, "Even the best stories were built like Fords fifteen years ago, while now there are probably forty or fifty young writers who see life freshly, render it clearly, and write without a thought of pandering to editorial prejudices." Sentimentality on the page was replaced by what O'Brien termed "saturation in the physical scene." Writers such as Ernest Hemingway and Ring Lardner "communicate to us with nearly complete disinterestedness as well as personal interest what the senses of sight and hearing have brought to them in the circles of the world in which they move." O'Brien went on to write, "[Hemingway] conceals the tenderness of his heart by an attitude of bravado . . . This is a very common and beautiful attitude in American youth since the war."

O'Brien questioned the number of American writers living in Paris during the 1920s, worrying that so many artists living in close proximity created "sterile inbreeding"—a certain sameness in their fiction.

The Best American Short Stories gained some popularity, but fans of commercial fiction objected to O'Brien's "obscure" taste. Critics railed against his "dull, predictable" choices, stories that delivered anything but the "living truth" he promised in his forewords. They thought he was losing touch with the essence of American culture by living across the Atlantic. They also found his tone elitist. In almost every foreword he bemoaned the current fads of short fiction as well as the hazards of commercial editors and publishers. Some critics labeled Irvin S. Cobb, Katharine Fullerton Gerould, and Konrad Bercovici, whose work was featured in the book, "perverting" influences. One even reacted to the idea of an anthology of the short story: "Overindulgence in the short story is a dissipation which produces an inevitable reaction; it leaves the mind in a jerky state . . . the perfect short-story is like champagne, scarcely able to be taken in as the sole article of diet." O'Brien's response was "The public . . . is beginning to have an opinion of its own and much more discrimination than the editors and critics who wish to leg-islate for it."

O'Brien championed small literary journals, especially those in the Midwest, like *Prairie Schooner* and *The Midland*. In 1929 he wrote pre-sciently, "Two generations ago, Boston was the geographical centre of American literary life, one generation ago New York . . . and I suggest that the geographical centre to-day is Iowa City." Seven years later the Iowa Writers' Workshop, one of the country's best writing programs, was founded.

O'Brien and his wife had a son, Johnny, in 1924. Not long after, Romer was diagnosed with cancer and grew sick. In 1930 she passed away. Her death coincided with the onset of the Great Depression.

★ ★ ★

1921

SHERWOOD ANDERSON
BROTHERS

from *The Bookman*

SHERWOOD ANDERSON (1876–1941) was born in Camden, Ohio, and dropped out of school at fourteen. He worked a variety of jobs, joined the National Guard, and finally settled in Chicago. After serving in Cuba during the Spanish-American War, he found work selling ads and writing copy for an advertising agency and later as a sales manager in Ohio. He often told friends that he was a businessman until the day he abruptly stopped dictating a letter, left his office — and soon his family — and never went back.

Anderson is the author of the renowned story collection *Winesburg, Ohio,* as well as poetry, essays, criticism, and novels, including *Dark Laughter, Tar, A Midwest Childhood,* and *A Storyteller's Life.* His unadorned style and modernist stories about alienation in small-town America influenced countless future writers. Anderson spoke out against the plot found in so much of the fiction of his time: "'The Poison Plot,' I called it in conversation with my friends as the plot notion did seem to poison all story telling. What was wanted was form, no plot, an altogether more elusive and difficult thing to come at . . . The Short Story is a result of a sudden passion. It is an idea grasped whole as one would grasp an apple in an orchard. All my own stories have been written in one sitting."

When Anderson and his wife moved to New Orleans, they hosted William Faulkner and Edmund Wilson. Anderson portrayed the city in *Dark Laughter.* The book was a bestseller, his only one while he was alive.

Anderson was an early supporter of Ernest Hemingway, who was outraged when critics compared his style to his mentor's. When one critic named Anderson "America's most interesting writer," Hemingway quickly wrote a novel, *The Torrents of Spring,* which spoofed Anderson's work, and the friendship was over.

Throughout his career, series editor Edward O'Brien referred to Anderson as having made "the most permanent contribution to the American short story." Anderson died in 1941 while on a cruise to South America.

★

I AM AT MY house in the country and it is late October. It rains. Back of my house is a forest and in front there is a road and beyond that open fields. The country is one of low hills, flattening suddenly into plains. Some twenty miles away, across the flat country, lies the huge city, Chicago.

On this rainy day the leaves of the trees that line the road before my window are falling like rain, the yellow, red, and golden leaves fall straight down heavily. The rain beats them brutally down. They are denied a last golden flash across the sky. In October leaves should be carried away, out over the plains, in a wind. They should go dancing away.

Yesterday morning I arose at daybreak and went for a walk. There was a heavy fog and I lost myself in it. I went down into the plains and returned to the hills and everywhere the fog was as a wall before me. Out of it trees sprang suddenly, grotesquely, as in a city street late at night people come suddenly out of the darkness into the circle of light under a street lamp. Above there was the light of day forcing itself slowly into the fog. The fog moved slowly. The tops of trees moved slowly. Under the trees the fog was dense, purple. It was like smoke lying in the streets of a factory town.

An old man came up to me in the fog. I know him well. The people here call him insane. "He is a little cracked," they say. He lives alone in a little house buried deep in the forest and has a small dog he carries always in his arms. On many mornings I have met him walking on the road and he has told me of men and women who were his brothers and sisters, his cousins, aunts, uncles, brothers-in-law. The notion has possession of him. He cannot draw close to people near at hand so he gets hold of a name out of a newspaper and his mind plays with it. One morning he told me he was a cousin to the man named Cox who at the time when I write is a candidate for the presidency. On another morning he told me that Caruso the singer had married a woman who was his sister-in-law. "She is my wife's sister," he said, holding the little dog closely. His gray watery eyes looked appealingly up to me. He wanted me to believe. "My wife was a sweet slim girl," he declared. "We lived together in a big house and in the morning walked about arm in arm. Now her sister has married Caruso the singer. He is of my family now." As some one had told me the old man had never been married I went away wondering.

One morning in early September I came upon him sitting under a tree beside a path near his house. The dog barked at me and then ran and crept into his arms. At that time the Chicago newspapers were filled

with the story of a millionaire who had got into trouble with his wife because of an intimacy with an actress. The old man told me the actress
was his sister. He is sixty years old and the actress whose story appeared
in the newspapers is twenty, but he spoke of their childhood together.
"You would not realize it to see us now but we were poor then," he said.
"It's true. We lived in a little house on the side of a hill. Once when there
was a storm the wind nearly swept our house away. How the wind blew.
Our father was a carpenter and he built strong houses for other people
but our own house he did not build very strongly." He shook his head
sorrowfully. "My sister the actress has got into trouble. Our house is not
built very strongly," he said as I went away along the path.

For a month, two months, the Chicago newspapers, that are delivered
every morning in our village, have been filled with the story of a murder. A man there has murdered his wife and there seems no reason for
the deed. The tale runs something like this—

The man, who is now on trial in the courts and will no doubt be
hanged, worked in a bicycle factory where he was a foreman, and lived
with his wife and his wife's mother in an apartment in Thirty-Second
Street. He loved a girl who worked in the office of the factory where he
was employed. She came from a town in Iowa and when she first came
to the city lived with her aunt who has since died. To the foreman, a
heavy stolid-looking man with gray eyes, she seemed the most beautiful
woman in the world. Her desk was by a window at an angle of the factory, a sort of wing of the building, and the foreman, down in the shop,
had a desk by another window. He sat at his desk making out sheets
containing the record of the work done by each man in his department.
When he looked up he could see the girl sitting at work at her desk. The
notion got into his head that she was peculiarly lovely. He did not think
of trying to draw close to her or of winning her love. He looked at her as
one might look at a star or across a country of low hills in October when
the leaves of the trees are all red and yellow gold. "She is a pure, virginal
thing," he thought vaguely. "What can she be thinking about as she sits
there by the window at work?"

In fancy the foreman took the girl from Iowa home with him to his
apartment in Thirty-Second Street and into the presence of his wife and
his mother-in-law. All day in the shop and during the evening at home
he carried her figure about with him in his mind. As he stood by a window in his apartment and looked out toward the Illinois Central railroad tracks and beyond the tracks to the lake, the girl was there beside
him. Down below women walked in the street and in every woman he

saw there was something of the Iowa girl. One woman walked as she did, another made a gesture with her hand that reminded of her. All the women he saw except only his wife and his mother-in-law were like the girl he had taken inside himself.

The two women in his own house puzzled and confused him. They became suddenly unlovely and commonplace. His wife in particular was like some strange unlovely growth that had attached itself to his body.

In the evening after the day at the factory he went home to his own place and had dinner. He had always been a silent man and when he did not talk no one minded. After dinner he, with his wife, went to a picture show. When they came home his wife's mother sat under an electric light reading. There were two children and his wife expected another. They came into the apartment and sat down. The climb up two flights of stairs had wearied his wife. She sat in a chair beside her mother groaning with weariness.

The mother-in-law was the soul of goodness. She took the place of a servant in the home and got no pay. When her daughter wanted to go to a picture show she waved her hand and smiled. "Go on," she said. "I don't want to go. I'd rather sit here." She got a book and sat reading. The little boy of nine awoke and cried. He wanted to sit on the po-po. The mother-in-law attended to that.

After the man and his wife came home the three people sat in silence for an hour or two before bedtime. The man pretended to read a newspaper. He looked at his hands. Although he had washed them carefully grease from the bicycle frames left dark stains under the nails. He thought of the Iowa girl and of her white quick hands playing over the keys of a typewriter. He felt dirty and uncomfortable.

The girl at the factory knew the foreman had fallen in love with her and the thought excited her a little. Since her aunt's death she had gone to live in a rooming house and had nothing to do in the evening. Although the foreman meant nothing to her she could in a way use him. To her he became a symbol. Sometimes he came into the office and stood for a moment by the door. His large hands were covered with black grease. She looked at him without seeing. In his place in her imagination stood a tall slender young man. Of the foreman she saw only the gray eyes that began to burn with a strange fire. The eyes expressed eagerness, a humble and devout eagerness. In the presence of a man with such eyes she felt she need not be afraid.

She wanted a lover who would come to her with such a look in his eyes. Occasionally, perhaps once in two weeks, she stayed a little late at the office, pretending to have work that must be finished. Through the window she could see the foreman, waiting. When every one had gone she closed her desk and went into the street. At the same moment the foreman came out at the factory door.

They walked together along the street, a half-dozen blocks, to where she got aboard her car. The factory was in a place called South Chicago and as they went along evening was coming on. The streets were lined with small unpainted frame houses and dirty-faced children ran screaming in the dusty roadway. They crossed over a bridge. Two abandoned coal barges lay rotting in the stream.

He went along by her side walking heavily, striving to conceal his hands. He had scrubbed them carefully before leaving the factory but they seemed to him like heavy dirty pieces of waste matter hanging at his side. Their walking together happened but a few times and during one summer. "It's hot," he said. He never spoke to her of anything but the weather. "It's hot," he said; "I think it may rain."

She dreamed of the lover who would some time come, a tall fair young man, a rich man owning houses and lands. The workingman who walked beside her had nothing to do with her conception of love. She walked with him, stayed at the office until the others had gone to walk unobserved with him, because of his eyes, because of the eager thing in his eyes that was at the same time humble, that bowed down to her. In his presence there was no danger, could be no danger. He would never attempt to approach too closely, to touch her with his hands. She was safe with him.

In his apartment in the evening the man sat under the electric light with his wife and his mother-in-law. In the next room his two children were asleep. In a short time his wife would have another child. He had been with her to a picture show and presently they would get into bed together.

He would lie awake thinking, would hear the creaking of the springs of a bed from where, in another room, his mother-in-law was crawling under the sheets. Life was too intimate. He would lie awake eager, expectant — expecting what?

Nothing. Presently one of the children would cry. It wanted to get out of bed and sit on the po-po. Nothing strange or unusual or lovely would or could happen. Life was too close, intimate. Nothing that could happen in the apartment could in any way stir him. The things his wife might say, her occasional half-hearted outbursts of passion, the goodness of his stout mother-in-law who did the work of a servant without pay—

He sat in the apartment under the electric light pretending to read a newspaper—thinking. He looked at his hands. They were large, shapeless, a workingman's hands.

The figure of the girl from Iowa walked about the room. With her he went out of the apartment and walked in silence through miles of streets. It was not necessary to say words. He walked with her by a sea, along the crest of a mountain. The night was clear and silent and the stars shone. She also was a star. It was not necessary to say words.

Her eyes were like stars and her lips were like soft hills rising out of dim, star-lit plains. "She is unattainable, she is far off like the stars," he thought. "She is unattainable like the stars but unlike the stars she breathes, she lives, like myself she has being."

One evening, some six weeks ago, the man who worked as foreman in the bicycle factory killed his wife and he is now in the courts being tried for murder. Every day the newspapers are filled with the story. On the evening of the murder he had taken his wife as usual to a picture show and they started home at nine. In Thirty-Second Street, at a corner near their apartment building, the figure of a man darted suddenly out of an alleyway and then darted back again. That incident may have put the idea of killing his wife into the man's head.

They got to the entrance to the apartment building and stepped into a dark hallway. Then quite suddenly and apparently without thought the man took a knife out of his pocket. "Suppose that man who darted into the alleyway had intended to kill us," he thought. Opening the knife he whirled about and struck his wife. He struck twice, a dozen times— madly. There was a scream and his wife's body fell.

The janitor had neglected to light the gas in the lower hallway. Afterward, the foreman decided that was the reason he did it, that and the fact that the dark slinking figure of a man darted out of an alleyway and then darted back again. "Surely," he told himself, "I could never have done it had the gas been lighted."

He stood in the hallway thinking. His wife was dead and with her had died her unborn child. There was a sound of doors opening in the apartments above. For several minutes nothing happened. His wife and her unborn child were dead—that was all.

He ran upstairs thinking quickly. In the darkness on the lower stairway he had put the knife back into his pocket and, as it turned out later, there was no blood on his hands or on his clothes. The knife he later washed carefully in the bathroom, when the excitement had died down a little. He told everyone the same story. "There has been a holdup," he explained. "A man came slinking out of an alleyway and followed me and my wife home. He followed us into the hallway of the building and there was no light." The janitor had neglected to light the gas. Well there had been a struggle and in the darkness his wife had been killed. He could not tell how it had happened. "There was no light. The janitor had neglected to light the gas," he kept saying.

For a day or two they did not question him specially and he had time to get rid of the knife. He took a long walk and threw it away into the river in South Chicago where the two abandoned coal barges lay rotting under the bridge, the bridge he had crossed when on the summer evenings he walked to the street car with the girl who was virginal and pure, who was far off and unattainable, like a star and yet not like a star.

And then he was arrested and right away he confessed—told everything. He said he did not know why he had killed his wife and was careful to say nothing of the girl at the office. The newspapers tried to discover the motive for the crime. They are still trying. Some one had seen him on the few evenings when he walked with the girl and she was dragged into the affair and had her picture printed in the paper. That has been annoying for her, as of course she has been able to prove she had nothing to do with the man.

Yesterday morning a heavy fog lay over our village here at the edge of the city and I went for a long walk in the early morning. As I returned out of the lowlands into our hill country I met the old man whose family has so many and such strange ramifications. For a time he walked beside me holding the little dog in his arms. It was cold and the dog whined and shivered. In the fog the old man's face was indistinct. It moved slowly back and forth with the fog banks of the upper air and with the tops of trees. He spoke of the man who has killed his wife and whose name is being shouted in the pages of the city newspapers that come to our village each morning. As he walked beside me he launched into a long tale concerning a life he and his brother, who had now become a murderer, had once lived together. "He is my brother," he said over and over, shaking his head. He seemed afraid I would not believe. There was a fact that must be established. "We were boys together, that man and I," he began again. "You see we played together in a barn back of our father's house. Our father went away to sea in a ship. That is the way our names became confused. You understand that. We have different names but we are brothers. We had the same father. We played together in a barn back of our father's house. All day we lay together in the hay in the barn and it was warm there."

In the fog the slender body of the old man became like a little gnarled tree. Then it became a thing suspended in air. It swung back and forth like a body hanging on the gallows. The face beseeched me to believe the story the lips were trying to tell. In my mind everything concerning the relationship of men and women became confused, a muddle. The spirit of the man who had killed his wife came into the body of the little old man there by the roadside. It was striving to tell me the story it would never be able to tell in the courtroom in the city, in the presence of the judge. The whole story of mankind's loneliness, of the effort to reach out to unattainable beauty tried to get itself expressed from the lips of a mumbling old man, crazed with loneliness, who stood by the side of a country road on a foggy morning holding a little dog in his arms.

The arms of the old man held the dog so closely that it began to whine with pain. A sort of convulsion shook his body. The soul seemed striving to wrench itself out of the body, to fly away through the fog down across the plain to the city, to the singer, the politician, the millionaire, the murderer, to its brothers, cousins, sisters, down in the city. The intensity of the old man's desire was terrible and in sympathy my body began to tremble. His arms tightened about the body of the little dog so that it screamed with pain. I stepped forward and tore the arms away and the dog fell to the ground and lay whining. No doubt it had been injured. Perhaps ribs had been crushed. The old man stared at the dog lying at his feet as in the hallway of the apartment building the worker from the bicycle factory had stared at his dead wife. "We are brothers," he said again. "We have different names but we are brothers. Our father you understand went off to sea."

I am sitting in my house in the country and it rains. Before my eyes the hills fall suddenly away and there are the flat plains and beyond the plains the city. An hour ago the old man of the house in the forest went past my door and the little dog was not with him. It may be that as we talked in the fog he crushed the life out of his companion. It may be that the dog like the workman's wife and her unborn child is now dead.

The leaves of the trees that line the road before my window are falling like rain — the yellow, red, and golden leaves fall straight down, heavily. The rain beats them brutally down. They are denied a last golden flash across the sky. In October leaves should be carried away, out over the plains, in a wind. They should go dancing away.

1923

ERNEST HEMINGWAY
MY OLD MAN

ERNEST HEMINGWAY (1899–1961) was born in Oak Park, Illinois. He worked as a reporter in Kansas City and after serving as an ambulance driver on the Italian front in World War I returned to Illinois, and eventually Chicago, where he befriended Sherwood Anderson. Hemingway later settled in Paris. In 1923 a small French press published his first book, *Three Stories and Ten Poems*. Anderson persuaded his American publisher to acquire Hemingway's story collection *In Our Time*, published in 1925.

Hemingway wrote with distinct understatement, compressed language, and hidden pathos, qualities that continue to be emulated in short fiction today. Series editor Edward O'Brien once recalled a conversation with Hemingway in Paris, when the writer complained that he had tried "to help people to do something in their own way and then find that they merely imitated him. [Hemingway] used to lament that it was the very passages in his work over which he had labored hardest and which seemed to him to reveal his own weakness that other writers copied as tricks."

Among Hemingway's best-known novels are *The Sun Also Rises*, *A Farewell to Arms*, and *The Old Man and the Sea*, which was awarded the Nobel Prize. In his writing he explored themes of war and love and nature. In 1961 he committed suicide in his house in Ketchum, Idaho.

★

I GUESS LOOKING AT it, now, my old man was cut out for a fat guy, one of those regular little roly fat guys you see around, but he sure never got that way, except a little toward the last, and then it wasn't his fault, he was riding over the jumps only and he could afford to carry plenty of weight then. I remember the way he'd pull on a rubber shirt over a couple of jerseys and a big sweat shirt over that, and get me to run with him in the forenoon in the hot sun. He'd have, maybe, taken a trial trip with one of Razzo's skins early in the morning after just getting in from Torino at four o'clock in the morning and beating it out to the stables in a cab and then with the dew all over everything and the sun just starting to get going, I'd help him pull off his boots and he'd get into a pair of sneakers and all these sweaters and we'd start out.

"Come on, kid," he'd say, stepping up and down on his toes in front of the jock's dressing room, "let's get moving."

Then we'd start off jogging around the infield once, maybe, with him ahead, running nice, and then turn out the gate and along one of those roads with all the trees along both sides of them that run out from San Siro. I'd go ahead of him when we hit the road and I could run pretty stout and I'd look around and he'd be jogging easy just behind me and after a little while I'd look around again and he'd begun to sweat. Sweating heavy and he'd just be dogging it along with his eyes on my back, but when he'd catch me looking at him he'd grin and say, "Sweating plenty?" When my old man grinned, nobody could help but grin too. We'd keep right on running out toward the mountains and then my old man would yell, "Hey, Joe!" and I'd look back and he'd be sitting under a tree with a towel he'd had around his waist wrapped around his neck.

I'd come back and sit down beside him and he'd pull a rope out of his pocket and start skipping rope out in the sun with the sweat pouring off his face and him skipping rope out in the white dust with the rope going cloppetty, cloppetty, clop, clop, clop, and the sun hotter, and him working harder up and down a patch of the road. Say, it was a treat to see my old man skip rope, too. He could whirr it fast or lop it slow and fancy. Say, you ought to have seen wops look at us sometimes, when they'd come by, going into town walking along with big white steers hauling the cart. They sure looked as though they thought the old man was nuts. He'd start the rope whirring till they'd stop dead still and watch him, then give the steers a cluck and a poke with the goad and get going again.

When I'd sit watching him working out in the hot sun I sure felt fond of him. He sure was fun and he done his work so hard and he'd finish up with a regular whirring that'd drive the sweat out on his face like water and then sling the rope at the tree and come over and sit down with me and lean back against the tree with the towel and a sweater wrapped around his neck.

"Sure is hell keeping it down, Joe," he'd say and lean back and shut his eyes and breathe long and deep, "it ain't like when you're a kid." Then he'd get up before he started to cool and we'd jog along back to the stables. That's the way it was keeping down to weight. He was worried all the time. Most jocks can just about ride off all they want to. A jock loses about a kilo every time he rides, but my old man was sort of dried out and he couldn't keep down his kilos without all that running.

I remember once at San Siro, Regoli, a little wop, that was riding for Buzoni, came out across the paddock going to the bar for something cool; and flicking his boots with his whip, after he'd just weighed in and my old man had just weighed in too, and came out with the saddle under his arm looking red-faced and tired and too big for his silks and he stood there looking at young Regoli standing up to the outdoors bar, cool and kid-looking, and I says, "What's the matter, Dad?" 'cause I thought maybe Regoli had bumped him or something and he just looked at Regoli and said, "Oh, to hell with it," and went on to the dressing room.

Well, it would have been all right, maybe, if we'd stayed in Milan and ridden at Milan and Torino, 'cause if there ever were any easy courses, it's those two. "Pianola, Joe," my old man said when he dismounted in the winning stall after what the wops thought was a hell of a steeplechase. I asked him once. "This course rides itself. It's the pace you're going at, that makes riding the jumps dangerous, Joe. We ain't going any pace here, and they ain't any really bad jumps either. But it's the pace always — not the jumps that makes the trouble."

San Siro was the swellest course I'd ever seen but the old man said it was a dog's life. Going back and forth between Mirafiore and San Siro and riding just about every day in the week with a train ride every other night.

I was nuts about the horses, too. There's something about it, when they come out and go up the track to the post. Sort of dancy and tight looking with the jock keeping a tight hold on them and maybe easing off a little and letting them run a little going up. Then once they were at the barrier it got me worse than anything. Especially at San Siro with that big green infield and the mountains way off and the fat wop starter with his big whip and the jocks fiddling them around and then the barrier snapping up and that bell going off and them all getting off in a bunch and then commencing to string out. You know the way a bunch of skins gets off. If you're up in the stand with a pair of glasses all you see is them plunging off and then that bell goes off and it seems like it rings for a thousand years and then they come sweeping round the turn. There wasn't ever anything like it for me.

But my old man said one day, in the dressing room, when he was getting into his street clothes, "None of these things are horses, Joe. They'd

kill that bunch of skates for their hides and hoofs up at Paris." That was
the day he'd won the Premio Commercio with Lantorna shooting her
out of the field the last hundred meters like pulling a cork out of a bottle.

It was right after the Premio Commercio that we pulled out and left
Italy. My old man and Holbrook and a fat wop in a straw hat that kept
wiping his face with a handkerchief were having an argument at a table
in the Galleria. They were all talking French and the two of them were
after my old man about something. Finally he didn't say anything any
more but just sat there and looked at Holbrook, and the two of them
kept after him, first one talking and then the other, and the fat wop always butting in on Holbrook.

"You go out and buy me a *Sportsman,* will you, Joe?" my old man said,
and handed me a couple of soldi without looking away from Holbrook.

So I went out of the Galleria and walked over to in front of the Scala
and bought a paper, and came back and stood a little way away because I
didn't want to butt in and my old man was sitting back in his chair looking down at his coffee and fooling with a spoon and Holbrook and the
big wop were standing and the big wop was wiping his face and shaking
his head. And I came up and my old man acted just as though the two
of them weren't standing there and said, "Want an ice, Joe?" Holbrook
looked down at my old man and said slow and careful, "You son of a
bitch," and he and the fat wop went out through the tables.

My old man sat there and sort of smiled at me, but his face was white
and he looked sick as hell and I was scared and felt sick inside because I
knew something had happened and I didn't see how anybody could call
my old man a son of a bitch, and get away with it. My old man opened
up the *Sportsman* and studied the handicaps for a while and then he
said, "You got to take a lot of things in this world, Joe." And three days
later we left Milan for good on the Turin train for Paris, after an auction
sale out in front of Turner's stables of everything we couldn't get into a
trunk and a suit case.

We got into Paris early in the morning in a long, dirty station the old
man told me was the Gare de Lyon. Paris was an awful big town after
Milan. Seems like in Milan everybody is going somewhere and all the
trams run somewhere and there ain't any sort of a mix-up, but Paris is
all balled up and they never do straighten it out. I got to like it, though,
part of it, anyway, and say it's got the best race courses in the world.
Seems as though that were the thing that keeps it all going and about
the only thing you can figure on is that every day the buses will be going out to whatever track they're running at, going right out through

everything to the track. I never really got to know Paris well, because I just came in about once or twice a week with the old man from Maisons and he always sat at the Café de la Paix on the Opera side with the rest of the gang from Maisons and I guess that's one of the busiest parts of the town. But, say, it is funny that a big town like Paris wouldn't have a Galleria, isn't it?

Well, we went out to live at Maisons-Lafitte, where just about everybody lives except the gang at Chantilly, with a Mrs. Meyers that runs a boarding house. Maisons is about the swellest place to live I've ever seen in all my life. The town ain't so much, but there's a lake and a swell forest that we used to go off bumming in all day, a couple of us kids, and my old man made me a sling shot and we got a lot of things with it but the best one was a magpie. Young Dick Atkinson shot a rabbit with it one day and we put it under a tree and were all sitting around and Dick had some cigarettes and all of a sudden the rabbit jumped up and beat it into the brush and we chased it but we couldn't find it. Gee, we had fun at Maisons. Mrs. Meyers used to give me lunch in the morning and I'd be gone all day. I learned to talk French quick. It's an easy language.

As soon as we got to Maisons, my old man wrote to Milan for his license and he was pretty worried till it came. He used to sit around the Café de Paris in Maisons with the gang, there were lots of guys he'd known when he rode up at Paris, before the war, lived at Maisons, and there's a lot of time to sit around because the work around a racing stable, for the jocks, that is, is all cleaned up by nine o'clock in the morning. They take the first batch of skins out to gallop them at 5.30 in the morning and they work the second lot at 8 o'clock. That means getting up early all right and going to bed early, too. If a jock's riding for somebody too, he can't go boozing around because the trainer always has an eye on him if he's a kid and if he ain't a kid he's always got an eye on himself. So mostly if a jock ain't working he sits around the Café de Paris with the gang and they can all sit around about two or three hours in front of some drink like a vermouth and seltz and they talk and tell stories and shoot pool and it's sort of like a club or the Galleria in Milan. Only it ain't really like the Galleria because there everybody is going by all the time and there's everybody around at the tables.

Well, my old man got his license all right. They sent it through to him without a word and he rode a couple of times. Amiens, up country and that sort of thing, but he didn't seem to get any engagement. Everybody liked him and whenever I'd come in to the Café in the forenoon I'd find somebody drinking with him because my old man wasn't tight like most of these jockeys that have got the first dollar they made riding at the World's Fair in St. Louis in nineteen ought four. That's what my old man would say when he'd kid George Burns. But it seemed like everybody steered clear of giving my old man any mounts.

We went out to wherever they were running every day with the car from Maisons and that was the most fun of all. I was glad when the horses came back from Deauville and the summer. Even though it meant no more bumming in the woods, 'cause then we'd ride to Enghien or Tremblay or St. Cloud and watch them from the trainers' and jockeys' stand. I sure learned about racing from going out with that gang and the fun of it was going every day.

I remember once out at St. Cloud. It was a big two hundred thousand franc race with seven entries and Kzar a big favorite. I went around to the paddock to see the horses with my old man and you never saw such horses. This Kzar is a great big yellow horse that looks like just nothing but run. I never saw such a horse. He was being led around the paddocks with his head down and when he went by me I felt all hollow inside he was so beautiful. There never was such a wonderful, lean, running built horse. And he went around the paddock putting his feet just so and quiet and careful and moving easy like he knew just what he had to do and not jerking and standing up on his legs and getting wild eyed like you see these selling platers with a shot of dope in them. The crowd was so thick I couldn't see him again except just his legs going by and some yellow and my old man started out through the crowd and I followed him over to the jock's dressing room back in the trees and there was a big crowd around there, too, but the man at the door in a derby nodded to my old man and we got in and everybody was sitting around and getting dressed and pulling shirts over their heads and pulling boots on and it all smelled hot and sweaty and linimenty and outside was the crowd looking in.

The old man went over and sat down beside George Gardner that was getting into his pants and said, "What's the dope, George?" just in an ordinary tone of voice 'cause there ain't any use him feeling around because George either can tell him or he can't tell him.

"He won't win," George says very low, leaning over and buttoning the bottoms of his pants.

"Who will?" my old man says, leaning over close so nobody can hear.

"Kircubbin," George says, "and if he does, save me a couple of tickets."

My old man says something in a regular voice to George and George says, "Don't ever bet on anything, I tell you," kidding like, and we beat it out and through all the crowd that was looking in over to the 100 franc mutuel machine. But I knew something big was up because George is Kzar's jockey. On the way he gets one of the yellow odds-sheets with the starting prices on and Kzar is only paying 5 for 10, Cefisidote is next at 3 to 1 and fifth down the list this Kircubbin at 8 to 1. My old man bets five thousand on Kircubbin to win and puts on a thousand to place and we went around back of the grandstand to go up the stairs and get a place to watch the race.

We were jammed in tight and first a man in a long coat with a gray tall hat and a whip folded up in his hand came out and then one after another the horses, with the jocks up and a stable boy holding the bridle on each side and walking along, followed the old guy. That big yellow horse Kzar came first. He didn't look so big when you first looked at him until you saw the length of his legs and the whole way he's built and the way he moves. Gosh, I never saw such a horse. George Gardner was riding him and they moved along slow, back of the old guy in the gray tall hat that walked along like he was the ring master in a circus. Back of Kzar, moving along smooth and yellow in the sun, was a good looking black with a nice head with Tommy Archibald riding him; and after the black was a string of five more horses all moving along slow in a procession past the grandstand and the pesage. My old man said the black was Kircubbin and I took a good look at him and he was a nice looking horse, all right, but nothing like Kzar.

Everybody cheered Kzar when he went by and he sure was one swell-looking horse. The procession of them went around on the other side past the pelouse and then back up to the near end of the course and the circus master had the stable boys turn them loose one after another so they could gallop by the stands on their way up to the post and let everybody have a good look at them. They weren't at the post hardly any time at all when the gong started and you could see them way off across the infield all in a bunch starting on the first swing like a lot of little toy horses. I was watching them through the glasses and Kzar was running well back, with one of the bays making the pace. They swept down and around and came pounding past and Kzar was way back when they passed us and this Kircubbin horse in front and going smooth. Gee, it's awful when they go by you and then you have to watch them go farther away and get smaller and smaller and then all bunched up on the turns and then come around towards into the stretch and you feel like swearing and goddamming worse and worse. Finally they made the last turn and came into the straightaway with this Kircubbin horse way out in front. Everybody was looking funny and saying "Kzar" in sort of a sick way and them pounding nearer down the stretch, and then something came out of the pack right into my glasses like a horse-headed yellow streak and everybody began to yell "Kzar" as though they were crazy. Kzar came on faster than I'd ever seen anything in my life and pulled up on Kircubbin that was going fast as any black horse could go with the jock flogging hell out of him with the gad and they were right dead neck and neck for a second but Kzar seemed going about twice as fast with those great jumps and that head out—but it was while they were neck and neck that they passed the winning post and when the numbers went up in the slots the first one was 2 and that meant Kircubbin had won.

I felt all trembly and funny inside, and then we were all jammed in with the people going downstairs to stand in front of the board where they'd post what Kircubbin paid. Honest, watching the race I'd forgot how much my old man had bet on Kircubbin. I'd wanted Kzar to win so damned bad. But now it was all over it was swell to know we had the winner.

"Wasn't it a swell race, Dad?" I said to him. He looked at me sort of funny with his derby on the back of his head. "George Gardner's a swell jockey, all right," he said. "It sure took a great jock to keep that Kzar horse from winning."

Of course I knew it was funny all the time. But my old man saying that right out like that sure took the kick all out of it for me and I didn't get the real kick back again ever, even when they posted the numbers up on the board and the bell rang to pay off and we saw that Kircubbin paid 67.50 for 10. All round people were saying, "Poor Kzar! Poor Kzar!" And I thought, I wish I were a jockey and could have rode him instead of that son of a bitch. And that was funny, thinking of George Gardner as a son of a bitch because I'd always liked him and besides he'd given us the winner, but I guess that's what he is, all right.

My old man had a big lot of money after that race and he took to coming into Paris oftener. If they raced at Tremblay he'd have them drop him in town on their way back to Maisons, and he and I'd sit out in front of the Café de la Paix and watch the people go by. It's funny sitting there. There's streams of people going by and all sorts of guys come up and want to sell you things, and I loved to sit there with my old man. That was when we'd have the most fun. Guys would come by selling funny rabbits that jumped if you squeezed a bulb and they'd come up to us and my old man would kid with them. He could talk French just like

English and all those kind of guys knew him 'cause you can always tell
a jockey — and then we always sat at the same table and they got used to
seeing us there. There were guys selling matrimonial papers and girls
selling rubber eggs that when you squeezed them a rooster came out of
them and one old wormy-looking guy that went by with postcards of
Paris, showing them to everybody, and, of course, nobody ever bought
any, and then he would come back and show the under side of the pack
and they would all be smutty postcards and lots of people would dig
down and buy them. Gee, I remember the funny people that used to go
by. Girls around supper time looking for somebody to take them out to
eat and they'd speak to my old man and he'd make some joke at them
in French and they'd pat me on the head and go on. Once there was an
American woman sitting with her kid daughter at the next table to us
and they were both eating ices and I kept looking at the girl and she was
awfully good looking and I smiled at her and she smiled at me but that
was all that ever came of it because I looked for her mother and her every day and I made up ways that I was going to speak to her and I wondered if I got to know her if her mother would let me take her out to Auteuil or Tremblay but I never saw either of them again. Anyway, I guess
it wouldn't have been any good, anyway, because looking back on it I remember the way I thought out would be best to speak to her was to say,
"Pardon me, but perhaps I can give you a winner at Enghien today?"
and, after all, maybe she would have thought I was a tout instead of really trying to give her a winner.

We'd sit at the Café de la Paix, my old man and me, and we had a big
drag with the waiter because my old man drank whisky and it cost five
francs, and that meant a good tip when the saucers were counted up. My
old man was drinking more than I'd ever seen him, but he wasn't riding at all now and besides he said that whisky kept his weight down. But
I noticed he was putting it on, all right, just the same. He'd busted away
from his old gang out at Maisons and seemed to like just sitting around
on the boulevard with me. But he was dropping money every day at the
track. He'd feel sort of doleful after the last race, if he'd lost on the day,
until we'd get to our table and he'd have his first whisky and then he'd be
fine.

He'd be reading the *Paris-Sport* and he'd look over at me and say,
"Where's your girl, Joe?" to kid me on account I had told him about the
girl that day at the next table. And I'd get red, but I liked being kidded
about her. It gave me a good feeling. "Keep your eye peeled for her, Joe,"
he'd say, "she'll be back." He'd ask me questions about things and some

of the things I'd say he'd laugh. And then he'd get started talking about things. About riding down in Egypt, or at St. Moritz on the ice before my mother died, and about during the war when they had regular races down in the south of France without any purses, or betting or crowd or anything just to keep the breed up. Regular races with the jocks riding hell out of the horses. Gee, I could listen to my old man talk by the hour, especially when he'd had a couple or so of drinks. He'd tell me about when he was a boy in Kentucky and going coon hunting, and the old days in the States before everything went on the bum there. And he'd say, "Joe, when we've got a decent stake, you're going back there to the States and go to school."

"What've I got to go back there to go to school for when everything's on the bum there?" I'd ask him. "That's different," he'd say and get the waiter over and pay the pile of saucers and we'd get a taxi to the Gare St. Lazare and get on the train out to Maisons.

One day at Auteuil, after a selling steeplechase, my old man bought in the winner for 30,000 francs. He had to bid a little to get him but the stable let the horse go finally and my old man had his permit and his colors in a week. Gee, I felt proud when my old man was an owner. He fixed it up for stable space with Charles Drake and cut out coming in to Paris, and started his running and sweating out again, and him and I were the whole stable gang. Our horse's name was Gilford, he was Irish bred and a nice, sweet jumper. My old man figured that training him and riding him, himself, he was a good investment. I was proud of everything and I thought Gilford was as good a horse as Kzar. He was a good, solid jumper, a bay, with plenty of speed on the flat, if you asked him for it, and he was a nice-looking horse, too. Gee, I was fond of him. The first time he started with my old man up, he finished third in a 2,500 meter hurdle race and when my old man got off him, all sweating and happy in the place stall, and went in to weigh, I felt as proud of him as though it was the first race he'd ever placed in. You see, when a guy ain't been riding for a long time, you can't make yourself really believe that he has ever rode. The whole thing was different now, 'cause down in Milan, even big races never seemed to make any difference to my old man, if he won he wasn't ever excited or anything, and now it was so I couldn't hardly sleep the night before a race and I knew my old man was excited, too, even if he didn't show it. Riding for yourself makes an awful difference.

Second time Gilford and my old man started, was a rainy Sunday at Auteuil, in the Prix du Marat, a 4,500 meter steeplechase. As soon as he'd gone out I beat it up in the stand with the new glasses my old man had bought for me to watch them. They started way over at the far end of the course and there was some trouble at the barrier. Something with goggle blinders on was making a great fuss and rearing around and busted the barrier once, but I could see my old man in our black jacket, with a white cross and a black cap, sitting up on Gilford, and patting him with his hand. Then they were off in a jump and out of sight behind the trees and the gong going for dear life and the parimutuel wickets rattling down. Gosh, I was so excited, I was afraid to look at them, but I fixed the glasses on the place where they would come out back of the trees and then out they came with the old black jacket going third and they all sailing over the jump like birds. Then they went out of sight again and then they came pounding out and down the hill and all going nice and sweet and easy and taking the fence smooth in a bunch, and moving away from us all solid. Looked as though you could walk across on their backs they were all so bunched and going so smooth. Then they bellied over the big double Bullfinch and something came down. I couldn't see who it was, but in a minute the horse was up and galloping free and the field, all bunched still, sweeping around the long left turn into the straightaway. They jumped the stone wall and came jammed down the stretch toward the big water-jump right in front of the stands. I saw them coming and hollered at my old man as he went by, and he was leading by about a length and riding way out, and light as a monkey, and they were racing for the water-jump. They took off over the big hedge of the water-jump in a pack and then there was a crash, and two horses pulled sideways out off it, and kept on going, and three others were piled up. I couldn't see my old man anywhere. One horse kneed himself up and the jock had hold of the bridle and mounted and went slamming on after the place money. The other horse was up and away by himself, jerking his head and galloping with the bridle rein hanging and the jock staggered over to one side of the track against the fence. Then Gilford rolled over to one side off my old man and got up and started to run on three legs with his off hoof dangling and there was my old man laying there on the grass flat out with his face up and blood all over the side of his head. I ran down the stand and bumped into a jam of people and got to the rail and a cop grabbed me and held me and two big stretcher-bearers were going out after my old man and around on the other side of the course I saw three horses, strung way out, coming out of the trees and taking the jump. My old man was dead when they brought him in and while a doctor was listening to his heart with a thing plugged in his ears, I heard a shot up the track that meant they'd killed Gilford. I lay down beside my old man, when they carried the stretcher into the hospital room, and hung onto the stretcher and cried and cried, and he looked so white and gone and so awfully dead, and I couldn't help feeling that if my old man was dead maybe they didn't need to have shot Gilford. His hoof might have got well. I don't know. I loved my old man so much.

Then a couple of guys came in and one of them patted me on the back and then went over and looked at my old man and then pulled a sheet off the cot and spread it over him; and the other was telephoning in French for them to send the ambulance to take him out to Maisons. And I couldn't stop crying, crying and choking, sort of, and George Gardner came in and sat down beside me on the floor and put his arm around me and says, "Come on, Joe, old boy. Get up and we'll go out and wait for the ambulance." George and I went out to the gate and I was trying to stop bawling and George wiped off my face with his handkerchief and we were standing back a little ways while the crowd was going out of the gate and a couple of guys stopped near us while we were waiting for the crowd to get through the gate and one of them was counting a bunch of mutuel tickets and he said, "Well, Butler got his, all right."

The other guy said, "I don't give a good goddam if he did, the crook. He had it coming to him on the stuff he's pulled."

"I'll say he had," said the other guy, and tore the bunch of tickets in two.

And George Gardner looked at me to see if I'd heard and I had all right and he said, "Don't you listen to what those bums said, Joe. Your old man was one swell guy."

But I don't know. Seems like when they get started they don't leave a guy nothing.

1925

RING LARDNER
HAIRCUT

from *Liberty*

RING LARDNER (1885–1933) was born in Niles, Michigan. After writing for newspapers for many years, he published *You Know Me Al,* a novel written as letters from a minor-league baseball player. Series editor Martha Foley wrote, "Hiding behind the seeming good humor of light entertainment . . . is a terrific bitterness. Lardner hates his people. He cynically strips them to show them as cruel, vicious and stupid."

Groucho Marx once revealed that Lardner preferred to write in hotel rooms, with the blinds drawn so he would not be seen. Lardner published numerous story collections, including *How to Write Short Stories* and *The Love Nest.* He wrote during Prohibition, and in speakeasies he befriended a variety of people, from prizefighters to actors. His work achieved both commercial success and literary acclaim.

Lardner had an impact on both F. Scott Fitzgerald and Ernest Hemingway. He and Fitzgerald became friends, although Fitzgerald once wrote, "Whatever Ring's achievement was it fell short of the achievement he was capable of, and this because of a cynical attitude toward his work." Still, Foley called Lardner "a master of black humor." He died at the age of forty-eight in New York.

★

I GOT ANOTHER BARBER that comes over from Carterville and helps me out Saturdays, but the rest of the time I can get along all right alone. You can see for yourself that this ain't no New York City and besides that, the most of the boys works all day and don't have no leisure to drop in here and get themselves prettied up.

You're a newcomer, ain't you? I thought I hadn't seen you round before. I hope you like it good enough to stay. As I say, we ain't no New York City or Chicago, but we have pretty good times. Not as good, though, since Jim Kendall got killed. When he was alive, him and Hod

Meyers used to keep this town in an uproar. I bet they was more laughin'
done here than any town its size in America.

Jim was comical, and Hod was pretty near a match for him. Since
Jim's gone, Hod tries to hold his end up just the same as ever, but it's
tough goin' when you ain't got nobody to kind of work with.

They used to be plenty fun in here Saturdays. This place is jam-
packed Saturdays, from four o'clock on. Jim and Hod would show up
right after their supper, round six o'clock. Jim would set himself down
in that big chair, nearest the blue spittoon. Whoever had been settin' in
that chair, why they'd get up when Jim come in and give it to him.

You'd have thought it was a reserved seat like they have sometimes in
a theayter. Hod would generally always stand or walk up and down, or
some Saturdays, of course, he'd be settin' in this chair part of the time,
gettin' a haircut.

Well, Jim would set there a w'ile without openin' his mouth only to
spit, and then finally he'd say to me, "Whitey,"— my right name, that is,
my right first name, is Dick, but everybody round here calls me Whitey
—Jim would say, "Whitey, your nose looks like a rosebud tonight. You
must of been drinkin' some of your aw de cologne."

So I'd say, "No, Jim, but you look like you'd been drinkin' somethin'
of that kind or somethin' worse."

Jim would have to laugh at that, but then he'd speak up and say, "No, I
ain't had nothin' to drink, but that ain't sayin' I wouldn't like somethin'.
I wouldn't even mind if it was wood alcohol."

Then Hod Meyers would say, "Neither would your wife." That would
set everybody to laughin' because Jim and his wife wasn't on very good
terms. She'd of divorced him only they wasn't no chance to get alimony
and she didn't have no way to take care of herself and the kids. She
couldn't never understand Jim. He *was* kind of rough, but a good fella at
heart.

Him and Hod had all kinds of sport with Milt Sheppard. I don't suppose you've seen Milt. Well, he's got an Adam's apple that looks more
like a mushmelon. So I'd be shavin' Milt and when I start to shave down
here on his neck, Hod would holler, "Hey, Whitey, wait a minute! Before
you cut into it, let's make up a pool and see who can guess closest to the
number of seeds."

And Jim would say, "If Milt hadn't of been so hoggish, he'd of ordered
a half a cantaloupe instead of a whole one and it might not of stuck in
his throat."

All the boys would roar at this and Milt himself would force a smile, though the joke was on him. Jim certainly was a card!

There's his shavin' mug, settin' on the shelf, right next to Charley Vail's. "Charles M. Vail." That's the druggist. He comes in regular for his shave, three times a week. And Jim's is the cup next to Charley's. "James H. Kendall." Jim won't need no shavin' mug no more, but I'll leave it there just the same for old time's sake. Jim certainly was a character!

Years ago, Jim used to travel for a canned goods concern over in Carterville. They sold canned goods. Jim had the whole northern half of the state and was on the road five days out of every week. He'd drop in here Saturdays and tell his experiences for that week. It was rich.

I guess he paid more attention to playin' jokes than makin' sales. Finally the concern let him out and he come right home here and told everybody he'd been fired instead of sayin' he'd resigned like most fellas would of.

It was a Saturday and the shop was full and Jim got up out of that chair and says, "Gentlemen, I got an important announcement to make. I been fired from my job."

Well, they asked him if he was in earnest and he said he was and nobody could think of nothin' to say till Jim finally broke the ice himself. He says, "I been sellin' canned goods and now I'm canned goods myself."

You see, the concern he'd been workin' for was a factory that made canned goods. Over in Carterville. And now Jim said he was canned himself. He was certainly a card!

Jim had a great trick that he used to play w'ile he was travelin'. For instance, he'd be ridin' on a train and they'd come to some little town like, well, like, we'll say, like Benton. Jim would look out the train window and read the signs on the stores.

For instance, they'd be a sign, "Henry Smith, Dry Goods." Well, Jim would write down the name and the name of the town and when he got to wherever he was goin' he'd mail back a postal card to Henry Smith at Benton and not sign no name to it, but he'd write on the card, well, somethin' like "Ask your wife about that book agent that spent the afternoon last week," or "Ask your Missus who kept her from gettin' lonesome the last time you was in Carterville." And he'd sign the card, "A Friend."

Of course, he never knew what really come of none of these jokes, but he could picture what *probably* happened and that was enough.

Jim didn't work very steady after he lost his position with the Carterville people. What he did earn, doin' odd jobs round town, why he spent pretty near all of it on gin and his family might of starved if the stores hadn't of carried them along. Jim's wife tried her hand at dressmakin', but they ain't nobody goin' to get rich makin' dresses in this town.

As I say, she'd of divorced Jim, only she seen that she couldn't support herself and the kids and she was always hopin' that some day Jim would cut out his habits and give her more than two or three dollars a week.

They was a time when she would go to whoever he was workin' for and ask them to give her his wages, but after she done this once or twice, he beat her to it by borrowin' most of his pay in advance. He told it all round town, how he had outfoxed his Missus. He certainly was a caution!

But he wasn't satisfied with just outwittin' her. He was sore the way she had acted, tryin' to grab off his pay. And he made up his mind he'd get even. Well, he waited till Evans's Circus was advertised to come to town. Then he told his wife and two kiddies that he was goin' to take them to the circus. The day of the circus, he told them he would get the tickets and meet them outside the entrance to the tent.

Well, he didn't have no intentions of bein' there or buyin' tickets or nothin'. He got full of gin and laid round Wright's poolroom all day. His wife and kids waited and waited and of course he didn't show up. His wife didn't have a dime with her, or nowhere else, I guess. So she finally had to tell the kids it was all off and they cried like they wasn't never goin' to stop.

Well, it seems, w'ile they was cryin', Doc Stair came along and he asked what was the matter, but Mrs. Kendall was stubborn and wouldn't tell him, but the kids told him and he insisted on takin' them and their mother in to the show. Jim found this out afterwards and it was one reason why he had it in for Doc Stair.

Doc Stair come here about a year and a half ago. He's a mighty handsome young fella and his clothes always look like he has them made to order. He goes to Detroit two or three times a year and w'ile he's there he must have a tailor take his measure and then make him a suit to order. They cost pretty near twice as much, but they fit a whole lot better than if you just bought them in a store.

For a w'ile everybody was wonderin' why a young doctor like Doc Stair should come to a town like this where we already got old Doc Gamble and Doc Foote that's both been here for years and all the practice in town was already divided between the two of them.

Then they was a story got round that Doc Stair's gal had throwed him over, a gal up in the Northern Peninsula somewheres, and the reason he come here was to hide himself away and forget it. He said himself that he thought they wasn't nothin' like general practice in a place like ours to fit a man to be a good all round doctor. And that's why he'd came.

Anyways, it wasn't long before he was makin' enough to live on, though they tell me that he never dunned nobody for what they owed him, and the folks here certainly has got the owin' habit, even in my business. If I had all that was comin' to me for just shaves alone, I could go to Carterville and put up at the Mercer for a week and see a different picture every night. For instance, they's old George Purdy—but I guess I shouldn't ought to be gossipin'.

Well, last year, our coroner died, died of the flu. Ken Beatty, that was his name. He was the coroner. So they had to choose another man to be coroner in his place and they picked Doc Stair. He laughed at first and said he didn't want it, but they made him take it. It ain't no job that any-body would fight for and what a man makes out of it in a year would just about buy seeds for their garden. Doc's the kind, though, that can't say no to nothin' if you keep at him long enough.

But I was goin' to tell you about a poor boy we got here in town— Paul Dickson. He fell out of a tree when he was about ten years old. Lit on his head and it done somethin' to him and he ain't never been right. No harm in him, but just silly. Jim Kendall used to call him cuckoo; that's a name Jim had for anybody that was off their head, only he called people's head their bean. That was another of his gags, callin' head bean and callin' crazy people cuckoo. Only poor Paul ain't crazy, but just silly.

You can imagine that Jim used to have all kinds of fun with Paul. He'd send him to the White Front Garage for a left-handed monkey wrench. Of course they ain't they no such a thing as a left-handed monkey wrench.

And once we had a kind of a fair here and they was a baseball game between the fats and the leans and before the game started Jim called Paul over and sent him way down to Schrader's hardware store to get a key for the pitcher's box.

They wasn't nothin' in the way of gags that Jim couldn't think up, when he put his mind to it.

Poor Paul was always kind of suspicious of people, maybe on account of how Jim had kept foolin' him. Paul wouldn't have much to do with anybody only his own mother and Doc Stair and a girl here in town named Julie Gregg. That is, she ain't a girl no more, but pretty near thirty or over.

When Doc first came to town, Paul seemed to feel like here was a real friend and he hung around Doc's office most of the w'ile; the only time he wasn't there was when he'd go home to eat or sleep or when he seen Julie Gregg doin' her shoppin'.

When he looked out Doc's window and seen her, he'd run downstairs and join her and tag along with her to the different stores. The poor boy was crazy about Julie and she always treated him mighty nice and made him feel like he was welcome, though of course it wasn't nothin' but pity on her side.

Doc done all he could to improve Paul's mind and he told me once that he really thought the boy was gettin' better, that they was times when he was as bright and sensible as anybody else.

But I was goin' to tell you about Julie Gregg. Old Man Gregg was in the lumber business, but got to drinkin' and lost the most of his money and when he died, he didn't leave nothin' but the house and just enough insurance for the girl to skimp along on.

Her mother was a kind of a half invalid and didn't hardly ever leave the house. Julie wanted to sell the place and move somewheres else after the old man died, but the mother said she was born here and would die here. It was tough on Julie, as the young people round this town — well, she's too good for them.

She's been away to school and Chicago and New York and different places and they ain't no subject she can't talk on, where you take the rest of the young folks here and you mention anything to them outside of Gloria Swanson or Tommy Meighan and they think you're delirious. Did you see Gloria in *Wages of Virtue*? You missed somethin'!

Well, Doc Stair hadn't been here more than a week when he come in one day to get shaved and I recognized who he was as he had been pointed out to me, so I told him about my old lady. She's been ailin' for a couple years and either Doc Gamble or Doc Foote, neither one, seemed to be helpin' her. So he said he would come out and see her, but if she was able to get out herself, it would be better to bring her to his office where he could make a complete examination.

So I took her to his office and w'ile I was waitin' for her in the reception room, in come Julie Gregg. When somebody comes in Doc Stair's office, they's a bell that rings in his inside office so he can tell they's somebody to see him.

So he left my old lady inside and come out to the front office and that's the first time him and Julie met and I guess it was what they call love at first sight. But it wasn't fifty-fifty. This young fella was the slickest lookin' fella she'd ever seen in this town and she went wild over him. To him she was just a young lady that wanted to see the doctor.

She'd came on about the same business I had. Her mother had been doctorin' for years with Doc Gamble and Doc Foote and without no results. So she'd heard they was a new doc in town and decided to give him a try. He promised to call and see her mother that same day.

I said a minute ago that it was love at first sight on her part. I'm not only judgin' by how she acted afterwards but how she looked at him that first day in his office. I ain't no mind reader, but it was wrote all over her face that she was gone.

Now Jim Kendall, besides bein' a jokesmith and a pretty good drinker, well, Jim was quite a lady-killer. I guess he run pretty wild durin' the time he was on the road for them Carterville people, and besides that, he'd had a couple little affairs of the heart right here in town. As I say, his wife could of divorced him, only she couldn't.

But Jim was like the majority of men, and women, too, I guess. He wanted what he couldn't get. He wanted Julie Gregg and worked his head off tryin' to land her. Only he'd of said bean instead of head.

Well, Jim's habits and his jokes didn't appeal to Julie and of course he was a married man, so he didn't have no more chance than, well, than a rabbit. That's an expression of Jim's himself. When somebody didn't have no chance to get elected or somethin', Jim would always say they didn't have no more chance than a rabbit.

He didn't make no bones about how he felt. Right in here, more than once, in front of the whole crowd, he said he was stuck on Julie and anybody that could get her for him was welcome to his house and his wife and kids included. But she wouldn't have nothin' to do with him; wouldn't even speak to him on the street. He finally seen he wasn't gettin' nowheres with his usual line so he decided to try the rough stuff. He went right up to her house one evenin' and when she opened the door he forced his way in and grabbed her. But she broke loose and before he could stop her, she run in the next room and locked the door and phoned to Joe Barnes. Joe's the marshal. Jim could hear who she was phonin' to and he beat it before Joe got there.

Joe was an old friend of Julie's pa. Joe went to Jim the next day and told him what would happen if he ever done it again.

I don't know how the news of this little affair leaked out. Chances is that Joe Barnes told his wife and she told somebody else's wife and they told their husband. Anyways, it did leak out and Hod Meyers had the

nerve to kid Jim about it, right here in this shop. Jim didn't deny nothin'
and kind of laughed it off and said for us all to wait; that lots of people
had tried to make a monkey out of him, but he always got even.

Meanw'ile everybody in town was wise to Julie's bein' wild mad over
the Doc. I don't suppose she had any idea how her face changed when
him and her was together; of course she couldn't of, or she'd of kept
away from him. And she didn't know that we was all noticin' how many
times she made excuses to go up to his office or pass it on the other side
of the street and look up in his window to see if he was there. I felt sorry
for her and so did most other people.

Hod Meyers kept rubbin' it into Jim about how the Doc had cut him
out. Jim didn't pay no attention to the kiddin' and you could see he was
plannin' one of his jokes.

One trick Jim had was the knack of changin' his voice. He could make
you think he was a girl talkin' and he could mimic any man's voice. To
show you how good he was along this line, I'll tell you the joke he played
on me once.

You know, in most towns of any size, when a man is dead and needs a
shave, why the barber that shaves him soaks him five dollars for the job;
that is, he don't soak *him,* but whoever ordered the shave. I just charge
three dollars because personally I don't mind much shavin' a dead person. They lay a whole lot stiller than live customers. The only thing is
that you don't feel like talkin' to them and you get kind of lonesome.

Well, about the coldest day we ever had here, two years ago last winter, the phone rung at the house w'ile I was home to dinner and I answered the phone and it was a woman's voice and she said she was Mrs.
John Scott and her husband was dead and would I come out and shave
him.

Old John had always been a good customer of mine. But they live
seven miles out in the country, on the Streeter road. Still I didn't see
how I could say no.

So I said I would be there, but would have to come in a jitney and it
might cost three or four dollars besides the price of the shave. So she,
or the voice, it said that was all right, so I got Frank Abbott to drive me
out to the place and when I got there, who should open the door but old
John himself! He wasn't no more dead than, well, than a rabbit.

It didn't take no private detective to figure out who had played me
this little joke. Nobody could of thought it up but Jim Kendall. He certainly was a card!

I tell you this incident just to show you how he could disguise his voice and make you believe it was somebody else talkin'. I'd of swore it was Mrs. Scott had called me. Anyways, some woman.

Well, Jim waited till he had Doc Stair's voice down pat; then he went after revenge.

He called Julie up on a night when he knew Doc was over in Carterville. She never questioned but what it was Doc's voice. Jim said he must see her that night; he couldn't wait no longer to tell her somethin'. She was all excited and told him to come to the house. But he said he was expectin' an important long distance call and wouldn't she please forget her manners for once and come to his office. He said they couldn't nothin' hurt her and nobody would see her and he just *must* talk to her a little w'ile. Well, poor Julie fell for it.

Doc always keeps a night light in his office, so it looked to Julie like they was somebody there.

Meanw'ile Jim Kendall had went to Wright's poolroom, where they was a whole gang amusin' themselves. The most of them had drank plenty of gin, and they was a rough bunch even when sober. They was always strong for Jim's jokes and when he told them to come with him and see some fun they give up their card games and pool games and followed along.

Doc's office is on the second floor. Right outside his door they's a flight of stairs leadin' to the floor above. Jim and his gang hid in the dark behind these stairs.

Well, Julie come up to Doc's door and rung the bell and they was nothin' doin'. She rung it again and she rung it seven or eight times. Then she tried the door and found it locked. Then Jim made some kind of noise and she heard it and waited a minute, and then she says, "Is that you, Ralph?" Ralph is Doc's first name.

They was no answer and it must of came to her all of a sudden that she'd been bunked. She pretty near fell downstairs and the whole gang after her. They chased her all the way home, hollerin', "Is that you, Ralph?" and "Oh, Ralphie, dear, is that you?" Jim says he couldn't holler it himself, as he was laughin' too hard.

Poor Julie! She didn't show up here on Main Street for a long, long time afterward.

And of course Jim and his gang told everybody in town, everybody but Doc Stair. They was scared to tell him, and he might of never knowed only for Paul Dickson. The poor cuckoo, as Jim called him, he was here in the shop one night when Jim was still gloatin' yet over what

he'd done to Julie. And Paul took in as much of it as he could understand and he run to Doc with the story.

It's a cinch Doc went up in the air and swore he'd make Jim suffer.
But it was a kind of a delicate thing, because if it got out that he had beat
Jim up, Julie was bound to hear of it and then she'd know that Doc knew
and of course knowin' that he knew would make it worse for her than
ever. He was goin' to do somethin', but it took a lot of figurin'.

Well, it was a couple days later when Jim was here in the shop again,
and so was the cuckoo. Jim was goin' duck-shootin' the next day and
had come in lookin' for Hod Meyers to go with him. I happened to
know that Hod had went over to Carterville and wouldn't be home till
the end of the week. So Jim said he hated to go alone and he guessed he
would call it off. Then poor Paul spoke up and said if Jim would take
him he would go along. Jim thought a w'ile and then he said, well, he
guessed a half-wit was better than nothin'.

I suppose he was plottin' to get Paul out in the boat and play some
joke on him, like pushin' him in the water. Anyways, he said Paul could
go. He asked him had he ever shot a duck and Paul said no, he'd never
even had a gun in his hands. So Jim said he could set in the boat and
watch him and if he behaved himself, he might lend him his gun for a
couple of shots. They made a date to meet in the mornin' and that's the
last I seen of Jim alive.

Next mornin', I hadn't been open more than ten minutes when Doc
Stair come in. He looked kind of nervous. He asked me had I seen Paul
Dickson. I said no, but I knew where he was, out duck-shootin' with Jim
Kendall. So Doc says that's what he had heard, and he couldn't under-
stand it because Paul had told him he wouldn't never have no more to
do with Jim as long as he lived.

He said Paul had told him about the joke Jim had played on Julie. He
said Paul had asked him what he thought of the joke and the Doc had
told him that anybody that would do a thing like that ought not to be let
live.

I said it had been a kind of a raw thing, but Jim just couldn't resist
no kind of joke, no matter how raw. I said I thought he was all right at
heart, but just bubblin' over with mischief. Doc turned and walked out.

At noon he got a phone call from old John Scott. The lake where Jim
and Paul had went shootin' is on John's place. Paul had came runnin' up
to the house a few minutes before and said they'd been an accident. Jim
had shot a few ducks and then give the gun to Paul and told him to try

his luck. Paul hadn't never handled a gun and he was nervous. He was shakin' so hard that he couldn't control the gun. He let fire and Jim sunk back in the boat, dead.

Doc Stair, bein' the coroner, jumped in Frank Abbott's flivver and rushed out to Scott's farm. Paul and old John was down on the shore of the lake. Paul had rowed the boat to shore, but they'd left the body in it, waitin' for Doc to come.

Doc examined the body and said they might as well fetch it back to town. They was no use leavin' it there or callin' a jury, as it was a plain case of accidental shootin'.

Personally I wouldn't never leave a person shoot a gun in the same boat I was in unless I was sure they knew somethin' about guns. Jim was a sucker to leave a new beginner have his gun, let alone a half-wit. It probably served Jim right, what he got. But still we miss him round here. He certainly was a card!

Comb it wet or dry?

1930-1940

IN 1930, THE SAME YEAR THAT HIS WIFE DIED, SERIES
editor Edward O'Brien met Ruth Gorgel, a poor sixteen-year-old German girl. To the surprise and dismay of his family and friends, he married her soon after. They had two daughters, and O'Brien began to travel yet more in order to drum up work and money to support his growing family.

He became a highly public figure, both in England, where he often hosted visiting Rhodes Scholars, and in the United States, where he traveled on grueling lecture tours. He once wrote to Ruth that he rarely had time to go to the bathroom or enjoy more than fifteen minutes to himself. He was treated like a celebrity and juggled dozens of interviews, lectures, and business lunches, sometimes daily. He was asked in one interview how he found the time to read so many stories. He replied that over time, his reading speed had increased. He also said, "You don't have to swallow an oyster to know that it's bad."

He continued to live in England, removed from the daily realities of the Depression. He hardly mentioned the dire situation in the United States in his forewords. He did take note, though, when sales of the series began to plummet. His *Best American* and *Best British* story volumes were combined in 1934 as a result of low sales of both. Smaller magazines began to go under. In the 1930s, just three weekly general-interest magazines maintained a circulation of over one million: *The Saturday Evening Post, Liberty,* and *Collier's*. But "glossy" magazines — especially women's magazines, many of which featured fiction — held their ground.

During the Depression, southern writing, often dark and agrarian, came to the fore. In 1931 O'Brien wrote, "The old pretentiousness is gone. The false sentiment is gone. The 'hard-boiled mask' is gone. The reader is now confronted with two or three people and a situation." He went on: "The American scene is dusty and colorless. Its beauty and meaning depend on line and mass rather than on colour and decorative detail. The beauty of American life is not exterior. It is a hidden beauty which requires patient search to reward the finder."

Also during this time, stories became more political and socially conscious. Writers like Theodore Dreiser, Erskine Caldwell, Meridel LeSueur, and John Steinbeck explored injustices associated with class, gender, and race. O'Brien did not hide his political preferences, at least when it came to short fiction. In 1935 he admitted, "During the past four or five years, it is on the left rather than on the right that I have found the most fruitful interpretation of American life by the short story writer."

Some critics continued to clamor for O'Brien to choose stories with more intrigue and plot. In 1936 he responded: "What I do object to is the short story that exists for the sake of the plot. The plot, after all, is merely a skeleton which the story clothes. The story which exists for the sake of the plot is merely a grinning and repulsive skeleton without flesh and blood."

One "small" magazine that was started during this time made a significant impact on the publishing world: *Story*. Martha Foley and her husband, Whit Burnett, founded the magazine while they were serving as foreign correspondents in Vienna. Foley wrote, "We did not plan to spend our lives at ephemeral day-to-day reporting. We wanted to produce literature." Foley and Burnett's first idea was to present *Story* as a catalogue of potential new writers for fiction editors. The first publication, sixty-seven mimeographed copies, opened with their statement of purpose: "[*Story* will] present short narratives of significance by no matter whom and coming from no matter where ... [it will be] a sort of proof-book of hitherto unpublished manuscripts." Foley and Burnett were soon flooded with submissions, and *Story* became a bona fide bimonthly magazine.

O'Brien was a fan of Whit Burnett's own fiction and was enthusiastic about *Story* right away. His support bolstered the magazine's reputation and visibility. Random House contacted Foley and Burnett and offered to publish *Story* when the two returned to the United States. The new publishing house, primarily a reprint house at the time, drew a flood of new talent with the publication of *Story*. Foley and Burnett were the first to publish a number of writers who went on to achieve major success:

Charles Bukowski, Erskine Caldwell, Tennessee Williams, J. D. Salinger, William Saroyan, and John Cheever, among others.

In 1936 *Story* announced its plan to begin publishing longer stories, coining the English word *novella:* "We have gone somewhat far afield, and are bringing back the ancient and traditional Italian word novella for this neglected but highly important and eminently readable literary form." There was and still is much disagreement over the "official" length of a novella. Stephen King once called the genre "an ill-defined and disreputable literary banana republic."

O'Brien visited Hollywood, where he met Edwin Knopf, the brother of Alfred Knopf, Romer's American publisher. Edwin Knopf headed a major department at MGM, and after a luncheon party with Clark Gable, Spencer Tracy, Luise Rainer, Greta Garbo, and two producers—"I think it was a psychological test to see how I would act"—Knopf offered O'Brien work as MGM's "European Scenario Editor." The job would mean instant affluence and an even higher profile. O'Brien took the job but continued his work with the story anthology and his many other editorial projects. His grueling schedule became even worse. He allowed himself only weekday evenings, Saturdays, and Sunday mornings for nonfilm work.

★ ★ ★

1931

F. SCOTT FITZGERALD
BABYLON REVISITED

from *The Saturday Evening Post*

F. SCOTT FITZGERALD (1896–1940) was born in St. Paul, Minnesota, and went to Princeton University. While training in army boot camp, he wrote a draft of his first novel, *This Side of Paradise*. His next two books were collections of short stories: *Flappers and Philosophers* and *Tales of the Jazz Age*. Fitzgerald became renowned as a fictional chronicler of the Jazz Age as well as a keen social critic.

Series editor Edward O'Brien did not select many of Fitzgerald's short stories for *The Best American Short Stories*, which angered Fitzgerald, who called O'Brien "the world's greatest admirer of mediocre short stories."

In the midst of his career, Fitzgerald's wife, Zelda, had struggles with mental illness. Fitzgerald himself soon became ill, and he suffered financially. He tried unsuccessfully to make a living by becoming a screenwriter in Hollywood.

Fitzgerald's most influential later books were *The Great Gatsby* and *The Last Tycoon*, left incomplete when he died at the age of forty-four. *The Great Gatsby* earned tepid reviews and its sales were meager at first. At his funeral, Dorothy Parker looked down at him in his coffin and, taking a line from *The Great Gatsby*, said, "You poor son of a bitch!" Only after his death did the book garner greater admiration and more positive reviews. Its republication made it one of the most popular American novels of the century.

★

AND WHERE'S MR. Campbell?" Charlie asked.

"Gone to Switzerland. Mr. Campbell's a pretty sick man, Mr. Wales."

"I'm sorry to hear that. And George Hardt?" Charlie inquired.

"Back in America, gone to work."

"And where is the snow bird?"

"He was in here last week. Anyway, his friend, Mr. Schaeffer, is in Paris."

Two familiar names from the long list of a year and a half ago. Charlie scribbled an address in his notebook and tore out the page.

"If you see Mr. Schaeffer, give him this," he said. "It's my brother-in-law's address. I haven't settled on a hotel yet."

He was not really disappointed to find Paris was so empty. But the stillness in the bar was strange, almost portentous.

It was not an American bar any more—he felt polite in it, and not as if he owned it. It had gone back into France. He felt the stillness from the moment he got out of the taxi and saw the doorman, usually in a frenzy of activity at this hour, gossiping with a *chasseur* by the servants' entrance.

Passing through the corridor, he heard only a single, bored voice in the once-clamorous women's room. When he turned into the bar he traveled the twenty feet of green carpet with his eyes fixed straight ahead by old habit; and then, with his foot firmly on the rail, he turned and surveyed the room, encountering only a single pair of eyes that fluttered up from a newspaper in the corner. Charlie asked for the head barman, Paul, who in the latter days of the bull market had come to work in his own custom-built car—disembarking, however, with due nicety at the nearest corner. But Paul was at his country house to-day and Alix was giving him his information.

"No, no more. I'm going slow these days."

Alix congratulated him: "Hope you stick to it, Mr. Wales. You were going pretty strong a couple of years ago."

"I'll stick to it all right," Charlie assured him. "I've stuck to it for over a year and a half now."

"How do you find conditions in America?"

"I haven't been to America for months. I'm in business in Prague, representing a couple of concerns there. They don't know about me down there." He smiled faintly. "Remember the night of George Hardt's bachelor dinner here? . . . By the way, what's become of Claude Fessenden?"

Alix lowered his voice confidentially: "He's in Paris, but he doesn't come here any more. Paul doesn't allow it. He ran up a bill of thirty thousand francs, charging all his drinks and his lunches, and usually his dinner, for more than a year. And when Paul finally told him he had to pay, he gave him a bad check."

Alix pressed his lips together and shook his head.

"I don't understand it, such a dandy fellow. Now he's all bloated up—" He made a plump apple of his hands.

A thin world, resting on a common weakness, shredded away now like tissue paper. Turning, Charlie saw a group of effeminate young men installing themselves in a corner.

"Nothing affects them," he thought. "Stocks rise and fall, people loaf or work, but they go on forever." The place oppressed him. He called for the dice and shook with Alix for the drink.

"Here for long, Mr. Wales?"

"I'm here for four or five days to see my little girl."

"Oh-h! You have a little girl?"

Outside, the fire-red, gas-blue, ghost-green signs shone smokily through the tranquil rain. It was late afternoon and the streets were in movement; the *bistros* gleamed. At the corner of the Boulevard des Capucines he took a taxi. The Place de la Concorde moved by in pink majesty; they crossed the logical Seine, and Charlie felt the sudden provincial quality of the left bank.

"I spoiled this city for myself," he thought. "I didn't realize it, but the days came along one after another, and then two years were gone, and everything was gone, and I was gone."

He was thirty-five, a handsome man, with the Irish mobility of his face sobered by a deep wrinkle between his eyes. As he rang his brother-in-law's bell in the Rue Palatine, the wrinkle deepened till it pulled down his brows; he felt a cramping sensation in his belly. From behind the maid who opened the door darted a lovely little girl of nine who shrieked "Daddy!" and flew up, struggling like a fish, into his arms. She pulled his head around by one ear and set her cheek against his.

"My old pie," he said.

"Oh, daddy, daddy, daddy, daddy, dads, dads, dads!"

She drew him into the salon, where the family waited, a boy and girl his daughter's age, his sister-in-law and her husband. He greeted Marion with his voice pitched carefully to avoid either feigned enthusiasm or dislike, but her response was more frankly tepid, and she minimized her expression of unalterable distrust by directing her regard toward his child. The two men clasped hands in a friendly way and Lincoln Peters rested his for a moment on Charlie's shoulder.

The room was warm and comfortably American. The three children moved intimately about, playing through the yellow oblongs that led to other rooms; the cheer of six o'clock spoke in the eager smacks of the fire and the sounds of French activity in the kitchen. But Charlie did not relax; his heart sat up rigidly in his body and he drew confidence from his daughter, who from time to time came close to him, holding in her arms the doll he had brought.

"Really extremely well," he declared in answer to Lincoln's question. "There's a lot of business there that isn't moving at all, but we're doing even better than ever. In fact, damn well. I'm bringing my sister over from America next month to keep house for me. My income last year was bigger than it was when I had money. You see, the Czechs—"

His boasting was for a specific purpose; but after a moment, seeing a faint restiveness in Lincoln's eye, he changed the subject:

"Those are fine children of yours, well brought up, good manners."

"We think Honoria's a great little girl too."

Marion Peters came back into the little salon. She was a tall woman with worried eyes, who had once possessed a fresh American loveliness. Charlie had never been sensitive to it and was always surprised when people spoke of how pretty she had been. From the first there had been an instinctive antipathy between them.

"Well, how do you find Honoria?" she asked.

"Wonderful. I was astonished how much she's grown in ten months. All the children are looking well."

"We haven't had a doctor for a year. How do you like being back in Paris?"

"It seems very funny to see so few Americans around."

"I'm delighted," Marion said vehemently. "Now at least you can go into a store without their assuming you're a millionaire. We've suffered like everybody, but on the whole it's a good deal pleasanter."

"But it was nice while it lasted," Charlie said. "We were a sort of royalty, almost infallible, with a sort of magic around us. In the bar this afternoon"—he stumbled, seeing his mistake—"there wasn't a man I knew."

She looked at him keenly. "I should think you'd have had enough of bars."

"I only stayed a minute. I take one drink every afternoon, and no more."

"Don't you want a cocktail before dinner?" Lincoln asked.

"I take only one drink every afternoon, and I've had that."

"I hope you keep to it," said Marion.

Her dislike was evident in the coldness with which she spoke, but Charlie only smiled; he had larger plans. Her very aggressiveness gave him an advantage, and he knew enough to wait. He wanted them to initiate the discussion of what they knew had brought him to Paris.

Honoria was to spend the following afternoon with him. At dinner he couldn't decide whether she was most like him or her mother. Fortunate if she didn't combine the traits of both that had brought them to disaster. A great wave of protectiveness went over him. He thought he knew what to do for her. He believed in character; he wanted to jump back a whole generation and trust in character again as the eternally valuable element. Everything wore out now. Parents expected genius, or at least brilliance, and both the forcing of children and the fear of forcing them, the fear of warping natural abilities, were poor substitutes for that long, careful watchfulness, that checking and balancing and reckoning of accounts, the end of which was that there should be no slipping below a certain level of duty and integrity.

That was what the elders had been unable to teach plausibly since the break between the generations ten or twelve years ago.

He left soon after dinner, but not to go home. He was curious to see Paris by night with clearer and more judicious eyes. He bought a *strapontin* for the Casino and watched Josephine Baker go through her chocolate arabesques.

After an hour he left and strolled toward Montmartre, up the Rue Pigalle into the Place Blanche. The rain had stopped and there were a few people in evening clothes disembarking from taxis in front of cabarets, and *cocottes* prowling singly or in pairs, and many Negroes. He passed a lighted door from which issued music, and stopped with the sense of familiarity; it was Bricktop's, where he had parted with so many hours and so much money. A few doors farther on he found another ancient rendezvous and incautiously put his head inside. Immediately an eager orchestra burst into sound, a pair of professional dancers leaped to their feet and a maître d'hôtel swooped toward him, crying, "Crowd just arriving, sir!" But he withdrew quickly.

"You have to be damn drunk," he thought.

Zelli's was closed, the bleak and sinister cheap hotels surrounding it were dark; up in the Rue Blanche there was more light and a local, colloquial French crowd. The Poet's Cave had disappeared, but the two great mouths of the Café of Heaven and the Café of Hell still yawned — even devoured, as he watched, the meager contents of a tourist bus — a German, a Japanese, and an American couple who glanced at him with frightened eyes.

So much for the effort and ingenuity of Montmartre. All the catering to vice and waste was on an utterly childish scale, and he suddenly realized the meaning of the word "dissipate"—to dissipate into thin air; to make nothing out of something. In the little hours of the night every move from place to place was an enormous human jump, an increase of paying for the privilege of slower and slower motion.

He remembered thousand-franc notes given to an orchestra for playing a single number, hundred-franc notes tossed to a doorman for calling a cab.

But it hadn't been given for nothing.

It had been given, even the most wildly squandered sum, as an offering to destiny that he might not remember the things most worth remembering, the things that now he would always remember—his child taken from his control, his wife escaped to a grave in Vermont.

In the glare of a *brasserie* a woman spoke to him. He bought her some eggs and coffee, and then, eluding her encouraging stare, gave her a twenty-franc note and took a taxi to his hotel.

II

He woke upon a fine fall day—football weather. The depression of yesterday was gone and he liked the people on the streets. At noon he sat opposite Honoria at the Grand Vatel, the only restaurant he could think of not reminiscent of champagne dinners and long luncheons that began at two and ended in a blurred and vague twilight.

"Now, how about vegetables? Oughtn't you to have some vegetables?"

"Well, yes."

"Here's *épinards* and *chou-fleur* and carrots and *haricots*."

"I'd like *choux-fleurs*."

"Wouldn't you like to have two vegetables?"

"I usually only have one at lunch."

The waiter was pretending to be inordinately fond of children. "*Qu'elle est mignonne la petite? Elle parle exactement comme une française.*"

"How about dessert? Shall we wait and see?"

The waiter disappeared. Honoria looked at him expectantly.

"What are we going to do?"

"First we're going to that toy store in the Rue Saint-Honoré and buy you anything you like. And then we're going to the vaudeville at the Empire."

She hesitated. "I like it about the vaudeville, but not the toy store."

"Why not?"

"Well, you brought me this doll." She had it with her. "And I've got lots of things. And we're not rich any more, are we?"

"We never were. But to-day you are to have anything you want."

"All right," she agreed resignedly.

He had always been fond of her, but when there had been her mother and a French nurse he had been inclined to be strict; now he extended himself, reached out for a new tolerance; he must be both parents to her and not shut any of her out of communication.

"I want to get to know you," he said gravely. "First let me introduce myself. My name is Charles J. Wales, of Prague."

"Oh, daddy!" her voice cracked with laughter.

"And who are you, please?" he persisted, and she accepted a rôle immediately: "Honoria Wales, Rue Palatine, Paris."

"Married or single?"

"No, not married. Single."

He indicated the doll. "But I see you have a child, madame."

Unwilling to disinherit it, she took it to her heart and thought quickly: "Yes, I've been married, but I'm not married now. My husband is dead."

He went on quickly, "And the child's name?"

"Simone. That's after my best friend at school."

"I'm very pleased that you're doing so well at school."

"I'm third this month," she boasted. "Elsie"—that was her cousin—"is only about eighteenth, and Richard is about at the bottom."

"You like Richard and Elsie, don't you?"

"Oh, yes. I like Richard quite well and I like her all right."

Cautiously and casually he asked: "And Aunt Marion and Uncle Lincoln—which do you like best?"

"Oh, Uncle Lincoln, I guess."

He was increasingly aware of her presence. As they came in, a murmur of "What an adorable child" followed them, and now the people at the next table bent all their silences upon her, staring as if she were something no more conscious than a flower.

"Why don't I live with you?" she asked suddenly. "Because mamma's dead?"

"You must stay here and learn more French. It would have been hard for daddy to take care of you so well."

"I don't really need much taking care of any more. I do everything for myself."

Going out of the restaurant, a man and a woman unexpectedly hailed him.

"Well, the old Wales!"

"Hello there, Lorraine . . . Dunc."

Sudden ghosts out of the past: Duncan Schaeffer, a friend from college. Lorraine Quarrles, a lovely, pale blond of thirty; one of a crowd who had helped them make months into days in the lavish times of two years ago.

"My husband couldn't come this year," she said, in answer to his question. "We're poor as hell. So he gave me two hundred a month and told me I could do my worst on that . . . This your little girl?"

"What about sitting down?" Duncan asked.

"Can't do it." He was glad for an excuse. As always, he felt Lorraine's passionate, provocative attraction, but his own rhythm was different now.

"Well, how about dinner?" she asked.

"I'm not free. Give me your address and let me call you."

"Charlie, I believe you're sober," she said judicially. "I honestly believe he's sober, Dunc. Pinch him and see if he's sober."

Charlie indicated Honoria with his head. They both laughed.

"What's your address?" said Duncan skeptically.

He hesitated, unwilling to give the name of his hotel.

"I'm not settled yet. I'd better call you. We're going to see the vaudeville at the Empire."

"There! That's what I want to do," Lorraine said. "I want to see some clowns and acrobats and jugglers. That's just what we'll do, Dunc."

"We've got to do an errand first," said Charlie. "Perhaps we'll see you there."

"All right, you snob . . . Good-by, beautiful little girl."

"Good-by." Honoria bobbed politely.

Somehow, an unwelcome encounter, Charlie thought. They liked him because he was functioning, because he was serious; they wanted to see him, because he was stronger than they were now, because they wanted to draw a certain sustenance from his strength.

At the Empire, Honoria proudly refused to sit upon her father's folded coat. She was already an individual with a code of her own, and Charlie was more and more absorbed by the desire of putting a little of himself into her before she crystallized utterly. It was hopeless to try to know her in so short a time.

Between the acts they came upon Duncan and Lorraine in the lobby where the band was playing.

"Have a drink?"

"All right, but not up at the bar. We'll take a table."

"The perfect father."

Listening abstractedly to Lorraine, Charlie watched Honoria's eyes leave them all, and he followed them wistfully about the room, wondering what they saw. He met them and she smiled.

"I liked that lemonade," she said.

What had she said? What had he expected? Going home in a taxi afterward, he pulled her over until her head rested against his chest.

"Darling, do you ever think about your mother?"

"Yes, sometimes," she answered vaguely.

"I don't want you to forget her. Have you got a picture of her?"

"Yes, I think so. Anyhow, Aunt Marion has. Why don't you want me to forget her?"

"She loved you very much."

"I loved her too."

They were silent for a moment.

"Daddy, I want to come and live with you," she said suddenly.

His heart leaped; he had wanted it to come like this.

"Aren't you perfectly happy?"

"Yes, but I love you better than anybody. And you love me better than anybody, don't you, now that mummy's dead?"

"Of course I do. But you won't always like me best, honey. You'll grow up and meet somebody your own age and go marry him and forget you ever had a daddy."

"Yes, that's true," she agreed tranquilly.

He didn't go in. He was coming back at nine o'clock and he wanted to keep himself fresh and new for the thing he must say then.

"When you're safe inside, just show yourself in that window."

"All right. Good-by, dads, dads, dads, dads."

He waited in the dark street until she appeared, all warm and glowing, in the window above and kissed her fingers out into the night.

III

They were waiting. Marion sat behind empty coffee cups in a dignified black dinner dress that just faintly suggested mourning. Lincoln was walking up and down with the animation of one who had already been talking. They were as anxious as he was to get into the question. He opened it almost immediately:

"I suppose you know what I want to see you about—why I really came to Paris."

Marion fiddled with the glass grapes on her necklace and frowned.

"I'm awfully anxious to have a home," he continued. "And I'm awfully anxious to have Honoria in it. I appreciate your taking in Honoria for her mother's sake, but things have changed now"—he hesitated and then continued strongly—"changed radically with me, and I want to ask you to reconsider the matter. It would be silly for me to deny that about two years ago I was acting badly—"

Marion looked up at him with hard eyes.

"—but all that's over. As I told you, I haven't had more than a drink a day for over a year, and I take that drink deliberately, so that the idea of alcohol won't get too big in my imagination. You see the idea?"

"No," said Marion succinctly.

"It's a sort of stunt I set myself. It keeps the matter in proportion."

"I get you," said Lincoln. "You don't want to admit it's got any attraction for you."

"Something like that. Sometimes I forget and don't take it. But I try to take it. Anyhow, I couldn't afford to drink in my position. The people I represent are more than satisfied with what I've done, and I'm bringing my sister over from Burlington to keep house for me, and I want awfully to have Honoria too. You know that even when her mother and I weren't getting along well I never let anything that happened touch Honoria. I know she's fond of me and I know I'm able to take care of her and—well, there you are. How do you feel about it?"

He knew that now he would have to take a beating. It would last an hour or two hours, and it would be difficult, but if he modulated his inevitable resentment to the chastened attitude of the reformed sinner, he might win his point in the end. "Keep your temper," he told himself. "You don't want to be justified. You want Honoria."

Lincoln spoke first: "We've been talking it over ever since we got your letter last month. We're happy to have Honoria here. She's a dear little thing, and we're glad to be able to help her, but of course that isn't the question—"

Marion interrupted suddenly. "How long are you going to stay sober, Charlie?" she asked.

"Permanently, I hope."

"How can anybody count on that?"

"You know I never did drink heavily until I gave up business and came over here with nothing to do. Then Helen and I began to run around with—"

"Please leave Helen out of it. I can't bear to hear you talk about her like that."

He stared at her grimly; he had never been certain how fond of each other the sisters were in life.

"My drinking only lasted about a year and a half—from the time we came over until I—collapsed."

"It was time enough."

"It was time enough," he agreed.

"My duty is entirely to Helen," she said. "I try to think what she would have wanted me to do. Frankly, from the night you did that terrible thing you haven't really existed for me. I can't help that. She was my sister."

"Yes."

"When she was dying she asked me to look out for Honoria. If you hadn't been in a sanitarium then, it might have helped matters."

He had no answer.

"I'll never in my life be able to forget the morning when Helen knocked at my door, soaked to the skin and shivering, and said you'd locked her out."

Charlie gripped the sides of the chair. This was more difficult than he expected; he wanted to launch out into a long expostulation and explanation, but he only said: "The night I locked her out—" and she interrupted, "I don't feel up to going over that again."

After a moment's silence Lincoln said: "We're getting off the subject. You want Marion to set aside her legal guardianship and give you Honoria. I think the main point for her is whether she has confidence in you or not."

"I don't blame Marion," Charlie said slowly, "but I think she can have entire confidence in me. I had a good record up to three years ago. Of course, it's within human possibilities I might go wrong any time. But if we wait much longer I'll lose Honoria's childhood and my chance for a home. I'll simply lose her, don't you see?"

"Yes, I see," said Lincoln.

"Why didn't you think of all this before?" Marion asked.

"I suppose I did, from time to time, but Helen and I were getting along badly. When I consented to the guardianship, I was flat on my back in a sanitarium and the market had cleaned me out of every sou. I knew I'd acted badly, and I thought if it would bring any peace to Helen, I'd agree to anything. But now it's different. I'm well, I'm functioning, I'm behaving damn well, so far as —"

"Please don't swear at me," Marion said.

He looked at her, startled. With each remark the force of her dislike became more and more apparent. She had built up all her fear of life into one wall and faced it toward him. This trivial reproof was possibly the result of some trouble with the cook several hours before. Charlie became increasingly alarmed at leaving Honoria in this atmosphere of hostility against himself; sooner or later it would come out, in a word here, a shake of the head there, and some of that distrust would be irrevocably implanted in Honoria. But he pulled his temper down out of his face and shut it up inside him; he had won a point, for Lincoln realized the absurdity of Marion's remark and asked her lightly since when she had objected to the word "damn."

"Another thing," Charlie said: "I'm able to give her certain advantages now. I'm going to take a French governess to Prague with me. I've got a lease on a new apartment —"

He stopped, realizing that he was blundering. They couldn't be expected to accept with equanimity the fact that his income was again twice as large as their own.

"I suppose you can give her more luxuries than we can," said Marion. "When you were throwing away money we were living along watching every ten francs . . . I suppose you'll start doing it again."

"Oh, no," he said. "I've learned. I worked hard for ten years, you know — until I got lucky in the market, like so many people. Terribly lucky. It didn't seem any use working any more, so I quit. It won't happen again."

There was a long silence. All of them felt their nerves straining, and for the first time in a year Charlie wanted a drink. He was sure now that Lincoln Peters wanted him to have his child.

Marion shuddered suddenly; part of her saw that Charlie's feet were planted on the earth now, and her own maternal feeling recognized the naturalness of his desire; but she had lived for a long time with a prejudice — a prejudice founded on a curious disbelief in her sister's happiness, and which, in the shock of one terrible night, had turned to hatred for him. It had all happened at a point in her life where the discouragement of ill-health and adverse circumstances made it necessary for her to believe in tangible villainy and a tangible villain.

"I can't help what I think!" she cried out suddenly. "How much you were responsible for Helen's death, I don't know. It's something you'll have to square with your own conscience."

An electric current of agony surged through him; for a moment he was almost on his feet, an unuttered sound echoing in his throat. He hung on to himself for a moment, another moment.

"Hold on there," said Lincoln uncomfortably. "I never thought you were responsible for that."

"Helen died of heart trouble," Charlie said dully.

"Yes, heart trouble." Marion spoke as if the phrase had another meaning for her.

Then, in the flatness that followed her outburst, she saw him plainly and she knew he had somehow arrived at control over the situation. Glancing at her husband, she found no help from him, and as abruptly as if it were a matter of no importance, she threw up the sponge.

"Do what you like!" she cried, springing up from her chair. "She's your child. I'm not the person to stand in your way. I think if it were my child I'd rather see her—" She managed to check herself. "You two decide it. I can't stand this. I'm sick. I'm going to bed."

She hurried from the room; after a moment Lincoln said:

"This has been a hard day for her. You know how strongly she feels—" His voice was almost apologetic: "When a woman gets an idea in her head."

"Of course."

"It's going to be all right. I think she sees now that you—can provide for the child, and so we can't very well stand in your way or Honoria's way."

"Thank you, Lincoln."

"I'd better go along and see how she is."

"I'm going."

He was still trembling when he reached the street, but a walk down the Rue Bonaparte to the quais set him up, and as he crossed the Seine, dotted with many cold moons, he felt exultant. But back in his room he couldn't sleep. The image of Helen haunted him. Helen whom he had loved so until they had senselessly begun to abuse each other's love and tear it into shreds. On that terrible February night that Marion remembered so vividly, a slow quarrel that had gone on for hours. There was a scene at the Florida, and then he attempted to take her home, and then Helen kissed Ted Wilder at a table, and what she had hysterically said. Charlie's departure and, on his arrival home, his turning the key in the lock in wild anger. How could he know she would arrive an hour later alone, that there would be a snowstorm in which she wandered about in slippers for an hour, too confused to find a taxi? Then the aftermath, her escaping pneumonia by a miracle, and all the attendant horror. They were "reconciled," but that was the beginning of the end, and Marion, who had seen with her own eyes and who imagined it to be one of many scenes from her sister's martyrdom, never forgot.

Going over it again brought Helen nearer, and in the white, soft light that steals upon half sleep near morning he found himself talking to her again. She said that he was perfectly right about Honoria and that she wanted Honoria to be with him. She said she was glad he was being good and doing better. She said a lot of other things — very friendly things — but she was in a swing in a white dress, and swinging faster and faster all the time, so that at the end he could not hear clearly all that she said.

IV

He woke up feeling happy. The door of the world was open again. He made plans, vistas, futures for Honoria and himself, but suddenly he grew sad, remembering all the plans he and Helen had made. She had not planned to die. The present was the thing — work to do and some-one to love. But not to love too much, for Charlie had read in D. H. Law-rence about the injury that a father can do to a daughter or a mother to a son by attaching them too closely. Afterward, out in the world, the child would seek in the marriage partner the same blind tenderness and, fail-ing in all human probability to find it, develop a grudge against love and life.

It was another bright, crisp day. He called Lincoln Peters at the bank where he worked and asked if he could count on taking Honoria when he left for Prague. Lincoln agreed that there was no reason for delay. One thing — the legal guardianship. Marion wanted to retain that a while longer. She was upset by the whole matter, and it would oil things if she felt that the situation was still in her control for another year. Charlie agreed, wanting only the tangible, visible child.

Then the question of a governess. Charlie sat in a gloomy agency and talked to a buxom Breton peasant whom he knew he couldn't endure. There were others whom he could see tomorrow.

He lunched with Lincoln Peters at the Griffon, trying to keep down his exultation.

"There's nothing quite like your own child," Lincoln said. "But you understand how Marion feels too."

"She's forgotten how hard I worked for seven years there," Charlie said. "She just remembers one night."

"There's another thing." Lincoln hesitated. "While you and Helen were tearing around Europe throwing money away, we were just getting along. I didn't touch any of the prosperity because I never got ahead enough to carry anything but my insurance. I think Marion felt there was some kind of injustice in it — you not even working and getting richer and richer."

"It went just as quick as it came," said Charlie.

"A lot did. And a lot of it stayed in the hands of *chasseurs* and saxophone players and maîtres d'hôtel — well, the big party's over now. I just said that to explain Marion's feeling about those crazy years. If you drop in about six o'clock to-night before Marion's too tired, we'll settle the details on the spot."

Back at his hotel, Charlie took from his pocket a *pneumatique* that Lincoln had given him at luncheon. It had been redirected by Paul from the hotel bar.

> DEAR CHARLIE: You were so strange when we saw you the other day that I wondered if I did something to offend you. If so, I'm not conscious of it. In fact, I have thought about you too much for the last year, and it's always been in the back of my mind that I might see you if I came over here. We did have such good times that crazy spring, like the night you and I stole the butcher's tricycle, and the time we tried to call on the president and you had the old derby and the wire cane. Everybody seems so old lately, but I don't feel old a bit. Couldn't we get together some time to-day for old time's sake? I've got a vile hang-over for the moment, but will be feeling better this afternoon and will look for you about five at the bar.
>
> Always devotedly,
> LORRAINE.

His first feeling was one of awe that he had actually, in his mature years, stolen a tricycle and pedaled Lorraine all over the Étoile between the small hours and dawn. In retrospect it was a nightmare. Locking out Helen didn't fit in with any other act of his life, but the tricycle incident did — it was one of many. How many weeks or months of dissipation to arrive at that condition of utter irresponsibility?

He tried to picture how Lorraine had appeared to him then — very at-

tractive; so much so that Helen had been jealous. Yesterday, in the restaurant, she had seemed trite, blurred, worn away. He emphatically did
not want to see her, and he was glad no one knew at what hotel he was
staying. It was a relief to think of Honoria, to think of Sundays spent
with her and of saying good morning to her and of knowing she was
there in his house at night, breathing quietly in the darkness.

At five he took a taxi and bought presents for all the Peterses — a pi-
quant cloth doll, a box of Roman soldiers, flowers for Marion, big linen
handkerchiefs for Lincoln.

He saw, when he arrived in the apartment, that Marion had accepted
the inevitable. She greeted him now as though he were a recalcitrant
member of the family, rather than a menacing outsider. Honoria had
been told she was going, and Charlie was glad to see that her tact was
sufficient to conceal her excessive happiness. Only on his lap did she
whisper her delight and the question "When?" before she slipped away.

He and Marion were alone for a minute in the room, and on an impulse he spoke out boldly:

"Family quarrels are bitter things. They don't go according to my
rules. They're not like aches or wounds; they're more like splits in the
skin that won't heal because there's not enough material. I wish you and
I could be on better terms."

"Some things are hard to forget," she answered. "It's a question of
confidence. If you behave yourself in the future I won't have any criticism." There was no answer to this, and presently she asked, "When do
you propose to take her?"

"As soon as I can get a governess. I hoped the day after tomorrow."

"That's impossible. I've got to get her things in shape. Not before
Saturday."

He yielded. Coming back into the room, Lincoln offered him a drink.
"I'll take my daily whisky," he said.

It was warm here, it was a home, people together by a fire. The children felt very safe and important; the mother and father were serious,
watchful. They had things to do for the children more important than
his visit here. A spoonful of medicine was, after all, more important than
the strained relations between Marion and himself. They were not dull
people, but they were very much in the grip of life and circumstances,
and their gestures as they turned in a cramped space lacked largeness
and grace. He wondered if he couldn't do something to get Lincoln out
of that rut at the bank.

There was a long peal at the doorbell; the maid crossed the room and went down the corridor. The door opened upon another long ring, and then voices, and the three in the salon looked up expectantly; Lincoln moved to bring the corridor within his range of vision, and Marion rose. Then the maid came along the corridor, closely followed by the voices, which developed under the light into Duncan Schaeffer and Lorraine Quarrles.

They were gay, they were hilarious, they were roaring with laughter. For a moment Charlie was astounded; then he realized they had got the address he had left at the bar.

"Ah-h-h!" Duncan wagged his finger roguishly at Charlie. "Ah-h-h!"

They both slid down another cascade of laughter. Anxious and at a loss, Charlie shook hands with them quickly and presented them to Lincoln and Marion. Marion nodded, scarcely speaking. She had drawn back a step toward the fire; her little girl stood beside her, and Marion put an arm about her shoulder.

With growing annoyance at the intrusion, Charlie waited for them to explain themselves. After some concentration Duncan said:

"We came to take you to dinner. Lorraine and I insist that all this shi-shi, cagy business got to stop."

Charlie came closer to them, as if to force them backward down the corridor.

"Sorry, but I can't. Tell me where you'll be and we'll call you in half an hour."

This made no impression. Lorraine sat down suddenly on the side of a chair, and focusing her eyes on Richard, cried, "Oh, what a nice little boy! Come here, little boy." Richard glanced at his mother, but did not move. With a perceptible shrug of her shoulders, Lorraine turned back to Charlie:

"Come on out to dinner. Be yourself, Charlie. Come on."

"How about a little drink?" said Duncan to the room at large.

Lincoln Peters had been somewhat uneasily occupying himself by swinging Honoria from side to side with her feet off the ground.

"I'm sorry, but there isn't a thing in the house," he said. "We just this minute emptied the only bottle."

"All the more reason coming to dinner," Lorraine assured Charlie.

"I can't," said Charlie almost sharply. "You two go have dinner and I'll phone you."

"Oh, you will, will you?" Her voice became suddenly unpleasant. "All right, we'll go along. But I remember, when you used to hammer on my door, I used to be enough of a good sport to give you a drink. Come on, Dunc."

Still in slow motion, with blurred, angry faces, with uncertain feet, they retired along the corridor.

"Good night," Charlie said.

"Good night!" responded Lorraine emphatically.

When he went back into the salon Marion had not moved, only now her son was standing in the circle of her other arm. Lincoln was still swinging Honoria back and forth like a pendulum from side to side.

"What an outrage!" Charlie broke out. "What an absolute outrage!"

Neither of them answered. Charlie dropped into an armchair, picked up his drink, set it down again and said:

"People I haven't seen for two years having the colossal nerve —"

He broke off. Marion had made the sound "Oh!" in one swift, furious breath, turned her body from him with a jerk and left the room.

Lincoln set down Honoria carefully.

"You children go in and start your soup," he said, and when they obeyed, he said to Charlie:

"Marion's not well and she can't stand shocks. That kind of people make her really physically sick."

"I didn't tell them to come here. They wormed this address out of Paul at the bar. They deliberately —"

"Well, it's too bad. It doesn't help matters. Excuse me a minute."

Left alone, Charlie sat tense in his chair. In the next room he could hear the children eating, talking in monosyllables, already oblivious of the scene among their elders. He heard a murmur of conversation from a farther room and then the ticking bell of a phone picked up, and in a panic he moved to the other side of the room and out of earshot.

In a minute Lincoln came back. "Look here, Charlie. I think we'd better call off dinner for tonight. Marion's in bad shape."

"Is she angry with me?"

"Sort of," he said, almost roughly. "She's not strong and —"

"You mean she's changed her mind about Honoria?"

"She's pretty bitter right now. I don't know. You phone me at the bank to-morrow."

"I wish you'd explain to her I never dreamed these people would come here. I'm just as sore as you are."

"I couldn't explain anything to her now."

Charlie got up. He took his coat and hat and started down the corridor. Then he opened the door of the dining room and said in a strange voice, "Good night, children."

Honoria rose and ran around the table to hug him.

"Good night, sweetheart," he said vaguely, and then trying to make his voice more tender, trying to conciliate something, "Good night, dear children."

V

Charlie went directly to the bar with the furious idea of finding Lorraine and Duncan, but they were not there, and he realized that in any case there was nothing he could do. He had not touched his drink at the Peterses', and now he ordered a whisky-and-soda. Paul came over to say hello.

"It's a great change," he said sadly. "We do about half the business we did. So many fellows I hear about back in the States lost everything, maybe not in the first crash, but then in the second, and now when everything keeps going down. Your friend George Hardt lost every cent, I hear. Are you back in the States?"

"No, I'm in business in Prague."

"I heard that you lost a lot in the crash."

"I did," and he added grimly, "but I lost everything I wanted in the boom."

"Selling short."

"Something like that."

Again the memory of those days swept over him like a nightmare — the people they had met traveling; then people who couldn't add a row of figures or speak a coherent sentence. The little man Helen had consented to dance with at the ship's party, who had insulted her ten feet from the table; the human mosaic of pearls who sat behind them at the Russian ballet and, when the curtain rose on a scene, remarked to her companion: "Luffly; just luffly. Zomebody ought to baint a bicture of it." Men who locked their wives out in the snow, because the snow of twenty-nine wasn't real snow. If you didn't want it to be snow, you just paid some money.

He went to the phone and called the Peters apartment; Lincoln himself answered.

"I called up because, as you can imagine, this thing is on my mind. Has Marion said anything definite?"

"Marion's sick," Lincoln answered shortly. "I know this thing isn't altogether your fault, but I can't have her go to pieces about this. I'm afraid we'll have to let it slide for six months; I can't take the chance of working her up to this state again."

"I see."

"I'm sorry, Charlie."

He went back to his table. His whisky glass was empty, but he shook his head when Alix looked at it questioningly. There wasn't much he could do now except send Honoria some things; he would send her a lot of things tomorrow. He thought rather angrily that that was just money — he had given so many people money.

"No, no more," he said to another waiter. "What do I owe you?"

He would come back some day; they couldn't make him pay forever. But he wanted his child, and nothing was much good now, beside that fact. He wasn't young any more, with a lot of nice thoughts and dreams to have by himself. He was absolutely sure Helen wouldn't have wanted him to be so alone.

1933

KATHERINE ANNE PORTER
THE CRACKED LOOKING-GLASS

from *Scribner's Magazine*

KATHERINE ANNE PORTER (1890–1980) was born in Texas but ran away at sixteen. She later settled in Chicago, where she worked as an extra in movies. Then she returned to Texas and began work as a drama critic and society commentator for the *Fort Worth Critic*. She went on to live in New York, Mexico, Germany, and France.

Her first book was *Flowering Judas,* a story collection published to rave reviews. She was also the author of *Pale Horse, Pale Rider; The Leaning Tower;* and *Collected Stories,* which earned her the Pulitzer Prize and the National Book Award. In 1962 her only novel, *Ship of Fools,* was published. In 1977 she published *The Never-Ending Wrong,* a book about Sacco and Vanzetti.

Porter's work explored themes of justice and betrayal. She is considered to be one of the country's finest writers, although she struggled financially owing to moderate sales and the length of time it took her to produce new works. She taught at many different universities, including Stanford and the University of Michigan.

In an interview she said, "The thing is not to follow a pattern. Follow your own pattern of feeling and thought. The thing is to accept your own life and not try to live someone else's life. Look, the thumbprint is not like any other, and the thumbprint is what you must go by."

★

DENNIS HEARD ROSALEEN talking in the kitchen and a man's voice answering. He sat with his hands dangling over his knees, and thought for the hundredth time that sometimes Rosaleen's voice was company to him, and other days he wished all day long she didn't have so much to say about everything. More and more the years put a quietus on a man; there was no earthly sense in saying the same things over and over. Even thinking the same thoughts grew tiresome after a while. But Rosaleen was full of talk as ever. If not to him, to whatever passerby stopped for a minute, and if nobody stopped, she talked to the cats and to herself. If Dennis came near she merely raised her voice and went on with whatever she was saying, so it was nothing for her to shout suddenly, "Come out of that, now — how often have I told ye to keep off the table?" and the cats would scatter in all directions with guilty faces. "It's enough to make a man lep out of his shoes," Dennis would complain. "It's not meant for you, darlin'," Rosaleen would say, as if that cured everything, and if he didn't go away at once, she would start telling some kind of story. But today she kept shooing him out of the place and hadn't a kind word in her mouth, and Dennis in exile felt that everything and everybody was welcome in the place but himself. For the twentieth time he approached on tiptoe and listened at the parlor keyhole.

Rosaleen was saying: "Maybe his front legs might look a little stuffed for a living cat, but in the picture it's no great matter. I said to Kevin, 'You'll never paint that cat alive,' but Kevin did it, with house paint mixed in a saucer, and a small brush the way he could put in all them fine lines. His legs look like that because I wanted him pictured on the table, but it wasn't so, he was on my lap the whole time. He was a wonder after the mice, a born hunter bringing them in from morning till night —"

Dennis sat on the sofa in the parlor and thought: "There it is. There she goes telling it again." He wondered who the man was, a strange voice, but a loud and ready gabbler as if maybe he was trying to sell something. "It's a fine painting, Miz O'Toole," he said, "and who did you say the artist was?"

"A lad named Kevin, like my own brother he was, who went away to make his fortune," answered Rosaleen. "A house painter by trade."

"The spittin' image of a cat!" roared the voice. "It is so," said Rosaleen. "The Billy-cat to the life. The Nelly-cat here is own sister to him, and the Jimmy-cat and the Annie-cat and the Miekey-cat is nephews and nieces, and there's a great family look between all of them. It was the strangest thing happened to the Billy-cat, Mr. Pendleton. He sometimes didn't come in for his supper till after dark, he was so taken up with the hunting, and then one night he didn't come at all, nor the next day neither, nor the next, and me with him on my mind so I didn't get a wink of sleep. Then at midnight on the third night I did go to sleep, and the Billy-cat came into my room and lep upon my pillow and said: 'Up beyond the north field there's a maple tree with a great scar where the branch was taken away by the storm, and near to it is a flat stone, and there you'll find me. I was caught in a trap,' he says, 'wasn't set for me,' he says, 'but it got me all the same. And now be easy in your mind about me,' he says, 'because it's all over.' Then he went away, giving me a look over his shoulder like a human creature, and I woke up Dennis and told him. Surely as we live, Mr. Pendleton, it was all true. So Dennis went beyond the north field and brought him home and we buried him in the garden and cried over him." Her voice broke and lowered and Dennis shuddered for fear she was going to shed tears before this stranger.

"For God's *sake*, Miz O'Toole," said the loud-mouthed man, "you can't get around that now, can you? Why, that's the most remarkable thing I ever heard!"

Dennis rose, creaking a little, and hobbled around to the east side of the house in time to see a round man with a flabby red face climbing into a rusty old car with a sign painted on the door. "Always something, now," he commented, putting his head in at the kitchen door. "Always telling a tall tale!"

"Well," said Rosaleen, without the least shame, "he wanted a story so I gave him a good one. That's the Irish in me."

"Always making a thing more than it is," said Dennis. "That's the way it goes." Rosaleen turned a little edgy. "Out with ye!" she cried, and the cats never budged a whisker. "The kitchen's no place for a man! How often must I tell ye?"

"Well, hand me my hat, will you?" said Dennis, for his hat hung on a nail over the calendar and had hung there within easy reach ever since they had lived in the farm house. A few minutes later he wanted his pipe, lying on the lamp shelf where he always kept it. Next he had to have his barn boots at once, though he hadn't seen them for a month. At last he thought of something to say, and opened the door a few inches.

"Wherever have I been sitting unmolested for the past ten years?" he asked, looking at his easy chair with the pillow freshly plumped, side ways to the big table. "And today it's no place for me?"

"If ye grumble ye'll be sorry," said Rosaleen gayly, "and now clear out before I hurl something at ye!"

Dennis put his hat on the parlor table and his boots under the sofa, and sat on the front steps and lit his pipe. It would soon be cold weather, and he wished he had his old leather jacket off the hook on the kitchen door. Whatever was Rosaleen up to now? He decided that Rosaleen was always doing the Irish a great wrong by putting her own faults off on them. To be Irish, he felt, was to be like him, a sober, practical, thinking man, a lover of truth. Rosaleen couldn't see it at all. "It's just your head is like a stone!" she said to him once, pretending she was joking, but she meant it. She had never appreciated him, that was it. And neither had his first wife. Whatever he gave them, they always wanted something else. When he was young and poor his first wife wanted money. And when he was a steady man with money in the bank, his second wife wanted a young man full of life. "They're all born ingrates one way or another," he decided, and felt better at once, as if at last he had something solid to stand on. In October a man could get his death sitting on the steps like this, and little she cared! He clacked his teeth together and felt how they didn't fit any more, and his feet and hands seemed tied on him with strings.

All the while Rosaleen didn't look to be a year older. She might almost be doing it to spite him, except that she wasn't the spiteful kind. He'd be bound to say that for her. But she couldn't forget that her girlhood had been a great triumph in Ireland, and she was forever telling him tales about it, and telling them again. This youth of hers was clearer in his mind than his own. He couldn't remember one thing over another that had happened to him. His past lay like a great lump within him; there it was, he knew it all at once, when he thought of it, like a chest a man has packed away, knowing all that is in it without troubling to name or count the objects. All in a lump it had not been an easy life being named Dennis O'Toole in Bristol, England, where he was brought up and worked sooner than he was able at the first jobs he could find. And his English wife had never forgiven him for pulling her up by the roots and bringing her to New York, where his brothers and sisters were, and a better job. All the long years he had been first a waiter and then head waiter in a New York hotel had telescoped in his mind, somehow. It wasn't the best of hotels, to be sure, but still he was head waiter and there was good money in it, enough to buy this farm in Connecticut and have a little steady money coming in, and what more could Rosaleen ask?

He was not unhappy over his first wife's death a few years after they left England, because they had never really liked each other, and it seemed to him now that even before she was dead he had made up his mind, if she did die, never to marry again. He had held out on this until he was nearly fifty, when he met Rosaleen at a dance in the County Sligo hall far over on East 86th Street. She was a great tall rosy girl, a prize dancer, and the boys were fairly fighting over her. She led him a dance then for two years before she would have him. She said there was nothing against him except he came from Bristol, and the outland Irish had the name of people you couldn't trust. She couldn't say why—it was just a name they had, worse than Dublin people itself. No decent Sligo girl would marry a Dublin man if he was the last man on earth. Dennis didn't believe this, he'd never heard any such thing against the Dubliners; he thought a country girl would lep at the chance to marry a city man whatever. Rosaleen said, "Maybe," but he'd see whether she would lep to marry Bristol Irish. She was chambermaid in a rich woman's house, a fiend of darkness if there ever was one, said Rosaleen, and at first Dennis had been uneasy about the whole thing, fearing a young girl who had to work so hard might be marrying an older man for his money, but before the two years were up he had got over that notion.

It wasn't long after they were married Dennis began almost to wish sometimes he had let one of those strong-armed boys have her, but he had been fond of her, she was a fine good girl, and after she cooled down a little, he knew he could have never done better. The only thing was, he wished it had been Rosaleen he had married that first time in Bristol, and now they'd be settled better together, nearer an age. Thirty years was too much difference altogether. But he never said any such thing to Rosaleen. A man owes something to himself. He knocked out his pipe on the foot scraper and felt a real need to go in the kitchen and find a pipe cleaner.

Rosaleen said, "Come in and welcome!" He stood peering around wondering what she had been making. She warned him: "I'm off to milk now, and mind ye keep your eyes in your pocket. The cow, now—the creature! Pretty soon she'll be jumping the stone walls after the apples, and running wild through the fields roaring, and it's all for another calf only, the poor deceived thing!" Dennis said, "I don't see what deceit there is in that." "Oh, don't you now?" said Rosaleen, and gathered up her milk pails.

The kitchen was warm and Dennis felt at home again. The kettle was simmering for tea, the cats lay curled or sprawled as they chose, and Dennis sat within himself smiling a sunken smile, cleaning his pipe. In the barn Rosaleen looped up her purple gingham skirts and sat with her forehead pressed against the warm, calm side of the cow, drawing two thick streams of milk into the pail. She said to the cow: "It's no life, no life at all. A man of his years is no comfort to a woman," and went on with a slow murmur that was not complaining about the things of her life.

• • •

She wished sometimes they had never come to Connecticut where there was nobody to talk to but Rooshans and Polacks and Wops no better than Black Protestants when you come right down to it. And the natives were worse even. A picture of her neighbors up the hill came into her mind: a starved-looking woman in a blackish gray dress, and a jaundiced man with red-rimmed eyes, and their mizzle-witted boy. On Sundays they shambled by in their sad old shoes, walking to the meeting-house, but that was all the religion they had, thought Rosaleen, contemptuously. On week days they beat the poor boy and the animals, and fought between themselves. Never a feast-day, nor a bit of bright color in their clothes, nor a Christian look out of their eyes for a living soul. "It's just living in mortal sin from one day to the next," said Rosaleen. But it was Dennis getting old that took the heart out of her. And him with the grandest head of hair she had ever seen on a man. A fine man, oh, a fine man Dennis was in those days! Dennis rose before her eyes in his black suit and white gloves, a knowledgeable man who could tell the richest people the right things to order for a good dinner, such a gentleman in his stiff white shirt front, managing the waiters on the one hand and the customers on the other, and making good money at it. And now. No, she couldn't believe it was Dennis any more. Where was Dennis now? And where was Kevin? She was sorry now she had spited him about his girl. It had been all in fun, really, no harm meant. It was strange if you couldn't speak your heart out to a good friend. Kevin had showed her the picture of his girl, like a clap of thunder it came one day when Rosaleen hadn't even heard there was one. She was a waitress in New York, and if ever Rosaleen had laid eyes on a brassy, bold-faced hussy, the kind the boys make jokes about at home, the kind that comes out to New York and goes wrong, this was the one. "You're never never keeping steady with her, are you?" Rosaleen had cried out and the tears came into her eyes. "And why not?" asked Kevin, his chin square as a box. "We've been great now for three years. Who says a word against her says it against me." And there they were, not exactly quarrelling, but not friends for the moment, certainly, with Kevin putting the picture back in his pocket, saying: "There's the last of it between us. I was greatly wrong to tell ye!"

That night he was packing up his clothes before he went to bed, but came down afterward and sat on the steps with them, and they made it up by saying nothing, as if nothing had happened. "A man must do something with his life," Kevin explained. "There's always a place to be made in the world, and I'm off to New York, or Boston, maybe." Rosaleen said, "Write me a letter, don't forget, I'll be waiting." "The very day I know where I'll be," he promised her. They had parted with false wide smiles on their faces, arms around each other to the very gate. There had come a postcard from New York of the Woolworth Building, with a word on it: "This is my hotel. Kevin." And never another word in these five years. The wretch, the stump! After he had disappeared down the road with his suitcase strapped on his shoulders, Rosaleen had gone back in the house and had looked at herself in the square looking-glass beside the kitchen window. There was a ripple in the glass and a crack across the middle, and it was like seeing your face in water. "Before God I don't look like that," she said, hanging it on the nail again. "If I did, it's no wonder he was leaving. But I don't." She knew in her heart no good would come of him running off after that common-looking girl; but it was likely he'd find her out soon, and come back, for Kevin was nobody's fool. She waited and watched for Kevin to come back and confess she had been right, and he would say, "I'm sorry I hurt your feelings over somebody not fit to look at you!" But now it was five years. She hung a drapery of crochet lace over the frame on the Billy-cat's picture, and propped it up on a small table in the kitchen, and sometimes it gave her an excuse to mention Kevin's name again, though the sound of it was a crack on the ear drums to Dennis. "Don't speak of him," said Dennis, more than once. "He owed it to send us word. It's ingratitude I can't stand." Whatever was she going to do with Dennis now, she wondered, and sighed heavily into the flank of the cow. It wasn't being a wife at all to wrap a man in flannels like a baby and put hot water bottles to him. She got up sighing and kicked back the stool. "There you are now," she said to the cow.

She couldn't help feeling happy all at once at the sight of the lamp and the fire making everything cosy, and the smell of vanilla reminded her of perfume. She set the table with a white-fringed cloth while Dennis strained the milk. "Now Dennis, today's a big day, and we're having a feast for it."

"Is it All-Souls?" asked Dennis, who never looked at a calendar any more. What's a day, more or less? "It is not," said Rosaleen, "draw up your chair now." Dennis made another guess it was Christmas, and Rosaleen said it was a better day than Christmas, even. "I can't think what," said Dennis, looking at the glossy baked goose. "It's nobody's birthday that I mind." Rosaleen lifted the curtain of the corner shelves and brought out a cake like a mound of new snow blooming with candles. "Count them and see what day is this, will you?" she urged him. Dennis counted them with a waggling forefinger. "So it is, Rosaleen, so it is." They went on bandying words. It had slipped his mind entirely. Rosaleen wanted to know when hadn't it slipped his mind? For all he ever thought of it, they might never have had a wedding day at all. "That's not so," said Dennis. "I mind well I married you. It's the date that slips me."

"You might as well be English," said Rosaleen, "you might just as well." She glanced at the clock, and reminded him it was twenty-five years ago that morning at ten o'clock, and tonight the very hour they had sat down to their first married dinner together. Dennis thought maybe it was telling people what to eat and then watching them eat it all those years that had taken away his wish for food. "You know I can't eat cake," he said. "It upsets my stomach."

Rosaleen felt sure her cake wouldn't upset the stomach of a nursing child. Dennis knew better, any kind of cake sat on him like a stone. While the argument went on, they ate nearly all the goose which fairly melted on the tongue, and finished with wedges of cake and floods of tea, and Dennis had to admit he hadn't felt better in years. He looked at her sitting across the table from him and thought she was a very fine woman, noticed again her red hair and yellow eyelashes and big arms and strong big teeth, and wondered what she thought of him now he was no human good to her. Here he was, all gone, and he had been so for years, and he felt guilt sometimes before Rosaleen, who couldn't always understand how there comes a time when a man is finished, and there is no more to be done that way. Rosaleen poured out two small glasses of homemade cherry brandy. "I could feel like dancing itself this night, Dennis," she told him. "Do you remember the first time we met in Sligo Hall with the band playing?" She gave him another glass of brandy and took one herself and leaned over with her eyes shining as if she was telling him something he had never heard before.

"I remember a boy in Ireland was a great step-dancer, the best, and he was wild about me and I was a devil to him. Now what makes a girl like that, Dennis? He was a fine match, too, all the girls were glad of a chance with him, but I wasn't. He said to me a thousand times, 'Rosaleen, why won't ye dance with me just once?' And I'd say, 'Ye've plenty to dance with ye without my wasting my time.' And so it went for the summer long with him not dancing at all and everybody plaguing the living life out of him, till in the end I danced with him. Afterwards he walked home with me and a crowd of them, and there was a heaven full of stars and the dogs barking far off. Then I promised to keep steady with him, and was sorry for it the minute I promised. I was like that. We used to be the whole day getting ready for the dances, washing our hair and curling it and trying on our dresses and trimming them, laughing fit to kill about the boys and making up things to say to them. When my sister Honora was married they took me for the bride, Dennis, with my white dress ruffled to the heels and my hair with a wreath. Everybody drank my health for the belle of the ball, and said I would surely be the next bride. Honora said for me to save my blushes or I'd have none left for my own wedding. She was always jealous, Dennis, she's jealous of me to this day, you know that."

"Maybe so," said Dennis.

"There's no maybe about it," said Rosaleen. "But we had grand times together when we was little. I mind the time when my great-grandfather was ninety years old and on his deathbed. We watched by turns the night —"

"And he was a weary time on it," said Dennis, to show his interest. He was so sleepy he could hardly hold up his head.

"He was," said Rosaleen, "so this night Honora and I were watching, and we were yawning our hearts out of us, for there had been a great ball the night before. Our mother told us, 'Feel his feet from time to time, and when you feel the chill rising, you'll know he's near the end. He can't last out the night,' she said, 'but stay by him.' So there we were drinking tea and laughing together in whispers to keep awake, and the old man lying there with his chin propped on the quilt. 'Wait a minute,' says Honora, and felt his feet. 'They're getting cold,' she says, and went on telling me what she had said to Shane at the ball, how he was jealous of Terence and asks her can he trust her out of his sight. And Honora says to Shane, 'No, you cannot,' and oh, but he was roaring mad with anger! Then Honora stuffs her fist in her mouth to keep down the giggles. I felt great-grandfather's feet and they was like clay to the knees, and I says, 'Maybe we'd better call somebody'; but Honora says, 'Oh, there's a power of him left to get cold yet!' So we poured out tea and began to comb and braid each other's hair, and fell to whispering our secrets and laughing more. Then Honora put her hand under the quilt and said, 'Rosaleen, his stomach's cold, it's gone he must be by now.' Then great-grandfather opened the one eye full of rage and says, 'It's nothing of the kind, and to hell with ye!' We let out a great scream, and the others came flying in, and Honora cried out, 'Oh, he's dead and gone surely, God rest him!' And would you believe it, it was so. He was gone. And while the old women were washing him Honora and me sat down laughing and crying in the one breath ... and it was six months later to the very day great-grandfather came to me in the dream, the way I told you, and he was still after Honora and me for laughing in the watch. 'I've a great mind to thrash ye within an inch of your life,' he told me, 'only I'm wailing in Purgatory this minute for them last words to ye. Go and have an extra Mass said for the repose of me soul because it's by your misconduct I'm here at all,' he says to me. 'Get a move on now,' he said. 'And be damned to ye!'"

"And you woke up in a sweat," said Dennis, "and was off to Mass before daybreak." Rosaleen nodded her head. "Ah, Dennis, if I'd set my heart on that boy I need never have left Ireland. And when I think how it all came out with him. With me so far away, him struck on the head and left for dead in a ditch."

"You dreamed that," said Dennis.

"Surely I dreamed it, and it is so. When I was crying and crying over him" — Rosaleen was proud of her crying — "I didn't know then what good luck I would find here."

Dennis couldn't think what good luck she was talking about. "Let it pass, then," said Rosaleen. She went to the corner shelves again. "The man today was selling pipes," she said, "and I bought the finest he had." It was an imitation meerschaum pipe carved with a crested lion glaring out of a jungle and it was as big as a man's fist. Dennis said, "You must have paid a pretty penny for that." "It doesn't concern ye," said Rosaleen. "I wanted to give ye a pipe." Dennis said, "It's grand carving, I wonder if it'll draw at all." He filled it and lit it and said there wasn't much taste on a new one, for he was tired holding it up. "It is such a pipe as my father had once," Rosaleen said to encourage him, "and in no time it was fit to knock ye off your feet, so this'll be a fine pipe some day."

"And some day I'll be in my tomb," thought Dennis, bitterly, "and she'll find a man can keep her quiet."

When they were in bed Rosaleen took his head on her shoulder. "Dennis, I could cry for the wink of an eyelash. When I think how happy we were that wedding day."

"From the way you carried on," said Dennis, feeling very sly all of a sudden on that brandy, "I thought different."

"Go to sleep," said Rosaleen, prudishly. "That's no way to talk."

Dennis' head fell back like a bag of sand on the pillow. Rosaleen could not sleep, and lay thinking about marriage; not her own, for once you've given your word there's nothing to think about in it, but all other kinds of marriages, unhappy ones: where the husband drinks, or won't work, or mistreats his wife and the children. Where the wife runs away from home, or spoils the children or neglects them, or turns a perfect strumpet and flirts with other men: where a woman marries a man too young for her, and he feels cheated and strays after other women till it's just a disgrace: or take when a young girl marries an old man, even if he has money she's bound to be disappointed some way. If Dennis hadn't been such a good man, God knows what might have come out of it. She was lucky. It would break your heart to dwell on it. Her black mood closed down on her and she wanted to walk the floor holding her head and remembering every unhappy thing in the world. She had had nothing but disasters, one after another, and she couldn't get over them, no matter how long ago they happened. Once she had let entirely the wrong man kiss her, she had almost got into bad trouble with him, and even now her heart stopped on her when she thought how near she'd come to being a girl with no character. There was the Billy-cat and his good heart and his sad death, and it was mixed up with the time her father had been knocked down, by a runaway horse, when the drink was in him, and the time when she had to wear mended stockings to a big ball because that sneaky Honora had stolen the only good ones.

She wished now she'd had a dozen children instead of the one that died in two days. This half-forgotten child suddenly lived again in her, she began to weep for him with all the freshness of her first agony; now he would be a fine grown man and the dear love of her heart. The image of him floated before her eyes plain as day, and became Kevin, painting the barn and the pig sty all colors of the rainbow, the brush swinging in his hand like a bell. He would work like a wild man for days and then lie for days under the trees, idle as a tramp. The darling, the darling lad like her own son. A painter by trade was a nice living, but she couldn't bear the thought of him boarding around the country with the heathen Rooshans and Polacks and Wops with their liquor stills and their outlandish lingo. She said as much to Kevin.

"It's not a Christian way to live, and you a good County Sligo boy." So Kevin started to make jokes at her like any other Sligo boy. "I said to myself, that's a County Mayo woman if ever I clapped eyes on one." "Hold your tongue," said Rosaleen softly as a dove. "You're talking to a Sligo woman as if you didn't know it!"

"Is it so?" said Kevin in great astonishment. "Well, I'm glad of the mistake. The Mayo people are too proud for me." "And for me, too," said Rosaleen. "They beat the world for holding up their chins about nothing." "They do so," said Kevin, "but the Sligo people have a right to be proud." "And you've a right to live in a good Irish house," said Rosaleen, "so you'd best come with us." "I'd be proud of that as if I came from Mayo," said Kevin, and he went on slapping paint on Rosaleen's front gate. They stood there smiling at each other, feeling they had agreed enough, it was time to think of how to get the best of each other in the talk from now on. For more than a year they had tried to get the best of each other in the talk, and sometimes it was one and sometimes another, but a gay easy time and such a bubble of joy like a kettle singing. "You've been a sister to me, Rosaleen, I'll not forget ye while I have breath." He had said that the last night. Dennis muttered and snored a little. Rosaleen wanted to mourn about everything at the top of her voice, but it wouldn't do to wake Dennis. He was sleeping like the dead after all that goose.

Rosaleen said, "Dennis, I dreamed about Kevin in the night. There was a grave, an old one, but with fresh flowers on it, and a name on the headstone cut very clear but as if it was in another language and I couldn't make it out some way. You come up then and I said, 'Dennis, what grave is this?' and you answered me, 'That's Kevin's grave, don't you remember? And you put those flowers there yourself.' Then I said, 'Well, a grave it is then, and let's not think of it any more.' Now isn't it strange to think Kevin's been dead all this time and I didn't know it?"

Dennis said, "He's not fit to mention, going off as he did after all our kindness to him, and not a word from him."

"It was because he hadn't the power any more," said Rosaleen. "And ye mustn't be down on him now. I was wrong to put my judgment on him the way I did. Ah, but to think! Kevin dead and gone, and all these natives and foreigners living on, with the paint still on their barns and houses where Kevin put it! It's very bitter."

Grieving for Kevin, she drifted into thinking of the natives and foreigners who owned farms all around her. She was afraid for her life of them, she said, the way they looked at you out of their heathen faces, the foreigners bold as brass, the natives sly and mean. "The way they do be selling the drink to all, and burning each other in their beds and splitting each other's heads with axes," she complained. "The decent people aren't safe in their houses."

Yesterday she had seen that native Guy Richards going by wild-drunk again, fit to do any crime. He was a great offense to Rosaleen with his shaggy mustaches and his shirt in rags till the brawny skin showed through, a shame to the world, staring around with his sneering eyes; living by himself in a shack and having his cronies in for drink until you could hear them shouting at all hours and careering round the countryside like the devils from hell. He would pass by the house driving his bony gray horse at top speed, standing up in the rackety buggy singing in a voice like a power of scrap-iron falling, drunk as a lord before breakfast. Once when Rosaleen was standing in her doorway wearing a green checkerboard dress, he yelled at her: "Hey, Rosie, want to come for a ride?"

"The bold stump!" said Rosaleen to Dennis, "if ever he lays a finger on me I'll shoot him dead."

"If you mind your business by day," said Dennis in a shrivelled voice, "and bar the doors well by night, there'll be no call to shoot anybody."

"Little you know!" said Rosaleen. She had a series of visions of Richards laying a finger on her and herself shooting him dead in his tracks. "Whatever would I do without ye, Dennis?" she asked him that night, as they sat on the steps in a soft darkness full of fireflies and the sound of crickets. "When I think of all the kinds of men there are in the world. That Richards!"

"When a man is young he likes his fun," said Dennis amiably, beginning to yawn. "Young, is it?" said Rosaleen warm with anger. "The old crow! Fit to have children grown he is, the same as myself, and I'm a settled woman over her nonsense!" Dennis almost said, "I'll never call you old," but all at once he was irritable too. "Will you stop your gossiping?" he asked censoriously.

Rosaleen sat silent, without rancor, but there was no denying the old man was getting old, old. He got up as if he gathered his bones in his arms, and carried himself in the house. Somewhere inside of him there must be Dennis, but where? "The world is a wilderness," she informed the crickets and frogs and fireflies.

Richards never had offered to lay a finger on Rosaleen, but now and again he pulled up at the gate when he was not quite drunk, and sat with them afternoons on the doorstep, and there were signs in him of a nice-behaved man before the drink got him down. He would tell them stories of his life, and what a desperate wild fellow he had been, all in all. Not when he was a boy, though. As long as his mother lived he had never done a thing to hurt her feelings. She wasn't what you might call a rugged woman, the least thing made her sick, and she was so religious she prayed all day long under her breath at her work, and even while she ate.

He had belonged to a society called The Sons of Temperance, with all the boys in the countryside banded together under a vow never to touch strong drink in any form: "Not even for medicinal purposes," he would quote, raising his right hand and staring solemnly before him. Quite often he would burst into a rousing march tune which he remembered from the weekly singings they had held: "With flags of temperance flying, With banners white as snow," and he could still repeat almost word for word the favorite poem he had been called upon to recite at every meeting: "At midnight, in his guarded tent, The Turk lay dreaming of the hour—"

Rosaleen wanted to interrupt sometimes and tell him that had been no sort of life, he should have been young in Ireland. But she wouldn't say it. She sat stiffly beside Dennis and looked at Richards severely out of the corner of her eye, wondering if he remembered that time he had yelled "Hey, Rosie!" at her. It was enough to make a woman wild not to find a word in her mouth for such boldness. The cheek of him, pretending nothing had happened. One day she was racking her mind for some saying that would put him in his place, while he was telling about the clambakes his gang was always having down by the creek behind the rock pile, with a keg of home-brew beer; and the dances the Railroad Street outfit gave every Saturday night in Winston. "We're always up to some devilment," he said, looking straight at Rosaleen, and before she could say scat, the hellion had winked his near eye at her. She turned away with her mouth down at the corners; after a long minute, she said, "Good day to ye, Mr. Richards," cold as ice, and went in the house. She took down the looking-glass to see what kind of look she had on her, but the wavy place made her eyes broad and blurred as the palm of her hands, and she couldn't tell her nose from her mouth in the cracked seam . . .

The pipe salesman came back next month and brought a patent cooking pot that cooked vegetables perfectly without any water in them. "It's a lot healthier way of cooking, Miz O'Toole," Dennis heard his mouthy voice going thirteen to the dozen. "I'm telling you as a friend because you're a good customer of mine."

"Is it so?" thought Dennis, and his gall stirred within him.

"You'll find it's going to be a perfect God-send for your husband's health. Old folks need to be mighty careful what they eat, and you know better than I do, Miz O'Toole, that health begins or ends right in the kitchen. Now your husband don't look as stout as he might. It's because, tasty as your cooking is, you've been pouring all the good vitamins, the sunlit life-giving elements, right down the sink . . . Right down the sink, Miz O'Toole, is where you're pouring your husband's health and your own. And I say it's a shame, a good-looking woman like you wasting your time and strength standing over the cook-stove when all you've got to do from now on is just fill this scientific little contrivance with whatever you've planned for dinner and then go away and read a good book in your parlor while it's cooking — or curl your hair."

"My hair curls by nature," said Rosaleen. Dennis almost groaned aloud from his hiding-place.

"For the love of — why, Miz O'Toole, you don't mean to tell me that! When I first saw that hair, I said to myself, why, it's so perfect it looks to be artificial! I was just getting ready to ask you how you did it so I could tell my wife. Well, if your hair curls like that, without any vitamins at all, I want to come back and have a look at it after you've been cooking in this little pot for two weeks."

Rosaleen said, "Well, it's not my looks I'm thinking about. But my husband isn't up to himself, and that's the truth, Mr. Pendleton. Ah, it would have done your heart good to see that man in his younger days! Strong as an ox he was, the way no man dared to rouse his anger. I've seen my husband, many's the time, swing on a man with his fist and send him sprawling twenty feet, and that for the least thing, mind you! But Dennis could never hold his grudge for long, and the next instant you'd see him picking the man up and dusting him off like a brother, and saying, 'Now think no more of that.' He was too forgiving always. It was his great fault."

"And look at him, now," said Mr. Pendleton, sadly.

Dennis felt pretty hot around the ears. He stood forward at the corner of the house, listening. He had never weighed more than one hundred thirty pounds at his most, a tall thin man he had been always, a little proud of his elegant shape, and not since he left school in Bristol had he lifted his hand in anger against a creature, brute or human. "He was a fine man a woman could rely on, Mr. Pendleton," said Rosaleen, "and quick as a tiger with his fists."

"I might be dead and mouldering away to dust the way she talks," thought Dennis, "and there she is throwing away the money as if she was already a gay widow woman." He tottered out bent on speaking his mind and putting a stop to such foolishness. The salesman turned a floppy smile and shrewd little eyes upon him. "Hello, Mr. O'Toole," he said, with the manly cordiality he used for husbands. "I'm just leaving you a little birthday present with the Missis here." "It's not my birthday," said Dennis, sour as a lemon. "That's just a manner of speaking!" interrupted Rosaleen, merrily. "And now many thanks to ye, Mr. Pendleton."

"Many thanks to *you*, Miz O'Toole," answered the salesman, folding away nine dollars of good green money. No more was said except good day, and Rosaleen stood shading her eyes to watch the Ford walloping off down the hummocky lane. "That's a nice, decent family man," she told Dennis, as if rebuking his evil thoughts. "He travels out of New York, and he always has the latest thing and the best. He's full of admiration for ye, too, Dennis. He said he couldn't call to mind another man of your age as sound as you are."

"I heard him," said Dennis. "I know all he said."

"Well, then," said Rosaleen, serenely. "There's no good saying it over." She hurried to wash potatoes to cook in the pot that made the hair curl.

The winter piled in upon them, and the snow was shot through with blizzards. Dennis couldn't bear a breath of cold, and all but sat in the oven, rheumy and grunty, with his muffler on. Rosaleen began to feel as if she couldn't bear the feel of her clothes in the hot kitchen, and when she did the barn work she had one chill after another. She complained that her hands were gnawed to the bone with the cold. Did Dennis realize that now, or was he going to sit like a log all winter, and where was the lad he had promised her to help with the outside work?

Dennis sat wordless under her unreasonableness, thinking she had very little work for a strong-bodied woman, and the truth was she was blaming him for something he couldn't help. Still she said nothing he could take hold of, only nipping his head off when the kettle dried up or the fire went low. There would come a day when she would say outright, "It's no life here, I won't stay here any longer," and she would drag him back to a flat in New York, or even leave him, maybe. Would she? Would she do such a thing? Such a thought had never occurred to him before. He peered at her as if he watched through a keyhole. He tried to think of something to ease her mind, but no plan came. She would look at some harmless thing around the house, say — the calendar, and suddenly tear it off the wall and stuff it in the fire. "I hate the very sight of it," she would explain, and she was always hating the very sight of one thing or another, even the cow; almost, but not quite, the cats.

One morning she sat up very tired and forlorn, and began almost before Dennis could get an eye open: "I had a dream in the night that my sister Honora was sick and dying in her bed, and was calling for me."

She bowed her head on her hands and breathed brokenly to her very toes, and said, "It's only natural I must go to Boston to find out for myself how it is, isn't it?" Dennis, pulling on the chest protector she had knitted him for Christmas, said, "I suppose so. It looks that way."

Over the coffee pot she began making her plans. "I could go if only I had a coat. It should be a fur one against this weather. A coat is what I've needed all these years. If I had a coat I'd go this very day."

"You've a great coat with fur on it," said Dennis.

"A rag of a coat!" cried Rosaleen. "And I won't have Honora see me in it. She was jealous always, Dennis, she'd be glad to see me without a coat."

"If she's sick and dying maybe she won't notice," said Dennis.

Rosaleen agreed. "And maybe it will be better to buy one there, or in New York—something in the new style."

"It's long out of your way by New York," said Dennis. "There's shorter ways to Boston than that."

"It's by New York I'm going, because the trains are better," said Rosaleen, "and I want to go that way." There was a look on her face as if you could put her on the rack and she wouldn't yield. Dennis kept silence.

When the postman passed she asked him to leave word with the native family up the hill to send their lad down for a few days to help with the chores, at the same pay as before. And tomorrow morning, if it was all the same to him, she'd be driving in with him to the train. All day long, with her hair in curl papers, she worked getting her things together in the lazy old canvas bag. She put a ham on to bake and set bread and filled the closet off the kitchen with firewood. "Maybe there'll come a message saying Honora's better and I shan't have to go," she said several times, but her eyes were excited and she walked about so briskly the floor shook.

Late in the afternoon Guy Richards knocked, and floundered in stamping his big boots. He was almost sober, but he wasn't going to be for long. Rosaleen said, "I've sad news about my sister, she's on her deathbed maybe and I'm going to Boston."

"I hope it's nothing serious, Missis O'Toole," said Richards. "Let's drink her health in this," and he took out a bottle half full of desperate-looking drink. Dennis said he didn't mind. Richards said, "Will the lady join us?" and his eyes had the devil in them if Rosaleen had ever seen it. "I will not," she said. "I've something better to do." While they drank she sat fixing the hem of her dress, and began to tell again about the persons without number she'd known who came back from the dead to bring word about themselves, and Dennis himself would back her up in it. She told again the story of the Billy-cat, her voice warm and broken with the threat of tears.

Dennis swallowed his drink, leaned over and began to fumble with his shoelace, his face sunken to a handful of wrinkles, and thought right out plainly to himself: "There's not a word of truth in it, not a word. And she'll go on telling it to the world's end for God's truth." He felt helpless, as if he were involved in some disgraceful fraud. He wanted to speak up once for all and say, "It's a lie, Rosaleen, it's something you've made up, and now let's hear no more about it." But Richards, sitting there with his ears lengthened, stopped the words in Dennis' throat. The moment passed. Rosaleen said solemnly, "My dreams never renege on me, Mr. Richards. They're all I have to go by." "It never happened at all," said Dennis inside himself, stubbornly. "Only the Billy-cat got caught in a trap and I buried him." Could this really have been all? He had a nightmarish feeling that somewhere just out of his reach lay the truth about it, he couldn't swear for certain, yet he was *almost* willing to swear that this had been all. Richards got up saying he had to be getting on to a shindig at Winston. "I'll take you to the train tomorrow, Missis O'Toole," he said. "I love doing a good turn for the ladies."

Rosaleen said very stiffly, "I'll be going in with the letter-carrier, and many thanks just the same."

She tucked Dennis into bed with great tenderness and sat by him a few minutes, putting cold cream on her face. "It won't be for long," she told him, "and you're well taken care of the whole time. Maybe by the grace of God I'll find her recovered."

"Maybe she's not sick at all," Dennis wanted to say, and said instead, "I hope so." It was nothing to him. Everything else aside, it seemed a great fuss to be making over Honora, who might die when she liked for all Dennis would turn a hair.

Dennis hoped until the last minute that Rosaleen would come to her senses and give up the trip, but at the last minute there she was with her hat and the rag of a coat on, a streak of pink powder on her chin, pulling on her tan gloves that smelt of naphtha, flourishing a handkerchief that smelt of Azurea, and going every minute to the window, looking for the postman. "In this snow maybe he'll be late," she said in a trembling voice. "What if he didn't come at all?" She took a last glimpse of herself in the mirror. "One thing I must remember, Dennis," she said in another tone. "And that is to bring back a looking-glass that won't make my face look like a monster's."

"It's a good enough glass," said Dennis, "without throwing away money." The postman came only a few minutes late. Dennis kissed Rosaleen good-by and shut the kitchen door so he could not see her climbing into the car, but he heard her laughing.

"It's just a born liar she is," Dennis said to himself, sitting by the stove, and at once he felt he had leaped head-first into a very dark pit. His better self tried to argue it out with him. "Have you no shame," said Dennis's better self, "thinking such thoughts about your own wife?" The baser Dennis persisted. "It's not half she deserves," he answered sternly, "leaving me here by my lone, and for what?" That was the great question. Certainly not to run after Honora, living or dying or dead. Where then? For what on earth? Here he stopped thinking altogether. There wasn't a spark in his mind. He had a lump on his chest could surely be pneumonia if he had a cold, which he hadn't, specially. His feet ached until you'd swear it was rheumatism, only he never had it. Still, he wasn't thinking. He stayed in this condition for two days, and the underwitted lad from the native farm above did all the work, even to washing the dishes. Dennis ate pretty well, considering the grief he was under.

Rosaleen settled back in the plush seat and thought how she had always been a great traveller. A train was like home to her, with all the other people sitting near, and the smell of newspapers and some kind of nice-smelling furniture polish and the perfume from fur collars and the train dust and something over and above she couldn't place, but it was the smell of travel: fruit, maybe, or was it machinery? She bought chocolate bars, though she wasn't hungry, and a magazine of love stories, though she was never one for reading. She only wished to prove to herself she was once more on a train going somewhere.

She watched the people coming on or leaving at the stations, greeting, or kissing good-by, and it seemed a lucky sign she did not see a sad face anywhere. There was a cold sweet sunshine on the snow, and the city people didn't look all frozen and bundled up. Their faces looked smooth after the gnarled raw frost-bitten country faces. The Grand Central hadn't changed at all, with all the crowds whirling in every direction, and a noise that almost had a tune in it, it was so steady. She held on to her bag the colored men were trying to get away from her, and stood on the sidewalk trying to remember which direction was Broadway where the moving pictures were. She hadn't seen one for five years, it was high time now! She wished she had an hour to visit her old flat in 164th Street — just a turn around the block would be enough, but there wasn't time. An old resentment rose against Honora, who was a born spoilsport and would spoil this trip for her if she could. She walked on, getting her directions, brooding a little because she had been such a city girl once, thinking only of dress and a good time, and now she hardly knew one street from another. She went in to the first moving picture theatre she saw because she liked the name of it. "The Prince of Love," she said to herself. It was about two beautiful young things, a boy with black wavy hair and a girl with curly golden hair, who loved each other and had great troubles, but it all came well in the end, and all the time it was just one fine ballroom or garden after another, and such beautiful clothes! She sniffled a little in the Azurea-smelling handkerchief, and ate her chocolates, and reminded herself these two were really alive somewhere and looked just like that, but it was hard to believe living beings could be so beautiful.

After the dancing warm lights of the screen the street was cold and dark and ugly, with the slush and the roar and the millions of people all going somewhere in a great rush, but not one face she knew. She decided to go to Boston by boat the way she used in the old days when she visited Honora. She gazed into the shop windows thinking how the styles in underthings had changed till she could hardly believe her eyes, wondering what Dennis would say if she bought the green glove silk slip with the tea-colored lace. Ah, was he eating his ham now as she told him, and did the boy come to help as he had promised?

She ate ice cream with strawberry preserves on it, and bought a powder puff and decided there was time for another moving picture. It was called "The Lover King," and it was about a king in a disguise, a lovely young man with black wavy hair and eyes would melt in his head, who married a poor country girl who was more beautiful than all the princesses and ladies in the land. Music came out of the screen, and voices talking, and Rosaleen cried, for the love song went to her heart like a dagger.

Afterward there was just time to ride in a taxi to Christopher Street and catch the boat. She felt happier the minute she set foot on board, how she always loved a ship! She ate her supper thinking, "That boy didn't have much style to his waiting. Dennis would never have kept him on in the hotel"; and afterward sat in the lounge and listened to the radio until she almost fell asleep there before everybody. She stretched out in her narrow bunk and felt the engine pounding under her, and the grand steady beat shook the very marrow of her bones. The fog horn howled and bellowed through the darkness over the rush of water, and Rosaleen turned on her side. "Howl for me, that's the way I could cry in the night in that lost heathen place," for Connecticut seemed a thousand miles and a hundred years away by now. She fell asleep and had no dreams at all.

In the morning she felt this was a lucky sign. At Providence she took the train again, and as the meeting with Honora came nearer, she grew sunken and tired. "Always Honora making trouble," she thought, standing outside the station holding her bag and thinking it strange she hadn't remembered what a dreary ugly place Boston was; she couldn't remember any good times there. Taxicab drivers were yelling in her face. Maybe it would be a good thing to go to a church and light a candle for Honora. The taxi scampered through winding streets to the nearest church, with Rosaleen thinking what she wouldn't give to be able to ride around all day, and never walk at all!

She knelt near the high altar, and something surged up in her heart and pushed the tears out of her eyes. Prayers began to tumble over each other on her lips. How long it had been since she had seen the church as it should be, dressed for a feast with candles and flowers, smelling of incense and wax. The little doleful church in Winston, now who could really pray in it? "Have mercy on us," said Rosaleen, calling on fifty saints at once, "I confess . . ." She struck her breast three times, then got up suddenly, carrying her bag, and peered into the confessionals hoping she might find a priest in one of them. "It's too early or it's not the day, but I'll come back," she promised herself with tenderness. She lit the candle for Honora and went away feeling warm and quiet. She was blind and confused, too, and could not make up her mind what to do next. Where ever should she turn? It was a burning sin to spend money on taxicabs when there was always the hungry poor in the world, but she hailed one anyhow, and gave Honora's house number. Yes, there it was, just like in old times.

She read all the names pasted on slips above the bells, all the floors front and back, but Honora's name was not among them. The janitor had never heard of Mrs. Terence Gogarty, nor Mrs. Honora Gogarty, neither. Maybe it would be in the telephone book. There were many Gogartys but no Terence nor Honora. Rosaleen smothered down the impulse to tell the janitor, a good Irishman, how her dream had gone back on her. "Thank ye kindly, it's no great matter," she said, and stepped out into the street again. The wind hacked at her shoulders through the rag of a coat, the bag was too heavy altogether. Now what kind of nature was in Honora not to drop a line and say she had moved?

Walking about with her mind in a whirl, she came to a small dingy square with iron benches and some naked trees in it. Sitting, she began to shed tears again. When one handkerchief was wet she took out another, and the fresh perfume put new heart in her. She glanced around when a shadow fell on the corner of her eye, and there hunched on the other end of the bench was a scrap of a lad with freckles, his collar turned about his ears, his red hair wilted on his forehead under his bulging cap. He slanted his gooseberry eyes at her and said, "We've all something to cry for in this world, isn't it so?"

Rosaleen said, "I'm crying because I've come a long way for nothing." The boy said, "I knew you was a County Sligo woman the minute I clapped eyes on ye."

"God bless ye for that," said Rosaleen, "for I am." "I'm County Sligo myself, long ago, and curse the day I ever thought of leaving it," said the boy, with such anger Rosaleen dried her eyes once for all and turned to have a good look at him.

"Whatever makes ye say that now?" she asked him. "It's a good country, this. There's opportunity for all here." "So I've heard tell many's the countless times," said the boy. "There's all the opportunity in the wide world to shrivel with the hunger and walk the soles off your boots hunting the work, and there's a great chance of dying in the gutter at last. God forgive me the first thought I had of coming here."

"Ye haven't been out long?" asked Rosaleen. "Eleven months and five days the day," said the boy. He plunged his hands into his pockets and stared at the freezing mud clotted around his luckless shoes.

"And what might ye do by way of a living?" asked Rosaleen. "I'm an hostler," he said. "I used to work at the Dublin race tracks, even. No man can tell me about horses," he said proudly. "And it's good work if it's to be found."

Rosaleen looked attentively at his sharp red nose, frozen it was, and the stung look around his eyes, and the sharp bones sticking out at his wrists, and was surprised at herself for thinking, in the first glance, that he had the look of Kevin. She saw different now, but think if it had been Kevin! Better off to be dead and gone. "I'm perishing of hunger and cold," she told him, "and if I knew where there was a place to eat, we'd have some lunch, for it's late."

His eyes looked like he was drowning. "Would ye? I know a place!" and he leaped up as if he meant to run. They did almost run to the edge of the square and the far corner. It was a Coffee Pot and full of the smell of hot cakes. "We'll get our fill here," said Rosaleen, taking off her gloves, "though I'd never call it a grand place."

The boy ate one thing after another as if he could never stop: roast beef and potatoes and spaghetti and custard pie and coffee, and Rosaleen ordered a package of cigarettes. It was like this with her, she was fond of the smell of tobacco, her husband was a famous smoker, never without his pipe. "It's no use keeping it in," said the boy. "I haven't a penny, yesterday and today I didn't eat till now, and I've been fit to hang myself, or go to jail for a place to lay my head."

Rosaleen said, "I'm a woman doesn't have to think of money, I have all my heart desires, and a boy like yourself has a right to think nothing of a little loan will never be missed." She fumbled in her purse and brought out a ten-dollar bill, crumpled it and pushed it under the rim of his saucer so the man behind the counter wouldn't notice. "That's for luck in the new world," she said, smiling at him. "You might be Kevin or my own brother or my own little lad alone in the world, and it'll all come back to me if ever I need it."

The boy said, "I never thought to see this day," and put the money in his pocket. Rosaleen said, "I don't even know your name, think of that!"

"I'm a blight on the name of Sullivan," said he. "Hugh it is — Hugh Sullivan."

"That's a good enough name," said Rosaleen. "I've cousins named Sullivan in Dublin, but I never saw one of them. There was a man named Sullivan married my mother's sister, my aunt Brigid she was, and she went to live in Dublin. You're not related to the Dublin Sullivans, are ye!"

"I never heard of it, but maybe I am."

"Ye have the look of a Sullivan to me," said Rosaleen, "and they're cousins of mine, some of them." She ordered more coffee and he lit another cigarette, and she told him how she had come out more than twenty-five years past, a greenhorn like himself, and everything had turned out well for her and all her family here. Then she told about her husband, how he had been head-waiter and a moneyed man, but he was old now; about the farm, if there was some one to help her, they could make a good thing of it; and about Kevin and the way he had gone away and died and sent her news of it in a dream; and this led to the dream about Honora and here she was, the first time ever a dream had gone back on her. She went on to say there was always room for a strong willing boy in the country if he knew about horses, and how it was a shame for him to be tramping the streets with an empty stomach when there was everything to be had if he only knew which way to look for it. She leaned over and took him by the arm very urgently.

"You've a right to live in a good Irish house," she told him. "Why don't ye come home with me and live there like one of the family in peace and comfort?"

Hugh Sullivan stared at her out of his glazed green eyes down the edge of his sharp nose and a crafty look came over him. "'T would be dangerous," he said. "I'd hate to try it." "Dangerous, is it?" asked Rosaleen. "What danger is there in the peaceful countryside?" "It's not safe at all," said Hugh. "I was caught at it once in Dublin, and there was a holy row! A fine woman like yourself she was, and her husband peeking through a crack in the wall the whole time. Man, that was a scrape for ye!"

Rosaleen understood in her bones before her mind grasped it. "Whatever—" she began, and the blood boiled up in her face until it was like looking through a red veil. "Ye little whelp," she said, trying to get her breath, "so it's that kind ye are, is it? I might know you're from Dublin! Never in my whole life—" Her rage rose like a bonfire in her, and she stopped. "If I was looking for a man," she said, "I'd choose a *man* and not a half-baked little . . ." She took a deep breath and started again. "The *cheek* of ye," she said, "insulting a woman could be your mother. God keep me from it! It's plain you're just an ignorant greenhorn doesn't know the ways of decent people, and now be off—" She stood up and motioned to the man behind the counter. "Out of that door now—"

He stood up too, glancing around fearfully with his squinted eyes, and put out a hand as if he would try to make it up with her. "Not so loud now, woman—it's what any man might think the way ye're—"

Rosaleen said, "Hold your tongue or I'll tear it out of your head!" and her right arm went back in a business-like way. He ducked and shot past her, then collected himself and lounged out of reach. "Farewell to ye, County Sligo woman," he said tauntingly. "I'm from County Cork myself!" and darted through the door. Rosaleen shook so she could hardly find the money for the bill, and she couldn't see her way before her, hardly, but when the cold air struck her, her head cleared, and she could have almost put a curse on Honora for making all this trouble for her . . .

She took a train the short way home, for the taste of travel had soured on her altogether. She wanted to be home and nowhere else. That shameless boy, whatever was he thinking of? "Boys do be known for having evil minds in them," she told herself, and the blood fairly crinkled in her veins. But he had said, "A fine woman like yourself," and maybe he'd met too many bold ones, and thought they were all alike; maybe she had been too free in her ways because he was Irish and looked so sad and poor. But there it was, he was a mean sort, and he would have made love to her if she hadn't stopped him, maybe. It flashed over her and she saw it clear as day — Kevin had loved her all the time, and she had sent him away to that cheap girl who wasn't half good enough for him! And Kevin a sweet decent boy would have cut off his right hand rather than give her an improper word. Kevin had loved her and she had loved Kevin and, oh, she hadn't known it in time! She bowed herself back into the corner with her elbow on the windowsill, her old fur collar pulled up around her face and wept long and bitterly for Kevin, who would have stayed if she had said the word — and now he was gone and lost and dead. She would hide herself from the world and never speak to a soul again.

"Safe and sound she is, Dennis," Rosaleen told him. "She's been dangerous but it's past. I left her in health."

"That's good enough," said Dennis, without enthusiasm. He took off his cap with the ear flaps and ran his fingers through his downy white hair and put the cap on again and stood waiting to hear the wonders of the trip; but Rosaleen had no tales to tell and was full of homecoming.

"This kitchen is a disgrace," she said, putting things to rights. "But not for all the world would I live in the city, Dennis. It's a wild heartless place, full of criminals in every direction as far as the eye can reach. I was scared for my life the whole time. Light the lamp, will you?"

The native boy sat warming his great feet in the oven, and his teeth were chattering with something more than cold. He burst out: "I seed sumpin comin' up the road whiles ago. Black. Fust it went on all fours like a dawg and then it riz upon and walked longside of me on its hind legs. I was scairt, I was. I said Shoo! at it, and it went out, like a lamp."

"Maybe it was a dog," said Dennis.

"'Twarn't a dawg, neither," said the boy.

"Maybe 'twas a cat rising up to climb a fence," said Rosaleen.

"'Twarn't a cat, neither," said the boy. "'Twarn't nothin' I ever seed afore, nor *you*, neither."

"Never you mind about that," said Rosaleen. "I have seen it and many times, when I was a girl in Ireland. It's famous there, the way it come in a black lump and rolls along the path before you, but if you call on the Holy Name and make the sign of the Cross, it flees away. Eat your supper now, and sleep here the night; ye can't go out by your lone and the Evil waiting for ye."

She bedded him down in Kevin's room, and kept Dennis awake all hours telling him about the ghosts she'd seen in Sligo. The trip to Boston seemed to have gone out of her mind entirely.

In the morning, the boy's starveling black dog rose up at the opened kitchen door and stared sorrowfully at his master. The cats streamed out in a body, and silently, intently they chased him far up the road. The boy stood on the doorstep and began to tremble again. "The old woman told me to git back fer supper," he said blankly. "Howma *ever* gointa git back fer supper *now*? The ole man'll skin me alive."

Rosaleen wrapped her green wool shawl around her head and shoulders. "I'll go along with ye and tell what happened," she said. "They'll never harm ye when they know the straight of it." For he was shaking with fright until his knees buckled under him. "He's away in his mind," she thought, with pity. "Why can't they see it and let him be in peace?"

The steady slope of the lane ran on for nearly a mile, then turned into a bumpy trail leading to a forlorn house with broken-down steps and a litter of rubbish around them. The boy hung back more and more, and stopped short when the haggard, long-toothed woman in the gray dress came out carrying a stick of stove wood. The woman stopped short too, when she recognized Rosaleen, and a sly cold look came on her face.

"Good day," said Rosaleen. "Your boy saw a ghost in the road last night, and I didn't have the heart to send him out in the darkness. He slept safe in my house."

The woman gave a sharp dry bark, like a fox. "Ghosts!" she said. "From all I hear, there's more than ghosts around your house nights, Missis O'Toole." She wagged her head and her faded tan hair flew in strings. "A pretty specimen you are, Missis O'Toole, with your old husband and the young boys in your house and the travelling salesmen and the drunkards lolling on your doorstep all hours—"

"Hold your tongue before your lad here," said Rosaleen, the back of her neck beginning to crinkle. She was so taken by surprise she couldn't find a ready answer, but stood in her tracks listening.

"A pretty sight you are, Missis O'Toole," said the woman, raising her thin voice somewhat, but speaking with deadly cold slowness. "With your trips away from your husband and your loud colored dresses and your dyed hair—"

"May God strike you dead," said Rosaleen, raising her own voice suddenly. "If you say that of my hair! And for the rest may your evil tongue rot in your head with your teeth! I'll not waste words on ye! Here's your poor lad and may God pity him in your house, a blight on it! And if my own house is burnt over my head I'll know who did it!" She turned away and whirled back to call out, "May ye be ten years dying!"

"You can curse and swear, Missis O'Toole, but the whole countryside knows about you!" cried the other, brandishing her stick like a spear.

"Much good they'll get out of it!" shouted Rosaleen, striding away in a roaring fury. "Dyed, is it?" She raised her clinched fist and shook it at the world. "Oh, the liar!" and her rage was like a drum beating time for her marching legs. What was happening these days that everybody she met had dirty minds and dirty tongues in their heads? Oh, why wasn't she strong enough to strangle them all at once? Her eyes were so hot she couldn't close her lids over them, but went on staring and walking, until almost before she knew it she came in sight of her own house, sitting like a hen quietly in a nest of snow. She slowed down, her thumping heart eased a little, and she sat on a stone by the roadside to catch her breath and gather her wits before she must see Dennis. As she sat, it came to her that the Evil walking the roads at night in this place was the bitter lies people had been telling about her, who had been a good woman all this time when many another would have gone astray. It was no comfort now to remember all the times she might have done wrong and didn't. What was the good if she was being scandalized all the same? That lad in Boston now—the little whelp. She spat on the frozen earth and wiped her mouth. Then she put her elbows on her knees and her head in her hands, and thought, "So that's the way it is here, is it? That's what my life has come to, I'm a woman of bad fame with the neighbors."

Dwelling on this strange thought, little by little she began to feel better. Jealousy, of course, that was it. "Ah, what wouldn't that poor thing give to have my hair?" and she patted it tenderly. From the beginning it had been so, the women were jealous, because the men were everywhere after her, as if it was her fault! Well, let them talk. Let them. She knew in her heart what she was, and Dennis knew, and that was enough.

"Life is a dream," she said aloud, in a soft easy melancholy. "It's a mere dream." The thought and the words pleased her, and she gazed with pleasure at the loosened stones of the wall across the road, dark brown, with the thin shining coat of ice on them, in a comfortable daze until her feet began to feel chilled.

"Let me not sit here and take my death at my early time of life," she cautioned herself, getting up and wrapping her shawl carefully around her. She was thinking how this sad countryside needed some young hearts in it, and how she wished Kevin would come back to laugh with her at that woman up the hill; with him, she could just laugh in their faces! That dream about Honora now, it hadn't come true at all. Maybe the dream about Kevin wasn't true either. If one dream failed on you it would be foolish to think another mightn't fail you too: wouldn't it, wouldn't it? She smiled at Dennis sitting by the stove.

"What did the native people have to say this morning?" he asked, trying to pretend it was nothing much to him what they said.

"Oh, we exchanged the compliments of the season," said Rosaleen. "There was no call for more." She went about singing; her heart felt light as a leaf and she couldn't have told why if she died for it. But she was a good woman and she'd show them she was going to be one to her last day. Ah, she'd show them, the low-minded things.

In the evening they settled down by the stove, Dennis cleaning and greasing his boots, Rosaleen with the long tablecloth she'd been working on for fifteen years. Dennis kept wondering what had happened in Boston, or where ever she had been. He knew he would never hear the straight of it, but he wanted Rosaleen's story about it. And there she sat mum, putting a lot of useless stitches in something she would never use, even if she ever finished it, which she would not.

"Dennis," she said after a while. "I don't put the respect on dreams I once did."

"That's maybe a good thing," said Dennis, cautiously. "And why don't you?"

"All day long I've been thinking Kevin isn't dead at all, and we shall see him in this very house before long."

Dennis growled in his throat a little. "That's no sign at all," he said. And to show that he had a grudge against her he laid down his meerschaum pipe, stuffed his old briar and lit it instead. Rosaleen took no notice at all. Her embroidery had fallen on her knees and she was listening to the rattle and clatter of a buggy coming down the road, with Richards's voice roaring a song, "I've been working on the railroad, All the live-long day!" She stood up, taking hair pins out and putting them back, her hands trembling. Then she ran to the looking-glass and saw her face there, leaping into shapes fit to scare you. "Oh, Dennis," she cried out as if it was that thought had driven her out of her chair. "I forgot to buy a looking-glass, I forgot it altogether!"

"It's a good enough glass," repeated Dennis. The buggy clattered at the gate, the song halted. Ah, he was coming in, surely! It flashed through her mind a woman would have a ruined life with such a man, it was courting death and danger to let him set foot over the threshold.

She stopped herself from running to the door, hand on the knob even before his knock sounded. Then the wheels creaked and ground again, the song started up; if he thought of stopping he changed his mind and went on, off on his career to the Saturday night dance in Winston, with his rapscallion cronies.

Rosaleen didn't know what to expect, then, and then: surely he couldn't be stopping? Ah, surely he *couldn't* be going on? She sat down again with her heart just nowhere, and took up the tablecloth, but for a long time she couldn't see the stitches. She was wondering what had become of her life; every day she had thought something great was going to happen, and it was all just straying from one terrible disappointment to another. Here in the lamplight sat Dennis and the cats, beyond in the darkness and snow lay Winston and New York and Boston, and beyond that were far-off places full of life and gaiety she'd never seen nor even heard of, and beyond everything like a green field with morning sun on it lay youth and Ireland as if they were something she had dreamed, or made up in a story. Ah, what was there to remember, or to look forward to now? Without thinking at all, she leaned over and put her head on Dennis's knee. "Whyever," she asked him, in an ordinary voice, "did ye marry a woman like me?"

"Mind you don't turn over in that chair," said Dennis. "I knew well I could never do better." His bosom began to thaw and simmer. It was going to be all right with everything, he could see that.

She sat up and felt his sleeves carefully. "I want you to wrap up warm this bitter weather, Dennis," she told him. "With two pair of socks and the chest protector, for if anything happened to you, whatever would become of me in this world?"

"Let's not think of it," said Dennis, shuffling his feet.

"Let's not, then," said Rosaleen. "For I could cry if you crooked a finger at me."

1936

WILLIAM FAULKNER
THAT WILL BE FINE

from the *American Mercury*

WILLIAM FAULKNER'S biography in the 1943 volume of *The Best American Short Stories* reads:

> He grew up in Oxford, Mississippi, a descendant of a once-wealthy family. His schooling was intermittent and he spent most of his youth loafing around his father's livery stable. He wrote poetry, strongly influenced by Omar Khayyam and Swinburne, but, he says, it was no good except as an aid to love-making. Jolted out of his lazy life by the First World War, he joined the Canadian air force. After the war he turned to earning a living at odd jobs such as house-painting, selling books in a department store, and shoveling coal into a factory furnace. He started writing fiction and suddenly, he explains, "I discovered that writing was a mighty fine thing. It enables you to make men stand on their hind legs and cast a shadow."

Faulkner (1897–1962) published a book of poems, *The Marble Faun*, in 1924. He went to work for a newspaper in New Orleans, where he met and befriended Sherwood Anderson. After Anderson persuaded him to try writing fiction — and to write about the region he knew best — Faulkner published his first novel, *Soldier's Pay*, in 1926. He went on to publish a series of celebrated short stories, poems, and novels. Among his best-known books are *Absalom, Absalom!, As I Lay Dying, Light in August,* and *The Sound and the Fury.*

In his writing, Faulkner portrayed a character's subjective experience, his or her stream of consciousness, written in dialect. His work explored themes of race and class and featured a broad swath of characters of varying ages and backgrounds. His stories appeared six times in *The Best American Short Stories* during the 1930s alone. In 1949 he was awarded the Nobel Prize. William Faulkner died of a heart attack at the age of sixty-four.

★

I

We could hear the water running into the tub. We looked at the presents scattered over the bed where Mamma had wrapped them in the colored paper, with our names on them so Grandpa could tell who they belonged to easy when he would take them off the tree. There was a present for everybody except Grandpa because Mamma said that Grandpa is too old to get presents any more.

"This one is yours," I said.

"Sho now!" Rosie said. "You come on and get in that tub like your mamma tell you."

"I know what's in it," I said. "I could tell you if I wanted to."

Rosie looked at her present. "I reckon I kin wait twell hit be handed to me at the right time," she said.

"I'll tell you what's in it for a nickel," I said.

Rosie looked at her present. "I ain't got no nickel," she said. "But I will have Christmas morning when Mr. Rodney give me that dime."

"You'll know what's in it, anyway, then and you won't pay me," I said. "Go and ask Mamma to lend you a nickel."

Then Rosie grabbed me by the arm. "You come on and get in that tub," she said. "You and money! If you ain't rich time you twenty-one, hit will be because the law done abolished money or done abolished you."

So I went and bathed and came back, with the presents all scattered out across Mamma's and Papa's bed and you could almost smell it and tomorrow night they would begin to shoot the fireworks and then you could hear it too. It would be just tonight, and then tomorrow we would get on the train, except Papa, because he would have to stay at the livery stable until after Christmas Eve, and go to Grandpa's, and then tomorrow night and then it would be Christmas and Grandpa would take the presents off the tree and call out our names, and the one from me to Uncle Rodney that I bought with my own dime and so after a while Uncle Rodney would prize open Grandpa's desk and take a dose of Grandpa's tonic and maybe he would give me another quarter for helping him, like he did last Christmas, instead of just a nickel, like he would do last summer while he was visiting Mamma and us and we were doing business with Mrs. Tucker before Uncle Rodney went home and began to work for the Compress Association, and it would be fine. Or maybe even a half a dollar and it seemed to me like I just couldn't wait.

"Jesus, I can't hardly wait," I said.

"You which?" Rosie hollered. "Jesus?" she hollered. "Jesus? You let your mamma hear you cussing and I bound you'll wait. You talk to me about a nickel! For a nickel I'd tell her just what you said."

"If you'll pay me a nickel I'll tell her myself," I said.

"Get into that bed!" Rosie hollered. "A seven-year-old boy, cussing!"

"If you will promise not to tell her, I'll tell you what's in your present and you can pay me the nickel Christmas morning," I said.

"Get in that bed!" Rosie hollered. "You and your nickel! I bound if I thought any of you all was fixing to buy even a dime present for your grandpa, I'd put in a nickel of hit myself."

"Grandpa don't want presents," I said. "He's too old."

"Hah," Rosie said. "Too old, is he? Suppose everybody decided you was too young to have nickels: what would you think about that? Hah?"

So Rosie turned out the light and went out. But I could still see the presents by the firelight: the ones for Uncle Rodney and Grandma and Aunt Louisa and Aunt Louisa's husband Uncle Fred, and Cousin Louisa and Cousin Fred and the baby and Grandpa's cook and our cook, that was Rosie, and maybe somebody ought to give Grandpa a present only maybe it ought to be Aunt Louisa because she and Uncle Fred lived with Grandpa, or maybe Uncle Rodney ought to because he lived with Grandpa too. Uncle Rodney always gave Mamma and Papa a present but maybe it would be just a waste of his time and Grandpa's time both for Uncle Rodney to give Grandpa a present, because one time I asked Mamma why Grandpa always looked at the present Uncle Rodney gave her and Papa and got so mad, and Papa began to laugh and Mamma said Papa ought to be ashamed, that it wasn't Uncle Rodney's fault if his generosity was longer than his pocketbook, and Papa said Yes, it certainly wasn't Uncle Rodney's fault, he never knew a man to try harder to get money than Uncle Rodney did, that Uncle Rodney had tried every known plan to get it except work, and that if Mamma would just think back about two years she would remember one time when Uncle Rodney could have thanked his stars that there was one man in the connection whose generosity, or whatever Mamma wanted to call it, was at least five hundred dollars shorter than his pocketbook, and Mamma said she defied Papa to say that Uncle Rodney stole the money, that it had been malicious persecution and Papa knew it, and that Papa and most other men were prejudiced against Uncle Rodney, why she didn't know, and that if Papa begrudged having lent Uncle Rodney the five hundred dollars when the family's good name was at stake to say so and Grandpa would raise it somehow and pay Papa back, and then she began to cry and Papa said "All right, all right," and Mamma cried and said how Uncle Rodney was the baby and that must be why Papa hated him and Papa said "All right, all right; for God's sake, all right."

Because Mamma and Papa didn't know that Uncle Rodney had been handling his business all the time he was visiting us last summer, any more than the people in Mottstown knew that he was doing business last Christmas when I worked for him the first time and he paid me the quarter. Because he said that if he preferred to do business with ladies instead of men it wasn't anybody's business except his, not even Mr. Tucker's. He said how I never went around telling people about Papa's business and I said how everybody knew Papa was in the livery-stable business and so I didn't have to tell them, and Uncle Rodney said Well, that was what half of the nickel was for and did I want to keep on making the nickels or did I want him to hire somebody else? So I would go on ahead and watch through Mr. Tucker's fence until he came out to go to town and I would go along behind the fence to the corner and watch until Mr. Tucker was out of sight and then I would put my hat on top of the fence post and leave it there until I saw Mr. Tucker coming back. Only he never came back while I was there because Uncle Rodney would always be through before then, and he would come up and we would walk back home and he would tell Mamma how far we had walked that day and Mamma would say how good that was for Uncle Rodney's health. So he just paid me a nickel at home. It wasn't as much as the quarter when he was in business with the other lady in Mottstown Christmas, but that was just one time and he visited us all summer and so by that time I had a lot more than a quarter. And besides the other time was Christmas and he took a dose of Grandpa's tonic before he paid me the quarter and so maybe this time it might be even a half a dollar. I couldn't hardly wait.

II

But it got to be daylight at last and I put on my Sunday suit, and I would go to the front door and watch for the hack and then I would go to the kitchen and ask Rosie if it wasn't almost time and she would tell me the train wasn't even due for two hours yet. Only while she was telling me we heard the hack, and so I thought it was time for us to go and get on the train and it would be fine, and then we would go to Grandpa's and then it would be tonight and then tomorrow and maybe it would be a half a dollar this time and Jesus it would be fine. Then Mamma came running out without even her hat on and she said how it was two hours yet and she wasn't even dressed and John Paul said "Yessum," but Papa sent him and Papa said for John Paul to tell Mamma that Aunt Louisa was here and for Mamma to hurry. So we put the basket of presents into the hack and I rode on the box with John Paul and Mamma hollering from inside the hack about Aunt Louisa, and John Paul said that Aunt Louisa had come in a hired buggy and Papa took her to the hotel to eat breakfast because she left Mottstown before daylight even. And so maybe Aunt Louisa had come to Jefferson to help Mamma and Papa get a present for Grandpa.

"Because we have one for everybody else," I said, "I bought one for Uncle Rodney with my own money."

Then John Paul began to laugh and I said, "Why?" and he said it was at the notion of me giving Uncle Rodney anything that he would want to use, and I said, "Why?" and John Paul said because I was shaped like a man, and I said, "Why?" and John Paul said he bet Papa would like to give Uncle Rodney a present without even waiting for Christmas, and I said, "What?" and John Paul said, "A job of work." And I told John Paul how Uncle Rodney had been working all the time he was visiting us last summer, and John Paul quit laughing and said "Sho," he reckoned anything a man kept at all the time, night and day both, he would call it work no matter how much fun it started out to be, and I said, "Anyway, Uncle Rodney works now, he works in the office of the Compress Association," and John Paul laughed good then and said it would sholy take a whole association to compress Uncle Rodney. And then Mamma began to holler to go straight to the hotel, and John Paul said "Nome, Papa said to come straight to the livery stable and wait for him." And so we went to the hotel and Aunt Louisa and Papa came out and Papa helped Aunt Louisa into the hack and Aunt Louisa began to cry and Mamma hollering, "Louisa! Louisa! What is it? What has happened?" and Papa saying, "Wait now. Wait. Remember the nigger," and that meant John Paul, and so it must have been a present for Grandpa and it didn't come.

And then we didn't go on the train after all. We went to the stable and they already had the light road hack hitched up and waiting, and Mamma was crying now and saying how Papa never even had his Sunday clothes and Papa cussing now and saying, "Damn the clothes." If we didn't get to Uncle Rodney before the others caught him, Papa would just wear the clothes Uncle Rodney had on now. So we got into the road hack fast and Papa closed the curtains and then Mamma and Aunt Louisa could cry all right and Papa hollered to John Paul to go home and tell Rosie to pack his Sunday suit and take her to the train; anyway that would be fine for Rosie. So we didn't go on the train but we went fast, with Papa driving and saying Didn't anybody know where he was? and Aunt Louisa quit crying awhile and said how Uncle Rodney didn't come to supper last night, but right after supper he came in and how Aunt Louisa had a terrible feeling as soon as she heard his step in the hall and how Uncle Rodney wouldn't tell her until they were in his room and the door closed and then he said he must have two thousand dollars and Aunt Louisa said where in the world could she get two thousand dollars? and Uncle Rodney said, "Ask Fred"—that was Aunt Louisa's husband—"and George"—that was Papa; "tell them they would have to dig it up," and Aunt Louisa said she had that terrible feeling and she said, "Rodney! Rodney! What"—and Uncle Rodney begun to cuss and say, "Dammit, don't start sniveling and crying now," and Aunt Louisa said, "Rodney, what have you done now?" and then they both heard the knocking at the door and how Aunt Louisa looked at Uncle Rodney and she knew the truth before she even laid eyes on Mr. Pruitt and the sheriff, and how she said, "Don't tell Pa! Keep it from Pa! It will kill him . . ."

"Who?" Papa said. "Mister who?"

"Mr. Pruitt," Aunt Louisa said, crying again. "The president of the Compress Association. They moved to Mottstown last spring. You don't know him."

So she went down to the door and it was Mr. Pruitt and the sheriff. And how Aunt Louisa begged Mr. Pruitt for Grandpa's sake and how she gave Mr. Pruitt her oath that Uncle Rodney would stay right there in the house until Papa could get there, and Mr. Pruitt said how he hated it to happen at Christmas too and so for Grandpa's and Aunt Louisa's sake he would give them until the day after Christmas if Aunt Louisa would promise him that Uncle Rodney would not try to leave Mottstown. And how Mr. Pruitt showed her with her own eyes the check with Grandpa's name signed to it and how even Aunt Louisa could see that Grandpa's name had been—and then Mamma said, "Louisa! Louisa! Remember Georgie!" and that was me, and Papa cussed too, hollering, "How in damnation do you expect to keep it from him? By hiding the newspapers?" and Aunt Louisa cried again and said how everybody was bound to know it, that she didn't expect or hope that any of us could ever hold our heads up again, that all she hoped for was to keep it from Grandpa because it would kill him. She cried hard then and Papa had to stop at a branch and get down and soak his handkerchief for Mamma to wipe

Aunt Louisa's face with it and then Papa took the bottle of tonic out of the dash pocket and put a few drops on the handkerchief, and Aunt Louisa smelled it and then Papa took a dose of the tonic out of the bottle and Mamma said, "George!" and Papa drank some more of the tonic and then made like he was handing the bottle back for Mamma and Aunt Louisa to take a dose too and said, "I don't blame you. If I was a woman in this family I'd take to drink too. Now let me get this bond business straight."

"It was those road bonds of Ma's," Aunt Louisa said.

We were going fast again now because the horses had rested while Papa was wetting the handkerchief and taking the dose of tonic, and Papa was saying, "All right, what about the bonds?" when all of a sudden he jerked around in the seat and said, "Road bonds? Do you mean he took that damn screw driver and prized open your mother's desk too?"

Then Mamma said, "George! how can you?" only Aunt Louisa was talking now, quick now, not crying now, not yet, and Papa with his head turned over his shoulder and saying, did Aunt Louisa mean that that five hundred Papa had to pay out two years ago wasn't all of it? And Aunt Louisa said it was twenty-five hundred, only they didn't want Grandpa to find it out, and so Grandma put up her road bonds for security on the note, and how they said now that Uncle Rodney had redeemed Grandma's note and the road bonds from the bank with some of the Compress Association's bonds out of the safe in the Compress Association office, because when Mr. Pruitt found the Compress Association's bonds were missing he looked for them and found them in the bank and when he looked in the Compress Association's safe all he found was the check for two thousand dollars with Grandpa's name signed to it, and how Mr. Pruitt hadn't lived in Mottstown but a year but even he knew that Grandpa never signed that check and besides he looked in the bank again and Grandpa never had two thousand dollars in it, and how Mr. Pruitt said how he would wait until the day after Christmas if Aunt Louisa would give him her sworn oath that Uncle Rodney would not go away, and Aunt Louisa did it and then she went back upstairs to plead with Uncle Rodney to give Mr. Pruitt the bonds and she went into Uncle Rodney's room where she had left him, and the window was open and Uncle Rodney was gone.

"Damn Rodney!" Papa said. "The bonds! You mean, nobody knows where the bonds are?"

Now we were going fast because we were coming down the last hill and into the valley where Mottstown was. Soon we would begin to smell it again; it would be just today and then tonight and then it would be Christmas, and Aunt Louisa sitting there with her face white like a whitewashed fence that has been rained on and Papa said, "Who in hell ever gave him such a job anyway?" and Aunt Louisa said "Mr. Pruitt," and Papa said how even if Mr. Pruitt had only lived in Mottstown a few months, and then Aunt Louisa began to cry without even putting her handkerchief to her face this time and Mamma looked at Aunt Louisa and she began to cry too and Papa took out the whip and hit the team a belt with it even if they were going fast and he cussed. "Damnation to hell," Papa said. "I see. Pruitt's married."

Then we could see it too. There were holly wreaths in the windows like at home in Jefferson, and I said, "They shoot fireworks in Mottstown too like they do in Jefferson."

Aunt Louisa and Mamma were crying good now, and now it was Papa saying, "Here, here; remember Georgie," and that was me, and Aunt Louisa said, "Yes, yes! Painted common thing, traipsing up and down the streets all afternoon alone in a buggy, and the one and only time Mrs. Church called on her, and that was because of Mr. Pruitt's position alone, Mrs. Church found her without corsets on and Mrs. Church told me she smelled liquor on her breath."

And Papa saying "Here, here," and Aunt Louisa crying good and saying how it was Mrs. Pruitt that did it because Uncle Rodney was young and easy led because he never had had opportunities to meet a nice girl and marry her, and Papa was driving fast toward Grandpa's house and he said, "Marry? Rodney marry? What in hell pleasure would he get out of slipping out of his own house and waiting until after dark and slipping around to the back and climbing up the gutter and into a room where there wasn't anybody in it but his own wife?"

And so Mamma and Aunt Louisa were crying good when we got to Grandpa's.

III

And Uncle Rodney wasn't there. We came in, and Grandma said how Mandy, that was Grandpa's cook, hadn't come to cook breakfast and when Grandma sent Emmeline, that was Aunt Louisa's baby's nurse, down to Mandy's cabin in the back yard, the door was locked on the inside, but Mandy wouldn't answer and then Grandma went down there herself and Mandy wouldn't answer and so Cousin Fred climbed in the window and Mandy was gone and Uncle Fred had just got back from town then and he and Papa both hollered, "Locked? on the inside? and nobody in it?"

And then Uncle Fred told Papa to go in and keep Grandpa entertained and he would go and then Aunt Louisa grabbed Papa and Uncle Fred both and said she would keep Grandpa quiet and for both of them to go and find him, find him, and Papa said, "If only the fool hasn't tried to sell them to somebody," and Uncle Fred said, "Good God, man, don't you know that check was dated ten days ago?" And so we went in where Grandpa was reared back in his chair and saying how he hadn't expected Papa until tomorrow but, by God, he was glad to see somebody at last because he waked up this morning and his cook had quit and Louisa had chased off somewhere before daylight and now he couldn't even find Uncle Rodney to go down and bring his mail and a cigar or two back, and so, thank God, Christmas never came but once a year and so be damned if he wouldn't be glad when it was over, only he was laughing now because when he said that about Christmas before Christmas he always laughed, it wasn't until after Christmas that he didn't laugh when he said that about Christmas. Then Aunt Louisa got Grandpa's keys out of his pocket herself and opened the desk where Uncle Rodney would prize it open with a screw driver, and took out Grandpa's tonic and then Mamma said for me to go and find Cousin Fred and Cousin Louisa.

So Uncle Rodney wasn't there. Only at first I thought maybe it wouldn't be a quarter even, it wouldn't be nothing this time, so at first all I had to think about was that anyway it would be Christmas and that would be something anyway. Because I went on around the house, and so after a while Papa and Uncle Fred came out, and I could see them through the bushes knocking at Mandy's door and calling, "Rodney, Rodney," like that. Then I had to get back in the bushes because Uncle Fred had to pass right by me to go to the woodshed to get the axe to open Mandy's door. But they couldn't fool Uncle Rodney. If Mr. Tucker couldn't fool Uncle Rodney in Mr. Tucker's own house, Uncle Fred and Papa ought to have known they couldn't fool him right in his own papa's back yard. So I didn't even need to hear them. I just waited until after a while Uncle Fred came back out the broken door and came to the woodshed and took the axe and pulled the lock and hasp and steeple off the woodhouse door and went back and then Papa came out of Mandy's house and they nailed the woodhouse lock onto Mandy's door and locked it and they went around behind Mandy's house, and I could hear

Uncle Fred nailing the windows up. Then they went back to the house. But it didn't matter if Mandy was in the house too and couldn't get out, because the train came from Jefferson with Rosie and Papa's Sunday clothes on it and so Rosie was there to cook for Grandpa and us and so that was all right too.

But they couldn't fool Uncle Rodney. I could have told them that. I could have told them that sometimes Uncle Rodney even wanted to wait until after dark to even begin to do business. And so it was all right even if it was late in the afternoon before I could get away from Cousin Fred and Cousin Louisa. It was late; soon they would begin to shoot the fireworks downtown, and then we would be hearing it too, so I could just see his face a little between the slats where Papa and Uncle Fred had nailed up the back window; I could see his face where he hadn't shaved, and he was asking me why in hell it took me so long because he had heard the Jefferson train come before dinner, before eleven o'clock, and laughing about how Papa and Uncle Fred had nailed him up in the house to keep him when that was exactly what he wanted, and that I would have to slip out right after supper somehow and did I reckon I could manage it? And I said how last Christmas it had been a quarter, but I didn't have to slip out of the house that time, and he laughed, saying, "Quarter? Quarter?" did I ever see ten quarters all at once? and I never did, and he said for me to be there with the screw driver right after supper and I would see ten quarters, and to remember that even God didn't know where he is and so for me to get the hell away and stay away until I came back after dark with the screw driver.

And they couldn't fool me either. Because I had been watching the man all afternoon, even when he thought I was just playing and maybe because I was from Jefferson instead of Mottstown and so I wouldn't know who he was. But I did, because once when he was walking past the back fence and he stopped and lit his cigar again and I saw the badge under his coat when he struck the match and so I knew he was like Mr. Watts at Jefferson that catches the niggers. So I was playing by the fence and I could hear him stopping and looking at me and I played and he said, "Howdy, son. Santy Claus coming to see you tomorrow?"

"Yes, sir," I said.

"You're Miss Sarah's boy, from up at Jefferson, ain't you?" he said.

"Yes, sir," I said.

"Come to spend Christmas with your Grandpa, eh?" he said. "I wonder if your Uncle Rodney's at home this afternoon."

"No, sir," I said.

"Well, well, that's too bad," he said. "I wanted to see him a minute. He's downtown, I reckon?"

"No, sir," I said.

"Well, well," he said. "You mean he's gone away on a visit, maybe?"

"Yes, sir," I said.

"Well, well," he said. "That's too bad. I wanted to see him on a little business. But I reckon it can wait." Then he looked at me and then he said, "You're sure he's out of town, then?"

"Yes, sir," I said.

"Well, that was all I wanted to know," he said. "If you happen to mention this to your Aunt Louisa or your Uncle Fred you can tell them that was all I wanted to know."

"Yes, sir," I said. So he went away. And he didn't pass the house any more. I watched for him, but he didn't come back. So he couldn't fool me either.

IV

Then it began to get dark and they started to shoot the fireworks downtown. I could hear them, and soon we would be seeing the Roman candles and skyrockets and I would have the ten quarters then and I thought about the basket full of presents and I thought how maybe I could go on downtown when I got through working for Uncle Rodney and buy a present for Grandpa with a dime out of the ten quarters and give it to him tomorrow and maybe, because nobody else had given him a present, Grandpa might give me a quarter too instead of the dime tomorrow, and that would be twenty-one quarters, except for the dime, and that would be fine sure enough. But I didn't have time to do that. We ate supper, and Rosie had to cook that too, and Mamma and Aunt Louisa with powder on their faces where they had been crying, and Grandpa; it was Papa helping him take a dose of tonic every now and then all afternoon while Uncle Fred was downtown, and Uncle Fred came back and Papa came out in the hall and Uncle Fred said he had looked everywhere, in the bank and in the Compress, and how Mr. Pruitt had helped him but they couldn't find a sign either of them or of the money, because Uncle Fred was afraid because one night last week Uncle Rodney hired a rig and went somewhere and Uncle Fred found out Uncle Rodney drove over to the main line at Kingston and caught the fast train to

Memphis, and Papa said, "Damnation," and Uncle Fred said, "By God, we will go down there after supper and sweat it out of him, because at least we have got him. I told Pruitt that and he said that if we hold to him, he will hold off and give us a chance."

So Uncle Fred and Papa and Grandpa came in to supper together, with Grandpa between them saying, "Christmas don't come but once a year, thank God, so hooray for it," and Papa and Uncle Fred saying, "Now you are all right, Pa; straight ahead now, Pa," and Grandpa would go straight ahead awhile and then begin to holler, "Where in hell is that damn boy?" and that meant Uncle Rodney, and that Grandpa was a good mind to go downtown himself and haul Uncle Rodney out of that damn poolhall and make him come home and see his kinfolks. And so we ate supper and Mamma said she would take the children upstairs and Aunt Louisa said, "No," Emmeline could put us to bed, and so we went up the back stairs, and Emmeline said how she had done already had to cook breakfast extra today and if folks thought she was going to waste all her Christmas doing extra work they never had the sense she give them credit for and that this looked like to her it was a good house to be away from nohow, and so we went into the room and then after a while I went back down the back stairs and I remembered where to find the screw driver too. Then I could hear the firecrackers plain from downtown, and the moon was shining now but I could still see the Roman candles and the skyrockets running up the sky. Then Uncle Rodney's hand came out of the crack in the shutter and took the screw driver. I couldn't see his face now and it wasn't laughing exactly, it didn't sound exactly like laughing, it was just the way he breathed behind the shutter. Because they couldn't fool him.

"All right," he said. "Now that's ten quarters. But wait. Are you sure nobody knows where I am?"

"Yes, sir," I said. "I waited by the fence until he come and asked me."

"Which one?" Uncle Rodney said.

"The one that wears the badge," I said.

Then Uncle Rodney cussed. But it wasn't mad cussing. It sounded just like it sounded when he was laughing except the words.

"He said if you were out of town on a visit, and I said, Yes, sir," I said.

"Good," Uncle Rodney said. "By God, some day you will be as good a business man as I am. And I won't make you a liar much longer, either. So now you have got ten quarters, haven't you?"

"No," I said. "I haven't got them yet."

Then he cussed again, and I said, "I will hold my cap up and you can drop them in it and they won't spill then."

Then he cussed hard, only it wasn't loud. "Only I'm not going to give you ten quarters," he said, and I begun to say, "You said—" and Uncle Rodney said, "Because I am going to give you twenty."

And I said, "Yes, sir," and he told me how to find the right house, and what to do when I found it. Only there wasn't any paper to carry this time because Uncle Rodney said how this was a twenty-quarter job, and so it was too important to put on paper and besides I wouldn't need a paper because I would not know them anyhow, and his voice coming hissing down from behind the shutter where I couldn't see him and still sounding like when he cussed while he was saying how Papa and Uncle Fred had done him a favor by nailing up the door and window and they didn't even have sense enough to know it.

"Start at the corner of the house and count three windows. Then throw the handful of gravel against the window. Then when the window opens—never mind who it will be, you won't know anyway—just say who you are and then say 'He will be at the corner with the buggy in ten minutes. Bring the jewelry.' Now you say it," Uncle Rodney said.

"He will be at the corner with the buggy in ten minutes. Bring the jewelry," I said.

"Say 'Bring all the jewelry,'" Uncle Rodney said.

"Bring all the jewelry," I said.

"Good," Uncle Rodney said. Then he said, "Well? What are you waiting on?"

"For the twenty quarters," I said.

Uncle Rodney cussed again. "Do you expect me to pay you before you have done the work?" he said.

"You said about a buggy," I said. "Maybe you will forget to pay me before you go and you might not get back until after we go back home. And besides, that day last summer when we couldn't do any business with Mrs. Tucker because she was sick and you wouldn't pay me the nickel because you said it wasn't your fault Mrs. Tucker was sick."

Then Uncle Rodney cussed hard and quiet behind the crack and then he said, "Listen. I haven't got the twenty quarters now. I haven't even got one quarter now. And the only way I can get any is to get out of here and finish this business. And I can't finish this business tonight unless you do your work. See? I'll be right behind you. I'll be waiting right there at the corner in the buggy when you come back. Now, go on. Hurry."

V

So I went on across the yard, only the moon was bright now and I walked behind the fence until I got to the street. And I could hear the firecrackers and I could see the Roman candles and skyrockets sliding up the sky, but the fireworks were all downtown, and so all I could see along the street was the candles and wreaths in the windows. So I came to the lane, went up the lane to the stable, and I could hear the horse in the stable, but I didn't know whether it was the right stable or not; but pretty soon Uncle Rodney kind of jumped around the corner of the stable and said, "Here you are," and he showed me where to stand and listen toward the house and he went back into the stable. But I couldn't hear anything but Uncle Rodney harnessing the horse, and then he whistled and I went back and he had the horse already hitched to the buggy and I said, "Whose horse and buggy is this; it's a lot skinnier than Grandpa's horse?" And Uncle Rodney said, "It's my horse now, only damn this moonlight to hell." Then I went back down the lane to the street and there wasn't anybody coming so I waved my arm in the moonlight, and the buggy came up and I got in and we went fast. The side curtains were up and so I couldn't see the skyrockets and Roman candles from town, but I could hear the firecrackers and I thought maybe we were going through town and maybe Uncle Rodney would stop and give me some of the twenty quarters and I could buy Grandpa a present for tomorrow, but we didn't; Uncle Rodney just raised the side curtain without stopping and then I could see the house, the two magnolia trees, but we didn't stop until we came to the corner.

"Now," Uncle Rodney said, "when the window opens, say 'He will be at the corner in ten minutes. Bring *all* the jewelry.' Never mind who it will be. You don't want to know who it is. You want to even forget what house it is. See?"

"Yes, sir," I said. "And then you will pay me the—"

"Yes!" he said, cussing. "Yes! Get out of here quick!"

So I got out and the buggy went on and I went back up the street. And the house was dark all right except for one light, so it was the right one, besides the two trees. So I went across the yard and counted the three windows and I was just about to throw the gravel when a lady ran out from behind a bush and grabbed me. She kept on trying to say something, only I couldn't tell what it was, and besides she never had time to say very much anyhow because a man ran out from behind another bush and grabbed us both. Only he grabbed her by the mouth, because I could tell that from the kind of slobbering noise she made while she was fighting to get loose.

"Well, boy?" he said. "What is it? Are you the one?"

"I work for Uncle Rodney," I said.

"Then you're the one," he said. Now the lady was fighting and slobbering sure enough, but he held her by the mouth. "All right. What is it?"

Only I didn't know Uncle Rodney ever did business with men. But maybe after he began to work in the Compress Association he had to. And then he had told me I would not know them anyway, so maybe that was what he meant.

"He says to be at the corner in ten minutes," I said. "And to bring all the jewelry. He said for me to say that twice. Bring all the jewelry."

The lady was slobbering and fighting worse than ever now, so maybe he had to turn me loose so he could hold her with both hands.

"Bring all the jewelry," he said, holding the lady with both hands now. "That's a good idea. That's fine. I don't blame him for telling you to say that twice. All right. Now you go back to the corner and wait and when he comes, tell him this: 'She says to come and help carry it.' Say that to him twice, too. Understand?"

"Then I'll get my twenty quarters," I said.

"Twenty quarters, hah?" the man said, holding the lady. "That's what you are to get, is it? That's not enough. You tell him this, too: 'She says to give you a piece of the jewelry.' Understand?"

"I just want my twenty quarters," I said.

Then he and the lady went back behind the bushes again and I went on, too, back toward the corner, and I could see the Roman candles and skyrockets again from toward town and I could hear the firecrackers, and then the buggy came back and Uncle Rodney was hissing again behind the curtain like when he was behind the slats on Mandy's window.

"Well?" he said.

"She said for you to come and help carry it," I said.

"What?" Uncle Rodney said. "She said he's not there?"

"No, sir. She said for you to come and help carry it. For me to say that twice." Then I said, "Where's my twenty quarters?" because he had already jumped out of the buggy and jumped across the walk into the shadow of some bushes. So I went into the bushes too and said, "You said you would give—"

"All right; all right!" Uncle Rodney said. He was kind of squatting along the bushes; I could hear him breathing. "I'll give them to you tomorrow. I'll give you thirty quarters tomorrow. Now you get to hell on home. And if they have been down to Mandy's house, you don't know anything. Run, now. Hurry."

"I'd rather have the twenty quarters tonight," I said.

He was squatting fast along in the shadow of the bushes, and I was right behind him, because when he whirled around he almost touched me, but I jumped back out of the bushes in time and he stood there cussing at me and then he stooped down and I saw it was a stick in his hand and I turned and ran. Then he went on, squatting along in the shadow, and then I went back to the buggy, because the day after Christmas we would go back to Jefferson, and so if Uncle Rodney didn't get back before then I would not see him again until next summer and then maybe he would be in business with another lady and my twenty quarters would be like my nickel that time when Mrs. Tucker was sick. So I waited by the buggy and I could watch the skyrockets and the Roman candles and I could hear the firecrackers from town, only it was late now and so maybe all the stores would be closed and so I couldn't buy Grandpa a present, even when Uncle Rodney came back and gave me my twenty quarters. So I was listening to the firecrackers and thinking about how maybe I could tell Grandpa that I had wanted to buy him a present and so maybe he might give me fifteen cents instead of a dime anyway, when all of a sudden they started shooting firecrackers back at the house where Uncle Rodney had gone. Only they just shot five of them fast, and when they didn't shoot any more I thought that maybe in a minute they would shoot the skyrockets and Roman candles too. But they didn't. They just shot the five firecrackers right quick and then stopped, and I stood by the buggy and then folks began to come out of the houses and holler at one another and then I began to see men running toward the house where Uncle Rodney had gone, and then a man came out of the yard fast and went up the street toward Grandpa's and I thought at first it was Uncle Rodney and that he had forgotten the buggy, until I saw that it wasn't.

But Uncle Rodney never came back and so I went on toward the yard to where the men were, because I could still watch the buggy too and see Uncle Rodney if he came back out of the bushes, and I came to the yard and I saw six men carrying something long and then two other men ran up and stopped me and one of them said, "Hell-fire, it's one of those kids, the one from Jefferson." And I could see then that what the men were carrying was a window blind with something wrapped in a quilt on it and so I thought at first that they had come to help Uncle

Rodney carry the jewelry, only I didn't see Uncle Rodney anywhere, and then one of the men said, "Who? One of the kids? Hell-fire, somebody take him on home."

So the man picked me up, but I said I had to wait on Uncle Rodney, and the man said that Uncle Rodney would be all right, and I said, "But I want to wait for him here," and then one of the men behind us said, "Damn it, get him on out of here," and we went on. I was riding on the man's back and then I could look back and see the six men in the moonlight carrying the blind with the bundle on it, and I said did it belong to Uncle Rodney? and the man said, "No, if it belonged to anybody now it belonged to Grandpa." And so then I knew what it was.

"It's a side of beef," I said. "You are going to take it to Grandpa." Then the other man made a funny sound and the one I was riding on said, "Yes, you might call it a side of beef," and I said, "It's a Christmas present for Grandpa. Who is it going to be from? Is it from Uncle Rodney?"

"No," the man said. "Not from him. Call it from the men of Mottstown. From all the husbands in Mottstown."

VI

Then we came in sight of Grandpa's house. And now the lights were all on, even on the porch, and I could see folks in the hall, I could see ladies with shawls over their heads, and some more of them going up the walk toward the porch, and then I could hear somebody in the house that sounded like singing and then Papa came out of the house and came down the walk to the gate and we came up and the man put me down and I saw Rosie waiting at the gate too. Only it didn't sound like singing now because there wasn't any music with it, and so maybe it was Aunt Louisa again and so maybe she didn't like Christmas now any better than Grandpa said he didn't like it.

"It's a present for Grandpa," I said.

"Yes," Papa said. "You go on with Rosie and go to bed. Mamma will be there soon. But you be a good boy until she comes. You mind Rosie. All right, Rosie. Take him on. Hurry."

"Yo don't need to tell me that," Rosie said. She took my hand. "Come on."

Only we didn't go back into the yard, because Rosie came out the gate and we went up the street. And then I thought maybe we were going around the back to dodge the people and we didn't do that, either. We just went on up the street, and I said, "Where are we going?"

And Rosie said, "We gonter sleep at a lady's house name Mrs. Jordon."

So we went on. I didn't say anything. Because Papa had forgotten to say anything about my slipping out of the house yet and so maybe if I went on to bed and stayed quiet he would forget about it until tomorrow too. And besides, the main thing was to get a holt of Uncle Rodney and get my twenty quarters before we went back home, and so maybe that would be all right tomorrow too. So we went on and Rosie said, "Yonder's the house," and we went in the yard and then all of a sudden Rosie saw the possum. It was in a persimmon tree in Mrs. Jordon's yard and I could see it against the moonlight too, and I hollered, "Run! Run and get Mrs. Jordon's ladder!"

And Rosie said, "Ladder my foot! You going to bed!"

But I didn't wait. I began to run toward the house, with Rosie running behind me and hollering, "You, Georgie! You come back here!" But I didn't stop. We could get the ladder and get the possum and give it to Grandpa along with the side of meat and it wouldn't cost even a dime and then maybe Grandpa might even give me a quarter too, and then when I got the twenty quarters from Uncle Rodney I would have twenty-one quarters and that will be fine.

1940-1950

THE NEW YORKER WAS ESTABLISHED IN 1925, AND IN its early years published short stories that were typically comic. The magazine's reputation for publishing only humor caused critics to pay less attention to its stories, although pieces by Dorothy Parker, Emily Hahn, and Morley Callaghan did appear in *The Best American Short Stories* over the years. In 1940 Katharine White, fiction editor for the magazine, decided to publish an anthology of stories. In a memo to her boss, White wrote, "What this book should be, as I see it, is a distinguished collection of short stories which, though we didn't set out to do it, we seemed to have amassed during the years. It would be mostly savage, serious, moving, or just well-written fiction with some that are funny in part."

White's anthology brought the desired recognition. In 1941 alone, series editor Edward O'Brien chose three stories from the magazine to appear in *The Best American Short Stories*. Four appeared in the next volume. O'Brien's vision meshed with White's definition of a "*New Yorker* short story," a story that traces a development of character or situation "free of the burden of plot."

O'Brien died in 1941 of a heart attack. His mother was probably the only one who knew of the heart condition that had plagued him most of his life. She had stayed near him, to the despair of his wives, throughout the years, most likely to monitor his health and well-being. His death was widely reported, even during this time of war.

A decade before his death, O'Brien had suggested to Martha Foley that she and Whit Burnett would be the logical successors for his job should anything happen to him. When he died, Houghton Mifflin approached Foley about taking over the job, and in 1941 she parted ways with both Burnett and *Story* and began editing the series.

Like O'Brien, Foley had grown up in Boston. She had dropped out of Boston University, become a copy editor in New York and, soon after, a journalist in California. Like Burnett, she wrote fiction. O'Brien had chosen many of her stories to appear in *The Best American Short Stories.* Foley was an ardent feminist and socialist; when she was twenty, she was arrested and jailed for protesting about women's rights at a rally for President Woodrow Wilson. She had bright red hair and smoked from a cigarette holder.

When she took the helm of the series, she defined a good short story more loosely than O'Brien had: "A good short story is a story which is not too long and which gives the reader the feeling he has undergone a memorable experience." Perhaps, given O'Brien's mixed reception in his early years of overseeing the series, this generality served as insurance against future critics.

Foley paid tribute to O'Brien in each foreword. She also supported small and regional magazines. She was equally opposed to commercialism and agreed that the series should be a vehicle to promote literary stories. She wrote, "Unfortunately most people never see these [literary] magazines because few ever appear on newsstands, owing to a monopolistic distribution system and the usurpation of all the media by advertisers in the last half-century." Though the general popularity of short stories had begun to wane, Foley noted that the overall literary quality had improved. In her first foreword, she declared that "the lifelessly plotted story, with the forced happy or trick ending, is dying, slowly but surely dying."

Foley's reading process was less orderly than O'Brien's. She kept a supply of colored index cards and on each wrote the author's name, the title of the story, the name and date of the magazine, and a few words to jog her memory about the story itself. Those she found superlative were given orange cards; those "quite good" got blue cards; "above average" stories got white. "The others I try to forget." She read in fits and starts, never on regular days, and often she found herself weeks behind.

Foley had a keen eye for fictional trends. In 1943 came "a multitude of stories obviously written with the word 'escape' in the minds of their authors and often so labeled by the editors seeking them. And, because their authors are so desperately and self-consciously in flight from any reality, the stories themselves lack significance." She later noted in that year a preponderance of "non-realistic" or fantasy stories, some with overtones of "mysticism": "In modern atom-bomb-inventing, air-plane-traveling, electrically powered United States of America the new-est widespread literary development is, of all things, a re-emergence of the old-fashioned ghost story!" She observed that writing had become more sentimental after the war: "Writers are no longer afraid of their emotions." Foley posited, as O'Brien had, that the best writing about a war comes a generation later: "It often has been noted that the great sto-ries of the last World War were not written until after the conflict had ended. There had to come a distillation of the profound events writers, like their countries, had undergone."

Foley championed the rise of "minority literature," especially black writers. She also kept a close eye on opportunities for women in fiction, as well as on the role of female characters. She was offered a job host-ing a feminist radio talk show, and her speech coach, Ludwig Donath, a well-known Austrian actor, connected her with a Viennese friend who rented Foley a small seaside house in Santa Monica. Here she met Ber-thold Brecht, Thomas Mann, and Charlie Chaplin. Foley wrote about the Chaplins' visits to her friend's house, about Oona Chaplin "silently knitting afghans." She later regaled friends with stories about Greta Garbo and their occasional lunches of "cottage cheese and a salad" while discussing Garbo's childhood.

Foley guessed that TV would threaten magazine and book readership and deplete audiences at movie theaters. Writers such as Gore Vidal and Horton Foote began to earn decent money — and fame — by writing tele-plays. J. D. Salinger, whose first story had been published in *Story,* never allowed the televising of any of his stories. When Foley chided him, say-ing, "If all good writers take your attitude, television will be as bad as Hollywood," Salinger replied, "The writing was on the wall before the wall was even there."

★　★　★

NANCY HALE

THOSE ARE AS BROTHERS

from *Mademoiselle*

NANCY HALE (1908–1988) was born in Boston, the daughter of two renowned painters. She studied as a painter but also pursued writing and published her first story in the *Boston Herald* when she was only eleven. After she married, she moved to New York and became a writer and editor for *Vogue*. She later became the first female news reporter for the *New York Times*. At the same time she wrote the novel *The Young Die Good,* as well as short stories, some about women struggling to maintain their independence. She divorced and moved with her new husband to Charlottesville, Virginia. At this time she wrote her best-known novel, *The Prodigal Women*. She also published many stories in *The New Yorker;* in 1961 alone, she sold the magazine twelve stories.

Hale's husband taught at the University of Virginia while William Faulkner was writer in residence there, and Hale and Faulkner socialized frequently. In an essay she described meeting Faulkner for the first time at a cocktail party and saying to him, "The first sip of whiskey is much the best, isn't it?" to which he replied, "Uhh-huuh . . . Why, down home, when I come in of an evenin', and walk in by the fire, and sit down there with a drink of whiskey in my hand, I tell you there's nothin in the world like that first sip runnin down my throat.'" She wrote, "We were off. After that we never had any silences when we met at parties. Simple, sensuous experience was what Faulkner wanted to talk about . . . the sounds of tree toads at night in summer, the way it smells when you wake up to fine snow."

Hale, the founder of the Virginia Center for the Creative Arts, won a Benjamin Franklin Award for short story authors, an O. Henry Award, and a Henry H. Bellamann Award for literature.

★

T HE LONG, CLEAR American summer passed slowly, dreaming over the Connecticut Valley and the sound, square houses under the elms and the broad, living fields, and over the people there that came and went and lay and sat still, with purpose and without, but free; moving in and out of their houses of their own free will, free to perceive the passage of the days through the different summer months and the smells and the sun and the rain and the high days and the brooding days, as was their right; without fear and without apprehension.

On the front lawn of the white house on the riverbank, the two little boys came out every morning and dug holes and hammered nails into boards and pushed around the express-wagon filled with rocks. Their skins were filled with the sun, with the season, and they played all day, humming tuneless songs under their breath.

Up the road at the gardener's cottage of the big house where nobody lived, the gardener, who was unmarried, a short stout man who was a Jewish refugee, tended the borders of the garden and painted the long white fence and worked on the driveway; in the summer-morning sun he sang, too, in German, as he did his slow, neat work. In the evenings after supper when it was dusk and the only light left was in the red sky on the other side of the river, he would come walking down the road to the house on the riverbank, to call on the German governess who took care of the two little boys. His footsteps could be heard walking, hard and quick, down the road. Fräulein would be sitting on the stone front steps. He would stop short in the road in front of her, dressed in his clean clothes, his body round and compact, and his black hair brushed down, and bow. "Good evening," he said. Fräulein said, "How are you?" Then he would come and sit beside her on the steps and the conversation would continue in German, because although he could understand sufficient English, Mr. Loeb could talk hardly any.

Fräulein was friendly to him because she was a friendly woman, but always a little superior because he was a Jew and she belonged to a family of small merchants in Cologne. She was sorry for him because he was a refugee and because he had been in a concentration camp in Germany, and it was necessary to be kind to those who had suffered under that Hitler, but a Jew was a Jew; there were right German names and wrong German names; Fräulein's name was Strasser. She did not mind speaking her mind to him on the subject of the Nazis who were ruining Germany. There were no other Germans about, in this place, as there were in the winter in New York, who might be on the other side; to them she had only praise to speak of Hitler, for her family was still in Cologne and people suffered at home for what was said by their relatives in America — if it came to the wrong ears. But Mr. Loeb was a Jew and safe to talk to, to tell exactly what she thought of those people, those

Nazis. He never said anything much back, just listened and nodded; his face was round and florid.

In the evenings Mrs. Mason, the children's mother, sat in a garden chair out on the lawn and listened to the crickets in the marshes and watched the red fade beyond the river. Or, if it was one of the nights when she could not enjoy the evening sounds, the smells, when a little of the tension and fear clung to her mind and twisted it about, she would sit inside the living-room, on one of the chintz-covered chairs under a light with a book. She read all sorts of books — novels, detective stories, and the papers and magazines that were full of the news about Europe. On the bad nights, the nights when peace was not quite at her command, she noticed that whatever she read seemed curiously to be written about her . . . to fit her situation, no matter what it was meant to be about. And especially all the books, the articles, about the Nazis. She did not know if it was morbid of her, but she could not help feeling *he* had stood for the thing that was the Nazis, that spirit, and she had been a country being conquered, a country dominated by those methods. It was so like; so very like. When she read of those tortured in concentration camps, of those dispossessed and smashed to the Nazi will, she knew she felt as those people felt. She had been through a thing that was the same in microcosm. Her life was a tiny scale model of the thing that was happening in Europe: the ruthless swallowing the helpless. By a miracle, by an overlooked shred of courage, she had escaped and was free here. She was a refugee like that man out there talking to Fräulein who had escaped, too, by another miracle, for only miracles saved people from that spirit. In refuge, peace and assurance were coming back slowly like strength to a sick body, and the fear, the terror that was once everything, was draining away drop by drop with the days of safety. The same thing must be happening to him, the man out there; confidence and a quietly beating heart, in this calm summer country where there was nothing any more to fear.

Only the habit of fear; only the uncontrollably quickened pulse for no reason, the fear that came out of nothing because fear was a poison in the blood and passed in and out of the heart again and again and again before it was finally worked out, if it ever was. Perhaps, she thought, it never was. If you were infected virulently enough with that poison perhaps it never left you, but recurred forever like some tropical fevers, forever part of you and in your blood though you were a thousand miles away from the source. He was nearly a thousand miles away, too, and there would be no reason, no need, ever to see him again; but perhaps the fear would stay with her though there was nothing left to fear.

As the summer wandered by, the young man from across the river came over more and more often to see Mrs. Mason. He had a boat with an outboard motor; she would hear it buzzing across the water, and the sound of the motor cut as he drew near to the dock; there would be silence while he tied up, and then he would come walking up the lawn, very tall with his fair hair cut short all over, catching the light from the sunset in the quiet dusk.

"Hello, Fräulein," he would say as he came up the steps. "Hello, Mr. Loeb."

Mr. Loeb always got to his feet and bowed smartly. Fräulein said, "Good evening, Mr. Worthington." Then the screen door would slam and the sound of German being spoken quietly would begin again and he would walk into the living-room and grin at Mrs. Mason.

He used to sit in the chintz-covered chair with his long legs stuck out in front of him, smoking cigarettes. Sometimes he took her out on the smooth, dark river in his boat. Once they struck a log in the darkness on the water and she started violently and cried out. "What are you afraid of?" he asked her. "You're so lovely, I don't see why you should ever be afraid of anything."

It was impossible to explain to him that she was not afraid of the log, nor of the water, nor of anything; that it was only a reflex which she was helpless to control, without reason; just fear. "You know I'd take care of you, if anything ever happened, don't you?" he said. "If you'd just let me." And she knew he would, but that did not make any difference. Nobody could help because nobody could possibly understand the irrationality, the uncontrollability, of fear when it was like this, in the blood. Any help had to come from within, the self-learning through days, perhaps years, of peace: that nothing of all that which was over would ever happen again. Talking to it was no good; no young man's protectiveness penetrated to it; it had to learn slowly by itself.

The young man was falling in love with Mrs. Mason through that long summer. But it was inconceivable that she should fall in love with him. No matter how kind and strong he was, no matter how much more often she saw him each day — how good he was, how there was none of that spirit in him — it was inconceivable that her muscles could ever grow slack enough for her to look at him quietly, a man, and fall in love with him. She had been naked once, and vulnerable to everything that had happened to her; now, and perhaps forever, something in her clutched the coverings of tension, of reserve, of aloneness, having learned what happened when they were dropped. Her mind could say that it would not happen with this young man, who was all gentleness and generosity; but the inner thing did not believe that; it believed nothing except what it had learned.

When they sat on the lawn, smoking in the twilight, or inside in the big cool living-room, the German talk went on quietly on the front steps. Mr. Loeb was a quiet man, and Fräulein did most of the talking. When she had said her say about the Nazis, Fräulein told him about the children — how Hugh was as good as an angel and Dicky was just so different, a sweet child but always up to something. The big June-bugs and the moths banged against the screen door, and the light from the house came soft and yellow through the door and lay upon the stone slabs of the steps.

After a while, when she knew him pretty well, Fräulein told him about that Mr. Mason, what a bad man he was and how glad she was that they did not live with him any more.

"That poor lady," she said. "She took plenty of unhappiness from him, I can tell you. My, what a place! I can't tell you what a man he was. You wouldn't believe it. She never said anything, but I knew what went on. I don't mean maybe beating her, I know husbands get mad sometimes and beat their wives, that's all right, but that man! I tried to keep my babies from seeing the things that used to happen, and she helped me to do it. Not that I ever discussed it with her. She's that kind of lady, very proud, and I never saw her cry, only heard her sometimes, nights when he was very bad. She had such a look in her eyes in those days; she doesn't have it any more. I can tell you I'm glad she got rid of him. In this country it's very easy to divorce, you know."

"Yes," Mr. Loeb said quietly, in the darkness.

"Well, she's got rid of him now and I'm glad. It would have killed her, a life like that, and my poor babies, what would have happened to them? She's got rid of him, thank God, and now she can just forget about him and be happy."

Mr. Loeb said nothing. He didn't smoke because he was saving money out of what he earned as a gardener. He just sat there in the darkness, and he smelled a little of sweat. Fräulein made allowances for his smell, knowing that he was a laborer.

In the middle of the summer Hugh had a birthday and there was a big cake with seven candles, and one to grow on. Mr. Worthington came across the river for the little party, and both children were allowed to sit up till ten. After supper Mr. Loeb came walking down the road as usual, and Mrs. Mason called him in.

"Won't you have a piece of cake," she said, holding out a plate to him. "Here's a piece with a candle."

Mr. Loeb made his bow and took the plate. Mrs. Mason smiled at him and he smiled at her and they did not say anything.

"We're going to play games in the living-room," Mrs. Mason said. "Do you know any games, Mr. Loeb?"

The children were wild with excitement and ran round and round the room. Mr. Worthington showed Hugh a game with a piece of paper and a pencil, where he could guess any number of a total if he knew the right-hand numbers of the other lines. It was very mysterious. Dicky didn't understand it at all, and stamped and yelled to make them stop and do something else.

"I show you," Mr. Loeb said and hesitated. He asked Fräulein how to say something in English.

"He shows you a card-trick," Fräulein said. Mr. Loeb's face was round and red and smiling. He took the pack of cards Mrs. Mason held out to him and drew out two aces.

"You see," he said to Hugh. "This is the farmer's cow." He pointed to the ace of hearts. "And this is Mrs. Sisson's cow." Mrs. Sisson owned the big place where Mr. Loeb was gardener. The card was the ace of clubs.

"Now I put them back again," Mr. Loeb said, shuffling the pack. "Now. Which cow you want to see? The farmer's cow? Mrs. Sisson's cow?"

Hugh deliberated, standing on one leg.

"Mrs. Sisson's cow," he decided.

"Then go to the barn and look for it!" cried Mr. Loeb.

The children were enchanted. They screamed and rolled on the floor; Dicky kept crying, "Go to the barn and look for it!" Everybody was laughing.

"That was a very nice trick," Mrs. Mason said when the laughter stopped.

The children, after a while, fell to playing with the cards on the floor. Their two little round butts stuck up in the air, and their two little boys' heads were close together.

Mr. Loeb finished his cake and took out a folded handkerchief and wiped his mouth. He put the plate down carefully on the desk near him.

"Thank you very much," he said to Mrs. Mason. He was still standing up, politely. Now he moved toward the door.

"Don't go away," she said. "Stay and talk. Sit down, please. You're part of the party."

"Thank you very much," he said.

"Understand you had a bad time with those Nazi fellows," Mr. Worthington said, being very friendly. "Were you really in one of the concentration camps?"

"Yes, I was. It was very bad."

"I was in Germany once," Mr. Worthington said. "The thing I kept noticing was, they were such damned bad losers. One night I went out drinking beer with a lot of fellows, me and a Frenchman I knew. They seemed all right guys. But about two in the morning when we'd all drunk a lot of beer one of them said, 'Let's have a foot-race.' Down the main street there, it was all quiet. Well, we started, and in a minute or two the Frenchman was way in front, and I was just behind. They just quit. Started walking along. Wouldn't admit they'd been racing. But if they'd been ahead, you can bet they'd have rubbed it in. They want to be on top, that's it, and they take it out on the fellow underneath. If *they* get licked, they won't admit they were playing at all."

"Yes," said Mr. Loeb.

"You'd see fellows pick fights all the time, late at night, but you never saw them pick a fight unless they thought they could win. I played a lot of tennis over there and, of course, you know, American tennis . . . They just wouldn't play again. Fellow over here would say, 'Let's play a return match and I'll lick you.' Not them."

"Yes," said Mr. Loeb.

"Those concentration camps, now. Just the fellows on top doing it to the fellows underneath . . . It must have been a job keeping your courage up."

"I did not keep my courage up," Mr. Loeb said.

Mr. Worthington looked embarrassed.

"I don't blame you," he said. "The things you hear about those places; they break your spirit, I guess."

"Yes," Mr. Loeb said.

Fräulein sat under the light with her hair parted smoothly from the middle. She looked from Mr. Worthington to Mr. Loeb with self-assured eyes, not entirely understanding nor especially interested. Mr. Worthington twisted his long legs around one side of his chair.

"Anyway," he said, "it's all over for you and I bet you're damned glad.

You can just forget about all that stuff. This is a free country and you can do what you please and nobody can hurt you. It's all over now and finished for you."

"For many it is not," Mr. Loeb said after a few moments.

"Yeah, that's right. Poor devils."

"But," Mr. Loeb said hesitantly, "I have thought, I do not know how you say it; the more and more that are all the time — surrendered?"

"How do you mean?"

"He means oppressed," Mrs. Mason said. Mr. Loeb bowed to her.

"The more and more that are oppressed all the time, the more there are who know together the same thing, who have it together. When it is time and something happens to make it possible, there is something that all of these have had together and that will make them fight together. And now Frenchmen, too, Belgians, too, Flemings. If you have been in a concentration camp, it is more together than that you might be of different countries. I speak very badly," Mr. Loeb said.

"No," Mrs. Mason said. "A common cause."

"Please?" Mr. Loeb asked. Fräulein spoke to him in German.

"I do not think that it is what you call cause, just. But knowing the concentration camps together. And what happens. That they were all crying together and no — courage. It makes them love."

"I don't see what you mean, exactly," Mr. Worthington said.

"I do," said Mrs. Mason. "They all remember the same thing together."

"Yes," Mr. Loeb said.

It seemed to her for a minute that she saw a sea of faces upturned, with the same look in all the thousands of them, the anguish, the terrible humiliation, the fear. It was a vast and growing sea, a great host of the tortured and the outcast, who had known ultimate fear instead of death and had been together in the valley of living hell. Separately each of them had known fear, had felt it burning in their veins, but now that they were all together the common fear became something else, larger, because there were so many millions of them, because they were not alone; it was set in dignity like a brand of brotherhood upon their lifted faces. And there were more of them, and more of them; if there were any more they would be the largest part of all the people on earth; this part would be strong by its numbers, and unshakeable because of its suffering shared. This was something she had never thought of before.

· · ·

The children were sent off to bed at last, and Mrs. Mason went up to say good night to them. They lay in the two cot-beds holding still while they said their prayers and then releasing into a last, wild activity before the light should be turned out on them. She pushed them back under their sheets and kissed them. When she came downstairs again Mr. Worthington was sitting alone in the living-room and the German voices were coming in softly through the screen door, from the warm darkness outside.

"Hello," Mr. Worthington said.

"Hello," she said. He reached out and took her hand as she passed where he sat, and kissed it. She stood still for a minute, and smiled at him.

"I love you from now," he said. She went on looking at his face, bent over her hand but with his eyes looking up at her. After a minute the consciousness of what he said, where she was, the consciousness of herself came back over her and she drew away her hand. But for a moment she had lived in freedom, without watching herself.

In August Mrs. Sisson came back from California and opened the big house, and Mr. Loeb was much busier, doing all the things that Mrs. Sisson wanted done. Mrs. Sisson was a woman of fifty with black hair and a tall strong figure, who was very particular and liked her big place tended to perfection. Mrs. Mason knew her only slightly—to wave to when Mrs. Sisson drove along the road in her black car with her initials on the Connecticut license plate, and to speak to in a neighborly way when they met in the village. Sometimes now Fräulein started to tell her things about Mrs. Sisson, how badly she treated all her servants, that she didn't even feed them properly, and had had three different waitresses in just the time she had been back.

"Nobody wants to work for a woman like that," Fräulein said.

But Mrs. Mason thought she ought not to listen to gossip, and did not let Fräulein talk about it much.

One afternoon when she came out of the house, Mr. Loeb was standing at the gate, talking to Fräulein. The two little boys were playing at the end of the lawn. Mr. Loeb was talking very fast in German, his voice much higher than usual, and Fräulein was looking at him and from time to time saying something in her usual calm voice. Mrs. Mason walked to the gate.

"Hello, Mr. Loeb," she said.

Mr. Loeb made his bow, but he seemed distracted. His eyes were tense and his face was even redder than usual. Mrs. Mason thought he looked almost as if he were going to cry. He turned to her and began to speak in English but stumbled and was silent.

"That Mrs. Sisson," Fräulein said. "She says to him she will report him to the Refugee Committee in New York so that he will never be able to get a job again."

"What did he do?"

"Nothing! She talked to him the way she talks to all the people who work for her, she bawled him out, he doesn't paint the fence quick enough, she says he's too slow. He's a foolish man, he pays attention to what she says. I tell him he ought to shrug his shoulders, what does he care, as long as he gets his pay."

"I cannot have her speak to me that way!" Mr. Loeb broke out. "I cannot have her call me those things she says. I cannot . . ."

"He pays attention," Fräulein said. "He gets his feelings hurt too easy. I tell him, what does he care what she says? She's nothing. But he says to her, she can't speak to him that way, he cannot have her speak to him that way, he cannot stay and work for her if she talks like that. So she says all right, she's going to report him to the Refugee Committee."

"What can she say?"

"She was terrible angry," Mr. Loeb said. "She will say I do not work. She will say I am a no-good worker. She will say I speak to her fresh."

He looked at Mrs. Mason with his frightened eyes, and she nodded at him. Their eyes met and she nodded again, but more slowly this time.

"I'll go up and talk to her," Mrs. Mason said. She did not feel at all afraid to do that, suddenly. She was not thinking about how she felt.

Fräulein shrugged.

"I don't think it makes any difference, you excuse me, Mrs. Mason. That Mrs. Sisson, she doesn't want Mr. Loeb to work for her any more because he talks back to her, and she writes the letter anyway."

"I'll write to the Refugee Committee, too," she said. "I'll tell them that I know all about Mr. Loeb and he's a good worker and a nice man. But I'll go up and talk to her anyway."

Mr. Loeb leaned against the fence and looked at her. She came out and walked past him into the road.

"Thank you very much," Mr. Loeb said in his foreign, formal voice.

She smiled at him. The tension had gone away from his eyes, the look of fear that she recognized had gone.

"You don't have to worry, you know," she said. "I wouldn't ever let anything happen to you."

EUDORA WELTY

THE WHOLE WORLD KNOWS

from *Harper's Bazaar*

EUDORA WELTY (1909–2001) was born in Jackson, Mississippi. She attended graduate school at Columbia University during the Great Depression, but was unable to find a job in New York, so she moved back to Jackson and began work at a radio station and a newspaper. She later took a job as a publicist with the Works Progress Administration, gathering material that documented stories about the people of Mississippi. At the same time she assembled a group of writers and composers, which she called the Night-Blooming Cereus Club.

In 1941 Welty roomed with Katherine Anne Porter and the two became great friends. *A Curtain of Green,* published the same year, was Welty's first collection of short stories. She won a Guggenheim Fellowship grant, which enabled her to travel to Europe. She later lectured at Harvard University and gathered her speeches in *One Writer's Beginnings.* Her works of fiction include *Delta Wedding, The Ponder Heart, Collected Stories,* and *Losing Battles.* Series editor Martha Foley described Welty's fiction as "gentler, less macabre in her presentation of grotesque characters than many of her Southern contemporaries."

Welty won a Pulitzer Prize for *The Optimist's Daughter.* Over the course of her career, she also received numerous O. Henry Awards, a National Book Award, a National Medal of Arts, and the French Chevalier de la Légion d'Honneur, among many other honors.

★

MOTHER SAID, WHERE *have you been, son? — Nowhere, mother. — I wish you wouldn't look so unhappy, son. You could come back to me, now. — I can't do that, mother. I have to stay in Sabina.*

When I locked the door of the Sabina Bank I rolled down my sleeves and stood for some time looking out at a cotton field across the way until the whiteness nearly put me to sleep and then woke me up like a light turned on in my face. Dugan had been gone a few minutes or so. I got in my car and drove it up the street, turned it around in the foot of Jinny's driveway (there went Dugan), and drove down again. I backed in a cotton field at the other end of the pavement, turned, and made the same trip. You know — the thing everybody does every day.

There was Maideen Summers on the corner waving a little colored handkerchief. She was at first the only stranger — then finally not much of one. When I didn't remember to stop I saw the handkerchief slowly fall still. I turned again, and picked her up.

"Dragging Main?" she said. She was eighteen years old. She promptly told you all those things. "Look! Grown-up and citified," she said, and held both hands toward me. She had brand new white cotton gloves on — they shone. Maideen would ride beside me and talk about things I didn't mind hearing about — the ice plant, where she kept the books. Fred Killigrew her boss, the way working in Sabina seemed after the country and junior college. Her first job — her mother could hardly believe it, she said. It was so easy, too, out in the world, and nice, with getting her ride home with me sometimes like this and not on the dusty bus — except Mr. Killigrew sometimes wanted her to do something at the last minute — guess what today — and so on.

She said, "This sure is nice. I didn't think you saw me, Ran, not at first."

I told her my eyes had gone bad. She looked sorry. I drove, idling along, up and down Main Street a few times more. Each time the same people, Miss Callie Hudson and all, the people standing in the store doors or riding in the other cars, waved at my car, and to them all, Maideen waved back — her little blue handkerchief was busy. Their avidity would be far beyond her. She waved at them as she did at me.

"Are you tired out like you were yesterday? Today's just as hot."

She knew what anybody in Sabina told her; and for four or five afternoons I had picked her up and taken her up and down the street a few turns, bought her a Coca-Cola and driven her home out by the Old Murray Forks somewhere, and she had never said a word except a kind one, like this. She was kind; her company was the next thing to being alone.

I drove her home and then drove back to the room I had at Mrs. Judge O'Leary's — usually, but on this day, there at the end of the pavement, I turned up the cut to the Stark place. I couldn't stand it any longer.

Maideen didn't say anything until we reached the top of the drive and stopped, and I got out and opened her door.

"Do you want to take me in yonder?" she said. "Please, I'd just as soon you wouldn't."

All at once her voice came all over me. It had a kind of humility.

"Sure. Let's go in and see Jinny. Why not?" I couldn't stand it any longer, that was why. "I'm going and taking you."

It wasn't as if Colonel Waters didn't say to me every afternoon, Come on home with me, boy — argue, while he forced that big Panama down on his head — no sense in your not sleeping cool, with one of our fans turned on you. Mabel says so, Mabel has something to say to you — and he waited a minute in the door before he left, and held his cane (the one Dugan and I had gone in together to buy him because he was president), up in the air as if he threatened me with comfort, until I answered him No Sir.

With Maideen, I walked around the baked yard to the porch, under the heavy heads, the too-bright blooms that hang down like fruits from the trees — crape myrtles. Jinny's mama, I saw, put her face to her bedroom window first thing, to show she'd marched right upstairs at the sight of Randall MacLain coming to her door, bringing who-on-earth with him too. After daring to leave her daughter and right on Easter Sunday before church. Now right back to her door, big as you please. And her daughter Jinny, Virginia, who once Shared His Bed, sent straight into the arms of Trash by what he did. One thing — it was Jinny's family home after all, her mother still kept alive to run it, *grand* old Mrs. Stark, and this outrage right under her nose. The curtain fell back, as on a triumph.

"I've never been invited to the Stark home," Maideen said, and I began to smile. I felt curiously lighthearted. Lilies must have been in bloom somewhere near, and I took a full breath of their water smell as determinedly as if then consciousness might go, or might not.

Out in the front hall, Jinny stood with her legs apart, cutting off locks of her hair at the mirror. The locks fell at her feet. She had on boy's shorts. She looked up at me and said "How do you like it?" She grinned, as if she had been preparing for me, and then she looked past my shoulder. She would know, with her quickness like foreknowledge, that I would come back when this summer got too much for me, and that I would just as soon bring a stranger if I could find one, somebody who didn't know a thing, into the house with me when I came.

I remember Maideen looked down at her gloves, and seemed to decide to keep them on. Jinny hollered at Tellie to bring in some cokes. A spell of remoteness, a feeling of lightness, had hold of me still, and as we all stood on that thin light matting in the Stark hall that seems to billow a little if you take a step, and with Jinny's hair lying on it, I saw us all in the mirror. And I could almost hear it being told right across me — our story, the fragment of what happened, Jinny's and my story, as if it were being told — told in the clear voice of Maideen, rushing, unquestioning — the town words. Oh, this is what Maideen Summers was — telling what she looked at, repeating what she listened to — she was like an outlandish little bird, being taught, some each day, to sing a song *people* made ... He walked out on her and moved three blocks away down the street. Now everybody's wondering when he'll try to go back. They say Jinny MacLain's got her sweetheart there. Under her mama's nose. Good thing her father's dead and she has no brothers. Sure, it's Lonnie Dugan, the other one at the bank, and you knew from the start, if it wasn't Ran, who else in Sabina would there be for Jinny Stark? They don't say how it happened, does anybody know? At the circle, at the table, at Mrs. Judge's, at Sunday School, they say, they say she will marry the sweetheart if he'll marry her, but Ran will kill someone if she does. And there's Ran's papa died of drink, remember, remember? They say Ran will do something bad. He won't divorce her but he will do something bad. Maybe kill them all. They say Jinny's not scared. And oh you know, they say, they run into each other every day of the world, all three. Poor things! But it's no surprise. There'll be no surprises. How could they help it if they wanted to help it, how could you get away from anything here? You can't get away in Sabina. Away from anything.

Maideen held the tinkling glass in her white glove and said to Jinny, "I look too tacky and mussed when I work all day to be coming in anybody's strange house."

She looked like *Jinny* — she was an awkward version of Jinny. Jinny, "I look too tacky and mussed when I work all day to be always revealed contamination. I knew it after the fact, so to speak — and was just a bit pleased with myself." I don't mean there was anything of mockery in Maideen's little face — no — but something of Jinny that went back early — to whatever original and young my Jinny would never be now. The breeze from that slow ceiling fan lifted their hair from their temples, like the same hand — Maideen's brown hair long and Jinny's brown hair short, ruined — she ruined it herself, as she liked doing.

Maideen was so still, so polite, but she glowed with something she didn't know about, there in the room with Jinny. She took on a great deal of unsuspected value. It was like a kind of maturity all at once. They sat down in wicker chairs and talked to each other. With them side by side and talking back and forth, it seemed to reward my soul for Maideen to protest her fitness to be in the house. I would not have minded how bedraggled she would ever get herself. I relaxed, leaned back in my chair and smoked cigarettes. But I had to contain my sudden interest; it seemed almost too funny to be true, their resemblance. I was delighted with myself, most of all, to have been the one to make it evident. I looked from Jinny to Maideen (of course *she* didn't guess) and back to Jinny and almost expected praise — praise from somewhere — for my true vision.

There were knocking sounds from outside — croquet again. Jinny was guiding us to the open door (we walked on her hair) where they were slowly moving across the shade of the backyard — Doc Short, Vera and Red Lassiter, and the two same schoolteachers — with Lonnie Dugan striking a ball through the wicket. I watched through the doorway and the crowd seemed to have dwindled a little. I could not think who was out. It was myself.

Mother said, Son, you're walking around in a dream.

Bella, Mrs. Judge O'Leary's little dog, panted sorrowfully all the time — she was sick. I always went out in the yard and spoke to her. Poor Bella, how do you do, lady? Is it hot, do they leave you alone?

Mother said, Where have you been, son? — Not anywhere, mother. — I wish you wouldn't look so peaked. And you keep things from me, son. — I haven't been anywhere, where would I go? — If you came back with me, everything would be just like it was before. I know you won't eat at Mrs. Judge's table, not her biscuit.

When the bank opened, Miss Callie Hudson came up to my window and hollered, Randall, when are you coming back to your precious wife? You forgive her, now, you hear? That's no way to do, bear grudges. Your mother never bore your father a grudge in her life, and he made her life right hard, I tell you, how do you suppose he made her life? She didn't bear him a grudge. We're all human on earth. Where's little old Lonnie, now, has he stepped out, or you done something to him? I still think of him as a boy in knee breeches and Buster Brown bob, riding the ice wagon, stealing ice — your lifelong playmate, Jinny's lifelong playmate — a little common but so smart. Ah, I'm a woman that's been clear around the world in my rocking chair, and I tell you we all get surprises now and then. But you march on back to your wife, Ran MacLain. You hear? It's a thing of the flesh, not the spirit, it'll pass. Jinny'll get over this in three, four months maybe. You hear me? And you go back *nice*. No striking about now and doing anything we'll all be shamed to hear

about. I know you won't. I knew your father, was crazy about your father, just as long as he could recognize me, love your mother. Sweetest
people in the world, most happily mated people in the world. Go home
and tell your mother I said so. And you march back to that precious
wife. March back and have you some chirren. How long has it been?
How long? What day was it you tore the house down, Christmas or Easter? I said Easter, Mr. Hudson said Christmas — who was right? My Circle declares she'll get a divorce and marry Lonnie but I say not. Thing of
the flesh, I told Mr. Hudson. Won't last. And they've known each other
a hundred years! The Missionary Circle said you'd kill him and I said,
You all, who are you talking about? If it's Ran MacLain that I knew in
his buggy, I said he's the last person I know to take on to that extent. I
laughed. And little Jinny. I had to laugh at her. Says — I couldn't help it.
I says, How did it happen, Jinny, tell old Miss Callie, you monkey, and
she says, Oh Miss Callie, I don't know — it just happened, she says, sort
of across the bridge table. I says across the bridge table my foot. Jinny
told me yesterday on the street, Oh, she says, I just saw Ran. I hope Ran
won't cherish it against me, Jinny says. I have to write my checks on
the Sabina Bank, and Lonnie Dugan works in it, right next to Ran. And
we're all grown up, not little children any more. And I says I know, how
could you get away from each other if you tried, you could not. It's an
endless circle. That's what a thing of the flesh is. And you won't get away
from that in Sabina or hope to. Even our little town. Jinny was never
scared of the Devil himself as a growing girl, and shouldn't be now. And
Lonnie Dugan won't ever quit at the bank, will he? Can't quit. But as I
said to Mr. Hudson — they're in separate *cages*. All right, I said to Mr.
Hudson, look. Jinny was unfaithful to Ran — that's what it *was*. There
you have what it's all *about*. That's the brunt of it. Face it, I told Mr.
Hudson. You're a train man — just a station agent, you're out of things. I
don't know how many *times*.

But I'd go back to my lawful spouse! Miss Callie hollers at me through
the bars. You or I or the man in the moon got no business living in that
little hot upstairs room with a western exposure at Mrs. Judge O'Leary's
for all the pride on earth, not in August.

After work I was always staying to cut the grass in Mrs. Judge's backyard, so it would be cooler for Bella. It kept the fleas away from her a little. None of it did much good. The heat held on. After I went back to the
Starks, the men were playing, still playing croquet with a few little girls,
and the women had taken off to themselves, stretched out on the screen
porch. They called Maideen, I sent her in to them. It was the long Mis-

sissippi evening, the waiting till it was cool enough to eat. The voice of Jinny's mama carried — I heard it — her reminiscent one — but the evening was quiet, very hot and still.

Somebody called, You're dead on Lonnie. It was just a little Williams girl in pigtails.

I may have answered with a joke. I felt lighthearted, almost not serious at all, really addressing a child, as I lifted my mallet — the one with the red band that had always been mine. I brought Dugan to earth with it. He went down and shook the ground, fanning the air as he went. He toppled and sighed. Then I beat his whole length and his head with that soft girl's hair and all the schemes, beat him without stopping my mallet till every bone and little bone, all the way down to the little bones in the hand, flew to pieces. I beat Lonnie Dugan till there was nothing to know there. And I proved the male body — it has a too certain, too special shape to it not to be hurt — could be finished and done away with — with one good loud blow after another — Jinny could be taught that. I looked at Dugan down there. And his blue eyes remained unharmed. Just as sometimes bubbles a child blows seem the most impervious things, and grass blades will go through them and they still reflect the world, give it back unbroken. Dugan I declare was dead.

"Now watch."

Dugan said that. He spoke with no pain. Of course he never felt pain, never had time to. But that absurd, boyish tone of *competition* was in his voice. It had always been a mystery, now it was a deceit. Dugan — born nothing. Dugan — the other boy at the dance, the other man in the bank, the other sweetheart in Sabina, Jinny's other man — it was together he and I made up the choice. Even then it was hard to believe — we were the choice in everything. But if that was over, settled — how could it open again, the destroyed mouth of Dugan? And I heard him say "Now watch." He was dead on the ruined grass. But he had risen up. Just then he gave one of the fat little Williams girls a spank. I could see it and not hear it, the most familiar sound in the world.

There was that breathless stillness, and the sky changing the way a hand would pass over it. And I should have called it out *then* — All is disgrace! Human beings' cries would swell in the last of evening like this and cross the grass in the yard before the light changes, if only they cried. Our grass in August is like the floor under the sea, and we walk on it slowly playing, and the sky turns green before dark. We don't say anything the others remember.

But at our feet the shadows faded out light into the pale twilight and the locusts sang in long waves, O-E, O-E. Sweat ran down my back, arms, and legs, branching like some upside-down tree.

Then, "You'll all come in!" They were calling from the porch — the well-known yellow lamps suddenly all went on. They called us in their shrill women's voices, Jinny and all and her mama. "Fools, you're playing in the dark! Come to supper!"

Somebody bumped into me in the sudden blindness of the yard. We laughed at their voracious voices. Across the dark the porch of women waited. It was like a long boat to me, or a box lighted up from within. But I was hungry.

I'd go down to Mrs. Judge O'Leary's to sleep in my little western room — that's the house where Mrs. Judge and the three other Sabina schoolteachers sit on the porch. Each evening to avoid them I ran through porch and hall both, like a man through the pouring rain. In the big dark backyard, full of pecan trees, moonlit, Bella opened her eyes and looked at me. They showed the moon. If she drank water, she vomited it up — yet she went with effort to her pan and drank again. I held her. Poor Bella. I thought she suffered from a tumor, and stayed with her most of the night.

Mother said, Son, I noticed that old pistol of your father's in your nice coat pocket, what do you want with that old thing, your father never cared for it. Not any robbers coming to the bank that I know of. Son, if you'd just saved your money you could take yourself a little trip to the coast. I'd go with you. They always have a breeze at Gulfport, nearly always.

When you get to Jinny's, there are yuccas and bare ground — it looks like some old playground, with the house back out of sight. Just the sharp, over-grown yuccas with up and down them rays of spiderwebs glinting in the light — as if they wore dresses. And back up in the shade is a little stone statue, all pockmarked now, of a dancing girl with a finger to her chin. Jinny stole that from a Vicksburg park once and her mama let her keep it.

Maideen said, "Are you taking me in yonder? I wish you wouldn't."

I looked down and saw my hand on the gate, and said "Wait. I've lost a button." I showed my loose sleeve to Maideen. I felt all at once solemn — fateful — ready to shed tears.

"Why, I'll sew you one on, if you stop by my house," Maideen said. She touched my sleeve for an instant. A chameleon ran up a leaf, and held there panting. "Then Mama can see you. She'd be so glad to have you stay to supper."

I opened the little old gate. I caught a whiff of the sour pears on the ground, the smell of August. I had not told Maideen I was ever coming to supper at any time, or seeing her mama.

"Oh, Jinny can sew it on now," I said.

"Oh, I can?" Jinny said. She had of course been listening to me all the time from the half-hidden path. She looked out from under her shade-hat. She has the face, she has the threatening stare of a prankster — about to curtsey to you. Don't you think it's the look of a woman that loves dogs and horses best, and long trips away she never takes? "Come in before I forget, then," Jinny said.

We went ahead of Maideen. There in the flower beds walked the same robins, where the sprinkler had been. Once again, we went in the house by the back door. We took hands. We stepped on Tellie's patch of mint — the yellow cat went around the corner — the back door knob was as hot as the hand to the touch, and on the step, impeding the feet of two people going in together, the fruit jars with the laborious cuttings rooting in water — "Watch out for Mama's —!" That had happened a thousand times, the way we went in. As a thousand bees droned and burrowed in the pears that lay on the ground.

As Mama Stark almost ran over me, she shrank with a cry, and started abruptly up the stairs — bosom lifted — her shadow trotted up beside her like a nosy bear. But she could never get to the top without turning. She came down again and held up a finger at me. Her voice . . . Randall. Let me tell you about a hand I held yesterday. My partner was Amanda Mackey and you know she always plays her own hand with no more regard for her partner than you have. Well, she opened with a spade and Fanny doubled. I held: a singleton spade five clubs to the king queen five hearts to the king and two little diamonds. I said two clubs, Gert Gish two diamonds, Amanda two spades, all passed. And when I laid down my hand Amanda said, *O partner!* Why didn't you bid your hearts! I said Hardly. At the level of three with the opponents doubling for a takeout. It developed of course she was two suited — six spades to the ace jack and four hearts to the ace jack ten, also my ace of clubs. Now Randall. It would have been just as easy for Amanda when she opened her mouth a second time to bid three hearts. But no! She could see only her own hand and so she took us down two, and we could have made five hearts. Now do *you* think I should have bid three hearts? — I said, You were justified not to, Mama Stark, and she gave me a nod. Then she glared as if I had slapped her. How well she could turn up her discontent to outrage again, and go on upstairs.

We turned, Jinny leading me, into the little back study, "Mama's office," with the landscape wall-paper and the desk full-up with its immediacy of Daughters of the Confederacy correspondence. Tellie sashayed in with the work basket and then just waited, eyeing and placing us and eyeing the placing herself between us.

"Put it down, Tellie. Now you go on. Pull your mouth in, you hear me?" Jinny took the fancy little basket and flicked it open and fished in it. She found a button that belonged to me, and glanced up at Tellie.

"I hear you's a mess." Tellie went out.

Jinny looked at me. She pulled my hand up and I shot. I fired point blank at Jinny — more than once. It was close range — between us suddenly there was barely room for the pistol to come up. And she only stood threading the needle, her hand not deviating, not even shaken at the noise. The little heart-shaped gold and china clock on the mantel was striking — the pistol's noise had not drowned that. I looked at Jinny and I saw her childish breasts, little pouting excuses for breasts, all sprung with bright holes where my bullets had gone. But Jinny did not feel it, the noise had veered off at the silly clock, and she threaded the needle. She made her little face of success. Her thread always went in its tiny hole.

"Hold still," Jinny muttered softly between fixed lips. She far from acknowledged her pain — anything but sorrow and pain. Just as when she was angry, she sang some faraway song. For domestic talk her voice would lower to a pitch of utter disparagement. Disparagement that had all my life elated me. The little cheat. I waited unable to move again while she sewed dartingly at my sleeve; the sleeve to my helpless hand. As if I counted my breaths now I slowly exhaled fury and inhaled simple dismay that she was not dead on earth. She bit the thread. I was unsteady when her mouth withdrew. The cheat.

I could not, dared not say goodby to Jinny any more, and "Go get in the croquet," she told me. She walked to the mirror in the hall, and began cutting at her hair.

I know Vera Lassiter darted in the room and her face lighted. "Mercy me," she said, and in her mischief came up and fingered Jinny's hair, the short soft curls. "Who're you being now? Somebody's little brother?"

But Jinny stood there at her mirrored face half smiling, so touchingly desirable, so sweet, so tender, vulnerable, touching to me I could hardly bear it, again I could not.

Old Tellie spat into the stove and clanged down an iron lid as I went out through the kitchen. She had spent so much time, twenty-seven years, saying she had brought Jinny into this world: "Born in dis hand."

"No use for you atall you don't whup her. Been de matter wid you? Where you *been*?"

I found Maideen waiting out in the swing, and took her arm and led her down to the croquet where we all played Jinny's game.

Dear God wipe it clean. Wipe it clean, wipe it out. Don't let it be.

At last Mrs. Judge O'Leary caught hold of me in the hall. Do me a favor. Ran, do me a favor and put Bella out of her misery. None of these school teachers any better at it than I would be. And Judge too tenderhearted. You do it. Just do it and don't tell us, hear?

Where have you been, son? — Nowhere, mother, nowhere. — If you were back under my roof I would have things just the way they were. Son, I wish you would just speak to me, and promise —

And I was getting tired, oh so tired, of Mr. Killigrew. I felt cornered when Maideen spoke, kindly as ever, about the workings of the ice house. Now I knew her mother's maiden name. God help me, the name Parsons was laid on my head like the top teetering crown of a pile of things to remember. Not to forget, the name of Parsons.

I remember your wedding, Old Lady Hartford said at my window, poking her finger through the bars. Never knew it would turn out like this, the prettiest wedding in my memory. If you had all *this* money, you could leave town.

Maideen believed so openly — I believe she told Miss Callie — that I wanted to take her somewhere sometime by herself and have a nice time — like other people — but that I put it off till I was free. Still, she had eyes to see, we would run into Jinny every time, Jinny and Lonnie Dugan and the crowd. Of course I couldn't help that, not in Sabina. And then always having to take the little Williams girl home at night. She was the bridge player; that was a game Maideen had never learned to play. Maideen — I never kissed her.

But the Sunday came when I took her over to Vicksburg.

Already on the road I began to miss my bridge. We could get our old game now, Jinny, Dugan, myself and often the little Williams child, who was really a remarkable player, for a Williams. Mama Stark of course would insist on walking out in stately displeasure, we were all very forward children indeed if we thought she would be our fourth, holding no brief for what a single one of us had done. So the game was actually a better one.

Maideen never interrupted our silence with a word. She turned the pages of a magazine. Now and then she lifted her eyes to me, but I could not let her see that I saw her wondering. I would win every night and take their money. Then at home I would be sick, going outdoors so the teachers would not wonder. "Now you really must get little Maideen home. Her mother will be thinking something awful's happened to her. Won't she, Maideen?"—Jinny's voice. "I'll ride with you"—the little Williams. Maideen would not have begun to cry in Jinny's house for anything. I could trust her. Did she want to? She wasn't *dumb*.

She would get stupefied for sleep. She would lean farther and farther over in her chair. She would never have a rum and coke with us, but she would be simply dead for sleep. She slept sitting up in the car going home, where her mama, now large-eyed, maiden name Parsons, sat up listening. I would wake her up to say I had got her home at last. The little Williams girl would be chatting away in the back seat, there and back wide awake as an owl.

Vicksburg: nineteen miles over the gravel and the thirteen little swamp bridges and the Big Black. Suddenly all sensation returned.

Sabina I had looked at till I saw nothing. Till the street was a pencil mark on the sky, a little stick. Maybe outside my eyes a real roofline clamped down still, Main Street was there the same, four red-brick scallops, branchy trees, one little cross, but if I saw it, it was not with love, it was a pencil mark on the sky. Sabina wasn't there to me. If some indelible red false-fronts joined one to the other like a little toy train went by —I did not think of my childhood any more. Sabina had held in my soul to constriction. It was never to be its little street again.

I stopped my car at the foot of Vicksburg, under the wall, by the canal. There was a dazzling light, a water-marked light. I woke Maideen and asked her if she were thirsty. She smoothed her dress and lifted her head at the sounds of a city, the traffic on cobblestones just behind the wall. I watched the water-taxi come, chopping over the canal strip at us, absurd as a rocking horse.

"Duck your head," I said to Maideen.

"In here?"

Very near across the water the island rose glittering against the sunset—a waste of willow trees, yellow and green strands that seemed to weave loosely one upon the other, like a basket that let the light spill out uncontrollably. We shaded our eyes to ride across the water. We all stood up bending our heads under the low top. The Negro who ran the put-put never spoke once, "Get in" or "Get out." "Where are we going?" Maideen said. In two minutes we were touching the barge. Old ramshackle floating saloon fifty years old, with its twin joined to it, for colored.

Nobody was inside but the one man — a silent, relegated place like a barn. I let him bring some rum cokes out to the only table, the card table out on the back where the two cane chairs were. The sun was going down on the island side, and making Vicksburg alight on the other. East and West were in our eyes.

"Don't make me drink it. I don't want to drink it," Maideen said.

"Go on and drink it."

"You drink if you like it. Don't make me drink it."

"You drink it too."

I looked at her take some of it, and sit shading her eyes. There were wasps dipping from the ledge over the old screen door and skimming her hair. There was a smell of fish and of the floating roots fringing the island. The card table smelled warmly of its oilcloth top and of endless deals. A load of Negroes came over on the water-taxi and stepped out with tin buckets. They were sulphur yellow all over, thickly coated with cottonseed meal, and disappeared in the colored barge at the other end, in single file, as if they were sentenced to it.

"Sure enough, I don't want to drink it."

"You drink it. It doesn't taste bad."

Inside, in the dim saloon, two men with black spurred cocks under their arms had appeared. Without noise they each set a muddy boot on the rail and drank, the cocks hypnotically still. They got off the barge on the island side, where they disappeared in the hot blur of willow branches. They might never be seen again.

The heat trembled on the water and on the other side wavered the edges of the old white buildings and concrete slabbed bluffs. From the barge, Vicksburg looked like an image of itself in a tarnished mirror — like its portrait at a sad time of life.

A short cowboy in boots and his girl came in, walking alike. They dropped a nickel in the nickelodeon, and came together.

The canal had no visible waves, yet trembled slightly beneath us; I was aware of it like the sound of a winter fire in the room.

"You don't ever dance, do you?" Maideen said.

It was a long time before we left. All kinds of people had come out to the barge, and the white side and the nigger side filled up. When we left it was good-dark.

The lights twinkled sparsely on the shore — old sheds and warehouses, long dark walls. High up on the ramparts of town some old iron bells were ringing.

"Are you a Catholic?" I asked her suddenly, and I bent my head to hear her answer.

"No."

I looked at her — I made it plain she had disappointed some hope of mine — for she had; I could not tell you now what hope.

"We're all Baptists. Why, are you a Catholic?" Oh, nobody was a Catholic in Sabina.

"No."

Without touching her except momently with my knee I walked her ahead of me up the steep uneven way, to where my car was parked listing sharply downhill. Inside, she could not shut her door. I stood outside and looked, it hung heavily and she had drunk three or four drinks, all I had made her take. Now she could not shut her door. "I'll fall out, I'll fall in your arms. I'll fall, catch me."

"No you won't. Shut it hard. Shut it. All your might."

At last. I leaned against her shut door, spent for a moment.

I grated up the steep cobbles, turned and followed the river road high along the bluff, turned again off into a deep rutted dirt way under shaggy banks, dark and circling and down-rushing.

"Don't lean against my arm," I said. "Sit up and get some air."

"I don't want to," she said in her soft voice that I could hardly understand any more.

"You want to lie down?"

"No. I don't want to lie down."

"Get some air."

"Don't make me lie down. I don't want to do anything, anything at all."

"You're drunk."

"I don't want to do a thing from now and on till evermore."

We circled down. The sounds of the river tossing and dizzying and teasing its great trash could be heard through the dark now. It made the noise of a moving wall, and up it fishes and reptiles and uprooted trees and man's throwaways played and climbed all alike in a splashing like innocence. A great wave of smell beat at my face. The track had come down deep as a tunnel. We were on the floor of the world. The trees met and matted overhead, the cedars came together, and through them the stars of Vicksburg looked sifted and fine as seed, so high and so far. There was the sound of a shot, somewhere, somewhere.

"Yonder's the river," she said. "I see it — the Mississippi River."

"You don't see it. We're not that close."

"I see it, I see it."

"Haven't you ever seen it before? You baby."

"Before? No, I never have seen the Mississippi River before. I thought we were on it on the boat."

"Look, the road has ended."

"Why does it come this far and stop?"

"How should I know? What do they come down here for?"

"Why do they?"

"There are all kinds of people in the world." Far away somebody was burning something.

"Do you mean bad people and niggers and all? Ones that hide? Moonshiners?"

"Oh, fishermen. River men. Cock fighters. You're waked up."

"I think we're lost," she said.

Mother said, if I thought you'd ever go back to that Jinny Stark, I couldn't hold up my head. — No, mother, I'll never go back. — The whole world knows what she did to you.

"You dreamed we're lost. We'll go somewhere where you can lie down a little."

"You can't get lost in Sabina."

"After you lie down a little you'll be all right again, you can get up. We'll go somewhere where you can lie down."

"I don't want to lie down."

"Did you know a car would back up a hill as steep as this?"

"You'll be killed."

"I bet nobody ever saw such a crazy thing. Do you think anybody ever saw such a crazy thing?"

We were almost straight up and down, hanging on the bluff and the tail end bumping and lifting us and swaying from side to side. At last we were up. If I had not drunk that last drink maybe I would not have made such startling maneuvers and would not have bragged so loud. The car had leaned straight over that glimpse of the river, over the brink as sweetly as you ever saw a hummingbird over a flower.

We drove a long way. All among the statues in the dark park, the re-peating stances, the stone rifles again and again on lost hills, the spiral-staired and condemned towers.

I looked for the moon, which would be in the last quarter. There she was. The air was not darkness but faint light, and floating sound — the breath of all the people in the world who were breathing out into the night looking at the moon, knowing her quarter.

We rode in wilderness under the lifting moon, Maideen keeping very still, sighing faintly as if she longed for something herself, for sleep — for going the other way. A coon, white as a ghost, crossed the road, passed a gypsy camp — all sleeping.

Off the road, under the hanging moss, a light burned in a white-washed tree. It showed a circle of whitewashed cabins, dark, and all around and keeping the trees back, a fence of white palings. Sunset Oaks. A little nigger boy leaned on the gate this late at night, wearing an engineer's cap.

Yet it did not seem far. I pulled in, and paid.

"One step up," I told her at the door.

I sat on the bed, the old iron bed with rods. I think I said, "Get your dress off."

She had her head turned away. The naked light hung far down in the room — a long cord that looked as if something had stretched it. She turned, then, with tender shoulders bent toward the chair, as if in confidence toward that, the old wreck of a thing that tonight held her little white dress.

I turned out the light that hung down, and the room filled with the pale night like a bucket let down a well. It was never dark enough, the enormous sky flashing with its August light rushing into the emptiest rooms, the loneliest windows. The month of falling stars. I hate the time of year this is.

If we lay together any on the bed, almost immediately I was propped up against the hard rods with my back pressing them, and sighing — deep sigh after deep sigh. I heard myself.

"Get up," I said. "I want the whole bed. You don't need to be here." And I showed I had the pistol. I lay back holding it toward me and trying to frown her away, the way I used to lie still cherishing a dream in the morning and Jinny would pull me out of it.

Maideen had been pulling or caressing my arm, but she had no strength in her hands at all. She rose up and stood in the space before my eyes, so plain there in the lighted night. She was disarrayed. There was blood on her, blood and disgrace. Or perhaps there wasn't. I did not remember anything about it. For a moment I saw her double.

"Get away from me," I said.

While she was speaking to me I could hear only the noises of the place we were in — of frogs and nightbirds, a booted step in the heavy tangle all around, and the little idiot nigger running up and down the fence, up and down, as far as it went and back, sounding the palings with his stick.

"This is my grandfather's dueling pistol — one of a pair. Very valuable."

"Don't, Ran. Don't do that, Ran. Don't do it. Please don't do it."

I knew I had spoken to her again in order to lie. It was my father's pistol he'd never cared for. When she spoke, I didn't hear what she said; I was reading her lips, the way people being told good-by do conscientiously through train windows. I had the pistol pointing toward my face and did not swerve it. Outside, it sounded as though the little nigger at the gate was keeping that up forever — running a stick along the fence, up and down, to the end and back again.

Poor Bella, it was so hot for her. She lay that day with shut eyes, her narrow little forehead creased. Her nose was dry as a thrown-away rind. The weather was only making her suffer more. She never had a long thick coat, was the one good thing. She was just any kind of a dog. The kind I liked best.

I tried to think. What had happened? No — what had not happened? Something had not happened. The world was not going on. Or, you understand, it went on but somewhere it had stopped being real, and I had walked on, like a tight-rope walker without any rope. How far? Where should I have fallen? Hate. Discovery and hate. Then, right after . . . Destruction was not real, disgrace not real, nor death. They all got up again, Jinny and Dugan got up . . .

Up and down, the little idiot nigger. He was having a good time at that. I wondered, when would that stop? Then that stopped.

I put the pistol's mouth in my own. It tasted, the taste of the whole machinery of it. And then instead it was my own mouth put to the pistol's, quick as a little baby's maybe, whose hunger goes on every minute — who can't be reassured or gratified, ever, quite in time enough. There was Maideen still, white in her petticoat.

"Don't do it, Ran. Please don't do it."

Urgently I made it — made the awful sound.

And immediately she said, "Now, you see. It didn't work. Now you see. Hand that old thing to me, I'll keep that."

She took it from me. She took it over to the chair, as if she were possessed of some long-tried way to deal with it, and disposed of it in the fold of her clothes. She came back and sat down on the edge of the bed.

In a minute she put her hand out again, differently — and touched my shoulder. Then I met it, hard, with my face, the small, bony, freckled (I knew) hand that I hated (I knew), and kissed it and bit it until my lips and tongue tasted salt tears and salt blood — that the hand was not Jinny's. Then I lay back in the bed a long time, up against the rods.

"You're so stuck up," she said.

I lay there and after a while my eyes began to close and I saw her again. She lay there plain as the day by the side of me, quietly weeping for herself. The kind of soft, restful, meditative sobs a child will venture long after punishment.

So I slept.

How was I to know she would hurt herself like this?

Now — where is Jinny?

1948

JOHN CHEEVER
THE ENORMOUS RADIO

from *The New Yorker*

JOHN CHEEVER (1912–1982) was born in Quincy, Massachusetts. He was expelled from Thayer Academy and described the event in his first published
story, which was bought by Malcolm Cowley, an editor of the *New Republic*.

Cheever moved to New York City during the Depression and continued to
write, publishing stories in *The New Yorker* and *Story*. One day he walked a
manuscript into the *Story* office. He had until then spelled his first name Jon.
Series editor Martha Foley looked at the cover of his story and told him, "You
are going to spend the rest of your life correcting proofs," so he changed it to
John.

Cheever said in an interview, "I don't work with plots. I work with intuition,
apprehension, dreams, concepts. Characters and events come simultaneously
to me. Plot implies narrative and a lot of crap. It is a calculated attempt to hold
the reader's interest at the sacrifice of moral conviction."

Cheever met the woman who would become his wife while riding in an elevator. "We went together for a couple of years before we got married," he said.
"Nobody got married in those years, then there was a period where everybody
got married, then nobody got married again." Cheever is known for his insight-
ful portrayals of marriage and suburban life as well as for depicting the tension
between a character's inner and outer worlds.

In 1958 Cheever won the National Book Award for *The Wapshot Chronicle*.
The Stories of John Cheever won the 1979 Pulitzer Prize for Fiction and a National Book Critics Circle Award, and its first paperback edition won the 1981
National Book Award. Shortly before he died of cancer, Cheever was awarded
the National Medal for Literature by the American Academy of Arts and Letters.

★

JIM AND IRENE Westcott were the kind of people who seem to
strike that satisfactory average of income, endeavor, and respecta-
bility that is reached by the statistical reports in college alumni bulle-

tins. They were the parents of two young children, they had been married nine years, they lived on the twelfth floor of an apartment house in the East Seventies between Fifth and Madison Avenues, they went to the theatre on an average of 10.3 times a year, and they hoped someday to live in Westchester. Irene Westcott was a pleasant, rather plain girl with soft brown hair and a wide, fine forehead upon which nothing at all had been written, and in the cold weather she wore a coat of fitch skins dyed to resemble mink. You could not say that Jim Westcott, at thirty-seven, looked younger than he was, but you could at least say of him that he seemed to feel younger. He wore his graying hair cut very short, he dressed in the kind of clothes his class had worn at Andover, and his manner was earnest, vehement, and intentionally naïve. The Westcotts differed from their friends, their classmates, and their neighbors only in an interest they shared in serious music. They went to a great many concerts — although they seldom mentioned this to anyone — and they spent a good deal of time listening to music on the radio.

Their radio was an old instrument, sensitive, unpredictable, and beyond repair. Neither of them understood the mechanics of radio — or of any of the other appliances that surrounded them — and when the instrument faltered, Jim would strike the side of the cabinet with his hand. This sometimes helped. One Sunday afternoon, in the middle of a Schubert quartet, the music faded away altogether. Jim struck the cabinet repeatedly, but there was no response; the Schubert was lost to them forever. He promised to buy Irene a new radio, and on Monday when he came home from work he told her that he had got one. He refused to describe it, and said it would be a surprise for her when it came.

The radio was delivered at the kitchen door the following afternoon, and with the assistance of her maid and the handyman Irene uncrated it and brought it into the living room. She was struck at once with the physical ugliness of the large gumwood cabinet. Irene was proud of her living room, she had chosen its furnishings and colors as carefully as she chose her clothes, and now it seemed to her that the new radio stood among her intimate possessions like an aggressive intruder. She was confounded by the number of dials and switches on the instrument panel, and she studied them thoroughly before she put the plug into a wall socket and turned the radio on. The dials flooded with a malevolent green light, and in the distance she heard the music of a piano quintet. The quintet was in the distance for only an instant; it bore down upon her with a speed greater than light and filled the apartment with the noise of music amplified so mightily that it knocked a china orna-

ment from a table to the floor. She rushed to the instrument and reduced the volume. The violent forces that were snared in the ugly gumwood cabinet made her uneasy. Her children came home from school
then, and she took them to the Park. It was not until later in the afternoon that she was able to return to the radio.

The maid had given the children their suppers and was supervising
their baths when Irene turned on the radio, reduced the volume, and sat
down to listen to a Mozart quintet that she knew and enjoyed. The music came through clearly. The new instrument had a much purer tone,
she thought, than the old one. She decided that tone was most important and that she could conceal the cabinet behind a sofa. But as soon as
she had made her peace with the radio, the interference began. A crackling sound like the noise of a burning powder fuse began to accompany
the singing of the strings. Beyond the music, there was a rustling that
reminded Irene unpleasantly of the sea, and as the quintet progressed,
these noises were joined by many others. She tried all the dials and
switches but nothing dimmed the interference, and she sat down, disappointed and bewildered, and tried to trace the flight of the melody.
The elevator shaft in her building ran beside the living-room wall, and
it was the noise of the elevator that gave her a clue to the character of
the static. The rattling of the elevator cables and the opening and closing of the elevator doors were reproduced in her loudspeaker, and, realizing that the radio was sensitive to electrical currents of all sorts, she
began to discern through the Mozart the ringing of telephone bells, the
dialing of phones, and the lamentation of a vacuum cleaner. By listening
more carefully, she was able to distinguish doorbells, elevator bells, electric razors, and Waring mixers, whose sounds had been picked up from
the apartments that surrounded hers and transmitted through her loudspeaker. The powerful and ugly instrument, with its mistaken sensitivity to discord, was more than she could hope to master, so she turned
the thing off and went into the nursery to see her children.

When Jim Westcott came home that night, he went to the radio con-
fidently and worked the controls. He had the same sort of experience
Irene had had. A man was speaking on the station Jim had chosen, and
his voice swung instantly from the distance into a force so powerful that
it shook the apartment. Jim turned the volume control and reduced the
voice. Then, a minute or two later, the interference began. The ringing of telephones and doorbells set in, joined by the rasp of the elevator doors and the whir of cooking appliances. The character of the noise
had changed since Irene had tried the radio earlier; the last of the elec-

tric razors was being unplugged, the vacuum cleaners had all been re-turned to their closets, and the static reflected that change in pace that overtakes the city after the sun goes down. He fiddled with the knobs but couldn't get rid of the noises, so he turned the radio off and told Irene that in the morning he'd call the people who had sold it to him and give them hell.

The following afternoon, when Irene returned to the apartment from a luncheon date, the maid told her that a man had come and fixed the radio. Irene went into the living room before she took off her hat or her furs and tried the instrument. From the loudspeaker came a record-ing of the "Missouri Waltz." It reminded her of the thin, scratchy music from an old-fashioned phonograph that she sometimes heard across the lake where she spent her summers. She waited until the waltz had fin-ished, expecting an explanation of the recording, but there was none. The music was followed by silence, and then the plaintive and scratchy record was repeated. She turned the dial and got a satisfactory burst of Caucasian music — the thump of bare feet in the dust and the rattle of coin jewelry — but in the background she could hear the ringing of bells and a confusion of voices. Her children came home from school then, and she turned off the radio and went to the nursery.

When Jim came home that night, he was tired, and he took a bath and changed his clothes. Then he joined Irene in the living room. He had just turned on the radio when the maid announced dinner, so he left it on, and he and Irene went to the table.

Jim was too tired to make even a pretense of sociability, and there was nothing about the dinner to hold Irene's interest, so her attention wan-dered from the food to the deposits of silver polish on the candlesticks and from there to the music in the other room. She listened for a few moments to a Chopin prelude and then was surprised to hear a man's voice break in. "For Christ's sake, Kathy," he said, "do you always have to play the piano when I get home?" The music stopped abruptly. "It's the only chance I have," a woman said. "I'm at the office all day." "So am I," the man said. He added something obscene about an upright pi-ano, and slammed a door. The passionate and melancholy music began again.

"Did you hear that?" Irene asked.

"What?" Jim was eating his dessert.

"The radio. A man said something while the music was still going on —something dirty."

"It's probably a play."

"I don't think it *is* a play," Irene said.

They left the table and took their coffee into the living room. Irene asked Jim to try another station. He turned the knob. "Have you seen my garters?" a man asked. "Button me up," a woman said. "Have you seen my garters?" the man said again. "Just button me up and I'll find your garters," the woman said. Jim shifted to another station. "I wish you wouldn't leave apple cores in the ashtrays," a man said. "I hate the smell."

"This is strange," Jim said.

"Isn't it?" Irene said.

Jim turned the knob again. "'On the coast of Coromandel where the early pumpkins blow,'" a woman with a pronounced English accent said, "'in the middle of the woods lived the Yonghy-Bonghy-Bò. Two old chairs, and half a candle, one old jug without a handle . . .'"

"My God!" Irene cried. "That's the Sweeneys' nurse."

"'These were all his worldly goods,'" the British voice continued.

"Turn that thing off," Irene said. "Maybe they can hear *us*." Jim switched the radio off. "That was Miss Armstrong, the Sweeneys' nurse," Irene said. "She must be reading to the little girl. They live in 17-B. I've talked with Miss Armstrong in the Park. I know her voice very well. We must be getting other people's apartments."

"That's impossible," Jim said.

"Well, that was the Sweeneys' nurse," Irene said hotly. "I know her voice. I know it very well. I'm wondering if they can hear us."

Jim turned the switch. First from a distance and then nearer, nearer, as if borne on the wind, came the pure accents of the Sweeneys' nurse again: "'Lady Jingly! Lady Jingly!'" she said, "'Sitting where the pumpkins blow, will you come and be my wife, said the Yonghy-Bonghy-Bò . . .'"

Jim went over to the radio and said "Hello" loudly into the speaker.

"'I am tired of living singly,'" the nurse went on, "'on this coast so wild and shingly, I'm a-weary of my life; if you'll come and be my wife, quite serene would be my life . . .'"

"I guess she can't hear us," Irene said. "Try something else."

Jim turned to another station, and the living room was filled with the uproar of a cocktail party that had overshot its mark. Someone was playing the piano and singing the Whiffenpoof Song, and the voices that surrounded the piano were vehement and happy. "Eat some more sandwiches," a woman shrieked. There were screams of laughter and a dish of some sort crashed to the floor.

"Those must be the Hutchinsons, in 15-B," Irene said. "I knew they were giving a party this afternoon. I saw her in the liquor store. Isn't this too divine? Try something else. See if you can get those people in 18-C."

The Westcotts overheard that evening a monologue on salmon fishing in Canada, a bridge game, running comments on home movies of what had apparently been a fortnight at Sea Island, and a bitter family quarrel about an overdraft at the bank. They turned off the radio at midnight and went to bed, weak with laughter. Sometime in the night, their son began to call for a glass of water and Irene got one and took it to his room. It was very early. All the lights in the neighborhood were extinguished, and from the boy's window she could see the empty street. She went into the living room and tried the radio. There was some faint coughing, a moan, and then a man spoke. "Are you all right, darling?" he asked. "Yes," a woman said wearily. "Yes, I'm all right, I guess," and then she added with great feeling, "But, you know, Charlie, I don't feel like myself any more. Sometimes there are about fifteen or twenty minutes in the week when I feel like myself. I don't like to go to another doctor, because the doctor's bills are so awful already, but I just don't feel like myself, Charlie. I just never feel like myself." They were not young, Irene thought. She guessed from the timbre of their voices that they were middle-aged. The restrained melancholy of the dialogue and the draft from the bedroom window made her shiver, and she went back to bed.

The following morning, Irene cooked breakfast for the family — the maid didn't come up from her room in the basement until ten — braided her daughter's hair, and waited at the door until her children and her husband had been carried away in the elevator. Then she went into the living room and tried the radio. "I don't want to go to school," a child screamed. "I hate school. I won't go to school. I hate school." "You will go to school," an enraged woman said. "We paid eight hundred dollars to get you into that school and you'll go if it kills you." The next number on the dial produced the worn record of the "Missouri Waltz." Irene shifted the control and invaded the privacy of several breakfast tables. She overheard demonstrations of indigestion, carnal love, abysmal vanity, faith, and despair. Irene's life was nearly as simple and sheltered as it appeared to be, and the forthright and sometimes brutal language that came from the loudspeaker that morning astonished and troubled her. She continued to listen until her maid came in. Then she turned off the radio quickly, since this insight, she realized, was a furtive one.

Irene had a luncheon date with a friend that day, and she left her apartment at a little after twelve. There were a number of women in the elevator when it stopped at her floor. She stared at their handsome and impassive faces, their furs, and the cloth flowers in their hats. Which one of them had been to Sea Island, she wondered. Which one had overdrawn her bank account? The elevator stopped at the tenth floor and a woman with a pair of Skye terriers joined them. Her hair was rigged high on her head and she wore a mink cape. She was humming the "Missouri Waltz."

Irene had two Martinis at lunch, and she looked searchingly at her friend and wondered what her secrets were. They had intended to go shopping after lunch, but Irene excused herself and went home. She told the maid that she was not to be disturbed; then she went into the living room, closed the doors, and switched on the radio. She heard, in the course of the afternoon, the halting conversation of a woman entertaining her aunt, the hysterical conclusion of a luncheon party, and a hostess briefing her maid about some cocktail guests. "Don't give the best Scotch to anyone who hasn't white hair," the hostess said. "See if you can get rid of that liver paste before you pass those hot things, and could you lend me five dollars? I want to tip the elevator man."

As the afternoon waned, the conversation increased in intensity. From where Irene sat, she could see the open sky above the East River. There were hundreds of clouds in the sky, as though the south wind had broken the winter into pieces and were blowing it north, and on her radio she could hear the arrival of cocktail guests and the return of children and businessmen from their schools and offices. "I found a good-sized diamond on the bathroom floor this morning," a woman said. "It must have fallen out of that bracelet Mrs. Dunston was wearing last night." "We'll sell it," a man said. "Take it down to the jeweller on Madison Avenue and sell it. Mrs. Dunston won't know the difference, and we could use a couple of hundred bucks . . ." " 'Oranges and lemons, say the bells of St. Clement's,' " the Sweeneys' nurse sang. " 'Half-pence and far-things, say the bells of St. Martin's. When will you pay me? say the bells at old Bailey . . .' " "It's not a hat," a woman cried, and at her back roared a cocktail party. "It's not a hat, it's a love affair. That's what Walter Florell said. He said it's not a hat, it's a love affair," and then, in a lower voice, the same woman added, "Talk to somebody, for Christ's sake, honey, talk to somebody. If she catches you standing here not talking to anybody, she'll take us off her invitation list, and I love these parties."

The Westcotts were going out for dinner that night, and when Jim came home, Irene was dressing. She seemed sad and vague, and he

brought her a drink. They were dining with friends in the neighborhood, and they walked to where they were going. The sky was broad
and filled with light. It was one of those splendid spring evenings that
excite memory and desire, and the air that touched their hands and
faces felt very soft. A Salvation Army band was on the corner playing
"Jesus Is Sweeter." Irene drew on her husband's arm and held him there
for a minute, to hear the music. "They're really such nice people, aren't
they?" she said. "They have such nice faces. Actually, they're so much
nicer than a lot of the people we know." She took a bill from her purse
and walked over and dropped it into the tambourine. There was in her
face, when she returned to her husband, a look of radiant melancholy
that he was not familiar with. And her conduct at the dinner party that
night seemed strange to him, too. She interrupted her hostess rudely
and stared at the people across the table from her with an intensity for
which she would have punished her children.

It was still mild when they walked home from the party, and Irene
looked up at the spring stars. "'How far that little candle throws its
beams,'" she exclaimed. "'So shines a good deed in a naughty world.'"
She waited that night until Jim had fallen asleep, and then went into the
living room and turned on the radio.

Jim came home at about six the next night. Emma, the maid, let him
in, and he had taken off his hat and was taking off his coat when Irene
ran into the hall. Her face was shining with tears and her hair was disordered. "Go up to 16-C, Jim!" she screamed. "Don't take off your coat.
Go up to 16-C. Mr. Osborn's beating his wife. They've been quarrelling
since four o'clock, and now he's hitting her. Go up and stop him."

From the radio in the living room, Jim heard screams, obscenities,
and thuds. "You know you don't have to listen to this sort of thing," he
said. He strode into the living room and turned the switch. "It's inde-
cent," he said. "It's like looking in windows. You know you don't have to
listen to this sort of thing. You can turn it off."

"Oh, it's so horrible, it's so dreadful," Irene was sobbing. "I've been
listening all day, and it's so depressing."

"Well, if it's so depressing, why do you listen to it? I bought this
damned radio to give you some pleasure," he said. "I paid a great deal of
money for it. I thought it might make you happy. I wanted to make you
happy."

"Don't, don't, don't, don't quarrel with me," she moaned, and laid
her head on his shoulder. "All the others have been quarrelling all day.
Everybody's been quarrelling. They're all worried about money. Mrs.

Hutchinson's mother is dying of cancer in Florida and they don't have enough money to send her to the Mayo Clinic. At least, Mr. Hutchinson says they don't have enough money. And some woman in this building is having an affair with the handyman — with that hideous handyman. It's too disgusting. And Mrs. Melville has heart trouble and Mr. Hendricks is going to lose his job in April and Mrs. Hendricks is horrid about the whole thing and that girl who plays the "Missouri Waltz" is a whore, a common whore, and the elevator man has tuberculosis and Mr. Osborn has been beating Mrs. Osborn." She wailed, she trembled with grief and checked the stream of tears down her face with the heel of her palm.

"Well, why do you have to listen?" Jim asked again. "Why do you have to listen to this stuff if it makes you so miserable?"

"Oh, don't don't don't," she cried. "Life is too terrible, too sordid and awful. But we've never been like that, have we, darling? Have we? I mean we've always been good and decent and loving to one another, haven't we? And we have two children, two beautiful children. Our lives aren't sordid, are they, darling? Are they?" She flung her arms around his neck and drew his face down to hers. "We're happy, aren't we, darling? We are happy, aren't we?"

"Of course we're happy," he said tiredly. He began to surrender his resentment. "Of course we're happy. I'll have that damned radio fixed or taken away tomorrow." He stroked her soft hair. "My poor girl," he said.

"You love me, don't you?" she asked. "And we're not hypocritical or worried about money or dishonest, are we?"

"No, darling," he said.

A man came in the morning and fixed the radio. Irene turned it on cautiously and was happy to hear a California-wine commercial and a recording of Beethoven's Ninth Symphony, including Schiller's "Ode to Joy." She kept the radio on all day and nothing untoward came from the speaker.

A Spanish suite was being played when Jim came home. "Is everything all right?" he asked. His face was pale, she thought. They had some cocktails and went in to dinner to the "Anvil Chorus" from "Il Trovatore." This was followed by Debussy's "La Mer."

"I paid the bill for the radio today," Jim said. "It cost four hundred dollars. I hope you'll get some enjoyment out of it."

"Oh, I'm sure I will," Irene said.

"Four hundred dollars is a good deal more than I can afford," he went on. "I wanted to get something that you'd enjoy. It's the last extravagance we'll be able to indulge in this year. I see that you haven't paid your clothing bills yet. I saw them on your dressing table." He looked directly at her. "Why did you tell me you'd paid them? Why did you lie to me?"

"I just didn't want you to worry, Jim," she said. She drank some water. "I'll be able to pay my bills out of this month's allowance. There were the slipcovers last month, and that party."

"You've got to learn to handle the money I give you a little more intelligently, Irene," he said. "You've got to understand that we won't have as much money this year as we had last. I had a very sobering talk with Mitchell today. No one is buying anything. We are spending all our time promoting new issues, and you know how long that takes. I'm not getting any younger, you know. I'm thirty-seven. My hair will be gray next year. I haven't done as well as I'd hoped to do. And I don't suppose things will get any better."

"Yes, dear," she said.

"We've got to start cutting down," Jim said. "We've got to think of the children. To be perfectly frank with you, I worry about money a great deal. I'm not at all sure of the future. No one is. If anything should happen to me, there's the insurance, but that wouldn't go very far today. I've worked awfully hard to give you and the children a comfortable life," he said bitterly. "I don't like to see all of my energies, all of my youth, wasted on fur coats and radios and slipcovers and—"

"Please, Jim," she said. "Please. They'll hear us."

"*Who'll* hear us? Emma can't hear us."

"The radio."

"Oh, I'm sick!" he shouted. "I'm sick to death of your apprehensiveness. The radio can't hear us. Nobody can hear us. And what if they can hear us? Who cares?"

Irene got up from the table and went into the living room. Jim went to the door and shouted at her from there. "Why are you so Christly all of a sudden? What's turned you overnight into a convent girl? You stole your mother's jewelry before they probated her will. You never gave your sister a cent of that money that was intended for her—not even when she needed it. You made Grace Howland's life miserable, and where was all your piety and your virtue when you went to that abortionist? I'll never forget how cool you were. You packed your bag and went off to have that child murdered as if you were going to Nassau. If you'd had any reasons, if you'd had any good reasons—"

Irene stood for a minute before the hideous cabinet, disgraced and sickened, but she held her hand on the switch before she extinguished the music and the voices, hoping that the instrument might speak to her kindly, that she might hear the Sweeneys' nurse. Jim continued to shout at her from the door. The voice on the radio was suave and noncommittal. "An early-morning railroad disaster in Tokyo," the loudspeaker said, "killed twenty-nine people. A fire in a Catholic hospital near Buffalo for the care of blind children was extinguished early this morning by nuns. The temperature is forty-seven. The humidity is eighty-nine."

1950-1960

IN 1951 SERIES EDITOR MARTHA FOLEY WROTE, "OUR
tragedy today is a general and universal physical fear so long sustained
by now that we can even bear it. There are no longer problems of the
spirit. There is only the question: When will I be blown up?" The Cold
War saw a return to formulaic, or "safer" and more sentimental, fiction,
the kind popular during and just after both world wars. Foley saw "little reason for the upsurge of conservatism in the country to also be reflected in the few remaining publications for the creative writer. Here is
where change and experiment should be." Many stories featured children or adults from a child's point of view. Also common were stories
with a religious bent or, as Foley called it, "religiosity because of its artificial nature."

Still, some writers began to explore new territory with fresh voices.
Bernard Malamud attracted notice, along with Philip Roth, Saul Bellow, and Harvey Swados. As Foley noted, "Once it was the New England
writer that predominated, then came the Middle Western, then the
Southern, and now it is the Jewish." Indeed, Jewish writers introduced a
new comic sensibility and energy in the 1950s and 1960s.

Perhaps because of the "Hollywoodization" of short fiction and a
growing disdain for writers who were thought to have sold out, certain
writers became fiercely private and, as they grew more successful, denied Foley permission to reprint their stories in the series. After grant-
ing permission for Foley to reprint "A Girl I Knew," J. D. Salinger refused all future requests for permission, even though Foley had first
published his fiction in *Story*. These refusals had the unexpected effect
of benefiting other writers. Vladimir Nabokov refused Foley permission
to reprint a story, and at the last minute she replaced his with "Will You

Please Be Quiet, Please?" by Raymond Carver. It was Carver's first appearance in the series. He wrote, "People used to call it that—simply,
'The Foley Collection' . . . the day the anthology came in the mail I took
it to bed to read and just to look at, you know, and hold it, but I did
more looking and holding than actual reading. I fell asleep and woke up
the next morning with the book there in bed beside me, with my wife."

Foley had a contentious relationship with Houghton Mifflin. Her editors grew frustrated by how frequently she missed deadlines and wondered about the breadth of her taste. They suggested that she share the
editorship with two other people, but she refused and threatened to take
the series to another house. She frequently demanded early payments;
she struggled financially throughout her life and felt that she was never
paid enough for her work. In order to support herself and her son, she
taught fiction writing at Columbia University. She became known for
her pragmatism—she insisted that everything the students wrote be
submitted to magazines. She passed along her insights about the writing life; her student Barbara Probst Solomon explained, "She advised
the women writers not to fall in love with writers and spend [their] lives
typing their manuscripts for them." Despite her editorship, her teaching
job, and miscellaneous freelance assignments, Foley continued to struggle financially, and in 1959 the IRS issued a tax lien and levy on her roy-
alties. From then on, 20 percent of her earnings went directly to the U.S.
government. Years later Foley wrote, "[My editor] once figured out that
I receive far less than a cleaning woman for my time and work."

★ ★ ★

1957

TILLIE OLSEN

I STAND HERE IRONING

from the *Pacific Spectator*

TILLIE OLSEN (1912–2007) was born in Nebraska, the daughter of Russian Jewish immigrants. She dropped out of high school at fifteen and worked as a waitress, factory worker, and maid. She became politically active and eventually joined the American Communist Party. She later moved to San Francisco, which became her home for most of her life.

Tell Me a Riddle, Olsen's first book, was a collection of short stories mostly narrated by mothers. Olsen wrote relatively little during her career, but her stories did bring awareness of the plight of exploited people.

Olsen taught at colleges such as Amherst College and Stanford University and was the recipient of nine honorary degrees, a Guggenheim Fellowship, National Endowment for the Arts fellowships, and the Rea Award for the Short Story, in 1994, for a lifetime of achievement. She died at the age of ninety-four.

★

I STAND HERE IRONING, and what you asked of me moves tormented back and forth with the iron.

"I wish you would manage the time to come in and talk with me about your daughter. I'm sure you can help me understand her. She's a youngster who needs help and whom I'm deeply interested in helping."

"Who needs help?" Even if I came what good would it do? You think because I am her mother I have a key, or that in some way you could use me as a key? She has lived for nineteen years. There is all that life that has happened outside of me, beyond me.

And when is there time to remember, to sift, to weigh, to estimate, to total? I will start and there will be an interruption and I will have to gather it all together again. Or I will become engulfed with all I did or did not do, with what should have been and what cannot be helped.

She was a beautiful baby. The first and only one of our five that was beautiful at birth. You do not guess how new and uneasy her tenancy in her now-loveliness. You did not know her all those years she was thought homely, or see her poring over her baby pictures, making me tell her over and over how beautiful she had been — and would be, I would tell her — and was now, to the seeing eye. But the seeing eyes were few or nonexistent. Including mine.

I nursed her. They feel that's important nowadays. I nursed all the children, but with her, with all the fierce rigidity of first motherhood, I did like the books said. Though her cries battered me to trembling and my breasts ached with swollenness, I waited till the clock decreed.

Why do I put that first? I do not even know if it matters, or if it explains anything.

She was a beautiful baby. She blew shining bubbles of sound. She loved motion, loved light, loved color and music and textures. She would lie on the floor in her blue overalls patting the surface so hard in ecstasy her hands and feet would blur. She was a miracle to me, but when she was eight months old I had to leave her daytimes with the woman downstairs to whom she was no miracle at all, for I worked or looked for work and for Emily's father, who "could no longer endure" (he wrote in his goodbye note) "sharing want with us."

I was nineteen. It was the pre-relief, pre-WPA world of the depression. I would start running as soon as I got off the streetcar, running up the stairs, the place smelling sour, and awake or asleep to startle awake, when she saw me she would break into a clogged weeping that could not be comforted, a weeping I can hear yet.

After a while I found a job hashing at night so I could be with her days, and it was better. But it came to where I had to bring her to his family and leave her.

It took a long time to raise the money for her fare back. Then she got chicken pox and I had to wait longer. When she finally came, I hardly knew her, walking quick and nervous like her father, looking like her father, thin, and dressed in a shoddy red that yellowed her skin and glared at the pockmarks. All the baby loveliness gone.

She was two. Old enough for nursery school they said, and I did not know then what I know now — the fatigue of the long day, and the lacerations of group life in the kinds of nurseries that are only parking places for children.

Except that it would have made no difference if I had known. It was the only place there was. It was the only way we could be together, the only way I could hold a job.

And even without knowing, I knew. I knew the teacher that was evil because all these years it has curdled into my memory, the little boy hunched in the corner, her rasp, "Why aren't you outside, because Alvin hits you? That's no reason, go out, coward." I knew Emily hated it even if she did not clutch and implore "Don't go, Mommy" like the other children, mornings.

She always had a reason why we should stay home. Momma, you look sick, Momma. I feel sick. Momma, the teachers aren't there today, they're sick. Momma there was a fire there last night. Momma it's a holiday today, no school, they told me.

But never a direct protest, never rebellion. I think of our others in their three-, four-year-oldness—the explosions, the tempers, the denunciations, the demands—and I feel suddenly ill. I stop the ironing. What in me demanded that goodness in her? And what was the cost, the cost to her of such goodness?

The old man living in the back once said in his gentle way, "You should smile at Emily more when you look at her." What *was* in my face when I looked at her? I loved her. There were all the acts of love.

It was only with the others I remembered what he said, so that it was the face of joy, and not of care or tightness or worry I turned to them —but never to Emily. She does not smile easily, let alone almost always, as her brothers and sisters do. Her face is closed and somber, but when she wants, how fluid. You must have seen it in her pantomimes, you spoke of her rare gift for comedy on the stage that rouses a laughter out of the audience so dear they applaud and applaud and do not want to let her go.

Where does it come from, that comedy? There was none of it in her when she came back to me that second time, after I had had to send her away again. She had a new daddy now to learn to love, and I think perhaps it was a better time. Except when we left her alone nights, telling ourselves she was old enough.

"Can't you go some other time, Mommy, like tomorrow?" she would ask. "Will it be just a little while you'll be gone?"

The time we came back, the front door open, the clock on the floor in the hall. She rigid, awake. "It wasn't just a little while. I didn't cry. I called you a little, just three times, and then I went downstairs to open the door so you could come faster. The clock talked loud, I threw it away, it scared me, what it talked."

She said the clock talked loud again that night I went to the hospital to have Susan. She was delirious with the fever that comes before red measles, but she was fully conscious all the week I was gone and the week after we were home when she could not come near the baby or me.

She did not get well. She stayed skeleton-thin, not wanting to eat, and night after night she had nightmares. She would call for me, and I would sleepily call back, "You're all right, darling, go to sleep, it's just a dream," and if she still called, in a sterner voice, "Now go to sleep, Emily, there's nothing to hurt you." Twice, only twice, when I had to get up for Susan anyhow, I went in to sit with her.

Now when it is too late (as if she would let me hold and comfort her like I do the others) I get up and go to her at her moan or restless stirring. "Are you awake? Can I get you something?" And the answer is always the same: "No, I'm all right, go back to sleep, Mother."

They persuaded me at the clinic to send her away to a convalescent home in the country where "she can have the kind of food and care you can't manage for her, and you'll be free to concentrate on the new baby." They still send children to that place. I see pictures on the society page of sleek young women planning affairs to raise money for it, or dancing at the affairs, or decorating Easter eggs or filling Christmas stockings for the children.

They never have a picture of the children so I do not know if they still wear those gigantic red bows and the ravaged looks on the every other Sunday when parents can come to visit "unless otherwise notified"—as we were notified the first six weeks.

Oh it is a handsome place, green lawns and tall trees and fluted flower beds. High up on the balconies of each cottage the children stand, the girls in their red bows and white dresses, the boys in white suits and giant red ties. The parents stand below shrieking up to be heard and the children shriek down to be heard, and between them the invisible wall "Not to Be Contaminated by Parental Germs or Physical Affection."

There was a tiny girl who always stood hand in hand with Emily. Her parents never came. One visit she was gone. "They moved her to Rose Cottage," Emily shouted in explanation. "They don't like you to love anybody here."

She wrote once a week, the labored writing of a seven-year-old. "I am fine. How is the baby. If I write my letter nicely I will have a star. Love." There never was a star. We wrote every other day, letters she could never hold or keep but only hear read—once. "We simply do not have room for children to keep any personal possessions," they patiently explained when we pieced one Sunday's shrieking together to plead how much it would mean to Emily to keep her letters and cards.

Each visit she looked frailer. "She isn't eating," they told us. (They had runny eggs for breakfast or mush with lumps, Emily said later, I'd hold it in my mouth and not swallow. Nothing ever tasted good, just when they had chicken.)

It took us eight months to get her released home, and only the fact that she gained back so little of her seven lost pounds convinced the social worker.

I used to try to hold and love her after she came back, but her body would stay stiff, and after a while she'd push away. She ate little. Food sickened her, and I think much of life too. Oh she had physical lightness and brightness, twinkling by on skates, bouncing like a ball up and down up and down over the jump rope, skimming over the hill; but these were momentary.

She fretted about her appearance, thin and dark and foreign-looking at a time when every little girl was supposed to look or thought she should look a chubby blond replica of Shirley Temple. The doorbell sometimes rang for her, but no one seemed to come and play in the house or be a best friend. Maybe because we moved so much.

There was a boy she loved painfully through two school semesters. Months later she told me how she had taken pennies from my purse to buy him candy. "Licorice was his favorite and I brought him some every day, but he still liked Jennifer better'n me. Why Mommy why?" A question I could never answer.

School was a worry to her. She was not glib or quick in a world where glibness and quickness were easily confused with ability to learn. To her overworked and exasperated teachers she was an overconscientious "slow learner" who kept trying to catch up and was absent entirely too often.

I let her be absent, though sometimes the illness was imaginary. How different from my now-strictness about attendance with the others. I wasn't working. We had a new baby, I was home anyhow. Sometimes, after Susan grew old enough, I would keep her home from school, too, to have them all together.

Mostly Emily had asthma, and her breathing, harsh and labored, would fill the house with a curiously tranquil sound. I would bring the two old dresser mirrors and her boxes of collections to her bed. She would select beads and single earrings, bottle tops and shells, dried flowers and pebbles, old postcards and scraps, all sorts of oddments; then she and Susan would play Kingdom, setting up landscapes and furniture, peopling them with action.

Those were the only times of peaceful companionship between her and Susan. I have edged away from it, that poisonous feeling between them, that terrible balancing of hurts and needs I had to do between them, and did so badly, those earlier years.

Oh there are conflicts between the others too, each one human, needing, demanding, hurting, taking — but only between Emily and Susan, no, Emily toward Susan that corroding resentment. It seems so obvious on the surface, yet it is not obvious. Susan, the second child, Susan, golden and curly-haired and chubby, quick and articulate and assured, everything in appearance and manner Emily was not; Susan, not able to resist Emily's precious things, losing or sometimes clumsily breaking them; Susan telling jokes and riddles to company for applause while Emily sat silent (to say to me later: that was *my* riddle, Mother, I told it to Susan); Susan, who for all the five years' difference in age was just a year behind Emily in developing physically.

I am glad for that slow physical development that widened the difference between her and her contemporaries, though she suffered over it. She was too vulnerable for that terrible world of youthful competition, of preening and parading, of constant measuring of yourself against every other, of envy, "If I had that copper hair," or "If I had that skin ..." She tormented herself enough about not looking like the others, there was enough of the unsureness, the having to be conscious of words before you speak, the constant caring — What are they thinking of me? What kind of an impression am I making? — there was enough without having it all magnified unendurably by the merciless physical drives.

Ronnie is calling. He is wet and I change him. It is rare there is such a cry now. That time of motherhood is almost behind me when the ear is not one's own but must always be racked and listening for the child cry, the child call. We sit for a while and I hold him, looking out over the city spread in charcoal with its soft aisles of light. "Shuggily" he breathes. A funny word, a family word, inherited from Emily, invented by her to say comfort.

In this and other ways she leaves her seal, I say aloud. And startle at my saying it. What do I mean? What did I start to gather together, to try and make coherent? I was at the terrible, growing years. War years. I do not remember them well. I was working, there were four smaller ones now, there was not time for her. She had to help be a mother, and housekeeper, and shopper. She had to set her seal. Mornings of crisis and near-hysteria trying to get lunches packed, hair combed, coats and shoes found, everyone to school or Child Care on time, the baby ready for transportation. And always the paper scribbled on by a smaller one, the book looked at by Susan then mislaid, the homework not done. Running out to that huge school where she was one, she was lost, she was a drop; suffering over the unpreparedness, stammering and unsure in her classes.

There was so little time left at night after the kids were bedded down. She would struggle over books, always eating (it was in those years she developed her enormous appetite that is legendary in our family) and I would be ironing, or preparing food for the next day, or writing V-mail to Bill, or tending the baby. Sometimes, to make me laugh, or out of her despair, she would imitate happenings or types at school.

I think I said once, "Why don't you do something like this in the school amateur show?" One morning she phoned me at work, hardly understandable through the weeping: "Mother, I did it. I won, I won; they gave me first prize; they clapped and clapped and wouldn't let me go."

Now suddenly she was Somebody, and as imprisoned in her difference as in anonymity.

She began to be asked to perform at other high schools, even in colleges, then at city and statewide affairs. The first one we went to, I only recognized her that first moment when thin, shy, she almost drowned herself into the curtains. Then: Was this Emily? The control, the command, the convulsing and deadly clowning, the spell, then the roaring, stamping audience, unwilling to let this rare and precious laughter out of their lives.

Afterwards: You ought to do something about her with a gift like that — but without money or knowing how, what does one do? We have left it all to her, and the gift has as often eddied inside, clogged and clotted, as been used and growing.

She is coming. She runs up the stairs two at a time with her light graceful step, and I know she is happy tonight. Whatever it was that occasioned your call did not happen today.

"Aren't you ever going to finish the ironing, Mother? Whistler painted his mother in a rocker. I'd have to paint mine standing over an ironing board." This is one of her communicative nights and she tells me everything and nothing as she fixes herself a plate of food out of the icebox.

She is so lovely. Why did you want me to come in at all? Why were you concerned? She will find her way.

She starts up the stairs to bed. "Don't get me up with the rest in the morning." "But I thought you were having midterms." "Oh, those," she comes back in and says quite lightly, "in a couple of years when we'll all be atom-dead they won't matter a bit."

She has said it before. She believes it. But because I have been dredging the past, and all that compounds a human being is so heavy and meaningful in me, I cannot endure it tonight.

I will never total it all. I will never come in to say: She was a child seldom smiled at. Her father left me before she was a year old. I had to work her first six years when there was work, or I sent her home and to his relatives. There were years she had care she hated. She was dark and thin and foreign-looking in a world where the prestige went to blondness and curly hair and dimples, she was slow where glibness was prized. She was a child of anxious, not proud, love. We were poor and could not afford for her the soil of easy growth. I was a young mother, I was a distracted mother. There were the other children pushing up, demanding. Her younger sister was all that she was not. She did not like me to touch her. She kept too much in herself, her life was such she had to keep too much in herself. My wisdom came too late. She has much to her and probably nothing will come of it. She is a child of her age, of depression, of war, of fear.

Let her be. So all that is in her will not bloom — but in how many does it? There is still enough left to live by. Only help her to believe — help make it so there is cause for her to believe that she is more than this dress on the ironing board, helpless before the iron.

1958

JAMES BALDWIN
SONNY'S BLUES

from *Partisan Review*

JAMES BALDWIN (1924–1987), the stepson of a pastor, grew up in Harlem. As a teenager, he worked at small jobs in Greenwich Village while he began writing. He grew frustrated by the treatment of blacks and gays in the United States, so left home and moved to Paris. There he became politically active.

Baldwin's first novel, *Go Tell It on the Mountain,* brought him great acclaim. His next novels were *Giovanni's Room, Another Country,* and *Tell Me How Long the Train's Been Gone.* Baldwin's fiction portrayed characters faced with discrimination because of their race or sexuality, as well as the upheaval of the 1960s. Series editor Martha Foley called him "the most important American black writer since Richard Wright."

Baldwin was made a Commandeur de la Légion d'Honneur by the French government in 1986. He died at age sixty-three in St.-Paul-de-Vence, France.

★

I READ ABOUT IT in the paper, in the subway, on my way to work. I read it, and I couldn't believe it, and I read it again. Then perhaps I just stared at it, at the newsprint spelling out his name, spelling out the story. I stared at it in the swinging lights of the subway car, and in the faces and bodies of the people, and in my own face, trapped in the darkness which roared outside.

It was not to be believed and I kept telling myself that as I walked from the subway station to the high school. And at the same time I couldn't doubt it. I was scared, scared for Sonny. He became real to me again. A great block of ice got settled in my belly and kept melting there slowly all day long, while I taught my classes algebra. It was a special kind of ice. It kept melting, sending trickles of ice water all up and down my veins, but it never got less. Sometimes it hardened and seemed to expand until I felt my guts were going to come spilling out or that I was

going to choke or scream. This would always be at a moment when I
was remembering some specific thing Sonny had once said or done.

When he was about as old as the boys in my classes his face had been
bright and open, there was a lot of copper in it; and he'd had wonderfully direct brown eyes, and great gentleness and privacy. I wondered
what he looked like now. He had been picked up, the evening before, in
a raid on an apartment downtown, for peddling and using heroin.

I couldn't believe it: but what I mean by that is that I couldn't find
any room for it anywhere inside me. I had kept it outside me for a long
time. I hadn't wanted to know. I had had suspicions, but I didn't name
them, I kept putting them away. I told myself that Sonny was wild, but
he wasn't crazy. And he'd always been a good boy, he hadn't ever turned
hard or evil or disrespectful, the way kids can, so quick, so quick, especially in Harlem. I didn't want to believe that I'd ever see my brother going down, coming to nothing, all that light in his face gone out, in the
condition I'd already seen so many others. Yet it had happened and here
I was, talking about algebra to a lot of boys who might, every one of
them for all I knew, be popping off needles every time they went to the
head. Maybe it did more for them than algebra could.

I was sure that the first time Sonny had ever had horse, he couldn't
have been much older than these boys were now. These boys, now, were
living as we'd been living then, they were growing up with a rush and
their heads bumped abruptly against the low ceiling of their actual possibilities. They were filled with rage. All they really knew were two dark-
nesses, the darkness of their lives, which was now closing in on them,
and the darkness of the movies, which had blinded them to that other
darkness, and in which they now, vindictively, dreamed, at once more
together than they were at any other time, and more alone.

When the last bell rang, the last class ended, I let out my breath. It
seemed I'd been holding it for all that time. My clothes were wet — I may
have looked as though I'd been sitting in a steam bath, all dressed up, all
afternoon. I sat alone in the classroom a long time. I listened to the boys
outside, downstairs, shouting and cursing and laughing. Their laughter struck me for perhaps the first time. It was not the joyous laughter
which — God knows why — one associates with children. It was mocking and insular, its intent was to denigrate. It was disenchanted, and in
this, also, lay the authority of their curses. Perhaps I was listening to
them because I was thinking about my brother and in them I heard my
brother. And myself.

One boy was whistling a tune, at once very complicated and very simple, it seemed to be pouring out of him as though he were a bird, and it sounded very cool and moving through all that harsh, bright air, only just holding its own through all those other sounds.

I stood up and walked over to the window and looked down into the courtyard. It was the beginning of the spring and the sap was rising in the boys. A teacher passed through them every now and again, quickly, as though he or she couldn't wait to get out of that courtyard, to get those boys out of their sight and off their minds. I started collecting my stuff. I thought I'd better get home and talk to Isabel.

The courtyard was almost deserted by the time I got downstairs. I saw this boy standing in the shadow of a doorway, looking just like Sonny. I almost called his name. Then I saw that it wasn't Sonny, but somebody we used to know, a boy from around our block. He'd been Sonny's friend. He'd never been mine, having been too young for me, and, anyway, I'd never liked him. And now, even though he was a grown-up man, he still hung around that block, still spent hours on the street corner, was always high and raggy. I used to run into him from time to time and he'd often work around to asking me for a quarter or fifty cents. He always had some real good excuse, too, and I always gave it to him, I don't know why.

But now, abruptly, I hated him. I couldn't stand the way he looked at me, partly like a dog, partly like a cunning child. I wanted to ask him what the hell he was doing in the school courtyard.

He sort of shuffled over to me, and he said, "I see you got the papers. So you already know about it."

"You mean about Sonny? Yes, I already know about it. How come they didn't get you?"

He grinned. It made him repulsive and it also brought to mind what he'd looked like as a kid. "I wasn't there. I stay away from them people."

"Good for you." I offered him a cigarette and I watched him through the smoke. "You come all the way down here just to tell me about Sonny?"

"That's right." He was sort of shaking his head and his eyes looked strange, as though they were about to cross. The bright sun deadened his damp dark brown skin and it made his eyes look yellow and showed up the dirt in his conked hair. He smelled funky. I moved a little away from him and I said, "Well, thanks. But I already know about it and I got to get home."

"I'll walk you a little ways," he said. We started walking. There were a couple of kids still loitering in the courtyard and one of them said good night to me and looked strangely at the boy beside me.

"What're you going to do?" he asked me. "I mean, about Sonny?"

"Look. I haven't seen Sonny for over a year, I'm not sure I'm going to do anything. Anyway, what the hell *can* I do?"

"That's right," he said quickly, "ain't nothing you can do. Can't much help old Sonny no more, I guess."

It was what I was thinking and so it seemed to me he had no right to say it.

"I'm surprised at Sonny, though," he went on—he had a funny way of talking, he looked straight ahead as though he were talking to himself —"I thought Sonny was a smart boy, I thought he was too smart to get hung."

"I guess he thought so too," I said sharply, "and that's how he got hung. And how about you? You're pretty goddamn smart, I bet."

Then he looked directly at me, just for a minute. "I ain't smart," he said. "If I was smart, I'd have reached for a pistol a long time ago."

"Look. Don't tell *me* your sad story, if it was up to me, I'd give you one." Then I felt guilty—guilty, probably, for never having supposed that the poor bastard *had* a story of his own, much less a sad one, and I asked, quickly, "What's going to happen to him now?"

He didn't answer this. He was off by himself some place. "Funny thing," he said, and from his tone we might have been discussing the quickest way to get to Brooklyn, "when I saw the papers this morning, the first thing I asked myself was if I had anything to do with it. I felt sort of responsible."

I began to listen more carefully. The subway station was on the corner, just before us, and I stopped. He stopped, too. We were in front of a bar and he ducked slightly, peering in, but whoever he was looking for didn't seem to be there. The juke box was blasting away with something black and bouncy and I half watched the barmaid as she danced her way from the juke box to her place behind the bar. And I watched her face as she laughingly responded to something someone said to her, still keeping time to the music. When she smiled one saw the little girl, one sensed the doomed, still-struggling woman beneath the battered face of the semi-whore.

"I never *give* Sonny nothing," the boy said finally, "but a long time ago I come to school high and Sonny asked me how it felt." He paused, I couldn't bear to watch him, I watched the barmaid, and I listened to the music which seemed to be causing the pavement to shake. "I told him it felt great." The music stopped, the barmaid paused and watched the juke box until the music began again. "It did."

All this was carrying me some place I didn't want to go. I certainly didn't want to know how it felt. It filled everything, the people, the houses, the music, the dark, quicksilver barmaid, with menace; and this menace was their reality.

"What's going to happen to him now?" I asked again.

"They'll send him away some place and they'll try to cure him." He shook his head. "Maybe he'll even think he's kicked the habit. Then they'll let him loose"— He gestured, throwing his cigarette into the gutter. "That's all."

"What do you mean, that's *all*?"

But I knew what he meant.

"I *mean*, that's *all*." He turned his head and looked at me, pulling down the corners of his mouth. "Don't you know what I mean?" he asked, softly.

"How the hell *would* I know what you mean?" I almost whispered it, I don't know why.

"That's right," he said to the air, "how would *he* know what I mean?" He turned toward me again, patient and calm, and yet I somehow felt him shaking, shaking as though he were going to fall apart. I felt that ice in my guts again, the dread I'd felt all afternoon; and again I watched the barmaid, moving about the bar, washing glasses, and singing. "Listen. They'll let him out and then it'll just start all over again. That's what I mean."

"You mean — they'll let him out. And then he'll just start working his way back in again. You mean he'll never kick the habit. Is that what you mean?"

"That's right," he said, cheerfully. "*You* see what I mean."

"Tell me," I said at last, "why does he want to die? He must want to die, he's killing himself, why does he want to die?"

He looked at me in surprise. He licked his lips. "He don't want to die. He wants to live. Don't nobody want to die, ever."

Then I wanted to ask him — too many things. He could not have answered, or if he had, I could not have borne the answers. I started walking. "Well, I guess it's none of my business."

"It's going to be rough on old Sonny," he said. We reached the subway station. "This is your station?" he asked. I nodded. I took one step down. "Damn!" he said, suddenly. I looked up at him. He grinned again.

"Damn if I didn't leave all my money home. You ain't got a dollar on you, have you? Just for a couple of days, is all."

All at once something inside gave and threatened to come pouring out of me. I didn't hate him any more. I felt that in another moment I'd start crying like a child.

"Sure," I said. "Don't sweat." I looked in my wallet and didn't have a dollar, I only had a five. "Here," I said. "That hold you?"

He didn't look at it—he didn't want to look at it. A terrible, closed look came over his face, as though he were keeping the number on the bill a secret from him and me. "Thanks," he said, and now he was dying to see me go. "Don't worry about Sonny. Maybe I'll write him or something."

"Sure," I said. "You do that. So long."

"Be seeing you," he said. I went on down the steps.

And I didn't write Sonny or send him anything for a long time. When I finally did, it was just after my little girl died, he wrote me back a letter which made me feel like a bastard.

Here's what he said:

Dear brother,

You don't know how much I needed to hear from you. I wanted to write you many a time but I dug how much I must have hurt you and so I didn't write. But now I feel like a man who's been trying to climb up out of some deep, real deep and funky hole and just saw the sun up there, outside. I got to get outside.

I can't tell you much about how I got here. I mean I don't know how to tell you. I guess I was afraid of something or I was trying to escape from something and you know I have never been very strong in the head (smile). I'm glad Mama and Daddy are dead and can't see what's happened to their son and I swear if I'd known what I was doing I would never have hurt you so, you and a lot of other fine people who were nice to me and who believed in me.

I don't want you to think it had anything to do with me being a musician. It's more than that. Or maybe less than that. I can't get anything straight in my head down here and I try not to think about what's going to happen to me when I get outside again. Sometime I think I'm going to flip and never get outside and sometime I think I'll come straight back. I tell you one thing, though, I'd rather blow my brains out than go through this again. But that's what they all say, so they tell me. If I tell you when I'm

coming to New York and if you could meet me, I sure would appreciate it.
Give my love to Isabel and the kids and I was sure sorry to hear about little
Gracie. I wish I could be like Mama and say the Lord's will be done, but I
don't know it seems to me that trouble is the one thing that never does get
stopped and I don't know what good it does to blame it on the Lord. But
maybe it does some good if you believe it.

Your brother,
SONNY

Then I kept in constant touch with him and I sent him whatever I could and I went to meet him when he came back to New York. When I saw him many things I thought I had forgotten came flooding back to me. This was because I had begun, finally, to wonder about Sonny, about the life that Sonny lived inside. This life, whatever it was, had made him older and thinner and it had deepened the distant stillness in which he had always moved. He looked very unlike my baby brother. Yet, when he smiled, when we shook hands, the baby brother I'd never known looked out from the depths of his private life, like an animal waiting to be coaxed into the light.

"How you been keeping?" he asked me.

"All right. And you?"

"Just fine." He was smiling all over his face. "It's good to see you again."

"It's good to see you."

The seven years' difference in our ages lay between us like a chasm: I wondered if these years would ever operate between us as a bridge. I was remembering, and it made it hard to catch my breath, that I had been there when he was born; and I had heard the first words he had ever spoken. When he started to walk, he walked from our mother straight to me. I caught him just before he fell when he took the first steps he ever took in this world.

"How's Isabel?"

"Just fine. She's dying to see you."

"And the boys?"

"They're fine, too. They're anxious to see their uncle."

"Oh, come on. You know they don't remember me."

"Are you kidding? Of course they remember you."

He grinned again. We got into a taxi. We had a lot to say to each other, far too much to know how to begin.

As the taxi began to move, I asked, "You still want to go to India?"

He laughed. "You still remember that. Hell, no. This place is Indian enough for me."

"It used to belong to them," I said.

And he laughed again. "They damn sure knew what they were doing when they got rid of it."

Years ago, when he was around fourteen, he'd been all hipped on the idea of going to India. He read books about people sitting on rocks, naked, in all kinds of weather, but mostly bad, naturally, and walking barefoot through hot coals and arriving at wisdom. I used to say that it sounded to me as though they were getting away from wisdom as fast as they could. I think he sort of looked down on me for that.

"Do you mind," he asked, "if we have the driver drive alongside the park? On the west side—I haven't seen the city in so long."

"Of course not," I said. I was afraid that I might sound as though I were humoring him, but I hoped he wouldn't take it that way.

So we drove along, between the green of the park and the stony, life-less elegance of hotels and apartment buildings, toward the vivid, killing streets of our childhood. These streets hadn't changed, though housing projects jutted up out of them now like rocks in the middle of a boil-ing sea. Most of the houses in which we had grown up had vanished, as had the stores from which we had stolen, the basements in which we had first tried sex, the rooftops from which we had hurled tin cans and bricks. But houses exactly like the houses of our past yet dominated the landscape, boys exactly like the boys we once had been found them-selves smothering in these houses, came down into the streets for light and air and found themselves encircled by disaster. Some escaped the trap, most didn't. Those who got out always left something of them-selves behind, as some animals amputate a leg and leave it in the trap. It might be said, perhaps, that I had escaped, after all, I was a school-teacher; or that Sonny had, he hadn't lived in Harlem for years. Yet, as the cab moved uptown through streets which seemed, with a rush, to darken with dark people, and as I covertly studied Sonny's face, it came to me that what we both were seeking through our separate cab windows was that part of ourselves which had been left behind. It's al-ways at the hour of trouble and confrontation that the missing member aches.

We hit 110th Street and started rolling up Lenox Avenue. And I'd known this avenue all my life, but it seemed to me again, as it had seemed on the day I'd first heard about Sonny's trouble, filled with a hidden menace which was its very breath of life.

"We almost there," said Sonny.

"Almost." We were both too nervous to say anything more.

We live in a housing project. It hasn't been up long. A few days after it was up it seemed uninhabitably new, now, of course, it's already rundown. It looks like a parody of the good, clean, faceless life — God knows the people who live in it do their best to make it a parody. The beat-looking grass lying around isn't enough to make their lives green, the hedges will never hold out the streets, and they know it. The big windows fool no one, they aren't big enough to make space out of no space. They don't bother with the windows, they watch the TV screen instead. The playground is most popular with the children who don't play at jacks, or skip rope, or roller skate, or swing, and they can be found in it after dark. We moved in partly because it's not too far from where I teach, and partly for the kids; but it's really just like the houses in which Sonny and I grew up. The same things happen, they'll have the same things to remember. The moment Sonny and I started into the house I had the feeling that I was simply bringing him back into the danger he had almost died trying to escape.

Sonny has never been talkative. So I don't know why I was sure he'd be dying to talk to me when supper was over the first night. Everything went fine, the oldest boy remembered him, and the youngest boy liked him, and Sonny had remembered to bring something for each of them; and Isabel, who is really much nicer than I am, more open and giving, had gone to a lot of trouble about dinner and was genuinely glad to see him. And she's always been able to tease Sonny in a way that I haven't. It was nice to see her face so vivid again and to hear her laugh and watch her make Sonny laugh. She wasn't, or, anyway, she didn't seem to be, at all uneasy or embarrassed. She chatted as though there were no subject which had to be avoided and she got Sonny past his first, faint stiffness. And thank God she was there, for I was filled with that icy dread again. Everything I did seemed awkward to me, and everything I said sounded freighted with hidden meaning. I was trying to remember everything I'd heard about dope addiction and I couldn't help watching Sonny for signs. I wasn't doing it out of malice. I was trying to find out something about my brother. I was dying to hear him tell me he was safe.

"Safe!" my father grunted, whenever Mama suggested trying to move to a neighborhood which might be safer for children. "Safe, hell! Ain't no place safe for kids, nor nobody."

He always went on like this, but he wasn't, ever, really as bad as he sounded, not even on weekends, when he got drunk. As a matter of fact, he was always on the lookout for "something a little better," but he died before he found it. He died suddenly, during a drunken weekend in the middle of the war, when Sonny was fifteen. He and Sonny hadn't ever got on too well. And this was partly because Sonny was the apple of his father's eye. It was because he loved Sonny so much, and was frightened for him, that he was always fighting with him. It doesn't do any good to fight with Sonny. Sonny just moves back, inside himself, where he can't be reached. But the principal reason that they never hit it off is that they were so much alike. Daddy was big and rough and loud-talking, just the opposite of Sonny, but they both had — that same privacy.

Mama tried to tell me something about this, just after Daddy died. I was home on leave from the army.

This was the last time I ever saw my mother alive. Just the same, this picture gets all mixed up in my mind with pictures I had of her when she was younger. The way I always see her is the way she used to be on a Sunday afternoon, say, when the old folks were talking after the big Sunday dinner. I always see her wearing pale blue. She'd be sitting on the sofa. And my father would be sitting in the easy chair, not far from her. And the living room would be full of church folks and relatives. There they sit, in chairs all around the living room, and the night is creeping up outside, but nobody knows it yet. You can see the darkness growing against the windowpanes and you hear the street noises every now and again, or maybe the jangling beat of a tambourine from one of the churches close by, but it's real quiet in the room. For a moment nobody's talking, but every face looks darkening, like the sky outside. And my mother rocks a little from the waist, and my father's eyes are closed. Everyone is looking at something a child can't see. For a minute they've forgotten the children. Maybe a kid is lying on the rug, half asleep. Maybe somebody's got a kid in his lap and is absent-mindedly stroking the kid's head. Maybe there's a kid, quiet and big-eyed, curled up in a big chair in the corner. The silence, the darkness coming, and the darkness in the faces frightens the child obscurely. He hopes that the hand which strokes his forehead will never stop — will never die. He hopes that there will never come a time when the old folks won't be sitting around the living room, talking about where they've come from, and what they've seen, and what's happened to them and their kinfolk.

But something deep and watchful in the child knows that this is bound to end, is already ending. In a moment someone will get up and turn on the light. Then the old folks will remember the children and they won't talk any more that day. And when light fills the room, the child is filled with darkness. He knows that every time this happens he's moved just a little closer to that darkness outside. The darkness outside is what the old folks have been talking about. It's what they've come from. It's what they endure. The child knows that they won't talk any more because if he knows too much about what's happened to *them,* he'll know too much too soon, about what's going to happen to *him.*

The last time I talked to my mother, I remember I was restless. I wanted to get out and see Isabel. We weren't married then and we had a lot to straighten out between us.

There Mama sat, in black, by the window. She was humming an old church song, "Lord, you brought me from a long ways off." Sonny was out somewhere. Mama kept watching the streets.

"I don't know," she said, "if I'll ever see you again, after you go off from here. But I hope you'll remember the things I tried to teach you."

"Don't talk like that," I said, and smiled. "You'll be here a long time yet."

She smiled, too, but she said nothing. She was quiet for a long time. And I said, "Mama, don't you worry about nothing. I'll be writing all the time, and you be getting the checks . . ."

"I want to talk to you about your brother," she said, suddenly. "If anything happens to me he ain't going to have nobody to look out for him."

"Mama," I said, "ain't nothing going to happen to you *or* Sonny. Sonny's all right. He's a good boy and he's got good sense."

"It ain't a question of his being a good boy," Mama said, "nor of his having good sense. It ain't only the bad ones, nor yet the dumb ones that gets sucked under." She stopped, looking at me. "Your daddy once had a brother," she said, and she smiled in a way that made me feel she was in pain. "You didn't never know that, did you?"

"No," I said, "I never knew that," and I watched her face.

"Oh, yes," she said, "your daddy had a brother." She looked out of the window again. "I know you never saw your daddy cry. But *I* did — many a time, through all these years."

I asked her, "What happened to his brother? How come nobody's ever talked about him?"

This was the first time I ever saw my mother look old.

"His brother got killed," she said, "when he was just a little younger than you are now. I knew him. He was a fine boy. He was maybe a little full of the devil, but he didn't mean nobody no harm."

Then she stopped and the room was silent, exactly as it had sometimes been on those Sunday afternoons. Mama kept looking out into the streets.

"He used to have a job in the mill," she said, "and, like all young folks, he just liked to perform on Saturday nights. Saturday nights, him and your father would drift around to different places, go to dances and things like that, or just sit around with people they knew, and your father's brother would sing, he had a fine voice, and play along with himself on his guitar. Well, this particular Saturday night, him and your father was coming home from some place, and they were both a little drunk and there was a moon that night, it was bright like day. Your father's brother was feeling kind of good, and he was whistling to himself, and he had his guitar slung over his shoulder. They was coming down a hill and beneath them was a road that turned off from the highway. Well, your father's brother, being always kind of frisky, decided to run down this hill, and he did, with that guitar banging and clanging behind him, and he ran across the road, and he was making water behind a tree. And your father was sort of amused at him and he was still coming down the hill, kind of slow. Then he heard a car motor and that same minute his brother stepped from behind the tree, into the road, in the moonlight. And he started to cross the road. And your father started to run down the hill, he says he don't know why. This car was full of white men. They was all drunk, and when they seen your father's brother they let out a great whoop and holler and they aimed the car straight at him. They was having fun, they just wanted to scare him, the way they do sometimes, you know. But they was drunk. And I guess the boy, being drunk, too, and scared, kind of lost his head. By the time he jumped it was too late. Your father says he heard his brother scream when the car rolled over him, and he heard the wood of that guitar when it give, and he heard them strings go flying, and he heard them white men shouting, and the car kept on a-going and it ain't stopped till this day. And, time your father got down the hill, his brother weren't nothing but blood and pulp."

Tears were gleaming on my mother's face. There wasn't anything I could say.

"He never mentioned it," she said, "because I never let him mention it before you children. Your daddy was like a crazy man that night and for many a night thereafter. He says he never in his life seen anything as dark as that road after the lights of that car had gone away. Weren't nothing, weren't nobody on that road, just your daddy and his brother and that busted guitar. Oh, yes. Your daddy never did really get right again. Till the day he died he weren't sure but that every white man he saw was the man that killed his brother."

She stopped and took out her handkerchief and dried her eyes and looked at me.

"I ain't telling you all this," she said, "to make you scared or bitter or to make you hate nobody. I'm telling you this because you got a brother. And the world ain't changed."

I guess I didn't want to believe this. I guess she saw this in my face. She turned away from me, toward the window again, searching those streets.

"But I praise my Redeemer," she said at last, "that He called your daddy home before me. I ain't saying it to throw no flowers at myself, but, I declare, it keeps me from feeling too cast down to know I helped your father get safely through this world. Your father always acted like he was the roughest, strongest man on earth. And everybody took him to be like that. But if he hadn't had *me* there—to see his tears!"

She was crying again. Still, I couldn't move. I said, "Lord, Lord, Mama, I didn't know it was like that."

"Oh, honey," she said, "there's a lot that you don't know. But you are going to find it out." She stood up from the window and came over to me. "You got to hold on to your brother," she said, "and don't let him fall, no matter what it looks like is happening to him and no matter how evil you gets with him. You going to be evil with him many a time. But don't you forget what I told you, you hear?"

"I won't forget," I said. "Don't you worry, I won't forget. I won't let nothing happen to Sonny."

My mother smiled as though she were amused at something she saw in my face. Then, "You may not be able to stop nothing from happening. But you got to let him know you's *there*."

Two days later I was married, and then I was gone. And I had a lot of things on my mind and I pretty well forgot my promise to Mama until I got shipped home on a special furlough for her funeral.

And after the funeral, with just Sonny and me alone in the empty kitchen, I tried to find out something about him.

"What do you want to do?" I asked him.

"I'm going to be a musician," he said.

For he had graduated, in the time I had been away, from dancing to the juke box to finding out who was playing what, and what they were doing with it, and he had bought himself a set of drums.

"You mean, you want to be a drummer?" I somehow had the feeling that being a drummer might be all right for other people but not for my brother Sonny.

"I don't think," he said, looking at me very gravely, "that I'll ever be a good drummer. But I think I can play a piano."

I frowned. I'd never played the role of the older brother quite so seriously before, had scarcely ever, in fact, *asked* Sonny a damn thing. I sensed myself in the presence of something I didn't really know how to handle, didn't understand. So I made my frown a little deeper as I asked: "What kind of musician do you want to be?"

He grinned. "How many kinds do you think there are?"

"Be *serious*," I said.

He laughed, throwing his head back, and then looked at me. "I *am* serious."

"Well, then, for Christ's sake, stop kidding around and answer a serious question. I mean, do you want to be a concert pianist, you want to play classical music and all that, or — or what?" Long before I finished he was laughing again. "For Christ's *sake*, Sonny!"

He sobered, but with difficulty. "I'm sorry. But you sound so — *scared!*" and he was off again.

"Well, you may think it's funny now, baby, but it's not going to be so funny when you have to make your living at it, let me tell you *that*." I was furious because I knew he was laughing at me and I didn't know why.

"No," he said, very sober now, and afraid, perhaps, that he'd hurt me, "I don't want to be a classical pianist. That isn't what interests me. I mean"— he paused, looking hard at me, as though his eyes would help me to understand, and then gestured helplessly, as though perhaps his hand would help —"I mean, I'll have a lot of studying to do, and I'll have to study *everything*, but, I mean, I want to play *with* — jazz musicians." He stopped. "I want to play jazz," he said.

Well, the word had never before sounded as heavy, as real, as it sounded that afternoon in Sonny's mouth. I just looked at him and I was probably frowning a real frown by this time. I simply couldn't see why on earth he'd want to spend his time hanging around night clubs, clowning around on bandstands, while people pushed each other around a dance floor. It seemed — beneath him, somehow. I had never thought about it before, had never been forced to, but I suppose I had always put jazz musicians in a class with what Daddy called "good-time people."

"Are you *serious*?"

"Hell, *yes*, I'm serious."

He looked more helpless than ever, and annoyed, and deeply hurt.

I suggested, helpfully: "You mean — like Louis Armstrong?"

His face closed as though I'd struck him. "No. I'm not talking about none of that old-time, down-home crap."

"Well, look, Sonny, I'm sorry, don't get mad. I just don't altogether get it, that's all. Name somebody — you know, a jazz musician you admire."

"Bird."

"Who?"

"Bird! Charlie Parker! Don't they teach you nothing in the goddamn army?"

I lit a cigarette. I was surprised and then a little amused to discover I was trembling. "I've been out of touch," I said. "You'll have to be patient with me. Now. Who's this Parker character?"

"He's just one of the greatest jazz musicians alive," said Sonny, sullenly, his hands in his pockets, his back to me. "Maybe *the* greatest," he added, bitterly, "that's probably why *you* never heard of him."

"All right," I said, "I'm ignorant. I'm sorry. I'll go out and buy all the cat's records right away, all right?"

"It don't," said Sonny, with dignity, "make any difference to me. I don't care what you listen to. Don't do me no favors."

I was beginning to realize that I'd never seen him so upset before. With another part of my mind I was thinking that this would probably turn out to be one of those things kids go through and that I shouldn't make it seem important by pushing it too hard. Still, I didn't think it would do any harm to ask: "Doesn't all this take a lot of time? Can you make a living at it?"

He turned back to me and half leaned, half sat, on the kitchen table. "Everything takes time," he said, "and — well, yes, sure, I can make a living at it. But what I don't seem to be able to make you understand is that it's the only thing I want to do."

"Well, Sonny," I said, gently, "you know people can't always do exactly what they *want* to do —"

"*No,* I don't know that," said Sonny, surprising me. "I think people *ought* to do what they want to do, what else are they alive for?"

"You getting to be a big boy," I said desperately, "it's time you started thinking about your future."

"I'm thinking about my future," said Sonny grimly. "I think about it all the time."

I gave up. I decided, if he didn't change his mind, that we could always talk about it later. "In the meantime," I said, "you got to finish school." We had already decided that he'd have to move in with Isabel and her folks. I knew this wasn't the ideal arrangement because Isabel's folks are inclined to be dicty and they hadn't especially wanted Isabel to marry me. But I didn't know what else to do. "And we have to get you fixed up at Isabel's."

There was a long silence. He moved from the kitchen table to the window. "That's a terrible idea. You know it yourself."

"Do you have a *better* idea?"

He just walked up and down the kitchen for a minute. He was as tall as I was. He had started to shave. I suddenly had the feeling that I didn't know him at all.

He stopped at the kitchen table and picked up my cigarettes. Looking at me with a kind of mocking, amused defiance, he put one between his lips. "You mind?"

"You smoking already?"

He lit the cigarette and nodded, watching me through the smoke. "I just wanted to see if I'd have the courage to smoke in front of you." He grinned and blew a great cloud of smoke to the ceiling. "It was easy." He looked at my face. "Come on, now. I bet you was smoking at my age, tell the truth."

I didn't say anything but the truth was on my face, and he laughed. But now there was something very strained in his laugh. "Sure. And I bet that ain't all you was doing."

He was frightening me a little. "Cut the crap," I said. "We already decided that you was going to go and live at Isabel's. Now what's got into you all of a sudden?"

"*You* decided it," he pointed out. "*I* didn't decide nothing." He stopped in front of me, leaning against the stove, arms loosely folded. "Look, brother. I don't want to stay in Harlem no more, I really don't." He was very earnest. He looked at me, then over toward the kitchen window. There was something in his eyes I'd never seen before, some thoughtfulness, some worry all his own. He rubbed the muscle of one arm. "It's time I was getting out of here."

"Where do you want to *go,* Sonny?"

"I want to join the army. Or the navy, I don't care. If I say I'm old enough, they'll believe me."

Then I got mad. It was because I was so scared. "You must be crazy.

You goddamn fool, what the hell do you want to go and join the *army* for?"

"I just told you. To get out of Harlem."

"Sonny, you haven't even finished *school*. And if you really want to be a musician, how do you expect to study if you're in the *army*?"

He looked at me, trapped, and in anguish. "There's ways. I might be able to work out some kind of deal. Anyway, I'll have the G.I. Bill when I come out."

"*If* you come out." We stared at each other. "Sonny, please. Be reasonable. I know the setup is far from perfect. But we got to do the best we can."

"I ain't learning nothing in school," he said. "Even when I go." He turned away from me and opened the window and threw his cigarette out into the narrow alley. I watched his back. "At least, I ain't learning nothing you'd want me to learn." He slammed the window so hard I thought the glass would fly out, and turned back to me. "And I'm sick of the stink of these garbage cans!"

"Sonny," I said, "I know how you feel. But if you don't finish school now, you're going to be sorry later that you didn't." I grabbed him by the shoulders. "And you only got another year. It ain't so bad. And I'll come back and I swear I'll help you do *whatever* you want to do. Just try to put up with it till I come back. Will you please do that? For me?"

He didn't answer and he wouldn't look at me.

"Sonny. You hear me?"

He pulled away. "I hear you. But you never hear anything *I* say."

I didn't know what to say to that. He looked out of the window and then back at me. "OK," he said, and sighed. "I'll try."

Then I said, trying to cheer him up a little, "They got a piano at Isabel's. You can practice on it."

And as a matter of fact, it did cheer him up for a minute. "That's right," he said to himself. "I forgot that." His face relaxed a little. But the worry, the thoughtfulness, played on it still, the way shadows play on a face which is staring into the fire.

But I thought I'd never hear the end of that piano. At first, Isabel would write me, saying how nice it was that Sonny was so serious about his music and how, as soon as he came in from school, or wherever he had been when he was supposed to be at school, he went straight to that piano and stayed there until suppertime. And, after supper, he went back to that piano and stayed there until everybody went to bed. He was at that piano all day Saturday and all day Sunday. Then he bought a record player and started playing records. He'd play one record over and over again, all day long sometimes, and he'd improvise along with it on the piano. Or he'd play one section of the record, one chord, one change, one progression, then he'd do it on the piano. Then back to the record. Then back to the piano.

Well, I really don't know how they stood it. Isabel finally confessed that it wasn't like living with a person at all, it was like living with sound. And the sound didn't make any sense to her, didn't make any sense to any of them — naturally. They began, in a way, to be afflicted by this presence that was living in their home. It was as though Sonny were some sort of god, or monster. He moved in an atmosphere which wasn't like theirs at all. They fed him and he ate, he washed himself, he walked in and out of their door; he certainly wasn't nasty or unpleasant or rude, Sonny isn't any of those things; but it was as though he were all wrapped up in some cloud, some fire, some vision all his own; and there wasn't any way to reach him.

At the same time, he wasn't really a man yet, he was still a child, and they had to watch out for him in all kinds of ways. They certainly couldn't throw him out. Neither did they dare to make a great scene about that piano because even they dimly sensed, as I sensed, from so many thousands of miles away, that Sonny was at that piano playing for his life.

But he hadn't been going to school. One day a letter came from the school board and Isabel's mother got it — there had, apparently, been other letters but Sonny had torn them up. This day, when Sonny came in, Isabel's mother showed him the letter and asked where he'd been spending his time. And she finally got it out of him that he'd been down in Greenwich Village, with musicians and other characters, in a white girl's apartment. And this scared her and she started to scream at him and what came up, once she began — though she denies it to this day — was what sacrifices they were making to give Sonny a decent home and how little he appreciated it.

Sonny didn't play the piano that day. By evening, Isabel's mother had calmed down but then there was the old man to deal with, and Isabel herself. Isabel says she did her best to be calm but she broke down and started crying. She says she just watched Sonny's face. She could tell, by watching him, what was happening with him. And what was happening was that they penetrated his cloud, they had reached him. Even if their fingers had been a thousand times more gentle than human fingers ever are, he could hardly help feeling that they had stripped him naked and were spitting on that nakedness. For he also had to see that his presence, that music, which was life or death to him, had been torture for them and that they had endured it, not at all for his sake, but only for mine. And Sonny couldn't take that. He can take it a little better today than he could then but he's still not very good at it and, frankly, I don't know anybody who is.

The silence of the next few days must have been louder than the sound of all the music ever played since time began. One morning, before she went to work, Isabel was in his room for something and she suddenly realized that all of his records were gone. And she knew for certain that he was gone. And he was. He went as far as the navy would carry him. He finally sent me a postcard from some place in Greece and that was the first I knew that Sonny was still alive. I didn't see him any more until we were both back in New York and the war had long been over.

He was a man by then, of course, but I wasn't willing to see it. He came by the house from time to time, but we fought almost every time we met. I didn't like the way he carried himself, loose and dreamlike all the time, and I didn't like his friends, and his music seemed to be merely an excuse for the life he led. It sounded just that weird and disordered.

Then we had a fight, a pretty awful fight, and I didn't see him for months. By and by I looked him up where he was living, in a furnished room in the Village, and I tried to make it up. But there were lots of other people in the room and Sonny just lay on his bed, and he wouldn't come downstairs with me, and he treated these other people as though they were his family and I weren't. So I got mad and then he got mad, and then I told him that he might just as well be dead as live the way he was living. Then he stood up and he told me not to worry about him any more in life, that he *was* dead as far as I was concerned. Then he pushed me to the door and the other people looked on as though nothing were happening, and he slammed the door behind me. I stood in the hallway, staring at the door. I heard somebody laugh in the room and then the tears came to my eyes. I started down the steps, whistling to keep from crying, I kept whistling to myself, "You going to need me, baby, one of these cold, rainy days."

I read about Sonny's trouble in the spring. Little Grace died in the fall. She was a beautiful little girl. But she only lived a little over two years.

She died of polio and she suffered. She had a slight fever for a couple of days, but it didn't seem like anything and we just kept her in bed. And we would certainly have called the doctor, but the fever dropped, she seemed to be all right. So we thought it had just been a cold. Then, one day, she was up, playing; Isabel was in the kitchen fixing lunch for the two boys when they'd come in from school, and she heard Grace fall down in the living room. When you have a lot of children you don't always start running when one of them falls, unless they start screaming or something. And, this time, Grace was quiet. Yet, Isabel says that when she heard that *thump* and then that silence, something happened in her to make her afraid. And she ran to the living room and there was little Grace on the floor, all twisted up, and the reason she hadn't screamed was that she couldn't get her breath. And when she did scream, it was the worst sound, Isabel says, that she'd ever heard in all her life, and she still hears it sometimes in her dreams. Isabel will sometimes wake me up with a low, moaning, strangled sound and I have to be quick to awaken her and hold her to me and where Isabel is weeping against me seems a mortal wound.

I think I may have written Sonny the very day that little Grace was buried. I was sitting in the living room in the dark, by myself, and I suddenly thought of Sonny. My trouble made his real.

One Saturday afternoon, when Sonny had been living with us, or, anyway, been in our house, for nearly two weeks, I found myself wandering aimlessly about the living room, drinking from a can of beer, and trying to work up the courage to search Sonny's room. He was out, he was usually out whenever I was home, and Isabel had taken the children to see their grandparents. Suddenly I was standing still in front of the living room window, watching Seventh Avenue. The idea of searching Sonny's room made me still. I scarcely dared to admit to myself what I'd be searching for. I didn't know what I'd do if I found it. Or if I didn't.

On the sidewalk across from me, near the entrance to a barbecue joint, some people were holding an old-fashioned revival meeting. The barbecue cook, wearing a dirty white apron, his conked hair reddish and metallic in the pale sun and a cigarette between his lips, stood in the doorway, watching them. Kids and older people paused in their errands and stood there, along with some older men and a couple of very tough-looking women who watched everything that happened on the avenue, as though they owned it, or were maybe owned by it. Well, they were watching this, too. The revival was being carried on by three sisters in black, and a brother. All they had were their voices and their Bibles and a tambourine. The brother was testifying and while he testified two of the sisters stood together, seeming to say Amen, and the third sister walked around with the tambourine outstretched and a couple of people dropped coins into it. Then the brother's testimony ended and the sister who had been taking up the collection dumped the coins into her palm and transferred them to the pocket of her long black robe. Then she raised both hands, striking the tambourine against the air, and then against one hand, and she started to sing. And the two other sisters and the brother joined in.

It was strange, suddenly, to watch, though I had been seeing these street meetings all my life. So, of course, had everybody else down there. Yet, they paused and watched and listened and I stood still at the window. "Tis the old ship of Zion," they sang, and the sister with the tambourine kept a steady, jangling beat, "it has rescued many a thousand!" Not a soul under the sound of their voices was hearing this song for the first time, not one of them had been rescued. Nor had they seen much in the way of rescue work being done around them. Neither did they especially believe in the holiness of the three sisters and the brother, they knew too much about them, knew where they lived, and how. The woman with the tambourine, whose voice dominated the air, whose face was bright with joy, was divided by very little from the woman who stood watching her, a cigarette between her heavy, chapped lips, her hair a cuckoo's nest, her face scarred and swollen from many beatings, and her black eyes glittering like coal. Perhaps they both knew this, which was why, when, as rarely, they addressed each other, they addressed each other as Sister. As the singing filled the air the watching, listening faces underwent a change, the eyes focusing on something within; the music seemed to soothe a poison out of them; and time seemed, nearly, to fall away from the sullen, belligerent, battered faces, as though they were fleeing back to their first condition, while dreaming of their last. The barbecue cook half shook his head and smiled, and dropped his cigarette and disappeared into his joint. A man fumbled in his pockets for change and stood holding it in his hand impatiently, as though he had just remembered a pressing appointment further up the avenue. He looked furious. Then I saw Sonny, standing on the edge of the crowd. He was carrying a wide, flat notebook with a green cover, and it made him look, from where I was standing, almost like a schoolboy. The coppery sun brought out the copper in his skin, he was very faintly smiling, standing very still. Then the singing stopped, the tambourine turned into a collection plate again. The furious man dropped in his coins and vanished, so did a couple of the women, and Sonny dropped some change in the plate, looking directly at the woman with a little smile. He started across the avenue, toward the house. He has a slow, loping walk, something like the way Harlem hipsters walk, only he's imposed on this his own half-beat. I had never really noticed it before.

I stayed at the window, both relieved and apprehensive. As Sonny disappeared from my sight, they began singing again. And they were still singing when his key turned in the lock.

"Hey," he said.

"Hey, yourself. You want some beer?"

"No. Well, maybe." But he came up to the window and stood beside me, looking out. "What a warm voice," he said.

They were singing "If I could only hear my mother pray again!"

"Yes," I said, "and she can sure beat that tambourine."

"But what a terrible song," he said, and laughed. He dropped his notebook on the sofa and disappeared into the kitchen. "Where's Isabel and the kids?"

"I think they went to see their grandparents. You hungry?"

"No." He came back into the living room with his can of beer. "You want to come someplace with me tonight?"

I sensed, I don't know how, that I couldn't possibly say No. "Sure. Where?"

He sat down on the sofa and picked up his notebook and started leafing through it. "I'm going to sit in with some fellows in a joint in the Village."

"You mean, you're going to play, tonight?"

"That's right." He took a swallow of his beer and moved back to the window. He gave me a sidelong look. "If you can stand it."

"I'll try," I said.

He smiled to himself and we both watched as the meeting across the way broke up. The three sisters and the brother, heads bowed, were singing "God be with you till we meet again." The faces around them were very quiet. Then the song ended. The small crowd dispersed. We watched the three women and the lone man walk slowly up the avenue.

"When she was singing before," said Sonny, abruptly, "her voice reminded me for a minute of what heroin feels like sometimes — when it's in your veins. It makes you feel sort of warm and cool at the same time. And distant. And — and sure." He sipped his beer, very deliberately not looking at me. I watched his face. "It makes you feel — in control. Sometimes you've got to have that feeling."

"Do you?" I sat down slowly in the easy chair.

"Sometimes." He went to the sofa and picked up his notebook again. "Some people do."

"In order," I asked, "to play?" And my voice was very ugly, full of contempt and anger.

"Well" — he looked at me with great, troubled eyes, as though, in fact, he hoped his eyes would tell me things he could never otherwise say — "they *think so*. And *if* they think so — !"

"And what do *you* think?" I asked.

He sat on the sofa and put his can of beer on the floor. "I don't know," he said, and I couldn't be sure if he were answering my question or pursuing his thoughts. His face didn't tell me. "It's not so much to *play*. It's to *stand* it, to be able to make it at all. On any level." He frowned and smiled. "In order to keep from shaking to pieces."

"But these friends of yours," I said, "they seem to shake themselves to pieces pretty goddamn fast."

"Maybe." He played with the notebook. And something told me that I should curb my tongue, that Sonny was doing his best to talk, that I should listen. "But of course you only know the ones that've gone to pieces. Some don't — or at least they haven't *yet* and that's just about all *any* of us can say." He paused. "And then there are some who just live, really, in hell, and they know it and they see what's happening and they go right on. I don't know." He sighed, dropped the notebook, folded his arms. "Some guys, you can tell from the way they play, they on something *all* the time. And you can see that, well, it makes something real for them. But of course," he picked up his beer from the floor and sipped it and put the can down again, "they *want* to, too, you've got to see that. Even some of them that say they don't — *some*, not all."

"And what about you?" I asked — I couldn't help it. "What about you? Do *you* want to?"

He stood up and walked to the window and remained silent for a long time. Then he sighed. "Me," he said. Then: "While I was downstairs before, on my way here, listening to that woman sing, it struck me all of a sudden how much suffering she must have had to go through — to sing like that. It's *repulsive* to think you have to suffer that much."

I said: "But there's no way not to suffer — is there, Sonny?"

"I believe not," he said, and smiled, "but that's never stopped anyone from trying." He looked at me. "Has it?" I realized, with this mocking look, that there stood between us, forever, beyond the power of time or forgiveness, the fact that I had held silence — so long! — when he had needed human speech to help him. He turned back to the window. "No, there's no way not to suffer. But you try all kinds of ways to keep from drowning in it, to keep on top of it, and to make it seem — well, like *you*. Like you did something, all right, and now you're suffering for it. You know?" I said nothing. "Well, you know," he said, impatiently, "why *do* people suffer? Maybe it's better to do something to give it a reason, *any* reason."

"But we just agreed," I said, "that there's no way not to suffer. Isn't it better, then, just to — take it?"

"But nobody just takes it," Sonny cried, "that's what I'm telling you! *Everybody* tries not to. You're just hung up on the *way* some people try — it's not *your* way!"

The hair on my face began to itch, my face felt wet. "That's not true," I said, "that's not true. I don't give a damn what other people do, I don't even care how they suffer. I just care how *you* suffer." And he looked at me. "Please believe me," I said, "I don't want to see you — die — trying not to suffer."

"I won't," he said, flatly, "die trying not to suffer. At least, not any faster than anybody else."

"But there's no need," I said, trying to laugh, "is there? in killing yourself."

I wanted to say more, but I couldn't. I wanted to talk about will power and how life could be — well, beautiful. I wanted to say that it was all within; but was it? Or, rather, wasn't that exactly the trouble? And I wanted to promise that I would never fail him again. But it would all have sounded — empty words and lies.

So I made the promise to myself and prayed that I would keep it.

"It's terrible sometimes, inside," he said, "that's what's the trouble. You walk these streets, black and funky and cold, and there's not really a living ass to talk to, and there's nothing shaking, and there's no way of getting it out — that storm inside. You can't talk it and you can't make love with it, and when you finally try to get with it and play it, you realize *nobody's* listening. So *you've* got to listen. You got to find a way to listen."

And then he walked away from the window and sat on the sofa again, as though all the wind had suddenly been knocked out of him. "Sometimes you'll do *anything* to play, even cut your mother's throat." He laughed and looked at me. "Or your brother's." Then he sobered. "Or your own." Then: "Don't worry. I'm all right now and I think I'll *be* all right. But I can't forget—where I've been. I don't mean just the physical place I've been, I mean where I've *been*. And *what* I've been."

"What have you been, Sonny?" I asked.

He smiled—but sat sideways on the sofa, his elbow resting on the back, his fingers playing with his mouth and chin, not looking at me. "I've been something I didn't recognize, didn't know I could be. Didn't know anybody could be." He stopped, looking inward, looking help-lessly young, looking old. "I'm not talking about it now because I feel *guilty* or anything like that—maybe it would be better if I did, I don't know. Anyway, I can't really talk about it. Not to you, not to anybody," and now he turned and faced me. "Sometimes, you know, and it was ac-tually when I was most *out* of the world, I felt that I was in it, that I was *with* it, really, and I could play or I didn't really have to *play*, it just came out of me, it was there. And I don't know how I played, thinking about it now, but I know I did awful things, those times, sometimes, to peo-ple. Or it wasn't that I *did* anything to them—it was that they weren't real." He picked up the beer can; it was empty; he rolled it between his palms: "And other times—well, I needed a fix, I needed to find a place to lean, I needed to clear a space to *listen*—and I couldn't find it, and I —went crazy, I did terrible things to *me*, I was terrible *for* me." He be-gan pressing the beer can between his hands, I watched the metal be-gin to give. It glittered, as he played with it, like a knife, and I was afraid he would cut himself, but I said nothing. "Oh well. I can never tell you. I was all by myself at the bottom of something, stinking and sweating and crying and shaking, and I smelled it, you know? *my* stink, and I thought I'd die if I couldn't get away from it and yet, all the same, I knew that everything I was doing was just locking me in with it. And I didn't know," he paused, still flattening the beer can, "I didn't know, I still *don't* know, something kept telling me that maybe it was good to smell your own stink, but I didn't think that *that* was what I'd been trying to do —and—who can stand it?" and he abruptly dropped the ruined beer can, looking at me with a small, still smile, and then rose, walking to the window as though it were the lodestone rock. I watched his face, he watched the avenue. "I couldn't tell you when Mama died—but the rea-son I wanted to leave Harlem so bad was to get away from drugs. And then, when I ran away, that's what I was running from—really. When I came back, nothing had changed, *I* hadn't changed, I was just—older." And he stopped, drumming with his fingers on the windowpane. The sun had vanished, soon darkness would fall. I watched his face. "It can come again," he said, almost as though speaking to himself. Then he turned to me. "It can come again," he repeated. "I just want you to know that."

"All right," I said, at last. "So it can come again. All right."

He smiled, but the smile was sorrowful. "I had to try to tell you," he said.

"Yes," I said. "I understand that."

"You're my brother," he said, looking straight at me, and not smiling at all.

"Yes," I repeated, "yes. I understand that."

He turned back to the window, looking out. "All that hatred down there," he said, "all that hatred and misery and love. It's a wonder it doesn't blow the avenue apart."

We went to the only night club on a short, dark street, downtown. We squeezed through the narrow, chattering, jam-packed bar to the entrance of the big room, where the bandstand was. And we stood there for a moment, for the lights were very dim in this room and we couldn't see. Then, "Hello, boy," said a voice and an enormous black man, much older than Sonny or myself, erupted out of all that atmospheric lighting and put an arm around Sonny's shoulder. "I been sitting right here," he said, "waiting for you."

He had a big voice, too, and heads in the darkness turned toward us.

Sonny grinned and pulled a little away, and said, "Creole, this is my brother. I told you about him."

Creole shook my hand. "I'm glad to meet you, son," he said, and it was clear that he was glad to meet me *there,* for Sonny's sake. And he smiled, "You got a real musician in *your* family," and he took his arm from Sonny's shoulder and slapped him, lightly, affectionately, with the back of his hand.

"Well. Now I've heard it all," said a voice behind us. This was another musician, and a friend of Sonny's, a coal-black, cheerful-looking man, built close to the ground. He immediately began confiding to me, at the top of his lungs, the most terrible things about Sonny, his teeth gleaming like a lighthouse and his laugh coming up out of him like the beginning of an earthquake. And it turned out that everyone at the bar knew Sonny, or almost everyone; some were musicians, working there, or nearby, or not working, some were simply hangers-on, and some were there to hear Sonny play. I was introduced to all of them and they were all very polite to me. Yet, it was clear that, for them, I was only Sonny's brother. Here, I was in Sonny's world. Or, rather: his kingdom. Here, it was not even a question that his veins bore royal blood.

They were going to play soon and Creole installed me, by myself, at a table in a dark corner. Then I watched them, Creole, and the little black man, and Sonny, and the others, while they horsed around, standing just below the bandstand. The light from the bandstand spilled just a little short of them and, watching them laughing and gesturing and moving about, I had the feeling that they, nevertheless, were being most careful not to step into that circle of light too suddenly: that if they moved into the light too suddenly, without thinking, they would perish in flame. Then, while I watched, one of them, the small, black man, moved into the light and crossed the bandstand and started fooling around with his drums. Then — being funny and being, also, extremely ceremonious — Creole took Sonny by the arm and led him to the piano. A woman's voice called Sonny's name and a few hands started clapping. And Sonny, also being funny and being ceremonious, and so touched, I think, that he could have cried, but neither hiding it nor showing it, riding it like a man, grinned, and put both hands to his heart and bowed from the waist.

Creole then went to the bass fiddle and a lean, very bright-skinned brown man jumped up on the bandstand and picked up his horn. So there they were, and the atmosphere on the bandstand and in the room began to change and tighten. Someone stepped up to the microphone and announced them. Then there were all kinds of murmurs. Some people at the bar shushed others. The waitress ran around, frantically getting in the last orders, guys and chicks got closer to each other, and the lights on the bandstand, on the quartet, turned to a kind of indigo. Then they all looked different there. Creole looked about him for the last time, as though he were making certain that all his chickens were in the coop, and then he jumped and struck the fiddle. And there they were.

All I know about music is that not many people ever really hear it. And even then, on the rare occasions when something opens within, and the music enters, what we mainly hear, or hear corroborated, are personal, private, vanishing evocations. But the man who creates the music is hearing something else, is dealing with the roar rising from the void and imposing order on it as it hits the air. What is evoked in him, then, is of another order, more terrible because it has no words, and triumphant, too, for that same reason. And his triumph, when he triumphs, is ours. I just watched Sonny's face. His face was troubled, he was working hard, but he wasn't with it. And I had the feeling that, in a way, everyone on the bandstand was waiting for him, both waiting for him and pushing him along. But as I began to watch Creole, I realized that it was Creole who held them all back. He had them on a short rein. Up there, keeping the beat with his whole body, wailing on the fiddle, with his eyes half closed, he was listening to everything, but he was listening to Sonny. He was having a dialogue with Sonny. He wanted Sonny to leave the shore line and strike out for the deep water. He was Sonny's witness that deep water and drowning were not the same thing —he had been there, and he knew. And he wanted Sonny to know. He was waiting for Sonny to do the things on the keys which would let Creole know that Sonny was in the water.

And, while Creole listened, Sonny moved, deep within, exactly like someone in torment. I had never before thought of how awful the relationship must be between the musician and his instrument. He has to fill it, this instrument, with the breath of life, his own. He has to make it do what he wants it to do. And a piano is just a piano. It's made out of so much wood and wires and little hammers and big ones, and ivory. While there's only so much you can do with it, the only way to find this out is to try to try and make it do everything.

And Sonny hadn't been near a piano for over a year. And he wasn't on much better terms with his life, not the life that stretched before him now. He and the piano stammered, started one way, got scared, stopped; started another way, panicked, marked time, started again; then seemed to have found a direction, panicked again, got stuck. And the face I saw on Sonny I'd never seen before. Everything had been burned out of it, and, at the same time, things usually hidden were being burned in, by the fire and fury of the battle which was occurring in him up there.

Yet, watching Creole's face as they neared the end of the first set, I had the feeling that something had happened, something I hadn't heard. Then they finished, there was scattered applause, and then, without an instant's warning, Creole started into something else, it was almost sardonic, it was "Am I Blue." And, as though he had been commanded, Sonny began to play. Something began to happen. And Creole let out the reins. The dry, low, black man said something awful on the drums, Creole answered, and the drums talked back. Then the horn insisted, sweet and high, slightly detached perhaps, and Creole listened, commenting now and then, dry, and driving, beautiful and calm and old. Then they all came together again, and Sonny was part of the family again. I could tell this from his face. He seemed to have found, right there beneath his fingers, a damn brand-new piano. It seemed that he couldn't get over it. Then, for a while, just being happy with Sonny, they seemed to be agreeing with him that brand-new pianos certainly were a gas.

Then Creole stepped forward to remind them that what they were playing was the blues. He hit something in all of them, he hit something in me, myself and the music tightened and deepened, apprehension began to beat the air. Creole began to tell us what the blues were all about. They were not about anything very new. He and his boys up there were keeping it new, at the risk of ruin, destruction, madness, and death, in order to find new ways to make us listen. For, while the tale of how we suffer, and how we are delighted, and how we may triumph is never new, it always must be heard. There isn't any other tale to tell, it's the only light we've got in all this darkness.

And this tale, according to that face, that body, those strong hands on those strings, has another aspect in every country, and a new depth in every generation. Listen, Creole seemed to be saying, listen. Now these are Sonny's blues. He made the little black man on the drums know it, and the bright, brown man on the horn. Creole wasn't trying any longer to get Sonny in the water. He was wishing him Godspeed. Then he stepped back, very slowly, filling the air with the immense suggestion that Sonny speak for himself.

Then they all gathered around Sonny and Sonny played. Every now and again one of them seemed to say, Amen. Sonny's fingers filled the air with life, his life. But that life contained so many others. And Sonny went all the way back, he really began with the spare, flat statement of the opening phrase of the song. Then he began to make it his. It was very beautiful because it wasn't hurried and it was no longer a lament. I seemed to hear with what burning he had made it his, with what burning we had yet to make it ours, how we could cease lamenting. Freedom lurked around us and I understood, at last, that he could help us to be free if we would listen, that he would never be free until we did. Yet, there was no battle in his face now. I heard what he had gone through, and would continue to go through until he came to rest in earth. He had made it his: that long line, of which we knew only Mama and Daddy. And he was giving it back, as everything must be given back, so that, passing through death, it can live forever. I saw my mother's face again, and felt, for the first time, how the stones of the road she had walked on must have bruised her feet. I saw the moonlit road where my father's brother died. And it brought something else back to me, and carried me past it, I saw my little girl again and felt Isabel's tears again, and I felt my own tears begin to rise. And I was yet aware that this was only a moment, that the world waited outside, as hungry as a tiger, and that trouble stretched above us, longer than the sky.

Then it was over. Creole and Sonny let out their breath, both soaking wet, and grinning. There was a lot of applause and some of it was real. In the dark, the girl came by and I asked her to take drinks to the bandstand. There was a long pause, while they talked up there in the indigo light and after a while I saw the girl put a Scotch and milk on top of the piano for Sonny. He didn't seem to notice it, but just before they started playing again, he sipped from it and looked toward me, and nodded. Then he put it back on top of the piano. For me, then, as they began to play again, it glowed and shook above my brother's head like the very cup of trembling.

1959

PHILIP ROTH
THE CONVERSION OF THE JEWS

from *The Paris Review*

In 1997 PHILIP ROTH won the Pulitzer Prize for *American Pastoral*. In 1998 he received the National Medal of Arts at the White House and in 2002 the highest award of the American Academy of Arts and Letters, the Gold Medal in Fiction, previously awarded to John Dos Passos, William Faulkner, and Saul Bellow, among others. He has twice won the National Book Award, in 1960 for his first book, *Goodbye, Columbus,* and in 1996 for *Sabbath's Theater.* He has also twice won the National Book Critics Circle Award and three times won the PEN/Faulkner Award. In 2005 *The Plot Against America* received the Society of American Historians' prize for "the outstanding historical novel on an American theme for 2003–2004" and the W. H. Smith Award for the Best Book of the Year, making Roth the first writer in the forty-six-year history of the prize to win it twice.

In 2005 Roth became the third living American writer to have his works published in a comprehensive, definitive edition by the Library of America. In consecutive years he won the PEN/Nabokov Award (2006) and the PEN/Bellow Award (2007). In 2011 he received the National Humanities Medal at the White House, and he was later named the fourth recipient of the Man Booker International Prize. In 2012 he won Spain's highest honor, the Prince of Asturias Award, and in 2013 he received France's highest honor, Chevalier de la Légion d'Honneur.

★

"Y OU'RE A REAL one for opening your mouth in the first place," Itzie said. "What do you open your mouth all the time for?"

"I didn't bring it up, Itz, I didn't," Ozzie said.

"What do you care about Jesus Christ for anyway?"

"I didn't bring up Jesus Christ. He did. I didn't even know what he was talking about. Jesus is historical, he kept saying. Jesus is historical." Ozzie mimicked the monumental voice of Rabbi Binder.

"Jesus was a person that lived like you and me," Ozzie continued. "That's what Binder said—"

"Yeah? . . . So what! What do I give two cents whether he lived or not. And what do you gotta open your mouth!" Itzie Lieberman favored closed-mouthedness, especially when it came to Ozzie Freedman's questions. Mrs. Freedman had to see Rabbi Binder twice before about Ozzie's questions and this Wednesday at four-thirty would be the third time. Itzie preferred to keep *his* mother in the kitchen; he settled for behind-the-back subtleties such as gestures, faces, snarls and other less delicate barnyard noises.

"He was a real person, Jesus, but he wasn't like God, and we don't believe he is God." Slowly, Ozzie was explaining Rabbi Binder's position to Itzie, who had been absent from Hebrew School the previous afternoon.

"The Catholics," Itzie said helpfully, "they believe in Jesus Christ, that he's God." Itzie Lieberman used "the Catholics" in its broadest sense—to include the Protestants.

Ozzie received Itzie's remark with a tiny head bob, as though it were a footnote, and went on. "His mother was Mary, and his father probably was Joseph," Ozzie said. "But the New Testament says his real father was God."

"His *real* father?"

"Yeah," Ozzie said, "that's the big thing, his father's supposed to be God."

"Bull."

"That's what Rabbi Binder says, that it's impossible—"

"Sure it's impossible. That stuff's all bull. To have a baby you gotta get laid," Itzie theologized. "Mary hadda get laid."

"That's what Binder says: 'The only way a woman can have a baby is to have intercourse with a man.'"

"He said *that,* Ozz?" For a moment it appeared that Itzie had put the theological question aside. "He said that, intercourse?" A little curled smile shaped itself in the lower half of Itzie's face like a pink mustache. "What you guys do, Ozz, you laugh or something?"

"I raised my hand."

"Yeah? Whatja say?"

"That's when I asked the question."

Itzie's face lit up. "Whatja ask about—intercourse?"

"No, I asked the question about God, how if He could create the heaven and earth in six days, and make all the animals and the fish and the light in six days—the light especially, that's what always gets me, that He could make the light. Making fish and animals, that's pretty good—"

"That's damn good." Itzie's appreciation was honest but unimaginative: it was as though God had just pitched a one-hitter.

"But making light . . . I mean when you think about it, it's really something," Ozzie said. "Anyway, I asked Binder if He could make all that in six days, and He could *pick* the six days he wanted right out of nowhere, why couldn't He let a woman have a baby without having intercourse."

"You said intercourse, Ozz, to Binder?"

"Yeah."

"Right in class?"

"Yeah."

Itzie smacked the side of his head.

"I mean, no kidding around," Ozzie said, "that'd really be nothing. After all that other stuff, that'd practically be nothing."

Itzie considered a moment. "What'd Binder say?"

"He started all over again explaining how Jesus was historical and how he lived like you and me but he wasn't God. So I said I under*stood* that. What I wanted to know was different."

What Ozzie wanted to know was always different. The first time he had wanted to know how Rabbi Binder could call the Jews "The Chosen People" if the Declaration of Independence claimed all men to be created equal. Rabbi Binder tried to distinguish for him between political equality and spiritual legitimacy, but what Ozzie wanted to know, he insisted vehemently, was different. That was the first time his mother had to come.

Then there was the plane crash. Fifty-eight people had been killed in a plane crash at La Guardia. In studying a casualty list in the newspaper his mother had discovered among the list of those dead eight Jewish names (his grandmother had nine but she counted Miller as a Jewish name); because of the eight she said the plane crash was "a tragedy." During free-discussion time on Wednesday Ozzie had brought to Rabbi Binder's attention this matter of "some of his relations" always picking out the Jewish names. Rabbi Binder had begun to explain cultural unity and some other things when Ozzie stood up at his seat and said that what he wanted to know was different. Rabbi Binder insisted that he sit down and it was then that Ozzie shouted that he wished all fifty-eight were Jews. That was the second time his mother came.

"And he kept explaining about Jesus being historical, and so I kept asking him. No kidding, Itz, he was trying to make me look stupid."

"So what he finally do?"

"Finally he starts screaming that I was deliberately simple-minded and a wise guy, and that my mother had to come, and this was the last time. And that I'd never get bar-mitzvahed if he could help it. Then, Itz, then he starts talking in that voice like a statue, real slow and deep, and he says that I better think over what I said about the Lord. He told me to go to his office and think it over." Ozzie leaned his body towards Itzie. "Itz, I thought it over for a solid hour, and now I'm convinced God could do it."

Ozzie had planned to confess his latest transgression to his mother as soon as she came home from work. But it was a Friday night in November and already dark, and when Mrs. Freedman came through the door she tossed off her coat, kissed Ozzie quickly on the face, and went to the kitchen table to light the three yellow candles, two for the Sabbath and one for Ozzie's father.

When his mother lit the candles she would move her two arms slowly towards her, dragging them through the air, as though persuading people whose minds were half made up. And her eyes would get glassy with tears. Even when his father was alive Ozzie remembered that her eyes had gotten glassy, so it didn't have anything to do with his dying. It had something to do with lighting the candles.

As she touched the flaming match to the unlit wick of a Sabbath candle, the phone rang, and Ozzie, standing only a foot from it, plucked it off the receiver and held it muffled to his chest. When his mother lit candles Ozzie felt there should be no noise; even breathing, if you could manage it, should be softened. Ozzie pressed the phone to his breast and watched his mother dragging whatever she was dragging, and he felt his own eyes get glassy. His mother was a round, tired, gray-haired penguin of a woman whose gray skin had begun to feel the tug of gravity and the weight of her own history. Even when she was dressed up she didn't look like a chosen person. But when she lit candles she looked like something better; like a woman who knew momentarily that God could do anything.

After a few mysterious minutes she was finished. Ozzie hung up the phone and walked to the kitchen table where she was beginning to lay the two places for the four-course Sabbath meal. He told her that she would have to see Rabbi Binder next Wednesday at four-thirty, and then he told her why. For the first time in their life together she hit Ozzie across the face with her hand.

All through the chopped liver and chicken soup parts of the dinner Ozzie cried; he didn't have any appetite for the rest.

On Wednesday, in the largest of the three basement classrooms of the synagogue, Rabbi Marvin Binder, a tall, handsome, broad-shouldered man of thirty with thick strong-fibered black hair, removed his watch from his pocket and saw that it was four o'clock. At the rear of the room Yakov Blotnik, the seventy-one-year-old custodian, slowly polished the large window, mumbling to himself, unaware that it was four o'clock or six o'clock, Monday or Wednesday. To most of the students Yakov Blotnik's mumbling, along with his brown curly beard, scythe nose, and two heel-trailing black cats, made of him an object of wonder, a foreigner, a relic, towards whom they were alternately fearful and disrespectful. To Ozzie the mumbling had always seemed a monotonous, curious prayer; what made it curious was that old Blotnik had been mumbling so steadily for so many years, Ozzie suspected he had memorized the prayers and forgotten all about God.

"It is now free-discussion time," Rabbi Binder said. "Feel free to talk about any Jewish matter at all — religion, family, politics, sports —"

There was silence. It was a gusty, clouded November afternoon and it did not seem as though there ever was or could be a thing called baseball. So nobody this week said a word about that hero from the past, Hank Greenberg — which limited free discussion considerably.

And the soul-battering Ozzie Freedman had just received from Rabbi Binder had imposed its limitation. When it was Ozzie's turn to read aloud from the Hebrew book the rabbi had asked him petulantly why he didn't read more rapidly. He was showing no progress. Ozzie said he could read faster but that if he did he was sure not to understand what he was reading. Nevertheless, at the rabbi's repeated suggestion Ozzie tried, and showed a great talent, but in the midst of a long passage he stopped short and said he didn't understand a word he was reading, and started in again at a drag-footed pace. Then came the soul-battering.

Consequently when free-discussion time rolled around none of the students felt too free. The rabbi's invitation was answered only by the mumbling of feeble old Blotnik.

"Isn't there anything at all you would like to discuss?" Rabbi Binder asked again, looking at his watch. "No questions or comments?"

There was a small grumble from the third row. The rabbi requested that Ozzie rise and give the rest of the class the advantage of his thought.

Ozzie rose. "I forget it now," he said, and sat down in his place.

Rabbi Binder advanced a seat towards Ozzie and poised himself on the edge of the desk. It was Itzie's desk and the rabbi's frame only a dagger's-length away from his face snapped him to sitting attention.

"Stand up again, Oscar," Rabbi Binder said calmly, "and try to assemble your thoughts."

Ozzie stood up. All his classmates turned in their seats and watched as he gave an unconvincing scratch to his forehead.

"I can't assemble any," he announced, and plunked himself down.

"Stand up!" Rabbi Binder advanced from Itzie's desk to the one directly in front of Ozzie; when the rabbinical back was turned Itzie gave it five-fingers off the tip of his nose, causing a small titter in the room. Rabbi Binder was too absorbed in squelching Ozzie's nonsense once and for all to bother with titters. "Stand up, Oscar. What's your question about?"

Ozzie pulled a word out of the air. It was the handiest word. "Religion."

"Oh, now you remember?"

"Yes."

"What is it?"

Trapped, Ozzie blurted the first thing that came to him. "Why can't He make anything He wants to make!"

As Rabbi Binder prepared an answer, a final answer, Itzie, ten feet behind him, raised one finger on his left hand, gestured it meaningfully towards the rabbi's back, and brought the house down.

Binder twisted quickly to see what had happened and in the midst of the commotion Ozzie shouted into the rabbi's back what he couldn't have shouted to his face. It was a loud, toneless sound that had the timbre of something stored inside for about six days.

"You don't know! You don't know anything about God!"

The rabbi spun back towards Ozzie. "What?"

"You don't know — you don't —"

"Apologize, Oscar, apologize!" It was a threat.

"You don't —"

Rabbi Binder's hand flicked out at Ozzie's cheek. Perhaps it had only been meant to clamp the boy's mouth shut, but Ozzie ducked and the palm caught him squarely on the nose.

The blood came in a short, red spurt on to Ozzie's shirt front.

The next moment was all confusion. Ozzie screamed, "You bastard, you bastard!" and broke for the classroom door. Rabbi Binder lurched a step backwards, as though his own blood had started flowing violently in the opposite direction, then gave a clumsy lurch forward and bolted out the door after Ozzie. The class followed after the rabbi's huge blue-suited back, and before old Blotnik could turn from his window, the room was empty and everyone was headed full speed up the three flights leading to the roof.

If one should compare the light of day to the life of man: sunrise to birth; sunset — the dropping down over the edge — to death; then as Ozzie Freedman wiggled through the trapdoor of the synagogue roof, his feet kicking backwards bronco-style at Rabbi Binder's outstretched arms — at that moment the day was fifty years old. As a rule, fifty or fifty-five reflects accurately the age of late afternoons in November, for it is in that month, during those hours, that one's awareness of light seems no longer a matter of seeing, but of hearing: light begins clicking away. In fact, as Ozzie locked shut the trapdoor in the rabbi's face, the sharp click of the bolt into the lock might momentarily have been mistaken for the sound of the heavier gray that had just throbbed through the sky.

With all his weight Ozzie kneeled on the locked door; any instant he was certain that Rabbi Binder's shoulder would fling it open, splintering the wood into shrapnel and catapulting his body into the sky. But the door did not move and below him he heard only the rumble of feet, first loud then dim, like thunder rolling away.

A question shot through his brain. "Can this be *me*?" For a thirteen-year-old who had just labeled his religious leader a bastard, twice, it was not an improper question. Louder and louder the question came to him —"Is it me? Is it me?"—until he discovered himself no longer kneeling, but racing crazily towards the edge of the roof, his eyes crying, his throat screaming, and his arms flying everywhichway as though not his own.

"Is it me? Is it me Me ME Me ME! It has to be me—but is it!"

It is the question a thief must ask himself the night he jimmies open his first window, and it is said to be the question with which bridegrooms quiz themselves before the altar.

In the few wild seconds it took Ozzie's body to propel him to the edge of the roof, his self-examination began to grow fuzzy. Gazing down at the street, he became confused as to the problem beneath the question: was it, is-it-me-who-called-Binder-a-bastard? or, is-it-me-prancing-around-on-the-roof? However, the scene below settled all, for there is an instant in any action when whether it is you or somebody else is academic. The thief crams the money in his pockets and scoots out the window. The bridegroom signs the hotel register for two. And the boy on the roof finds a streetful of people gaping at him, necks stretched backwards, faces up, as though he were the ceiling of the Hayden Planetarium. Suddenly you know it's you.

"Oscar! Oscar Freedman!" A voice rose from the center of the crowd, a voice that, could it have been seen, would have looked like the writing on a scroll. "Oscar Freedman, get down from there. Immediately!" Rabbi Binder was pointing one arm stiffly up at him; and at the end of that arm, one finger aimed menacingly. It was the attitude of a dictator, but one — the eyes confessed all — whose personal valet had spit neatly in his face.

Ozzie didn't answer. Only for a blink's length did he look towards Rabbi Binder. Instead his eyes began to fit together the world beneath him, to sort out people from places, friends from enemies, participants from spectators. In little jagged starlike clusters his friends stood around Rabbi Binder, who was still pointing. The topmost point on a star compounded not of angels but of five adolescent boys was Itzie. What a world it was, with those stars below, Rabbi Binder below . . . Ozzie, who a moment earlier hadn't been able to control his own body, started to feel the meaning of the word control: he felt Peace and he felt Power.

"Oscar Freedman, I'll give you three to come down."

Few dictators give their subjects three to do anything; but, as always, Rabbi Binder only looked dictatorial.

"Are you ready, Oscar?"

Ozzie nodded his head yes, although he had no intention in the world — the lower one or the celestial one he'd just entered — of coming down even if Rabbi Binder should give him a million.

"All right then," said Rabbi Binder. He ran a hand through his black Samson hair as though it were the gesture prescribed for uttering the first digit. Then, with his other hand cutting a circle out of the small piece of sky around him, he spoke. "One!"

There was no thunder. On the contrary, at that moment, as though "one" was the cue for which he had been waiting, the world's least thunderous person appeared on the synagogue steps. He did not so much come out the synagogue door as lean out, onto the darkening air. He clutched at the doorknob with one hand and looked up at the roof.

"Oy!"

Yakov Blotnik's old mind hobbled slowly, as if on crutches, and though he couldn't decide precisely what the boy was doing on the roof, he knew it wasn't good — that is, it wasn't-good-for-the-Jews. For Yakov Blotnik life had fractionated itself simply: things were either good-for-the-Jews or no-good-for-the-Jews.

He smacked his free hand to his in-sucked cheek, gently. "Oy, Gut!" And then quickly as he was able, he jacked down his head and surveyed the street. There was Rabbi Binder (like a man at an auction with only three dollars in his pocket, he had just delivered a shaky "Two!"); there were the students, and that was all. So far it-wasn't-so-bad-for-the-Jews. But the boy had to come down immediately, before anybody saw. The problem: how to get the boy off the roof?

Anybody who has ever had a cat on the roof knows how to get him down. You call the fire department. Or first you call the operator and you ask her for the fire department. And the next thing there is great jamming of brakes and clanging of bells and shouting of instructions. And then the cat is off the roof. You do the same thing to get a boy off the roof.

That is, you do the same thing if you are Yakov Blotnik and you once had a cat on the roof.

When the engines, all four of them, arrived, Rabbi Binder had four times given Ozzie the count of three. The big hook-and-ladder swung around the corner and one of the firemen leaped from it, plunging headlong towards the yellow fire hydrant in front of the synagogue. With a huge wrench he began to unscrew the top nozzle. Rabbi Binder raced over to him and pulled at his shoulder.

"There's no fire . . ."

The fireman mumbled back over his shoulder and, heatedly, continued working at the nozzle.

"But there's no fire, there's no fire . . ." Binder shouted. When the fireman mumbled again, the rabbi grasped his face with both hands and pointed it up at the roof.

To Ozzie it looked as though Rabbi Binder was trying to tug the fireman's head out of his body, like a cork from a bottle. He had to giggle at the picture they made: it was a family portrait — rabbi in black skullcap, fireman in red fire hat, and the little yellow hydrant squatting beside like a kid brother, bareheaded. From the edge of the roof Ozzie waved at the portrait, a one-handed, flapping, mocking wave; in doing it his right foot slipped from under him. Rabbi Binder covered his eyes with his hands.

Firemen work fast. Before Ozzie had even regained his balance, a big, round, yellowed net was being held on the synagogue lawn. The firemen who held it looked up at Ozzie with stern, feelingless faces.

One of the firemen turned his head towards Rabbi Binder. "What, is the kid nuts or something?"

Rabbi Binder unpeeled his hands from his eyes, slowly, painfully, as if they were tape. Then he checked: nothing on the sidewalk, no dents in the net.

"Is he gonna jump, or what?" the fireman shouted.

In a voice not at all like a statue, Rabbi Binder finally answered. "Yes. Yes, I think so . . . He's been threatening to . . ."

Threatening to? Why, the reason he was on the roof, Ozzie remembered, was to get away; he hadn't even thought about jumping. He had just run to get away, and the truth was that he hadn't really headed for the roof as much as he'd been chased there.

"What's his name, the kid?"

"Freedman," Rabbi Binder answered. "Oscar Freedman."

The fireman looked up at Ozzie. "What is it with you, Oscar? You gonna jump, or what?"

Ozzie did not answer. Frankly, the question had just arisen.

"Look, Oscar, if you're gonna jump, jump — and if you're not gonna jump, don't jump. But don't waste our time, willya?"

Ozzie looked at the fireman and then at Rabbi Binder. He wanted to see Rabbi Binder cover his eyes one more time.

"I'm going to jump."

And then he scampered around the edge of the roof to the corner, where there was no net below, and he flapped his arms at his sides, swishing the air and smacking his palms to his trousers on the downbeat. He began screaming like some kind of engine, "Wheeeee . . . wheeeeee," and leaning way out over the edge with the upper half of his body. The firemen whipped around to cover the ground with the net. Rabbi Binder mumbled a few words to somebody and covered his eyes. Everything happened quickly, jerkily, as in a silent movie. The crowd, which had arrived with the fire engines, gave out a long, Fourth-of-July fireworks oooh-aahhh. In the excitement no one had paid the crowd much heed, except, of course, Yakov Blotnik, who swung from the doorknob counting heads. "Fier und tsvansik . . . finf und tsvansik . . . Oy, Gut!" It wasn't like this with the cat.

Rabbi Binder peeked through his fingers, checked the sidewalk and net. Empty. But there was Ozzie racing to the other corner. The firemen

raced with him but were unable to keep up. Whenever Ozzie wanted to
he might jump and splatter himself upon the sidewalk, and by the time
the firemen scooted to the spot all they could do with their net would be
to cover the mess.

"Wheeeee . . . wheeeee . . ."

"Hey, Oscar," the winded fireman yelled, "what the hell is this, a game
or something?"

"Wheeeee . . . wheeeee . . ."

"Hey, Oscar —"

But he was off now to the other corner, flapping his wings fiercely.
Rabbi Binder couldn't take it any longer — the fire engines from nowhere, the screaming suicidal boy, the net. He fell to his knees, exhausted, and with his hands curled together in front of his chest like a
little dome, he pleaded, "Oscar, stop it, Oscar. Don't jump, Oscar. Please
come down . . . Please don't jump."

And further back in the crowd a single voice, a single young voice,
shouted a lone word to the boy on the roof.

"Jump!"

It was Itzie. Ozzie momentarily stopped flapping.

"Go ahead, Ozz — jump!" Itzie broke off his point of the star and courageously, with the inspiration not of a wise-guy but of a disciple, stood
alone. "Jump, Ozz, jump!"

Still on his knees, his hands still curled, Rabbi Binder twisted his
body back. He looked at Itzie, then, agonizingly, back to Ozzie.

"OSCAR, DON'T JUMP! PLEASE, DON'T JUMP . . . please please . . ."

"Jump!" This time it wasn't Itzie but another point of the star. By the
time Mrs. Freedman arrived to keep her four-thirty appointment with
Rabbi Binder, the whole little upside-down heaven was shouting and
pleading for Ozzie to jump, and Rabbi Binder no longer was pleading
with him not to jump, but was crying into the dome of his hands.

Understandably Mrs. Freedman couldn't figure out what her son was
doing on the roof. So she asked.

"Ozzie, my Ozzie, what are you doing? My Ozzie, what is it?"

Ozzie stopped wheeeeeing and slowed his arms down to a cruising
flap, the kind birds use in soft winds, but he did not answer. He stood
against the low, clouded, darkening sky — light clicked down swiftly
now, as on a small gear — flapping softly and gazing down at the small
bundle of a woman who was his mother.

"What are you doing, Ozzie?" She turned towards the kneeling Rabbi

Binder and rushed so close that only a paper-thickness of dusk lay between her stomach and his shoulders.

"What is my baby doing?"

Rabbi Binder gaped at her but he too was mute. All that moved was the dome of his hands; it shook back and forth like a weak pulse.

"Rabbi, get him down! He'll kill himself. Get him down, my only baby . . ."

"I can't," Rabbi Binder said, "I can't . . ." and he turned his handsome head towards the crowd of boys behind him. "It's them. Listen to them."

And for the first time Mrs. Freedman saw the crowd of boys, and she heard what they were yelling.

"He's doing it for them. He won't listen to me. It's them." Rabbi Binder spoke like one in a trance.

"For them?"

"Yes."

"Why for them?"

"They want him to . . ."

Mrs. Freedman raised her two arms upward as though she were conducting the sky. "For them he's doing it!" And then in a gesture older than pyramids, older than prophets and floods, her arms came slapping down to her sides. "A martyr I have. Look!" She tilted her head to the roof. Ozzie was still flapping softly. "My martyr."

"Oscar, come down, *please,*" Rabbi Binder groaned.

In a startlingly even voice Mrs. Freedman called to the boy on the roof. "Ozzie, come down, Ozzie. Don't be a martyr, my baby."

As though it were a litany, Rabbi Binder repeated her words. "Don't be a martyr, my baby. Don't be a martyr."

"Gawhead, Ozz—*be* a Martin!" It was Itzie. "Be a Martin, be a Martin," and all the voices joined in singing for Martindom, whatever *it* was. "Be a Martin, be a Martin . . ."

Somehow when you're on a roof the darker it gets the less you can hear. All Ozzie knew was that two groups wanted two new things: his friends were spirited and musical about what they wanted; his mother and the rabbi were even-toned, chanting, about what they didn't want. The rabbi's voice was without tears now and so was his mother's.

The big net stared up at Ozzie like a sightless eye. The big, clouded sky pushed down. From beneath it looked like a gray corrugated board. Suddenly, looking up into that unsympathetic sky, Ozzie realized all the strangeness of what these people, his friends, were asking: they wanted him to jump, to kill himself; they were singing about it now — it made them that happy. And there was an even greater strangeness: Rabbi Binder was on his knees, trembling. If there was a question to be asked now it was not "Is it me?" but rather "Is it us? . . . Is it us?"

Being on the roof, it turned out, was a serious thing. If he jumped would the singing become dancing? Would it? What would jumping stop? Yearningly, Ozzie wished he could rip open the sky, plunge his hands through, and pull out the sun; and on the sun, like a coin, would be stamped JUMP or DON'T JUMP.

Ozzie's knees rocked and sagged a little under him as though they were setting him for a dive. His arms tightened, stiffened, froze, from shoulders to fingernails. He felt as if each part of his body were going to vote as to whether he should kill himself or not — and each part as though it were independent of *him*.

The light took an unexpected click down and the new darkness, like a gag, hushed the friends singing for this and the mother and rabbi chanting for that.

Ozzie stopped counting votes, and in a curiously high voice, like one who wasn't prepared for speech, he spoke.

"Mamma?"

"Yes, Oscar."

"Mamma, get down on your knees, like Rabbi Binder."

"Oscar —"

"Get down on your knees," he said, "or I'll jump."

Ozzie heard a whimper, then a quick rustling, and when he looked down where his mother had stood he saw the top of a head and beneath that a circle of dress. She was kneeling beside Rabbi Binder.

He spoke again. "Everybody kneel." There was the sound of everybody kneeling.

Ozzie looked around. With one hand he pointed towards the synagogue entrance. "Make *him* kneel."

There was a noise, not of kneeling, but of body-and-cloth stretching. Ozzie could hear Rabbi Binder saying in a gruff whisper, ". . . or he'll *kill* himself," and when next he looked there was Yakov Blotnik off the doorknob and for the first time in his life upon his knees in the Gentile posture of prayer.

As for the firemen — it is not as difficult as one might imagine to hold a net taut while you are kneeling.

Ozzie looked around again; and then he called to Rabbi Binder.

"Rabbi?"

"Yes, Oscar."

"Rabbi Binder, do you believe in God?"

"Yes."

"Do you believe God can do Anything?" Ozzie leaned his head out into the darkness. "Anything?"

"Oscar, I think—"

"Tell me you believe God can do Anything."

There was a second's hesitation. Then: "God can do Anything."

"Tell me you believe God can make a child without intercourse."

"He can."

"Tell me!"

"God," Rabbi Binder admitted, "can make a child without intercourse."

"Mamma, you tell me."

"God can make a child without intercourse," his mother said.

"Make *him* tell me." There was no doubt who *him* was.

In a few moments Ozzie heard an old comical voice say something to the increasing darkness about God.

Next, Ozzie made everybody say it. And then he made them all say they believed in Jesus Christ—first one at a time, then all together.

When the catechizing was through it was the beginning of evening. From the street it sounded as if the boy on the roof might have sighed.

"Ozzie?" A woman's voice dared to speak. "You'll come down now?"

There was no answer, but the woman waited, and when a voice finally did speak it was thin and crying, and exhausted as that of an old man who has just finished pulling the bells.

"Mamma, don't you see—you shouldn't hit me. He shouldn't hit me. You shouldn't hit me about God, Mamma. You should never hit anybody about God—"

"Ozzie, please come down now."

"Promise me, Mamma, promise me you'll never hit anybody about God."

He had asked only his mother, but for some reason everyone kneeling in the street promised he would never hit anybody about God.

Once again there was silence.

"I can come down now, Mamma," the boy on the roof finally said. He turned his head both ways as though checking the traffic lights. "Now I can come down . . ."

And he did, right into the center of the yellow net that glowed in the evening's edge like an overgrown halo.

1960-1970

IN KEEPING WITH SERIES EDITOR MARTHA FOLEY'S
notion that the best writing about war usually arrives years later, little reference to Vietnam was made in the fiction that appeared in *The
Best American Short Stories* during the 1960s. As after World War II,
stories about fantasy and the supernatural, as well as dreams, crowded
magazines. "Ghosts, talking animals, werewolves and the like . . . [and]
dreams," Foley wrote. "Not, thank heaven, the old device of a character
having an extraordinary adventure and waking up to find it was only a
dream but dreams as a more tangible part of the story."

During this time writers also began to explore the hidden complexities of the 1950s "happy family." Two very different writers were included frequently in the series in these years: John Updike, who was
criticized for featuring too little violence in his work, and Joyce Carol
Oates, who was criticized for featuring too much.

With the rise of a new counterculture came a new sexual frankness
in short fiction. Foley wrote, "The editors of this volume do not believe
in censorship, and the stories here represented have been chosen for
their literary merits only. Actually, the stories in this volume happen to
be more restrained in their use of sex than most of the pieces appearing."

Feminism, increasingly part of the zeitgeist, was slow to catch on in
the short stories that appeared in popular magazines. Women's magazines ran commercial fiction, typically written by men and featuring benign male characters. Foley wrote, "But women can be bitches in their
stories. An editor explained that although her readers were nearly all
women she had to be careful not to print anything derogatory about
male characters. There can be no wonderful villains as in all fiction of

yore. 'Our publisher and top executives are men. They wouldn't like it.' I, personally, refuse to believe that modern men, even publishers, have become so namby-pamby."

Over the years Foley had maintained a strained friendship with her ex-husband, Whit Burnett, arguing frequently over the support of their son. In 1962 she asked Houghton Mifflin to omit *Story* from the list of magazines at the back of *The Best American Short Stories* and refused to read it in consideration for the series. An editor at Houghton Mifflin secretly read the magazine each year to assure that no potential candidates were being omitted.

In 1966 Foley broke her pelvic bone and retired from Columbia. She began instead teaching a small group of adult students at the Gramercy Park Hotel on Wednesday afternoons. She regaled students with tales of her work as a reporter and her crusade for women's rights, anecdotes about Paris in the twenties and her years as an editor. She talked openly to her students and friends about writers whom she had disliked —"Oh, Hemingway. Hemingway was such a mean bastard. He never did a nice thing for anybody in his life." One of her favorite tales involved Ray Bradbury. She had chosen a story of his to appear in *The Best American Short Stories* and soon after got a telegram refusing permission to reprint it. Later she learned that he'd been arguing with a girlfriend, who, without his knowledge, had in fact been the one to send the telegram to Foley.

Foley eventually moved to Maine to live with her brother, who died two days after she arrived. He left no will, and she moved back to New York while his estate was settled. She endured a string of more bad luck: her apartment building in Manhattan burned down, she broke an ankle, "two burglaries [took place] in my apartment, one committed by a man who threatened to kill me (I was too frightened to ask if he wrote short stories)." Although she rarely spoke of it, her son, David, had struggles of his own. Her work began to suffer; the list of magazines at the back of the book became hopelessly outdated. Editors at Houghton Mifflin continued to question her taste: "Not only are the stories of mediocre quality, but there is an overwhelming preoccupation with death, old age, senility, disease, alcoholism in the aged."

In 1967 Foley moved to New Canaan, Connecticut, and seemed optimistic that her luck would change. She wrote, "I am very happy here. I have a few acres of woods and garden and river and a small contemporary house that is a work of art."

★ ★ ★

1962

FLANNERY O'CONNOR
EVERYTHING THAT RISES MUST CONVERGE

from *New World Writing*

FLANNERY O'CONNOR (1925–1964) was born in Savannah, Georgia, and grew up on a farm where peacocks were raised. Later she attended the Writers' Workshop at the University of Iowa. She became a star there and "scared the boys to death with her irony," as one biographer put it.

O'Connor believed that "a writer with Christian concerns needed to take ever more violent means to get her vision across to [her audience]." Her fiction explored themes of original sin, guilt, and isolation. She published two collections of stories, *A Good Man Is Hard to Find* and *Everything That Rises Must Converge,* and two novels, *Wise Blood* and *The Violent Bear It Away.* O'Connor displayed a uniquely dark humor meant to emphasize her characters' spiritual deficits, the parts where, as she said, "the good is under construction."

O'Connor suffered from lupus for much of her life and died at the age of thirty-nine from complications of the disease. *The Collected Stories of Flannery O'Connor* won the National Book Award in 1972.

★

HER DOCTOR HAD told Julian's mother that she must lose twenty pounds on account of her blood pressure, so on Wednesday nights Julian had to take her downtown on the bus for a reducing class at the Y. The reducing class was designed for working girls over fifty, who weighed from 165 to 200 pounds. His mother was one of the slimmer ones, but she said ladies did not tell their age or weight. She would not ride on the buses by herself at night since they had been integrated, and because the reducing class was one of her few pleasures, necessary for her health, and *free,* she said Julian could at least put himself out to take her, considering all she did for him. Julian did not like to consider all she did for him, but every Wednesday night he braced himself and took her.

She was almost ready to go, standing before the hall mirror, putting on her hat, while he, his hands behind him, appeared pinned to the door frame, waiting like Saint Sebastian for the arrows to begin piercing him. The hat was new and had cost her seven dollars and a half. She kept saying, "Maybe I shouldn't have paid that for it. No, I shouldn't have. I'll take it off and return it tomorrow. I shouldn't have bought it."

Julian raised his eyes to heaven. "Yes, you should have bought it," he said. "Put it on and let's go." It was a hideous hat. A purple velvet flap came down on one side of it and stood up on the other; the rest of it was green and looked like a cushion with the stuffing out. He decided it was less comical than jaunty and pathetic. Everything that gave her pleasure was small and depressed him.

She lifted the hat one more time and set it down slowly on top of her head. Two wings of gray hair protruded on either side of her florid face, but her eyes, sky-blue, were as innocent and untouched by experience as they must have been when she was ten. Were it not that she was a widow who had struggled fiercely to feed and clothe and put him through school and who was supporting him still, "until he got on his feet," she might have been a little girl that he had to take to town.

"It's all right, it's all right," he said. "Let's go." He opened the door himself and started down the walk to get her going. The sky was a dying violet and the houses stood out darkly against it, bulbous liver-colored monstrosities of a uniform ugliness though no two were alike. Since this had been a fashionable neighborhood forty years ago, his mother persisted in thinking they did well to have an apartment in it. Each house had a narrow collar of dirt around it in which sat, usually, a grubby child. Julian walked with his hands in his pockets, his head down and thrust forward and his eyes glazed with the determination to make himself completely numb during the time he would be sacrificed to her pleasure.

The door closed and he turned to find the dumpy figure, surmounted by the atrocious hat, coming toward him. "Well," she said, "you only live once and paying a little more for it, I at least won't meet myself coming and going."

"Some day I'll start making money," Julian said gloomily — he knew he never would —"and you can have one of those jokes whenever you take the fit." But first they would move. He visualized a place where the nearest neighbors would be three miles away on either side.

"I think you're doing fine," she said, drawing on her gloves. "You've only been out of school a year. Rome wasn't built in a day."

She was one of the few members of the Y reducing class who arrived in hat and gloves and who had a son who had been to college. "It takes time," she said, "and the world is in such a mess. This hat looked better on me than any of the others, though when she brought it out I said, 'Take that thing back. I wouldn't have it on my head,' and she said, 'Now wait till you see it on,' and when she put it on me, I said, 'We-ull,' and she said, 'If you ask me, that hat does something for you and you do something for the hat, and besides,' she said, 'with that hat, you won't meet yourself coming and going.'"

Julian thought he could have stood his lot better if she had been selfish, if she had been an old hag who drank and screamed at him. He walked along, saturated in depression, as if in the midst of his martyrdom he had lost his faith. Catching sight of his long, hopeless, irritated face, she stopped suddenly with a grief-stricken look, and pulled back on his arm. "Wait on me," she said. "I'm going back to the house and take this thing off and tomorrow I'm going to return it. I was out of my head. I can pay the gas bill with that seven-fifty."

He caught her arm in a vicious grip. "You are not going to take it back," he said. "I like it."

"Well," she said, "I don't think I ought . . ."

"Shut up and enjoy it," he muttered, more depressed than ever.

"With the world in the mess it's in," she said, "it's a wonder we can enjoy anything. I tell you, the bottom rail is on the top."

Julian sighed.

"Of course," she said, "if you know who you are, you can go anywhere." She said this every time he took her to the reducing class. "Most of them in it are not our kind of people," she said, "but I can be gracious to anybody. I know who I am."

"They don't give a damn for your graciousness," Julian said savagely. "Knowing who you are is good for one generation only. You haven't the foggiest idea where you stand now or who you are."

She stopped and allowed her eyes to flash at him. "I most certainly do know who I am," she said, "and if you don't know who you are, I'm ashamed of you."

"Oh hell," Julian said.

"Your great-grandfather was a former governor of this state," she said. "Your grandfather was a prosperous landowner. Your grandmother was a Godhigh."

"Will you look around you," he said tensely, "and see where you are now?" and he swept his arm jerkily out to indicate the neighborhood, which the growing darkness at least made less dingy.

"You remain what you are," she said. "Your great-grandfather had a plantation and two hundred slaves."

"There are no more slaves," he said irritably.

"They were better off when they were," she said. He groaned to see that she was off on that topic. She rolled onto it every few days like a train on an open track. He knew every stop, every junction, every swamp along the way, and knew the exact point at which her conclusion would roll majestically into the station: "It's ridiculous. It's simply not realistic. They should rise, yes, but on their own side of the fence."

"Let's skip it," Julian said.

"The ones I feel sorry for," she said, "are the ones that are half white. They're tragic."

"Will you skip it?"

"Suppose we were half white. We would certainly have mixed feelings."

"I have mixed feelings now," he groaned.

"Well let's talk about something pleasant," she said. "I remember going to Grandpa's when I was a little girl. Then the house had double stairways that went up to what was really the second floor — all the cooking was done on the first. I used to like to stay down in the kitchen on account of the way the walls smelled. I would sit with my nose pressed against the plaster and take deep breaths. Actually the place belonged to the Godhighs but your grandfather Chestny paid the mortgage and saved it for them. They were in reduced circumstances," she said, "but reduced or not, they never forgot who they were."

"Doubtless that decayed mansion reminded them," Julian muttered. He never spoke of it without contempt or thought of it without longing. He had seen it once when he was a child before it had been sold. The double stairways had rotted and been torn down. Negroes were living in it. But it remained in his mind as his mother had known it. It appeared in his dreams regularly. He would stand on the wide porch, listening to the rustle of oak leaves, then wander through the high-ceilinged hall into the parlor that opened onto it and gaze at the worn rugs and faded draperies. It occurred to him that it was he, not she, who could have appreciated it. He preferred its threadbare elegance to anything he could name and it was because of it that all the neighborhoods they had lived in had been a torment to him — whereas she had hardly known the difference. She called her insensitivity "being adjustable."

"And I remember the old darky who was my nurse, Caroline. There was no better person in the world. I've always had a great respect for my colored friends," she said. "I'd do anything in the world for them and they'd..."

"Will you for God's sake get off that subject?" Julian said. When he got on a bus by himself, he made it a point to sit down beside a Negro, in reparation as it were for his mother's sins.

"You're mighty touchy tonight," she said. "Do you feel all right?"

"Yes I feel all right," he said. "Now lay off."

She pursed her lips. "Well, you certainly are in a vile humor," she observed. "I just won't speak to you at all."

They had reached the bus stop. There was no bus in sight and Julian, his hands still jammed in his pockets and his head thrust forward, scowled down the empty street. The frustration of having to wait on the bus as well as ride on it began to creep up his neck like a hot hand. The presence of his mother was borne in upon him as she gave a pained sigh. He looked at her bleakly. She was holding herself very erect under the preposterous hat, wearing it like a banner of her imaginary dignity. There was in him an evil urge to break her spirit. He suddenly unloosened his tie and pulled it off and put it in his pocket.

She stiffened. "Why must you look like *that* when you take me to town?" she said. "Why must you deliberately embarrass me?"

"If you'll never learn where you are," he said, "you can at least learn where I am."

"You look like a — thug," she said.

"Then I must be one," he murmured.

"I'll just go home," she said. "I will not bother you. If you can't do a little thing like that for me..."

Rolling his eyes upward, he put his tie back on. "Restored to my class," he muttered. He thrust his face toward her and hissed, "True culture is in the mind, the *mind*," he said, and tapped his head, "the mind."

"It's in the heart," she said, "and in how you do things and how you do things is because of who you *are*."

"Nobody in the damn bus cares who you are."

"I care who I am," she said icily.

The lighted bus appeared on top of the next hill and as it approached, they moved out into the street to meet it. He put his hand under her elbow and hoisted her up on the creaking step. She entered with a little smile, as if she were going into a drawing room where everyone had been waiting for her. While he put in the tokens, she sat down on one of the broad front seats for three which faced the aisle. A thin woman with protruding teeth and long yellow hair was sitting on the end of it. His mother moved up beside her and left room for Julian beside herself. He sat down and looked at the floor across the aisle where a pair of thin feet in red and white canvas sandals were planted.

His mother immediately began a general conversation meant to attract anyone who felt like talking. "Can it get any hotter?" she said and removed from her purse a folding fan, black with a Japanese scene on it, which she began to flutter before her.

"I reckon it might could," the woman with the protruding teeth said, "but I know for a fact my apartment couldn't get no hotter."

"It must get the afternoon sun," his mother said. She sat forward and looked up and down the bus. It was half filled. Everybody was white. "I see we have the bus to ourselves," she said. Julian cringed.

"For a change," said the woman across the aisle, the owner of the red and white canvas sandals. "I come on one the other day and they were thick as fleas—up front and all through."

"The world is in a mess everywhere," his mother said. "I don't know how we've let it get in this fix."

"What gets my goat is all those boys from good families stealing automobile tires," the woman with the protruding teeth said. "I told my boy, I said you may not be rich but you been raised right and if I ever catch you in any such mess, they can send you on to the reformatory. Be exactly where you belong."

"Training tells," his mother said. "Is your boy in high school?"

"Ninth grade," the woman said.

"My son just finished college last year. He wants to write but he's selling typewriters until he gets started," his mother said.

The woman leaned forward and peered at Julian. He threw her such a malevolent look that she subsided against the seat. On the floor across the aisle there was an abandoned newspaper. He got up and got it and opened it out in front of him. His mother discreetly continued the conversation in a lower tone but the woman across the aisle said in a loud voice, "Well that's nice. Selling typewriters is close to writing. He can go right from one to the other."

"I tell him," his mother said, "that Rome wasn't built in a day."

Behind the newspaper Julian was withdrawing into the inner compartment of his mind where he spent most of his time. This was a kind of mental bubble in which he established himself when he could not bear to be a part of what was going on around him. From it he could see out and judge but in it he was safe from any kind of penetration from without. It was the only place where he felt free of the general idiocy of his fellows. His mother had never entered it but from it he could see her with absolute clarity.

The old lady was clever enough and he thought that if she had started from any of the right premises, more might have been expected of her. She lived according to the laws of her own fantasy world, outside of which he had never seen her set foot. The law of it was to sacrifice herself for him after she had first created the necessity to do so by making a mess of things. If he had permitted her sacrifices, it was only because her lack of foresight had made them necessary. All of her life had been a struggle to act like a Chestny without the Chestny goods, and to give him everything she thought a Chestny ought to have; but since, said she, it was fun to struggle, why complain? And when you had won, as she had won, what fun to look back on the hard times! He could not forgive her that she had enjoyed the struggle and that she thought *she* had won.

What she meant when she said she had won was that she had brought him up successfully and had sent him to college and that he had turned out so well — good-looking (her teeth had gone unfilled so that his could be straightened), intelligent (he realized he was too intelligent to be a success), and with a future ahead of him (there was of course no future ahead of him). She excused his gloominess on the grounds that he was still growing up and his radical ideas on his lack of practical experience. She said he didn't yet know a thing about "life," that he hadn't even entered the real world — when already he was as disenchanted with it as a man of fifty.

The further irony of all this was that in spite of her, he had turned out so well. In spite of going to only a third-rate college, he had, on his own initiative, come out with a first-rate education; in spite of growing up dominated by a small mind, he had ended up with a large one; in spite of all her foolish views, he was free of prejudice and unafraid to face facts. Most miraculous of all, instead of being blinded by love for her as she was for him, he had cut himself emotionally free of her and could see her with complete objectivity. He was not dominated by mother.

The bus stopped with a sudden jerk and shook him from his meditation. A woman from the back lurched forward with little steps and barely escaped falling in his newspaper as she righted herself. She got off and a large Negro got on. Julian kept his paper lowered to watch. It gave him a certain satisfaction to see injustice in daily operation. It confirmed his view that with a few exceptions there was no one worth knowing within a radius of three hundred miles. The Negro was well dressed and carried a briefcase. He looked around and then sat down on the other end of the seat where the woman with the red and white canvas sandals was sitting. He immediately unfolded a newspaper and obscured himself behind it. Julian's mother's elbow at once prodded insistently into his ribs. "Now you see why I won't ride on these buses by myself," she whispered.

The woman with the red and white canvas sandals had risen at the same time the Negro sat down and had gone farther back in the bus and taken the seat of the woman who had got off. His mother leaned forward and cast her an approving look.

Julian rose, crossed the aisle, and sat down in the place of the woman with the canvas sandals. From this position, he looked serenely across at his mother. Her face had turned an angry red. He stared at her, making his eyes the eyes of a stranger. He felt his tension suddenly lift as if he had openly declared war on her.

He would have liked to get in conversation with the Negro and to talk with him about art or politics or any subject that would be above the comprehension of those around them, but the man remained entrenched behind his paper. He was either ignoring the change of seating or had never noticed it. There was no way for Julian to convey his sympathy.

His mother kept her eyes fixed reproachfully on his face. The woman with the protruding teeth was looking at him avidly as if he were a type of monster new to her.

"Do you have a light?" he asked the Negro.

Without looking away from his paper, the man reached in his pocket and handed him a packet of matches.

"Thanks," Julian said. For a moment he held the matches foolishly. A No Smoking sign looked down upon him from over the door. This alone would not have deterred him; he had no cigarettes. He had quit smoking some months before because he could not afford it. "Sorry," he muttered and handed back the matches. The Negro lowered the paper and gave him an annoyed look. He took the matches and raised the paper again.

His mother continued to gaze at him but she did not take advantage of his momentary discomfort. Her eyes retained their battered look. Her face seemed to be unnaturally red, as if her blood pressure had risen. Julian allowed no glimmer of sympathy to show on his face. Having got the advantage, he wanted desperately to keep it and carry it through. He would have liked to teach her a lesson that would last her a while, but there seemed no way to continue the point. The Negro refused to come out from behind his paper.

Julian folded his arms and looked stolidly before him, facing her but as if he did not see her, as if he had ceased to recognize her existence. He visualized a scene in which, the bus having reached their stop, he would remain in his seat and when she said, "Aren't you going to get off?" he would look at her as at a stranger who had rashly addressed him. The corner they got off on was usually deserted, but it was well lighted and it would not hurt her to walk by herself the four blocks to the Y. He decided to wait until the time came and then decide whether or not he would let her get off by herself. He would have to be at the Y at ten to bring her back, but he could leave her wondering if he was going to show up. There was no reason for her to think she could always depend on him.

He retired again into the high-ceilinged room sparsely settled with large pieces of antique furniture. His soul expanded momentarily but then he became aware of his mother across from him and the vision shriveled. He studied her coldly. Her feet in little pumps dangled like a child's and did not quite reach the floor. She was training on him an exaggerated look of reproach. He felt completely detached from her. At that moment he could with pleasure have slapped her as he would have slapped a particularly obnoxious child in his charge.

He began to imagine various unlikely ways by which he could teach her a lesson. He might make friends with some distinguished Negro professor or lawyer and bring him home to spend the evening. He would be entirely justified but her blood pressure would rise to 300. He could not push her to the extent of making her have a stroke, and moreover, he had never been successful at making any Negro friends. He had tried to strike up an acquaintance on the bus with some of the better types, with ones that looked like professors or ministers or lawyers. One morning he had sat down next to a distinguished-looking dark brown man who had answered his questions with a sonorous solemnity but who had turned out to be an undertaker. Another day he had sat down beside a cigar-smoking Negro with a diamond ring on his finger, but after a few stilted pleasantries, the Negro had rung the buzzer and risen, slipping two lottery tickets into Julian's hand as he climbed over him to leave.

He imagined his mother lying desperately ill and his being able to secure only a Negro doctor for her. He toyed with that idea for a few minutes and then dropped it for a momentary vision of himself participating as a sympathizer in a sit-in demonstration. This was possible but he did not linger with it. Instead, he approached the ultimate horror. He brought home a beautiful suspiciously Negroid woman. Prepare yourself, he said. There is nothing you can do about it. This is the woman I've chosen. She's intelligent, dignified, even good, and she's suffered and she hasn't thought it *fun*. Now persecute us, go ahead and persecute us. Drive her out of here, but remember, you're driving me too. His eyes were narrowed and through the indignation he had generated, he saw his mother across the aisle, purple-faced, shrunken to the dwarflike proportions of her moral nature, sitting like a mummy beneath the ridiculous banner of her hat.

He was tilted out of his fantasy again as the bus stopped. The door opened with a sucking hiss and out of the dark a large, gaily dressed, sullen-looking colored woman got on with a little boy. The child, who might have been four, had on a short plaid suit and a Tyrolean hat with a blue feather in it. Julian hoped that he would sit down beside him and that the woman would push in beside his mother. He could think of no better arrangement.

As she waited for her tokens, the woman was surveying the seating possibilities — he hoped with the idea of sitting where she was least wanted. There was something familiar-looking about her but Julian could not place what it was. She was a giant of a woman. Her face was set not only to meet opposition but to seek it out. The downward tilt of her large lower lip was like a warning sign: DON'T TAMPER WITH ME. Her bulging figure was encased in a green crepe dress and her feet overflowed in red shoes. She had on a hideous hat. A purple velvet flap came down on one side of it and stood up on the other; the rest of it was green and looked like a cushion with the stuffing out. She carried a mammoth red pocketbook that bulged throughout as if it were stuffed with rocks.

To Julian's disappointment, the little boy climbed up on the empty seat beside his mother. His mother lumped all children, black and white, into the common category "cute," and she thought little Negroes were on the whole cuter than the little white children. She smiled at the little boy as he climbed on the seat.

Meanwhile the woman was bearing down upon the empty seat beside Julian. To his annoyance, she squeezed herself into it. He saw his mother's face change as the woman settled herself next to him and he realized with satisfaction that this was more objectionable to her than it was to him. Her face seemed almost gray and there was a look of dull recognition in her eyes, as if suddenly she had sickened at some awful confrontation. Julian saw that it was because she and the woman had, in a sense, swapped sons. Though his mother would not realize the symbolic significance of this, she would feel it. His amusement showed plainly on his face.

The woman next to him muttered something unintelligible to herself. He was conscious of a kind of bristling next to him, a muted growling like that of an angry cat. He could not see anything but the red pocketbook upright on the bulging green thighs. He visualized the woman as she had stood waiting for her tokens — the ponderous figure, rising from the red shoes upward over the solid hips, the mammoth bosom, haughty face, to the green and purple hat.

His eyes widened.

The vision of the two hats, identical, broke upon him with the radiance of a brilliant sunrise. His face was suddenly lit with joy. He could not believe that Fate had thrust upon his mother such a lesson. He gave a loud chuckle so that she would look at him and see that he saw. She turned her eyes on him slowly. The blue in them seemed to have turned a bruised purple. For a moment he had an uncomfortable sense of her innocence, but it lasted only a second before principle rescued him. Justice entitled him to laugh. His grin hardened until it said to her as plainly as if he were saying aloud: Your punishment exactly fits your pettiness. This should teach you a permanent lesson.

Her eyes shifted to the woman. She seemed unable to bear looking at him and to find the woman preferable. He became conscious again of the bristling presence at his side. The woman was rumbling like a volcano about to become active. His mother's mouth began to twitch slightly at one corner. With a sinking heart, he saw incipient signs of recovery on her face and realized that this was going to strike her suddenly as funny and was going to be no lesson at all. She kept her eyes on the woman and an amused smile came over her face as if the woman were a monkey that had stolen her hat. The little Negro was looking up at her with large fascinated eyes. He had been trying to attract her attention for some time.

"Carver!" the woman said suddenly. "Come heah!"

When he saw that the spotlight was on him at last, Carver drew his feet up and turned himself toward Julian's mother and giggled.

"Carver!" the woman said. "You heah me? Come heah!"

Carver slid down from the seat but remained squatting with his back against the base of it, his head turned slyly around toward Julian's mother, who was smiling at him. The woman reached a hand across the aisle and snatched him to her. He righted himself and hung back-wards on her knees, grinning at Julian's mother. "Isn't he cute?" Julian's mother said to the woman with the protruding teeth.

"I reckon he is," the woman said without conviction.

The Negress yanked him upright but he eased out of her grip and shot across the aisle and scrambled, giggling wildly, onto the seat beside his love.

"I think he likes me," Julian's mother said, and smiled at the woman. It was the smile she used when she was being particularly gracious to an inferior. Julian saw everything lost. The lesson had rolled off her like rain on a roof.

The woman stood up and yanked the little boy off the seat as if she were snatching him from contagion. Julian could feel the rage in her at having no weapon like his mother's smile. She gave the child a sharp slap across his leg. He howled once and then thrust his head into her stomach and kicked his feet against her shins. "Be-have," she said vehemently.

The bus stopped and the Negro who had been reading the newspa-per got off. The woman moved over and set the little boy down with a thump between herself and Julian. She held him firmly by the knee. In a moment he put his hands in front of his face and peeped at Julian's mother through his fingers.

"I see yoooooooo!" she said and put her hand in front of her face and peeped at him.

The woman slapped his hand down. "Quit yo' foolishness," she said, "before I knock the living Jesus out of you!"

Julian was thankful that the next stop was theirs. He reached up and pulled the cord. The woman reached up and pulled it at the same time. Oh my God, he thought. He had the terrible intuition that when they got off the bus together, his mother would open her purse and give the little boy a nickel. The gesture would be as natural to her as breathing. The bus stopped and the woman got up and lunged to the front, drag-ging the child, who wished to stay on, after her. Julian and his mother got up and followed. As they neared the door, Julian tried to relieve her of her pocketbook.

"No," she murmured, "I want to give the little boy a nickel."

"No!" Julian hissed. "No!"

She smiled down at the child and opened her bag. The bus door opened and the woman picked him up by the arm and descended with him, hanging at her hip. Once in the street she set him down and shook him.

Julian's mother had to close her purse while she got down the bus step but as soon as her feet were on the ground, she opened it again and began to rummage inside. "I can't find but a penny," she whispered, "but it looks like a new one."

"Don't do it!" Julian said fiercely between his teeth. There was a streetlight on the corner and she hurried to get under it so that she could better see into her pocketbook. The woman was heading off rapidly down the street with the child still hanging backward on her hand.

"Oh little boy!" Julian's mother called and took a few quick steps and caught up with them just beyond the lamppost. "Here's a bright new penny for you," and she held out the coin, which shone bronze in the dim light.

The huge woman turned and for a moment stood, her shoulders lifted and her face frozen with frustrated rage, and stared at Julian's mother. Then all at once she seemed to explode like a piece of machinery that had been given one ounce of pressure too much. Julian saw the black fist swing out with the red pocketbook. He shut his eyes and cringed as he heard the woman shout, "He don't take nobody's pennies!" When he opened his eyes, the woman was disappearing down the street with the little boy staring wide-eyed over her shoulder. Julian's mother was sitting on the sidewalk.

"I told you not to do that," Julian said angrily. "I told you not to do that!"

He stood over her for a minute, gritting his teeth. Her legs were stretched out in front of her and her hat was on her lap. He squatted down and looked her in the face. It was totally expressionless. "You got exactly what you deserved," he said. "Now get up."

He picked up her pocketbook and put what had fallen out back in it. He picked the hat up off her lap. The penny caught his eye on the sidewalk and he picked that up and let it drop before her eyes into the purse. Then he stood up and leaned over and held his hand out to pull her up. She remained immobile. He sighed. Rising above them on either side were black apartment buildings, marked with irregular rectangles of light. At the end of the block a man came out of a door and walked off in the opposite direction. "All right," he said, "suppose somebody happens by and wants to know why you're sitting on the sidewalk?"

She took the hand and, breathing hard, pulled heavily up on it and then stood for a moment, swaying slightly as if the spots of light in the darkness were circling around her. Her eyes, shadowed and confused, finally settled on his face. He did not try to conceal his irritation. "I hope this teaches you a lesson," he said. She leaned forward and her eyes raked his face. She seemed trying to determine his identity. Then, as if she found nothing familiar about him, she started off with a headlong movement in the wrong direction.

"Aren't you going on to the Y?" he asked.

"Home," she muttered.

"Well, are we walking?"

For answer she kept going. Julian followed along, his hands behind him. He saw no reason to let the lesson she had had go without backing it up with an explanation of its meaning. She might as well be made to understand what had happened to her. "Don't think that was just an uppity Negro woman," he said. "That was the whole colored race which will no longer take your condescending pennies. That was your black double. She can wear the same hat as you, and to be sure," he added gratuitously (because he thought it was funny), "it looked better on her than it did on you. What all this means," he said, "is that the old world is gone. The old manners are obsolete and your graciousness is not worth a damn." He thought bitterly of the house that had been lost for him. "You aren't who you think you are," he said.

She continued to plow ahead, paying no attention to him. Her hair had come undone on one side. She dropped her pocketbook and took no notice. He stooped and picked it up and handed it to her but she did not take it.

"You needn't act as if the world has come to an end," he said, "because it hasn't. From now on you've got to live in a new world and face a few realities for a change. Buck up," he said, "it won't kill you."

She was breathing fast.

"Let's wait on the bus," he said.

"Home," she said thickly.

"I hate to see you behave like this," he said. "Just like a child. I should be able to expect more of you." He decided to stop where he was and make her stop and wait for a bus. "I'm not going any farther," he said, stopping. "We're going on the bus."

She continued to go on as if she had not heard him. He took a few steps and caught her arm and stopped her. He looked into her face and caught his breath. He was looking into a face he had never seen before. "Tell Grandpapa to come get me," she said.

He stared, stricken.

"Tell Caroline to come get me," she said.

Stunned, he let her go and she lurched forward again, walking as if one leg were shorter than the other. A tide of darkness seemed to be sweeping her from him. "Mother!" he cried. "Darling, sweetheart, wait!" Crumpling, she fell to the pavement. He dashed forward and fell at her side, crying, "Mamma, Mamma!" He turned her over. Her face was fiercely distorted. One eye, large and staring, moved slightly to the left as if it had become unmoored. The other remained fixed on him, raked his face again, found nothing and closed.

"Wait here, wait here!" he cried and jumped up and began to run for help toward a cluster of lights he saw in the distance ahead of him. "Help, help!" he shouted, but his voice was thin, scarcely a thread of sound. The lights drifted farther away the faster he ran and his feet moved numbly as if they carried him nowhere. The tide of darkness seemed to sweep him back to her, postponing from moment to moment his entry into the world of guilt and sorrow.

1962

JOHN UPDIKE
PIGEON FEATHERS

from *The New Yorker*

JOHN UPDIKE (1932–2009) was born in Pennsylvania and graduated from Harvard University. After a few years away, he returned to Massachusetts, where he lived for the rest of his life.

In 1959 Updike appeared in *The Best American Short Stories* for the first time with the story "A Gift from the City." His stories continued to appear in every succeeding decade until his death. When Anne Tyler was guest editor of the series, she said that Updike's fiction reminded her of "those tiny paintings that, when you examine certain details under a magnifying glass, appear to swell and take over a room." Updike defined his own style as an attempt "to give the mundane its beautiful due."

Updike was the author of numerous books, including the celebrated Rabbit novels, *Couples, In the Beauty of the Lilies,* and *Bech at Bay.* His novels won the National Book Award, the Pulitzer Prize, the American Book Award, the National Book Critics Circle Award, and the William Dean Howells Medal from the American Academy of Arts and Letters. In 1998 he received the National Book Foundation Medal for Distinguished Contribution to American Letters.

At the time of his death from lung cancer at the age of seventy-six, he was working on a novel about Saint Paul and the beginnings of Christianity.

★

WHEN THEY MOVED to Firetown, things were upset, displaced, rearranged. A red cane-back sofa that had been the chief piece in the living room at Olinger was here banished, too big for the narrow country parlor, to the barn, and shrouded under a tarpaulin. Never again would David lie on its length all afternoon eating raisins and reading mystery novels and science fiction and P. G. Wodehouse. The blue wing chair that had stood for years in the ghostly, immaculate guest bedroom in town, gazing through windows curtained with dotted swiss at the telephone wires and horse-chestnut trees and opposite houses, was here established importantly in front of the smutty little fireplace that supplied, in those first cold April days, their only heat. As a child, David had always been afraid of the guest bedroom — it was there that he, lying sick with the measles, had seen a black rod the size of a yardstick jog along at a slight slant beside the edge of the bed, and vanish when he screamed — and it was disquieting to have one of the elements of its haunted atmosphere basking by the fire, in the center of the family, growing sooty with use. The books that at home had gathered dust in the case beside the piano were here hastily stacked, all out of order, in the shelves that the carpenters had built low along one wall. David, at fourteen, had been more moved than a mover; like the furniture, he had to find a new place, and on the Saturday of the second week tried to work off some of his disorientation by arranging the books.

It was a collection obscurely depressing to him, mostly books his mother had acquired when she was young: college anthologies of Greek plays and Romantic poetry; Will Durant's *Story of Philosophy;* a soft-leather set of Shakespeare with string bookmarks sewed to the bindings; *Green Mansions,* boxed and illustrated with woodcuts; *I, the Tiger,* by Manuel Komroff; novels by names like Galsworthy and Ellen Glasgow and Irvin S. Cobb and Sinclair Lewis and "Elizabeth." The odor of faded taste made him feel the ominous gap between himself and his parents, the insulting gulf of time that existed before he was born. Suddenly he was tempted to dip into this time. From the heaps of books around him on the broad old floorboards, he picked up Volume II of a four-volume set of *An Outline of History,* by H. G. Wells. The book's red binding had faded to orange-pink on the spine. When he lifted the cover, there was a sweetish, atticlike smell, and his mother's maiden name written in unfamiliar handwriting on the flyleaf — an upright, bold, yet careful signature, bearing a faint relation to the quick scrunched backslant that flowed with marvelous consistency across her shopping lists and budget accounts and notes on Christmas cards to college friends from this same, vaguely menacing long ago.

He leafed through, pausing at drawings, done in an old-fashioned stippled style, of bas-reliefs, masks, Romans without pupils in their eyes, articles of ancient costume, fragments of pottery found in unearthed homes. The print was determinedly legible, and smug, like a lesson book. As he bent over the pages, yellow at the edges, they were like rectangles of dusty glass through which he looked down into unreal and irrelevant worlds. He could see things sluggishly move, and an unpleasant fullness came into his throat. His mother and grandmother fussed in the kitchen; the puppy, which they had just acquired, "for protection in the country," was cowering, with a sporadic panicked scrabble of claws, under the dining table that in their old home had been reserved for special days but that here was used for every meal.

Then, before he could halt his eyes, David slipped into Wells's account of Jesus. He had been an obscure political agitator, a kind of hobo, in a minor colony of the Roman Empire. By an accident impossible to reconstruct, he (the small *h* horrified David) survived his own crucifixion and presumably died a few weeks later. A religion was founded on the freakish incident. The credulous imagination of the times retrospectively assigned miracles and supernatural pretensions to Jesus; a myth grew, and then a church, whose theology at most points was in direct contradiction of the simple, rather communistic teachings of the Galilean.

It was as if a stone that for weeks and even years had been gathering weight in the web of David's nerves snapped them, plunged through the page, and a hundred layers of paper underneath. These fantastic falsehoods (plainly untrue; churches stood everywhere, the entire nation was founded "under God") did not at first frighten him; it was the fact that they had been permitted to exist in an actual human brain. This was the initial impact — that at a definite spot in time and space a brain black with the denial of Christ's divinity had been suffered to exist; that the universe had not spit out this ball of tar but allowed it to continue in its blasphemy, to grow old, win honors, wear a hat, write books that, if true, collapsed everything into a jumble of horror. The world outside the deep-silled windows — a rutted lawn, a whitewashed barn, a walnut tree frothy with fresh green — seemed a haven from which he was forever sealed off. Hot washrags seemed pressed against his cheeks.

He read the account again. He tried to supply out of his ignorance objections that would defeat the complacent march of these black words, and found none. Survivals and misunderstandings more farfetched were reported daily in the papers. But none of them caused churches to be built in every town. He tried to work backward through the churches, from their brave high fronts through their shabby, ill-attended interiors back into the events at Jerusalem, and felt himself surrounded by shifting gray shadows, centuries of history, where he knew nothing. The thread dissolved in his hands. Had Christ ever come to him, David Kern, and said, "Here. Feel the wound in My side"? No; but prayers had been answered. What prayers? He had prayed that Rudy Mohn, whom he had purposely tripped so he cracked his head on their radiator, not die, and he had not died. But for all the blood, it was just a cut; Rudy came back the same day, wearing a bandage and repeating the same teasing words. He could never have died. Again, David had prayed for two separate photographs of movie stars he had sent away for to arrive tomorrow, and though they did not, they did arrive, some days later, together, popping through the clacking letter slot like a rebuke from God's mouth: *I answer your prayers in My way, in My time.* After that, he had made his prayers less definite, less susceptible of being twisted into a scolding. But what a tiny, ridiculous coincidence this was, after all, to throw into battle against H. G. Wells's engines of knowledge! Indeed, it proved the enemy's point: Hope bases vast premises on foolish accidents, and reads a word where in fact only a scribble exists.

His father came home. They had supper. It got dark. He had to go to the bathroom, and took a flashlight down through the wet grass to the outhouse. For once, his fear of spiders there felt trivial. He set the flashlight, burning, beside him, and an insect alighted on its lens, a tiny insect, a mosquito or flea, so fragile and fine that the weak light projected its X-ray onto the wall boards: the faint rim of its wings, the blurred strokes, magnified, of its long hinged legs, the dark cone at the heart of its anatomy. The tremor must be its heart beating. Without warning, David was visited by an exact vision of death: a long hole in the ground, no wider than your body, down which you are drawn while the white faces above recede. You try to reach them but your arms are pinned. Shovels pour dirt into your face. There you will be forever, in an upright position, blind and silent, and in time no one will remember you, and you will never be called. As strata of rock shift, your fingers elongate, and your teeth are distended sidewise in a great underground grimace indistinguishable from a strip of chalk. And the earth tumbles on, and the sun expires, and unaltering darkness reigns where once there were stars.

Sweat broke out on his back. His mind seemed to rebound off of a solidness. Such extinction was not another threat, a graver sort of danger, a kind of pain; it was qualitatively different. It was not even a conception that could be voluntarily pictured; it entered you from outside. His protesting nerves swarmed on its surface like lichen on a meteor. The skin of his chest was soaked with the effort of rejection. At the same time that the fear was dense and internal, it was dense and all around him; a tide of clay had swept up to the stars; space was crushed into a mass. When he stood up, automatically hunching his shoulders to keep his head away from the spider webs, it was with a numb sense of being cramped between two huge volumes of rigidity. That he had even this small freedom to move surprised him. In the narrow shelter of that rank shack, adjusting his pants, he felt — his first spark of comfort — too small to be crushed.

But in the open, as the beam of the flashlight skidded with frightened quickness across the remote surfaces of the barn wall and the grape arbor and the giant pine that stood by the path to the woods, the terror descended. He raced up through the clinging grass pursued not by one of the wild animals the woods might hold, or one of the goblins his superstitious grandmother had communicated to his childhood, but by specters out of science fiction, where gigantic cinder moons fill half the turquoise sky. As David ran, a gray planet rolled inches behind his neck. If he looked back, he would be buried. And in the momentum of his terror, hideous possibilities — the dilation of the sun, the triumph of the insects — wheeled out of the vacuum of make-believe and added their weight to his impending oblivion.

He wrenched the door open; the lamps within the house flared. The wicks burning here and there seemed to mirror one another. His mother was washing the dishes in a little pan of heated pump water; Granmom fluttered near her elbow apprehensively. In the living room — the downstairs of the little square house was two long rooms — his father sat in front of the black fireplace restlessly folding and unfolding a newspaper.

David took from the shelf, where he had placed it this afternoon, the great unabridged Webster's Dictionary that his grandfather had owned. He turned the big thin pages, floppy as cloth, to the entry he wanted, and read:

soul . . . 1. An entity conceived as the essence, substance, animating principle, or actuating cause of life, or of the individual life, esp. of life manifested in physical activities; the vehicle of individual existence, separate in nature from the body and usually held to be separable in existence.

The definition went on, into Greek and Egyptian conceptions, but David stopped short on the treacherous edge of antiquity. He needed to read no farther. The careful overlapping words shingled a temporary shelter for him. "Usually held to be separable in existence"— what could be fairer, more judicious, surer?

Upstairs, he seemed to be lifted above his fears. The sheets on his bed were clean. Granmom had ironed them with a pair of flatirons saved from the Olinger attic; she plucked them hot off the stove alternately, with a wooden handle called a goose. It was a wonder, to see how she managed. In the next room, his parents made comforting scratching noises as they carried a little lamp back and forth. Their door was open a crack, so he saw the light shift and swing. Surely there would be, in the last five minutes, in the last second, a crack of light, showing the door from the dark room to another, full of light. Thinking of it this vividly frightened him. His own dying, in a specific bed in a specific room, specific walls mottled with wallpaper, the dry whistle of his breathing, the murmuring doctors, the nervous relatives going in and out, but for him no way out but down into the funnel. Never touch a doorknob again. A whisper, and his parents' light was blown out. David prayed to be reassured. Though the experiment frightened him, he lifted his hands high into the darkness above his face and begged Christ to touch them. Not hard or long; the faintest, quickest grip would be final for a lifetime. His hands waited in the air, itself a substance, which seemed to move through his fingers; or was it the pressure of his pulse? He returned his hands to beneath the covers uncertain if they had been touched or not. For would not Christ's touch *be* infinitely gentle?

Through all the eddies of its aftermath, David clung to this thought about his revelation of extinction: that there, in the outhouse, he had struck a solidness *qualitatively different,* a rock of horror firm enough to support any height of construction. All he needed was a little help; a word, a gesture, a nod of certainty and he would be sealed in, safe. The assurance from the dictionary had melted in the night. Today was Sunday, a hot fair day. Across a mile of clear air the church bells called, *Celebrate, celebrate.* Only Daddy went. He put on a coat over his rolled-up shirtsleeves and got into the little old black Plymouth parked by the barn and went off, with the same pained, hurried grimness of all his actions. His churning wheels, as he shifted too hastily into second, raised plumes of red dust on the dirt road. Mother walked to the far field, to see what bushes needed cutting. David, though he usually preferred to stay in the house, went with her. The puppy followed at a distance, whining as it picked its way through the stubble but floundering off timidly if one of them went back to pick it up and carry it. When they reached the crest of the far field, his mother asked, "David, what's troubling you?"

"Nothing. Why?"

She looked at him sharply. The greening woods cross-hatched the space beyond her half-gray hair. Then she turned her profile, and gestured toward the house, which they had left a half mile behind them. "See how it sits in the land? They don't know how to build with the land any more. Pop always said the foundations were set with the compass. We must try to get a compass and see. It's supposed to face due south; but south feels a little more *that* way to me." From the side, as she said these things, she seemed handsome and young. The smooth sweep of her hair over her ear seemed white with a purity and calm that made her feel foreign to him. He had never regarded his parents as consolers of his troubles; from the beginning they had seemed to have more troubles than he. Their confusion had flattered him into an illusion of strength; so now on this high clear ridge he jealously guarded the menace all around them, blowing like a breeze on his fingertips, the possibility of all this wide scenery sinking into darkness. The strange fact that though she came to look at the brush she carried no clippers, for she had a fixed prejudice against working on Sundays, was the only consolation he allowed her to offer.

As they walked back, the puppy whimpering after them, the rising dust behind a distant line of trees announced that Daddy was speeding home from church. When they reached the house he was there. He had brought back the Sunday paper and the vehement remark "Dobson's too intelligent for these farmers. They just sit there with their mouths open and don't hear a thing he's saying."

David hid in the funny papers and sports section until one-thirty. At two, the catechetical class met at the Firetown church. He had transferred from the catechetical class of the Lutheran church in Olinger, a humiliating comedown. In Olinger they met on Wednesday nights, spiffy and spruce, in the atmosphere of a dance. Afterward, blessed by the brick-faced minister from whose lips the word "Christ" fell like a burning stone, the more daring of them went with their Bibles to a luncheonette and smoked. Here in Firetown, the girls were dull white cows and the boys narrow-faced brown goats in old men's suits, herded on Sunday afternoons into a threadbare church basement that smelled of stale hay. Because his father had taken the car on one of his countless errands to Olinger, David walked, grateful for the open air and the silence. The catechetical class embarrassed him, but today he placed hope in it, as the source of the nod, the gesture, that was all he needed.

Reverend Dobson was a delicate young man with great dark eyes and small white shapely hands that flickered like protesting doves when he preached; he seemed a bit misplaced in the Lutheran ministry. This was his first call. It was a split parish; he served another rural church twelve miles away. His iridescent green Ford, new six months ago, was spattered to the windows with red mud and rattled from bouncing on the rude back roads, where he frequently got lost, to the malicious satisfaction of many. But David's mother liked him, and, more pertinent to his success, the Haiers, the sleek family of feed merchants and innkeepers and tractor salesmen who dominated the Firetown church, liked him. David liked him, and felt liked in turn; sometimes in class, after some special stupidity, Dobson directed toward him out of those wide black eyes a mild look of disbelief, a look that, though flattering, was also delicately disquieting.

Catechetical instruction consisted of reading aloud from a work booklet answers to problems prepared during the week, problems like "I am the———, the———, and the———, saith the Lord." Then there was a question period in which no one ever asked any questions. Today's theme was the last third of the Apostles' Creed. When the time came for questions, David blushed and asked, "About the Resurrection of the Body — are we conscious between the time when we die and the Day of Judgment?"

Dobson blinked, and his fine little mouth pursed, suggesting that David was making difficult things more difficult. The faces of the other students went blank, as if an indiscretion had been committed.

"No, I suppose not," Reverend Dobson said.

"Well, where is our soul, then, in this gap?"

The sense grew, in the class, of a naughtiness occurring. Dobson's shy eyes watered, as if he were straining to keep up the formality of attention, and one of the girls, the fattest, simpered toward her twin, who was a little less fat. Their chairs were arranged in a rough circle. The current running around the circle panicked David. Did everybody know something he didn't know?

"I suppose you could say our souls are asleep," Dobson said.

"And then they wake up, and there is the earth like it always is, and all the people who have ever lived? Where will Heaven be?"

Anita Haier giggled. Dobson gazed at David intently, but with an awkward, puzzled flicker of forgiveness, as if there existed a secret between them that David was violating. But David knew of no secret. All he wanted was to hear Dobson repeat the words he said every Sunday morning. This he would not do. As if these words were unworthy of the conversational voice.

"David, you might think of Heaven this way: as the way the goodness Abraham Lincoln did lives after him."

"But is Lincoln conscious of it living on?" He blushed no longer with embarrassment but in anger; he had walked here in good faith and was being made a fool.

"Is he conscious now? I would have to say no; but I don't think it matters." Dobson's voice had a coward's firmness; he was hostile now.

"You don't?"

"Not in the eyes of God, no." The unction, the stunning impudence, of this reply sprang tears of outrage in David's eyes. He bowed them to his book, where short words like Duty, Love, Obey, Honor were stacked in the form of a cross.

"Were there any other questions, David?" Dobson asked with renewed gentleness. The others were rustling, collecting their books.

"No." He made his voice firm, though he could not bring up his eyes.

"Did I answer your question fully enough?"

"Yes."

In the minister's silence the shame that should have been his crept over David; the burden and fever of being a fraud were placed upon *him,* who was innocent, and it seemed, he knew, a confession of this guilt that on the way out he was unable to face Dobson's stirred gaze, though he felt it probing the side of his head.

Anita Haier's father gave him a ride down the highway as far as the dirt road. David said he wanted to walk the rest, and figured that his offer was accepted because Mr. Haier did not want to dirty his bright blue Buick with dust. This was all right; everything was all right, as long as it was clear. His indignation at being betrayed, at seeing Christianity betrayed, had hardened him. The straight dirt road reflected his hardness. Pink stones thrust up through its packed surface. The April sun beat down from the center of the afternoon half of the sky; already it had some of summer's heat. Already the fringes of weeds at the edges of the road were bedraggled with dust. From the reviving grass and scruff of the fields he walked between, insects were sending up a monotonous, automatic chant. In the distance a tiny figure in his father's coat was walking along the edge of the woods. His mother. He wondered what joy she found in such walks; to him the brown stretches of slowly rising and falling land expressed only a huge exhaustion.

Flushed with fresh air and happiness, she returned from her walk earlier than he had expected, and surprised him at his grandfather's Bible. It was a stumpy black book, the boards worn thin where the old man's fingers had held them; the spine hung by one weak hinge of fabric. David had been looking for the passage where Jesus says to the one thief on the cross "Today shalt thou be with me in paradise." He had never tried reading the Bible for himself before. What was so embarrassing about being caught at it was that he detested the apparatus of piety. Fusty churches, creaking hymns, ugly Sunday-school teachers and their stupid leaflets — he hated everything about them but the promise they held out, a promise that in the most perverse way, as if the homeliest crone in the kingdom were given the prince's hand, made every good and real thing, ball games and jokes and big-breasted girls, possible. He couldn't explain this to his mother. Her solicitude was upon him.

"David, what are you doing at Granpop's Bible?"

"Trying to read it. This is supposed to be a Christian country, isn't it?"

She sat down on the green sofa that used to be in the sun parlor at Olinger, under the fancy mirror. A little smile still lingered on her face from the walk. "David, I wish you'd talk to me."

"What about?"

"About whatever it is that's troubling you. Your father and I have both noticed it."

"I asked Reverend Dobson about Heaven and he said it was like Abraham Lincoln's goodness living after him."

He waited for the shock to strike her. "Yes?" she said, expecting more.

"That's all."

"And why didn't you like it?"

"Well; don't you see? It amounts to saying there isn't any Heaven at all."

"I don't see that it amounts to that. What do you want Heaven to be?"

"Well, I don't know. I want it to be *some*thing. I thought *he'd* tell me what it was. I thought that was his job." He was becoming angry, sensing her surprise at him. She had assumed that Heaven had faded from his head years ago. She had imagined that he had already entered, in the secrecy of silence, the conspiracy that he now knew to be all around him.

"David," she asked gently, "don't you ever want to rest?"

"No. Not forever."

"David, you're so young. When you get older, you'll feel differently."

"Grandpa didn't. Look how tattered this book is."

"I never understood your grandfather."

"Well, I don't understand ministers who say it's like Lincoln's memory going on and on. Suppose you're not Lincoln?"

"I think Reverend Dobson made a mistake. You must try to forgive him."

"It's not a *question* of his making a mistake! It's a question of dying and never moving or seeing or hearing anything ever again."

"But"—in exasperation—"darling, it's so *greedy* of you to want more. When God has given us this wonderful April day, and given us this farm, and you have your whole life ahead of you—"

"You think, then, that there is God?"

"Of course I do"—with deep relief that smoothed her features into a reposeful oval. He was standing, and above her, too near for his comfort. He was afraid she would reach out and touch him.

"He made everything? You feel that?"

"Yes."

"Then who made Him?"

"Why, Man. Man." The happiness of this answer lit up her face radiantly, until she saw his gesture of disgust.

"Well that amounts to saying there is none."

Her hand reached for his wrist but he backed away. "David, it's a mystery. A miracle. It's a miracle more beautiful than any Reverend Dobson could have told you about. You don't say houses don't exist because Man made them."

"No. God has to be different."

"But, David, you have the *evidence*. Look out the window at the sun; at the fields."

"Mother, good grief. Don't you see"—he gasped away the roughness in his throat—"if when we die there's nothing, all your sun and fields and what not are all, ah, *horror*? It's just an ocean of horror."

"But David, it's not. It's so clearly not that." And she made an urgent opening gesture with her hands that expressed, with its suggestion of a willingness to receive his helplessness, all her grace, her gentleness, her love of beauty gathered into a passive intensity that made him intensely hate her. He would not be wooed away from the truth. *I am the Way, the Truth*—

"No," he told her. "Just let me alone."

He found his tennis ball behind the piano and went outside to throw it against the side of the house. There was a patch high up where the brown stucco that had been laid over the sandstone masonry was crumbling away; he kept trying with the tennis ball to chip more pieces off. Superimposed upon his deep ache was a smaller but more immediate worry that he had hurt his mother. He heard his father's car rattling on the straightaway, and went into the house, to make peace before he arrived. To his relief, she was not giving off the stifling damp heat of her anger but instead was cool, decisive, maternal. She handed him an old green book, her college text of Plato.

"I want you to read the Parable of the Cave," she said.

"All right," he said, though he knew it would do no good. Some story by a dead Greek just vague enough to please her. "Don't worry about it, Mother."

"I *am* worried. Honestly, David, I'm sure there will be something for us. As you get older, these things seem to matter a great deal less."

"That may be. It's a dismal thought, though."

His father bumped at the door. The locks and jambs stuck here. But before Granmom could totter to the catch and let him in, he had knocked it open. Although Mother usually kept her talks with David a confidence, a treasure between them, she called instantly, "George, David is worried about death!"

He came to the doorway of the living room, his shirt pocket bristling with pencils, holding in one hand a pint box of melting ice cream and in the other the knife with which he was about to divide it into four sections, their Sunday treat. "Is the kid worried about death? Don't give it a thought, David. I'll be lucky if I live till tomorrow, and I'm not worried. If they'd taken a buckshot gun and shot me in the cradle I'd be better off. The *world'd* be better off. Hell, I think death is a wonderful thing. I look forward to it. Get the garbage out of the way. If I had the man here who invented death, I'd pin a medal on him."

"Hush, George. You'll frighten the child worse than he is."

This was not true; he never frightened David. There was no harm in his father, no harm at all. Indeed, in the man's steep self-disgust the boy felt a kind of ally. A distant ally. He saw his position with a certain strategic coldness. Nowhere in the world of other people would he find the hint, the nod, he needed to begin to build his fortress against death. They none of them believed. He was alone. In a deep hole.

In the months that followed, his position changed little. School was some comfort. All those sexy, perfumed people, wisecracking, chewing gum, all of them doomed to die, and none of them noticing. In their company David felt that they would carry him along into the bright, cheap paradise reserved for them. In any crowd, the fear ebbed a little; he had reasoned that somewhere in the world there must exist a few people who believed what was necessary, and the larger the crowd, the greater the chance that he was near such a soul, within calling distance, if only he was not too ignorant, too ill-equipped, to spot him. The sight of clergymen cheered him; whatever they themselves thought, their collars were still a sign that somewhere, at some time, someone had recognized that we cannot, *cannot,* submit to death. The sermon topics posted outside churches, the flip hurried pieties of disc jockeys, the cartoons in magazines showing angels or devils — on such scraps he kept alive the possibility of hope.

For the rest, he tried to drown his hopelessness in clatter and jostle. The pinball machine at the luncheonette was a merciful distraction; as he bent over its buzzing, flashing board of flippers and cushions, the weight and constriction in his chest lightened and loosened. He was grateful for all the time his father wasted in Olinger. Every delay postponed the moment when they must ride together down the dirt road into the heart of the dark farmland, where the only light was the kerosene lamp waiting on the dining room table, a light that made their food shadowy, scrabbled, sinister.

He lost his appetite for reading. He was afraid of being ambushed again. In mystery novels people died like dolls being discarded; in science fiction enormities of space and time conspired to crush the humans; and even in P. G. Wodehouse he felt a hollowness, a turning away from reality that was implicitly bitter and became explicit in the comic figures of futile clergymen. All gaiety seemed minced out on the skin of a void. All quiet hours seemed invitations to dread.

School stopped. His father took the car in the opposite direction, to a construction job where he had been hired for the summer as a timekeeper, and David was stranded in the middle of acres of heat and greenery and blowing pollen and the strange, mechanical humming that lay invisibly in the weeds and alfalfa and dry orchard grass.

For his fifteenth birthday his parents gave him, with jokes about his being a hillbilly now, a Remington .22. It was somewhat like a pinball machine to take it out to the old kiln in the woods, where they dumped their trash, and set up tin cans on the kiln's sandstone shoulder and shoot them off one by one. He'd take the puppy, who had grown long legs and a rich coat of reddish fur — he was part chow. Copper hated the gun but loved David enough to accompany him. When the flat acrid crack rang out, he would race in terrified circles that would tighten and tighten until they brought him, shivering, against David's legs. Depending upon his mood, David would shoot again or drop to his knees and comfort the dog. Giving this comfort to a degree returned comfort to him. The dog's ears, laid flat against his skull in fear, were folded so intricately, so — he groped for the concept — *surely.* Where the dull-studded collar made his fur stand up, each hair showed a root of soft white under the length, black-tipped, of the metal color that had given the dog its name. In his agitation Copper panted through nostrils that were elegant slits, like two healed cuts, or like the keyholes of a dainty lock of black, grained wood. His whole whorling, knotted, jointed body was a wealth of such embellishments. And in the smell of the dog's hair David seemed to descend through many finely differentiated layers of earth: mulch, soil, sand, clay, and the glittering mineral base.

But when he returned to the house, and saw the books arranged on the low shelves, fear returned. The four adamant volumes of Wells like four thin bricks, the green Plato that had puzzled him with its queer softness and tangled purity, the dead Galsworthy and "Elizabeth," Grandpa's mammoth dictionary, Grandpa's Bible, the Bible that he himself had received on becoming a member of the Firetown Lutheran Church — at the sight of these, the memory of his fear reawakened and came around him. He had grown stiff and stupid in its embrace. His parents tried to think of ways to entertain him.

"David, I have a job for you to do," his mother said one evening at the table.

"What?"

"If you're going to take that tone perhaps we'd better not talk."

"What tone? I didn't take any tone."

"Your grandmother thinks there are too many pigeons in the barn."

"Why?" David turned to look at his grandmother, but she sat there staring at the orange flame of the burning lamp with her usual expression of bewilderment.

Mother shouted, "Mom, he wants to know why?"

Granmom made a jerky, irritable motion with her bad hand, as if generating the force for utterance, and said, "They foul the furniture."

"That's right," Mother said. "She's afraid for that old Olinger furniture that we'll never use. David, she's been after me for a month about those poor pigeons. She wants you to shoot them."

"I don't want to kill anything especially," David said.

Daddy said, "The kid's like you are, Elsie. He's too good for this world. Kill or be killed, that's my motto."

His mother said loudly, "Mother, he doesn't want to do it."

"Not?" The old lady's eyes distended as if in horror, and her claw descended slowly to her lap.

"Oh, I'll do it, I'll do it tomorrow," David snapped, and a pleasant crisp taste entered his mouth with the decision.

"And I had thought, when Boyer's men made the hay, it would be better if the barn doesn't look like a rookery," his mother added needlessly.

A barn, in day, is a small night. The splinters of light between the dry shingles pierce the high roof like stars, and the rafters and crossbeams and built-in ladders seem, until your eyes adjust, as mysterious as the branches of a haunted forest. David entered silently, the gun in one hand. Copper whined desperately at the door, too frightened to come in with the gun yet unwilling to leave the boy. David stealthily turned, said, "Go away," shut the door on the dog, and slipped the bolt across. It was a door within a door; the double door for wagons and tractors was as high and wide as the face of a house.

The smell of old straw scratched his sinuses. The red sofa, half hidden under its white-splotched tarpaulin, seemed assimilated into this smell, sunk in it, buried. The mouths of empty bins gaped like caves. Rusty oddments of farming—coils of baling wire, some spare tines for a harrow, a handleless shovel—hung on nails driven here and there in the thick wood. He stood stock-still a minute; it took a while to separate the cooing of the pigeons from the rustling in his ears. When he had focused on the cooing, it flooded the vast interior with its throaty, bubbling outpour: there seemed no other sound. They were up behind the beams. What light there was leaked through the shingles and the dirty glass windows at the far end and the small round holes, about as big as basketballs, high on the opposite stone side walls, under the ridge of the roof.

A pigeon appeared in one of these holes, on the side toward the house. It flew in, with a battering of wings, from the outside, and waited there, silhouetted against its pinched bit of sky, preening and cooing in a throbbing, thrilled, tentative way. David tiptoed four steps to the side, rested his gun against the lowest rung of a ladder pegged between two upright beams, and lowered the gunsight into the bird's tiny, jauntily cocked head. The slap of the report seemed to come off the stone wall behind him, and the pigeon did not fall. Neither did it fly. Instead it stuck in the round hole, pirouetting rapidly and nodding its head as if in frantic agreement. David shot the bolt back and forth and had aimed again before the spent cartridge stopped jingling on the boards by his feet. He eased the tip of the sight a little lower, into the bird's breast, and took care to squeeze the trigger with perfect evenness. The slow contraction of his hand abruptly sprang the bullet; for a half second there was doubt, and then the pigeon fell like a handful of rags, skimming down the barn wall into the layer of straw that coated the floor of the mow on this side.

Now others shook loose from the rafters, and whirled in the dim air with a great blurred hurtle of feathers and noise. They would go for the hole; he fixed his sights on the little moon of blue, and when a pigeon came to it, shot him as he was walking the ten inches or so of stone that would carry him into the open air. This pigeon lay down in that tunnel of stone, unable to fall either one way or the other, although he was alive enough to lift one wing and cloud the light. It would sink back, and he would suddenly lift it again, the feathers flaring. His body blocked that exit. David raced to the other side of the barn's main aisle, where a similar ladder was symmetrically placed, and rested his gun on the same rung. Three birds came together to this hole; he got one, and two got through. The rest resettled in the rafters.

There was a shallow triangular space behind the crossbeams supporting the roof. It was here they roosted and hid. But either the space was too small, or they were curious, for now that his eyes were at home in the dusty gloom David could see little dabs of gray popping in and out. The cooing was shriller now; its apprehensive tremolo made the whole volume of air seem liquid. He noticed one little smudge of a head that was especially persistent in peeking out; he marked the place, and fixed his gun on it, and when the head appeared again, had his finger tightened in advance on the trigger. A parcel of fluff slipped off the beam and fell the barn's height onto a canvas covering some Olinger furniture, and where its head had peeked out there was a fresh prick of light in the shingles.

Standing in the center of the floor, fully master now, disdaining to steady the barrel with anything but his arm, he killed two more that way. He felt like a beautiful avenger. Out of the shadowy ragged infinity of the vast barn roof these impudent things dared to thrust their heads, presumed to dirty its starred silence with their filthy timorous life, and he cut them off, tucked them back neatly into the silence. He had the sensations of a creator; these little smudges and flickers that he was clever to see and even cleverer to hit in the dim recesses of the rafters — out of each of them he was making a full bird. A tiny peek, probe, dab of life, when he hit it, blossomed into a dead enemy, falling with good, final weight.

The imperfection of the second pigeon he had shot, who was still lifting his wing now and then up in the round hole, nagged him. He put a new clip into the stock. Hugging the gun against his body, he climbed the ladder. The barrel sight scratched his ear; he had a sharp, bright vision, like a color slide, of shooting himself and being found tumbled on the barn floor among his prey. He locked his arm around the top rung —a fragile, gnawed rod braced between uprights—and shot into the bird's body from a flat angle. The wing folded, but the impact did not, as he had hoped, push the bird out of the hole. He fired again, and again, and still the little body, lighter than air when alive, was too heavy to budge from its high grave. From up here he could see green trees and a brown corner of the house through the hole. Clammy with the cobwebs that gathered between the rungs, he pumped a full clip of eight bullets into the stubborn shadow, with no success. He climbed down, and was struck by the silence in the barn. The remaining pigeons must have escaped out the other hole. That was all right; he was tired of it.

He stepped with his rifle into the light. His mother was coming to meet him, and it amused him to see her shy away from the carelessly held gun. "You took a chip out of the house," she said. "What were those last shots about?"

"One of them died up in that little round window and I was trying to shoot it down."

"Copper's hiding behind the piano and won't come out. I had to leave him."

"Well, don't blame me. *I* didn't want to shoot the poor devils."

"Don't smirk. You look like your father. How many did you get?"

"Six."

She went into the barn, and he followed. She listened to the silence. Her hair was scraggly, perhaps from tussling with the dog. "I don't suppose the others will be back," she said wearily. "Indeed, I don't know why I let Mother talk me into it. Their cooing was such a comforting noise." She began to gather up the dead birds. Though he didn't want to touch them, David went into the mow and picked up by its tepid, horny, coral-colored feet the first bird he had killed. Its wings unfolded disconcertingly, as if the creature had been held together by threads that now were slit. It did not weigh much. He retrieved the one on the other side of the barn; his mother got the three in the middle, and led the way across the road to the little southern slope of land that went down toward the foundations of the vanished tobacco shed. The ground was too steep to plant or mow; wild strawberries grew in the tangled grass. She put her burden down and said, "We'll have to bury them. The dog will go wild."

He put his two down on her three; the slick feathers let the bodies slide liquidly on one another. He asked, "Shall I get you the shovel?"

"Get it for yourself; *you* bury them. They're your kill," she said. "And be sure to make the hole deep enough so he won't dig them up."

While he went to the tool shed for the shovel, she went into the house. Unlike her, she did not look up, either at the orchard to the right of her or at the meadow on her left, but instead held her head rigidly, tilted a little, as if listening to the ground.

He dug the hole, in a spot where there were no strawberry plants, before he studied the pigeons. He had never seen a bird this close before. The feathers were more wonderful than dog's hair; for each filament was shaped within the shape of the feather, and the feathers in turn were trimmed to fit a pattern that flowed without error across the bird's body. He lost himself in the geometrical tides as the feathers now broadened and stiffened to make an edge for flight, now softened and constricted to cup warmth around the mute flesh. And across the surface of the infinitely adjusted yet somehow effortless mechanics of the feathers played idle designs of color, no two alike, designs executed, it seemed, in a controlled rapture, with a joy that hung level in the air above and behind him. Yet these birds bred in the millions and were exterminated as pests. Into the fragrant, open earth he dropped one broadly banded in shades of slate blue, and on top of it another, mottled all over with rhythmic patches of lilac and gray. The next was almost wholly white, yet with a salmon glaze at the throat. As he fitted the last two, still pliant, on the top, and stood up, crusty coverings were lifted from him, and with a feminine, slipping sensation along his nerves that seemed to give the air hands, he was robed in this certainty: that the God who had lavished such craft upon these worthless birds would not destroy His whole Creation by refusing to let David live forever.

1967

RAYMOND CARVER
WILL YOU PLEASE BE QUIET, PLEASE?

from *December*

RAYMOND CARVER (1938–1988) was born in Oregon and grew up in Yakima, Washington. His father worked in a sawmill and his mother as a waitress and a retail clerk. In his early twenties Carver attended a creative writing course taught by John Gardner, who became an important force in Carver's work. Carver later studied at the Iowa Writers' Workshop.

His first story to appear in *The Best American Short Stories* was "Will You Please Be Quiet, Please?" But it was not until 1982 that another story, "Cathedral," was selected.

Carver's style has been described as minimalist. His reaction was, "There's something about 'minimalist' that smacks of smallness of vision and execution that I don't like." This impression has been put into discussion and correction since the publication of *Beginners,* the original version of the book *What We Talk About When We Talk About Love,* which had caused him to be categorized as a minimalist.

Carver is the author of five collections of stories and was nominated for the National Book Award, the National Book Critics Circle Award, and the Pulitzer Prize. He also wrote six books of poems published posthumously in *All of Us,* his collected poems. In 1983 he received the Mildred and Harold Strauss Living Award, and he was inducted into the American Academy and Institute of Arts and Letters in 1988. He also received two NEA grants, a Guggenheim Fellowship, and an honorary doctor of letters degree from the University of Hartford. After a ten-year relationship, he and the writer Tess Gallagher celebrated their marriage in July 1988. Raymond Carver died at fifty from lung cancer on August 2, 1988.

★

W HEN HE WAS 18 and left home for the first time, in the fall, Ralph Wyman had been advised by his father, principal of Jefferson Elementary School in Weaverville and trumpet-player in the Elks' Club Auxiliary Band, that life today was a serious matter; something that required strength and direction in a young person just setting out. A difficult journey, everyone knew that, but nevertheless a comprehensible one, he believed.

But in college Ralph's goals were still hazy and undefined. He first thought he wanted to be a doctor, or a lawyer, and he took pre-medical courses and courses in history of jurisprudence and business-law before he decided he had neither the emotional detachment necessary for medicine, nor the ability for sustained reading and memorization in the *Corpus Iuris Civilis,* as well as the more modern texts on property and inheritance. Though he continued to take classes here and there in the sciences and in the Department of Business, he also took some lower-division classes in history and philosophy and English. He continually felt he was on the brink of some kind of momentous discovery about himself. But it never came. It was during this time, his lowest ebb, as he jokingly referred back to it later, that he believed he almost became an alcoholic; he was in a fraternity and he used to get drunk every night. He drank so much, in fact, that he even acquired something of a reputation; guys called him Jackson, after the bartender at The Keg, and he sat every day in the cafeteria with a deck of cards playing poker solitaire, or bridge, if someone happened along. His grades were down and he was thinking of dropping out of school entirely and joining the air force.

Then, in his third year, he came under the influence of a particularly fascinating and persuasive literature teacher. Dr. Maxwell was his name; Ralph would never forget him. He was a handsome, graceful man in his early forties, with exquisite manners and with just the trace of a slight southern drawl to his voice. He had been educated at Vanderbilt, had studied in Europe, and later had had something to do with one or two literary magazines in New York. Almost overnight, it seemed to him, Ralph decided on teaching as a career. He stopped drinking so much and began to bear down on his studies. Within a year he was elected to Omega Psi, the national journalism fraternity; he became a member of the English Club; was invited to come with his cello, which he hadn't played in three years, and join in a student chamber music group just forming; and he ran successfully for Secretary of the Senior Class. He also started going out with Marian Ross that year; a pale, slender girl he had become acquainted with in a Chaucer class.

She wore her hair long and liked high-necked sweaters in the winter; and summer and winter she always went around with a leather purse on a long strap swinging from her shoulder. Her eyes were large and seemed to take in everything at a glance; if she got excited over something, they flashed and widened even more. He liked going out with her in the evenings. They went to The Keg, and a few other nightspots where everyone else went, but they never let their going together, or their subsequent engagement that next summer, interfere with their studies. They were serious students, and both sets of parents eventually gave their approval of the match. They did their student-teaching at the same high school in Chico the next spring, and went through graduation exercises together in June. They married in St. James Episcopal Church two weeks later. Both of them held hands the night before their wedding and pledged solemnly to preserve forever the excitement and the mystery of marriage.

For their honeymoon they drove to Guadalajara; and while they both enjoyed visiting the old decayed churches and the poorly lighted museums, and the several afternoons they spent shopping and exploring in the marketplace (which swarmed with flies), Ralph secretly felt a little appalled and at the same time let down by the squalor and promiscuity of the people; he was only too glad to get back to more civilized California. Even so, Marian had seemed to enjoy it, and he would always remember one scene in particular. It was late afternoon, almost evening, and Marian was leaning motionless on her arms over the iron-worked balustrade of their rented, second-floor *casa* as he came up the dusty road below. Her hair was long and hung down in front over her shoulders, and she was looking away from him, staring at something toward the horizon. She wore a white blouse with a bright red scarf at the throat, and he could see her breasts pushing against her front. He had a bottle of dark, unlabeled wine under his arm, and the whole incident reminded him of something from a play, or a movie. Thinking back on it later, it was always a little vaguely disturbing for some reason.

Before they had left for their six-week honeymoon, they had accepted teaching positions at a high school in Eureka, in the northern part of the state near the ocean. They waited a year to make certain that the school and the weather, and the people themselves were exactly what they wanted to settle down to, and then made a substantial down-payment on a house in the Fire Hill district. He felt, without really thinking about it, that they understood each other perfectly; as well, anyway, as any two people could understand one another. More, he understood himself; his capacities, his limitations. He knew where he was going and how to get there.

In eight years they had two children, Dorothea and Robert, who were now five and four years old. A few months after Robert, Marian had accepted at mid-term a part-time position as a French and English teacher at Harris Junior College, at the edge of town. The position had become full-time and permanent that next fall, and Ralph had stayed on, happily, at the high school. In the time they had been married, they had had only one serious disturbance, and that was long ago: two years ago that winter to be exact. It was something they had never talked about since it happened, but, try as he might, Ralph couldn't help thinking about it sometimes. On occasion, and then when he was least prepared, the whole ghastly scene leaped into his mind. Looked at rationally and in its proper, historical perspective, it seemed impossible and monstrous; an event of such personal magnitude for Ralph that he still couldn't entirely accept it as something that had once happened to Marian and himself: he had taken it into his head one night at a party that Marian had betrayed him with Mitchell Anderson, a friend. In a fit of uncontrollable rage, he had struck Marian with his fist, knocking her sideways against the kitchen table and onto the floor.

It was a Sunday night in November. The children were in bed. Ralph was sleepy, and he still had a dozen themes from his twelfth-grade class in accelerated English to correct before tomorrow morning. He sat on the edge of the couch, leaning forward with his red pencil over a space he'd cleared on the coffee table. He had the papers separated into two stacks, and one of the papers folded open in front of him. He caught himself blinking his eyes, and again felt irritated with the Franklins. Harold and Sarah Franklin. They'd stopped over early in the afternoon for cocktails and stayed on into the evening. Otherwise, Ralph would have finished hours ago, as he'd planned. He'd been sleepy, too, he remembered, the whole time they were here. He'd sat in the big leather chair by the fireplace and once he recalled letting his head sink back against the warm leather of the chair and starting to close his eyes when Franklin had cleared his throat loudly. Too loudly. He didn't feel comfortable with Franklin anymore. Harold Franklin was a big, forthright man with bushy eyebrows who caught you and held you with his eyes when he spoke. He looked like he never combed his hair, his suits were always baggy, and Ralph thought his ties hideous, but he was one of the few men on the staff at Harris Junior College who had his Ph.D. At 35 he was head of the combined History and Social Science Department. Two years ago he and Sarah had been witness to a large part of Ralph's humiliation. That occasion had never later been brought up by any of them, of course, and in a few weeks, the next time they'd seen one another, it was as though nothing had happened. Still, since then, Ralph couldn't help feeling a little uneasy when he was around them.

He could hear the radio playing softly in the kitchen, where Marian was ironing. He stared a while longer at the paper in front of him, then gathered up all of the papers, turned off the lamp, and walked out to the kitchen.

"Finished, love?" Marian said with a smile. She was sitting on a tall stool, ironing one of Robert's shirts. She sat the iron up on its end as if she'd been waiting for him.

"Damn it, no," he said with an exaggerated grimace, tossing the papers on the table. "What the hell the Franklins come by here for anyway?"

She laughed; bright, pleasant. It made him feel better. She held up her face to be kissed, and he gave her a little peck on the cheek. He pulled out a chair from the table and sat down, leaned back on the legs and looked at her. She smiled again, and then lowered her eyes.

"I'm already half-asleep," he said.

"Coffee," she said, reaching over and laying the back of her hand against the electric percolator.

He nodded.

She took a long drag from the cigarette she'd had burning in the ashtray, smoked it a minute while she stared at the floor, and then put it back in the ashtray. She looked up at him, and a smile started at the corners of her mouth. She was tall and limber, with a good bust, narrow hips, and wide, gleaming eyes.

"Ralph, do you remember that party?" she asked, still looking at him.

He shifted in the chair and said, "Which party? You mean that one two or three years ago?"

She nodded.

He waited a minute and asked, when she didn't say anything else, "What about it? Now that you brought it up, honey, what about it?" Then: "He kissed you after all, that night, didn't he? . . . Did he try to kiss you, or didn't he?"

"I didn't say that," she said. "I was just thinking about it and I asked you; that's all."

"Well, he did, didn't he? Come on, Marian, we're just talking, aren't we?"

"I'm afraid it'd make you angry, Ralph."

"It won't make me angry, Marian. It was a long time ago, wasn't it? I won't be angry . . . Well?"

"Well, yes," she said slowly, "he did kiss me a few times." She smiled tentatively, gauging his reaction.

His first impulse was to return her smile, and then he felt himself blushing and said defensively, "You told me before he didn't. You said he only put his arm around you while he was driving."

He stared at her. It all came back to him again; the way she looked coming in the back door that night; eyes bright, trying to tell him . . . something, he didn't hear. He hit her in the mouth, at the last instant pulling to avoid her nose, knocked her against the table where she sat down hard on the floor. "What did you do that for?" she'd asked dreamily, her eyes still bright, and her mouth dripping blood. "Where were you all night?" he'd yelled, teetering over her, his legs watery and trembling. He'd drawn back his fist again but already sorry for the first blow, the blood he'd caused. "I wasn't gone all night," she'd said, turning her head back and forth heavily. "I didn't do anything. Why did you hit me?"

Ralph passed his open hand over his forehead, shut his eyes for a minute. "I guess I lost my head that night, all right. We were both in the wrong. You for leaving the party with Mitchell Anderson, and I for losing my head. I'm sorry."

"I'm sorry, too," she said. "Even so," she grinned, "you didn't have to knock hell out of me."

"I don't know — maybe I should've done more." He looked at her, and then they both had to laugh.

"How did we ever get onto this?" she asked.

"You brought it up," he said.

She shook her head. "The Franklins being here made me think of it, I guess." She pulled in her upper lip and stared at the floor. In a minute she straightened her shoulders and looked up. "If you'll move this ironing board for me, love, I'll make us a hot drink. A buttered rum: now how does that sound?"

"Good."

She went into the living room and turned on the lamp, bent to pick up a magazine by the endtable. He watched her hips under the plaid woolen skirt. She moved in front of the window by the large dining room table and stood looking out at the street light. She smoothed her palm down over her right hip, then began tucking in her blouse with the fingers of her right hand. He wondered what she was thinking. A car went by outside, and she continued to stand in front of the window.

After he stood the ironing board in its alcove on the porch, he sat down again and said, when she came into the room, "Well, what else went on between you and Mitchell Anderson that night? It's all right to talk about it now."

Anderson had left Harris less than two years ago to accept a position as Associate Professor of Speech and Drama at a new, four-year college the state was getting underway in southwestern California. He was in his early thirties, like everyone else they knew; a slender, moustached man with a rough, slightly pocked face; he was a casual, eccentric dresser and sometimes, Marian had told Ralph, laughing, he wore a green velvet smoking jacket to school. The girls in his classes were crazy about him, she said. He had thin, dark hair which he combed forward to cover the balding spot on the top of his head. Both he and his wife, Emily, a costume designer, had done a lot of acting and directing in Little Theater in the Bay Area before coming to Eureka. As a person, though, someone he liked to be around, it was something different as far as Ralph was concerned. Thinking about it, he decided he hadn't liked him from the beginning, and he was glad he was gone.

"What else?" he asked.

"Nothing," she said. "I'd rather not talk about it now, Ralph, if you don't mind. I was thinking about something else."

"What?"

"Oh . . . about the children, the dress I want Dorothea to have for next Easter; that sort of thing. Silly, unrelated things. And about the class I'm going to have tomorrow. Walt Whitman. Some of the kids didn't approve when I told them there was a, a bit of speculation Whitman was — how should I say it? — attracted to certain men." She laughed. "Really, Ralph, nothing else happened. I'm sorry I ever said anything about it."

"Okay."

He got up and went to the bathroom to wash cold water over his face. When he came out he leaned against the wall by the refrigerator and watched her measure out the sugar into the two cups and then stir in the rum. The water was boiling on the stove. The clock on the wall behind the table said 9:45.

"Look, honey, it's been brought up now," he said. "It was two or three years ago; there's no reason at all I can think of we can't talk about it if we want to, is there?"

"There's really nothing to talk about, Ralph."

"I'd like to know," he said vaguely.

"Know what?"

"Whatever else he did besides kiss you. We're adults. We haven't seen the Andersons in . . . a year at least. We'll probably never see them again. It happened a long time ago; as I see it, there's no reason whatever we can't talk about it." He was a little surprised at the level, reasoning quality in his voice. He sat down and looked at the tablecloth, and then looked up at her again. "Well?"

"Well," she said, laughing a little, tilting her head to one side, remembering. "No, Ralph, really; I'm not trying to be coy about it either: I'd just rather not."

"For Christ's sake, Marian! Now I mean it," he said, "if you don't tell me, it will make me angry."

She turned off the gas under the water and put her hand out on the stool; then sat down again, hooking her heels over the bottom step. She leaned forward, resting her arms across her knees. She picked at something on her skirt and then looked up.

"You remember Emily'd already gone home with the Beattys, and for some reason Mitchell had stayed on. He looked a little out of sorts that night to begin with. I don't know, maybe they weren't getting along . . . But I don't know that. But there were you and I, the Franklins, and Mitchell Anderson left. All of us a little drunk, if I remember rightly. I'm not sure how it happened, Ralph, but Mitchell and I just happened to find ourselves alone together in the kitchen for a minute. There was no whiskey left, only two or three bottles of that white wine we had. It must've been close to one o'clock because Mitchell said, 'If we hurry we can make it before the liquor store closes.' You know how he can be so theatrical when he wants? Softshoe stuff, facial expressions. . . ? Anyway, he was very witty about it all. At least it seemed that way at the time. And very drunk, too, I might add. So was I, for that matter . . . It was an impulse, Ralph, I swear. I don't know why I did it, don't ask me, but when he said, 'Let's go'—I agreed. We went out the back, where his car was parked. We went just like we were: we didn't even get our coats out of the closet. We thought we'd just be gone a few minutes. I guess we thought no one would miss us . . . I don't know what we thought . . . I don't know *why* I went, Ralph. It was an impulse, that's all that I can say. It was a wrong impulse." She paused. "It was my fault that night, Ralph, and I'm sorry. I shouldn't have done anything like that, I know that."

"Christ!" the word leaped out. "But you've always been that way, Marian!"

"That isn't true!"

His mind filled with a swarm of tiny accusations, and he tried to focus on one in particular. He looked down at his hands and noticed they
had the same lifeless feeling as they did when he woke up mornings. He
picked up the red pencil lying on the table, and then put it down again.

"I'm listening," he said.

"You're angry," she said. "You're swearing and getting all upset, Ralph.
For nothing, nothing, honey! . . . There's nothing else."

"Go on."

"*What* is the matter with us anyway? How did we ever get onto this
subject?"

"Go on, Marian."

"That's all, Ralph. I've told you. We went for a ride . . . We talked.
He kissed me. I still don't see how we could've been gone three hours;
whatever it was you said."

He remembered again the waiting, the unbearable weakness that
spread down through his legs when they'd been gone an hour, two
hours. It made him lean weakly against the corner of the house after
he'd gone outside; for a breath of air he said vaguely, pulling into his
coat, but really so that the embarrassed Franklins could themselves
leave without any more embarrassment; without having to take leave of
the absent host, or the vanished hostess. From the corner of the house,
standing behind the rose trellis in the soft, crumbly dirt, he watched
the Franklins get into their car and drive away. Anger and frustration
clogged inside him, then separated into little units of humiliation that
jumped against his stomach. He waited. Gradually the horror drained
away as he stood there, until finally nothing was left but a vast, empty
realization of betrayal. He went into the house and sat at this same table,
and he remembered his shoulder began to twitch and he couldn't stop it
even when he squeezed it with his fingers. An hour later, or two hours —
what difference did it make then? — she'd come in.

"Tell me the rest, Marian." And he knew there was more now. He felt
a slight fluttering start up in his stomach, and suddenly he didn't want
to know any more. "No. Do whatever you want. If you don't want to talk
about it, Marian, that's all right. Do whatever you want to, Marian. Actually, I guess I'd just as soon leave it at that."

He worked his shoulders against the smooth, solid chairback, then
balanced unsteadily on the two back legs. He thought fleetingly that he
would have been someplace else tonight, doing something else at this
very moment, if he hadn't married. He glanced around the kitchen. He
began to perspire and leaned forward, setting all the legs on the floor.

He took one of her cigarettes from the pack on the table. His hands were trembling as he struck the match.

"Ralph. You won't be angry, will you? Ralph? We're just talking. You won't, will you?" She had moved over to a chair at the table.

"I won't."

"Promise?"

"Promise."

She lit a cigarette. He had suddenly a great desire to see Robert and Dorothea; to get them up out of bed, heavy and turning in their sleep, and hold each of them on a knee, jiggle them until they woke up and began to laugh. He absently began to trace with his finger the outline of one of the tiny black coaches in the beige tablecloth. There were four miniature white prancing horses pulling each of the tiny coaches. The figure driving the horses had his arm up and was wearing a tall hat. Suitcases were strapped down on top of the coach, and what looked like a kerosene lamp hung from the side.

"We went straight to the liquor store, and I waited in the car till he came out. He had a sack in one hand and one of those plastic bags of ice in the other. He weaved a little getting into the car. I hadn't realized he was so drunk until we started driving again, and I noticed the way he was driving; terribly slow, and all hunched over the wheel with his eyes staring. We were talking about a lot of things that didn't make sense . . . I can't remember . . . Nietzsche . . . and Strindberg; he was directing *Miss Julie* second semester, you know, and something about Norman Mailer stabbing his wife in the breast a long time ago, and how he thought Mailer was going downhill anyway—a lot of crazy things like that. Then, I'll swear before God it was an accident, Ralph, he didn't know what he was doing, he made a wrong turn and we somehow wound up out by the golf course, right near Jane Van Eaton's. In fact, we pulled into her driveway to turn around and when we did Mitchell said to me, 'We might as well open one of these bottles.' He did, he opened it, and then he drove a little farther on down the road that goes around the green, you know, and comes out by the park? Actually, not too far from the Franklins' . . . And then he stopped for a minute in the middle of the road with his lights on, and we each took a drink out of the bottle. Then he said, said he'd hate to think of me being stabbed in the breast. I guess he was still thinking about Mailer's wife. And then . . . I can't say it, Ralph . . . I know you'd get angry."

"I won't get angry, Marian," he said slowly. His thoughts seemed to move lazily, as if he were in a dream, and he was able to take in only one thing at a time she was telling him. At the same time he noticed a peculiar alertness taking hold of his body.

"Go on. Then what, Marian?"

"You aren't angry, are you? Ralph?"

"No. But I'm getting interested, though."

They both had to laugh, and for a minute everything was all right. He leaned across the table to light another cigarette for her, and they smiled at each other; just like any other night. He struck another match, held it a while, and then brought the match, almost to burn his fingers, up under the end of the cigarette that protruded at an angle from his lips. He dropped the burned match into the ashtray and stared at it before looking up.

"Go on."

"I don't know ... things seemed to happen fast after that. He drove up the road a little and turned off someplace, I don't know, maybe right onto the green ... and started kissing me. Then he said, said he'd like to kiss my breast. I said I didn't think we should. I said, 'What about Emily?' He said I didn't know her. He got the car going again, and then he stopped again and just sort of slumped over and put his head on my lap. God! It sounds so vulgar now, I know, but it didn't seem that way at all then. I felt like, like I was losing my innocence somehow, Ralph. For the first time — that night I realized I was really, really doing something wrong, something I wasn't supposed to do and that might hurt people. I shouldn't be there, I felt. And I felt ... like it was the first time in my life I'd ever *intentionally* done anything wrong or hurtful and gone on doing it, knowing I shouldn't be. Do you know what I mean, Ralph? Like some of the characters in Henry James? I felt that way. Like ... for the first time ... my innocence ... something was happening."

"You can dispense with that shit," he cut in. "Get off it, Marian! Go on! Then what? Did he caress you? Did he? Did he try to feel you up, Marian? Tell me!"

And then she hurried on, trying to get over the hard spots quickly, and he sat with his hands folded on the table and watched her lips out of which dropped the frightful words. His eyes skipped around the kitchen — stove, cupboards, toaster, radio, coffeepot, window, curtains, refrigerator, breadbox, napkin holder, stove, cupboards, toaster ... back to her face. Her dark eyes glistened under the overhead light. He felt a peculiar desire for her flicker through his thighs at what she was leading up to, and at the same time he had to check an urge to stand up yelling, smash his fist into her face.

" 'Shall we have a go at it?' he said."

"Shall we have a go at it?" Ralph repeated.

"I'm to blame. If anyone should, should be blamed for it, I'm to blame. He said he'd leave it all up to me, I could . . . could do . . . whatever I wanted." Tears welled out of her eyes, started down her cheeks. She looked down at the table, blinked rapidly.

He shut his eyes. He saw a barren field under a heavy, gray sky; a fog moving in across the far end. He shook his head, tried to admit other possibilities, other conclusions. He tried to bring back that night two years ago, imagine himself coming into the kitchen just as she and Mitchell were at the door, hear himself telling her in a hearty voice, Oh no, no; you're not going out for liquor with that Mitchell Anderson! He's drunk, and he isn't a good driver to boot. You've got to go to bed now and get up with little Robert and Dorothea in the morning . . . Stop! Stop where you are.

He opened his eyes, raised his eyebrows as if he were just waking up. She had a hand up over her face and was crying silently, her shoulders rounded and moving in little jerks.

"Why did you go with him, Marian?" he asked desperately.

She shook her head without looking up.

Then, suddenly, he knew. His mind buckled. *Cuckold.* For a minute he could only stare helplessly at his hands. Then he wanted to pass it off somehow, say it was all right, it was two years ago, adults, etc. He wanted to forgive: *I forgive you.* But he could not forgive. He couldn't forgive her this. His thoughts skittered around the Middle Ages, touched on Arthur and Guinevere, surged on to the outraged husbandry of the eighteenth-century dramatists, came to a sullen halt with Karenin. But what had any of them to do with him? What were they? They were nothing. Nothing. Figments. They did not exist. Their discoveries, their disintegrations, adjustments, did not at all relate to him. No relation. What then? What did it all mean? What is the nature of a book? his mind roared.

"Christ!" he said, springing up from the table. "*Jesus Christ.* Christ, no, Marian!"

"No, no," she said, throwing her head back.

"You let him!"

"No, no, Ralph."

"You let him! Didn't you? Didn't you? Answer me!" he yelled. "Did he come in you? Did you let him come in you? That s-s-swine," he said, his teeth chattering. "That bastard."

"Listen, listen to me, Ralph. I swear to you he didn't, he didn't come. He didn't come in me." She rocked from side to side in the chair, shaking her head.

"You wouldn't let him! That's it, isn't it? Yes, yes, you had your scruples. What'd you do — catch it in your hands? Oh God! God *damn* you!"

"God!" she said, getting up, holding out her hands. "Are we crazy, Ralph? Have we lost our minds? Ralph? Forgive me, Ralph. Forgive —"

"Don't touch me! Get away from me, Marian."

"In God's name, Ralph! Ralph! Please, Ralph. For the children's sake, Ralph. Don't go, Ralph. Please don't go, Ralph!" Her eyes were white and large, and she began to pant in her fright. She tried to head him off, but he took her by the shoulder and pushed her out of the way.

"Forgive me, Ralph! *Please.* Ralph!"

He slammed the kitchen door, started across the porch. Behind him, she jerked open the door, clattered over the dustpan as she rushed onto the porch. She took his arm at the porch door, but he shook her loose. "Ralph!" But he jumped down the steps onto the walk.

When he was across the driveway and walking rapidly down the sidewalk, he could hear her at the door yelling for him. Her voice seemed to be coming through a kind of murk. He looked back: she was still calling, limned against the doorway. My God, he thought, what a sideshow it was. Fat men and bearded ladies.

2.

He had to stop and lean against a car for a few minutes before going on. But two well-dressed couples were coming down the sidewalk toward him, and the man on the outside, near the curb, was telling a story in a loud voice. The others were already laughing. Ralph pushed off from the car and crossed the street. In a few minutes he came to Blake's, where he stopped some afternoons for a beer with Dick Koenig before picking up the children from nursery school.

It was dark inside. The air was warm and heavy with the odor of beer and seemed to catch at the top of his throat and make it hard for him to swallow. Candles flickered dimly in long-necked wine bottles at some of the tables along the left wall when he closed the door. He glimpsed shadowy figures of men and women talking with their heads close together. One of the couples, near the door, stopped talking and looked up at him. A box-like fixture in the ceiling revolved overhead, throwing out pale red and green lights. Two men sat at the end of the bar, and a dark cutout of a man leaned over the jukebox in the corner, his hands splayed out on each side of the glass.

The man is going to play something. Ralph stands in the center of the floor, watches him. He sways, rubs his wrist against his forehead, and starts out.

"Ralph! — Mr. Wyman, sir!"

He stopped, looked around. David Parks was calling to him from behind the bar. Ralph walked over, leaned heavily against the bar before sliding onto a stool.

"Should I draw one, Mr. Wyman?" He had the glass in his hand, smiling.

He worked evenings and weekends for Charley Blake. He was 26, married, had two children, babies. He attended Harris Junior College on a football scholarship, and worked besides. He had three mouths to feed now, along with his own. Four mouths altogether. Not like it used to be. David Parks. He had a white bar towel slung over his shoulder.

Ralph nodded, watched him fill the glass.

He held the glass at an angle under the tap, slowly straightened it as the glass filled, closed the tap, and cut off the head with a smooth, professional air. He wiped the towel across the gleaming surface of the bar and set the glass in front of Ralph, still smiling.

"How's it going, Mr. Wyman? Didn't hear you come in." He put his foot up on a shelf under the bar. "Who's going to win the game next week, Mr. Wyman?"

Ralph shook his head, brought the beer to his lips. His shoulders ached with fatigue from being held rigid the last hour.

David Parks coughed faintly. "I'll buy you one, Mr. Wyman. This one's on me." He put his leg down, nodded assurance, and reached under his apron into his pocket.

"Here. I have it right here." Ralph pulled out some change, examined it in his hand from the light cast by a bare bulb on a stand next to the cash register. A quarter, nickel, two dimes, pennies. He laid down the quarter and stood up, pushing the change back into his pocket. The man was still in front of the jukebox, leaning his weight on one leg. The phone rang.

Ralph opened the door.

"Mr. Wyman! Mr. Wyman, for you, sir."

Outside he turned around, trying to decide what to do. He wanted to be alone, but at the same time he thought he'd feel better if other people were around. Not here though. His heart was fluttering, as if he'd been running. The door opened behind him and a man and woman came out. Ralph stepped out of the way and they got into a car parked at the curb. He recognized the woman as the receptionist at the children's dentist. He started off walking.

He walked to the end of the block, crossed the street, and walked another block before he decided to head downtown. It was eight or ten blocks and he walked hurriedly, his hands balled into his pockets, his shoes smacking the pavement. He kept blinking his eyes and thought it incredible he could still feel tired and fogged after all that had happened. He shook his head. He would have liked to sit someplace for a while and think about it, but he knew he could not sit, could not yet think about it. He remembered a man he saw once sitting on a curb in Arcata: an old man with a growth of beard and a brown wool cap who just sat there with his arms between his legs. But a minute later it snapped into his mind, and for the first time he tried to get a clear look at it; himself, Marian, the children — his world. But it was impossible. He wondered if anyone could ever stand back far enough from life to see it whole, all in one piece. He thought of an enormous French tapestry they'd seen two or three years ago that took up one wall of a room in the De Young Museum. He tried to imagine how all this would seem twenty years from now, but there was nothing. He couldn't picture the children any older, and when he tried to think about Marian and himself, there was only a blank space. Then, for a minute, he felt profoundly indifferent, somehow above it, as if it did not concern him. He thought of Marian without any emotion at all. He remembered her as he had seen her a little while ago; face crumpled, tears running off her nose. Then Marian on the floor, holding onto the chair, blood on her teeth: "Why did you hit me?" . . . Marian reaching under her dress to unfasten her garter belt . . . She raises her dress slowly as she leans back in the seat.

He stopped and thought he was going to be sick. He moved off onto the edge of a lawn. He cleared his throat several times and kept swallowing, looked up as a car of yelling teenagers went by and gave him a long blast on their musical horn. Yes, there was a vast amount of evil loose in the world, he thought, and it only awaited an opportunity, the propitious moment to manifest itself . . . But that was an academic notion. A kind of retreat. He spat ahead of him on the walk and put his heel on it. He mustn't let himself find solace in that kind of thinking. Not now. Not anymore, if he could help it. If he was going to think about it — and he knew he must, sooner or later tonight — he must begin simply, from the essentials: with the fact that his wife had let herself be fucked, yes, fucked, by another man. And this, this he *knew* was evil: he felt it in his bones.

He came to Second Street, the part of town people called Two Street. It started here at Shelton, under the street light where the old rooming houses ended, and ran for four or five blocks on down to the pier, where fishing boats tied up. He'd been down here once, two years ago, to a second-hand store to look through the dusty shelves of old books. There was a liquor store across the street, and he could see a man standing outside in front of the glass door, looking at a newspaper.

Ralph crossed under the street light, read the headlines on the newspaper the man had been looking at, and went inside. A bell over the door tinkled. He hadn't noticed a bell that tinkled over a door since he was a child. He bought some cigarettes and went out again.

He walked down the street, looking in the windows. All the places were closed for the night, or vacated. Some of the windows had signs taped inside: a dance, a Shrine Circus that had come and gone last summer, an election—Vote For Fred C. Walters, Councilman. One of the windows he looked through had sinks and pipe-joints scattered around on a table. Everything dark. He came to a Vic Tanney Gym where he could see light coming under the curtains pulled across a big window. He could hear water splashing in the pool inside, and the hollow echo of voices calling across the water.

There was more light now, coming from the bars and cafés on both sides of the street. More people, groups of three or four but now and then a man by himself, or a woman in slacks walking rapidly. He stopped in front of the window of one place and watched some Negroes shooting pool. Gray cigarette smoke drifted around the lights over the table. One of the Negroes, who was chalking his cue, had his hat on and a cigarette in his mouth. He said something to another Negro, looked intently at the balls, and slowly leaned over the table.

He walked on, stopped in front of Jim's Oyster House. He had never been here before, had never been to any of these places before. Over the door the name was in yellow light bulbs: JIM'S OYSTER HOUSE. Above the lights, fixed to an iron grill, a huge neon-lighted clam shell with a man's legs sticking out. The torso was hidden in the shell and the legs flashed red, on and off. Ralph lit another cigarette from the one he had, and pushed open the door.

It was crowded. A lot of people were bunched on the floor, their arms wrapped around each other or hanging loosely on someone's shoulders. The men in the band were just getting up from their chairs for an intermission. He had to excuse himself several times trying to get to the bar, and once a drunken woman took hold of his coat. There were no stools and he had to stand at the end of the bar between a coast guardsman and a shrunken-faced man in denims. Neither of them spoke. The coast guardsman had his white cap off and his elbows propped out in front of him, a hand on each side of his face. He stared at his glass without looking up. The other man shook his head and then pointed with his narrow chin two or three times at the coast guardsman. Ralph put his arm up and signaled the bartender. Once, Ralph thought he heard the shrunken-faced man say something, but he didn't answer.

In the mirror he could see the men in the band get up from the table where they'd been sitting. Ralph picked up his glass, turned around, and leaned back against the bar. He closed his eyes and opened them. Someone unplugged the jukebox, and the music ground to a stop. The musicians wore white shirts and dark slacks with little string ties around their necks. There was a fireplace with blue gas flames behind a stack of metal logs, and the band platform was to the side, a few feet away. One of the men plucked the strings of his electric guitar, said something to the others with a grin, and leaned back in his chair. They began to play.

The music was country, or western, and not as bad as Ralph had imagined. He raised his glass and drained it. Down the bar he could hear a woman say angrily, "Well there's going to be trouble, that's all I've got to say about it!" The musicians came to the end of the number and swung into another. One of the men, the bass player, came to the microphone and began to sing, but Ralph couldn't understand the words.

When the band took another intermission, he looked around for the toilet. He could make out some doors opening and closing at the far end of the bar, and headed in that direction, staggering a little. Over one of the doors was a rack of antlers. He saw a man go in, and he saw another man catch the door and come out. Inside, waiting in line behind three or four others, he found himself staring at the penciled picture of a huge pair of female thighs and pubic area on the wall over the pocket-comb machine. Underneath the drawing was scrawled, Eat ME, and a little lower down someone had added Betty M. Eats It — RA 52275. The man ahead of him moved up, and Ralph took two steps forward, his eyes still fastened on the drawing. Finally, he moved up over the bowl and urinated so hard it was like a bolt going down through his legs. He sighed luxuriously when he was through, leaned forward and let his head rest against the wall. His life was changed from tonight on. Were there many other men, he wondered drunkenly, who could look at one singular event in their lives and perceive the workings of the catastrophe that hereinafter sets their lives on a different course? Are there many who can perceive the necessary changes and adjustments that must necessarily and inevitably follow? Probably so, he decided after a minute's reflection. He stood there a while longer, and then he looked down: he'd urinated on his fingers.

He moved over to the wash basin, ran water over his hands without using the dirty bar of soap. As he was unrolling the towel, he suddenly leaned over and put his face up close to the pitted mirror, looked into his eyes. A face: that was all. Hardly even familiar. There seemed nothing fixed or permanent about it. His nose just hung there, occupying a space, spotted with several tiny blackheads he hadn't noticed before. His skin was slightly chapped on the inside of one cheek. His lips . . . like any other lips. Only his eyes under the narrow eyebrows seemed out of the ordinary, like shiny glass objects. They moved as he moved, followed him around the mirror, looked out at him steadily when he looked straight in. He put his finger up to the mirror and touched the glass, moved away as a man tried to get past him to the sink.

As he was going out the door he noticed another door he hadn't seen at the end of a short, narrow corridor. He went over to it and looked through the glass plate in the door at four card-players around a green felt table. It seemed still and restful inside. He couldn't hear anything, and the silent movements of the men appeared languorous and heavy with meaning. He leaned against the glass, watching. One of the men at the table, the man dealing, looked up at him and stared until he moved away. He weaved back to the bar and thought how the scene reminded him of Cézanne's Card-Players. But did it really?

There was a flourish of guitars and people began whistling and clapping. A plump, middle-aged woman in a white evening dress was being helped onto the platform. She kept trying to pull back and was shaking her head and laughing. Finally she took the mike and made a little curtsy. The people whistled and stamped their feet. He thought of the scene in the card room. No, they didn't remind him of the Cézanne; that was certain. He suddenly had an enormous desire to watch them play, be in the same room with them. He could watch, even if he didn't play. He'd seen some empty chairs along the wall. He leaned against the bar, took out his wallet, keeping his hands up over the sides as he looked to see how much he had. He had eighteen dollars — just in case he was asked to play a hand or two. Without thinking anymore about it, he worked his way to the back. Behind him, the woman began to sing in a low, drowsy voice. Ralph stepped into the corridor, and then pushed open the door to the card room.

The man who'd looked up at him was still dealing.

"Decided to join us?" he said, sweeping Ralph with his eyes and looking down at the table again. Two of the others raised their eyes for an instant then looked back at the cards flashing around the table. As they picked up their cards, the man sitting with his back to Ralph, a short, fat man who breathed heavily through his nose, turned around in his chair and glared at him, and Ralph moved back a step.

"Benny, bring another chair!" the dealer called to an old man sweeping under a table that had the chairs turned up on the top.

"That's all right," Ralph said. "I'll just watch a few hands."

"Suit yourself."

He sat down in a chair against the wall, a few feet away from the table. No one spoke. The only sounds were the *clat-clat* of the chips as the men dropped them into the center of the table, and the shuffle and sharp flicking of the cards. The dealer was a large man, thirty or so; he wore a white shirt, open at the collar, and with the sleeves turned back once exposing the forearms covered with black, curling hair. But his small hands were white and delicate-looking, and there was a gold band on his ring finger. Around the table a tall, white-haired man with a cigar, the fat man, and a small dark man with a gray suit and a tie. An Italian, Ralph thought. He smoked one cigarette after another, and when he swallowed, the tie over his Adam's apple moved up and down. The old man, Benny, was wiping with a cloth around the cash register near the door. It was warm and quiet. Now and then Ralph could hear a horn blare out in the street. He drew a long breath and closed his eyes, opened them when he heard steps.

"Want anything to drink?" Benny asked, carrying a chair to the table.

Ralph said he'd have something; bourbon and water. He gave him a dollar and pulled out of his coat. Benny took the coat and hung it up by the door as he went out. Two of the men moved their chairs and Ralph sat down across from the dealer.

"How's it going?" he said to Ralph, not looking up.

For a minute Ralph wasn't sure whether it was directed at him. "All right," he said.

Then, as Ralph watched the other men play their cards, the dealer said gently, still not looking at him, "Low ball or five card. Table stakes, five dollar limit on raises."

Ralph nodded, and when the hand was finished he bought fifteen dollars' worth of blue chips.

He watched the cards as they flashed around the table, picked up his as he'd seen the tall, white-haired man do; sliding one card under the corner of another as each card fell face down in front of him. He raised his eyes once and looked at the expressionless faces of the others. He wondered if it'd ever happened to any of them. In half an hour he had won two hands and without counting the small pile of chips in front of him, he thought he must still have fifteen or even twenty dollars.

Benny brought a tray of drinks, and Ralph paid for his with a chip. He took out his handkerchief and wiped the perspiration from his face, aware how tired he was. But he felt better for some reason. He had come a long way since that evening. But it was only . . . a few hours ago. And had he really come so far? Was anything different, or anything resolved?

"You in or out?" the fat man asked. "Clyde, what's the bet, for Christ's sake?" he said to the dealer.

"Three dollars."

"In," Ralph said. "I'm in." He put three chips into the pot. "I have to be going though . . . another hand or so."

The dealer looked up and then back at his cards.

The Italian said: "Stick around. You really want some action we can go to my place when we finish here."

"No, that's all right. Enough action tonight . . . I just have to be going pretty soon." He shifted in the chair, glanced at their faces, and then fixed upon a small green plaque on the wall behind the table. "You know," he said, "I just found out tonight. My wife, my wife played around with another guy two years ago. Can you imagine?" He cleared his throat.

One of the men snickered; the Italian. The fat man said, "You can't trust 'em, that's all. Women are no damn good!"

No one else said anything; the tall, white-haired man laid down his cards and lit his cigar that had gone out. He stared at Ralph as he puffed, then shook out the match and picked up his cards.

The dealer looked up again, resting his open hands palms-up on the table. "You work here in town?" he said to Ralph. "I haven't seen you around."

"I live here. I, I just haven't gotten around much." He felt drained, oddly relaxed.

"We playing or not?" the fat man said. "Clyde?"

"Hold your shirt," the dealer said.

"For Christ's sake," the white-haired man said quietly, holding onto each word, "I've never seen such cards."

"I'm in three dollars," the fat man said. "Who's going to stay?"

Ralph couldn't remember his hole card. His neck was stiff, and he fought against the desire to close his eyes. He'd never been so tired. All the joints and bones and muscles in his body seemed to radiate and call to his attention. He looked at his card; a seven of clubs. His next card, face-up, was an ace. He started to drop out. He edged in his chair, picked up his glass but it was empty.

"Benny!" the dealer said sharply.

His next card was a king. The betting went up to the five dollar limit. More royalty; the Queen of Diamonds. He looked once more at his hole card to see if he might somehow have been mistaken: the seven of clubs.

Benny came back with another tray of drinks and said, "They're closing in ten minutes, Clyde."

The next card, the Jack of Spades, fell on top of Ralph's queen. Ralph stared. The white-haired man turned over his cards. For the first time the dealer gazed straight into Ralph's eyes, and Ralph felt his toes pull back in his shoes as the man's eyes pierced through to, what seemed to Ralph, his craven heart.

"I'll bet two dollars to see it," the fat man said.

A shiver traced up and down Ralph's spine. He hesitated, and then, in a grand gesture, called, and recklessly raised five dollars, his last chips.

The tall, white-haired man edged his chair closer to the table.

The dealer had a pair of eights showing. Still looking at Ralph, he picked ten chips off one of the stacks in front of him. He spread them in two groups of five near the pile at the center of the table.

"Call."

The Italian hesitated, and then swallowed and turned over his cards. He looked at the dealer's cards, and then he looked at Ralph's.

The fat man smacked his cards down and glared at Ralph.

All of them watched as Ralph turned over his card and lurched up from the table.

Outside, in the alley, he took out his wallet again, let his fingers number the bills he had left: two dollars, and some change in his pocket. Enough for something to eat. Ham and eggs, perhaps. But he wasn't hungry. He leaned back against the damp brick wall of the building, trying to think.

A car turned into the alley, stopped, and backed out again. He started walking. He went past the front of the Oyster House again, going back the way he'd come. He stayed close to the buildings, out of the way of the loud groups of men and women streaming up and down the sidewalk. He heard a woman in a long coat say to the man she was with, "It isn't that way at all, Bruce. You don't understand."

He stopped when he came to the liquor store. Inside he moved up to the counter and stared at the long, orderly rows of bottles. He bought a half-pint of rum and some more cigarettes. The palm trees on the label of the bottle, the large drooping fronds with the lagoon in the background, had caught his eye. The clerk, a thin, bald man wearing suspenders, put the rum in a paper sack without a word and rang up the sale. Ralph could feel the man's eyes on him as he stood in front of the magazine rack, swaying a little and looking at the covers. Once he glanced up in the mirror over his head and caught the man staring at him from behind the counter; his arms were folded over his chest and his bald head gleamed in the reflected light. Finally the man turned off one of the lights in the back of the store and said, "Closing it up, buddy."

Outside again, Ralph turned around once and started down another street, toward the pier; he thought he'd like to see the water with the lights reflected on it. He wondered how far he would drop tonight before he began to level off. He opened the sack as he walked, broke the seal on the little bottle, and stopped in a doorway to take a long drink. He could hardly taste it. He crossed some old streetcar tracks and turned onto another, darker street. He could already hear the waves splashing under the pier.

As he came up to the front of a dark, wooden building, he heard someone move in the doorway. A heavy Negro in a leather jacket stepped out in front of him and said, "Just a minute there, man. Where you think you're goin'?"

As Ralph tried to move around him, frightened, the man said, "Christ, man, that's my feet you're steppin' on!"

Before he could move away the Negro hit him hard in the stomach, and when Ralph groaned and bent over, the man hit him in the nose with his open hand, knocking him back against the wall where he sat down in a rush of pain and dizziness. He had one leg turned under, trying to raise himself up, when the Negro slapped him on the cheek and knocked him sprawling onto the pavement. He was aware of a hand slipping into his pants-pocket over the hip, felt his wallet slide out. He groaned and tried to sit up again as the man neatly stripped his watch over his hand. He kicked the wet sack of broken glass, and then sprinted down the street.

Ralph got his legs under him again. As if from a great distance he heard someone yell, "There's a man hurt over here!" and he struggled up to his feet. Then he heard someone running toward him over the pavement, and a car pulled up to the curb, a car door slammed. He wanted to say, It's all right, please, it's all right, as a man came up to him and stopped a few feet away, watching. But the words seemed to ball in his throat and something like a gasp escaped his lips. He tried to draw a breath and the air piled up in his throat again, as if there were an obstruction in the passage; and then the noise broke even louder through his nose and mouth. He leaned his shoulder against the doorway and wept. In the few seconds he stood there, shaking, his mind seemed to empty out, and a vast sense of wonderment flowed through him as he thought again of Marian, why she had betrayed him. Then, as a policeman with a big flashlight walked over to him, he brought himself up with a shudder and became silent.

3.

Birds darted overhead in the graying mist. He still couldn't see them, but he could hear their sharp *jueet-jueet*. He stopped and looked up, kept his eyes fixed in one place; then he saw them, no larger than his hand, dozens of them, wheeling and darting just under the heavy overcast. He wondered if they were seabirds, birds that only came in off the ocean this time of morning. He'd never seen any birds around Eureka in the winter except now and then a big, lumbering seagull. He remembered once, a long time ago, walking into an old abandoned house — the Marshall place, near Uncle Jack's in Springfield, Oregon — how the sparrows kept flying in and out of the broken windows, flying around the rafters where they had their nests, and then flying out the windows again, trying to lead him away.

It was getting light. The overcast seemed to be lifting and was turning light-gray with patches of white clouds showing through here and there. The street was black with the mist that was still falling, and he had to be careful not to step on the snails that trailed across the damp sidewalk.

A car with its lights on slowed down as it went past, but he didn't look up. Another car passed. In a minute, another. He looked: four men, two in front, two in the back. One of the men in the back seat, wearing a hat, turned around and looked at him through the back window.

Mill workers. The first shift of plywood mill workers going to work at Georgia-Pacific. It was Monday morning. He turned the corner, walked past Blake's; dark, the Venetian blinds pulled over the windows and two empty beer bottles someone had left standing like sentinels beside the door. It was cold, and he walked slowly, crossing his arms now and then and rubbing his shoulders.

He'd refused the policeman's offer of a ride home. He couldn't think of a more shabby ending to the night than riding home in the early morning in a black and white police car. After the doctor at Redwood Memorial Hospital had examined him, felt around over his neck with his fingers while Ralph had sat with his eyes closed, the doctor had made two X-rays and then put Merthiolate and a small bandage on his cheek. Then the policemen had taken him to the station where for two hours he'd had to look at photographs in large manila folders of Negro men. Finally, he had told the officer, "I'm sorry, but I'm afraid everyone looks pretty much alike right now." The man had shrugged, closed the folder. "They come and go," he'd said, staring at Ralph. "Sometimes it's hard to nail them on the right charge due to lack of proper identification. If we bring in some suspects we'll have you back here to help identify." He stared at Ralph a minute longer, then nodded curtly.

He came up the street to his house. He could see his front porch light on, but the rest of the house was dark. He crossed the lawn and went around to the back. He turned the knob, and the door opened quietly. He stepped onto the porch and shut the door. He waited a moment, then opened the kitchen door.

The house was quiet. There was the tall stool beside the draining board. There was the table where they'd sat. How long ago? He remembered he'd just gotten up off the couch, where he'd been working, and come into the kitchen and sat down . . . He looked at the clock over the stove: 7:00 a.m. He could see the dining room table with the lace cloth, the heavy glass centerpiece of red flamingos, their wings opened. The draperies behind the table were open. Had she stood at that window watching for him? He moved over to the door and stepped onto the living room carpet. Her coat was thrown over the couch, and in the pale light he could make out a large ashtray full of her cork cigarette ends on one of the cushions. He noticed the phone directory open on the coffee table as he went by. He stopped at the partially open door to their bedroom. For an instant he resisted the impulse to look in on her, and then with his finger he pushed open the door a few inches. She was sleeping, her head off the pillow, turned toward the wall, and her hair black against the sheet. The covers were bunched around her shoulders and had pulled up from the foot of the bed. She was on her side, her secret body slightly bent at the hips, her thighs closed together protectively. He stared for a minute. What, after all, should he do? Pack his things, now, and leave? Go to a hotel room until he can make other arrangements? Sleep on the extra bed in the little storage room upstairs? How should a man act, given the circumstances? The things that had been said last night. There was no undoing that — nor the other. There was no going back, but what course was he to follow now?

In the kitchen he laid his head down on his arms over the table. How should a man act? *How should a man act?* It kept repeating itself. Not just now, in this situation, for today and tomorrow, but every day on this earth. He felt suddenly there was an answer, that he somehow held the answer himself and that it was very nearly out if only he could think about it a little longer. Then he heard Robert and Dorothea stirring. He sat up slowly and tried to smile as they came into the kitchen.

"Daddy, daddy," they both said, running over to him in their pajamas.

"Tell us a story, daddy," Robert said, getting onto his lap.

"He can't tell us a story now," Dorothea said. "It's *too* early in the morning, isn't it, daddy?"

"What's that on your face, daddy?" Robert said, pointing at the bandage.

"Let me see!" Dorothea said. "Let me see, daddy."

"*Poor* daddy," Robert said.

"What *did* you do to your face, daddy?"

"It's nothing," Ralph said. "It's all right, sweetheart. Here, get down, Robert, I hear your mother."

Ralph stepped into the bathroom and locked the door.

"Is your father here?" he heard Marian ask the children. "Where is he, in the bathroom? Ralph?"

"Mama, mama!" Dorothea exclaimed. "Daddy has a big, big bandage on his face!"

"Ralph," she turned the knob. "Ralph, let me in, please, darling. Ralph? Please let me in, darling, I want to see you. Ralph? Please?"

"Go away, Marian. Just let me alone a while, all right?"

"Please, Ralph, open the door for a minute, darling. I just want to see you, Ralph. Ralph? The children said you were hurt. What's wrong, darling? . . . Ralph?"

"Will you please be quiet, please?"

She waited at the door for a minute, turned the knob again, and then he could hear her moving around the kitchen, getting the children breakfast, trying to answer their questions.

He looked at himself in the mirror, then pulled off the bandage and tried gently with warm water and a cloth to wipe off some of the red stain. In a minute or two he gave it up. He turned away from the mirror and sat down heavily on the edge of the bathtub, began to unlace his shoes. No cowardly Aegisthus waiting for him here, no Clytemnestra. He sat there with a shoe in his hand and looked at the white, streamlined clipper ships making their way across the pale blue of the plastic shower curtain. He unbuttoned his shirt, leaned over the bathtub with a sigh, and dropped in the plug. He opened the hot water handle, and the steam rose.

As he stood naked a minute on the smooth tile before getting into the water, he gathered in his fingers the slack flesh over his ribs, looked at himself again in the clouded mirror. He started when Marian called his name.

"Ralph. The children are in their room playing ... I called Von Williams and said you wouldn't be in today, and I'm going to stay home." She waited and then said, "I have a nice breakfast on the stove for you, darling, when you're through with your bath ... Ralph?"

"It's all right, Marian. I'm not hungry."

"Ralph ... Come out, darling."

He stayed in the bathroom until he heard her upstairs over the bathroom in the children's room. She was telling them: settle down and get dressed; didn't they want to play with Warren and Jeannie?

He went through the house and into the bedroom where he shut the door. He looked at the bed before he crawled in. He lay on his back and stared at the ceiling. *How should a man act?* It had assumed immense importance in his mind, was far more crucial and requiring of an answer than the other thing, the event two years ago ... He remembered he'd just gotten up off the couch in the living room where he'd been working, and come into the kitchen and sat down ... The light ornament in the ceiling began to sway. He snapped open his eyes and turned onto his side as Marian came into the room.

She took off her robe and sat down on the edge of the bed. She put her hand under the covers and began gently stroking the lower part of his back. "Ralph," she murmured.

He tensed at her cold fingers, and then, gradually, he relaxed. He imagined he was floating on his back in the heavy, milky water of Juniper Lake, where he'd spent one summer years ago, and someone was calling to him, Come in, Ralph, Come in. But he kept on floating and didn't answer, and the soft rising waves laved his body.

He woke again as her hand moved over his hip. Then it traced his groin before flattening itself against his stomach. She was in bed now, pressing the length of her body against his and moving gently back and forth with him. He waited a minute, and then he turned to her and their eyes met.

Her eyes were filled and seemed to contain layer upon layer of shimmering color and reflection, thicker and more opaque farther in, and almost transparent at the lustrous surface. Then, as he gazed even deeper, he glimpsed in first one pupil and then the other, the cameo-like, perfect reflection of his own strange and familiar face. He continued to stare, marveling at the changes he dimly felt taking place inside him.

1969

JOYCE CAROL OATES
BY THE RIVER

from *December*

JOYCE CAROL OATES was born in Lockport, New York, in 1938 and was raised on her parents' farm. She was fourteen when her grandmother gave her her first typewriter. Oates went on a scholarship to Syracuse University, where she majored in English.

After Oates stumbled upon the fact that one of her stories had been cited in the honor roll of *The Best American Short Stories,* she assembled the fourteen stories in her first book, *By the North Gate.* It was the first of almost seventy books. In addition to short stories and novels, she regularly publishes poems, plays, literary criticism, and essays. Of her prolific nature, she once said, "A writer who has published as many books as I have has developed, of necessity, a hide like a rhino's, while inside there dwells a frail, hopeful butterfly of a spirit." Among her numerous awards are the National Book Award, the Rea Award, the PEN/Malamud Award, the Bram Stoker Award, and five lifetime achievement awards.

Oates was once asked, "What is the function of violence in your work?" She replied, "Given the number of pages I have written, and the 'violent' incidents dispersed throughout them, I rather doubt that I am a violent writer in any meaningful sense of the word . . . Real life is much more chaotic."

Oates has taught at Princeton University since 1978.

★

HELEN THOUGHT: "AM I in love again, some new kind of love? Is that why I'm here?"

She was sitting in the waiting room of the Yellow Bus Lines station; she knew the big old room with its dirty tile floor and its solitary telephone booth in the corner and its candy machine and cigarette machine and popcorn machine by heart. Everything was familiar, though she had been gone for four months, even the old woman with the dyed red hair who sold tickets and had been selling them there, behind that counter, for as long as Helen could remember. Years ago, before Helen's marriage, she and her girl friends would be driven in to town by someone's father and after they tired of walking around town they would stroll over to the bus station to watch the buses unload. They were anxious to see who was getting off, but few of the passengers who got off stayed in Oriskany—they were just passing through, stopping for a rest and a drink, and their faces seemed to say that they didn't think much of the town. Nor did they seem to think much of the girls from the country who stood around in their colorful dresses and smiled shyly at strangers, not knowing any better: they were taught to be kind to people, to smile first, you never knew who it might be. So now Helen was back in Oriskany, but this time she had come in on a bus herself. Had ridden alone, all the way from the city of Derby, all alone, and was waiting for her father to pick her up so she could go back to her old life without any more fuss.

It was hot. Flies crawled languidly around; a woman with a small sickly-faced baby had to keep waving them away. The old woman selling tickets looked at Helen as if her eyes were drawn irresistibly that way, as if she knew every nasty rumor and wanted to let Helen know that she knew. Helen's forehead broke out in perspiration and she stood, abruptly, wanting to dislodge that old woman's stare. She went over to the candy machine but did not look at the candy bars; she looked at herself in the mirror. Her own reflection always made her feel better. Whatever went on inside her head—and right now she felt nervous about something—had nothing to do with the way she looked, her smooth gentle skin and the faint freckles on her forehead and nose and the cool, innocent green of her eyes; she was just a girl from the country and anyone in town would know that, even if they didn't know her personally, one of those easy, friendly girls who hummed to themselves and seemed always to be glancing up as if expecting something pleasant. Her light brown hair curled back lazily toward her ears, cut short now because it was the style; in high school she had worn it long. She watched her eyes in the mirror. No alarm there really. She would be back home in an hour or so. Not her husband's home, of course, but her parents' home. And her face in the mirror was the face she had always seen—twenty-two she was now, and to her that seemed very old, but she looked no different from the way she had looked on her wedding day five years ago.

But it was stupid to try to link together those two Helens, she thought. She went back to the row of seats and sat heavily. If the old woman was still watching, she did not care. A sailor in a soiled white uniform sat nearby, smoking, watching her but not with too much interest; he had other girls to recall. Helen opened her purse and looked inside at nothing and closed it again. The man she had been living with in the city for four months had told her it was stupid — no, he had not used that word; he said something fancy like "immature" — to confuse herself with the child she had been, married woman as she was now, and a mother, adulterous married woman ... and the word *adulterous* made her lips turn up in a slow bemused smile, the first flash of incredulous pride one might feel when told at last the disease that is going to be fatal. For there were so many diseases and only one way out of the world, only one death and so many ways to get to it. They were like doors, Helen thought dreamily. You walked down a hallway like those in movies, in huge wealthy homes, crystal chandeliers and marble floors and ... great sweeping lawns ... and doors all along those hallways; if you picked the wrong door you had to go through it. She was dreamy, drowsy. When thought became too much for her — when he had pestered her so much about marrying him, divorcing her husband and marrying him, always him! — she had felt so sleepy she could not listen. If she was not interested in a word her mind wouldn't hear it but made it blurred and strange, like words half-heard in dreams or through some thick substance like water. You didn't have to hear a word if you didn't want to.

So she had telephoned her father the night before and told him the three-fifteen bus and now it was three-thirty; where was he? Over the telephone he had sounded slow and solemn, it could have been a stranger's voice. Helen had never liked telephones because you could not see smiles or gestures and talking like that made her tired. Listening to her father, she had felt for the first time since she had run away and left them all behind — husband, baby girl, family, in-laws, the minister, the dreary sun-bleached look of the land — that she had perhaps died and only imagined she was running away. Nobody here trusted the city; it was too big. Helen had wanted to go there all her life, not being afraid of anything, and so she had gone, and was coming back; but it was an odd feeling, this dreamy ghostliness, as if she were really dead and coming back in a form that only looked like herself ... She was bored, thinking of this, and crossed her bare legs. The sailor crushed out a cigarette in the dirty tin ashtray and their eyes met. Helen felt a little smile tug at her lips. That was the trouble, she knew men too well. She knew their eyes and their gestures — like the sailor rubbing thoughtfully at his chin, now, as if he hadn't shaved well enough but really liked to feel his own skin. She knew them too well and had never figured out why: her sister,

four years older, wasn't like that. But to Helen the same man one hundred times or one hundred men, different men, seemed the same. It was
wrong, of course, because she had been taught it and believed what she
had been taught; but she could not understand the difference. The sailor
watched her but she looked away, half-closing her eyes. She had no time
for him. Her father should be here now, he would be here in a few minutes, so there was no time; she would be home in an hour. When she
thought of her father the ugly bus station with its odor of tobacco and
spilled soft drinks seemed to fade away — she remembered his voice the
night before, how gentle and soft she had felt listening to that voice,
giving in to the protection he represented. She had endured his rough
hands, as a child, because she knew they protected her, and all her life
they had protected her. There had always been trouble, sometimes the
kind you laughed about later and sometimes not, that was one of the
reasons she had married Paul, and before Paul there had been others —
just boys who didn't count, who had no jobs and thought mainly about
their cars. She had called her father from a roadhouse sixty miles away
once, when she was fifteen; she and her best friend Annie had gotten
mixed up with some men they had met at a picnic. That had been frightening, Helen thought, but now she could have handled them. She gave
everyone too much, that was her trouble. Her father had said that. Even
her mother. Lent money to girls at the telephone company where she'd
worked; lent her girl friends clothes; would run outside when some man
drove up and blew his horn, not bothering to get out and knock at the
door the way he should. She liked to make other people happy, what was
wrong with that? Was she too lazy to care? Her head had begun to ache.

Always her thoughts ran one way, fast and innocent, but her body
did other things. It got warm, nervous, it could not relax. Was she afraid
of what her father's face would tell her? She pushed that idea away, it
was nonsense. If she had to think of something, let it be of that muddy
spring day when her family had first moved to this part of the country, into an old farmhouse her father had bought at a "bargain." At that
time the road out in front of the house had been no more than a single
dirt lane . . . now it was wider, covered with black top that smelled ugly
and made your eyesight shimmer and sweat with confusion in the summer. Yes, that big old house. Nothing about it would have changed. She
did not think of her own house, her husband's house, because it mixed
her up too much right now. Maybe she would go back and maybe not.
She did not think of him — if she wanted to go back she would, he would

take her in. When she tried to think of what had brought her back, it was never her husband — so much younger, quicker, happier than the man she had just left — and not the little girl, either, but something to do with her family's house and that misty, warm day seventeen years ago when they had first moved in. So one morning when that man left for work her thoughts had turned back to home and she had sat at the breakfast table for an hour or so, not clearing off the dishes, looking at the coffee left in his cup as if it were a forlorn reminder of him — a man she was even beginning to forget. She knew then that she did not belong there in the city. It wasn't that she had stopped loving this man — she never stopped loving anyone who needed her, and he had needed her more than anyone — it was something else, something she did not understand. Not her husband, not her baby, not even the look of the river way off down the hill, through the trees that got so solemn and intricate with their bare branches in winter. Those things she loved, she hadn't stopped loving them because she had had to love this new man more . . . but something else made her get up and run into the next room and look through the bureau drawers and the closet, as if looking for something. That evening, when he returned, she explained to him that she was going back. He was over forty, she wasn't sure how much, and it had always been his hesitant, apologetic manner that made her love him, the odor of failure about him that mixed with the odor of the drinking he could not stop, even though he had "cut down" now with her help. Why were so many men afraid, why did they think so much? He did something that had to do with keeping books, was that nervous work? He was an attractive man but that wasn't what Helen had seen in him. It was his staring at her when they had first met, and the way he had run his hand through his thinning hair, telling her in that gesture that he wanted her and wanted to be young enough to tell her so. That had been four months ago. The months all rushed to Helen's mind in the memory she had of his keen intelligent baffled eyes, and the tears she had had to see in them when she went out to call her father . . .

Now, back in Oriskany, she would think of him no more.

A few minutes later her father came. Was that really him? she thought. Her heart beat furiously. If blood drained out of her face she would look mottled and sick, as if she had a rash . . . how she hated that! Though he had seen her at once, though the bus station was nearly empty, her father hesitated until she stood and ran to him. "Pa," she said, "I'm so glad to see you." It might have been years ago and he was just going to drive back home now, finished with his business in town, and Helen fourteen or fifteen, waiting to go back with him.

"I'll get your suitcase," he said. The sailor was reading a magazine, no longer interested. Helen watched her father nervously. What was wrong? He stooped, taking hold of the suitcase handle, but he did not straighten fast enough. Just a heartbeat too slow. Why was that? Helen took a tissue already stained with lipstick and dabbed it on her forehead.

On the way home he drove oddly, as if the steering wheel, heated by the sun, were too painful for him to hold. "No more trouble with the car, huh?" Helen said.

"It's all right," he said. They were nearly out of town already. Helen saw few people she knew. "Why are you looking around?" her father said. His voice was pleasant and his eyes fastened seriously upon the road, as if he did not dare look elsewhere.

"Oh, just looking," Helen said. "How is Davey?"

Waiting for her father to answer — he always took his time — Helen arranged her skirt nervously beneath her. Davey was her sister's baby, could he be sick? She had forgotten to ask about him the night before. "Nothing's wrong with Davey, is there, Pa?" she said.

"No, nothing."

"I thought Ma might come, maybe," Helen said.

"No."

"Didn't she want to? Mad at me, huh?"

In the past her mother's dissatisfaction with her had always ranged Helen and her father together; Helen could tell by a glance of her father's when this was so. But he did not look away from the road. They were passing the new high school, the consolidated high school Helen had attended for a year. No one had known what *consolidated* meant or was interested in knowing. Helen frowned at the dark brick and there came to her mind, out of nowhere, the word *adulterous,* for it too had been a word she had not understood for years. A word out of the Bible. It was like a mosquito bothering her at night, or a stain on her dress — the kind she would have to hide without seeming to, letting her hand fall accidentally over it. For some reason the peculiar smell of the old car, the rattling sun shades above the windshield, the same old khaki blanket they used for a seat cover did not comfort her and let her mind get drowsy, to push that word away.

She was not sleepy, but she said she was.

"Yes, honey. Why don't you lay back and try to sleep, then," her father said.

He glanced toward her. She felt relieved at once, made simple and safe. She slid over and leaned her head against her father's shoulder. "Bus ride was long, I hate bus rides," she said. "I used to like them."

"You can sleep till we get home."

"Is Ma mad?"

"No."

His shoulder wasn't as comfortable as it should have been. But she closed her eyes, trying to force sleep. She remembered that April day they had come here — their moving to the house that was new to them, a house of their own they would have to share with no one else, but a house it turned out had things wrong with it, secret things, that had made Helen's father furious. She could not remember the city and the house they had lived in there, but she had been old enough to sense the simplicity of the country and the eagerness of her parents, and then the angry perplexity that had followed. The family was big — six children then, before Arthur died at ten — and half an hour after they had moved in the house was crowded and shabby. And she remembered being frightened at something and her father picking her up right in the middle of moving, and not asking her why she cried — her mother had always asked her that, as if there were a reason — but rocked her and comforted her with his rough hands. And she could remember how the house had looked so well: the ballooning curtains in the windows, the first things her mother had put up. The gusty spring air, already too warm, smelling of good earth and the Eden River not too far behind them, and leaves, sunlight, wind; and the sagging porch piled with cartons and bundles and pieces of furniture from the old house. In that old dark house in the city, the grandparents had died — her mother's parents — and Helen did not remember them at all except as her father summoned them back, recalling with hatred his wife's father — some little confused argument they had had years ago, that he should have won. That old man had died and the house had gone to the bank somewhere mysterious, and her father had brought them all out here to the country. A new world, a new life. A farm. And four boys to help, and the promise of such good soil . . .

Her father turned the wheel sharply. "Rabbit run acrost," he said. He had this strange air of apology for whatever he did, even if it was something gentle; he hated to kill animals, even weasels and hawks. Helen wanted to cover his right hand with hers, that thickened, dirt-creased hand that could never be made clean. But she said, stirring a little as if he had woken her, "Then why didn't Ma want to come?"

They were taking a long, slow curve. Helen knew without looking up which curve this was, between two wheat fields that belonged to one of the old, old families, those prosperous men who drove broken-down pickup trucks and dressed no better than their own hired hands, but who had money, much money, not just in one bank but in many. "Yes, they're money people," Helen remembered her father saying, years ago. Passing someone's pasture. Those ugly red cows meant nothing to Helen, but they meant something to her father. And so after her father had said that — they had been out for a drive after church — her mother got sharp and impatient and the ride was ruined. That was years ago, Helen's father had been a young man then, with a raw, waiting, untested look, with muscular arms and shoulders that needed only to be directed to their work. "They're money people," he had said, and that had ruined the ride, as if by magic. It had been as if the air itself had changed, the direction of the wind changing and easing to them from the river that was often stagnant in August and September, and not from the green land. With an effort, Helen remembered that she had been thinking about her mother. Why did her mind push her into the past so often these days, she only twenty-two (that was not old, not really) and going to begin a new life? Once she got home and took a bath and washed out the things in the suitcase, and got some rest, and took a walk down by the river as she had as a child, skipping stones across it, and sat around the round kitchen table with the old oil cloth cover to listen to their advice ("You got to grow up, now. You ain't fifteen anymore"— that had been her mother, last time), then she would decide what to do. Make her decision about her husband and the baby and there would be nothing left to think about.

"Why didn't Ma come?"

"I didn't want her to," he said.

Helen swallowed, without meaning to. His shoulder was thin and hard against the side of her face. Were those same muscles still there, or had they become worn away like the soil that was sucked down into the river every year, stolen from them, so that the farm Helen's father had bought turned out to be a kind of joke on him? Or were they a different kind of muscle, hard and compressed like steel, drawn into themselves from years of resisting violence?

"How come?" Helen said.

He did not answer. She shut her eyes tight and distracting, eerie images came to her, stars exploding and shadowy figures like those in movies — she had gone to the movies all the time in the city, often taking in the first show at eleven in the morning; not because she was lonely or had nothing to do but because she liked movies. Five-twenty and he would come up the stairs, grimacing a little with the strange inexplicable pain in his chest: and there Helen would be, back from downtown, dressed up and her hair shining and her face ripe and fresh as a child's, not because she was proud of the look in his eyes but because she knew she could make that pain of his abate for a while. And so why had she left him, when he had needed her more than anyone? "Pa, is something wrong?" she said, as if the recollection of that other man's invisible pain were in some way connected with her father.

He reached down vaguely and touched her hand. She was surprised at this. The movie images vanished — those beautiful people she had wanted to believe in, as she had wanted to believe in God and the saints in their movie-world heaven — and she opened her eyes. The sun was bright. It had been too bright all summer. Helen's mind felt sharp and nervous as if pricked by tiny needles, but when she tried to think of what they could be no explanation came to her. She would be home soon, she would be able to rest. Tomorrow she could get in touch with Paul. Things could begin where they had left off — Paul had always loved her so much, and he had always understood her, had known what she was like. "Ma isn't sick, is she?" Helen said suddenly. "No," said her father. He released her fingers to take hold of the steering wheel again. Another curve. Off to the side, if she bothered to look, the river had swung toward them — low at this time of year, covered in places with a fine brown-green layer of scum. She did not bother to look.

"We moved out here seventeen years ago," her father said. He cleared his throat: the gesture of a man unaccustomed to speech. "You don't remember that."

"Yes, I do," Helen said. "I remember that."

"You don't, you were just a baby."

"Pa, I remember it. I remember you carrying the big rug in the house, you and Eddie. And I started to cry and you picked me up. I was such a big baby, always crying . . . And Ma came out and chased me inside so I wouldn't bother you."

"You don't remember that," her father said. He was driving jerkily, pressing down on the gas pedal and then letting it up, as if new thoughts continually struck him. What was wrong with him? Helen had an idea she didn't like: he was older now, he was going to become an old man.

If she had been afraid of the dark, upstairs in that big old farmhouse in the room she shared with her sister, all she had had to do was to think of him. He had a way of sitting at the supper table that was so still, so silent, that you knew nothing could budge him. Nothing could frighten him. So, as a child, and even now that she was grown up, it helped her to think of her father's face—those pale surprised green eyes that could be simple or cunning, depending upon the light, and the lines working themselves in deeper every year around his mouth, and the hard angle of his jaw going back to the ear, burned by the sun and then tanned by it, turned into leather, then going pale again in the winter. The sun could not burn its color deep enough into that skin, which was almost as fair as Helen's. At Sunday school she and the other children had been told to think of Christ when they were afraid, but the Christ she saw on the little Bible bookmark cards and calendars was no one to protect you. That was a man who would be your cousin, maybe, some cousin you liked but saw rarely, but he looked so given over to thinking and trusting that he could not be of much help; not like her father. When he and the boys came in from the fields with the sweat drenching their clothes and their faces looking as if they were dissolving with heat, you could still see the solid flesh beneath, the skeleton that hung onto its muscles and would never get old, never die. The boys—her brothers, all older—had liked her well enough, Helen being the baby, and her sister had watched her most of the time, and her mother had liked her too—or did her mother like anyone, having been brought up by German-speaking parents who had had no time to teach her love? But it had always been her father she had run to. She had started knowing men by knowing him. She could read things in his face that taught her about the faces of other men, the slowness or quickness of their thoughts, if they were beginning to be impatient, or were pleased and didn't want to show it yet. Was it for this she had come home?—And the thought surprised her so that she sat up, because she did not understand. Was it for this she had come home? "Pa," she said, "like I told you on the telephone, I don't know why I did it. I don't know why I went. That's all right, isn't it? I mean, I'm sorry for it, isn't that enough? Did you talk to Paul?"

"Paul? Why Paul?"

"What?"

"You haven't asked about him until now, so why now?"

"What do you mean? He's my husband, isn't he? Did you talk to him?"

"He came over to the house almost every night for two weeks. Three weeks," he said. Helen could not understand the queer chatty tone of his voice. "Then off and on, all the time. No, I didn't tell him you were coming."

"But why not?" Helen laughed nervously. "Don't you like him?"

"You know I like him. You know that. But if I told him he'd of gone down to get you, not me."

"Not if I said it was you I wanted . . ."

"I didn't want him to know. Your mother doesn't know either."

"What? You mean you didn't tell her?" Helen looked at the side of his face. It was rigid and bloodless behind the tan, as if something inside were shrinking away and leaving just his voice. "You mean you didn't even tell Ma? She doesn't know I'm coming?"

"No."

The nervous prickling in her brain returned suddenly. Helen rubbed her forehead.

"Pa," she said gently, "why didn't you tell anybody? You're ashamed of me, huh?"

He drove on slowly. They were following the bends of the river, that wide shallow meandering river the boys said wasn't worth fishing in any longer. One of its tributaries branched out suddenly — Mud Creek, it was called, all mud and bullfrogs and dragonflies and weeds — and they drove over it on a rickety wooden bridge that thumped beneath them. "Pa," Helen said carefully, "you said you weren't mad, on the phone. And I wrote you that letter explaining. I wanted to write some more, but you know . . . I don't write much, never even wrote to Annie when she moved away. I never forgot about you or anything, or Ma . . . I thought about the baby, too, and Paul, but Paul could always take care of himself. He's smart. He really is. I was in the store with him one time and he was arguing with some salesmen and got the best of them; he never learned all that from his father. The whole family is smart, though, aren't they?"

"The Hendrikses? Sure. You don't get money without brains."

"Yes, and they got money too, Paul never had to worry. In a house like his parents' house nothing gets lost or broken. You know? It isn't like it was at ours, when we were all kids. That's part of it — when Paul's father built us our house I was real pleased and real happy, but then something of them came in with it too. Everything is spost to be clean and put in its place, and after you have a baby you get so tired . . . but his mother was always real nice to me. I don't complain about them. I like them all real well."

"Money people always act nice," her father said. "Why shouldn't they?"

"Oh, Pa!" Helen said, tapping at his arm. "What do you mean by that? You always been nicer than anybody I know, that's the truth. Real nice. A lot of them with those big farms, like Paul's father, and that tractor store they got—they complain a lot. They do. You just don't hear about it. And when that baby got polio, over in the Rapids—that real big farm, you know what I mean?—the McGuires. How do you think they felt? They got troubles just like everybody else."

Then her father did a strange thing: here they were seven or eight miles from home, no house near, and he stopped the car. "Want to rest for a minute," he said. Yet he kept staring out the windshield as if he were still driving.

"What's wrong?"

"Sun on the hood of the car . . ."

Helen tugged at the collar of her dress, pulling it away from her damp neck. When had the heat ever bothered her father before? She remembered going out to the farthest field with water for him, before he had given up that part of the farm. And he would take the jug from her and lift it to his lips and it would seem to Helen, the sweet child Helen standing in the dusty corn, that the water flowed into her magnificent father and enlivened him as if it were secret blood of her own she had given him. And his chest would swell, his reddened arms eager with muscle emerging out from his rolled-up sleeves, and his eyes now wiped of sweat and exhaustion . . . The vision pleased and confused her, for what had it to do with the man now beside her? She stared at him and saw that his nose was queerly white and that there were many tiny red veins about it, hardly more than pen lines; and his hair was thinning and jagged, growing back stiffly from his forehead as if he had brushed it back impatiently with his hand once too often. When Eddie, the oldest boy, moved away now and lost to them, had pushed their father hard in the chest and knocked him back against the supper table, that same amazed white look had come to his face, starting at his nose.

"I was thinking if, if we got home now, I could help Ma with supper," Helen said. She touched her father's arm as if to waken him. "It's real hot, she'd like some help."

"She doesn't know you're coming."

"But I . . . I could help anyway." She tried to smile, watching his face for a hint of something: many times in the past he had looked stern but could be made to break into a smile, finally, if she teased him long enough. "But didn't Ma hear you talk on the phone? Wasn't she there?"

"She was there."

"Well, but then . . ."

"I told her you just talked. Never said nothing about coming home."

The heat had begun to make Helen dizzy. Her father opened the door on his side. "Let's get out for a minute, go down by the river," he said. Helen slid across and got out. The ground felt uncertain beneath her feet. Her father was walking and saying something and she had to run to catch up with him. He said: "We moved out here seventeen years ago. There were six of us then, but you don't remember. Then the boy died. And you don't remember your mother's parents and their house, that goddam stinking house, and how I did all the work for him in his store. You remember the store down front? The dirty sawdust floor and the old women coming in for sausage, enough to make you want to puke, and pig's feet and brains out of cows or guts or what the hell they were that people ate in that neighborhood. I could puke for all my life and not get clean of it. You just got born then. And we were dirt to your mother's people, just dirt. I was dirt. And when they died somebody else got the house, it was all owned by somebody else, and so we said how it was for the best and we'd come out here and start all over. You don't remember it or know nothing about us."

"What's wrong, Pa?" Helen said. She took his arm as they descended the weedy bank. "You talk so funny, did you get something to drink before you came to the bus station? You never said these things before. I thought it wasn't just meat, but a grocery store, like the one in . . ."

"And we came out here," he said loudly, interrupting her, "and bought that son of a bitch of a house with the roof half rotted through and the well all shot to hell . . . and those bastards never looked at us, never believed we were real people. The Hendrikses too. They were like all of them. They looked through me in town, do you know that? Like you look through a window. They didn't see me. It was because hillbilly families were in that house, came and went, pulled out in the middle of the night owing everybody money; they all thought we were like that. I said, we were poor but we weren't hillbillies. I said, do I talk like a hillbilly? We come from the city. But nobody gave a damn. You could go up to them and shout in their faces and they wouldn't hear you, not even when they started losing money themselves. I prayed to God during them bad times that they'd all lose what they had, every bastard one of them, that Swede with the fancy cattle most of all! I prayed to God to bring them down to me so they could see me, my children as good as theirs, and me a harder worker than any of them—if you work till you feel like dying you done the best you can do, whatever money you get.

I'd of told them that. I wanted to come into their world even if I had to be on the bottom of it, just so long as they gave me a name . . ."

"Pa, you been drinking," Helen said softly.

"I had it all fixed, what I'd tell them," he said. They were down by the river bank now. Fishermen had cleared a little area and stuck Y-shaped branches into the dried mud, to rest their poles on. Helen's father prodded one of the little sticks with his foot and then did something Helen had never seen anyone do in her life, not even boys — he brought his foot down on it and smashed it.

"You oughtn't of done that," Helen said. "Why'd you do that?"

"And I kept on and on; it was seventeen years. I never talked about it to anyone. Your mother and me never had much to say, you know that. She was like her father. — You remember that first day? It was spring, nice and warm, and the wind came along when we were moving the stuff in and was so different from that smell in the city — my God! It was a whole new world here."

"I remember it," Helen said. She was staring out at the shallow muddy river. Across the way birds were sunning themselves stupidly on flat, white rocks covered with dried moss like veils.

"You don't remember nothing!" her father said angrily. "Nothing! You were the only one of them I loved, because you didn't remember. It was all for you. First I did it for me, myself, to show that bastard father of hers that was dead — then those other bastards, those big farms around us — but then for you, for you. You were the baby. I said to God that when you grew up it'd be you in one of them big houses with everything fixed and painted all the time, and new machinery, and driving around in a nice car not this thing we got. I said I would do that for you or die."

"That's real nice, Pa," Helen said nervously, "but I never . . . I never knew nothing about it, or . . . I was happy enough any way I was. I liked it at home, I got along with Ma better than anybody did. And I liked Paul too, I didn't marry him just because you told me to. I mean, you never pushed me around. I wanted to marry him all by myself, because he loved me. I was always happy, Pa. If Paul didn't have the store coming to him, and that land and all, I'd have married him anyway — You oughtn't to worked all that hard for me."

In spite of the heat she felt suddenly chilled. On either side of them tall grass shrank back from the cleared, patted area, stiff and dried with August heat. These weeds gathered upon themselves in a brittle tumult back where the vines and foliage of trees began, the weeds dead and whitened and the vines a glossy, rich green, as if sucking life out of the water into which they drooped. All along the river bank trees and bushes leaned out and showed a yard or two of dead, whitish brown where the waterline had once been. This river bent so often you could never see far along it. Only a mile or so. Then foliage began, confused and unmoving. What were they doing here, she and her father? A thought came to Helen and frightened her—she was not used to thinking—that they ought not to be here, that this was some other kind of slow, patient world where time didn't care at all for her or her girl's face or her generosity of love, but would push right past her and go on to touch the faces of other people.

"Pa, let's go home. Let's go home," she said.

Her father bent and put his hands into the river. He brought them dripping to his face. "That's dirty there, Pa," she said. A mad dry buzzing started up somewhere—hornets or wasps. Helen looked around but saw nothing.

"God listened and didn't say yes or no," her father said. He was squatting at the river and now looked back at her, his chin creasing. The back of his shirt was wet. "If I could read him right it was something like this—that I was caught in myself and them money people caught in themselves and God Himself caught in what he was and so couldn't be anything else. Then I never thought about God again."

"I think about God," Helen said. "I do. People should think about God then they wouldn't have wars and things . . ."

"No, I never bothered about God again," he said slowly. "If he was up there or not it never had nothing to do with me. A hailstorm that knocked down the wheat, or a drought—what the hell? Whose fault? It wasn't God's no more than mine so I let him out of it. I knew I was in it all on my own. Then after a while it got better, year by year. We paid off the farm and the new machines. You were in school then, in town. And when we went into the church they said hello to us sometimes, because we outlasted them hillbillies by ten years. And now Mike ain't doing bad on his own place, got a nice car, and me and Bill get enough out of the farm so it ain't too bad, I mean it ain't too bad. But it wasn't money I wanted!"

He was staring at her. She saw something in his face that mixed with the buzzing of the hornets and fascinated her so that she could not move, could not even try to tease him into smiling too. "It wasn't never money I wanted," he said.

"Pa, why don't we go home?"

"I don't know what it was, exactly," he said, still squatting. His hands touched the ground idly. "I tried to think of it, last night when you called and all night long and driving in to town, today. I tried to think of it."

"I guess I'm awful tired from that bus. I . . . I don't feel good," Helen said.

"Why did you leave with that man?"

"What? Oh," she said, touching the tip of one of the weeds, "I met him at Paul's cousin's place, where they got that real nice tavern and a dance hall . . ."

"Why did you run away with him?"

"I don't know, I told you in the letter. I wrote it to you, Pa. He acted so nice and liked me so, he still does, he loves me so much . . . And he was always so sad and tired, he made me think of . . . you, Pa . . . but not really, because he's not strong like you and couldn't ever do work like you. And if he loved me that much I had to go with him."

"Then why did you come back?"

"Come back?" Helen tried to smile out across the water. Sluggish, ugly water, this river that disappointed everyone, so familiar to her that she could not really get used to a house without a river or a creek somewhere behind it, flowing along night and day: perhaps that was what she had missed in the city?

"I came back because . . . because . . ."

And she shredded the weed in her cold fingers, but no words came to her. She watched them fall. No words came to her, her mind had turned hollow and cold, she had come too far down to this river bank but it was not a mistake any more than the way the river kept moving was a mistake; it just happened.

Her father got slowly to his feet and she saw in his hand a knife she had been seeing all her life. Her eyes seized upon it and her mind tried to remember: where had she seen it last, whose was it, her father's or her brother's? He came to her and touched her shoulder as if waking her, and they looked at each other, Helen so terrified by now that she was no longer afraid but only curious with the mute marble-like curiosity of a child, and her father stern and silent until a rush of hatred transformed his face into a mass of wrinkles, the skin mottled red and white. He did not raise the knife but slammed it into her chest, up to the hilt, so that his whitened fist struck her body and her blood exploded out upon it.

Afterward, he washed the knife in the dirty water and put it away. He squatted and looked out over the river, then his thighs began to ache and he sat on the ground, a few feet from her body. He sat there for hours as if waiting for some idea to come to him. Then the water began to darken, very slowly, and the sky darkened a little while later, as if belonging to another, separate time, the same thing as always, and he had to turn his mind with an effort to the next thing he must do.

1970-1980

THE 1970S SAW CONTINUED FRANKNESS ABOUT SEX in short fiction, although a scarcity of love stories. Many characters confused love and lust, perhaps unsurprisingly, given the sexual revolution and the mood of experimentation. This was the "Me Decade," as Tom Wolfe called it.

Some writers began to experiment with surrealism and new forms. Series editor Martha Foley believed that "a danger confronting the experimental writer is to forget that style and content should be indivisible." Influential magazines that published cutting-edge fiction, such as *Ontario Review, Fiction International,* and *New Letters,* were founded at this time. Donald Barthelme's stories appeared five times in the series, but Foley's taste clearly tended toward realism. She never chose stories by John Barth and only two by Robert Coover.

From 1958 to 1971 Foley's son was listed as coeditor of *The Best American Short Stories,* although many people were skeptical about his actual involvement. David was an aspiring painter and was known as a lost soul. He died in 1971 as a result of addiction. His death sent Foley into a deep depression from which she never fully recovered. In 1975 she moved to a two-room apartment in Northampton, Massachusetts, and became isolated. She was barely able to survive on the $6,000 a year that she earned as the series editor. Again and again she was criticized for her narrowing tastes and predictable choices — Joyce Carol Oates appeared seven times in thirteen years, Peter Taylor six times in ten years.

In 1977 Foley died of heart disease. There was no memorial service or funeral for her. She had named no next of kin and had no living relatives. She left many of her own short stories incomplete, as well as the manuscript for a novel and a draft of a memoir, which was finished by Jay Neugeboren and published as *The Story of Story Magazine* in 1980.

None of the in-house editors at Houghton Mifflin could agree on how the series should continue. Heated discussions about creating a panel of judges and arguments about whom to approach to fill it ensued. The editors finally decided to ask the critic and editor Ted Solotaroff to oversee the series, but he said no. He did propose that they invite a different writer to steer the volume each year. Houghton Mifflin agreed, and Solotaroff signed on as the first guest editor.

Shannon Ravenel, a young editor who had known Foley at Houghton Mifflin, was asked to serve as the annual series editor. Ravenel had grown up in South Carolina, mostly in Charleston. She said, "I had a mixed raising in 'low country' and 'up country' South Carolina." An avid reader since childhood, she had sought work in publishing; "In college (Hollins — all girls) my major (English literature) professor and advisor, Louis Rubin, told me I should NOT go back to Charleston, get married and spend my life socializing and belonging to the Junior League. He told me that I should be an editor (I liked 'workshopping' my fellow creative writing students' work much better than I liked writing my own)." After college Ravenel had moved to Boston and gotten a job in Houghton Mifflin's trade editorial department as a secretary. "And three or four years into it I was beginning to scratch my way into an editorial job by asking if I might read the literary magazines that the department subscribed to that nobody else seemed to read. Doing that, I 'discovered' a couple of new writers that Houghton Mifflin eventually published and I was on my way. I also had the gall to suggest a few stories to the venerable Martha Foley who told me to mind my own business!"

Years later, after Ravenel married and moved to St. Louis, "far from the publishing world which I sorely missed." She accepted Houghton's offer to become the new series editor. She would choose 120 stories, from which Solotaroff would select 20. "The first year in my role as series editor," she said,

> I had no magazines, as Ms. Foley had died so recently and the subscriptions were still all in her name (and in her apartment). I scuttled around and found as many as I could in the college and university libraries in St. Louis and managed to submit the tear sheets of 120 of my favorite stories to Mr. Solotaroff, from which he selected his 20 "Best."

Martha Foley had listed many, many other selected titles in the back matter of her volumes — she read all stories published in English, by writers both American and not, and had several categories for her listings. I decided that since the book's title was *Best AMERICAN Short Stories,* I would read only work by North American (I read as many Canadian magazines as I could persuade to give me subscriptions) writers and list only 100 "Other Distinguished American Stories" in my back matter.

Ravenel secretly dreaded the complexities of working with a guest editor but admitted that "there is nothing like success to change the directions of one's ambitions." Sales of the book quadrupled once the guest editors came on board.

Many writers who were approached for the role of guest editor declined. When asked, Peter Taylor wrote, "I'd love to read those stories and select my favorites, but then I know too well how I would put off writing the preface. And finally I would do a hurried, lousy job of it! The trouble with being old and wise is that you know everything about yourself too well." That same year Walker Percy replied, "It's an honor, but I've got too much to do to read all those stories. You might be interested to know that we have a little book club that meets biweekly. We read and discuss 3 or 4 short stories. Just finished Raymond Carver's 1986 BASS. Going to Anne Tyler next."

★ ★ ★

1975

DONALD BARTHELME
THE SCHOOL

from *The New Yorker*

DONALD BARTHELME (1931–1989) was born in Philadelphia but grew up in Houston, where he began writing for the *Houston Post*. He was drafted into the U.S. Army and arrived in Korea on the day that the Korean Armistice Agreement, ending the Korean War, was signed. When he returned to Houston, he spent time listening to black jazz musicians in the city's clubs, which influenced his later writing.

Barthelme published eleven short story collections in addition to four novels, a children's book, and nonfiction. He contributed regularly to *The New Yorker* and lived in both New York and Houston, where he taught at the University of Houston; he was known for forbidding his students to write about the weather. He won a National Book Award for his children's book, *The Slightly Irregular Fire Engine;* a Guggenheim Fellowship; a National Institute of Arts and Letters Award; and many other honors.

Barthelme's stories gained momentum by their accumulation of detail rather than by any traditionally structured plot. Critic George Wicks called Barthelme "the leading American practitioner of surrealism today . . . whose fiction continues the investigations of consciousness and experiments in expression that began with Dada and surrealism a half century ago."

★

WELL, WE HAD all these children out planting trees, see, because we figured that . . . that was part of their education, to see how, you know, the root systems . . . and also the sense of responsibility, taking care of things, being individually responsible. You know what I mean. And the trees all died. They were orange trees. I don't know why they died, they just died. Something wrong with the soil possibly or maybe the stuff we got from the nursery wasn't the best. We complained about it. So we've got thirty kids there, each kid had his or her own little

tree to plant, and we've got these thirty dead trees. All these kids looking at these little brown sticks, it was depressing.

It wouldn't have been so bad except that . . . Before that, just a couple of weeks before the thing with the trees, the snakes all died. But I
think that the snakes — well, the reason that the snakes kicked off was
that . . . you remember, the boiler was shut off for four days because of
the strike, and that was explicable. It was something you could explain
to the kids because of the strike. I mean, none of their parents would let
them cross the picket line and they knew there was a strike going on and
what it meant. So when things got started up again and we found the
snakes they weren't too disturbed.

With the herb gardens it was probably a case of overwatering, and at
least now they know not to overwater. The children were very conscien-
tious with the herb gardens and some of them probably . . . you know,
slipped them a little extra water when we weren't looking. Or maybe . . .
well, I don't like to think about sabotage, although it did occur to us. I
mean, it was something that crossed our minds. We were thinking that
way probably because before that the gerbils had died, and the white
mice had died, and the salamander . . . well, now they know not to carry
them around in plastic bags.

Of course we *expected* the tropical fish to die, that was no surprise.
Those numbers, you look at them crooked and they're belly-up on the
surface. But the lesson plan called for a tropical-fish input at that point,
there was nothing we could do, it happens every year, you just have to
hurry past it.

We weren't even supposed to have a puppy.

We weren't even supposed to have one, it was just a puppy the Mur-
doch girl found under a Gristede's truck one day and she was afraid the
truck would run over it when the driver had finished making his delivery, so she stuck it in her knapsack and brought it to school with her. So
we had this puppy. As soon as I saw the puppy I thought, Oh Christ, I
bet it will live for about two weeks and then . . . And that's what it did. It
wasn't supposed to be in the classroom at all, there's some kind of regu-
lation about it, but you can't tell them they can't have a puppy when the
puppy is already there, right in front of them, running around on the
floor and yap yap yapping. They named it Edgar — that is, they named
it after me. They had a lot of fun running after it and yelling, "Here, Edgar! Nice Edgar!" Then they'd laugh like hell. They enjoyed the ambi-
guity. I enjoyed it myself. I don't mind being kidded. They made a little

house for it in the supply closet and all that. I don't know what it died of. Distemper, I guess. It probably hadn't had any shots. I got it out of there before the kids got to school. I checked the supply closet each morning, routinely, because I knew what was going to happen. I gave it to the custodian.

And then there was this Korean orphan that the class adopted through the Help the Children program, all the kids brought in a quarter a month, that was the idea. It was an unfortunate thing, the kid's name was Kim and maybe we adopted him too late or something. The cause of death was not stated in the letter we got, they suggested we adopt another child instead and sent us some interesting case histories, but we didn't have the heart. The class took it pretty hard, they began (I think; nobody ever said anything to me directly) to feel that maybe there was something wrong with the school. But I don't think there's anything wrong with the school, particularly, I've seen better and I've seen worse. It was just a run of bad luck. We had an extraordinary number of parents passing away, for instance. There were I think two heart attacks and two suicides, one drowning, and four killed together in a car accident. One stroke. And we had the usual heavy mortality rate among the grandparents, or maybe it was heavier this year, it seemed so. And finally the tragedy.

The tragedy occurred when Matthew Wein and Tony Mavrogordo were playing over where they're excavating for the new federal office building. There were all these big wooden beams stacked, you know, at the edge of the excavation. There's a court case coming out of that, the parents are claiming that the beams were poorly stacked. I don't know what's true and what's not. It's been a strange year.

I forgot to mention Billy Brandt's father, who was knifed fatally when he grappled with a masked intruder in his home.

One day, we had a discussion in class. They asked me, where did they go? The trees, the salamander, the tropical fish, Edgar, the poppas and mommas, Matthew and Tony, where did they go? And I said, I don't know, I don't know. And they said, who knows? and I said, nobody knows. And they said, is death that which gives meaning to life? And I said no, life is that which gives meaning to life. Then they said, but isn't death, considered as a fundamental datum, the means by which the taken-for-granted mundanity of the everyday may be transcended in the direction of —

I said, yes, maybe.

They said, we don't like it.

I said, that's sound.

They said, it's a bloody shame!

I said, it is.

They said, will you make love now with Helen (our teaching assistant) so that we can see how it is done? We know you like Helen.

I do like Helen but I said that I would not.

We've heard so much about it, they said, but we've never seen it.

I said I would be fired and that it was never, or almost never, done as a demonstration. Helen looked out of the window.

They said, please, please make love with Helen, we require an assertion of value, we are frightened.

I said that they shouldn't be frightened (although I am often frightened) and that there was value everywhere. Helen came and embraced me. I kissed her a few times on the brow. We held each other. The children were excited. Then there was a knock on the door, I opened the door, and the new gerbil walked in. The children cheered wildly.

1978

STANLEY ELKIN
THE CONVENTIONAL WISDOM

from *American Review*

STANLEY ELKIN (1930–1995) was born in Brooklyn, where his father sold costume jewelry, and was raised in Chicago. After two years in the U.S. Army, he taught in the English Department of Washington University in St. Louis, where he remained for the rest of his life.

Elkin was the author of more than a dozen works of fiction, including *Mrs. Ted Bliss, Van Gogh's Room at Arles, The MacGuffin, The Magic Kingdom,* and *Criers and Kibitzers, Kibitzers and Criers.* His novel *George Mills* won the National Book Critics Circle Award in 1982, and he was nominated three times for the National Book Award. Critic Josh Greenfeld called the author "at once a bright satirist, a bleak absurdist and a deadly moralist."

In 1972 Elkin was diagnosed with multiple sclerosis. He died at the age of sixty-five of heart failure. He had just completed the novel *Mrs. Ted Bliss,* for which he posthumously received his second National Book Critics Circle Award.

★

ELLERBEE HAD BEEN having a bad time of it. He'd had financial reversals. Change would slip out of his pockets and slide down into the crevices of other people's furniture. He dropped deposit bottles and lost money in pay phones and vending machines. He overtipped in dark taxicabs. He had many such financial reversals. He was stuck with Superbowl tickets when he was suddenly called out of town and with theater and opera tickets when the ice was too slick to move his car out of his driveway. But all this was small potatoes. His portfolio was a disgrace. He had gotten into mutual funds at the wrong time and out at a worse. His house, appraised for tax purposes at many thousands of dollars below its replacement cost, burned down, and recently his once flourishing liquor store, one of the largest in Minneapolis, had drawn the attentions of burly, hopped-up and armed deprivators, ski-masked, head-stockinged. Two of his clerks had been shot, one killed, the other crippled and brain damaged, during the most recent visitation by these marauders, and Ellerbee, feeling a sense of responsibility, took it upon himself to support his clerks' families. His wife reproached him for this which led to bad feeling between them.

"Weren't they insured?"

"I don't know, May. I suppose they had some insurance but how much could it have been? One was just a kid out of college."

"Whatshisname, the vegetable."

"Harold, May."

"What about whosis? He was no kid out of college."

"George died protecting my store, May."

"Some protection. The black bastards got away with over fourteen hundred bucks." When the police called to tell him of the very first robbery, May had asked if the men had been black. It hurt Ellerbee that this should have been her first question. "Who's going to protect you? The insurance companies red-lined that lousy neighborhood a year ago. We won't get a penny."

"I'm selling the store, May. I can't afford to run it anymore."

"Selling? Who'd buy it? *Selling!*"

"I'll see what I can get for it," Ellerbee said.

"Social Security pays them benefits," May said, picking up their quarrel again the next day. "Social Security pays up to the time the kids are eighteen years old, and they give it to the widow, too. Who do you think you are, anyway? We lose a house and have to move into one not half as good because it's all we can afford, and you want to keep on paying the salaries not only of two people who no longer work for you, but to pay them out of a business that you mean to sell! Let Social Security handle it."

Ellerbee, who had looked into it, answered May. "Harold started with me this year. Social Security pays according to what you've put into the system. Dorothy won't get three hundred a month, May. And George's girl is twenty. Evelyn won't even get that much."

"Idealist," May said. "Martyr."

"Leave off, will you, May? I'm responsible. I'm under an obligation."

"Responsible, under an obligation!"

"Indirectly. God damn it, yes. Indirectly. They worked for me, didn't they? It's a combat zone down there. I should have had security guards around the clock."

"Where are you going to get all this money? We've had financial reverses. You're selling the store. Where's this money coming from to sup-port three families?"

"We'll get it."

"*We'll* get it? There's no we'll about it, Mister. *You'll.* The stocks are in joint tenancy. You can't touch them, and I'm not signing a thing. Not a penny comes out of my mouth or off my back."

"All right, May," Ellerbee said. "I'll get it."

In fact Ellerbee had a buyer in mind — a syndicate that specialized in buying up business in decaying neighborhoods — liquor and drugstores, small groceries — and then put in ex-convicts as personnel, Green Be-rets from Vietnam, off-duty policemen, experts in the martial arts. Once the word was out, no one ever attempted to rob these places. The syn-dicate hiked the price of each item at least 20 percent — and got it. Eller-bee was fascinated and appalled by their strong-arm tactics. Indeed, he more than a little suspected that it was the syndicate itself which had been robbing him — all three times his store had been held up he had not been in it — to inspire him to sell, perhaps.

"We read about your trouble in the paper," Mr. Davis, the lawyer for the syndicate, had told him on the occasion of his first robbery. The thieves had gotten away with $300 and there was a four-line notice on the inside pages. "Terrible," he said, "terrible. A fine old neighborhood like this one. And it's the same all over America today. Everywhere it's the same story. Even in Kansas, even in Utah. They shoot you with bul-lets, they take your property. Terrible. The people I represent have the know-how to run businesses like yours in the spoiled neighborhoods." And then he had been offered a ridiculous price for his store and stock. Of course he turned it down. When he was robbed a second time, the lawyer didn't even bother to come in person. "Terrible. Terrible," he said. "Whoever said lightning doesn't strike twice in the same place was talking through his hat. I'm authorized to offer you ten thousand less than I did the last time." Ellerbee hung up on him.

Now, after his clerks had been shot, it was Ellerbee who called the lawyer. "Awful," the lawyer said. "Outrageous. A merchant shouldn't have to sit still for such things in a democracy."

They gave him even less than the insurance people had given him for his under-appraised home. Ellerbee accepted, but decided it was time he at least hint to Davis that he knew what was going on. "I'm selling," he said, "because I don't want anyone else to die."

"Wonderful," Davis said, "wonderful. There should be more Ameri-cans like you."

He deposited the money he got from the syndicate in a separate account so that his wife would have no claims on it and now, while he had no business to go to, he was able to spend more time in the hospital visiting Harold.

"How's Hal today, Mrs. Register?" he asked when he came into the room where the mindless quadraplegic was being cared for. Dorothy Register was a red-haired young woman in her early twenties. Ellerbee felt so terrible about what had happened, so guilty, that he had difficulty talking to her. He knew it would be impossible to visit Harold if he was going to run into his wife when he did so. It was for this reason, too, that he sent the checks rather than drop them off at the apartment, much as he wanted to see Hal's young son, Harold, Jr., in order to reassure the child that there was still a man around to take care of the boy and his young mother.

"Oh, Mr. Ellerbee," the woman wept. Harold seemed to smile at them through his brain damage.

"Please, Mrs. Register," said Ellerbee, "Harold shouldn't see you like this."

"Him? He doesn't understand a thing. You don't understand a thing, do you?" she said, turning on her husband sharply. When she made a move to poke at his eyes with a fork he didn't even blink. "Oh, Mr. Ellerbee," she said, turning away from her husband, "that's not the man I married. It's awful, but I don't feel anything for him. The only reason I come is that the doctors say I cheer him up. Though I can't see how. He smiles that way at his bedpan."

"Please, Mrs. Register," Ellerbee said softly. "You've got to be strong. There's little Hal."

"I know," she moaned, "I know." She wiped the tears from her eyes and sniffed and tossed her hair in a funny little way she had which Ellerbee found appealing. "I'm sorry," she said. "You've been very kind. I don't know what I would have done, what *we* would have done. I can't even thank you," she said helplessly.

"Oh don't think about it, there's no need," Ellerbee said quickly. "I'm not doing any more for you than I am for George Lesefario's widow." It was not a boast. Ellerbee had mentioned the older woman because he didn't want Mrs. Register to feel compromised. "It's company policy when these things happen," he said gruffly.

Dorothy Register nodded. "I heard," she said, "that you sold your store."

He hastened to reassure her. "Oh now listen," Ellerbee said, "you

mustn't give that a thought. The checks will continue. I'm getting another store. In a very lovely neighborhood. Near where we used to live
before our house burned down."

"Really?"

"Oh yes. I should be hearing about my loan any time now. I'll probably be in the new place before the month is out. Well," he said, "speaking of which, I'd better get going. There are some fixtures I'm supposed
to look at at the Wine and Spirits Mart." He waved to Harold.

"Mr. Ellerbee?"

"Mrs. Register?"

The tall redhead came close to him and put her hands on his shoulders. She made that funny little gesture with her hair again and Ellerbee almost died. She was about his own height and leaned forward and
kissed him on the mouth. Her fingernails grazed the back of his neck.
Tears came to Ellerbee's eyes and he turned away from her gently. He
hoped she hadn't seen the small lump in his trousers. He said good-bye
with his back to her.

The loan went through. The new store, as Ellerbee had said, was in
one of the finest neighborhoods in the city. In a small shopping mall
it was flanked by a good bookstore and a fine French restaurant. The
Ellerbees had often eaten there before their house burned to the ground.
There was an art cinema, a florist, and elegant haberdasher's and dress
shops. The liquor store, called High Spirits, a name Ellerbee decided to
keep after he bought the place, stocked, in addition to the usual gins,
Scotch, bourbons, vodkas, and blends, some really superior wines, and
Ellerbee was forced to become something of an expert in oenology. He
listened to his customers — doctors and lawyers, most of them — and in
this way was able to pick up a good deal.

The business flourished — doing so well that after only his second
month in the new location he no longer felt obliged to stay open on
Sundays — though his promise to his clerks' families, which he kept,
prevented him from making the inroads into his extravagant debt that
he would have liked. Mrs. Register began to come to the store to collect the weekly checks personally. "I thought I'd save you the stamp,"
she said each time. Though he enjoyed seeing her — she looked rather
like one of those splendid wives of the successful doctors who shopped
there — he thought he should discourage this. He made it clear to her
that he would be sending the checks.

Then she came and said that it was foolish, his continuing to pay her
husband's salary, that at least he ought to let her do something to earn it.

She saw that the suggestion made him uncomfortable and clarified what she meant.

"Oh, no," she said, "all I meant was that you ought to hire me. I was a hostess once. For that matter I could wait on trade."

"Well, I've plenty of help, Mrs. Register. Really. As I may have told you, I've kept on all the people who used to work for Anderson." Anderson was the man from whom he'd bought High Spirits.

"It's not as though you'd be hiring additional help. I'm costing you the money anyway."

It would have been pleasant to have the woman around, but Ellerbee nervously held his ground. "At a time like this," he said, "you ought to be with the boy."

"You're quite a guy," she said. It was the last time they saw each other. A few months later, while he was examining his bank statements, he realized that she had not been cashing his checks. He called her at once.

"I can't," she said. "I'm young. I'm strong." He remembered her fierce embrace in her husband's hospital room. "There's no reason for you to continue to send me those checks. I have a good job now. I can't accept them any longer." It was the last time they spoke.

And then he learned that George's widow was ill. He heard about it indirectly. One of his best customers — a psychiatrist — was beeped on the emergency Medi-Call he carried in his jacket, and asked for change to use Ellerbee's pay phone.

"That's not necessary, Doc," Ellerbee said, "use the phone behind my counter."

"Very kind," the psychiatrist said, and came back of the counter. He dialed his service. "Doctor Potter. What have you got for me, Nancy? What? She did *what*? Just a minute, let me get a pencil — Bill?" Ellerbee handed him a pencil. "Lesefario, right. I've got that. Give me the surgeon's number. Right. Thanks, Nancy."

"Excuse me, Doctor," Ellerbee said. "I hadn't meant to listen, but Lesefario, that's an unusual name. I know an Evelyn Lesefario."

"That's the one," said the medical man. "Oh," he said, "you're *that* Ellerbee. Well, she's been very depressed. She just tried to kill herself by eating a mile of dental floss."

"I hope she dies," his wife said.

"*May!*" said Ellerbee, shocked.

"It's what she wants, isn't it? I hope she gets what she wants."

"That's harsh, May."

"Yes? Harsh? You see how much good your checks did her? And another thing, how could she afford a high-priced man like Potter on what *you* were paying her?"

He went to visit the woman during her postoperative convalescence, and she introduced him to her sister, her twin she said, though the two women looked nothing alike and the twin seemed to be in her seventies, a good dozen years older than Mrs. Lesefario. "This is Mr. Ellerbee that my husband died protecting his liquor store from the niggers."

"Oh yes?" Mrs. Lesefario's sister said. "Very pleased. I heard so much about you."

"Look what she brought me," Mrs. Lesefario said, pointing to a large brown paper sack.

"Evelyn, don't. You'll strain your stitches. I'll show him." She opened the sack and took out a five-pound bag of sugar.

"Five pounds of sugar," the melancholic woman said.

"You don't come empty handed to a sick person," her sister said.

"She got it at Kroger's on special. Ninety-nine cents with the coupon," the manic-depressive said gloomily. "She says if I don't like it I can ·get peach halves."

Ellerbee, who did not want to flaunt his own gift in front of her sister, quietly put the dressing gown, still wrapped, on her tray table. He stayed for another half hour, and rose to go.

"Wait," Mrs. Lesefario said. "Nice try but not so fast."

"I'm sorry?" Ellerbee said.

"The ribbon."

"Ribbon?"

"On the fancy box. The ribbon, the string."

"Oh, your stitches. Sorry. I'll get it."

"I'm a would-be suicide," she said. "I tried it once, I could try it again. You don't bring dangerous ribbon to a desperate, unhappy woman."

In fact Mrs. Lesefario did die. Not of suicide, but of a low-grade infection she had picked up in the hospital and which festered along her stitches, undermining them, burning through them, opening her body like a package.

The Ellerbees were in the clear financially, but his wife's reactions to Ellerbee's efforts to provide for his clerks' families had soured their relationship. She had discovered Ellerbee's private account and accused him of dreadful things. He reminded her that it had been she who had insisted he would have to get the money for the women's support himself—that their joint tenancy was not to be disturbed. She ignored his arguments and accused him further. Ellerbee loved May and did what he could to placate her.

"How about a trip to Phoenix?" he suggested that spring. "The store's doing well and I have complete confidence in Kroll. What about it, May? You like Phoenix, and we haven't seen the folks in almost a year."

"Phoenix," she scoffed, "the *folks*. The way you coddle them. Any other grown man would be ashamed."

"They raised me, May."

"They raised you. Terrific. They aren't even your real parents. They only adopted you."

"They're the only parents I ever knew. They took me out of the Home when I was an infant."

"Look, you want to go to Phoenix, go. Take money out of your secret accounts and go."

"Please, May. There's no secret account. When Mrs. Lesefario died I transferred everything back into joint. Come on, sweetheart, you're awfully goddamn hard on me."

"Well," she said, drawing the word out. The tone was one she had used as a bride, and although Ellerbee had not often heard it since, it melted him. It was her signal of sudden conciliation, cute surrender, and he held out his arms and they embraced. They went off to the bedroom together.

"You know," May said afterwards, "it *would* be good to run out to Phoenix for a bit. Are you sure the help can manage?"

"Oh, sure, May, absolutely. They're a first-rate bunch." He spoke more forcefully than he felt, not because he had any lack of confidence in his employees, but because he was still disturbed by an image he had had during climax. Momentarily, fleetingly, he had imagined Mrs. Register beneath him.

In the store he was giving last-minute instructions to Kroll, the man who would be his manager during their vacation in Phoenix.

"I think the Californias," Ellerbee was saying. "Some of them beat several of even the more immodest French. Let's do a promotion of a few of the better Californias. What do you think?"

"They're a very competitive group of wines," Kroll said. "I think I'm in basic agreement."

Just then three men walked into the shop.

"Say," one called from the doorway, "you got something like a Closed sign I could hang in the door here?" Ellerbee stared at him. "Well you don't have to look at me as if I was nuts," the man said. "Lots of merchants keep them around. In case they get a sudden toothache or something they can whip out to the dentist. All right, if you ain't you ain't."

"I want," the second man said, coming up to the counter where Ellerbee stood with his manager, "to see your register receipts."

"What is this?" Kroll demanded.

"No, don't," Ellerbee said to Kroll. "Don't resist." He glanced toward the third man to see if he was the one holding the gun, but the man appeared merely to be browsing the bins of Scotch in the back. Evidently he hadn't even heard the first man, and clearly he could not have heard the second. Conceivably he could have been a customer. "Where's your gun?" Ellerbee asked the man at the counter.

"Oh gee," the man said, "I almost forgot. You got so many things to think about during a stick-up — the traffic flow, the timing, who stands where — you sometimes forget the basics. Here," he said, "here's my gun, in your kisser," and took an immense hand gun from his pocket and pointed it at Ellerbee's face.

Out of the corner of his eye Ellerbee saw Kroll's hands fly up. It was so blatant a gesture Ellerbee thought his manager might be trying to attract the customer's attention. If that was his idea it had worked, for the third man had turned away from the bins and was watching the activity at the counter. "Look," Ellerbee said, "I don't want anybody hurt."

"What's he say?" said the man at the door, who was also holding a pistol now.

"He don't want nobody hurt," the man at the counter said.

"Sure," said the man at the door, "it's costing him a fortune paying all them salaries to the widows. He's a good businessman all right."

"A better one than you," the man at the counter said to his confederate sharply. "He knows how to keep his mouth shut."

Why, they're white, Ellerbee thought. They're *white* men! He felt oddly justified and wished May were there to see.

"The register receipts," the man at the counter coaxed. Ellerbee's cash register kept a running total on what had been taken in. "Just punch Total Tab," the man instructed Kroll. "Let's see what we got." Kroll looked at Ellerbee and Ellerbee nodded. The man reached forward and tore off the tape. He whistled. "Nice little place you got here," he said.

"What'd we get? What'd we get?" the man at the door shouted.

Ellerbee cleared his throat. "Do you want to lock the door?" he asked. "So no one else comes in?" He glanced toward the third man.

"What, and have you kick the alarm while we're fucking around trying to figure which key opens the place?" said the man at the door. "You're a cutie. What'd we get? Let's see." He joined the man at the counter. "Holy smoke! Jackpot City! We're into four figures here." In his excitement he did a foolish thing. He set his revolver down on top of the appetizer table. It lay on the tins of caviar and smoked oysters, the imported cheeses and roasted peanuts. The third man was no more than four feet from the gun, and though Ellerbee saw that the man had caught the robber's mistake and that by taking one step toward the table he could have picked up the pistol and perhaps foiled the robbery, he made no move. Perhaps he's one of them, Ellerbee thought, or maybe he just doesn't want to get involved. Ellerbee couldn't remember ever having seen him. (By now, of course, he recognized all his repeat customers.) He still didn't know if he were a confederate or just an innocent bystander, but Ellerbee had had enough of violence and hoped that if he *were* a customer he wouldn't try anything dumb. He felt no animus toward the man at all. Kroll's face, however, was all scorn and loathing.

"Let's get to work," the man said who had first read the tape, and then to Kroll and Ellerbee, "Back up there. Go stand by the apéritifs."

The third man fell silently into step beside Ellerbee.

"Listen," Ellerbee explained as gently as he could, "you won't find that much cash in the drawer. A lot of our business is Master Charge. We take personal checks."

"Don't worry," the man said who had set his gun down (and who had taken it up again). "We know about the checks. We got a guy we can sell them to for — what is it, Ron, seventeen cents on the dollar?"

"Fourteen, and why don't you shut your mouth, will you? You want to jeopardize these people? What do you make it?"

Ellerbee went along with his sentiments. He wished the big-mouth would just take the money and not say anything more.

"Oh, jeopardize," the man said. "How jeopardized can you get? These people are way past jeopardized. About six hundred in cash, a fraction in checks. The rest is all credit card paper."

"Take it," Ron said.

"You won't be able to do anything with the charge slips," Kroll said.

"Oh yeah?" Ron's cohort said. "This is modern times, fellow. We got a way we launder Master Charge, BankAmericard, all of it."

Ron shook his head and Ellerbee glanced angrily at his manager.

The whole thing couldn't have taken four minutes. Ron's partner took a fifth of Chivas and a bottle of Lafitte '47. He's a doctor, Ellerbee thought.

"You got a bag?"

"A bag?" Ellerbee said.

"A bag, a paper bag, a doggy bag for the boodle."

"Behind the counter," Ellerbee said hopelessly.

The partner put the cash and the bottle of Chivas into one bag and handed it to Ron, and the wine, checks, and credit charges into a second bag which he held on to himself. They turned to go. They looked exactly like two satisfied customers. They were almost at the door when Ron's partner nudged Ron. "Oh, yeah," Ron said, and turned back to look at them. "My friend, Jay Ladlehaus, is right," he said, "you know too much."

Ellerbee heard two distinct shots before he fell.

When he came to, the third man was bending over him. "You're not hurt," Ellerbee said.

"Me? No."

The pain was terrific, diffuse, but fiercer than anything he had ever felt. He saw himself covered with blood. "Where's Kroll? The other man, my manager?"

"Kroll's all right."

"He is?"

"There, right beside you."

He tried to look. They must have blasted Ellerbee's throat away, half his spinal column. It was impossible for him to move his head. "I can't see him," he moaned.

"Kroll's fine." The man cradled Ellerbee's shoulders and neck and shifted him slightly. "There. See?" Kroll's eyes were shut. Oddly, both were blackened. He had fallen in such a way that he seemed to lie on both his arms, retracted behind him into the small of his back like a yoga. His mouth was open and his tongue floated in blood like meat in soup. A slight man, he seemed strangely bloated, and one shin, exposed to Ellerbee's vision where the trouser leg was hiked up above his sock, was discolored as thundercloud.

The man gently set Ellerbee down again. "Call an ambulance," Ellerbee wheezed through his broken throat.

"No, no. Kroll's fine."

"He's not conscious." It was as if his words were being mashed through the tines of a fork.

"He'll be all right. Kroll's fine."

"Then for *me*. Call one for *me*."

"It's too late for you," the man said.

"For Christ's sake, will you!" Ellerbee gasped. "I can't move. You could have grabbed that hoodlum's gun when he set it down. All right, you were scared, but some of this is your fault. You didn't lift a finger. At least call an ambulance."

"But you're dead," he said gently. "Kroll will recover. You passed away when you said 'move.'"

"Are you crazy? What are you talking about?"

"Do you feel pain?"

"What?"

"Pain. You don't feel any, do you?" Ellerbee stared at him. "Do you?"

He didn't. His pain was gone. "Who are you?" Ellerbee said.

"I'm an angel of death," the angel of death said.

"You're—"

"An angel of death."

Somehow he had left his body. He could see it lying next to Kroll's. "I'm dead? But if I'm dead—You mean there's really an afterlife?"

"Oh boy," the angel of death said.

They went to Heaven.

Ellerbee couldn't have said how they got there or how long it took, though he had the impression that time had passed, and distance. It was rather like a journey in films—a series of quick cuts, of montage. He was probably dreaming, he thought.

"It's what they all think," the angel of death said, "that they're dreaming. But that isn't so."

"I could have dreamed you said that," Ellerbee said, "that you read my mind."

"Yes."

"I could be dreaming all of it, the holdup, everything."

The angel of death looked at him.

"Hobgoblin . . . I could . . ." Ellerbee's voice—if it was a voice—trailed off.

"Look," the angel of death said, "I talk too much. I sound like a cabbie with an out-of-town fare. It's an occupational hazard."

"What?"

"*What?* Pride. The proprietary air. Showing off death like a booster. Thanatopography. 'If you look to your left you'll see where . . . Julius Caesar de dum de dum . . . Shakespeare da da da . . . And dead ahead our Father Adam heigh ho—' The tall buildings and the four-star sights. All that Baedeker reality of plaque place and high history. The Fields of

Homer and the Plains of Myth. Where whosis got locked in a star and all the Agriculture of the Periodic Table — the South Forty of the Universe, where Hydrogen first bloomed, where Lithium, Berylium, Zirconium, Niobium. Where Lead failed and Argon came a cropper. The furrows of gold, Bismuth's orchards . . . Still think you're dreaming?"

"No."

"Why not?"

"The language."

"Just so," the angel of death said. "When you were alive you had a vocabulary of perhaps seventeen or eighteen hundred words. Who am I?"

"An eschatological angel," Ellerbee said shyly.

"One hundred per cent," the angel of death said. "Why do we do that?"

"To heighten perception," Ellerbee said, and shuddered.

The angel of death nodded and said nothing more.

When they were close enough to make out the outlines of Heaven, the angel left him and Ellerbee, not questioning this, went on alone. From this distance it looked to Ellerbee rather like a theme park, but what struck him most forcibly was that it did not seem — for Heaven — very large.

He traveled as he would on Earth, distance familiar again, volume, mass, and dimension restored, ordinary. (*Quotidian,* Ellerbee thought.) Indeed, now that he was convinced of his death, nothing seemed particularly strange. If anything, it was all a little familiar. He began to miss May. She would have learned of his death by this time. Difficult as the last year had been, they had loved each other. It had been a good marriage. He regretted again that they had been unable to have children. Children — they would be teenagers now — would have been a comfort to his widow. She still had her looks. Perhaps she would remarry. He did not want her to be lonely.

He continued toward Heaven and now, only blocks away, he was able to perceive it in detail. It looked more like a theme park than ever. It was enclosed behind a high milky fence, the uprights smooth and round as the poles in subway trains. Beyond the fence were golden streets, a mixed architecture of minaret-spiked mosques, great cathedrals, the rounded domes of classical synagogues, tall pagodas like holy vertebrae, white frame churches with their beautiful steeples, even what Ellerbee took to be a storefront church. There were many mansions. But where were the people?

Just as he was wondering about this he heard the sound of a gorgeous chorus. It was making a joyful noise. "Oh dem golden slippers," the chorus sang, "Oh dem golden slippers." It's the Heavenly Choir, Ellerbee thought. They've actually got a Heavenly Choir. He went toward the fence and put his hands on the smooth posts and peered through into Heaven. He heard laughter and caught a glimpse of the running heels of children just disappearing around the corner of a golden street. They all wore shoes.

Ellerbee walked along the fence for about a mile and came to gates made out of pearl. The Pearly Gates, he thought. There are actually Pearly Gates.

An old man in a long white beard sat behind them, a key attached to a sort of cinch that went about his waist.

"Saint Peter?" Ellerbee ventured. The old man turned his shining countenance upon him. "Saint Peter," Ellerbee said again, "I'm Ellerbee."

"I'm Saint Peter," Saint Peter said.

"Gosh," Ellerbee said, "I can't get over it. It's all true."

"What is?"

"Everything. Heaven. The streets of gold, the Pearly Gates. You. Your key. The Heavenly Choir. The climate."

A soft breeze came up from inside Heaven and Ellerbee sniffed something wonderful in the perfect air. He looked toward the venerable old man.

"Ambrosia," the Saint said.

"There's actually ambrosia," Ellerbee said.

"You know," Saint Peter said, "you never get tired of it, you never even get used to it. He does that to whet our appetite."

"You eat in Heaven?"

"We eat manna."

"There's actually manna," Ellerbee said. An angel floated by on a fleecy cloud playing a harp. Ellerbee shook his head. He had never heard anything so beautiful. "Heaven is everything they say it is," he said.

"It's paradise," Saint Peter said.

Then Ellerbee saw an affecting sight. Nearby, husbands were reunited with wives, mothers with their small babes, daddies with their sons, brothers with sisters — all the intricate blood loyalties and enlisted loves. He understood all the relationships without being told — his heightened perception. What was most moving, however, were the old people, related or not, some just lifelong friends, people who had lived together or known one another much the greater part of their lives and then had lost each other. It was immensely touching to Ellerbee to see them gaze fondly into one another's eyes and then to watch them reach out and touch the patient, ancient faces, wrinkled and even withered but, Ellerbee could tell, unchanged in the loving eyes of the adoring beholder. If there were tears they were tears of joy, tears that melded inextricably with tender laughter. There was rejoicing, there were Hosannahs, there was dancing in the golden streets. "It's wonderful," Ellerbee muttered to himself. He didn't know where to look first. He would be staring at the beautiful flowing raiments of the angels — There are actually raiments, he thought, there are actually angels — so fine, he imagined, to the touch that just the caress of the cloth must have produced exquisite sensations not matched by anything in life, when something else would strike him. The perfectly proportioned angels' wings like discrete Gothic windows, the beautiful halos — There are actually halos — like golden quoits, or, in the distance, the lovely green pastures, delicious as fairway — all the perfectly banked turns of Heaven's geography. He saw philosophers deep in conversation. He saw kings and heroes. It was astonishing to him, like going to an exclusive restaurant one has only read about in columns and spotting, even at first glance, the celebrities one has read about, relaxed, passing the time of day, out in the open, up-front and sharing their high-echelon lives.

"This is for keeps?" he asked Saint Peter. "I mean it goes on like this?"

"World without end," Saint Peter said.

"Where's . . ."

"That's all right, say His name."

"God?" Ellerbee whispered.

Saint Peter looked around. "I don't see Him just . . . Oh, wait. *There!*" Ellerbee turned where the old Saint was pointing. He shaded his eyes. "There's no need," Saint Peter said.

"But the aura, the light."

"Let it shine."

He took his hand away fearfully and the light spilled into his eyes like soothing unguents. God was on His throne in the green pastures, Christ at His right Hand. To Ellerbee it looked like a picture taken at a summit conference.

"He's beautiful. I've never . . . It's ecstasy."

"And you're seeing Him from a pretty good distance. You should talk to Him sometime."

"People can talk to Him?"

"Certainly. He loves us."

There were tears in Ellerbee's eyes. He wished May no harm, but wanted her with him to see it all. "It's wonderful."

"We like it," Saint Peter said.

"Oh, I do too," Ellerbee said. "I'm going to be very happy here."

"Go to Hell," Saint Peter said beatifically.

Hell was the ultimate inner city. Its stinking sulfurous streets were unsafe. Everywhere Ellerbee looked he saw atrocities. Pointless, profitless muggings were commonplace; joyless rape that punished its victims and offered no relief to the perpetrator. Everything was contagious, cancer as common as a cold, plague the quotidian. There was stomachache, headache, toothache, earache. There was angina and indigestion and painful third-degree burning itch. Nerves like a hideous body hair grew long enough to trip over and lay raw and exposed as live wires or shoelaces that had come undone.

There was no handsomeness, no beauty, no one walked upright, no one had good posture. There was nothing to look at—although it was impossible to shut one's eyes—except the tumbled kaleidoscopic variations of warted deformity. This was one reason, Ellerbee supposed, that there was so little conversation in Hell. No one could stand to look at anyone else long enough. Occasionally two or three—lost souls? gargoyles? devils? demons?—of the damned, jumping about in the heat first on one foot then the other, would manage to stand with their backs to each other and perhaps get out a few words—a foul whining. But even this was rare and when it happened that a sufferer had the attention of a fellow sufferer he could howl out only a half-dozen or so words before breaking off in a piercing scream.

Ellerbee, constantly nauseated, eternally in pain, forever befouling himself, longed to find something to do, however tedious or make-work or awful. For a time he made paths through the smoldering cinders, but he had no tools and had to use his bare feet, moving the cinders to one side as a boy shuffles through fallen leaves hunting something lost. It was too painful. Then he thought he would make channels for the vomit and excrement and blood. It was too disgusting. He shouted for others to join him in work details—"Break up the fights, pile up the scabs"— even ministering to the less aggravated wounds, using his hands to wipe away the gangrenous drool since there was no fabric in Hell, all clothing consumed within minutes of arrival, flesh alone inconsumable, glowing and burning with his bones slow as phosphor. Calling out, suggesting in screams which may have been incoherent, all manner of pointless, arbitrary arrangements — that they organize the damned, that they count them. Demanding that their howls be synchronous.

No one stopped him. No one seemed to be in charge. He saw, that is, no Devil, no Arch-fiend. There were demons with cloven feet and scaly tails, with horns and pitchforks — They actually have horns, Ellerbee thought, there are actually pitchforks — but these seemed to have no more authority than he had himself, and when they were piqued to wrath by their own torment the jabs they made at the human damned with their sharp arsenal were no more painful — and no less — than anything else down there.

Then Ellerbee felt he understood something terrible — that the abortive rapes and fights and muggings were simply a refinement of his own attempts to socialize. They did it to make contact, to be friendly.

He was free to wander the vast burning meadows of Hell and to scale its fiery hills — and for many years he did — but it was much the same all over. What he was actually looking for was its Source, Hell's bright engine room, its storm-tossed bridge. It had no engine room, there was no bridge, its energy, all its dreadful combustion coming perhaps from the cumulative, collective agony of the inmates. Nothing could be done.

He was distracted, as he was sure they all were ("Been to Heaven?" he'd managed to gasp to an old man whose back was on fire and the man had nodded), by his memory of Paradise, his long-distance glimpse of God. It was unbearable to think of Heaven in his present condition, his memory of that spectacular place poisoned by the discrepancy between the exaltation of the angels and the plight of the damned. It was the old story of the disappointment of rising expectations. Still, without his bidding, thoughts of Paradise force-fed themselves almost constantly into his skull. They induced sadness, rage.

He remembered the impression he'd had of celebrity when he'd stood looking in at Heaven from beyond the Pearly Gates, and he thought to look out for the historic bad men, the celebrated damned, but either they were kept in a part of Hell he had not yet been or their sufferings had made them unrecognizable. If there were great men in Hell he did not see them and, curiously, no one ever boasted of his terrible deeds or notoriety. Indeed, except for the outbursts of violence, most of the damned behaved, considering their state, in a respectable fashion, even an exemplary one. Perhaps, Ellerbee thought, it was because they had not yet abandoned hope. (There was actually a sign: "Abandon Hope, All Who Enter Here." Ellerbee had read it.)

For several years he waited for May, for as long, that is, as he could remember her. Constant pain and perpetual despair chipped away at most of the memories he had of his life. It was possible to recall who and what he had been, but that was as fruitless as any other enterprise in the dark region. Ultimately, like everything else, it worked against him—Hell's fine print. It was best to forget. And that worked against him too.

He took the advice written above Hellgate. He abandoned hope, and with it memory, pity, pride, his projects, the sense he had of injustice —for a little while driving off, along with his sense of identity, even his broken recollection of glory. It was probably what they—whoever they were—wanted. Let them have it. Let them have the straight lines of their trade wind, trade route, through street, thrown stone vengeance. Let them have everything. Their pastels back and their blues and their greens, the recollection of gratified thirst, and the transient comfort of a sandwich and beer that had hit the spot, all the retrospective of good weather, a good night's sleep, a good joke, a good tune, a good time, the entire mosaic of small satisfactions that made up a life. Let them have his image of his parents and friends, the fading portrait of May he couldn't quite shake, the pleasure he'd had from work, from his body. Let them have all of it, his measly joy, his scrapbook past, his hope, too.

Which left only pure pain, the grand vocabulary they had given him to appreciate it, to discriminate and parse among the exquisite lesions and scored flesh and violated synapses, among the insulted nerves, joints, muscle and tissue, all the boiled kindling points of torment and the body's grief. That was all he was now, staggering Hiroshima'd flesh —a vessel of nausea, a pail of pain.

He continued thus for several years, his amnesia willed—There's Free Will, Ellerbee thought—shuffling Hell in his rote aphasia, his stripped self a sealed environment of indifference. There were years he did not think the name Ellerbee.

And even *that* did not assuage the panic of his burning theater'd, air raid warning'd, red alert afterlife. (And that was what they wanted, and he knew it, wanting as much as they did for him to persist in his tornado watch condition, fleeing with others through the crimped, cramped streets of mazy, refugee Hell, dragging his disaster-poster avatar like a wounded leg.) He existed like one plugged into superb equipment, interminably terminal—and changed his mind and tried it the other way again, taking back all he had surrendered, Hell's Indian giver, and dredged up from where he had left them the imperfect memories of his former self. (May he saw as she had once been, his breastless, awkward, shapeless childhood sweetheart.) And when that didn't work either — he gave it a few years — he went back to the other way, and then back again, shifting, quickly tiring of each tack as soon as he had taken it, changing fitfully, a man in bed in a hot, airless room rolling position, agressively altering the surfaces of his pillow. If he hoped — which he came to do whenever he reverted to Ellerbee — it was to go mad, but there was no madness in Hell — the terrific vocabulary of the damned, their poet's knack for rightly naming everything which was the fail-safe of Reason — and he could find peace nowhere.

He had been there sixty-two years, three generations, older now as a dead man than he had been as a living one. Sixty-two years of nightless days and dayless nights, of aggravated pain and cumulative grief, of escalate desperation, of not getting used to it, to any of it. Sixty-two years Hell's greenhorn, sixty-two years eluding the muggers and evading the rapists, all the joyless joy riders out for a night on his town, steering clear of the wild, stampeding, horizontal avalanche of the damned. And then, spinning out of the path of a charging, burning, screaming inmate, he accidentally backed into the smoldering ruin of a second. Ellerbee leaped away as their bodies touched.

"Ellerbee?"

Who? Ellerbee thought wildly. Who?

"Ellerbee?" the voice repeated.

How? Ellerbee wondered. How can he know me? In this form, how I look . . .

Ellerbee peered closely into the tormented face. It was one of the men who had held him up, not the one who had shot him but his accomplice, his murderer's accomplice. "Ladlehaus?" It was Ellerbee's vocabulary which had recognized him, for his face had changed almost completely in the sixty-two years, just as Ellerbee's had, just as it was Ladlehaus's vocabulary which had recognized Ellerbee.

"It is Ellerbee, isn't it?" the man said.

Ellerbee nodded and the man tried to smile, stretching his wounds, the scars which seamed his face, and breaking the knitting flesh, lined, caked as stool, braided as bowel.

"I died," he said, "of natural causes." Ellerbee stared at him. "Of leukemia, stroke, Hodgkin's disease, arteriosclerosis. I was blind the last thirteen years of my life. But I was almost a hundred. I lived to a ripe old age. I was in a Home eighteen years. Still in Minneapolis."

"I suppose," Ellerbee said, "you recall how *I* died."

"I do," Ladlehaus said. "Ron dropped you with one shot. That reminds me," he said. "You had a beautiful wife. May, right? I saw her photograph in the Minneapolis papers after the incident. There was tremendous coverage. There was a TV clip on the Six O'Clock News. They interviewed her. She was—" Ellerbee started to run. "Hey," the accomplice called after him. "Hey, wait."

He ran through the steamy corridors of the Underworld, plunging into Hell's white core, the brightest blazes, Temperature's moving parts. The pain was excruciating, but he knew that it was probably the only way he would shake Ladlehaus so he kept running. And then, exhausted, he came out the other side into an area like shoreline, burning surf. He waded through the flames lapping about his ankles and then, humiliated by fatigue and pain, he did something he had never done before.

He lay down in the fire. He lay down in the slimy excrement and noxious puddles, in the loose evidence of their spilled terror. A few damned souls paused to stare at him, their bad breath dropping over him like an awful steam. Their scabbed faces leaned down toward him, their poisoned blood leaking on him from imperfectly sealed wounds, their baked, hideous visages like blooms in nightmare. It was terrible. He turned over, turned face down in the shallow river of pus and shit. Someone shook him. He didn't move. A man straddled and penetrated him. He didn't move. His attacker groaned. "I can't," he panted, "I can't—I can't see myself in his *blisters*." That's why they do it, Ellerbee thought. The man grunted and dismounted and spat upon him. His fiery spittle burned into an open sore on Ellerbee's neck. He didn't move. "He's dead," the man howled. "I think he's dead. His blisters have gone out!"

He felt a pitchfork rake his back, then turn in the wound it had made as if the demon were trying to pry foreign matter from it.

"Did he die?" Ellerbee heard.

He had Free Will. He wouldn't move.

"Is he dead?"

"How did he do it?"

Hundreds pressed in on him, their collective stench like the swamps of men dead in earthquake, trench warfare—though Ellerbee knew that for all his vocabulary there were no proper analogies in Hell, only the mildest approximations. If he didn't move they would go away. He didn't move.

A pitchfork caught him under the armpit and turned him over.

"He's dead. I think so. I think he's dead."

"No. It can't be."

"I think."

"How? How did he do it?"

"Pull his cock. See."

"No. Make one of the women. If he isn't dead maybe he'll respond."

An ancient harridan stooped down and rubbed him between her palms. It was the first time he had been touched there by a woman in sixty-two years. He had Free Will, he had Free Will. But beneath her hot hands his penis began to smoke.

"Oh God," he screamed. "Leave me alone. Please," he begged. They gazed down at him like teammates over a fallen player.

"Faker," one hissed.

"Shirker," said another scornfully.

"He's not dead," a third cried. "I told you."

"There's no death here."

"World without end," said another.

"Get up," demanded someone else. "Run. Run through Hell. Flee your pain. Keep busy."

They started to lift him. "Let go," Ellerbee shouted. He rolled away from a demon poking at him with a pitchfork. He was on his hands and knees in Hell. Still on all fours he began to push himself up. He was on his knees.

"Looks like he's praying," said the one who had told him to run.

"No."

"Looks like it. I think so."

"How? What for?"

And he started to pray.

"Lord God of Ambush and Unconditional Surrender," he prayed. "Power Play God of Judo Leverage. Grand Guignol, Martial Artist—"

The others shrieked, backed away from him, cordoning Ellerbee off like a disaster area. Ellerbee, caught up, ignoring them, not even hearing them, continued his prayer.

"Browbeater," he prayed, "Bouncer Being, Boss of Bullies—this is Your servant, Ellerbee, sixty-two-year foetus in Eternity, tot, toddler, babe in Hell. Can You hear me? I know You exist because I saw You, avuncular in Your green pastures like an old man on a picnic. The angeled minarets I saw, the gold streets and marble temples and all the flashy summer palace architecture, all the gorgeous glory locked in Receivership, Your zoned Heaven in Holy Escrow. The miracle props— harps and Saints and Popes at tea. All of it—Your manna, Your ambrosia, Your Heavenly Host in their summer whites. So can You *hear* me, pick out my voice from all the others in this din bin? Come on, come on, Old Terrorist, God the Father, God the Godfather! The conventional wisdom is we can talk to You, that You love us, that—"

"I can hear you."

A great awed whine rose from the damned, moans, sharp cries. It was as if Ellerbee alone had not heard. He continued his prayer.

"I hear you," God repeated.

Ellerbee stopped.

God spoke. His voice was pitchless, almost without timbre, almost bland. "What do you want, Ellerbee?"

Confused, Ellerbee forgot the point of his prayer. He looked at the others, who were quiet now, perfectly still for once. Only the snap of localized fire could be heard. God was waiting. The damned watched Ellerbee fearfully. Hell burned beneath his knees. "An explanation," Ellerbee said.

"For openers," God roared, "I made the heavens and the earth! Were you there when I laid the foundations of the firmament? When I—"

Splinters of burning bone, incandescent as filament, glowed in the gouged places along Ellerbee's legs and knees where divots of his flesh had flared and fallen away. "An *explanation*," he cried out, "an *explanation!* None of this what-was-I-doing-when-You-pissed-the-oceans stuff, where I was when You colored the nigger and ignited Hell. I wasn't around when You elected the affinities. I wasn't there when You shaped shit and fashioned cancer. Were *You* there when I loved my neighbor as myself? When I never stole or bore false witness? I don't say when I never killed but when I never even raised a hand or pointed a finger in anger? Where were You when I picked up checks and popped for drinks all round? When I shelled out for charity and voted Yes on the bond issues? So no Job job, no nature in tooth and claw, please. An explanation!"

"You stayed open on the Sabbath!" God thundered.

"I what?"

"You stayed open on the Sabbath. When you were just getting started in your new location."

"You mean because I opened my store on Sundays? That's why?"

"You took My name in vain."

"I took . . ."

"That's right, that's right. You wanted an explanation, I'll give you an explanation. You wanted I/Thou, I'll give you I/Thou. You took It in vain. When your wife was nagging you because you wanted to keep those widows on the payroll. She mocked you when you said you were under an obligation and you said, 'Indirectly. G-d damn it, yes. Indirectly.' 'Come on, sweetheart,' you said, 'you're awfully g-d-damn hard on me.'"

"That's why I'm in Hell? *That's* why?"

"And what about the time you coveted your neighbor's wife? You had a big boner."

"I coveted no one, I was never unfaithful, I practically chased that woman away."

"You didn't honor your father and mother."

Ellerbee was stunned. "I did. I *always* honored my father and mother. I loved them very much. Just before I was killed we were planning a trip to Phoenix to see them."

"Oh, *them*. They only adopted you. I'm talking about your natural parents."

"I was in a Home. I was an *in*fant!"

"Sure, sure," God said.

"And *that's* why? *That's* why?"

"You went dancing. You wore zippers in your pants and drove automobiles. You smoked cigarettes and sold the demon rum."

"These are Your reasons? *This* is Your explanation?"

"You thought Heaven looked like a theme park!"

Ellerbee shook his head. Could this be happening? This pettiness signaled across the universe? But anything could happen, everything could, and Ellerbee began again to pray. "Lord," he prayed, "Heavenly Father, Dear God — maybe whatever is is right, and maybe whatever is is right isn't, but I've been around now, walking up and down in it, and everything is true. There is nothing that is not true. The philosopher's best idea and the conventional wisdom, too. So I am praying to You now in all humility, asking Your forgiveness and to grant one prayer."

"What is it?" God asked.

Ellerbee heard a strange noise and looked around. The damned, too, were on their knees — all the lost souls, all the gargoyles, all the demons, kneeling in fire, capitulate through Hell like a great ring of the conquered.

"What is it?" He asked.

"To kill us, to end Hell, to close the camp."

"Amen," said Ellerbee and all the damned in a single voice.

"Ha!" God scoffed and lighted up Hell's blazes like the surface of a star. Then God cursed and abused Ellerbee, and Ellerbee wouldn't have had it any other way. *He'd* damned him, no surrogate in Saint's clothing but the real McCoy Son of a Bitch God Whose memory Ellerbee would treasure and eternally repudiate forever, happily ever after, world without end.

But everything was true, even the conventional wisdom, perhaps especially the conventional wisdom — that which had made up Heaven like a shot in the dark and imagined into reality halos and Hell, gargoyles, gates of pearl, and the Pearl of Great Price, that had invented the horns of demons and cleft their feet and conceived angels riding clouds like cowboys on horseback, their harps at their sides like goofy guitars. Everything. Everything was. The self and what you did to protect it, learning the house odds, playing it safe — the honorable percentage baseball of existence.

Forever was a long time. Eternity was. He would seek out Ladlehaus, his murderer's accomplice, let bygones be bygones. They would get close to each other, close as family, closer. There was much to discuss in their fine new vocabularies. They would speak of Minneapolis, swap tales of the Twin Cities. They would talk of Ron, of others in the syndicate. And Ladlehaus had seen May, had caught her in what Ellerbee hoped was her grief on the Six O'Clock News. They would get close. And one day he would look for himself in Ladlehaus's glowing blisters.

1980-1990

SERIES EDITOR SHANNON RAVENEL SIMPLIFIED *THE BEST American Short Stories*. She got rid of most of the lists and of the series editor's foreword, keeping only the list of magazines and biographical notes. In 1987 she did, however, institute the contributors' notes, brief essays by the stories' authors describing their inspirations for their chosen pieces. Here they often revealed intimate truths about the writing process. Charles Baxter described "desk pounding, swearing, and pages flung into wastebaskets." Madison Smartt Bell admitted, "I still sometimes wish I could have made [this story] just a little shorter." Joy Williams wrote, "It is the unsayable which prompts writing in the first place."

Ravenel referred to the 1980s as "another golden age" for short stories. Because of the growing number of MFA programs and literary journals, the latter made possible by a larger budget for literature in the National Endowment for the Arts and stronger state arts councils, the amount of short fiction published each year increased. And story collections and anthologies were more frequently reviewed in magazines and newspapers. In 1977 Ravenel read 900 short stories, in 1989 over 2,000. She said, "The short story in the 1980s was *it.*"

Ravenel worked with such guest editors as Joyce Carol Oates, Hortense Calisher, Gail Godwin, Raymond Carver, and Ann Beattie. "Each of the guest editors was different," she noted. "John Updike wanted control over the Distinguished Others list. Anne Tyler wanted to know if I had a secret list of my own (I did) and how closely our two lists corresponded (80 percent). Stanley Elkin asked me to his home to discuss each of his selections and I argued him out of one and into a replacement." Her most memorable experience may have been with John Gardner:

> Just before it was time for me to send him the tear sheets of my 120 selected stories, I broke my leg (roller skating with my kids), but I managed to Xerox all the tear sheets, package up the originals, and get them off to Mr. Gardner by my deadline . . . Two weeks later, I had a phone call: John Gardner did not like a single one of the 120 stories I had sent him and wanted me to ship him the magazines so he could do his own reading and selection. Well. That year I had subscriptions to 151 magazines. Most of them were quarterlies, though many were monthly and at least one supplied 52 issues. So there was a huge pile in our basement that I was supposed to package up and mail to John Gardner. I did it, with my husband's help . . . As it turned out, John Gardner selected nine of my 120 and found another eleven on his own. The "100 Other Distinguished Short Stories" in the back of the 1981 volume are mine. All I can say is that all the rest of the volumes I edited were breezes in comparison.

In 1982 Ravenel cofounded Algonquin Books, devoted to publishing new writers. She also created the series *New Stories from the South*. She continued the tradition of supporting small magazines and new writers in *The Best American Short Stories:* Lynn Sharon Schwartz, Charles Baxter, Ethan Canin, Richard Ford, Amy Hempel, and Mona Simpson all appeared in the series early in their careers.

Divorce, addiction, and AIDS were concerns for writers in the 1980s. Others wrote of the psychological aftermath of the Vietnam War. Tim O'Brien's story "The Things They Carried" was an unforgettable indictment of that war. As Ravenel wrote, he "has taken the plainest kind of communication, the list, and turned the form itself into the theme of his powerful story."

In his introduction, guest editor John Gardner bemoaned the number of authors employing the present tense in their stories, writing that "the present tense turns out to be, itself, the message: One may with great sensitivity watch things happen . . . but one is silly to *expect* anything. Life, if one wishes to call it that, goes on: consciousness is all."

Minimalism — or as John Barth referred to it, "'K-Mart realism,' 'hick chic,' 'Diet-Pepsi minimalism' and 'post-Vietnam, post-literary, post-modernist blue-collar neo-early-Hemingwayism'" — was also popular in the 1980s, possibly due to a weariness from the war in Vietnam and the American culture of excess. In 1986 Anne Tyler wrote, "Even the sparest in style implies a torrent of additional details barely suppressed, bursting through the seams." Others recoiled at the trend. In 1988 guest editor Mark Helprin stated, "No better illumination of the pitfalls of the collective impulse exists than the school of the minimalists . . . Their characters always seem to have a health problem . . . How so many people can be sitting in so many diners, trailers, and pickup trucks with so many ingrown toenails, varicose veins, corns, bunions, boils . . . is the secret of the Sphinx."

★   ★   ★

1980

GRACE PALEY

FRIENDS

from *The New Yorker*

GRACE PALEY (1922–2007) was born in the Bronx. Her parents were Jewish socialists who had emigrated from the Ukraine. Paley's childhood was full of people and friendship and political arguments, all of which worked their way into her later writing.

Paley called herself a "somewhat combative pacifist and cooperative anarchist." Over the years she lobbied for pacifism and was jailed because of her protests against war and the maltreatment of women.

Paley wrote three collections of short stories, *The Little Disturbances of Man, Enormous Changes at the Last Minute,* and *Later the Same Day.* Her stories focused mostly on the daily lives of Jewish women living in New York. She said once, "I'm not writing a history of famous people. I am interested in a history of everyday life." *The Collected Stories of Grace Paley,* published in 1994, was a finalist for both the Pulitzer Prize and the National Book Award. From 1986 to 1988 Paley was New York's first official state author; she was also once poet laureate of Vermont.

Paley died at the age of eighty-four. Her obituary in the *New York Times* noted, "To read Ms. Paley's fiction is to be awash in the shouts and murmurs of secular Yiddishkeit, with its wild onrushing joy and twilight melancholy . . . Her stories, many of which are written in the first person and seem to start in mid-conversation, beg to be read aloud."

★

T O PUT US at our ease, to quiet our hearts as she lay dying, our dear friend Selena said, Life, after all, has not been an unrelieved horror — you know, I *did* have many wonderful years with her.

She pointed to a child who leaned out of a portrait on the wall — long brown hair, white pinafore, head and shoulders forward.

Eagerness, said Susan. Ann closed her eyes.

On the same wall three little girls were photographed in a schoolyard. They were in furious discussion; they were holding hands. Right in the middle of the coffee table, framed, in autumn colors, a handsome young woman of eighteen sat on an enormous horse — aloof, disinterested, a rider. One night this young woman, Selena's child, was found in a rooming house in a distant city, dead. The police called. They said, Do you have a daughter named Abby?

And with *him*, too, our friend Selena said. We had good times, Max and I. You know that.

There were no photographs of *him*. He was married to another woman and had a new, stalwart girl of about six, to whom no harm would ever come, her mother believed.

Our dear Selena had gotten out of bed. Heavily but with a comic dance, she soft-shoed to the bathroom, singing "Those were the days, my friend . . ."

Later that evening, Ann, Susan, and I were enduring our five-hour train ride home. After one hour of silence and one hour of coffee and the sandwiches Selena had given us (she actually stood, leaned her big soft excavated body against the kitchen table to make those sandwiches), Ann said, Well, we'll never see *her* again.

Who says? Anyway, listen, said Susan. Think of it. Abby isn't the only kid who died. What about that great guy, remember Bill Dalrymple — he was a noncooperator or a deserter? And Bob Simon. They were killed in automobile accidents. Matthew, Jeannie, Mike. Remember Al Lurie — he was murdered on Sixth Street — and that little kid Brenda, who O.D.'d on your roof, Ann? The tendency, I suppose, is to forget. You people don't remember them.

What do you mean, "you people"? Ann asked. You're talking to *us*.

I began to apologize for not knowing them all. Most of them were older than my kids, I said.

Of course, the child Abby was exactly in my time of knowing and in all my places of paying attention — the park, the school, our street. But oh! It's true! Selena's Abby was not the only one of the beloved generation of our children murdered by cars, lost to war, to drugs, to madness.

Selena's main problem, Ann said — you know, she didn't tell the truth. What?

A few hot human truthful words are powerful enough, Ann thinks, to steam all God's chemical mistakes and society's slimy lies out of her life. We all believe in that power, my friends and I, but sometimes . . . the heat.

Anyway, I always thought Selena had told us a lot. For instance, we knew she was an orphan. There were six, seven other children. She was the youngest. She was forty-two years old before someone informed her that her mother had *not* died in childbirthing her. It was some terrible sickness. And she had lived close to her mother's body — at her breast, in fact — until she was eight months old. Whew! said Selena. What a relief! I'd always felt I was the one who'd killed her.

Your family stinks, we told her. They really held you up for grief.

Oh, people, she said. Forget it. They did a lot of nice things for me, too. Me and Abby. Forget it. Who has the time?

That's what I mean, said Ann. Selena should have gone after them with an ax.

More information: Selena's two sisters brought her to a Home. They were ashamed that at sixteen and nineteen they could not take care of her. They kept hugging her. They were sure she'd cry. They took her to her room — not a room, a dormitory with about eight beds. This is your bed, Lena. This is your table for your things. This little drawer is for your toothbrush. All for me? she asked. No one else can use it? Only me. That's all? Artie can't come? Franky can't come? Right?

Believe me, Selena said, those were happy days at Home.

Facts, said Ann, just facts. Not necessarily the *truth*.

I don't think it's right to complain about the character of the dying or start hustling all their motives into the spotlight like that. Isn't it amazing enough, the bravery of that private inclusive intentional community?

It wouldn't help not to be brave, said Selena. You'll see.

She wanted to get back to bed. Susan moved to help her.

Thanks, our Selena said, leaning on another person for the first time in her entire life. The trouble is, when I stand, it hurts me here all down my back. Nothing they can do about it. All the chemotherapy. No more chemistry left in me to therapeut. Ha! Did you know before I came to New York and met you I used to work in that hospital? I was supervisor in gynecology. Nursing. They were my friends, the doctors. They weren't so snotty then. David Clark, big surgeon. He couldn't look at me last week. He kept saying, Lena . . . Lena . . . Like that. We were in North Africa the same year — '44, I think. I told him, Davy, I've been around a long enough time. I haven't missed too much. He knows it. But I didn't want to make him look at me. Ugh, my damn feet are a pain in the neck.

Recent research, said Susan, tells us that it's the neck that's a pain in the feet.

Always something new, said Selena, our dear friend.

On the way back to the bed, she stopped at her desk. There were about twenty snapshots scattered across it — the baby, the child, the young woman. Here, she said to me, take this one. It's a shot of Abby and your Richard in front of the school — third grade? What a day! The show those kids put on! What a bunch of kids! What's Richard doing now?

Oh, who knows? Horsing around someplace. Spain. These days, it's Spain. Who knows where he is? They're all the same.

Why did I say that? I knew exactly where he was. He writes. In fact, he found a broken phone and was able to call every day for a week — mostly to give orders to his brother but also to say, Are you O.K., Ma? How's your new boy friend, did he smile yet?

The kids, they're all the same, I said.

It was only politeness, I think, not to pour my boy's light, noisy face into that dark afternoon. Richard used to say in his early mean teens, You'd sell us down the river to keep Selena happy and innocent. It's true. Whenever Selena would say, I don't know, Abby has some peculiar friends, I'd answer for stupid comfort, You should see Richard's.

Still, he's in Spain, Selena said. At least you know that. It's probably interesting. He'll learn a lot. Richard is a wonderful boy, Faith. He acts like a wise guy but he's not. You know the night Abby died, when the police called me and told me? That was my first night's sleep in two years. I *knew* where she was.

Selena said this very matter-of-factly — just offering a few informative sentences.

But Ann, listening, said, Oh! — she called out to us all, Oh! — and began to sob. Her straightforwardness had become an arrow and gone right into her own heart.

Then a deep tear-drying breath: I want a picture, too, she said.

Yes. Yes, wait, I have one here someplace. Abby and Judy and that Spanish kid Victor. Where is it? Ah. Here!

Three nine-year-old children sat high on that long-armed sycamore in the park, dangling their legs on someone's patient head — smooth dark hair, parted in the middle. Was that head Kitty's?

Our dear friend laughed. Another great day, she said. Wasn't it? I remember you two sizing up the men. I *had* one at the time — I thought. Some joke. Here, take it. I have two copies. But you ought to get it enlarged. When this you see, remember me. Ha-ha. Well, girls — excuse me, I mean ladies — it's time for me to rest.

She took Susan's arm and continued that awful walk to her bed.

We didn't move. We had a long journey ahead of us and had expected a little more comforting before we set off.

No, she said. You'll only miss the express. I'm not in much pain. I've got lots of painkiller. See?

The tabletop was full of little bottles.

I just want to lie down and think of Abby.

It was true, the local could cost us an extra two hours at least. I looked at Ann. It had been hard for her to come at all. Still, we couldn't move. We stood there before Selena in a row. Three old friends. Selena pressed her lips together, ordered her eyes into cold distance.

I know that face. Once, years ago, when the children were children, it had been placed modestly in front of J. Hoffner, the principal of the elementary school.

He'd said, No! Without training you cannot tutor these kids. There are real problems. You have to know *how to teach*.

Our PTA had decided to offer some one-to-one tutorial help for the Spanish kids, who were stuck in crowded classrooms with exhausted teachers among little middle-class achievers. He had said, in a written communication to show seriousness and then in personal confrontation to *prove* seriousness, that he could not allow it. And the board of ed itself had said no. (All this no-ness was to lead to some terrible events in the schools and neighborhoods of our poor yes-requiring city.) But most of the women in our PTA were independent—by necessity and disposition. We were, in fact, the soft-speaking tough souls of anarchy.

I had Fridays off that year. At about 11 a.m. I'd bypass the principal's office and run up to the fourth floor. I'd take Robert Figueroa to the end of the hall, and we'd work away at storytelling for about twenty minutes. Then we would write the beautiful letters of the alphabet invented by smart foreigners long ago to fool time and distance.

That day, Selena and her stubborn face remained in the office for at least two hours. Finally, Mr. Hoffner, besieged, said that because she was a nurse, she would be allowed to help out by taking the littlest children to the modern difficult toilet. Some of them, he said, had just come from the barbarous hills beyond Maricao. Selena said O.K., she'd do that. In the toilet she taught the little girls which way to wipe, as she had taught her own little girl a couple of years earlier. At three o'clock she brought them home for cookies and milk. The children of that year ate cookies in her kitchen until the end of the sixth grade.

Now, what did we learn in that year of my Friday afternoons off? The following: Though the world cannot be changed by talking to one child at a time, it may at least be known.

Anyway, Selena placed into our eyes for long remembrance that useful stubborn face. She said, No. Listen to me, you people. Please. I don't have lots of time. What I want . . . I want to lie down and think about Abby. Nothing special. Just think about her, you know.

In the train Susan fell asleep immediately. She woke up from time to time, because the speed of the new wheels and the resistance of the old track gave us some terrible jolts. Once, she opened her eyes wide and said, You know, Ann's right. You don't get sick like that for nothing. I mean, she didn't even mention him.

Why should she? She hasn't even seen him, I said. Susan, you still have him-itis, the dread disease of females.

Yeah? And you don't? Anyway, he *was* around quite a bit. He was there every day, nearly, when the kid died.

Abby. I didn't like to hear "the kid." I wanted to say "Abby" the way I've said "Selena"—so those names can take thickness and strength and fall back into the world with their weight.

Abby, you know, was a wonderful child. She was in Richard's classes every class till high school. Goodhearted little girl from the beginning, noticeably kind—for a kid, I mean. Smart.

That's true, said Ann, very kind. She'd give away Selena's last shirt. Oh, yes, they were all wonderful little girls and wonderful little boys.

Chrissy *is* wonderful, Susan said.

She *is*, I said.

Middle kids aren't supposed to be, but she is. She put herself through college—I didn't have a cent—and now she has this fellowship. And, you know, she never did take any crap from boys. She's something.

Ann went swaying up the aisle to the bathroom. First she said, Oh, all of them—just wohunderful.

I loved Selena, Susan said, but she never talked to me enough. Maybe she talked to you women more, about things. Men.

Then Susan fell asleep.

Ann sat down opposite me. She looked straight into my eyes with a narrow squint. It often connotes accusation.

Be careful—you're wrecking your laugh lines, I said.

Screw you, she said. You're kidding around. Do you realize I don't know where Mickey is? You know, you've been lucky. You always have been. Since you were a little kid. Papa and Mama's darling.

As is usual in conversations, I said a couple of things out loud and kept a few structural remarks for interior mulling and righteousness. I thought: She's never even met my folks. I thought: What a rotten thing to say. Luck — isn't it something like an insult?

I said, Annie, I'm only forty-eight. There's lots of time for me to be totally wrecked — if I live, I mean.

Then I tried to knock wood, but we were sitting in plush and leaning on plastic. Wood! I shouted. Please, some wood! Anybody here have a matchstick?

Oh, shut up, she said. Anyway, death doesn't count.

I tried to think of a couple of sorrows as irreversible as death. But truthfully nothing in my life can compare to hers: a son, a boy of fifteen, who disappears before your very eyes into a darkness or a light behind his own, from which neither hugging nor hitting can bring him. If you shout, Come back, come back, he won't come. Mickey, Mickey, Mickey, we once screamed, as though he were twenty miles away instead of right in front of us in a kitchen chair; but he refused to return. And when he did, twelve hours later, he left immediately for California.

Well, some bad things have happened in my life, I said.

What? You were born a woman? Is that it?

She was, of course, mocking me this time, referring to an old discussion about feminism and Judaism. Actually, on the prism of isms, both of those do have to be looked at together once in a while.

Well, I said, my mother died a couple of years ago and I still feel it. I think *Ma* sometimes and I lose my breath. I miss her. You understand that. Your mother's seventy-six. You have to admit it's nice still having her.

She's very sick, Ann said. Half the time she's out of it.

I decided not to describe my mother's death. I could have done so and made Ann even more miserable. But I thought I'd save that for her next attack on me. These constrictions of her spirit were coming closer and closer together. Probably a great enmity was about to be born.

Susan's eyes opened. The death or dying of someone near or dear often makes people irritable, she stated. (She's been taking a course in relationships *and* interrelationships.) The real name of my seminar is Skills: Personal Friendship and Community. It's a very good course despite your snide remarks.

While we talked, a number of cities passed us, going in the opposite direction. I had tried to look at New London through the dusk of the windows. Now I was missing New Haven. The conductor explained, smiling: Lady, if the windows were clean, half of you'd be dead. The tracks are lined with sharpshooters.

Do you believe that? I hate people to talk that way.

He may be exaggerating, Susan said, but don't wash the window.

A man leaned across the aisle. Ladies, he said, I do believe it. According to what I hear of this part of the country, it don't seem unplausible.

Susan turned to see if he was worth engaging in political dialogue.

You've forgotten Selena already, Ann said. All of us have. Then you'll make this nice memorial service for her and everyone will stand up and say a few words and then we'll forget her again — for good. What'll you say at the memorial, Faith?

It's not right to talk like that. She's not dead yet, Annie.

Yes, she is, said Ann.

We discovered the next day that give or take an hour or two, Ann had been correct. It was a combination — David Clark, surgeon, said — of being sick unto real death and having a tabletop full of little bottles.

Now, why are you taking all those hormones? Susan had asked Selena a couple of years earlier. They were visiting New Orleans. It was Mardi Gras.

Oh, they're mostly vitamins, Selena said. Besides, I want to be young and beautiful. She made a joking pirouette.

Susan said, That's absolutely ridiculous.

But Susan's seven or eight years younger than Selena. What did she know? Because: People *do* want to be young and beautiful. When they meet in the street, male or female, if they're getting older they look at each other's faces a little ashamed. It's clear they want to say, Excuse me, I didn't mean to draw attention to mortality and gravity all at once. I didn't want to remind you, my dear friend, of our coming eviction, first from liveliness, then from life. To which, most of the time, the friend's eyes will courteously reply, My dear, it's nothing at all. I hardly noticed.

Luckily, I learned recently how to get out of that deep well of melancholy. Anyone can do it. You grab at roots of the littlest future, sometimes just stubs of conversation. Though some believe you miss a great deal of depth by not sinking down down down.

Susan, I asked, you still seeing Ed Flores?

Went back to his wife.

Lucky she didn't kill you, said Ann. I'd never fool around with a Spanish guy. They all have tough ladies back in the barrio.

No, said Susan, she's unusual. I met her at a meeting. We had an amazing talk. Luisa is a very fine woman. She's one of the office-worker organizers I told you about. She only needs him two more years, she says. Because the kids—they're girls—need to be watched a little in their neighborhood. The neighborhood is definitely not good. He's a good father but not such a great husband.

I'd call that a word to the wise.

Well, you know me—I don't want a husband. I like a male person around. I hate to do without. Anyway, listen to this. She, Luisa, whispers in my ear the other day, she whispers, Suzie, in two years you still want him, I promise you, you got him. Really, I may still want him then. He's only about forty-five now. Still got a lot of spunk. I'll have my degree in two years. Chrissy will be out of the house.

Two years! In two years we'll all be dead, said Ann.

I know she didn't mean all of us. She meant Mickey. That boy of hers would surely be killed in one of the drugstores or whorehouses of Chicago, New Orleans, San Francisco. I'm in a big beautiful city, he said when he called last month. Makes New York look like a garbage tank.

Mickey! Where?

Ha-ha, he said and hung up.

Soon he'd be picked up for vagrancy, dealing, small thievery, or simply screaming dirty words at night under a citizen's window. Then Ann would fly to the town or not fly to the town to disentangle him, depending on a confluence of financial reality and psychiatric advice.

How *is* Mickey? Selena had said. In fact, that was her first sentence when we came, solemn and embarrassed, into her sunny front room that was full of the light and shadow of windy courtyard trees. We said, each in her own way, How are you feeling, Selena? She said, O.K., first things first. Let's talk about important things. How's Richard? How's Tonto? How's John? How's Chrissy? How's Judy? How's Mickey?

I don't want to talk about Mickey, said Ann.

Oh, let's talk about him, talk about him, Selena said, taking Ann's hand. Let's all think before it's too late. How did it start? Oh, for God's sake talk about him.

Susan and I were smart enough to keep our mouths shut.

Nobody knows, nobody knows anything. Why? Where? Everybody has an idea, theories, and writes articles. Nobody knows.

Ann said this sternly. She didn't whine. She wouldn't lean too far into Selena's softness, but listening to Selena speak Mickey's name, she could sit in her chair more easily. I watched. It was interesting. Ann breathed deeply in and out the way we've learned in our Thursday-night yoga class. She was able to rest her body a little bit.

We were riding the rails of the trough called Park Avenue-in-the-Bronx. Susan had turned from us to talk to the man across the aisle. She was explaining that the war in Vietnam was not yet over and would not be, as far as she was concerned, until we repaired the dikes we'd bombed and paid for some of the hopeless ecological damage. He didn't see it that way. Fifty thousand American lives, our own boys — we'd paid, he said. He asked us if we agreed with Susan. Every word, we said.

You don't look like hippies. He laughed. Then his face changed. As the resident face-reader, I decided he was thinking: Adventure. He may have hit a mother lode of late counterculture in three opinionated left-wing ladies. That was the nice part of his face. The other part was the sly out-of-town-husband-in-New-York look.

I'd like to see you again, he said to Susan.

Oh? Well, come to dinner day after tomorrow. Only two of my kids will be home. You ought to have at least one decent meal in New York.

Kids? His face thought it over. Thanks. Sure, he said. I'll come.

Ann muttered, She's impossible. She did it again.

Oh, Susan's O.K., I said. She's just right in there. Isn't that good?

This is a long ride, said Ann.

Then we were in the darkness that precedes Grand Central.

We're irritable, Susan explained to her new pal. We're angry with our friend Selena for dying. The reason is, we want her to be present when we're dying. We all require a mother or mother-surrogate to fix our pillows on that final occasion, and we were counting on her to be that person.

I know just what you mean, he said. You'd like to have someone around. A little fuss, maybe.

Something like that. Right, Faith?

It always takes me a minute to slide under the style of her public-address system. I agreed. Yes.

The train stopped hard, in a grinding agony of opposing technologies.

Right. Wrong. Who cares? Ann said. She didn't have to die. She really wrecked everything.

Oh, Annie, I said.

Shut up, will you? Both of you, said Ann, nearly breaking our knees as she jammed past us and out of the train.

Then Susan, like a New York hostess, began to tell that man all our private troubles — the mistake of the World Trade Center, Westway, the decay of the South Bronx, the rage in Williamsburg. She rose with him on the escalator, gabbing into evening friendship and a happy night.

At home Anthony, my youngest son, said, Hello, you just missed Richard. He's in Paris now. He had to call collect.

Collect? From Paris?

He saw my sad face and made one of the herb teas used by his peer group to calm their overwrought natures. He does want to improve my pretty good health and spirits. His friends have a book that says a person should, if properly nutritioned, live forever. He wants me to give it a try. He also believes that the human race, its brains and good looks, will end in his time.

At about eleven-thirty he went out to live the pleasures of his eighteen-year-old nighttime life.

At 3 a.m. he found me washing the floors and making little apartment repairs.

More tea, Mom? he asked. He sat down to keep me company. O.K., Faith. I know you feel terrible. But how come Selena never realized about Abby?

Anthony, what the hell do I realize about you?

Come on, you had to be blind. I was just a little kid, and *I* saw. Honest to God, Ma.

Listen, Tonto. Basically Abby was O.K. She was. You don't know yet what their times can do to a person.

Here she goes with her goody-goodies — everything is so groovy wonderful far-out terrific. Next thing, you'll say people are darling and the world is *so* nice and round that Union Carbide will never blow it up.

I have never said anything as hopeful as that. And why to all our knowledge of that sad day did Tonto at 3 a.m. have to add the fact of the world?

The next night Max called from North Carolina. How's Selena? I'm flying up, he said. I have one early-morning appointment. Then I'm canceling everything.

At 7 a.m. Annie called. I had barely brushed my morning teeth. It was hard, she said. The whole damn thing. I don't mean Selena. All of us. In the train. None of you seemed real to me.

Real? Reality, huh? Listen, how about coming over for breakfast — I don't have to get going until after nine? I have this neat sourdough rye?

No, she said. Oh Christ, no. No!

·   ·   ·

I remember Ann's eyes and the hat she wore the day we first looked at each other. Our babies had just stepped howling out of the sandbox on their new walking legs. We picked them up. Over their sandy heads we smiled. I think a bond was sealed then, at least as useful as the vow we'd all sworn with husbands to whom we're no longer married. Hindsight, usually looked down upon, is probably as valuable as foresight, since it does include a few facts.

Meanwhile, Anthony's world—poor, dense, defenseless thing— rolls round and round. Living and dying are fastened to its surface and stuffed into its softer parts.

He was right to call my attention to its suffering and danger. He was right to harass my responsible nature. But I was right to invent for my friends and our children a report on these private deaths and the condition of our lifelong attachments.

1982

CHARLES BAXTER
HARMONY OF THE WORLD

from *Michigan Quarterly Review*

CHARLES BAXTER was born in 1947 in Minneapolis, and grew up "on forty acres of halfhearted farmland outside of Excelsior, Minnesota." He said, "I was very happy in elementary school, less happy in middle school, and very unhappy in high school." He earned his BA from Macalester College and his PhD in English from the University of Buffalo.

In 1983 Baxter submitted his first story collection, *Harmony of the World*, to an Association of Writers and Writing Programs competition. He explained, "They had already rejected the book at the Iowa contest and at a number of other fine high-rent locales. Don Barthelme was the judge of the AWP [Award] that year, and he liked my book enough to give it the prize."

Baxter is the author of the novels *First Light; Shadow Play; The Feast of Love,* which was nominated for the National Book Award; *Saul and Patsy;* and *The Soul Thief.* His story collections include *Through the Safety Net, A Relative Stranger, Believers, Gryphon,* and, most recently, *There's Something I Want You to Do.* His books on writing are *Burning Down the House: Essays on Fiction* and *The Art of Subtext: Beyond Plot.* He has also published three collections of poetry.

The *Atlantic* defined Baxter's signature themes as "revelations of the unexpected in the course of mundane day-to-day reality, the fleeting moments that indelibly shape a life, the moral and emotional quandaries that besiege us all."

Baxter has taught at Wayne State University, in the University of Michigan's MFA program in Ann Arbor, and at the Iowa Writers' Workshop. He now teaches at the University of Minnesota.

★

I

In the small Ohio town where I grew up, many homes had parlors that contained pianos, sideboards, and sofas, heavy objects signify-

ing gentility. These pianos were rarely tuned. They went flat in summer around the Fourth of July, and sharp in winter at Christmas. Ours
was a Story and Clark. On its music stand were copies of Stephen Foster
and Ethelbert Nevin favorites, along with one Chopin prelude that my
mother would practice for twenty minutes every three years. She had
no patience, but since she thought Ohio — all of it, every scrap — made
sense, she was happy and did not need to practice anything. Happiness
is not infectious, but somehow her happiness infected my father, a pharmacist, and then spread through the rest of the household. My whole
family was obstinately cheerful. I think of my two sisters, my brother,
and my parents as having artificial pasted-on smiles, like circus clowns.
They apparently thought cheer and good Christian words were univer-
sals, respected everywhere. The pianos were part of this cheer. They
played for celebrations and moments of pleasant pain. Or rather someone played them, but not too well, since excellent playing would have
been faintly antisocial. "Chopin," my mother said, shaking her head as
she stumbled through the prelude. "Why is he famous?"

When I was six, I received my first standing ovation. On the stage of
the community auditorium, where the temperature was about ninety-
four degrees, sweat fell from my forehead onto the piano keys, making their ivory surfaces slippery. At the conclusion of the piece, when
everyone stood up to applaud, I thought they were just being nice. My
playing had been mediocre; only my sweating had been extraordinary.
Two years later, they stood up again. When I was eleven, they cheered.
By that time I was astonishing these small-town audiences with Chopin
and Rachmaninoff recital chestnuts. I thought I was a genius, and read
biographies of Einstein. Already the townspeople were saying that I was
the best thing Parkersville had ever seen, *that I would put the place on
the map.* Mothers would send their children by to watch me practice.
The kids sat with their mouths open while I polished off another classic.

Like many musicians, I cannot remember ever playing badly, in
the sense of not knowing what I was doing. In high school, my identity was being sealed shut: My classmates called me El Señor Longhair,
even though I wore a crewcut, this being the 1950s. Whenever the town
needed a demonstration of local genius, it called upon me. There were
newspaper articles detailing my accomplishments, and I must have
heard the phrase "future concert career" at least two hundred times. My
parents smiled and smiled as I collected applause. My senior year, I gave
a solo recital and was hired for umpteen weddings and funerals. I was
good luck. On the Fourth of July the townspeople brought out a piano

to the city square so that I could improvise music between explosions at the fireworks display. Just before I left for college, I noticed that our neighbors wanted to come up to me, ostensibly for small talk but actually to touch me.

In college I made a shocking discovery: Other people existed in the world who were as talented as I was. If I sat down to play a Debussy etude, they would sit down and play Beethoven, only louder and faster than I had. I felt their breath on my neck. Apparently there were other small towns. In each of these small towns there was a genius. Perhaps some geniuses were not actually geniuses. I practiced constantly and began to specialize in the non-Germanic piano repertoire. I kept my eye out for students younger than I was, who might have flashier technique. At my senior recital I played Mozart, Chopin, Ravel, and Debussy, with encore pieces by Scriabin and Thomson. I managed to get the audience to stand up for the last time.

I was accepted into a large midwestern music school, famous for its high standards. Once there, I discovered that genius, to say nothing of talent, was a common commodity. Since I was only a middling composer, with no interesting musical ideas as such, I would have to make my career as a performer or teacher. But I didn't want to teach, and as a performer I lacked pizzazz. For the first time, it occurred to me that my life might be evolving into something unpleasant, something with the taste of stale bread.

I was beginning to meet performers with more confidence than I had, young musicians to whom doubt was as alien as proper etiquette. Often these people dressed like tramps, smelled, smoked constantly, were gay or sadistic. Whatever their imbalances, they were not genteel. *They did not represent small towns.* I was struck by their eyes. Their eyes seemed to proclaim, "The universe believes in me. It always has."

My piano teacher was a man I will call Luther Stecker. Every year he taught at the music school for six months. For the following six months he toured. He turned me away from the repertoire with which I was familiar and demanded that I learn several pieces by composers whom I had not often played, including Bach, Brahms, and Liszt. Each one of these composers discovered a weak point in me: I had trouble keeping up the consistent frenzy required by Liszt, the mathematical precision required by Bach, the unpianistic fingerings of Brahms.

I saw Stecker every week. While I played, he would doze off. When he woke, he would mumble some inaudible comment. He also coached a trio I participated in, and he spoke no more audibly then than he did during my private lesson.

I couldn't understand why, apart from his reputation, the school had hired him. Then I learned that in every Stecker student's life, the time came when the Master collected his thoughts, became blunt, and told the student exactly what his future would be. For me, the moment arrived on the third of November, 1966. I was playing sections of the Brahms Paganini Variations, a fiendish piece on which I had spent many hours. When I finished, I saw him sit up.

"Very good," he said, squinting at me. "You have talents."

There was a pause. I waited. "Thank you," I said.

"You have a nice house?" he asked.

"A nice house? No."

"You should get a nice house somewhere," he said, taking his handkerchief out of his pocket and waving it at me. "With windows. Windows with a view."

I didn't like the drift of his remarks. "I can't afford a house," I said.

"You will. A nice house. For you and your family."

I resolved to get to the heart of this. "Professor," I asked, "what did you think of my playing?"

"Excellent," he said. "That piece is very difficult."

"Thank you."

"Yes, technically excellent," he said, and my heart began to pound. "Intelligent phrasing. Not much for me to say. Yes. That piece has many notes," he added, enjoying the non sequitur.

I nodded. "Many notes."

"And you hit all of them accurately. Good pedal and good discipline. I like how you hit the notes."

I was dangling on his string, a little puppet.

"Thousands of notes, I suppose," he said, staring at my forehead, which was beginning to get damp, "and you hit all of them. You only forgot one thing."

"What?"

"The passion!" he roared. "You forgot the passion! You always forget it! Where is it? Did you leave it at home? You never bring it with you! Never! I listen to you and think of a robot playing! A smart robot, but a robot! No passion! Never ever ever!" He stopped shouting long enough to sneeze. "You *should* buy a house. You know why?"

"Why?"

"Because the only way you will ever praise God is with a family, that's why! Not with this piano! You are a fine student," he wound up, "but you make me sick! Why do you make me sick?"

He waited for me to answer.

"Why do you make me sick?" he shouted. "Answer me!"

"How can I possibly answer you?"

"By articulating words in English! Be courageous! Offer a suggestion! Why do you make me sick?"

I waited for a minute, the longest minute my life has seen or will ever see. "Passion," I said at last. "You said there wasn't enough passion. I thought there was. Perhaps not."

He nodded. "No. You are right. No passion. A corruption of music itself. Your playing is too gentle, too much good taste. To play the piano like a genius, you must have a bit of the fanatic. Just a bit. But it is essential. You have stubbornness and talent but no fanaticism. You don't have the salt on the rice. Without salt, the rice is inedible, no matter what its quality otherwise." He stood up. "I tell you this because sooner or later someone else will. You will have a life of disappointments if you stay in music. You may find a teacher who likes you. Good, good. *But you will never be taken up! Never!* You should buy a house, young man. With a beautiful view. Move to it. Don't stay here. You are close to success, but it is the difference between leaping the chasm and falling into it, one inch short. You are an inch short. You could come back for more lessons. You could graduate from here. But if you are truly intelligent, you will say good-bye. Good-bye." He looked down at the floor and did not offer me his hand.

I stood up and walked out of the room.

Becalmed, I drifted down and up the hallways of the building for half an hour. Then a friend of mine, a student of conducting from Bolivia, a Marxist named Juan Valparaiso, approached, and, ignoring my shallow breathing and cold sweat, started talking at once.

"Terrible, furious day!" he said.

"Yes."

"I am conducting *Benvenuto Cellini* overture this morning! All is going well until difficult flute entry. I instruct, with force, flutists. Soon all woodwinds are ignoring me." He raised his eyebrows and stroked his huge gaucho mustache. "Always! Always there are fascists in the woodwinds!"

"Fascists everywhere," I said.

"Horns bad, woodwinds worse. Demands of breath made for insanes. Pedro," he said, "you are appearing irresoluted. Sick?"

"Yes." I nodded. "Sick. I just came from Stecker. My playing makes *him* sick."

"He said that? That you are making him sick?"

"That's right. I play like a robot, he says."

"What will you do?" Juan asked me. "Kill him?"

"No." And then I knew. "I'm leaving the school."

"What? Is impossible!" Tears leaped instantly into Juan's eyes. "Cannot, Pedro. After one whipping? No! Disappointments everywhere here. Also outside in world. Must stick to it." He grabbed me by the shoulders. "Fascists put here on earth to break our hearts! Must live through. You cannot go." He looked around wildly. "Where could you go anyway?"

"I'm not sure," I said. "He said I would never amount to anything. I think he's right. But I could do something else." To prove that I could imagine options, I said, "I could work for a newspaper. You know, music criticism."

"Caterpillars!" Juan shouted, his tears falling onto my shirt. "Failures! Pathetic lives! Cannot, cannot! Who would hire you?"

I couldn't tell him for six months, until I was given a job in Knoxville on a part-time trial basis. But by then I was no longer writing letters to my musician friends. I had become anonymous. I worked in Knoxville for two years, then in Louisville — a great city for music — until I moved here, to this city I shall never name, in the middle of New York State, where I bought a house with a beautiful view.

In my home town, they still wonder what happened to me, but my smiling parents refuse to reveal my whereabouts.

II

Every newspaper has a command structure. Within that command structure, editors assign certain stories, but the writers must be given some freedom to snoop around and discover newsworthy material themselves. In this anonymous city, I was hired to review all the concerts of the symphony orchestra and to provide some hype articles during the week to boost the ticket sales for Friday's program. Since the owner of the paper was on the symphony board of trustees, writing about the orchestra and its programs was necessarily part of good journalistic citizenship. On my own, though, I initiated certain projects, wrote book reviews for the Sunday section, interviewed famous visiting musicians — some of them my ex-classmates — and during the summer I could fill in on all sorts of assignments, as long as I cleared what I did with the feature editor, Morris Cascadilla.

"You're the first serious musician we've ever had on the staff here," he announced to me when I arrived, suspicion and hope fighting for control on his face. "Just remember this: Be clear and concise. Assume they've got intelligence but no information. After that, you're on your own, except you should clear dicey stuff with me. And never forget the Maple Street angle."

The Maple Street angle was Cascadilla's equivalent to the Nixon administration's "How will it play in Peoria?" No matter what subject I wrote about, I was expected to make it relevant to Maple Street, the newspaper's mythical locus of middle-class values. I could write about electronic, aleatory, or post-Boulez music *if* I suggested that the city's daughters might be corrupted by it. Sometimes I found the Maple Street angle, and sometimes I couldn't. When I failed, Cascadilla would call me in, scowl at my copy and mutter, "All the Juilliard graduates in town will love this." Nevertheless, the Maple Street angle was a spiritual exercise in humility, and I did my best to find it week after week.

When I first learned that the orchestra was scheduled to play Paul Hindemith's *Harmony of the World* Symphony, I didn't think of Hindemith, but of Maple Street, that mythically harmonious place where I actually grew up.

III

Working on the paper left me some time for other activities. Unfortunately, there was nothing I knew how to do except play the piano and write reviews.

Certain musicians are very practical. Trumpet players (who love valves) tend to be good mechanics, and I have met a few composers who fly airplanes and can restore automobiles. Most performing violinists and pianists, however, are drained by the demands of their instruments and seldom learn how to do anything besides play. In daily life they are helpless and stricken. In midlife the smart ones force themselves to find hobbies. But the less fortunate come home to solitary apartments without pictures or other decorations, warm up their dinners in silence, read whatever books happen to be on the dinner table, and then go to bed.

I am speaking of myself here, of course. As time passed, and the vacuum of my life made it harder to breathe, I required more work. I fancied I was a tree, putting out additional leaves. I let it be known that I would play as an accompanist for voice students and other recitalists, if their schedules didn't interfere with my commitments for the paper.

One day I received a call at my desk. A quietly controlled female voice asked, "Is this Peter Jenkins?"

"Yes."

"Well," she said, pausing, as if she'd forgotten what she meant to tell me, "this is Karen Jensen. That's almost like Jenkins, isn't it?" I waited. "I'm a singer," she said, after a moment. "A soprano. I've just lost my accompanist and I'm planning on giving a recital in three months. They said you were available. Are you? What do you charge?"

I told her.

"Isn't that kind of steep? That's kind of steep. Well, I suppose . . . I can use somebody else until just before, and then I can use you. They say you're good. And I've read your reviews. I really admire the way you write!"

"Thank you."

"You get so much information into your reviews! Sometimes, when I read you, I imagine what you look like. Sometimes a person can make a mental picture. I just wish the paper would publish a photo or something of you."

"They want to," I said, "but I asked them to please don't."

"Even your voice sounds like your writing!" she said excitedly. "I can see you in front of me now. Can you play Fauré and Schubert? I mean, is there any composer or style you don't like and won't play?"

"No," I said. "I play anything."

"That's *wonderful!*" she said, as if I had confessed to a remarkable tolerance. "Some accompanists are so picky. 'I won't do this, I won't do that.' Well, *one* I know is like that. Anyhow, could we meet soon? Do you sight-read? Can we meet at the music school downtown? In a practice room? When are you free?"

I set up an appointment.

She was almost beautiful. Her deep eyes were accented by depressive bowls in quarter-moon shadow under them. Though she was only in her late twenties, she seemed slightly scorched by anxiety. She couldn't keep still. Her hands fluttered as they fixed her hair; she scratched nervously at her cheeks; and her eyes jumped every few seconds. Soon, however, she calmed down and began to look me in the eye, evaluating me. Then *I* turned away.

She wanted to test me out and had brought along her recital numbers, mostly standard fare: a Handel aria, Mozart, Schubert, and Fauré. The last set of songs, *Nine Epitaphs,* by an American composer I had never heard of, Theodore Chanler, was the only novelty.

"Who is this Chanler?" I asked, looking through the sheet music.

"I . . . I found it in the music library," she said. "I looked him up. He was born in Boston and died in 1961. There's a recording by Phyllis Curtin. Virgil Thomson says these are maybe the best American art songs ever written."

"Oh."

"They're kind of, you know, lugubrious. I mean they're all epitaphs written supposedly on tombstones, set to music. They're like portraits. I love them. Is it all right? Do you mind?"

"No, I don't mind."

We started through her program, beginning with Handel's "Un sospiretto d'un labbro pallido" from *Il Pastor fido.* I could immediately see why she was still in central New York State and why she would always be a student. She had a fine voice, clear and distinct, somewhat styled after Victoria de los Angeles (I thought), and her articulation was superb. If these achievements had been the whole story, she might have been a professional. But her pitch wobbled on sustained notes in a maddening way; the effect was not comic and would probably have gone unnoticed by most non-musicians, but to me the result was harrowing. She could sing perfectly for several measures and then she would miss a note by a semi-tone, which drove an invisible fingernail into my scalp. It was as though a gypsy's curse descended every five or six seconds, throwing her off pitch; then she was allowed to be a great singer until the curse descended again. Her loss of pitch was so regularized that I could see it coming and squirmed in anticipation. I felt as though I were in the presence of one of God's more complicated pranks.

Her choice of songs highlighted her failings. Their delicate textures were constantly broken by her lapses. When we arrived at the Chanler pieces, I thought I was accustomed to her, but I found I wasn't. The first song begins with the following verse, written by Walter de la Mare, who had crafted all the poems in archaic epitaph style:

> *Here lyeth our infant, Alice Rodd;*
> *She were so small,*

> *Scarce aught at all,*
> *But a mere breath of Sweetness sent from God.*

The vocal line for "She were so small" consists of four notes, the last two rising a half-step from the two before them. To work the passage requires a dead-eye accuracy of pitch:

Singing this line, Karen Jensen hit the D-sharp but missed the E and skidded up uncontrollably to F-sharp, which would sound all right to anyone who didn't have the music in front of his nose, as I did. Only a fellow-musician could be offended.

Infuriated, I began to feel that I could *not* participate in a recital with this woman. It would be humiliating to perform such lovely songs in this excruciating manner. I stopped playing, turned to her to tell her that I could not continue after all, and then I saw her bracelet.

I am not, on the whole, especially observant, a failing that probably accounts for my having missed the bracelet when we first met. But I saw it now: five silver canaries dangled down quietly from it, and, as it slipped back and forth, I saw her wrist and what I suddenly realized *would* be there — the parallel lines of her madness, etched in scar tissue.

The epitaphs finished, she asked me to work with her, and I agreed.

When we shook hands the canaries shook in tiny vibrations, as if pleased with my dutiful kindness, my charity, toward their mad mistress.

IV

Though Paul Hindemith's reputation once equaled Stravinsky's and Bartók's, it suffered after his death in 1963 an almost complete collapse. Only two of his orchestral works, the *Symphonic Metamorphoses on Themes of Weber* and the *Mathis der Maler* Symphony, are played with any frequency, thanks in part to their use of borrowed tunes. One hears his woodwind quintets and choral pieces now and again, but the works of which he was most proud—the ballet *Nobilissima Visione, Das Marienleben* (a song cycle) and the opera *Die Harmonie der Welt*—have fallen into total obscurity.

The reason for Hindemith's sudden loss of reputation was a mystery to me; I had always considered his craftsmanship if not his inspiration to be first-rate. When I saw that the *Harmony of the World* Symphony, almost never played, would be performed in our anonymous city, I told Cascadilla that I wanted to write a story for that week on how fame was gained and lost in the world of music. He thought that subject might be racy enough to interest the tone-deaf citizens of leafy and peaceful Maple Street, where no one is famous, if I made sure the story contained "the human element."

I read up on Hindemith, played his piano music, and listened to the recordings. I slowly found the music to be technically astute but emotionally arid, as if some problem of purely local interest kept the composer's gaze safely below the horizon. Technocratic and oddly timid, his work reminded me of a model train chugging through a tiny town where only models of people actually lived. In fact, Hindemith did have a lifelong obsession with train sets: In Berlin, his took up three rooms, and the composer wrote elaborate timetables so that the toys wouldn't collide.

But if Hindemith had a technocrat's intelligence, he also believed in the necessity of universal participation in musical activities. Listening was not enough. Even non-musical citizens could learn to sing and play, and he wrote music expressly for this purpose. He seems to have known that passive, drugged listening was a side effect of totalitarian environments and that elitist composers such as Schoenberg were engaged in antisocial Faustian projects that would bewilder and infuriate most audiences, leaving them isolated and thus eager to be drugged by a musical superman.

As the foremost anti-Nietzschean German composer of his day, therefore, Hindemith left Germany when his works could not be performed, thanks to the Third Reich; wrote textbooks with simple exercises; composed a requiem in memory of Franklin Roosevelt, set to words by Walt Whitman; and taught students, not all of them talented, in Ankara, New Haven, and Buffalo ("this caricature of a town"). As he passed through late middle age, he turned to a project he had contemplated all his life, an opera based on the career of the German astronomer Johannes Kepler, author of *De Harmonice Mundi*. This opera, a summary of Hindemith's ideas, would be called *Harmony of the World*. Hindemith worked out the themes first in a symphony, which bore the same title as the opera, and completed it in 1951. The more I thought about this project, the more it seemed anachronistic. Who believed in world harmony in 1951? Or thereafter? Such a symphony would have to pass beyond technical sophistication into divine inspiration, which Hindemith had never shown any evidence of possessing.

It occurred to me that Hindemith's lifelong sanity had perhaps given way in this case, toppled not by despair (as is conventional) but by faith in harmony.

V

For the next rehearsal, I drove to Karen Jensen's apartment, where there was, she said, a piano. I'd become curious about the styles of her insanity: I imagined a hamster cage in the kitchen, a doll-head mobile in the living room, and mottoes written with different colored inks on memo pads tacked up everywhere on the walls.

She greeted me at the door without her bracelet. When I looked at her wrist, she said, "Hmmm. I see that you noticed. A memento of adolescent despair." She sighed. "But it does frighten people off. Once you've tried to do something like that, people don't really trust you. I don't know why exactly. Don't want your blood on their hands or something. Well, come on in."

I was struck first by her forthrightness and second by her tiny apartment. Its style was much like the style in my house. She owned an attractive but worn-down sofa, a sideboard that supported an antique clock, one chair, a glass-top dinner table, and one nondescript poster on the wall. Trying to keep my advantage, I looked hard for telltale signs of insanity but found none. The piano was off in the corner, almost hidden, unlike those in the parlors back home.

"Very nice," I said.

"Well, thanks," she said. "It's not much. I'd like something bigger, but . . . where I work, I'm an administrative assistant, and they don't pay me very much. So that's why I live like a snail here. It's hardly big enough to move around in, right?" She wasn't looking at me. "I mean, I could almost pick it up and carry it away."

I nodded. "You just don't think like a rich person," I said, trying to be hearty. "They like to expand. They need room. Big houses, big cars, fat bodies."

"Oh, I know!" she said, laughing. "My uncle . . . would *you* like to stay for dinner? You look like you need a good meal. I mean, after the rehearsal. You're just skin and bones, Pet — May I call you Peter?"

"Sure." I sat down on the sofa and tried to think up an excuse. "I really can't stay, Miss Jensen. I have another rehearsal to go to later tonight. I wish I could."

"That's not it, is it?" she asked suddenly, looking down at me. "I don't believe you. I bet it's something else. I bet you're afraid of me."

"Why should I be afraid of you?"

She smiled and shrugged. "That's all right. You don't have to say anything. I know how it goes." She laughed once more, faintly. "I never found a man who could handle it. They want to show you *their* scars, you know? They don't want to see any on you, and if they discover any, they just run." She slapped her right hand into her forehead and then ran her fingers through her hair. "Well, shit. I didn't mean to do this *at all!* I mean, I admire you so much and everything, and here I am, running on like this. I guess we should get down to business, right? Since I'm paying you by the hour."

I smiled professionally and went to her piano.

Beneath the high-culture atmosphere that surrounds them, art songs have one subject: love. The permutations of love (lust, solitude, and loss) are present in abundance, of course, but for the most part they are simple vehicles for the expression of that one emotion. I was reminded of this as I played through the piano parts. As much as I concentrated on the music in front of me, I couldn't help but notice that my employer stood next to the piano, singing the words sometimes toward me, sometimes away. She was rather courageously forcing eye contact on me. She kept this up for an hour and a half until we came to the Chanler settings, when at last she turned slightly, singing to the walls.

As before, her voice broke out of control every five seconds, giving isolated words all the wrong shadings. The only way to endure it, I discovered, was to think of her singing as a postmodern phenomenon with its own conventions and rules. As the victim of necessity rather than accident, Karen Jensen was tolerable.

> *Here sleep I,*
> *Susannah Fry,*
> *No one near me,*
> *No one nigh:*
> *Alone, alone*
> *Under my stone,*
> *Dreaming on,*
> *Still dreaming on:*
> *Grass for my valance*
> *And coverlid,*
> *Dreaming on*
> *As I always did.*
> *"Weak in the head?"*
> *Maybe. Who knows?*
> *Susannah Fry*
> *Under the rose.*

There she was, facing away from me, burying Susannah Fry, and probably her own past and career into the bargain.

When we were done, she asked, "Sure you won't stay?"

"No, I don't think so."

"You really haven't another engagement, do you?"

"No," I admitted.

"I didn't think so. You were scared of me the moment you walked in the door. You thought I'd be crazy." She waited. "After all, only ugly girls live alone, right? And I'm not ugly."

"No, you aren't," I said. "You're quite attractive."

"Do you think so?" she asked, brightening. "It's so nice to hear that from you, even if you're just paying a compliment. I mean, it still means *something*." Then she surprised me. As I stood in the doorway, she got down on her knees in front of me and bowed her head in the style of one of her songs. "Please stay," she asked. Immediately she stood up and laughed. "But don't feel obliged to."

"Oh, no," I said, returning to her living room. "I've just changed my mind. Dinner sounds like a good idea."

After she had served and we had started to eat, she looked up at me and said, "You know, I'm not completely good." She paused. "At singing."

"What?" I stopped chewing. "Yes, you are. You're all right."

"Don't lie. I know I'm not. You know I'm not. Come on: Let's at least be honest. I think I have certain qualities of musicality, but my pitch is . . . you know. Uneven. You probably think it's awfully vain of me to put on these recitals like this. With nobody but friends and family coming."

"No, I don't."

"Well, I don't care what you say. It's . . . hmm, I don't know. People encourage me. And it's a discipline. Music's finally a discipline that rewards you. Privately, though. Well, that's what my mother says."

Carefully I said, "She may be right."

"Who cares if she is?" She laughed, her mouth full of food. "I enjoy doing it. Like I enjoy doing this. Listen, I don't want to seem forward or anything, but are you married?"

"No."

"I didn't think so." She picked up a string bean and eyed it suspiciously. "Why aren't you? You're not ugly. In fact you're all right looking. You obviously haven't been crazy. Are you gay or something?"

"No."

"No," she agreed, "you don't look gay. You don't even look very happy. You don't look very anything. Why is that?"

"I should be offended by this line of questioning."

"But you're not. You know why? Because I'm interested in you. I hardly know you, but I like you, what I can see. Don't you have any trust?"

"Yes," I said, finally.

"So answer my question. Why don't you look very anything?"

"Do you want to hear what my piano teacher once said?" I asked. "He said I wasn't enough of a fanatic. He said that to be one of the great ones you have to be a tiny bit crazy. Touched. And he said I wasn't. And when he said it, I knew all along he was right. I was waiting for someone to say what I already knew, and he was the one. I was too much a good citizen, he said. I wasn't possessed."

She rose, walked around the table to where I was sitting, and stood in front of me, looking down at my face. I knew that whatever she was going to do had been picked up, in attitude, from one of her songs. She touched the back of my arm with two fingers on her right hand. "Well," she said, "maybe you aren't possessed, but what would you think of me as another possession?"

VI

In 1618 at the age of seventy, Katherine Kepler, the mother of Johannes Kepler, was put on trial for witchcraft. The records indicate that her personality was so deranged, so deeply offensive to all, that if she were alive today she would *still* be called a witch. One of Kepler's biographers, Angus Armitage, notes that she was "evil-tempered" and possessed an interest in unnamed "outlandish things." Her trial lasted, on and off, for three years; by 1621, when she was acquitted, her personality had disintegrated completely. She died the following year.

At the age of six, Kepler's son Frederick died of smallpox. A few months later, Kepler's wife, Barbara, died of typhus. Two other children, Henry and Susanna, had died in infancy.

Like many another of his age, Kepler spent much of his adult life cultivating favor from the nobility. He was habitually penniless and was often reduced, as his correspondence shows, to begging for handouts. He was the victim of religious persecution, though luckier in this regard than some.

After he married for a second time, three more children died in infancy, a statistic that in theory carries less emotional weight than one might think, given the accepted levels of infant mortality for that era.

In 1619, despite the facts cited above, Kepler published *De Harmonice Mundi,* a text in which he set out to establish the correspondence between the laws of harmony and the disposition of planets in motion. In brief, Kepler argued that certain intervals, such as the octave, major and minor sixths, and major and minor thirds, were pleasurable, while other intervals were not. History indicated that mankind had always regarded certain intervals as unpleasant. Feeling that this set of universal tastes pointed to immutable laws, Kepler sought to map out the pleasurable intervals geometrically, and then to transfer that geometrical pattern to the order of the planets. The velocity of the planets, rather than their strict placement, constituted the harmony of the spheres. This velocity provided each planet with a note, what Armitage calls a "term in a mathematically determined relation."

In fact, each planet performed a short musical scale, set down by Kepler in staff notation. The length of the scale depended upon the eccentricity of the orbit; and its limiting notes could generally be shown to form a concord (except for Venus and the Earth with their nearly circular orbits, whose scales were of very constricted range) . . . At the Creation . . . complete concord prevailed and the morning stars sang together.

VII

We began to eat dinner together. Accustomed to solitude, we did not always engage in conversation. I would read the newspaper or ink in letters on my geometrically patterned crossword puzzles at my end of the table, while Karen would read detective novels or *Time* at hers. If she had cooked, I would clear and wash the dishes: if I had cooked, she did the cleaning. Experience and disappointments had made us methodical. She told me that she had once despised structured experiences governed by timetables, but that after several manic-depressive episodes she had learned to love regularity. This regularity included taking lithium at the same time — to the minute — each day.

The season being summer, we would pack towels and swimming suits after dinner and drive out to one of several public beaches, where we would swim until darkness came on. On calm evenings, Karen would drop her finger in the water and watch the waves lap outward. I favored immature splashing, or grabbing her by the arm and whirling her around me until I released her and she would spin back and fall into the water, laughing as she sank. One evening, we found a private beach, two hundred feet of sand all to ourselves, on a lake thirty miles out of town. Framed on both sides by woods and well-hidden from the highway, this beach had the additional advantage of being unpatrolled. We had no bathhouse in which to change, however, so Karen instructed me not to look as she walked about fifty feet away to a spot where she undressed and put on her suit.

Though we had been intimate for at least a week, I had still not seen her naked: Like a good Victorian, she demanded the shades be drawn, the lights out, and the covers pulled discreetly over us. But now, with the same methodical thoroughness, she wanted me to see her, so I looked, despite her warnings. She was bent over, under the tree boughs, the evening light breaking through the leaves and casting broken gold bands on her body. Her arms were delicate, the arms of a schoolgirl, I thought, an impression heightened by the paleness of her skin, but her breasts were full, at first making me think of Rubens's women, then of Renoir's, then of nothing at all. Slowly, knowing I was watching her, she pinned her hair up. Not her breasts or arms, but that expression of vague contentment as she looked out toward the water away from me: *That* made me feel a tingling below my heart, somewhere in an emotional center near my stomach. I wanted to pick her up and carry her somewhere, but with my knees wobbly it was all I could do to make my way over to where she stood and take her in my arms before she cried out. "Jesus," she said, shivering, "you gave me a surprise." I kissed her, waiting for inspiration to direct me on what to do next: Pick her up? Carry her? Make love to her on the sand? Wade into the water with her and swim out to the center of the lake, where we would drown together in a Lawrentian love-grip? But then we broke the kiss; she put on her swimsuit like a good citizen, and we swam for our usual fifteen minutes in silence. Afterward, we changed back into our clothes and drove home, muttering small talk. Behavior inspired by and demonstrating love embarrassed both of us. When I told her that she was beautiful and that I loved her, she patted me on the cheek and said, "Aw, how nice. You always try to say the right thing."

VIII

The Maple Street angle for *Harmony of the World* ran as follows: SYMPHONY OF FAITH IN A FAITHLESS AGE. Hindemith, I said, wished to confound the skeptics by composing a monument of faith. In an age of organized disharmony, of political chaos, he stood at the barricades defending tonality and traditional musical form. I carefully avoided any specific discussion of the musical materials of the symphony, which in the Schott orchestral score looked overcomplex and melodically ugly. From what I could tell without hearing the piece, Hindemith had employed stunning technique in order to disguise his lack of inspiration, though I did not say so in print. Instead, I wrote that the symphony's failure to win public support was probably the result of Hindemith's refusal to use musical gimmicks on the one hand and sticky sweet melodies on the other. I wrote that he had not been dismayed by the bad reviews *Harmony of the World* had received, which was untrue. I said he was a man of integrity. I did not say that men of integrity are often unable to express joy when the occasion demands. Cascadilla liked my article. "This guy sounds like me," he said, reading my copy. "I respect him." The article ran five days before the concert and was two pages away from the religion-and-faith section. Not long after, the symphony ticket office called me to say that my piece had caused a rush of ticket orders from ordinary folk, non-concert types, who wanted to hear this "religious symphony." The woman from the business office thanked me for my trouble. "Let's hope they like it," I said.

"Of course they will," she assured me. "You've told them to."

But they didn't. Despite all the oratory in the symphony, it was spiritually as dead as a lampshade. I could see why Hindemith had been shocked by the public reaction. Our audience applauded politely in discouragement, and then I heard an unusual sound for this anonymous city: one man, full of fun and conviction, booing loudly from the balcony. Booing the harmony of the world! He must be a Satanist! Don't intentions mean anything? So what if the harmony and joy were all counterfeit? The conductor came out for a bow, smiled at the booing man, and very soon the applause died away. I left the hall, feeling responsible. Arriving at the paper, I wrote a review of crushing dullness that reeked of bad faith. Goddamn Hindemith! Here he was, claiming to have seen God's workings, and they sounded like the workings of a steam engine or a trolley car. A fake symphony, with optimism the composer did not feel! I decided (but did not write) that *Harmony of the World* was just possibly the largest, most misconceived fiasco in modern music's history. It was a symphony that historically could not be written, by a man who was constitutionally not equipped to write it. In my review, I kept a civil pen: I said that the performance lacked "luster," "a certain necessary glow."

IX

"I'm worried about the recital tomorrow."

"Aw, don't worry. Here, kiss me. Right here."

"Aren't you listening? I'm worried."

"I'm singing. You're just accompanying me. Nobody's going to notice you. Move over a little, would you? Yeah, there. That pillow was forcing my head against the wall."

"Why aren't you worried?"

"Why should I be worried? I don't want to worry. I want to make love. Isn't that better than worrying?"

"Not if I'm worried."

"People won't notice *you*. By the way, have you noticed that when I kiss you on the stomach, you get goose bumps?"

"Yes. I think you're taking this pretty lightly. I mean, it's almost unprofessional."

"That's because I'm an amateur. A one-hundred-percent amateur. Always and totally. Even at this. But that doesn't mean I don't have my moments. Mmmmmm. That's better."

"I thought it would maybe help. But listen. I'm still worried."

"Uhhhn. Oh, wait a minute. Wait a minute. Oh, I get it."

"What?"

"I get it. You aren't worried about yourself. You're worried about me."

X

Forty people attended her recital, which was sponsored by the city university's music school, in which Karen was a sometime student. Somehow we made our way through the program, but when we came to the Chanler settings I suddenly wanted Karen to sing them perfectly. I wanted an angel to descend and to take away the gypsy's curse. But she sang as she always had — off pitch — and when she came to "Ann Poverty," I found myself in that odd region between rage and pity.

> *Stranger, here lies*
> *Ann Poverty;*
> *Such was her name*
> *And such was she.*
> *May Jesu pity*
> *Poverty.*

But I was losing my capacity for pity.

In the green room, her forty friends came back to congratulate her. I met them. They were all very nice. She smiled and laughed: There would be a party in an hour. Would I go? I declined. When we were alone, I said I was going back to my place.

"Why?" she asked. "Shouldn't you come to my party? You're my lover, after all. That *is* the word."

"Yes. But I don't want to go with you."

"Why?"

"Because of tonight's concert, that's why."

"What about it?"

"It wasn't very good, was it? I mean, it just wasn't."

"I thought it was all right. A few slips. It was pretty much what I was capable of. All those people said they liked it."

"Those people don't matter!" I said, my eyes watering with anger. "Only the music matters. Only the music is betrayed, they aren't. They don't know about pitch, most of them, I mean, Jesus, they aren't genuine musicians, so how would they know? Do you really think what we did tonight was good? It wasn't! It was a travesty! We ruined those songs! How can you stand to do that?"

"I don't ruin them. I sing them adequately. I project feeling. People get pleasure from them. That's enough."

"It's awful," I said, feeling the ecstatic liftoff into rage. "You're so close to being good, but you *aren't* good. Who cares what those ignoramuses think? They don't know what notes you're *supposed* to hit. It's that goddamn slippery pitch of yours. You're killing those songs. You just *drop* them like watermelons on the stage! It makes me sick! I couldn't have gone on for another day listening to you and your warbling! I'd die first."

She looked at me and nodded, her mouth set in a half-moue, half-smile of non-surprise. There may have been tears in her eyes, but I didn't see them. She looked at me as if she were listening hard to a long-distance call. "You're tired of me," she said.

"I'm not tired of you. I'm tired of hearing you sing! Your voice makes my flesh crawl! Do you know why? Can you tell me why you make me sick? Why do you make me sick? Never mind. I'm just glad this is over."

"You don't look glad. You look angry."

"And you look smug. Listen, why don't you go off to your party? Maybe there'll be a talent scout there. Or roses flung riotously at you. But don't give a recital like this again, please, okay? It's a public disgrace. It offends music. It offends *me.*"

I turned my back on her and walked out to my car.

XI

After the failure of *Harmony of the World,* Hindemith went on a strenuous tour that included Scandinavia. In Oslo, he was rehearsing the Philharmonic when he blinked his bright blue eyes twice, turned to the concertmaster, and said, "I don't know where I am." They took him away to a hospital; he had suffered a nervous breakdown.

XII

I slept until noon, having nothing to do at the paper and no reason to get up. At last, unable to sleep longer, I rose and walked to the kitchen to make coffee. I then took my cup to the picture window and looked down the hill to the trees of the conservation area, the view Stecker had once told me I should have.

The figure of a woman was hanging from one of the trees, a noose around her neck. I dropped my coffee cup and the hot coffee spilled out over my feet.

I ran out the back door in my pajamas and sprinted painfully down the hill's tall grass toward the tree. I was fifty feet away when I saw that it wasn't Karen, wasn't in fact a woman at all, but an effigy of sorts, with one of Karen's hats, a pillow head, and a dress hanging over a broomstick skeleton. Attached to the effigy was a note:

> In the old days, this might have been me. Not anymore. Still, I thought it'd make you think. And I'm not giving up singing, either. By the way, what your playing lacks is not fanaticism, but concentration. You can't seem to keep your mind on one thing for more than a minute at a time. *I* notice things, too. You aren't the only reviewer around here. Take good care of this doll, okay?
>
> XXXXX,
Karen

I took the doll up and dropped it in the clothes closet, where it stands to this hour.

Hindemith's biographer, Geoffrey Skelton, writes, "[On the stage] the episodic scenes from Kepler's life fail to achieve immediate dramatic coherence, and the basic theme remains obscure . . ."

She won't of course see me again. She won't talk to me on the phone, and she doesn't answer my letters. I am quite lucidly aware of what I have done. And I go on seeing doubles and reflections and wave motion everywhere. There is symmetry, harmony, after all. I suppose I should have been nice to her. That, too, is a discipline. I always tried to be nice to everyone else.

On his deathbed, Hindemith has Kepler sing:

> *Und muss sehn am End:*
> *Die grosse Harmonie, das ist der Tod.*
> *Absterben ist, sie zu bewirken, not.*
> *Im Leben hat sie keine Statte.*

 XIII

Hindemith's words may be correct. But Dante says that the residents of limbo, having never been baptized, will not see the face of God. This despite their having committed no sin, no active fault. In their fated locale they sigh, which keeps the air "forever trembling." No harmony for them, these guiltless souls. Through eternity, the residents of limbo — where one can imagine oneself if one cannot stand to imagine any part of hell — experience one of the most shocking of all the emotions that Dante names: "duol senza martíri," grief without torment. These sighs are rather like the sounds one hears drifting from front porches in small towns on soft summer nights.

1986

MONA SIMPSON
LAWNS

from the *Iowa Review*

MONA SIMPSON was born in 1957 in Green Bay, Wisconsin, and moved to Los Angeles as a young teenager. Her father was a recent immigrant from Syria and her mother the daughter of a mink farmer and the first person in her family to attend college. Simpson earned her BA from the University of California, Berkeley, and published her first stories in *Ploughshares, The Iowa Review,* and *Mademoiselle.* After earning her MFA from Columbia University, she worked as an editor for *The Paris Review.*

Simpson writes about the American class system through the lens of the family and its changing sociology. Alice Munro has called her families "amazing" and "heartbreaking . . . the sort who haven't turned up before in anything else I've read." John Ashberry wrote, "Simpson has a remarkable gift for transforming the homely cadences of plain American speech into something like poetry."

Simpson won the Whiting Prize for her first novel, *Anywhere but Here.* In 1992 she published a sequel titled *The Lost Father. Off Keck Road* won the *Chicago Tribune* Heartland Prize and was a finalist for the PEN/Faulkner Award. She has also been awarded a Literature Prize from the American Academy of Arts and Letters. Her most recent books are the novels *My Hollywood* and *Casebook.* Simpson lives in Santa Monica, California.

★

I STEAL. I'VE STOLEN books and money and even letters. Letters are great. I can't tell you the feeling walking down the street with twenty dollars in my purse, stolen earrings in my pocket. I don't get caught. That's the amazing thing. You're out on the sidewalk, other people all around, shopping, walking, and you've got it. You're out of the store, you've done this thing you're not supposed to do, but no one stops you. At first it's a rush. Like you're even for everything you didn't get before. But then you're left alone, no one even notices you. Nothing changes.

I work in the mailroom of my dormitory, Saturday mornings. I sort mail, put the letters in these long narrow cubbyholes. The insides of mailboxes. It's cool there when I stick in my arm.

I've stolen cash—these crisp, crackling, brand-new twenty-dollar bills the fathers and grandmothers send, sealed up in sheets of wax paper. Once I got a fifty. I've stolen presents, too. I got a sweater and a football. I didn't want the football, but after the package was messed up on the mail table, I had no choice, I had to take the whole thing in my day pack and throw it out on the other side of campus. I found a covered garbage can. It was miles away. Brand-new football.

Mostly, what I take are cookies. No evidence. They're edible. I can spot the coffee cans of chocolate chip. You can smell it right through the wrapping. A cool smell, like the inside of a pantry. Sometimes I eat straight through the can during my shift.

Tampering with the United States mail is a federal crime, I know. Listen, let me tell you, I know. I got a summons in my mailbox to go to the Employment Office next Wednesday. Sure I'm scared.

The university cops want to talk to me. Great. They think, "suspect" is the word they use, that one of us is throwing out mail instead of sorting it. Wonder who? Us is the others, I'm not the only sorter. I just work Saturdays, mail comes, you know, six days a week in this country. They'll never guess it's me.

They say this in the letter, they think it's out of *laziness*. Wanting to hurry up and get done, not spend the time. But I don't hurry. I'm really patient on Saturday mornings. I leave my dorm early, while Lauren's still asleep, I open the mailroom—it's this heavy door and I have my own key. When I get there, two bags are already on the table, sagging, waiting for me. Two old ladies. One's packages, one's mail. There's a small key opens the bank of doors, the little boxes from the inside. Through the glass part of every mail slot, I can see. The Astroturf field across the street over the parking lot, it's this light green. I watch the sky go from black to gray to blue while I'm there. Some days just stay foggy. Those are the best. I bring a cup of coffee in with me from the vending machine—don't want to wake Lauren up—and I get there at like seven-thirty or eight o'clock. I don't mind it then, my whole dorm's asleep. When I walk out it's as quiet as a football game day. It's eleven or twelve when you know everyone's up and walking that it gets bad being down there. That's why I start early. But I don't rush.

•   •   •

Once you open a letter, you can't just put it in a mailbox. The person's gonna say something. So I stash them in my pack and throw them out. Just people I know. Susan Brown I open, Annie Larsen, Larry Helprin. All the popular kids from my high school. These are kids who drove places together, took vacations, they all ski, they went to the prom in one big group. At morning nutrition — nutrition, it's your break at ten o'clock for donuts and stuff. California state law, you have to have it.

They used to meet outside on the far end of the math patio, all in one group. Some of them smoked. I've seen them look at each other, concerned at ten in the morning. One touched the inside of another's wrist, like grown-ups in trouble.

And now I know. Everything I thought those three years, worst years of my life, turns out to be true. The ones here get letters. Keri's at Santa Cruz, Lilly's in San Diego, Kevin's at Harvard, and Beth's at Stanford. And like from families, their letters talk about problems. They're each other's main lives. You always knew, looking at them in high school, they weren't just kids who had fun. They cared. They cared about things.

They're all worried about Lilly now. Larry and Annie are flying down to talk her into staying at school.

I saw Glenn the day I came to Berkeley. I was all unpacked and I was standing there leaning into the window of my father's car, saying, "Smile, Dad, jeez, at least try, would you?" He was crying because he was leaving. I'm thinking oh, my god, some of these other kids carrying in their trunks and backpacks are gonna see him, and then finally, he drives away and I was sad. That was the moment I was waiting for, him gone and me alone and there it was and I was sad. I took a walk through campus and I'd been walking for almost an hour and then I see Glenn, coming down on a little hill by the infirmary, riding one of those lawn mowers you sit on, with grass flying out of the side and he's smiling. Not at me but just smiling. Clouds and sky behind his hair, half of Tamalpais gone in fog. He was wearing this bright orange vest and I thought, fall's coming.

I saw him that night again in our dorm cafeteria. This's the first time I've been in love. I worry. I'm a bad person, but Glenn's the perfect guy, I mean for me at least, and he thinks he loves me and I've got to keep him from finding out about me. I'll die before I'll tell him. Glenn, OK, Glenn. He looks like Mick Jagger, but sweet, ten times sweeter. He looks like he's about ten years old. His father's a doctor over at UC Med. Gynecological surgeon.

First time we got together, a whole bunch of us were in Glenn's room drinking beer, Glenn and his roommate collect beer cans, they have them stacked up, we're watching TV and finally everybody else leaves. There's nothing on but those gray lines and Glenn turns over on his bed and asks me if I'd rub his back.

I couldn't believe this was happening to me. In high school, I was always ending up with the wrong guys, never the one I wanted. But I wanted it to be Glenn and I knew it was going to happen, I knew I didn't have to do anything. I just had to stay there. It would happen. I was sitting on his rear end, rubbing his back, going under his shirt with my hands.

All of a sudden, I was worried about my breath and what I smelled like. When I turned fourteen or fifteen, my father told me once that I didn't smell good. I slugged him when he said that and didn't talk to him for days, not that I cared about what I smelled like with my father. He was happy, though, kind of, that he could hurt me. That was the last time, though, I'll tell you.

Glenn's face was down in the pillow. I tried to sniff myself but I couldn't tell anything. And it went all right anyway.

I don't open Glenn's letters but I touch them. I hold them and smell them — none of his mail has any smell.

He doesn't get many letters. His parents live across the Bay in Marin County, they don't write. He gets letters from his grandmother in Michigan, plain, even handwriting on regular envelopes, a sticker with her return address printed on it, Rural Route #3, Guns Street, see, I got it memorized.

And he gets letters from Diane, Di, they call her. High school girlfriend. Has a pushy mother, wants her to be a scientist, but she already got a C in Chem 1A. I got an A+, not to brag. He never slept with her, though, she wouldn't, she's still a virgin down in San Diego. With Lilly. Maybe they even know each other.

Glenn and Di were popular kids in their high school. Redwood High. Now I'm one because of Glenn, popular. Because I'm his girlfriend, I know that's why. Not 'cause of me. I just know, OK, I'm not going to start fooling myself now. Please.

Her letters I hold up to the light, they've got fluorescent lights in there. She's supposed to be blond, you know, and pretty. Quiet. The soft type. And the envelopes. She writes on these sheer cream-colored envelopes and they get transparent and I can see her writing underneath, but not enough to read what it says, it's like those hockey lines painted under layers of ice.

I run my tongue along the place where his grandmother sealed the letter. A sharp, sweet gummy taste. Once I cut my tongue. That's what keeps me going to the bottom of the bag, I'm always wondering if there'll be a letter for Glenn. He doesn't get one every week. It's like a treasure. Cracker Jack prize. But I'd never open Glenn's mail. I kiss all four corners where his fingers will touch, opening it, before I put it in his box.

I brought home cookies for Lauren and me. Just a present. We'll eat 'em or Glenn'll eat 'em. I'll throw them out for all I care. They're chocolate chip with pecans. This was one good mother. A lucky can. I brought us coffee, too. I *bought* it.

Yeah, OK, so I'm in trouble. Wednesday, at ten-thirty, I got this notice I was supposed to appear. I had a class, Chem 1C, pre-med staple. Your critical thing. I never missed it before. I told Glenn I had a doctor's appointment.

OK, so I skip it anyway and I walk into this room and there's these two other guys, all work in the mailroom doing what I do, sorting. And we all sit there on chairs on this green carpet. I was staring at everybody's shoes. And there's a cop. University cop, I don't know what's the difference. He had this sagging, pear-shaped body. Like what my dad would have if he were fat, but he's not, he's thin. He walks slowly on the carpeting, his fingers hooked in his belt loops. I was watching his hips.

Anyway, he's accusing us all and he's trying to get one of us to admit we did it. No way.

"I hope one of you will come to me and tell the truth. Not a one of you knows anything about this? Come on, now."

I shake my head no and stare down at the three pairs of shoes. He says they're not going to do anything to the person who did it, right, wanna make a bet, they say they just want to know, but they'll take it back as soon as you tell them.

I don't care why I don't believe him. I know one thing for sure and that's they're not going to do anything to me as long as I say no, I didn't do it. That's what I said, no, I didn't do it, I don't know a thing about it. I just can't imagine where those missing packages could have gone, how letters got into garbage cans. Awful. I just don't know.

The cop had a map with X's on it every place they found mail. The garbage cans. He said there was a group of students trying to get an investigation. People's girlfriends sent cookies that never got here. Letters are missing. Money. These students put up Xeroxed posters on bulletin boards showing a garbage can stuffed with letters.

Why should I tell them, so they can throw me in jail? And kick me out of school? Four-point-oh average and I'm going to let them kick me out of school? They're sitting there telling us it's a felony. A federal crime. No way, I'm gonna go to medical school.

This tall, skinny guy with a blond mustache, Wallabees, looks kind of like a rabbit, he defended us. He's another sorter, works Monday/Wednesdays.

"We all do our jobs," he says. "None of us would do that." The rabbity guy looks at me and the other girl for support. So we're going to stick together. The other girl, a dark blonde chewing her lip, nodded. I loved that rabbity guy that second. I nodded too.

The cop looked down. Wide hips in the coffee-with-milk-colored pants. He sighed. I looked up at the rabbity guy. They let us all go.

I'm just going to keep saying no, not me, didn't do it and I just won't do it again. That's all. Won't do it anymore. So, this is Glenn's last chance for homemade cookies. I'm sure as hell not going to bake any.

I signed the form, said I didn't do it, I'm OK now. I'm safe. It turned out OK after all, it always does. I always think something terrible's going to happen and it doesn't. I'm lucky.

I'm afraid of cops. I was walking, just a little while ago, today, down Telegraph with Glenn, and these two policemen, not the one I'd met, other policemen, were coming in our direction. I started sweating a lot. I was sure until they passed us, I was sure it was all over, they were there for me. I always think that. But at the same time, I know it's just my imagination. I mean, I'm a four-point-oh student, I'm a nice girl just walking down the street with my boyfriend.

We were on our way to get Happy Burgers. When we turned the corner, about a block past the cops, I looked at Glenn and I was flooded with this feeling. It was raining a little and we were by People's Park. The trees were blowing and I was looking at all those little gardens coming up, held together with stakes and white string.

I wanted to say something to Glenn, give him something. I wanted to tell him something about me.

"I'm bad in bed," that's what I said, I just blurted it out like that. He just kind of looked at me, he was nervous, he just giggled. He didn't know what to say, I guess, but he sort of slung his arm around me and

I was so grateful and then we went in. He paid for my Happy Burger, I usually don't let him pay for me, but I did and it was the best goddamn hamburger I've ever eaten.

I want to tell him things.

I lie all the time, always have, but I keep track of each lie I've ever told Glenn and I'm always thinking of the things I can't tell him.

Glenn was a screwed up kid, kind of. He used to go in his backyard, his parents were inside the house I guess, and he'd find this big stick and start twirling around with it. He'd dance, he called it dancing, until if you came up and clapped in front of him, he wouldn't see you. He'd spin around with that stick until he fell down dead on the grass, unconscious, he said he did it to see the sky break up in pieces and spin. He did it sometimes with a tire swing, too. He told me when he was spinning like that, it felt like he was just hearing the earth spinning, that it really went that fast all the time but we just don't feel it. When he was twelve years old his parents took him in the city to a clinic to see a psychologist. And then he stopped. See, maybe I should go to a psychologist. I'd get better, too. He told me about that in bed one night. The ground feels so good when you fall, he said to me. I loved him for that.

"Does anything feel that good now?" I said.

"Sex sometimes. Maybe dancing."

Know what else he told me that night? He said, right before we went to sleep, he wasn't looking at me, he said he'd been thinking what would happen if I died, he said he thought how he'd be at my funeral, all my family and my friends from high school and my little brother would all be around at the front and he'd be at the edge in the cemetery, nobody'd even know who he was.

I was in that crack, breathing the air between the bed and the wall. Cold and dusty. Yeah, we're having sex. I don't know. It's good. Sweet. He says he loves me. I have to remind myself. I talk to myself in my head while we're doing it. I have to say, it's OK, this is just Glenn, this is who I want it to be and it's just like rubbing next to someone. It's just like pushing two hands together, so there's no air in between.

I cry sometimes with Glenn, I'm so grateful.

My mother called and woke me up this morning. Ms. I'm-going-to-be-perfect. Ms. Anything-wrong-is-your-own-fault. Ms. If-anything-bad-happens-you're-a-fool.

She says if she has time, she *might* come up and see my dorm room in the next few weeks. Help me organize my wardrobe, she says. She didn't bring me up here, my dad did. I wanted Danny to come along. I love Danny.

But my mother has *no* pity. She thinks she's got the answers. She's the one who's a lawyer, she's the one who went back to law school and stayed up late nights studying while she still made our lunch boxes. With gourmet cheese. She's proud of it, she tells you. She loves my dad, I guess. She thinks we're like this great family and she sits there at the dinner table bragging about us, to us. She Xeroxed my grade card first quarter with my Chemistry A+ so she's got it in her office and she's got the copy up on the refrigerator at home. She's sitting there telling all her friends that and I'm thinking, you don't know it, but I'm not one of you.

These people across the street from us. Little girl, Sarah, eight years old. Maybe seven. Her dad, he worked for the army, some kind of researcher, he decides he wants to get a sex-change operation. And he goes and does it, over at Stanford. My mom goes out, takes the dog for a walk, right. The mother *confides* in her. Says the thing she regrets most is she wants to have more children. The little girl, Sarah, eight years old, looks up at my mom and says, "Daddy's going to be an aunt."

Now that's sad, I think that's really sad. My mom thinks it's a good dinner table story, proving how much better we are than them. Yeah, I remember exactly what she said that night. "That's all Sarah's mother's got to worry about now is that she wants another child. Meanwhile, Daddy's becoming an aunt."

She should know about me.

So my dad comes to visit for the weekend. Glenn's dad came to speak at UC one night, he took Glenn out to dinner to a nice place, Glenn was glad to see him. Yeah, well. My dad. Comes to the dorm. Skulks around. This guy's a *businessman,* in a three-piece suit, and he acts inferior to the eighteen-year-old freshmen coming in the lobby. My dad. Makes me sick right now thinking of him standing there in the lobby and everybody seeing him. He was probably looking at the kids and looking jealous. Just standing there. Why? Don't ask me why, he's the one that's forty-two years old.

So he's standing there, nervous, probably sucking his hand, that's what he does when he's nervous, I'm always telling him not to. Finally, somebody takes him to my room. I'm not there, Lauren's gone, and he waits for I don't know how long.

When I come in he's standing with his back to the door, looking out

the window. I see him and right away I know it's him and I have this
urge to tiptoe away and he'll never see me.

My pink sweater, a nice sweater, a sweater I wore a lot in high school,
was over my chair, hanging on the back of it, and my father's got one
hand on the sweater shoulder and he's like rubbing the other hand
down an empty arm. He looks up at me, already scared and grateful
when I walk into the room. I feel like smashing him with a baseball bat.
Why can't he just stand up straight?

I drop my books on the bed and stand there while he hugs me.

"Hi, Daddy, what are you doing here?"

"I wanted to see you." He sits in my chair now, his legs crossed and
big, too big for this room, and he's still fingering the arm of my pink
sweater. "I missed you so I got away for the weekend," he says. "I have a
room up here at the Claremont Hotel."

So he's here for the weekend. He's just sitting in my dorm room and
I have to figure out what to do with him. He's not going to do anything.
He'd just sit there. And Lauren's coming back soon so I've got to get him
out. It's Friday afternoon and the weekend's shot. OK, so I'll go with
him. I'll go with him and get it over with.

But I'm not going to miss my date with Glenn Saturday night. No
way. I'd die before I'd cancel that. It's bad enough missing dinner in the
cafeteria tonight. Friday's eggplant, my favorite, and Friday nights are
usually easy, music on the stereos all down the hall. We usually work,
but work slow and talk and then we all meet in Glenn's room around
ten.

"Come, sit on my lap, honey." My dad like pulls me down and starts
bouncing me. *Bouncing me.* I stand up. "OK, we can go somewhere tonight and tomorrow morning, but I have to be back for tomorrow night.
I've got plans with people. And I've got to study, too."

"You can bring your books back to the hotel," he says. "I'm supposed
to be at a convention in San Francisco, but I wanted to see you. I have
work, too, we can call room service and both just work."

"I still have to be back by four tomorrow."

"All right."

"OK, just a minute." And he sat there in my chair while I called Glenn
and told him I wouldn't be there for dinner. I pulled the phone out into
the hall, it only stretches so far, and whispered. "Yeah, my father's here,"
I said, "he's got a conference in San Francisco. He just came by."

Glenn lowered his voice, sweet, and said, "Sounds fun."

My dad sat there, hunched over in my chair, while I changed my shirt

and put on deodorant. I put a nightgown in my shoulder pack and my
toothbrush and I took my chem book and we left. I knew I wouldn't
be back for a whole day. I was trying to calm myself, thinking, well, it's
only one day, that's nothing in my life. The halls were empty, it was five
o'clock, five-ten, everyone was down at dinner.

We walk outside and the cafeteria lights are on and I see everyone
moving around with their trays. Then my dad picks up my hand.

I yank it out. "Dad," I say, really mean.

"Honey, I'm your father." His voice trails off. "Other girls hold their
fathers' hands." It was dark enough for the lights to be on in the cafeteria, but it wasn't really dark out yet. The sky was blue. On the tennis
courts on top of the garage, two Chinese guys were playing. I heard that
thonk-pong and it sounded so carefree and I just wanted to be them. I'd
have even given up Glenn, Glenn-that-I-love-more-than-anything, at
that second, I would have given everything up just to be someone else,
someone new. I got into the car and slammed the door shut and turned
up the heat.

"Should we just go to the hotel and do our work? We can get a nice
dinner in the room."

"I'd rather go out," I said, looking down at my hands. He went where
I told him. I said the name of the restaurant and gave directions. Chez
Panisse and we ordered the most expensive stuff. Appetizers and two
desserts just for me. A hundred and twenty bucks for the two of us.

OK, this hotel room.

So, my dad's got the Bridal Suite. He claimed that was all they had.
Fat chance. Two-hundred-eighty-room hotel and all they've got left is
this deal with the canopy bed, no way. It's in the tower, you can almost
see it from the dorm. Makes me sick. From the bathroom, there's this
window, shaped like an arch, and it looks over all of Berkeley. You can
see the bridge lights. As soon as we got there, I locked myself in the
bathroom, I was so mad about that canopy bed. I took a long bath and
washed my hair. They had little soaps wrapped up there, shampoo, may
as well use them, he's paying for it. It's this deep old bathtub and wind
was coming in from outside and I felt like that window was just open,
no glass, just a hole cut out in the stone.

I was thinking of when I was little and what they taught us in cate-
chism. I thought a soul was inside your chest, this long horizontal trian-
gle with rounded edges, made out of some kind of white fog, some kind

of gas or vapor. I could be pregnant. I soaped myself all up and rinsed off with cold water. I'm lucky I never got pregnant, really lucky.

Other kids my age, Lauren, everybody, I know things they don't know. I know more for my age. Too much. Like I'm not a virgin. Lots of people are, you'd be surprised. I know about a lot of things being wrong and unfair, all kinds of stuff. It's like seeing a UFO, if I ever saw something like that, I'd never tell, I'd wish I'd never seen it.

My dad knocks on the door.

"What do you want?"

"Let me just come in and talk to you while you're in there."

"I'm done, I'll be right out. Just a minute." I took a long time toweling. No hurry, believe me. So I got into bed with my nightgown on and wet already from my hair. I turned away. Breathed against the wall. "Night."

My father hooks my hair over my ear and touches my shoulder. "Tired?"

I shrug.

"You really have to go back tomorrow? We could go to Marin or to the beach. Anything."

I hugged my knees up under my nightgown. "You should go to your conference, Dad."

I wake up in the middle of the night, I feel something's going on, and sure enough, my dad's down there, he's got my nightgown worked up like a frill around my neck and my legs hooked over his shoulders.

"Dad, stop it."

"I just wanted to make you feel good," he says, and looks up at me. "What's wrong? Don't you love me anymore?"

I never really told anybody. It's not exactly the kind of thing you can bring up over lunch. "So, I'm sleeping with my father. Oh, and let's split a dessert." Right.

I don't know, other people think my dad's handsome. They say he is. My mother thinks so, you should see her traipsing around the balcony when she gets in her romantic moods, which, on her professional lawyer schedule, are about once a year, thank god. It's pathetic. He thinks she's repulsive, though. I don't know that, that's what I think. But he loves me, that's for sure.

So next day, Saturday—that rabbity guy, Paul's his name, he did my shift for me—we go downtown and I got him to buy me this suit. Three hundred dollars from Saks. Oh, and I got shoes. So I stayed later with him because of the clothes, and I was a little happy because I thought at least now I'd have something good to wear with Glenn. My dad and I got brownie sundaes at Sweet Dreams and I got home by five. He was crying when he dropped me off.

"Don't cry, Dad. Please," I said. Jesus, how can you not hate someone who's always begging from you.

Lauren had Poly Styrene on the stereo and a candle lit in our room. I was never so glad to be home.

"Hey," Lauren said. She was on her bed with her legs propped up on the wall. She'd just shaved. She was rubbing in cream.

I flopped down on my bed. "Ohhhh," I said, grabbing the sides of the mattress.

"Hey, can you keep a secret about what I did today?" Lauren said. "I went to that therapist, up at Cowell."

"You have the greatest legs," I said, quiet. "Why don't you ever wear skirts?"

She stopped what she was doing and stood up. "You think they're good? I don't like the way they look, except in jeans." She looked down at them. "They're crooked, see?" She shook her head. "I don't want to think about it."

Then she went to her dresser and started rolling a joint. "Want some?"

"A little."

She lit up, lay back on her bed and held her arm out for me to come take the joint.

"So, she was this really great woman. Warm, kind of chubby. She knew instantly what kind of man Brent was." Lauren snapped her fingers. "Like that." Brent was the pool man Lauren had an affair with, home in LA.

I'm back in the room maybe an hour, putting on mascara, my jeans are on the bed, pressed, and the phone rings and it's my dad and I say, "Listen, just leave me alone."

"You don't care about me anymore."

"I just saw you. I have nothing to say. We just saw each other."

"What are you doing tonight?"

"Going out."

"Who are you seeing?"

"Glenn."

He sighs. "So you really like him, huh?"

"Yeah, I do and you should be glad. You should be glad I have a boy-friend." I pull the cord out into the hall and sit down on the floor there. There's this long pause.

"We're not going to end up together, are we?"

I felt like all the air's knocked out of me. I looked out the window and everything looked dead and still. The parked cars. The trees with pink toilet paper strung between the branches. The church all closed up across the street.

"No, we won't, Daddy."

He was crying. "I know, I know."

I hung up the phone and went back and sat in the hall. I'm scared, too. I don't know what'll happen.

I don't know. It's been going on I guess as long as I can remember. I mean, not the sex, but my father. When I was a little kid, tiny little kid, my dad came in before bed and said his prayers with me. He kneeled down by my bed and I was on my back. *Prayers*. He'd lift up my pajama top and put his hands on my breast. Little fried eggs, he said. One time with his tongue. Then one night, he pulled down the elastic of my pajama pants. He did it for an hour and then I came. Don't believe anything they ever tell you about kids not coming. That first time was the biggest I ever had and I didn't even know what it was then. It just kept going and going as if he were breaking me through layers and layers of glass and I felt like I'd slipped and let go and I didn't have myself anymore, he had me, and once I'd slipped like that I'd never be the same again.

We had this sprinkler on our back lawn, Danny and me used to run through it in summer and my dad'd be outside, working on the grass or the hedge or something and he'd squirt us with the hose. I used to wear a bathing suit bottom, no top—we were this modern family, our parents walked around the house naked after showers and then Danny and I ended up both being these modest kids, can't stand anyone to see us even in our underwear, I always dress facing the closet, Lauren teases me. We'd run through the sprinkler and my dad would come up and pat my bottom and the way he'd put his hand on my thigh, I felt like Danny could tell it was different than the way he touched him, I was like something he owned.

First time when I was nine, I remember, Dad and me were in the shower together. My mom might have even been in the house, they did that kind of stuff, it was supposed to be OK. Anyway, we're in the shower and I remember this look my dad had. Like he was daring me, knowing he knew more than I did. We're both under the shower. The water pasted his hair down on his head and he looked younger and weird. "Touch it. Don't be afraid of it," he says. And he grabs my thighs on the outside and pulls me close to him, pulling on my fat.

He waited till I was twelve to really do it. I don't know if you can call it rape, I was a good sport. The creepy thing is I know how it felt for him, I could see it on his face when he did it. He thought he was getting away with something. We were supposed to go hiking but right away that morning when we got into the car, he knew he was going to do it. He couldn't wait to get going. I said I didn't feel good, I had a cold, I wanted to stay home, but he made me go anyway and we hiked two miles and he set up the tent. He told me to take my clothes off and I undressed just like that, standing there in the woods. He's the one who was nervous and got us into the tent. I looked old for twelve, small but old. And right there on the ground, he spread my legs open and pulled my feet up and fucked me. I bled. I couldn't even breathe the tent was so small. He could have done anything. He could have killed me, he had me alone on this mountain.

I think about that sometimes when I'm alone with Glenn in my bed. It's so easy to hurt people. They just lie there and let you have them. I could reach out and choke Glenn to death, he'd be so shocked, he wouldn't stop me. You can just take what you want.

My dad thought he was getting away with something but he didn't. He was the one who fell in love, not me. And after that day, when we were back in the car, I was the one giving orders. From then on, I got what I wanted. He spent about twice as much money on me as on Danny and everyone knew it, Danny and my mom, too. How do you think I got good clothes and a good bike and a good stereo? My dad's not rich, you know. And I'm the one who got to go away to college even though it killed him. Says it's the saddest thing that ever happened in his life, me going away and leaving him. But when I was a little kid that day, he wasn't in love with me, not like he is now.

Only thing I'm sad about isn't either of my parents, it's Danny. Leaving Danny alone there with them. He used to send Danny out of the house. My mom'd be at work on a Saturday afternoon or something or even in the morning and my dad would kick my little brother out of his own house. Go out and play, Danny. Why doncha catch some rays. And Danny just went and got his glove and baseball from the closet and he'd go and throw it against the house, against the outside wall, in the driveway. I'd be in my room, I'd be like dead, I'd be wood, telling myself this doesn't count, no one has to know, I'll say I'm still a virgin, it's not really happening to me, I'm dead, I'm blank, I'm just letting time stop and pass, and then I'd hear the sock of the ball in the mitt and the slam of the screen door and I knew it was true, it was really happening.

Glenn's the one I want to tell. I can't ever tell Glenn.

I called my mom. Pay phone, collect, hour-long call. I don't know, I got real mad last night and I just told her. I thought when I came here, it'd just go away. But it's not going away. It makes me weird with Glenn. In the morning, with Glenn, when it's time to get up, I can't get up. I cry.

I knew it'd be bad. Poor Danny. Well, my mom says she might leave our dad. She cried for an hour, no joke, on the phone.

How could he *do* this to me, she kept yelping. To her. Everything's always to her.

But then she called an hour later, she'd talked to a psychiatrist already, she's kicked Dad out, and she arrives, just arrives here at Berkeley. But she was good. She says she's on my side, she'll help me, I don't know, I felt OK. She stayed in a hotel and she wanted to know if I wanted to stay there with her but I said no, I'd see her more in a week or something, I just wanted to go back to my dorm. She found this group. She says, just in San Jose, there's hundreds of families like ours, yeah, great, that's what I said. But there's groups. She's going to a group of other thick-o mothers like her, these wives who didn't catch on. She wanted me to go to a group of girls, yeah, molested girls, that's what they call them, but I said no, I have friends here already, she can do what she wants.

I talked to my dad, too, that's the sad thing, he feels like he's lost me and he wants to die and I don't know, he doesn't know what he's doing. He called in the middle of the night.

"Just tell me one thing, honey. Please tell me the truth. When did you stop?"

"Dad."

"Because I remember once you said I was the only person who ever understood you."

"I was ten years old."

"OK, OK. I'm sorry."

He didn't want to get off the phone. "You know, I love you, honey. I always will."

"Yeah, well."

My mom's got him lined up for a psychiatrist, too, she says he's lucky she's not sending him to jail. I *am* a lawyer, she keeps saying, as if we could forget. She'd pay for me to go to a shrink now, too, but I said no, forget it.

It's over. Glenn and I are, over. I feel like my dad's lost me everything. I sort of want to die now. I'm telling you I feel terrible. I told Glenn and that's it, it's over. I can't believe it either. Lauren says she's going to hit him.

I told him and we're not seeing each other anymore. Nope. He said he wanted to just think about everything for a few days. He said it had nothing to do with my father but he'd been feeling a little too settled lately. He said we don't have fun anymore, it's always so serious. That was Monday. So every meal after that, I sat with Lauren in the cafeteria and he's there on the other side, messing around with the guys. He sure didn't look like he was in any kind of agony. Wednesday, I saw Glenn over by the window in this food fight, slipping off his chair and I couldn't stand it, I got up and left and went to our room.

But I went and said I wanted to talk to Glenn that night, I didn't even have any dinner, and he said he wanted to be friends. He looked at me funny and I haven't heard from him. It's, I don't know, seven days, eight.

I know there are other guys. I live in a dorm full of them, or half full of them. Half girls. But I keep thinking of Glenn 'cause of happiness, that's what makes me want to hang on to him.

There was this one morning when we woke up in his room, it was light out already, white light all over the room. We were sticky and warm, the sheet was all tangled. His roommate, this little blond boy, was still sleeping. I watched his eyes open and he smiled and then he went down the hall to take a shower. Glenn was hugging me and it was nothing unusual, nothing special. We didn't screw. We were just there. We kissed, but slow, the way it is when your mouth is still bad from sleep.

I was happy that morning. I didn't have to do anything. We got dressed, went to breakfast, I don't know. Took a walk. He had to go to work at a certain time and I had that sleepy feeling from waking up with the sun on my head and he said he didn't want to say goodbye to me. There was that pang. One of those looks like as if at that second, we both felt the same way.

I shrugged. I could afford to be casual then. We didn't say goodbye. I walked with him to the shed by the Eucalyptus Grove. That's where they keep all the gardening tools, the rakes, the hoes, the mowers, big bags of grass seed slumped against the wall. It smelled like hay in there. Glenn changed into his uniform and we went to the North Side, up in front of the chancellor's manor, that thick perfect grass. And Glenn gave me a ride on the lawn mower, on the handlebars. It was bouncing over these little bumps in the lawn and I was hanging on to the handlebars, laughing. I couldn't see Glenn but I knew he was there behind me. I looked around at the buildings and the lawns, there's a fountain there, and one dog was drinking from it.

See, I can't help but remember things like that. Even now, I'd rather find some way, even though he's not asking for it, to forgive Glenn. I'd rather have it work out with him, because I want more days like that. I wish I could have a whole life like that. But I guess nobody does, not just me.

I saw him in the mailroom yesterday, we're both just standing there, each opening our little boxes, getting our mail — neither of us had any — I was hurt but I wanted to reach out and touch his face. He has this hard chin, it's pointy and all bone. Lauren says she wants to hit him.

I mean, I think of him spinning around in his backyard and that's why I love him and he should understand. I go over it all and think I should have just looked at him and said I can't believe you're doing this to me. Right there in the mailroom. Now when I think that, I think maybe if I'd said that, in those words, maybe it would be different.

But then I think of my father — he feels like there was a time when we had fun, when we were happy together. I mean, I can remember being in my little bed with Dad and maybe cracking jokes, maybe laughing, but he probably never heard Danny's baseball in his mitt the way I did or I don't know. I remember late in the afternoon, wearing my dad's navy-blue sweatshirt with a hood and riding bikes with him and Danny down to the diamond.

But that's over. I don't know if I'm sorry it happened. I mean I am, but it happened, that's all. It's just one of the things that happened to me in my life. But I would never go back, never. And what hurts so much is that maybe that's what Glenn is thinking about me.

I told Lauren last night. I had to. She kept asking me what happened with Glenn. She was so good, you couldn't believe it, she was great. We were talking late and this morning we drove down to go to House of Pancakes for breakfast, get something good instead of watery eggs for a change. And on the way, Lauren's driving, she just skids to a stop on this street, in front of this elementary school. "Come on," she says. It's early, but there's already people inside the windows.

We hooked our fingers in the metal fence. You know, one of those aluminum fences around a playground. There were pigeons standing on the painted game circles. Then a bell rang and all these kids came out, yelling, spilling into groups. This was a poor school, mostly black kids, Mexican kids, all in bright colors. There's a Nabisco factory nearby and the whole air smelled like blueberry muffins.

The girls were jump-roping and the boys were shoving and running and hanging on to the monkey bars. Lauren pinched her fingers on the back of my neck and pushed my head against the fence.

"Eight years old. Look at them. They're eight years old. One of their fathers is sleeping with one of those girls. Look at her. Do you blame her? Can you blame her? Because if you can forgive her you can forgive yourself."

"I'll kill him," I said.

"And I'll kill Glenn," Lauren says.

So we went and got pancakes. And drank coffee until it was time for class.

I saw Glenn yesterday. It was so weird after all this time. I just had lunch with Lauren. We picked up tickets for Talking Heads and I wanted to get back to the lab before class and I'm walking along and Glenn was working, you know, on the lawn in front of the Mobi Building. He was still gorgeous. I was just going to walk, but he yelled over at me.

"Hey, Jenny."

"Hi, Glenn."

He congratulated me, he heard about the NSF thing. We stood there. He has another girlfriend now. I don't know, when I looked at him and stood there by the lawn mower, it's chugging away, I felt the same as I always used to, that I loved him and all that, but he might just be one of those things you can't have. Like I should have been for my father and look at him now. Oh, I think he's better, they're all better, but I'm gone, he'll never have me again.

I'm glad they're there and I'm here, but it's strange, I feel more alone now. Glenn looked down at the little pile of grass by the lawn mower and said, "Well, kid, take care of yourself," and I said, "You too, 'bye," and started walking.

So, you know what's bad, though, I started taking stuff again. Little stuff from the mailroom. No packages and not people I know anymore.

But I take one letter a Saturday, I make it just one and someone I don't know. And I keep 'em and burn 'em with a match in the bathroom sink and wash the ashes down the drain. I wait until the end of the shift. I always expect it to be something exciting. The two so far were just everyday letters, just mundane, so that's all that's new, I-had-a-pork-chop-for-dinner letters.

But something happened today, I was in the middle, three-quarters way down the bag, still looking, I hadn't picked my letter for the day, I'm being really stern, I really mean just one, no more, and there's this little white envelope addressed to me. I sit there, trembling with it in my hand. It's the first one I've gotten all year. It was my name and address, typed out, and I just stared at it. There's no address. I got so nervous, I thought maybe it was from Glenn, of course, I wanted it to be from Glenn so bad, but then I knew it couldn't be, he's got that new girlfriend now, so I threw it in the garbage can right there, one of those with the swinging metal door, and then I finished my shift. My hands were sweating, I smudged the writing on one of the envelopes.

So all the letters are in boxes, I clean off the table, fold the bags up neat and close the door, ready to go. And then I thought, I don't have to keep looking at the garbage can, I'm allowed to take it back, that's my letter. And I fished it out, the thing practically lopped my arm off. And I had it and I held it a few minutes, wondering who it was from. Then I put it in my mailbox so I can go like everybody else and get mail.

1986

RICHARD FORD

COMMUNIST

from *Antaeus*

RICHARD FORD was born in Jackson, Mississippi, in 1944. At nineteen he worked as a switchman on the Missouri Pacific Railroad, and he later earned a BA from Michigan State University. Ford has experienced dyslexia all his life and has said, "Being a slow reader made me pore over sentences and possibly, helpfully, become more receptive to the 'poetical' aspects of written language."

Ford is known for the Bascombe books, which include *The Sportswriter, Independence Day* — winner of the Pulitzer Prize and the PEN/Faulkner Award — *The Lay of the Land,* and the recently published *Let Me Be Frank with You.* His short story collections include *Rock Springs* and *A Multitude of Sins.* He is Mellon Professor in the Humanities at Columbia University in New York.

In an interview, Ford said, "Fiction always uses language to refer the reader to lived life and to express life's consequence. This is true irrespective of how 'realistic' or how hermetic, self-referring, or abstract an individual story happens to be. It always takes us back to life."

Richard Ford lives in East Boothbay, Maine.

★

MY MOTHER ONCE had a boyfriend named Glen Baxter. This was in 1961. We — my mother and I — were living in the little house my father had left her up the Sun River, near Victory, Montana, west of Great Falls. My mother was thirty-one at the time. I was sixteen. Glen Baxter was somewhere in the middle, between us, though I cannot be exact about it.

We were living then off the proceeds of my father's life insurance policies, with my mother doing some part-time waitressing work up in Great Falls and going to the bars in the evenings, which I know is where she met Glen Baxter. Sometimes he would come back with her and stay in her room at night, or she would call up from town and explain that she was staying with him in his little place on Lewis Street by the GN yards. She gave me his number every time, but I never called it. I think she probably thought that what she was doing was terrible, but simply couldn't help herself. I thought it was all right, though. Regular life it seemed and still does. She was young, and I knew that even then.

Glen Baxter was a Communist and liked hunting, which he talked about a lot. Pheasants. Ducks. Deer. He killed all of them, he said. He had been to Vietnam as far back as then, and when he was in our house he often talked about shooting the animals over there — monkeys and beautiful parrots — using military guns just for sport. We did not know what Vietnam was then, and Glen, when he talked about that, referred to it only as "the Far East." I think now he must've been in the CIA and been disillusioned by something he saw or found out about and had been thrown out, but that kind of thing did not matter to us. He was a tall, dark-eyed man with thick black hair, and was usually in a good humor. He had gone halfway through college in Peoria, Illinois, he said, where he grew up. But when he was around our life he worked wheat farms as a ditcher, and stayed out of work winters and in the bars drinking with women like my mother, who had work and some money. It is not an uncommon life to lead in Montana.

What I want to explain happened in November. We had not been seeing Glen Baxter for some time. Two months had gone by. My mother knew other men, but she came home most days from work and stayed inside watching television in her bedroom and drinking beers. I asked about Glen once, and she said only that she didn't know where he was, and I assumed they had had a fight and that he was gone off on a flyer back to Illinois or Massachusetts, where he said he had relatives. I'll admit that I liked him. He had something on his mind always. He was a labor man as well as a Communist, and liked to say that the country was poisoned by the rich, and strong men would need to bring it to life again, and I liked that because my father had been a labor man, which was why we had a house to live in and money coming through. It was also true that I'd had a few boxing bouts by then — just with town boys and one with an Indian from Choteau — and there were some girlfriends I knew from that. I did not like my mother being around the house so much at night, and I wished Glen Baxter would come back, or that another man would come along and entertain her somewhere else.

At two o'clock on a Saturday, Glen drove up into our yard in a car. He had had a big brown Harley-Davidson that he rode most of the year, in his black-and-red irrigators and a baseball cap turned backwards. But this time he had a car, a blue Nash Ambassador. My mother and I went out on the porch when he stopped inside the olive trees my father had planted as a shelter belt, and my mother had a look on her face of not much pleasure. It was starting to be cold in earnest by then. Snow was down already onto the Fairfield Bench, though on this day a chinook was blowing, and it could as easily have been spring, though the sky above the Divide was turning over in silver and blue clouds of winter.

"We haven't seen you in a long time, I guess," my mother said coldly.

"My little retarded sister died," Glen said, standing at the door of his old car. He was wearing his orange VFW jacket and canvas shoes we called wino shoes, something I had never seen him wear before. He seemed to be in a good humor. "We buried her in Florida near the home."

"That's a good place," my mother said in a voice that meant she was a wronged party in something.

"I want to take this boy hunting today, Aileen," Glen said. "There's snow geese down now. But we have to go right away or they'll be gone to Idaho by tomorrow."

"He doesn't care to go," my mother said.

"Yes I do," I said and looked at her.

My mother frowned at me. "Why do you?"

"Why does he need a reason?" Glen Baxter said and grinned.

"I want him to have one, that's why." She looked at me oddly. "I think Glen's drunk, Les."

"No, I'm not drinking," Glen said, which was hardly ever true. He looked at both of us, and my mother bit down on the side of her lower lip and stared at me in a way to make you think she thought something was being put over on her and she didn't like you for it. She was pretty, though when she was mad her features were sharpened and less pretty by a long way. "All right then, I don't care," she said to no one in particular. "Hunt, kill, maim. Your father did that too." She turned to go back inside.

"Why don't you come with us, Aileen?" Glen was smiling still, pleased.

"To do what?" my mother said. She stopped and pulled a package of cigarettes out of her dress pocket and put one in her mouth.

"It's worth seeing."

"See dead animals?" my mother said.

"These geese are from Siberia, Aileen," Glen said. "They're not like a lot of geese. Maybe I'll buy us dinner later. What do you say?"

"Buy with what?" my mother said. To tell the truth, I didn't know why she was so mad at him. I would've thought she'd be glad to see him. But she just suddenly seemed to hate everything about him.

"I've got some money," Glen said. "Let me spend it on a pretty girl tonight."

"Find one of those and you're lucky," my mother said, turning away toward the front door.

"I've already found one," Glen Baxter said. But the door slammed behind her, and he looked at me then with a look I think now was helplessness, though I could not see a way to change anything.

My mother sat in the back seat of Glen's Nash and looked out the window while we drove. My double gun was in the seat between us beside Glen's Belgian pump, which he kept loaded with five shells in case, he said, he saw something beside the road he wanted to shoot. I had hunted rabbits before, and had ground-sluiced pheasants and other birds, but I had never been on an actual hunt before, one where you drove out to some special place and did it formally. And I was excited. I had a feeling that something important was about to happen to me and that this would be a day I would always remember.

My mother did not say anything for a long time, and neither did I. We drove up through Great Falls and out the other side toward Fort Benton, which was on the benchland where wheat was grown.

"Geese mate for life," my mother said, just out of the blue, as we were driving. "I hope you know that. They're special birds."

"I know that," Glen said in the front seat. "I have every respect for them."

"So where were you for three months?" she said. "I'm only curious."

"I was in the Big Hole for a while," Glen said, "and after that I went over to Douglas, Wyoming."

"What were you planning to do there?" my mother said.

"I wanted to find a job, but it didn't work out."

"I'm going to college," she said suddenly, and this was something I had never heard about before. I turned to look at her, but she was staring out her window and wouldn't see me.

"I knew French once," Glen said. "Rose's pink. Rouge's red." He glanced at me and smiled. "I think that's a wise idea, Aileen. When are you going to start?"

"I don't want Les to think he was raised by crazy people all his life," my mother said.

"Les ought to go himself," Glen said.

"After I go, he will."

"What do you say about that, Les?" Glen said, grinning.

"He says it's just fine," my mother said.

"It's just fine," I said.

Where Glen Baxter took us was out onto the high flat prairie that was disked for wheat and had high, high mountains out to the east, with lower heartbreak hills in between. It was, I remember, a day for blues in the sky, and down in the distance we could see the small town of Floweree and the state highway running past it toward Fort Benton and the high line. We drove out on top of the prairie on a muddy dirt road fenced on both sides, until we had gone about three miles, which is where Glen stopped.

"All right," he said, looking up in the rearview mirror at my mother. "You wouldn't think there was anything here, would you?"

"*We're* here," my mother said. "You brought us here."

"You'll be glad, though," Glen said, and seemed confident to me. I had looked around myself but could not see anything. No water or trees, nothing that seemed like a good place to hunt anything. Just wasted land. "There's a big lake out there, Les," Glen said. "You can't see it now from here because it's low. But the geese are there. You'll see."

"It's like the moon out here, I recognize that," my mother said, "only it's worse." She was staring out at the flat, disked wheatland as if she could actually see something in particular and wanted to know more about it. "How'd you find this place?"

"I came once on the wheat push," Glen said.

"And I'm sure the owner told you just to come back and hunt any time you like and bring anybody you wanted. Come one, come all. Is that it?"

"People shouldn't own land anyway," Glen said. "Anybody should be able to use it."

"Les, Glen's going to poach here," my mother said. "I just want you to know that, because that's a crime and the law will get you for it. If you're a man now, you're going to have to face the consequences."

"That's not true," Glen Baxter said, and looked gloomily out over the steering wheel down the muddy road toward the mountains. Though for myself I believed it was true, and didn't care. I didn't care about anything at that moment except seeing geese fly over me and shooting them down.

"Well, I'm certainly not going out there," my mother said. "I like towns better, and I already have enough trouble."

"That's okay," Glen said. "When the geese lift up you'll get to see them. That's all I wanted. Les and me'll go shoot them, won't we, Les?"

"Yes," I said, and I put my hand on my shotgun, which had been my father's and was heavy as rocks.

"Then we should go on," Glen said, "or we'll waste our light."

We got out of the car with our guns. Glen took off his canvas shoes and put on his pair of black irrigators out of the trunk. Then we crossed the barbed-wire fence and walked out into the high, tilled field toward nothing. I looked back at my mother when we were still not so far away, but I could only see the small, dark top of her head, low in the back seat of the Nash, staring out and thinking what I could not then begin to say.

On the walk toward the lake, Glen began talking to me. I had never been alone with him and knew little about him except what my mother said — that he drank too much, or other times that he was the nicest man she had ever known in the world and that someday a woman would marry him, though she didn't think it would be her. Glen told me as we walked that he wished he had finished college, but that it was too late now, that his mind was too old. He said he had liked "the Far East" very much, and that people there knew how to treat each other, and that he would go back someday but couldn't go now. He said also that he would like to live in Russia for a while and mentioned the names of people who had gone there, names I didn't know. He said it would be hard at first, because it was so different, but that pretty soon anyone would learn to like it and wouldn't want to live anywhere else, and that Russians treated Americans who came to live there like kings. There were Communists everywhere now, he said. You didn't know them, but they were there. Montana had a large number, and he was in touch with all of them. He said that Communists were always in danger and that he had to protect himself all the time. And when he said that he pulled back his VFW jacket and showed me the butt of a pistol he had stuck under his shirt against his bare skin. "There are people who want to kill me right now," he said, "and I would kill a man myself if I thought I had to." And we kept walking. Though in a while he said, "I don't think I know much about you, Les. But I'd like to. What do you like to do?"

"I like to box," I said. "My father did it. It's a good thing to know."

"I suppose you have to protect yourself too," Glen said.

"I know how to," I said.

"Do you like to watch TV?" Glen said, and smiled.

"Not much."

"I love to," Glen said. "I could watch it instead of eating if I had one."

I looked out straight ahead over the green tops of sage that grew at the edge of the disked field, hoping to see the lake Glen said was there. There was an airishness and a sweet smell that I thought might be the place we were going, but I couldn't see it. "How will we hunt these geese?" I said.

"It won't be hard," Glen said. "Most hunting isn't even hunting. It's only shooting. And that's what this will be. In Illinois you would dig holes in the ground to hide in and set out your decoys. Then the geese come to you, over and over again. But we don't have time for that here." He glanced at me. "You have to be sure the first time here."

"How do you know they're here now?" I asked. And I looked toward the Highwood Mountains twenty miles away, half in snow and half dark blue at the bottom. I could see the little town of Floweree then, looking shabby and dimly lighted in the distance. A red bar sign shone. A car moved slowly away from the scattered buildings.

"They always come November first," Glen said.

"Are we going to poach them?"

"Does it make any difference to you?" Glen asked.

"No, it doesn't."

"Well then we aren't," he said.

We walked then for a while without talking. I looked back once to see the Nash far and small in the flat distance. I couldn't see my mother, and I thought that she must've turned on the radio and gone to sleep, which she always did, letting it play all night in her bedroom. Behind the car the sun was nearing the rounded mountains southwest of us, and I knew that when the sun was gone it would be cold. I wished my mother had decided to come along with us, and I thought for a moment of how little I really knew her at all.

Glen walked with me another quarter mile, crossed another barbed-wire fence where sage was growing, then went a hundred yards through wheatgrass and spurge until the ground went up and formed a kind of long hillock bunker built by a farmer against the wind. And I realized the lake was just beyond us. I could hear the sound of a car horn blowing and a dog barking all the way down in the town, then the wind seemed to move and all I could hear then and after then were geese. So many geese, from the sound of them, though I still could not see even one. I stood and listened to the high-pitched shouting sound, a sound

I had never heard so close, a sound with size to it—though it was not loud. A sound that meant great numbers and that made your chest rise and your shoulders tighten with expectancy. It was a sound to make you feel separate from it and everything else, as if you were of no importance in the grand scheme of things.

"Do you hear them singing?" Glen asked. He held his hand up to make me stand still. And we both listened. "How many do you think, Les, just hearing?"

"A hundred," I said. "More than a hundred."

"Five thousand," Glen said. "More than you can believe when you see them. Go see."

I put down my gun and on my hands and knees crawled up the earthwork through the wheatgrass and thistle until I could see down to the lake and see the geese. And they were there, like a white bandage laid on the water, wide and long and continuous, a white expanse of snow geese, seventy yards from me, on the bank, but stretching onto the lake, which was large itself—a half mile across, with thick tules on the far side and wild plums farther and the blue mountain behind them.

"Do you see the big raft?" Glen said from below me, in a whisper.

"I see it," I said, still looking. It was such a thing to see, a view I had never seen and have not since.

"Are any on the land?" he said.

"Some are in the wheatgrass," I said, "but most are swimming."

"Good," Glen said. "They'll have to fly. But we can't wait for that now."

And I crawled backwards down the heel of land to where Glen was, and my gun. We were losing our light, and the air was purplish and cooling. I looked toward the car but couldn't see it, and I was no longer sure where it was below the lighted sky.

"Where do they fly to?" I said in a whisper, since I did not want anything to be ruined because of what I did or said. It was important to Glen to shoot the geese, and it was important to me.

"To the wheat," he said. "Or else they leave for good. I wish your mother had come, Les. Now she'll be sorry."

I could hear the geese quarreling and shouting on the lake surface. And I wondered if they knew we were here now. "She might be," I said with my heart pounding, but I didn't think she would be much.

It was a simple plan he had. I would stay behind the bunker, and he would crawl, on his belly with his gun through the wheatgrass as near to the geese as he could. Then he would simply stand up and shoot all the ones he could close up, both in the air and on the ground. And when all the others flew up, with luck some would turn toward me as they came into the wind, and then I could shoot them and turn them back to him, and he would shoot them again. He could kill ten, he said, if he was lucky, and I might kill four. It didn't seem hard.

"Don't show them your face," Glen said. "Wait till you think you can touch them, then stand up and shoot. To hesitate is lost in this."

"All right," I said. "I'll try it."

"Shoot one in the head, and then shoot another one," Glen said. "It won't be hard." He patted me on the arm and smiled. Then he took off his VFW jacket and put it on the ground, climbed up the side of the bunker, cradling his shotgun in his arms, and slid on his belly into the dry stalks of yellow grass out of my sight.

Then for the first time in that entire day I was alone. And I didn't mind it. I sat squat down in the grass, loaded my double gun, and took my other two shells out of my pocket to hold. I pushed the safety off and on to see that it was right. The wind rose a little then, scuffed the grass and made me shiver. It was not the warm chinook now, but a wind out of the north, the one geese flew away from if they could.

Then I thought about my mother in the car alone, and how much longer I would stay with her, and what it might mean to her for me to leave. And I wondered when Glen Baxter would die and if someone would kill him, or whether my mother would marry him and how I would feel about it. And though I didn't know why, it occurred to me then that Glen Baxter and I would not be friends when all was said and done, since I didn't care if he ever married my mother or didn't.

Then I thought about boxing and what my father had taught me about it. To tighten your fists hard. To strike out straight from the shoulder and never punch backing up. How to cut a punch by snapping your fist inwards, how to carry your chin low, and to step toward a man when he is falling so you can hit him again. And most important, to keep your eyes open when you are hitting in the face and causing damage, because you need to see what you're doing to encourage yourself, and because it is when you close your eyes that you stop hitting and get hurt badly. "Fly all over your man, Les," my father said. "When you see your chance, fly on him and hit him till he falls." That, I thought, would always be my attitude in things.

And then I heard the geese again, their voices in unison, louder and shouting, as if the wind had changed and put all new sounds in the cold air. And then a *boom*. And I knew Glen was in among them and had stood up to shoot. The noise of geese rose and grew worse, and my fingers burned where I held my gun too tight to the metal, and I put it down and opened my fist to make the burning stop so I could feel the trigger when the moment came. *Boom*, Glen shot again, and I heard him shuck a shell, and all the sounds out beyond the bunker seemed to be rising — the geese, the shots, the air itself going up. *Boom*, Glen shot another time, and I knew he was taking his careful time to make his shots good. And I held my gun and started to crawl up the bunker so as not to be surprised when the geese came over me and I could shoot.

From the top I saw Glen Baxter alone in the wheatgrass field, shooting at a white goose with black tips of wings that was on the ground not far from him, but trying to run and pull into the air. He shot it once more, and it fell over dead with its wings flapping.

Glen looked back at me and his face was distorted and strange. The air around him was full of white rising geese and he seemed to want them all. "Behind you, Les," he yelled at me and pointed. "They're all behind you now." I looked behind me, and there were geese in the air as far as I could see, more than I knew how many, moving so slowly, their wings wide out and working calmly and filling the air with noise, though their voices were not as loud or as shrill as I had thought they would be. And they were very close! Forty feet, some of them. The air around me vibrated and I could feel the wind from their wings and it seemed to me I could kill as many as the times I could shoot — a hundred or a thousand — and I raised my gun, put the muzzle on the head of a white goose and fired. It shuddered in the air, its wide feet sank below its belly, its wings cradled out to hold back air, and it fell straight down and landed with an awful sound, a noise a human would make, a thick, soft, *hump* noise. I looked up again and shot another goose, could hear the pellets hit its chest, but it didn't fall or even break its pattern for flying. *Boom*, Glen shot again. And then again. "Hey," I heard him shout. "Hey, hey." And there were geese flying over me, flying in line after line. I broke my gun and reloaded, and thought to myself as I did: I need confidence here, I need to be sure with this. I pointed at another goose and shot it in the head, and it fell the way the first one had, wings out, its belly down, and with the same thick noise of hitting. Then I sat down in the grass on the bunker and let geese fly over me.

By now the whole raft was in the air, all of it moving in a slow swirl above me and the lake and everywhere, finding the wind and heading

out south in long wavering lines that caught the last sun and turned to
silver as they gained a distance. It was a thing to see, I will tell you now.
Five thousand white geese all in the air around you, making a noise
like you have never heard before. And I thought to myself then: This
is something I will never see again. I will never forget this. And I was
right.

Glen Baxter shot twice more. One shot missed, but with the other he
hit a goose flying away from him and knocked it half-falling and -fly-
ing into the empty lake not far from shore, where it began to swim as
though it was fine and make its noise.

Glen stood in the stubbly grass, looking out at the goose, his gun lowered. "I didn't need to shoot that, did I, Les?"

"I don't know," I said, sitting on the little knoll of land, looking at the
goose swimming in the water.

"I don't know why I shoot 'em. They're so beautiful." He looked at
me.

"I don't know either," I said.

"Maybe there's nothing else to do with them." Glen stared at the
goose again and shook his head. "Maybe this is exactly what they're put
on earth for."

I did not know what to say because I did not know what he could
mean by that, though what I felt was embarrassment at the great number of geese there were, and a dulled feeling like a hunger because the
shooting had stopped and it was over for me now.

Glen began to pick up his geese, and I walked down to my two that
had fallen close together and were dead. One had hit with such an impact that its stomach had split and some of its inward parts were knocked
out. Though the other looked unhurt, its soft white belly turned up like
a pillow, its head and jagged bill teeth and its tiny black eyes looking as
if it were alive.

"What's happened to the hunters out here?" I heard a voice speak. It
was my mother, standing in her pink dress on the knoll above us, hugging her arms. She was smiling though she was cold. And I realized that
I had lost all thought of her in the shooting. "Who did all this shooting?
Is this your work, Les?"

"No," I said.

"Les is a hunter, though, Aileen," Glen said. "He takes his time." He
was holding two white geese by their necks, one in each hand, and he
was smiling. He and my mother seemed pleased.

"I see you didn't miss too many," my mother said and smiled. I could

tell she admired Glen for his geese, and that she had done some thinking in the car alone. "It *was* wonderful, Glen," she said. "I've never seen
anything like that. They were like snow."

"It's worth seeing once, isn't it?" Glen said. "I should've killed more,
but I got excited."

My mother looked at me then. "Where's yours, Les?"

"Here," I said and pointed to my two geese on the ground beside me.

My mother nodded in a nice way, and I think she liked everything
then and wanted the day to turn out right and for all of us to be happy.
"Six, then. You've got six in all."

"One's still out there," I said and motioned where the one goose was
swimming in circles on the water.

"Okay," my mother said and put her hand over her eyes to look.
"Where is it?"

Glen Baxter looked at me then with a strange smile, a smile that said
he wished I had never mentioned anything about the other goose. And
I wished I hadn't either. I looked up in the sky and could see the lines of
geese by the thousands shining silver in the light, and I wished we could
just leave and go home.

"That one's my mistake there," Glen Baxter said and grinned. "I
shouldn't have shot that one, Aileen. I got too excited."

My mother looked out on the lake for a minute, then looked at Glen
and back again. "Poor goose." She shook her head. "How will you get it,
Glen?"

"I can't get that one now," Glen said.

My mother looked at him. "What do you mean?" she said.

"I'm going to leave that one," Glen said.

"Well, no. You can't leave one," my mother said. "You shot it. You
have to get it. Isn't that a rule?"

"No," Glen said.

And my mother looked from Glen to me. "Wade out and get it, Glen,"
she said, in a sweet way, and my mother looked young then for some
reason, like a young girl, in her flimsy short-sleeved waitress dress, and
her skinny, bare legs in the wheatgrass.

"No." Glen Baxter looked down at his gun and shook his head. And
I didn't know why he wouldn't go, because it would've been easy. The
lake was shallow. And you could tell that anyone could've walked out a
long way before it got deep, and Glen had on his boots.

My mother looked at the white goose, which was not more than
thirty yards from the shore, its head up, moving in slow circles, its wings

settled and relaxed so you could see the black tips. "Wade out and get it, Glenny, won't you please?" she said. "They're special things."

"You don't understand the world, Aileen," Glen said. "This can happen. It doesn't matter."

"But that's so cruel, Glen," she said, and a sweet smile came on her lips.

"Raise up your own arms, Leeny," Glen said. "I can't see any angel's wings, can you, Les?" He looked at me, but I looked away.

"Then you go on and get it, Les," my mother said. "You weren't raised by crazy people." I started to go, but Glen Baxter suddenly grabbed me by my shoulder and pulled me back hard, so hard his fingers made bruises in my skin that I saw later.

"Nobody's going," he said. "This is over with now."

And my mother gave Glen a cold look then. "You don't have a heart, Glen," she said. "There's nothing to love in you. You're just a son of a bitch, that's all."

And Glen Baxter nodded at my mother as if he understood something that he had not understood before, but something that he was willing to know. "Fine," he said, "that's fine." And he took his big pistol out from against his belly, the big blue revolver I had only seen part of before and that he said protected him, and he pointed it out at the goose on the water, his arm straight away from him, and shot and missed. And then he shot and missed again. The goose made its noise once. And then he hit it dead, because there was no splash. And then he shot it three times more until the gun was empty and the goose's head was down and it was floating toward the middle of the lake where it was empty and dark blue. "Now who has a heart?" Glen said. But my mother was not there when he turned around. She had already started back to the car and was almost lost from sight in the darkness. And Glen smiled at me then and his face had a wild look on it. "Okay, Les?" he said.

"Okay," I said.

"There're limits to everything, right?"

"I guess so," I said.

"Your mother's a beautiful woman, but she's not the only beautiful woman in Montana." I did not say anything. And Glen Baxter suddenly said, "Here," and he held the pistol out at me. "Don't you want this? Don't you want to shoot me? Nobody thinks they'll die. But I'm ready for it right now." And I did not know what to do then. Though it is true that what I wanted to do was to hit him, hit him as hard in the face as I could, and see him on the ground, bleeding and crying and pleading for me to stop. Only at that moment he looked scared to me, and I had never seen a grown man scared before — though I have seen one since — and I felt sorry for him, as though he were already a dead man. And I did not end up hitting him at all.

A light can go out in the heart. All of this went on years ago, but I still can feel now how sad and remote the world was to me. Glen Baxter, I think now, was not a bad man, only a man scared of something he'd never seen before — something soft in himself — his life going a way he didn't like. A woman with a son. Who could blame him there? I don't know what makes people do what they do or call themselves what they call themselves, only that you have to live someone's life to be the expert.

My mother had tried to see the good side of things, tried to be hopeful in the situation she was handed, tried to look out for us both, and it hadn't worked. It was a strange time in her life then and after that, a time when she had to adjust to being an adult just when she was on the thin edge of things. Too much awareness too early in life was her problem, I think.

And what I felt was only that I had somehow been pushed out into the world, into the real life then, the one I hadn't lived yet. In a year I was gone to hard-rock mining and no-paycheck jobs and not to college. And I have thought more than once about my mother's saying that I had not been raised by crazy people, and I don't know what that could mean or what difference it could make, unless it means that love is a reliable commodity, and even that is not always true, as I have found out.

Late on the night that all this took place I was in bed when I heard my mother say, "Come outside, Les. Come and hear this." And I went out onto the front porch barefoot and in my underwear, where it was warm like spring, and there was a spring mist in the air. I could see the lights of the Fairfield Coach in the distance on its way up to Great Falls.

And I could hear geese, white birds in the sky, flying. They made their high-pitched sound like angry yells, and though I couldn't see them high up, it seemed to me they were everywhere. And my mother looked up and said, "Hear them?" I could smell her hair wet from the shower. "They leave with the moon," she said. "It's still half wild out here."

And I said, "I hear them," and I felt a chill come over my bare chest, and the hair stood up on my arms the way it does before a storm. And for a while we listened.

"When I first married your father, you know, we lived on a street called Bluebird Canyon, in California. And I thought that was the prettiest street and the prettiest name. I suppose no one brings you up like your first love. You don't mind if I say that, do you?" She looked at me hopefully.

"No," I said.

"We have to keep civilization alive somehow." And she pulled her little housecoat together because there was a cold vein in the air, a part of the cold that would be on us the next day. "I don't feel part of things tonight, I guess."

"It's all right," I said.

"Do you know where I'd like to go?" she said.

"No," I said. And I suppose I knew she was angry then, angry with life, but did not want to show me that.

"To the Straits of Juan de Fuca. Wouldn't that be something? Would you like that?"

"I'd like it," I said. And my mother looked off for a minute, as if she could see the Straits of Juan de Fuca out against the line of mountains, see the lights of things alive and a whole new world.

"I know you liked him," she said after a moment. "You and I both suffer fools too well."

"I didn't like him too much," I said. "I didn't really care."

"He'll fall on his face, I'm sure of that," she said. And I didn't say anything because I didn't care about Glen Baxter anymore, and was happy not to talk about him. "Would you tell me something if I asked you? Would you tell me the truth?"

"Yes," I said.

And my mother did not look at me. "Just tell the truth," she said.

"All right," I said.

"Do you think I'm still very feminine? I'm thirty-two years old now. You don't know what that means. But do you think I am?"

And I stood at the edge of the porch, with the olive trees before me, looking straight up into the mist where I could not see geese but could still hear them flying, could almost feel the air move below their white wings. And I felt the way you feel when you are on a trestle all alone and the train is coming, and you know you have to decide. And I said, "Yes, I do." Because that was the truth. And I tried to think of something else then and did not hear what my mother said after that.

And how old was I then? Sixteen. Sixteen is young, but it can also be a grown man. I am forty-one years old now, and I think about that time without regret, though my mother and I never talked in that way again, and I have not heard her voice now in a long, long time.

1988

ROBERT STONE
HELPING

from *The New Yorker*

ROBERT STONE (1937–2015) was born in Brooklyn, New York. His mother was schizophrenic, and after she was institutionalized, he lived for years in an orphanage. He later attended and won writing prizes at Archbishop Molloy High School, but he left before graduating.

Stone served in the navy during the mid-1950s and then attended New York University for a year while working as a copyboy at the *Daily News*. He eventually moved to California, where he attended Stanford University and met Beat Generation writers such as Ken Kesey.

Stone's first book is *A Hall of Mirrors,* which won the William Faulkner Foundation Award. Stone also created a screen adaptation of the work, which became the 1970 film *WUSA,* starring Paul Newman, Joanne Woodward, and Anthony Perkins. He won the National Book Award for Fiction in 1975 for his novel *Dog Soldiers.* His story collection *Bear and His Daughter* was a finalist for the Pulitzer Prize. Stone also received fellowships from the Guggenheim Foundation and the National Endowment for the Humanities, the Mildred and Harold Strauss Living Award, the John Dos Passos Prize for Literature, and the American Academy and Institute of Arts and Letters Award. His work often tells of politically related adventures in war-torn places like Jerusalem and Central America.

Stone taught writing at Johns Hopkins University Writing Seminars and Yale. His most recent novel is *Death of a Black-Haired Girl.* He died in 2015 at his home in Key West, Florida, at the age of seventy-seven.

★

O NE GRAY NOVEMBER day, Elliot went to Boston for the afternoon. The wet streets seemed cold and lonely. He sensed a broken promise in the city's elegance and verve. Old hopes tormented him like phantom limbs, but he did not drink. He had joined Alcoholics Anonymous fifteen months before.

Christmas came, childless, a festival of regret. His wife went to Mass and cooked a turkey. Sober, Elliot walked in the woods.

In January, blizzards swept down from the Arctic until the weather became too cold for snow. The Shawmut Valley grew quiet and crystalline. In the white silences, Elliot could hear the boards of his house contract and feel a shrinking in his bones. Each dusk, starveling deer came out of the wooded swamp behind the house to graze his orchard for whatever raccoons had uncovered and left behind. At night he lay beside his sleeping wife listening to the baying of dog packs running them down in the deep moon-shadowed snow.

Day in, day out, he was sober. At times it was almost stimulating. But he could not shake off the sensations he had felt in Boston. In his mind's eye he could see dead leaves rattling along brick gutters and savor that day's desperation. The brief outing had undermined him.

Sober, however, he remained, until the day a man named Blankenship came into his office at the state hospital for counseling. Blankenship had red hair, a brutal face, and a sneaking manner. He was a sponger and petty thief whom Elliot had seen a number of times before.

"I been having this dream," Blankenship announced loudly. His voice was not pleasant. His skin was unwholesome. Every time he got arrested the court sent him to the psychiatrists and the psychiatrists, who spoke little English, sent him to Elliot.

Blankenship had joined the Army after his first burglary but had never served east of the Rhine. After a few months in Wiesbaden, he had been discharged for reasons of unsuitability, but he told everyone he was a veteran of the Vietnam War. He went about in a tiger suit. Elliot had had enough of him.

"Dreams are boring," Elliot told him.

Blankenship was outraged. "Whaddaya mean?" he demanded.

During counseling sessions Elliot usually moved his chair into the middle of the room in order to seem accessible to his clients. Now he stayed securely behind his desk. He did not care to seem accessible to Blankenship. "What I said, Mr. Blankenship. Other people's dreams are boring. Didn't you ever hear that?"

"Boring?" Blankenship frowned. He seemed unable to imagine a meaning for the word.

Elliot picked up a pencil and set its point quivering on his desk-top blotter. He gazed into his client's slack-jawed face. The Blankenship family made their way through life as strolling litigants, and young Blankenship's specialty was slipping on ice cubes. Hauled off the pavement, he would hassle the doctors in Emergency for pain pills and hurry to a law clinic. The Blankenships had threatened suit against half the property owners in the southern part of the state. What they could not extort at law they stole. But even the Blankenship family had abandoned Blankenship. His last visit to the hospital had been subsequent to an arrest for lifting a case of hot-dog rolls from Woolworth's. He lived in a Goodwill depository bin in Wyndham.

"Now I suppose you want to tell me your dream? Is that right, Mr. Blankenship?"

Blankenship looked left and right like a dog surrendering eye contact. "Don't you want to hear it?" he asked humbly.

Elliot was unmoved. "Tell me something, Blankenship. Was your dream about Vietnam?"

At the mention of the word "Vietnam," Blankenship customarily broke into a broad smile. Now he looked guilty and guarded. He shrugged. "Ya."

"How come you have dreams about that place, Blankenship? You were never there."

"Whaddaya mean?" Blankenship began to say, but Elliot cut him off.

"You were never there, my man. You never saw the goddamn place. You have no business dreaming about it! You better cut it out!"

He had raised his voice to the extent that the secretary outside his open door paused at her word processor.

"Lemme alone," Blankenship said fearfully. "Some doctor you are."

"It's all right," Elliot assured him. "I'm not a doctor."

"Everybody's on my case," Blankenship said. His moods were volatile. He began to weep.

Elliot watched the tears roll down Blankenship's chapped, pitted cheeks. He cleared his throat. "Look, fella . . ." he began. He felt at a loss. He felt like telling Blankenship that things were tough all over.

Blankenship sniffed and telescoped his neck and after a moment looked at Elliot. His look was disconcertingly trustful; he was used to being counseled.

"Really, you know, it's ridiculous for you to tell me your problems have to do with Nam. You were never over there. It was me over there, Blankenship. Not you."

Blankenship leaned forward and put his forehead on his knees.

"Your troubles have to do with here and now," Elliot told his client. "Fantasies aren't helpful."

His voice sounded overripe and hypocritical in his own ears. What a dreadful business, he thought. What an awful job this is. Anger was driving him crazy.

Blankenship straightened up and spoke through his tears. "This dream . . ." he said. "I'm scared."

Elliot felt ready to endure a great deal in order not to hear Blankenship's dream.

"I'm not the one you see about that," he said. In the end he knew his duty. He sighed. "O.K. All right. Tell me about it."

"Yeah?" Blankenship asked with leaden sarcasm. "Yeah? You think dreams are friggin' boring!"

"No, no," Elliot said. He offered Blankenship a tissue and Blankenship took one. "That was sort of off the top of my head. I didn't really mean it."

Blankenship fixed his eyes on dreaming distance. "There's a feeling that goes with it. With the dream." Then he shook his head in revulsion and looked at Elliot as though he had only just awakened. "So what do you think? You think it's boring?"

"Of course not," Elliot said. "A physical feeling?"

"Ya. It's like I'm floating in rubber."

He watched Elliot stealthily, aware of quickened attention. Elliot had caught dengue in Vietnam and during his weeks of delirium had felt vaguely as though he were floating in rubber.

"What are you seeing in this dream?"

Blankenship only shook his head. Elliot suffered a brief but intense attack of rage.

"Hey, Blankenship," he said equably, "here I am, man. You can see I'm listening."

"What I saw was black," Blankenship said. He spoke in an odd tremolo. His behavior was quite different from anything Elliot had come to expect from him.

"Black? What was it?"

"Smoke. The sky maybe."

"The sky?" Elliot asked.

"It was all black. I was scared."

In a waking dream of his own, Elliot felt the muscles on his neck distend. He was looking up at a sky that was black, filled with smoke-swollen clouds, lit with fires, damped with blood and rain.

"What were you scared of?" he asked Blankenship.

"I don't know," Blankenship said.

Elliot could not drive the black sky from his inward eye. It was as though Blankenship's dream had infected his own mind.

"You don't know? You don't know what you were scared of?"

Blankenship's posture was rigid. Elliot, who knew the aspect of true fear, recognized it there in front of him.

"The Nam," Blankenship said.

"You're not even old enough," Elliot told him.

Blankenship sat trembling with joined palms between his thighs. His face was flushed and not in the least ennobled by pain. He had trouble with alcohol and drugs. He had trouble with everything.

"So wherever your black sky is, it isn't Vietnam."

Things were so unfair, Elliot thought. It was unfair of Blankenship to appropriate the condition of a Vietnam veteran. The trauma inducing his post-traumatic stress had been nothing more serious than his own birth, a routine procedure. Now, in addition to the poverty, anxiety, and confusion that would always be his life's lot, he had been visited with irony. It was all arbitrary and some people simply got elected. Everyone knew that who had been where Blankenship had not.

"Because, I assure you, Mr. Blankenship, you were never there."

"Whaddaya mean?" Blankenship asked.

When Blankenship was gone Elliot leafed through his file and saw that the psychiatrists had passed him upstairs without recording a diagnosis. Disproportionately angry, he went out to the secretary's desk.

"Nobody wrote up that last patient," he said. "I'm not supposed to see people without a diagnosis. The shrinks are just passing the buck."

The secretary was a tall, solemn redhead with prominent front teeth and a slight speech disorder. "Dr. Sayyid will have kittens if he hears you call him a shrink, Chas. He's already complained. He hates being called a shrink."

"Then he came to the wrong country," Elliot said. "He can go back to his own."

The woman giggled. "He *is* the doctor, Chas."

"Hates being called a shrink!" He threw the file on the secretary's table and stormed back toward his office. "That fucking little zip couldn't give you a decent haircut. He's a prescription clerk."

The secretary looked about her guiltily and shook her head. She was used to him.

Elliot succeeded in calming himself down after a while, but the image of the black sky remained with him. At first he thought he would be able to simply shrug the whole thing off. After a few minutes, he picked up his phone and dialed Blankenship's probation officer.

"The Vietnam thing is all he has," the probation officer explained. "I guess he picked it up around."

"His descriptions are vivid," Elliot said.

"You mean they sound authentic?"

"I mean he had me going today. He was ringing my bells."

"Good for Blanky. Think he believes it himself?"

"Yes," Elliot said. "He believes it himself now."

Elliot told the probation officer about Blankenship's current arrest, which was for showering illegally at midnight in the Wyndham Regional High School. He asked what probation knew about Blankenship's present relationship with his family.

"You kiddin'?" the P.O. asked. "They're all locked down. The whole family's inside. The old man's in Bridgewater. Little Donny's in San Quentin or somewhere. Their dog's in the pound."

Elliot had lunch alone in the hospital staff cafeteria. On the far side of the double-glazed windows, the day was darkening as an expected snowstorm gathered. Along Route 7, ancient elms stood frozen against the gray sky. When he had finished his sandwich and coffee, he sat staring out at the winter afternoon. His anger had given way to an insistent anxiety.

On the way back to his office, he stopped at the hospital gift shop for a copy of *Sports Illustrated* and a candy bar. When he was inside again, he closed the door and put his feet up. It was Friday and he had no appointments for the remainder of the day, nothing to do but write a few letters and read the office mail.

Elliot's cubicle in the social services department was windowless and lined with bookshelves. When he found himself unable to concentrate on the magazine and without any heart for his paperwork, he ran his eye over the row of books beside his chair. There were volumes by Heinrich Muller and Carlos Castaneda, Jones's life of Freud, and *The Golden Bough*. The books aroused a revulsion in Elliot. Their present uselessness repelled him.

Over and over again, detail by detail, he tried to recall his conversation with Blankenship.

"You were never there," he heard himself explaining. He was trying to get the whole incident straightened out after the fact. Something was wrong. Dread crept over him like a paralysis. He ate his candy bar without tasting it. He knew that the craving for sweets was itself a bad sign.

Blankenship had misappropriated someone else's dream and made it his own. It made no difference whether you had been there, after all. The dreams had crossed the ocean. They were in the air.

He took his glasses off and put them on his desk and sat with his arms folded, looking into the well of light from his desk lamp. There seemed to be nothing but whirl inside him. Unwelcome things came and went in his mind's eye. His heart beat faster. He could not control the headlong promiscuity of his thoughts.

It was possible to imagine larval dreams traveling in suspended animation undetectable in a host brain. They could be divided and regenerate like flatworms, hide in seams and bedding, in war stories, laughter, snapshots. They could rot your socks and turn your memory into a black-and-green blister. Green for the hills, black for the sky above. At daybreak they hung themselves up in rows like bats. At dusk they went out to look for dreamers.

Elliot put his jacket on and went into the outer office, where the secretary sat frowning into the measured sound and light of her machine. She must enjoy its sleekness and order, he thought. She was divorced. Four redheaded kids between ten and seventeen lived with her in an unpainted house across from Stop & Shop. Elliot liked her and had come to find her attractive. He managed a smile for her.

"Ethel, I think I'm going to pack it in," he declared. It seemed awkward to be leaving early without a reason.

"Jack wants to talk to you before you go, Chas."

Elliot looked at her blankly.

Then his colleague, Jack Sprague, having heard his voice, called from the adjoining cubicle. "Chas, what about Sunday's games? Shall I call you with the spread?"

"I don't know," Elliot said. "I'll phone you tomorrow."

"This is a big decision for him," Jack Sprague told the secretary. "He might lose twenty-five bucks."

At present, Elliot drew a slightly higher salary than Jack Sprague, although Jack had a Ph.D. and Elliot was simply an M.S.W. Different branches of the state government employed them.

"Twenty-five bucks," said the woman. "If you guys have no better use for twenty-five bucks, give it to me."

"Where are you off to, by the way?" Sprague asked.

Elliot began to answer, but for a moment no reply occurred to him. He shrugged. "I have to get back," he finally stammered. "I promised Grace."

"Was that Blankenship I saw leaving?"

Elliot nodded.

"It's February," Jack said. "How come he's not in Florida?"

"I don't know," Elliot said. He put on his coat and walked to the door. "I'll see you."

"Have a nice weekend," the secretary said. She and Sprague looked after him indulgently as he walked toward the main corridor.

"Are Chas and Grace going out on the town?" she said to Sprague. "What do you think?"

"That would be the day," Sprague said. "Tomorrow he'll come back over here and read all day. He spends every weekend holed up in this goddamn office while she does something or other at the church." He shook his head. "Every night he's at A.A. and she's home alone."

Ethel savored her overbite. "Jack," she said teasingly, "are you thinking what I think you're thinking? Shame on you."

"I'm thinking I'm glad I'm not him, that's what I'm thinking. That's as much as I'll say."

"Yeah, well, I don't care," Ethel said. "Two salaries and no kids, that's the way to go, boy."

Elliot went out through the automatic doors of the emergency bay and the cold closed over him. He walked across the hospital parking lot with his eyes on the pavement, his hands thrust deep in his overcoat pockets, skirting patches of shattered ice. There was no wind, but the motionless air stung; the metal frames of his glasses burned his skin. Curlicues of mud-brown ice coated the soiled snowbanks along the street. Although it was still afternoon, the street lights had come on.

The lock on his car door had frozen and he had to breathe on the keyhole to fit the key. When the engine turned over, Jussi Björling's recording of the Handel Largo filled the car interior. He snapped it off at once.

Halted at the first stoplight, he began to feel the want of a destination. The fear and impulse to flight that had got him out of the office faded, and he had no desire to go home. He was troubled by a peculiar impatience that might have been with time itself. It was as though he were waiting for something. The sensation made him feel anxious; it was unfamiliar but not altogether unpleasant. When the light changed he drove on, past the Gulf station and the firehouse and between the greens of Ilford Common. At the far end of the common he swung into the parking lot of the Packard Conway Library and stopped with the engine running. What he was experiencing, he thought, was the principle of possibility.

He turned off the engine and went out again into the cold. Behind the leaded library windows he could see the librarian pouring coffee in her tiny private office. The librarian was a Quaker of socialist principles named Candace Music, who was Elliot's cousin.

The Conway Library was all dark wood and etched mirrors, a Gothic saloon. Years before, out of work and booze-whipped, Elliot had gone to hide there. Because Candace was a classicist's widow and knew some Greek, she was one of the few people in the valley with whom Elliot had cared to speak in those days. Eventually, it had seemed to him that all their conversations tended toward Vietnam, so he had gone less and less often. Elliot was the only Vietnam veteran Candace knew well enough to chat with, and he had come to suspect that he was being probed for the edification of the East Ilford Friends Meeting. At that time he had still pretended to talk easily about his war and had prepared little discourses and picaresque anecdotes to recite on demand. Earnest seekers like Candace had caused him great secret distress.

Candace came out of her office to find him at the checkout desk. He watched her brow furrow with concern as she composed a smile. "Chas, what a surprise. You haven't been in for an age."

"Sure I have, Candace. I went to all the Wednesday films last fall. I work just across the road."

"I know, dear," Candace said. "I always seem to miss you."

A cozy fire burned in the hearth, an antique brass clock ticked along on the marble mantel above it. On a couch near the fireplace an old man sat upright, his mouth open, asleep among half a dozen soiled plastic bags. Two teenage girls whispered over their homework at a table under the largest window.

"Now that I'm here," he said, laughing, "I can't remember what I came to get."

"Stay and get warm," Candace told him. "Got a minute? Have a cup of coffee."

Elliot had nothing but time, but he quickly realized that he did not want to stay and pass it with Candace. He had no clear idea of why he had come to the library. Standing at the checkout desk, he accepted coffee. She attended him with an air of benign supervision, as though he were a Chinese peasant and she a medical missionary, like her father. Candace was tall and plain, more handsome in her middle sixties than she had ever been.

"Why don't we sit down?"

He allowed her to gentle him into a chair by the fire. They made a threesome with the sleeping old man.

"Have you given up translating, Chas? I hope not."

"Not at all," he said. Together they had once rendered a few fragments of Sophocles into verse. She was good at clever rhymes.

"You come in so rarely, Chas. Ted's books go to waste."

After her husband's death, Candace had donated his books to the Conway, where they reposed in a reading room inscribed to his memory, untouched among foreign-language volumes, local genealogies, and books in large type for the elderly.

"I have a study in the barn," he told Candace. "I work there. When I have time." The lie was absurd, but he felt the need of it.

"And you're working with Vietnam veterans," Candace declared.

"Supposedly," Elliot said. He was growing impatient with her nodding solicitude.

"Actually," he said, "I came in for the new Oxford *Classical World.* I thought you'd get it for the library and I could have a look before I spent my hard-earned cash."

Candace beamed. "You've come to the right place, Chas, I'm happy to say." He thought she looked disproportionately happy. "I have it."

"Good," Elliot said, standing. "I'll just take it, then. I can't really stay."

Candace took his cup and saucer and stood as he did. When the library telephone rang, she ignored it, reluctant to let him go. "How's Grace?" she asked.

"Fine," Elliot said. "Grace is well."

At the third ring she went to the desk. When her back was turned, he hesitated for a moment and then went outside.

The gray afternoon had softened into night, and it was snowing. The falling snow whirled like a furious mist in the headlight beams on Route 7 and settled implacably on Elliot's cheeks and eyelids. His heart, for no good reason, leaped up in childlike expectation. He had run away from a dream and encountered possibility. He felt in possession of a promise. He began to walk toward the roadside lights.

Only gradually did he begin to understand what had brought him there and what the happy anticipation was that fluttered in his breast. Drinking, he had started his evening from the Conway Library. He would arrive hung over in the early afternoon to browse and read. When the old pain rolled in with dusk, he would walk down to the Midway Tavern for a remedy. Standing in the snow outside the library, he realized that he had contrived to promise himself a drink.

Ahead, through the storm, he could see the beer signs in the Midway's window warm and welcoming. Snowflakes spun around his head like an excitement.

Outside the Midway's package store, he paused with his hand on the doorknob. There was an old man behind the counter whom Elliot remembered from his drinking days. When he was inside, he realized that the old man neither knew nor cared who he was. The package store was thick with dust; it was on the counter, the shelves, the bottles themselves. The old counterman looked dusty. Elliot bought a bottle of King William Scotch and put it in the inside pocket of his overcoat.

Passing the windows of the Midway Tavern, Elliot could see the ranks of bottles aglow behind the bar. The place was crowded with men leaving the afternoon shifts at the shoe and felt factories. No one turned to note him when he passed inside. There was a single stool vacant at the bar and he took it. His heart beat faster. Bruce Springsteen was on the jukebox.

The bartender was a club fighter from Pittsfield called Jackie G., with whom Elliot had often gossiped. Jackie G. greeted him as though he had been in the previous evening. "Say, babe?"

"How do," Elliot said.

A couple of men at the bar eyed his shirt and tie. Confronted with the bartender, he felt impelled to explain his presence. "Just thought I'd stop by," he told Jackie G. "Just thought I'd have one. Saw the light. The snow . . ." He chuckled expansively.

"Good move," the bartender said. "Scotch?"

"Double," Elliot said.

When he shoved two dollars forward along the bar, Jackie G. pushed one of the bills back to him. "Happy hour, babe."

"Ah," Elliot said. He watched Jackie pour the double. "Not a moment too soon."

For five minutes or so, Elliot sat in his car in the barn with the engine running and his Handel tape on full volume. He had driven over from East Ilford in a baroque ecstasy, swinging and swaying and singing along. When the tape ended, he turned off the engine and poured some Scotch into an apple juice container to store providentially beneath the car seat. Then he took the tape and the Scotch into the house with him. He was lying on the sofa in the dark living room, listening to the Largo, when he heard his wife's car in the driveway. By the time Grace had made her way up the icy back-porch steps, he was able to hide the Scotch and rinse his glass clean in the kitchen sink. The drinking life, he thought, was lived moment by moment.

Soon she was in the tiny cloakroom struggling off with her overcoat. In the process she knocked over a cross-country ski, which stood propped against the cloakroom wall. It had been more than a year since Elliot had used the skis.

She came into the kitchen and sat down at the table to take off her boots. Her lean, freckled face was flushed with the cold, but her eyes looked weary. "I wish you'd put those skis down in the barn," she told him. "You never use them."

"I always like to think," Elliot said, "that I'll start the morning off skiing."

"Well, you never do," she said. "How long have you been home?"

"Practically just walked in," he said. Her pointing out that he no longer skied in the morning enraged him. "I stopped at the Conway Library to get the new Oxford *Classical World.* Candace ordered it."

Her look grew troubled. She had caught something in his voice. With dread and bitter satisfaction, Elliot watched his wife detect the smell of whiskey.

"Oh God," she said. "I don't believe it."

Let's get it over with, he thought. Let's have the song and dance.

She sat up straight in her chair and looked at him in fear.

"Oh, Chas," she said, "how could you?"

For a moment he was tempted to try to explain it all.

"The fact is," Elliot told his wife, "I hate people who start the day cross-country skiing."

She shook her head in denial and leaned her forehead on her palm and cried.

He looked into the kitchen window and saw his own distorted image. "The fact is I think I'll start tomorrow morning by stringing head-high razor wire across Anderson's trail."

The Andersons were the Elliots' nearest neighbors. Loyall Anderson was a full professor of government at the state university, thirty miles away. Anderson and his wife were blond and both of them were over six feet tall. They had two blond children, who qualified for the gifted class in the local school but attended regular classes in token of the Andersons' opposition to elitism.

"Sure," Elliot said. "Stringing wire's good exercise. It's life-affirming in its own way."

The Andersons started each and every day with a brisk morning glide along a trail that they partly maintained. They skied well and presented a pleasing, wholesome sight. If, in the course of their adventure, they encountered a snowmobile, Darlene Anderson would affect to choke and cough, indicating her displeasure. If the snowmobile approached them from behind and the trail was narrow, the Andersons would decline to let it pass, asserting their statutory right-of-way.

"I don't want to hear your violent fantasies," Grace said.

Elliot was picturing razor wire, the Army kind. He was picturing the decapitated Andersons, their blood and jaunty ski caps bright on the white trail. He was picturing their severed heads, their earnest blue eyes and large white teeth reflecting the virginal morning snow. Although Elliot hated snowmobiles, he hated the Andersons far more.

He looked at his wife and saw that she had stopped crying. Her long, elegant face was rigid and lipless.

"Know what I mean? One string at Mommy and Daddy level for Loyall and Darlene. And a bitty wee string at kiddie level for Skippy and Samantha, those cunning little whizzes."

"Stop it," she said to him.

"Sorry," Elliot told her.

Stiff with shame, he went and took his bottle out of the cabinet into which he had thrust it and poured a drink. He was aware of her eyes on him. As he drank, a fragment from old Music's translation of *Medea* came into his mind. "Old friend, I have to weep. The gods and I went mad together and made things as they are." It was such a waste; eighteen months of struggle thrown away. But there was no way to get the stuff back in the bottle.

"I'm very sorry," he said. "You know I'm very sorry, don't you, Grace?"

The delectable Handel arias spun on in the next room.

"You must stop," she said. "You must make yourself stop before it takes over."

"It's out of my hands," Elliot said. He showed her his empty hands. "It's beyond me."

"You'll lose your job, Chas." She stood up at the table and leaned on it, staring wide-eyed at him. Drunk as he was, the panic in her voice frightened him. "You'll end up in jail again."

"One engages," Elliot said, "and then one sees."

"How can you have done it?" she demanded. "You promised me."

"First the promises," Elliot said, "and then the rest."

"Last time was supposed to be the last time," she said.

"Yes," he said, "I remember."

"I can't stand it," she said. "You reduce me to hysterics." She wrung her hands for him to see. "See? Here I am, I'm in hysterics."

"What can I say?" Elliot asked. He went to the bottle and refilled his glass. "Maybe you shouldn't watch."

"You want me to be forbearing, Chas? I'm not going to be."

"The last thing I want," Elliot said, "is an argument."

"I'll give you a fucking argument. You didn't have to drink. All you had to do was come home."

"That must have been the problem," he said.

Then he ducked, alert at the last possible second to the missile that came for him at hairline level. Covering up, he heard the shattering of glass, and a fine rain of crystals enveloped him. She had sailed the sugar bowl at him; it had smashed against the wall above his head and there was sugar and glass in his hair.

"You bastard!" she screamed. "You are undermining me!"

"You ought not to throw things at me," Elliot said. "I don't throw things at you."

He left her frozen into her follow-through and went into the living room to turn the music off. When he returned she was leaning back against the wall, rubbing her right elbow with her left hand. Her eyes were bright. She had picked up one of her boots from the middle of the kitchen floor and stood holding it.

"What the hell do you mean, that must have been the problem?"

He set his glass on the edge of the sink with an unsteady hand and turned to her. "What do I mean? I mean that most of the time I'm putting one foot in front of the other like a good soldier and I'm out of it from the neck up. But there are times when I don't think I will ever be dead enough — or dead long enough — to get the taste of this life off my teeth. That's what I mean!"

She looked at him dry-eyed. "Poor fella," she said.

"What you have to understand, Grace, is that this drink I'm having"— he raised the glass toward her in a gesture of salute —"is the only worthwhile thing I've done in the last year and a half. It's the only thing in my life that means jack shit, the closest thing to satisfaction I've had. Now how can you begrudge me that? It's the best I'm capable of."

"You'll go too far," she said to him. "You'll see."

"What's that, Grace? A threat to walk?" He was grinding his teeth. "Don't make me laugh. You, walk? You, the friend of the unfortunate?"

"Don't you hit me," she said when she looked at his face. "Don't you dare."

"You, the Christian Queen of Calvary, walk? Why, I don't believe that for a minute."

She ran a hand through her hair and bit her lip. "No, we stay," she said. Anger and distraction made her look young. Her cheeks blazed rosy against the general pallor of her skin. "In my family we stay until the fella dies. That's the tradition. We stay and pour it for them and they die."

He put his drink down and shook his head.

"I thought we'd come through," Grace said. "I was sure."

"No," Elliot said. "Not altogether."

They stood in silence for a minute. Elliot sat down at the oilcloth-covered table. Grace walked around it and poured herself a whiskey.

"You are undermining me, Chas. You are making things impossible for me and I just don't know." She drank and winced. "I'm not going to stay through another drunk. I'm telling you right now. I haven't got it in me. I'll die."

He did not want to look at her. He watched the flakes settle against the glass of the kitchen door. "Do what you feel the need of," he said.

"I just can't take it," she said. Her voice was not scolding but measured and reasonable. "It's February. And I went to court this morning and lost Vopotik."

Once again, he thought, my troubles are going to be obviated by those of the deserving poor. He said, "Which one was that?"

"Don't you remember them? The three-year-old with the broken fingers?"

He shrugged. Grace sipped her whiskey.

"I told you. I said I had a three-year-old with broken fingers, and you said, 'Maybe he owed somebody money.'"

"Yes," he said, "I remember now."

"You ought to see the Vopotiks, Chas. The woman is young and obese. She's so young that for a while I thought I could get to her as a juvenile. The guy is a biker. They believe the kid came from another planet to control their lives. They believe this literally, both of them."

"You shouldn't get involved that way," Elliot said. "You should leave it to the caseworkers."

"They scared their first caseworker all the way to California. They were following me to work."

"You didn't tell me."

"Are you kidding?" she asked. "Of course I didn't." To Elliot's surprise, his wife poured herself a second whiskey. "You know how they address the child? As 'dude.' She says to it, 'Hey, dude.'" Grace shuddered with loathing. "You can't imagine! The woman munching Twinkies. The kid smelling of shit. They're high morning, noon, and night, but you can't get anybody for that these days."

"People must really hate it," Elliot said, "when somebody tells them they're not treating their kids right."

"They definitely don't want to hear it," Grace said. "You're right." She sat stirring her drink, frowning into the glass. "The Vopotik child will die, I think."

"Surely not," Elliot said.

"This one I think will die," Grace said. She took a deep breath and puffed out her cheeks and looked at him forlornly. "The situation's extreme. Of course, sometimes you wonder whether it makes any difference. That's the big question, isn't it?"

"I would think," Elliot said, "that would be the one question you didn't ask."

"But you do," she said. "You wonder: Ought they to live at all? To continue the cycle?" She put a hand to her hair and shook her head as if in confusion. "Some of these folks, my God, the poor things cannot put Wednesday on top of Tuesday to save their lives."

"It's a trick," Elliot agreed, "a lot of them can't manage."

"And kids are small, they're handy and underfoot. They make noise. They can't hurt you back."

"I suppose child abuse is something people can do together," Elliot said.

"Some kids are obnoxious. No question about it."

"I wouldn't know," Elliot said.

"Maybe you should stop complaining. Maybe you're better off. Maybe your kids are better off unborn."

"Better off or not," Elliot said, "it looks like they'll stay that way."

"I mean our kids, of course," Grace said. "I'm not blaming you, understand? It's just that here we are with you drunk again and me losing Vopotik, so I thought why not get into the big unaskable questions." She got up and folded her arms and began to pace up and down the kitchen. "Oh," she said when her eye fell upon the bottle, "that's good stuff, Chas. You won't mind if I have another? I'll leave you enough to get loaded on."

Elliot watched her pour. So much pain, he thought; such anger and confusion. He was tired of pain, anger, and confusion; they were what had got him in trouble that very morning.

The liquor seemed to be giving him a perverse lucidity when all he now required was oblivion. His rage, especially, was intact in its salting of alcohol. Its contours were palpable and bleeding at the borders. Booze was good for rage. Booze could keep it burning through the darkest night.

"What happened in court?" he asked his wife.

She was leaning on one arm against the wall, her long, strong body flexed at the hip. Holding her glass, she stared angrily toward the invisible fields outside. "I lost the child," she said.

Elliot thought that a peculiar way of putting it. He said nothing.

"The court convened in an atmosphere of high hilarity. It may be Hate Month around here but it was buddy-buddy over at Ilford Courthouse. The room was full of bikers and bikers' lawyers. A colorful crowd. There was a lot of bonding." She drank and shivered. "They didn't think too well of me. They don't think too well of broads as lawyers. Neither does the judge. The judge has the common touch. He's one of the boys."

"Which judge?" Elliot asked.

"Buckley. A man of about sixty. Know him? Lots of veins on his nose?" Elliot shrugged.

"I thought I had done my homework," Grace told him. "But suddenly I had nothing but paper. No witnesses. It was Margolis at Valley Hospital who spotted the radiator burns. He called us in the first place. Suddenly he's got to keep his reservation for a campsite in St. John. So Buckley threw his deposition out." She began to chew on a fingernail. "The caseworkers have vanished — one's in L.A., the other's in Nepal. I went in there and got run over. I lost the child."

"It happens all the time," Elliot said. "Doesn't it?"

"This one shouldn't have been lost, Chas. These people aren't simply confused. They're weird. They stink."

"You go messing into anybody's life," Elliot said, "that's what you'll find."

"If the child stays in that house," she said, "he's going to die."

"You did your best," he told his wife. "Forget it."

She pushed the bottle away. She was holding a water glass that was almost a third full of whiskey.

"That's what the commissioner said."

Elliot was thinking of how she must have looked in court to the cherry-faced judge and the bikers and their lawyers. Like the schoolteachers who had tormented their childhoods, earnest and tight-assed, humorless and self-righteous. It was not surprising that things had gone against her.

He walked over to the window and faced his reflection again. "Your optimism always surprises me."

"My optimism? Where I grew up our principal cultural expression was the funeral. Whatever keeps me going, it isn't optimism."

"No?" he asked. "What is it?"

"I forget," she said.

"Maybe it's your religious perspective. Your sense of the divine plan."

She sighed in exasperation. "Look, I don't think I want to fight anymore. I'm sorry I threw the sugar at you. I'm not your keeper. Pick on someone your own size."

"Sometimes," Elliot said, "I try to imagine what it's like to believe that the sky is full of care and concern."

"You want to take everything from me, do you?" She stood leaning against the back of her chair. "That you can't take. It's the only part of my life you can't mess up."

He was thinking that if it had not been for her he might not have survived. There could be no forgiveness for that. "Your life? You've got all this piety strung out between Monadnock and Central America. And look at yourself. Look at your life."

"Yes," she said, "look at it."

"You should have been a nun. You don't know how to live."

"I know that," she said. "That's why I stopped doing counseling. Because I'd rather talk the law than life." She turned to him. "You got everything I had, Chas. What's left I absolutely require."

"I swear I would rather be a drunk," Elliot said, "than force myself to believe such trivial horseshit."

"Well, you're going to have to do it without a straight man," she said, "because this time I'm not going to be here for you. Believe it or not."

"I don't believe it," Elliot said. "Not my Grace."

"You're really good at this," she told him. "You make me feel ashamed of my own name."

"I love your name," he said.

The telephone rang. They let it ring three times, and then Elliot went over and answered it.

"Hey, who's that?" a good-humored voice on the phone demanded.

Elliot recited their phone number.

"Hey, I want to talk to your woman, man. Put her on."

"I'll give her a message," Elliot said.

"You put your woman on, man. Run and get her."

Elliot looked at the receiver. He shook his head. "Mr. Vopotik?"

"Never you fuckin' mind, man. I don't want to talk to you. I want to talk to the skinny bitch."

Elliot hung up.

"Is it him?" she asked.

"I guess so."

They waited for the phone to ring again and it shortly did.

"I'll talk to him," Grace said. But Elliot already had the phone.

"Who are you, asshole?" the voice inquired. "What's your fuckin' name, man?"

"Elliot," Elliot said.

"Hey, don't hang up on me, Elliot. I won't put up with that. I told you go get that skinny bitch, man. You go do it."

There were sounds of festivity in the background on the other end of the line—a stereo and drunken voices.

"Hey," the voice declared. "Hey, don't keep me waiting, man."

"What do you want to say to her?" Elliot asked.

"That's none of your fucking business, fool. Do what I told you."

"My wife is resting," Elliot said. "I'm taking her calls."

He was answered by a shout of rage. He put the phone aside for a moment and finished his glass of whiskey. When he picked it up again the man on the line was screaming at him. "That bitch tried to break up my family, man! She almost got away with it. You know what kind of pain my wife went through?"

"What kind?" Elliot asked.

For a few seconds he heard only the noise of the party. "Hey, you're not drunk, are you, fella?"

"Certainly not," Elliot insisted.

"You tell that skinny bitch she's gonna pay for what she did to my family, man. You tell her she can run but she can't hide. I don't care where you go—California, anywhere—I'll get to you."

"Now that I have you on the phone," Elliot said, "I'd like to ask you a couple of questions. Promise you won't get mad?"

"Stop it!" Grace said to him. She tried to wrench the phone from his grasp, but he clutched it to his chest.

"Do you keep a journal?" Elliot asked the man on the phone. "What's your hat size?"

"Maybe you think I can't get to you," the man said. "But I can get to you, man. I don't care who you are, I'll get to you. The brothers will get to you."

"Well, there's no need to go to California. You know where we live."

"For God's sake," Grace said.

"Fuckin' right," the man on the telephone said. "Fuckin' right I know."

"Come on over," Elliot said.

"How's that?" the man on the phone asked.

"I said come on over. We'll talk about space travel. Comets and stuff. We'll talk astral projection. The moons of Jupiter."

"You're making a mistake, fucker."

"Come on over," Elliot insisted. "Bring your fat wife and your beat-up kid. Don't be embarrassed if your head's a little small."

The telephone was full of music and shouting. Elliot held it away from his ear.

"Good work," Grace said to him when he had replaced the receiver.

"I hope he comes," Elliot said. "I'll pop him."

He went carefully down the cellar stairs, switched on the overhead light, and began searching among the spiderwebbed shadows and fouled fishing line for his shotgun. It took him fifteen minutes to find it and his cleaning case. While he was still downstairs, he heard the telephone ring again and his wife answer it. He came upstairs and spread his shooting gear across the kitchen table. "Was that him?"

She nodded wearily. "He called back to play us the chain saw."

"I've heard that melody before," Elliot said.

He assembled his cleaning rod and swabbed out the shotgun barrel. Grace watched him, a hand to her forehead. "God," she said. "What have I done? I'm so drunk."

"Most of the time," Elliot said, sighting down the barrel, "I'm helpless in the face of human misery. Tonight I'm ready to reach out."

"I'm finished," Grace said. "I'm through, Chas. I mean it."

Elliot rammed three red shells into the shotgun and pumped one forward into the breech with a satisfying report. "Me, I'm ready for some radical problem solving. I'm going to spray that no-neck Slovak all over the yard."

"He isn't a Slovak," Grace said. She stood in the middle of the kitchen with her eyes closed. Her face was chalk white.

"What do you mean?" Elliot demanded. "Certainly he's a Slovak."

"No he's not," Grace said.

"Fuck him anyway. I don't care what he is. I'll grease his ass."

He took a handful of deer shells from the box and stuffed them in his jacket pockets.

"I'm not going to stay with you. Chas. Do you understand me?"

Elliot walked to the window and peered out at his driveway. "He won't be alone. They travel in packs."

"For God's sake!" Grace cried, and in the next instant bolted for the downstairs bathroom. Elliot went out, turned off the porch light and switched on a spotlight over the barn door. Back inside, he could hear Grace in the toilet being sick. He turned off the light in the kitchen.

He was still standing by the window when she came up behind him. It seemed strange and fateful to be standing in the dark near her, holding the shotgun. He felt ready for anything.

"I can't leave you alone down here drunk with a loaded shotgun," she said. "How can I?"

"Go upstairs," he said.

"If I went upstairs it would mean I didn't care what happened. Do you understand? If I go it means I don't care anymore. Understand?"

"Stop asking me if I understand," Elliot said. "I understand fine."

"I can't think," she said in a sick voice. "Maybe I don't care. I don't know. I'm going upstairs."

"Good," Elliot said.

When she was upstairs, Elliot took his shotgun and the whiskey into the dark living room and sat down in an armchair beside one of the lace-curtained windows. The powerful barn light illuminated the length of his driveway and the whole of the back yard. From the window at which he sat, he commanded a view of several miles in the direction of East Ilford. The two-lane blacktop road that ran there was the only one along which an enemy could pass.

He drank and watched the snow, toying with the safety of his 12-gauge Remington. He felt neither anxious nor angry now but only impatient to be done with whatever the night would bring. Drunkenness and the silent rhythm of the falling snow combined to make him feel outside of time and syntax.

Sitting in the dark room, he found himself confronting Blankenship's dream. He saw the bunkers and wire of some long-lost perimeter. The rank smell of night came back to him, the dread evening and quick dusk, the mysteries of outer darkness: fear, combat, and death. Enervated by liquor, he began to cry. Elliot was sympathetic with other people's tears but ashamed of his own. He thought of his own tears as childish and excremental. He stifled whatever it was that had started them.

Now his whiskey tasted thin as water. Beyond the lightly frosted glass, illuminated snowflakes spun and settled sleepily on weighted pine boughs. He had found a life beyond the war after all, but in it he was still sitting in darkness, armed, enraged, waiting.

His eyes grew heavy as the snow came down. He felt as though he could be drawn up into the storm and he began to imagine that. He imagined his life with all its artifacts and appetites easing up the spout into white oblivion, everything obviated and foreclosed. He thought maybe he could go for that.

When he awakened, his left hand had gone numb against the trigger guard of his shotgun. The living room was full of pale, delicate light. He looked outside and saw that the storm was done with and the sky radiant and cloudless. The sun was still below the horizon.

Slowly Elliot got to his feet. The throbbing poison in his limbs served to remind him of the state of things. He finished the glass of whiskey on the windowsill beside his easy chair. Then he went to the hall closet to get a ski jacket, shouldered his shotgun, and went outside.

There were two cleared acres behind his house; beyond them a trail descended into a hollow of pine forest and frozen swamp. Across the hollow, white pastures stretched to the ridge line, lambent under the lightening sky. A line of skeletal elms weighted with snow marked the course of frozen Shawmut Brook.

He found a pair of ski goggles in a jacket pocket and put them on and set out toward the tree line, gripping the shotgun, step by careful step in the knee-deep snow. Two raucous crows wheeled high overhead, their cries exploding the morning's silence. When the sun came over the ridge, he stood where he was and took in a deep breath. The risen sun warmed his face and he closed his eyes. It was windless and very cold.

Only after he had stood there for a while did he realize how tired he had become. The weight of the gun taxed him. It seemed infinitely wearying to contemplate another single step in the snow. He opened his eyes and closed them again. With sunup the world had gone blazing blue and white, and even with his tinted goggles its whiteness dazzled him and made his head ache. Behind his eyes, the hypnagogic patterns formed a monsoon-heavy tropical sky. He yawned. More than anything, he wanted to lie down in the soft, pure snow. If he could do that, he was certain he could go to sleep at once.

He stood in the middle of the field and listened to the crows. Fear, anger, and sleep were the three primary conditions of life. He had learned that over there. Once he had thought fear the worst, but he had learned that the worst was anger. Nothing could fix it; neither alcohol nor medicine. It was a worm. It left him no peace. Sleep was the best.

He opened his eyes and pushed on until he came to the brow that overlooked the swamp. Just below, gliding along among the frozen cattails and bare scrub maple, was a man on skis. Elliot stopped to watch the man approach.

The skier's face was concealed by a red-and-blue ski mask. He wore snow goggles, a blue jumpsuit, and a red woolen Norwegian hat. As he came, he leaned into the turns of the trail, moving silently and gracefully along. At the foot of the slope on which Elliot stood, the man looked up, saw him, and slid to a halt. The man stood staring at him for a moment and then began to herringbone up the slope. In no time at all the skier stood no more than ten feet away, removing his goggles, and inside the woolen mask Elliot recognized the clear blue eyes of his neighbor, Professor Loyall Anderson. The shotgun Elliot was carrying seemed to grow heavier. He yawned and shook his head, trying unsuccessfully to clear it. The sight of Anderson's eyes gave him a little thrill of revulsion.

"What are you after?" the young professor asked him, nodding toward the shotgun Elliot was cradling.

"Whatever there is," Elliot said.

Anderson took a quick look at the distant pasture behind him and then turned back to Elliot. The mouth hole of the professor's mask filled with teeth. Elliot thought that Anderson's teeth were quite as he had imagined them earlier. "Well, Polonski's cows are locked up," the professor said. "So they at least are safe."

Elliot realized that the professor had made a joke and was smiling. "Yes," he agreed.

Professor Anderson and his wife had been the moving force behind an initiative to outlaw the discharge of firearms within the boundaries of East Ilford Township. The initiative had been defeated, because East Ilford was not that kind of town.

"I think I'll go over by the river," Elliot said. He said it only to have something to say, to fill the silence before Anderson spoke again. He was afraid of what Anderson might say to him and of what might happen.

"You know," Anderson said, "that's all bird sanctuary over there now."

"Sure," Elliot agreed.

Outfitted as he was, the professor attracted Elliot's anger in an elemental manner. The mask made him appear a kind of doll, a kachina figure or a marionette. His eyes and mouth, all on their own, were disagreeable.

Elliott began to wonder if Anderson could smell the whiskey on his breath. He pushed the little red bull's-eye safety button on his gun to Off.

"Seriously," Anderson said, "I'm always having to run hunters out of there. Some people don't understand the word 'posted.'"

"I would never do that," Elliot said, "I would be afraid."

Anderson nodded his head. He seemed to be laughing. "Would you?" he asked Elliot merrily.

In imagination, Elliot rested the tip of his shotgun barrel against Anderson's smiling teeth. If he fired a load of deer shot into them, he thought, they might make a noise like broken china. "Yes," Elliot said. "I wouldn't know who they were or where they'd been. They might resent my being alive. Telling them where they could shoot and where not."

Anderson's teeth remained in place. "That's pretty strange," he said. "I mean, to talk about resenting someone for being alive."

"It's all relative," Elliot said. "They might think, 'Why should he be alive when some brother of mine isn't?' Or they might think, 'Why should he be alive when I'm not?'"

"Oh," Anderson said.

"You see?" Elliot said. Facing Anderson, he took a long step backward. "All relative."

"Yes," Anderson said.

"That's so often true, isn't it?" Elliot asked. "Values are often relative."

"Yes," Anderson said. Elliot was relieved to see that he had stopped smiling.

"I've hardly slept, you know," Elliot told Professor Anderson. "Hardly at all. All night. I've been drinking."

"Oh," Anderson said. He licked his lips in the mouth of the mask. "You should get some rest."

"You're right," Elliot said.

"Well," Anderson said, "got to go now."

Elliot thought he sounded a little thick in the tongue. A little slow in the jaw.

"It's a nice day," Elliot said, wanting now to be agreeable.

"It's great," Anderson said, shuffling on his skis.

"Have a nice day," Elliot said.

"Yes," Anderson said, and pushed off.

Elliot rested the shotgun across his shoulders and watched Anderson withdraw through the frozen swamp. It was in fact a nice day, but Elliot took no comfort in the weather. He missed night and the falling snow.

As he walked back toward his house, he realized that now there would be whole days to get through, running before the antic energy of whiskey. The whiskey would drive him until he dropped. He shook his head in regret. "It's a revolution," he said aloud. He imagined himself talking to his wife.

Getting drunk was an insurrection, a revolution — a bad one. There would be outsize bogus emotions. There would be petty moral blackmail and cheap remorse. He had said dreadful things to his wife. He had bullied Anderson with his violence and unhappiness, and Anderson would not forgive him. There would be damn little justice and no mercy.

Nearly to the house, he was startled by the desperate feathered drumming of a pheasant's rush. He froze, and out of instinct brought the gun up in the direction of the sound. When he saw the bird break from its cover and take wing, he tracked it, took a breath, and fired once. The bird was a little flash of opulent color against the bright-blue sky. Elliot felt himself flying for a moment. The shot missed.

Lowering the gun, he remembered the deer shells he had loaded. A hit with the concentrated shot would have pulverized the bird, and he was glad he had missed. He wished no harm to any creature. Then he thought of himself wishing no harm to any creature and began to feel fond and sorry for himself. As soon as he grew aware of the emotion he was indulging, he suppressed it. Pissing and moaning, mourning and weeping, that was the nature of the drug.

The shot echoed from the distant hills. Smoke hung in the air. He turned and looked behind him and saw, far away across the pasture, the tiny blue-and-red figure of Professor Anderson motionless against the snow. Then Elliot turned again toward his house and took a few labored steps and looked up to see his wife at the bedroom window. She stood perfectly still, and the morning sun lit her nakedness. He stopped where he was. She had heard the shot and run to the window. What had she thought to see? Burnt rags and blood on the snow. How relieved was she now? How disappointed?

Elliot thought he could feel his wife trembling at the window. She was hugging herself. Her hands clasped her shoulders. Elliot took his snow goggles off and shaded his eyes with his hand. He stood in the field staring.

The length of the gun was between them, he thought. Somehow she had got out in front of it, to the wrong side of the wire. If he looked long enough he would find everything out there. He would find himself down the sight.

How beautiful she is, he thought. The effect was striking. The window was so clear because he had washed it himself, with vinegar. At the best of times he was a difficult, fussy man.

Elliot began to hope for forgiveness. He leaned the shotgun on his forearm and raised his left hand and waved to her. Show a hand, he thought. Please just show a hand.

He was cold, but it had got light. He wanted no more than the gesture. It seemed to him that he could build another day on it. Another day was all you needed. He raised his hand higher and waited.

DAVID WONG LOUIE

DISPLACEMENT

from Ploughshares

DAVID WONG LOUIE was born in 1954 and raised in New York. His parents were immigrants from China, his father entering under an assumed name and his mother, by way of Ellis Island, also claiming another's identity. They spoke only Cantonese, so that was his language too, until TV and kindergarten stole him. He earned a BA at Vassar and an MFA at Iowa and taught for many years at multiple schools before settling at UCLA, where he has worked for more than two decades.

Louie is the author of the novel *The Barbarians Are Coming* and the short story collection *Pangs of Love*, which won the *Los Angeles Times Book Review* First Fiction Award and the *Ploughshares* First Fiction Book Award and was a *New York Times Book Review* Notable Book and a *Voice Literary Supplement* Favorite. Louie's work shares an interest in identity, alienation—in the psychic dislocation at the intersection of race, class, desire, and obligation. His fiction is widely taught and anthologized. Among other honors he was awarded Lannan Writing Fellowship and a Lannan residency. He lives in Venice, California, with his wife and daughter.

★

M RS. CHOW HEARD the widow. She tried reading faster but kept stumbling over the same lines. She thought perhaps she was misreading them: "There comes, then, finally, the prospect of atomic war. If the war is ever to be carried to China, common sense tells us only atomic weapons could promise maximum loss with minimum damage."

When she heard the widow's wheelchair she tossed the copy of *Life* down on the couch, afraid she might be found out. The year was 1952.

Outside the kitchen, Chow was lathering the windows. He worked a soft brush in a circular motion. Inside, the widow was accusing Mrs. Chow of stealing her cookies. The widow had a handful of them clutched to her chest and brought one down hard against the table. She was counting. Chow waved, but Mrs. Chow only shook her head. He soaped up the last pane and disappeared.

Standing accused, Mrs. Chow wondered if this was what it was like when her parents faced the liberators who had come to reclaim her family's property in the name of the People. She imagined her mother's response to them: What people? All of my servants are clothed and decently fed.

The widow swept the cookies off the table as if they were a canasta trick won. She started counting again. Mrs. Chow and the widow had played out this scene many times before. As on other occasions, she didn't give the old woman the satisfaction of a plea, guilty or otherwise.

Mrs. Chow ignored the widow's busy blue hands. She fixed her gaze on the woman's milky eyes instead. Sight resided at the peripheries. Mornings, before she prepared the tub, emptied the pisspot, or fried the breakfast meat, Mrs. Chow cradled the widow's oily scalp and applied the yellow drops that preserved what vision was left in the cold, heaven-directed eyes.

"Is she watching?" said the widow. She tilted her big gray head sideways; a few degrees in any direction Mrs. Chow became a blur. In happier days Mrs. Chow might have positioned herself just right or left of center, neatly within a line of sight.

Mrs. Chow was thirty-five years old. After a decade-long separation from her husband she finally had entered the United States in 1950 under the joint auspices of the War Brides and Refugee Relief acts. She would agree she was a bride, but not a refugee, even though the Red Army had confiscated her home and turned it into a technical school. During the trouble she was away, safely studying in Hong Kong. Her parents, with all their wealth, could've easily escaped, but they were confident a few well-placed bribes among the Red hooligans would put an end to the foolishness. Mrs. Chow assumed her parents now were dead. She had seen pictures in *Life* of minor landlords tried and executed for lesser crimes against the People.

The widow's fondness for calling Mrs. Chow a thief began soon after the old woman broke her hip. At first Mrs. Chow blamed the widow's madness on pain displacement. She had read in a textbook that a malady in one part of the body could show up as a pain in another locale—sick kidneys, for instance, might surface as a mouthful of sore gums. The bad hip had weakened the widow's brain function. Mrs. Chow wanted to believe the crazy spells weren't the widow's fault, just as a baby soiling its diapers can't be blamed. But even a mother grows weary of changing them.

"I live with a thief under my roof," the widow said to the kitchen. "I could yell at her, but why waste my breath?"

When the widow was released from the hospital she returned to the house with a live-in nurse. Soon afterward her daughter paid a visit, and the widow told her she didn't want the nurse around anymore. "She can do me," the widow said, pointing in Mrs. Chow's direction. "She won't cost a cent. Besides, I don't like being touched that way by a person who knows what she's touching," she said of the nurse.

Nobody knew, but Mrs. Chow spoke a passable though highly accented English she had learned in British schools. Her teachers in Hong Kong always said that if she had the language when she came to the States she'd be treated better than other immigrants. Chow couldn't have agreed more. Once she arrived he started to teach her everything he knew in English. But that amounted to very little, considering he had been here for more than ten years. And what he had mastered came out crudely and strangely twisted. His phrases, built from a vocabulary of deference and accommodation, irritated Mrs. Chow for the way they resembled the obsequious blabber of her servants back home.

The Chows had been hired ostensibly to drive the widow to her canasta club, to clean the house, to do the shopping, and, since the bad hip, to oversee her personal hygiene. In return they lived rent-free upstairs in the children's rooms, three bedrooms and a large bath. Plenty of space, it would seem, except the widow wouldn't allow them to remove any of the toys and things from her children's cluttered rooms.

On weekends and Tuesday afternoons Chow borrowed the widow's tools and gardened for spending money. Friday nights, after they dropped the widow off at the canasta club, the Chows dined at Ming's and then went to the amusement park at the beach boardwalk. First and last, they got in line to ride the Milky Way. On the day the immigration authorities finally let Mrs. Chow go, before she even saw her new home, Chow took his bride to the boardwalk. He wanted to impress her with her new country. All that machinery, brainwork, and labor done for the sake of fun. He never tried the roller coaster before she arrived; he saved it for her. After that very first time he realized he was much happier with his feet on the ground. But not Mrs. Chow: Oh, this speed, this thrust at the sky, this UP! Oh, this raging, clattering, pushy country! So big! And since that first ride she looked forward to Friday nights and the wind whipping through her hair, stinging her eyes, blowing away the top layers of dailiness. On the longest, most dangerous descent her dry mouth would open to a silent O and she would thrust up her arms, as if she could fly away.

Some nights as the Chows waited in line, a gang of toughs out on a strut, trussed in denim and combs, would stop and visit: MacArthur, they said, will drain the Pacific; the H-bomb will wipe Korea clean of the Commies; the Chows were to blame for Pearl Harbor; the Chows, they claimed, were Red Chinese spies. On occasion, overextending his skimpy English, Chow mounted a defense: he had served in the U.S. Army; his citizenship was blessed by the Department of War; he was a member of the American Legion. The toughs would laugh at the way he talked. Mrs. Chow cringed at his habit of addressing them as "sirs."

"Get out, get out," the widow hissed. She brought her fist down on the table. Cookies broke, fell to the floor.

"Yes, Missus," said Mrs. Chow, thinking how she'd have to clean up the mess.

The widow, whose great-great-great-grandfather had been a central figure within the faction advocating Washington's coronation, was eighty-six years old. Each day Mrs. Chow dispensed medications that kept her alive. At times, though, Mrs. Chow wondered if the widow would notice if she were handed an extra blue pill or one less red.

Mrs. Chow filled an enamel-coated washbasin with warm water from the tap. "What's she doing?" said the widow. "Stealing my water now, is she?" Since Mrs. Chow first came into her service, the widow, with the exception of her hip, had avoided serious illness. But how she had aged: her ears were enlarged; the opalescence in her eyes had spread; her hands worked as if they were chipped from glass. Some nights, awake in their twin-size bed, Mrs. Chow would imagine old age as green liquid that seeped into a person's cells, where it coagulated and, with time, crumbled, caving in the cheeks and the breasts it had once supported. In the dark she fretted that fluids from the widow's old body had taken refuge in her youthful cells. On such nights she reached for Chow, touched him through the cool top sheet, and was comforted by the fit of her fingers in the shallows between his ribs.

Mrs. Chow knelt at the foot of the wheelchair and set the washbasin on the floor. The widow laughed. "Where did my little thief go?" She laughed again, her eyes closing, her head dropping to her shoulder. "Now she's after my water. Better see if the tap's still there." Mrs. Chow abruptly swung aside the wheelchair's footrests and slipped off the widow's matted cloth slippers and dunked her puffy blue feet into the water. It was the widow's nap time, and before she could be put to bed, her physician prescribed a warm foot bath to stimulate circulation; otherwise, in her sleep, her blood might settle comfortably in her toes.

Chow was talking long distance to the widow's daughter in Texas. Earlier the widow had told the daughter that the Chows were threatening again to leave. She apologized for her mother's latest spell of wildness. "Humor her," the daughter said. "She must've had another one of her little strokes."

Later Mrs. Chow told her husband she wanted to leave the widow. "My fingers," she said, snapping off the rubber gloves the magazine ads claimed would guarantee her beautiful hands into the next century. "I wasn't made for such work."

As a girl her parents had sent her to a Christian school for training in Western-style art. The authorities agreed she was talented. As expected she excelled there. Her portrait of the king was chosen to hang in the school cafeteria. When the colonial Minister of Education on a tour of the school saw her painting he requested a sitting with the gifted young artist.

A date was set. The rumors said a successful sitting would bring her the ultimate fame: a trip to London to paint the royal family. But a month before the great day she refused to do the minister's portrait. She gave no reason why; in fact, she stopped talking. The school administration was embarrassed, and her parents were furious. It was a great scandal; a mere child from a country at the edge of revolution but medieval in its affection for authority had snubbed the mighty British colonizers. She was sent home. Her parents first appealed to family pride, then they scolded and threatened her. She hid from them in a wardrobe, where her mother found her holding her fingers over lighted matches.

The great day came and went, no more momentous than the hundreds that preceded it. That night her father apologized to the world for raising such a child. With a bamboo cane he struck her outstretched hand—heaven help her if she let it fall one inch—and as her bones were young and still pliant, they didn't fracture or break, thus multiplying the blows she had to endure.

"Who'd want you now?" her mother said. Her parents sent her to live with a servant family. She could return home when she was invited. On those rare occasions she refused to go. Many years passed before she met Chow, who had come to the estate seeking work. They were married on the condition he take her far away. He left for America, promising to send for her when he had saved enough money for her passage. She returned to Hong Kong and worked as a secretary. Later she studied at the university.

Now as she talked about leaving the widow, it wasn't the chores or the old woman that she gave as the reason, though in the past she had complained the widow was a nuisance, an infantile brat born of an un-welcomed union. This time she said she had a project in mind, a great canvas of a yet undetermined subject. But that would come. Her imagi-nation would return, she said, once she was away from that house.

It was the morning of a late spring day. A silvery light filtered through the wall of eucalyptus and warmed the dew on the widow's roof, strik-ing the plums and acacia, irises and lilies, in such a way that, blended with the heavy air and the noise of a thousand birds, one sensed the uni-verse wasn't so vast, so cold, or so angry, and even Mrs. Chow suspected that it was a loving thing.

Mrs. Chow had finished her morning chores. She was in the bath-room rinsing the smell of bacon from her hands. She couldn't wash deep enough, however, to rid her fingertips of perfumes from the wid-ow's lotions and creams, which, over the course of months, had seeped indelibly into the whorls. But today her failure was less maddening. To-day she was confident the odors would eventually fade. She could afford to be patient. They were going to interview for an apartment of their very own.

"Is that new?" Chow asked, pointing to the blouse his wife had on. He adjusted his necktie against the starched collar of a white short-sleeved shirt, which billowed out from baggy, pin-striped slacks. His hair was slicked back with fragrant pomade.

"I think it's the daughter's," said Mrs. Chow. "She won't miss it." Mrs. Chow smoothed the silk undershirt against her stomach. She guessed the shirt was as old as she was; the daughter probably had worn it in her teens. Narrow at the hips and the bust, it fit Mrs. Chow nicely. Such a slight figure, she believed, wasn't fit for labor.

Chow saw no reason to leave the estate. He had found his wife what he thought was the ideal home, certainly not as grand as her parents' place, but one she'd feel comfortable in. Why move, he argued, when there were no approaching armies, no floods, no one telling them to go? Mrs. Chow understood. It was just that he was very Chinese, and very peasant. Sometimes she would tease him. If the early Chinese sojourn-ers who came to America were all Chows, she would say, the railroad wouldn't have been constructed, and Ohio would be all we know of California.

The Chows were riding in the widow's green Buick. As they approached the apartment building Mrs. Chow reapplied lipstick to her mouth.

It was a modern two-story stucco building, painted pink, surrounded by asphalt, with aluminum windows and a flat roof that met the sky like an engineer's level. Because their friends lived in the apartment in question the Chows were already familiar with its layout. They went to the manager's house at the rear of the property. Here the grounds were also asphalt. Very contemporary, no greenery anywhere. The closest things to trees were the clothesline's posts and crossbars.

The manager's house was a tiny replica of the main building. Chow knocked on the screen door. A radio was on and the smell of baking rushed past the wire mesh. A cat came to the door, followed by a girl. "I'm Velvet," she said. "This is High Noon." She gave the cat's orange tail a tug. "She did this to me," said Velvet, throwing a wicked look at the room behind her. She picked at her hair, ragged as tossed salad; someone apparently had cut it while the girl was in motion. She had gray, almost colorless eyes, which, taken with her hair, gave her the appearance of agitated smoke.

A large woman emerged from the back room carrying a basket of laundry. She wasn't fat, but large in the way horses are large. Her face was round and pink, with fierce little eyes and hair the color of olive oil and dripping wet. Her arms were thick and white, like soft tusks of ivory.

"It's the people from China," Velvet said.

The big woman nodded. "Open her up," she told the girl. "It's okay."

The front room was a mess, cluttered with evidence of frantic living. This was, perhaps, entropy in its final stages. The Chows sat on the couch. From all around her Mrs. Chow sensed a slow creep: the low ceiling seemed to be sinking, cat hairs clung to clothing, a fine spray from the fish tank moistened her bare arm.

No one said anything. It was as if they were sitting in a hospital waiting room. The girl watched the Chows. The large woman stared at a green radio at her elbow broadcasting news about the war. Every so often she looked suspiciously up at the Chows. "You know me," she said abruptly. "I'm Remora Cass."

On her left, suspended in a swing, was the biggest, ugliest baby Mrs. Chow had ever seen. It was dozing, arms dangling, great melon head flung so far back that it appeared to be all nostrils and chins. "A pig-boy," Mrs. Chow said in Chinese. Velvet jabbed two fingers into the ba-by's rubbery cheeks. Then she sprang back from the swing and executed a feral dance, all elbows and knees. She seemed incapable of holding her body still.

She caught Mrs. Chow's eye. "This is Ed," she said. "He has no hair." Mrs. Chow nodded.

"Quit," said Remora Cass, swatting at the girl as if she were a fly. Then the big woman looked Mrs. Chow in the eyes and said, "I know what you're thinking, and you're right. There's not a baby in the state bigger than Ed; eight pounds, twelve ounces at birth and he doubled that in-side a month." She stopped, bringing her palms heavily down on her knees, and shook her wet head. "You don't understand me, do you?"

Mrs. Chow was watching Velvet.

"Quit that!" Remora Cass slapped the girl's hand away from the ba-by's face.

"Times like this I'd say it's a blessing my Aunt Eleanor's deaf," said Remora Cass. "I've gotten pretty good with sign language." From her overstuffed chair she repeated in pantomime what she had said about the baby.

Velvet mimicked her mother's generous, sweeping movements. When Remora Cass caught sight of her she added a left jab to the girl's head to her repertoire of gestures. Velvet slipped the punch with practiced ease. But the blow struck the swing set. Everyone tensed. Ed flapped his arms and went on sleeping. "Leave us alone," said Remora Cass, "before I re-ally get mad."

The girl chased down the cat and skipped toward the door. "I'm bored anyway," she said.

Remora Cass asked the Chows questions, first about jobs and pets. Then she moved on to matters of politics and patriotism. "What's your feeling about the Red Chinese in Korea?"

A standard question. "Terrible," said Chow, giving his standard an-swer. "I'm sorry. Too much trouble."

Mrs. Chow sat by quietly. She admired Chow's effort. She had studied the language, but he did the talking; she wanted to move, but he had to plead their case; it was his kin back home who benefited from the new regime, but he had to badmouth it.

Remora Cass asked about children.

"No, no, no," Chow said, answering as his friend Bok had coached him. His face was slightly flushed from the question. Chow wanted children, many children. But whenever he discussed the matter with his wife, she answered that she already had one, meaning the old woman, of course, and that she was enough.

"Tell your wife later," the manager said, "what I'm about to tell you now. I don't care what jobs you do, just so long as you have them. What I say goes for the landlady. I'm willing to take a risk on you. Be nice to have nice quiet folks up there like Rikki and Bok. Rent paid up, I can live with anyone. Besides, I'm real partial to Chinese takeout. I know we'll do just right."

The baby moaned, rolling its head from side to side. His mother stared at him as if in all the world there were just the two of them.

Velvet came in holding a beach ball. She returned to her place beside the swing and started to hop, alternating legs, with the beach ball held to her head. "She must be in some kind of pain," Mrs. Chow said to her husband.

The girl mimicked the Chinese she heard. Mrs. Chow glared at Velvet, as if she were the widow during one of her spells. The look froze the girl, standing on one leg. Then she said, "Can Ed come out to play?"

Chow took hold of his wife's hand and squeezed it, as he did to brace himself before the roller coaster's forward plunge. Then in a single, well-rehearsed motion Remora Cass swept off her slipper and punched at the girl. Velvet masterfully side-stepped the slipper and let the beach ball fly. The slipper caught the swing set; the beach ball bounced off Ed's lap.

The collisions released charged particles into the air that seemed to hold everyone in a momentary state of paralysis. The baby's eyes peeled open, and he blinked at the ceiling. Soon his distended belly started rippling. He cried until he turned purple, then devoted his energy to maintaining that hue. Mrs. Chow had never heard anything as harrowing. She visualized his cry as large cubes forcing their way into her ears.

Remora Cass picked Ed up and bounced on the balls of her feet. "You better start running," she said to Velvet, who was already on her way out the door.

Remora Cass half smiled at the Chows over the baby's shoulder. "He'll quiet down sooner or later," she said.

Growing up, Mrs. Chow was the youngest of five girls. She had to endure the mothering of her sisters, who, at an early age, were already in training for their future roles. Each married in her teens, plucked in turn by a Portuguese, a German, a Brit, and a New Yorker. They had many babies. But Mrs. Chow thought little of her sisters' example. Even

when her parents made life unbearable she never indulged in the hope
that a man—foreign or domestic—or a child could save her from her unhappiness.

From the kitchen Remora Cass called Mrs. Chow. The big woman
was busy with her baking. The baby was slung over her shoulder. "Let's
try something," she said as she transferred the screaming Ed into Mrs.
Chow's arms.

Ed was a difficult package. Not only was he heavy and hot and sweaty
but he spat and squirmed like a sack of kittens. She tried to think of how
it was done. She tried to think of how a baby was held. She remembered
Romanesque Madonnas cradling their gentlemanly babies in art history
textbooks. If she could get his head up by hers, that would be a start.

Remora Cass told Mrs. Chow to try bouncing and showed her what
she meant. "Makes him think he's still inside," she said. Ed emitted a
long, sustained wail, then settled into a bout of hiccups. "You have a
nice touch with him. He won't do that for just anyone."

As the baby quieted, a pain rolled from the heel of Mrs. Chow's
brain, down through her pelvis, to a southern terminus at the backs of
her knees. She couldn't blame the baby entirely for her discomfort. He
wanted only to escape; animal instinct told him to leap from danger.

She was the one better equipped to escape. She imagined invading
soldiers murdering livestock and planting flags in the soil of her ances-
tral estate, as if it were itself a little nation; they make history by the
slaughter of generations of her family; they discover her in the wardrobe, striking matches; they ask where she has hidden her children, and
she tells them there are none; they say, good, they'll save ammunition,
but also too bad, so young and never to know the pleasure of children
(even if they'd have to murder them). Perhaps this would be the subject of her painting, a nonrepresentational canvas that hinted at a world
without light. Perhaps—

Ed interrupted her thought. He had developed a new trick. "Woop,
woop, woop," he went, thrusting his pelvis against her sternum in the
manner of an adult male in the act of mating. She called for Chow.

Remora Cass slid a cookie sheet into the oven and then stuck a bottle
of baby formula into Ed's mouth. He drained it instantly. "You do have a
way with him," said Remora Cass.

They walked into the front room. The baby was sleepy and dripping
curds on his mother's shoulder. Under the swing High Noon, the cat,
was licking the nipple of an abandoned bottle. "Scat!" she said. "Now
where's my wash gone to?" she asked the room. "What's she up to

now?" She scanned the little room, big feet planted in the deep brown shag carpet, hands on her beefy hips, baby slung over her shoulder like a pelt. "Velvet—" she started. That was all. Her jaw locked, her gums gleamed, her eyes rolled into her skull. Her head flopped backward, as if at the back of her neck there was a great hinge. Then she yawned, and the walls seemed to shake.

Remora Cass rubbed her eyes. "I'm bushed," she said.

Mrs. Chow went over to the screen door. Chow and the girl were at the clothesline. Except for their hands and legs, they were hidden behind a bed sheet. The girl's feet were in constant motion. From the basket her hands picked up pieces of laundry which Chow's hands then clipped to the line.

"Her daddy's hardly ever here," Remora Cass said. "Works all hours, he does. He has to." She patted Ed on the back, then rubbed her eyes again. "Looks like Velvet's found a friend. She won't do that with anyone. You two are naturals with my two. You should get some of your own." She looked over at Mrs. Chow and laughed. "Maybe it's best you didn't get that. Here." She set the baby on Mrs. Chow's shoulder. "This is what it's like when they're sleeping."

Before leaving, the Chows went to look at Rikki and Bok's apartment. They climbed up the stairs. No one was home. Rikki and Bok had barely started to pack. Bok's naked man, surrounded by an assortment of spears and arrows, was still hanging on the living room wall. Bok had paid good money for the photograph: an aboriginal gent stares into the camera, he's smiling, his teeth are good and large, and in his palms he's holding his sex out like a prize eel.

Mrs. Chow looked at the photograph for as long as it was discreetly possible before she averted her eyes and made her usual remark about Bok's tastes. Beyond the building's edge she saw the manager's cottage, bleached white in the sun. Outside the front door Remora Cass sat in a folding chair, her eyes shut, her pie-tin face turned up to catch the rays, while Velvet, her feet anchored to the asphalt, rolled her mother's hair in pink curlers. Between the big woman's legs the baby lay in a wicker basket. He was quietly rocking from side to side. Remora Cass's chest rose and fell in the rhythm of sleep.

Driving home, they passed the boardwalk, and Mrs. Chow asked if they might stop.

Chow refused to ride the roller coaster in the daytime, no matter how much Mrs. Chow teased. It was hard enough at night, when the heights from which the cars fell were lit by a few rows of bulbs. As he handed her an orange ticket, Chow said, "A drunk doesn't look in mirrors."

The Milky Way clattered into the terminus. After she boarded the ride, she watched Chow, who had wandered from the loading platform. and was standing beside a popcorn wagon, looking up at a billboard. His hands were deep in the pockets of his trousers, his legs crossed at the shins. That had been his pose, the brim of his hat low on his brow, as he waited for her finally to pass through the gates of Immigration.

"Go on," an old woman said. "You'll be glad you did." The old woman nudged her young charge toward the empty seat in Mrs. Chow's car. "Go on, she won't bite." The girl looked back at the old woman. "Grand-muth-ther!" she said, and then reluctantly climbed in beside Mrs. Chow.

Once the attendant strapped the girl in, she turned from her grandmother and stared at her new companion. The machine jerked away from the platform. They were climbing the first ascent when Mrs. Chow snuck a look at the girl. She was met by the clearest eyes she had ever known, eyes that didn't shy from the encounter. The girl's pupils, despite the bright sun, were fully dilated, stretched with fear. Now that she had Mrs. Chow's attention, she turned her gaze slowly toward the vertical track ahead. Mrs. Chow looked beyond the summit to the empty blue sky.

Within seconds they tumbled through that plane and plunged downward, the cars flung suddenly left and right, centrifugal force throwing Mrs. Chow against the girl's rigid body. She was surprised by Chow's absence.

It's gravity that makes the stomach fly, that causes the liver to flutter; it's the body catching up with the speed of falling. Until today, she had never known such sensations. Today there was a weightiness at her core, like a hard, concentrated pull inward, as if an incision had been made and a fist-sized magnet embedded.

Her arms flew up, two weak wings cutting the rush of wind. But it wasn't the old sensation this time, not the familiar embrace of the whole fleeting continent, but a grasp at something once there, now lost.

Chow had moved into position to see the riders' faces as they careened down the steepest stretch of track. Whenever he was up there with her, his eyes were clenched and his scream so wild and his grip on his life so tenuous that he never noticed her expression. At the top of the rise the cars seemed to stop momentarily, but then up and over, tumbling down, at what appeared, from his safe vantage point, a surprisingly slow speed. Arms shot up, the machine whooshed past him, preceded a split second earlier by the riders' collective scream. And for the first time Chow thought he heard her, she who loved this torture so, scream too.

As she was whipped skyward once more, her arms were wrapped around the little girl. Not in flight, not soaring, but anchored by another's being, as her parents stood against the liberators to protect their land.

Some curves, a gentle dip, one last sharp bend, and the ride rumbled to rest. The girl's breath was warm against Mrs. Chow's neck. For a moment longer she held on to the girl, whose small ribs were as thin as paintbrushes.

The Chows walked to the edge of the platform. He looked up at the billboard he had noticed earlier. It was a picture of an American woman with bright red hair, large red lips, and a slightly upturned nose; a fur was draped around her neck, pearls cut across her throat.

"What do you suppose they're selling?" he asked.

His wife pointed at the billboard. She read aloud what was printed there: "No other home permanent wave looks, feels, behaves so much like naturally curly hair."

She then gave a quick translation and asked what he thought of her curling her hair.

He made no reply. For some time now he couldn't lift his eyes from her.

"I won't do it," she said, "but what do you say?"

She turned away from him and stared a long time at the face on the billboard and then at the beach on the other side of the boardwalk and at the ocean, the Pacific Ocean, and at the horizon where all lines of sight converge, before she realized the land on the other side wouldn't come into view.

1990-2000

AT THE END OF 1989, SHANNON RAVENEL RESIGNED
as the series editor, moved to Chapel Hill, North Carolina, and continued her work with Algonquin Books. Again Houghton Mifflin had to
find a replacement. They chose Katrina Kenison, a young in-house editor. She said, "Reading wasn't something I did as a child, it was who I
was." After graduating from Smith College, Kenison

> got a job at Macy's selling lingerie . . . One day an article in the Sunday
> *New York Times* caught my eye: a feature about a small literary im-
> print of Houghton Mifflin Company being launched in New Haven,
> where we were living. I looked up the editor in chief in the phone
> book, typed a letter saying I would do anything, and mailed it to his
> home address. Within a week I was installed on a stool in the kitchen
> (the offices were in a newly renovated Victorian house), with scissors,
> a stack of news clippings, and a jar of rubber cement . . . It wasn't long
> before I was writing jacket copy, copy editing manuscripts, and read-
> ing the slush pile. And when I found a first novel that was good
> enough to publish, I was allowed to edit it.

She spent nine years working as an editor for Houghton Mifflin, first in
New Haven, then in New York, and finally in the Boston office.

Kenison's first son was only a month old when she became the fourth
series editor of *The Best American Short Stories*. She said, "I hired a baby
sitter, bought my first computer, and learned to use FileMaker Pro so I
could keep track of the more than 200 magazine subscriptions I'd suddenly inherited."

Ravenel told Kenison, "Read everything. Stay open-minded. Never
write someone off just because you've read twenty-five of his stories

and none of them has worked; the twenty-sixth might be wonderful."
When she sent her first volume of stories to Houghton Mifflin, Kenison included a letter suggesting that someone look into two new writers she had come across in her reading: Robert Olen Butler and Charles
D'Ambrosio.

Kenison reinstated the series editor's foreword. In her first foreword,
she defined her taste almost as broadly as Foley had: "A good story has
a way of announcing itself, rendering irrelevant any preconceived max-
ims of standards of excellence." She assured readers that any fears of the
homogenization of literary short fiction because of the proliferation of
writing programs were unfounded, that "our best fiction writers are in
no danger."

Like Foley, Kenison kept a file card for every story she read: "Title,
author, magazine, date, plot synopsis, opinion. I ripped out and filed the
stories I liked most and piled the magazines I was done with into boxes
in the basement to make room in my small home office for the next mail
delivery. Failing to stay on top of the tide was to drown in unread literary journals."

The 1990s saw a return to straight realism in literary fiction. Kenison noted that "this fiction was largely rooted in the middle range of
the American experience — a critic might have judged it 'safe,' a reader
might have gratefully called it a return to tradition, or to our roots."
These were also the years in which annual sales of *The Best American Short Stories* hit their peak. Kenison guessed that this return to the
mainstream "can be seen as a natural response to the antirealism of the
late sixties and seventies, the nonlinear, stylistically and structurally experimental fiction of the seventies, the minimalism and metafiction of
the eighties. American writers will always experiment, they will continue to nudge at the boundaries of the form, they will try anything
once — but the one generalization I'd venture to make is that realism was
and still is the bedrock of our literature."

Many short stories remained topical, although concerns were changing. The faltering state of our natural environment was addressed by
Rick Bass, while humankind's relationship to our wilderness was explored by Annie Proulx and T. C. Boyle. Stories by Jamaica Kincaid,
Akhil Sharma, and Lan Samantha Chang explored rituals of family and
love in other countries. Advances in technology crept into short fiction as well; the Internet, e-mail, and cell phones began to make appearances. Stories by realists such as Mary Gordon and Antonya Nelson
were published beside work by more voice-driven writers such as Denis

Johnson and Junot Díaz. The shadowy line between humor and desolation was explored with no small amount of irony by writers like Lorrie
Moore, Tim Gautreaux, and Thom Jones.

In 1996 Kenison noted the evaporation of federal arts funding and
the threat of technology to readers' leisure time. She began reading fiction on the Internet in 1997: "As I click from one Web site to another, I
feel rather like a dowser, my restless mouse the divining rod. There are
now scores of electronic magazines publishing literary fiction." There
was a new dilemma for editors of print literary journals: to remain print
or to migrate online?

As the turn of the century approached, Kenison worked with John
Updike to assemble *The Best American Short Stories of the Century*. She
said, "It was very striking to me as I began to read the early collections,
first of all what a different world it was in 1915 . . . John Updike said
when he was just starting out he supported his family just writing short
stories for *The New Yorker*. And that has changed. I don't think we'll
ever get back there . . . It's been a generation since anybody supported
themselves writing short stories for magazines."

★   ★   ★

1991

ALICE MUNRO
FRIEND OF MY YOUTH

from *The New Yorker*

ALICE MUNRO was born in Wingham, Ontario, in 1931 and raised on a fox farm. She attended the University of Western Ontario, where she published her first story, "The Dimensions of a Shadow."

Munro's first book, a collection of stories titled *Dance of the Happy Shades*, was awarded Canada's Governor General's Award. Munro went on to publish *Lives of Girls and Women* and *Who Do You Think You Are?*, which won another Governor General's Literary Award.

Munro's first appearance in *The Best American Short Stories* came in 1979 with a story titled "Spelling." The guest editor that year, Joyce Carol Oates, wrote, "In earlier works, Munro brought to near perfection the kind of story that summed up a life in carefully chosen scenes; here her tone is one of scrupulous meanness . . . Life is reduced to a gesture or two, and emotion is withheld."

Munro is known for her clarity of language and acute psychological realism. Many refer to her as "a Canadian Chekhov." Her stories are often set in small towns, where characters must reconcile societal demands with moral or emotional ambitions. These stories tell of small but critical occurrences that raise profound questions for both her characters and her readers.

In 2013 Munro, cited as a "master of the contemporary short story," was awarded the Nobel Prize in Literature. She is the first Canadian and the thirteenth woman to receive the Nobel Prize in Literature.

Munro has become a regular contributor to *The Best American Short Stories*. Her work has appeared in the series more times than that of Hemingway and Faulkner combined. She currently resides in Clinton, near her childhood home in southwestern Ontario.

★

I USED TO DREAM about my mother, and though the details in the dream varied, the surprise in it was always the same. The dream stopped, I suppose because it was too transparent in its hopefulness, too easy in its forgiveness.

In the dream I would be the age I really was, living the life I was really living, and I would discover that my mother was still alive. (The fact is, she died when I was in my early twenties and she in her early fifties.) Sometimes I would find myself in our old kitchen, where my mother would be rolling out pie crust on the table, or washing the dishes in the battered cream-colored dishpan with the red rim. But other times I would run into her on the street, in places where I would never have expected to see her. She might be walking through a handsome hotel lobby, or lining up in an airport. She would be looking quite well — not exactly youthful, not entirely untouched by the paralyzing disease that held her in its grip for a decade or more before her death, but so much better than I remembered that I would be astonished. Oh, I just have this little tremor in my arm, she would say, and a little stiffness up this side of my face. It is a nuisance but I get around.

I recovered, then, what in waking life I had lost — my mother's liveliness of face and voice before her throat muscles stiffened and a woeful, impersonal mask fastened itself over her features. How could I have forgotten this, I would think in the dream — the casual humor she had, not ironic but merry, the lightness and impatience and confidence. I would say that I was sorry I hadn't been to see her in such a long time — meaning not that I felt guilty but that I was sorry I had kept a bugbear in my mind, instead of this reality — and the strangest, kindest thing of all to me was her matter-of-fact reply.

Oh, well, she said, better late than never. I was sure I'd see you someday.

When my mother was a young woman with a soft, mischievous face and shiny, opaque silk stockings on her plump legs (I have seen a photograph of her, with her pupils), she went to teach at a one-room school, called Grieves' School, in the Ottawa Valley. The school was on a corner of the farm that belonged to the Grieves family — a very good farm for that country. Well-drained fields with none of the Precambrian rock shouldering through the soil, a little willow-edged river running alongside, a sugarbush, log barns, and a large, unornamented house whose wooden walls had never been painted but were left to weather. And when wood weathers in the Ottawa Valley, my mother said, I do not know why this is, but it never turns gray — it turns black. There must be something in the air, she said. She often spoke of the Ottawa Valley, which was her home — she had grown up about twenty miles away from Grieves' School — in a dogmatic, mystified way, emphasizing things about it that distinguished it from any other place on earth. Houses turn black, maple syrup has a taste no maple syrup produced elsewhere can equal, bears amble within sight of farmhouses. Of course, I was disappointed when I finally got to see this place. It was not a valley at all, if by that you mean a cleft between hills; it was a mixture of flat fields and low rocks and heavy brush and little lakes — a scrambled, disarranged sort of country with no easy harmony about it, not yielding readily to any description.

The log barns and unpainted house, common enough on poor farms, were not in the Grieveses' case a sign of poverty but of policy. They had the money but they did not spend it. That was what people told my mother. The Grieveses worked hard and they were far from ignorant, but they were very backward. They didn't have a car or electricity or a telephone or a tractor. Some people thought this was because they were Cameronians — they were the only people in the school district who were of that religion — but in fact their church, which they themselves always called the Reformed Presbyterian, did not forbid engines or electricity or any inventions of that sort, just card playing, dancing, movies, and, on Sundays, any other activity but the most unavoidable.

My mother could not say who the Cameronians were or why they were called that. Some freak religion from Scotland, she said, from the perch of her obedient and lighthearted Anglicanism. The teacher always boarded with the Grieveses, and my mother was a little daunted at the thought of going to live in that black house with its paralytic Sundays and coal-oil lamps and primitive notions. But she was engaged by that time, she wanted to work on her trousseau instead of running around the country having a good time, and she figured she could get home one Sunday out of three. (On Sundays at the Grieveses' house, you could light a fire for heat but not for cooking, you could not even boil the kettle to make tea, and you were not supposed to write a letter or swat a fly. But it turned out that my mother was exempt from these rules. "No, no," said Flora Grieves, laughing at her. "That doesn't mean you. You must just go on as you're used to doing." And after a while my mother had made friends with Flora to such an extent that she wasn't even going home on the Sundays when she'd planned to.)

Flora and Ellie were the two sisters left of the Grieves family. Ellie was married, to a man called Robert Deal, who lived there and worked the farm but had not changed its name to Deal's in anyone's mind. By the

way people spoke, my mother expected the Grieves sisters, and Robert
Deal, to be middle-aged at least, but Ellie, the younger sister, was only
about thirty, and Flora seven or eight years older. Robert Deal might be
in between.

The house was divided in an unexpected way. The married couple
didn't live with Flora. At the time of their marriage, she had given them
the parlor and the dining room, the front bedrooms and staircase, the
winter kitchen. There was no need to decide about the bathroom, because there wasn't one. Flora had the summer kitchen, with its open rafters and uncovered brick walls, the old pantry made into a narrow dining room and sitting room, and the two back bedrooms, one of which
was my mother's. The teacher was housed with Flora, in the poorer
part of the house. But my mother didn't mind. She immediately preferred Flora, and Flora's cheerfulness, to the silence and sickroom atmosphere of the front rooms. (In Flora's domain it was not even true
that all amusements were forbidden. She had a crokinole board—she
taught my mother how to play.)

The division had been made, of course, in the expectation that Robert and Ellie would have a family, and that they would need the room.
This hadn't happened. They had been married for more than a dozen
years and there had not been a live child. Time and again Ellie had been
pregnant, but two babies had been stillborn and the rest she had mis-
carried. During my mother's first year there, Ellie seemed to be staying in bed more and more of the time, and my mother thought that she
must be pregnant again, but there was no mention of it. Such people
would not mention it. You could not tell from the look of Ellie, when
she got up and walked around, because she showed a stretched and ruined though slack-chested shape. She carried a sickbed odor, and she
fretted in a childish way about everything. Flora took care of her and
did all the work. She washed the clothes and tidied up the rooms and
cooked the meals served in both sides of the house, and helped Robert
with the milking and separating. She was up before daylight and never
seemed to tire. The first spring my mother was there, a great housecleaning was embarked upon, during which Flora climbed the ladders
herself and carried down the storm windows, washed and stacked them
away, carried all the furniture out of one room after another so that
she could scrub the woodwork and varnish the floors. She washed every dish and glass that was sitting in the cupboards, supposedly clean
already. She scalded every pot and spoon. Such need and energy possessed her that she could hardly sleep—my mother would wake up to

the sound of stovepipes being taken down, or the broom, draped in a dish towel, whacking at the smoky cobwebs. Through the washed uncurtained windows came a torrent of unmerciful light. The cleanliness was devastating. My mother slept now on sheets that had been bleached and starched and that gave her a rash. Sick Ellie complained daily of the smell of varnish and cleansing powders. Flora's hands were raw. But her disposition remained topnotch. Her kerchief and apron and baggy overalls of Robert's that she donned for the climbing jobs gave her the air of a comedian — sportive, unpredictable.

My mother called her a whirling dervish.

"You're a regular whirling dervish, Flora," she said, and Flora halted. She wanted to know what was meant. My mother went ahead and explained, though she was a little afraid lest piety should be offended. (Not piety exactly — you could not call it that. Religious strictness.) Of course it wasn't. There was not a trace of nastiness or smug vigilance in Flora's observance of her religion. She had no fear of heathens — she had always lived in the midst of them. She liked the idea of being a dervish, and went to tell her sister.

"Do you know what the teacher says I am?"

Flora and Ellie were both dark-haired, dark-eyed women, tall and narrow-shouldered and long-legged. Ellie was a wreck, of course, but Flora was still superbly straight and graceful. She could look like a queen, my mother said — even riding into town in that cart they had. For church they used a buggy or a cutter, but when they went to town they often had to transport sacks of wool — they kept a few sheep — or produce, to sell, and they had to bring provisions home. The trip of a few miles was not made often. Robert rode in front, to drive the horse — Flora could drive a horse perfectly well, but it must always be the man who drove. Flora would be standing behind, holding on to the sacks. She rode to town and back standing up, keeping an easy balance, wearing her black hat. Almost ridiculous but not quite. A Gypsy queen, my mother thought she looked like, with her black hair and her skin that always looked slightly tanned, and her lithe and bold serenity. Of course, she lacked the gold bangles and the bright clothes. My mother envied her her slenderness, and her cheekbones.

Returning in the fall for her second year, my mother learned what was the matter with Ellie.

"My sister has a growth," Flora said. Nobody then spoke of cancer. My mother had heard that before. People suspected it. My mother

knew many people in the district by that time. She had made particular friends with a young woman who worked in the post office; she was
going to be one of my mother's bridesmaids. The story of Flora and Ellie and Robert — or all that people knew of it — had been told in various versions. My mother did not feel that she was listening to gossip,
because she was always on the alert for any disparaging remarks about
Flora — she would not put up with that. But indeed nobody offered any.
Everybody said that Flora had behaved like a saint. Even when she went
to extremes, as in dividing up the house — that was like a saint.

Robert had come to work at Grieves' some months before the girls'
father died. They knew him already, from church. (Oh, that church, my
mother said, having attended it once, out of curiosity — that drear building miles on the other side of town, no organ or piano and plain glass in
the windows and a doddery old minister with his hours-long sermon,
a man hitting a tuning fork for the singing.) Robert had come out from
Scotland and was on his way west. He had stopped with relatives or people he knew, members of the scanty congregation. To earn some money,
probably, he came to Grieves'. Soon he and Flora were engaged. They
could not go to dances or to card parties like other couples, but they
went for long walks. The chaperon — unofficially — was Ellie. Ellie was
then a wild tease, a long-haired, impudent, childish girl full of lolloping
energy. She would run up hills and smite the mullein stalks with a stick,
shouting and prancing and pretending to be a warrior on horseback.
That, or the horse itself. This when she was fifteen, sixteen years old.
Nobody but Flora could control her, and generally Flora just laughed at
her, being too used to her to wonder if she was quite right in the head.
They were wonderfully fond of each other. Ellie, with her long skinny
body, her long pale face, was like a copy of Flora — the kind of copy you
often see in families, in which, because of some carelessness or exag-
geration of features or coloring, the handsomeness of one person passes
into the plainness, or almost plainness, of another. But Ellie had no jealousy about this. She loved to comb out Flora's hair and pin it up. They
had great times, washing each other's hair. Ellie would press her face
into Flora's throat, like a colt nuzzling its mother. So when Robert laid
claim to Flora, or Flora to him — nobody knew how it was — Ellie had to
be included. She didn't show any spite toward Robert, but she pursued
and waylaid them on their walks; she sprung on them out of the bushes
or sneaked up behind them so softly that she could blow on their necks.
People saw her do it. And they heard of her jokes. She had always been
terrible for jokes, and sometimes it had gotten her into trouble with her

father, but Flora had protected her. Now she put thistles into Robert's bed. She set his place at the table with the knife and fork the wrong way around. She switched the milk pails to give him the old one with the hole in it. For Flora's sake, maybe, Robert humored her.

The father had made Flora and Robert set the wedding day a year ahead, and after he died they did not move it any closer. Robert went on living in the house. Nobody knew how to speak to Flora about this being scandalous, or looking scandalous. Flora would just ask why. Instead of putting the wedding ahead, she put it back—from next spring to early fall—so that there should be a full year between it and her father's death. A year from funeral to wedding—that seemed proper to her. She trusted fully in Robert's patience and in her own purity.

So she might. But in the winter a commotion started. There was Ellie, vomiting, weeping, running off and hiding in the haymow, howling when they found her and pulled her out, jumping to the barn floor, running around in circles, rolling in the snow. Ellie was deranged. Flora had to call the doctor. She told him that her sister's periods had stopped—could the backup of blood be driving her wild? Robert had had to catch her and tie her up, and together he and Flora had put her to bed. She would not take food, just whipped her head from side to side, howling. It looked as if she would die speechless. But somehow the truth came out. Not from the doctor, who could not get close enough to examine her, with all her thrashing about. Probably, Robert confessed. Flora finally got wind of the truth, through all her high-mindedness. Now there had to be a wedding, though not the one that had been planned.

No cake, no new clothes, no wedding trip, no congratulations. Just a shameful hurry-up visit to the manse. Some people, seeing the names in the paper, thought the editor must have got the sisters mixed up. They thought it must be Flora. A hurry-up wedding for Flora! But no. It was Flora who pressed Robert's suit—it must have been—and got Ellie out of bed and washed her and made her presentable. It would have been Flora who picked one geranium from the window plant and pinned it to her sister's dress. And Ellie hadn't torn it out. Ellie was meek now, no longer flailing or crying. She let Flora fix her up, she let herself be married, she was never wild from that day on.

Flora had the house divided. She herself helped Robert build the necessary partitions. The baby was carried full term—nobody even pretended that it was early—but it was born dead after a long, tearing labor. Perhaps Ellie had damaged it when she jumped from the barn beam and rolled in the snow and beat on herself. Even if she hadn't done that, people would have expected something to go wrong, with that child or maybe one that came later. God dealt out punishment for hurry-up marriages — not just Presbyterians but almost everybody else believed that. God rewarded lust with dead babies, idiots, harelips and withered limbs and clubfeet.

In this case the punishment continued. Ellie had one miscarriage after another, then another stillbirth and more miscarriages. She was constantly pregnant, and the pregnancies were full of vomiting fits that lasted for days, headaches, cramps, dizzy spells. The miscarriages were as agonizing as full-term births. Ellie could not do her own work. She walked around holding on to chairs. Her numb silence passed off, and she became a complainer. If anybody came to visit, she would talk about the peculiarities of her headaches or describe her latest fainting fit, or even — in front of men, in front of unmarried girls or children — go into bloody detail about what Flora called her "disappointments." When people changed the subject or dragged the children away, she turned sullen. She demanded new medicine, reviled the doctor, nagged Flora. She accused Flora of washing the dishes with a great clang and clatter, out of spite, of pulling her — Ellie's — hair when she combed it out, of stingily substituting water-and-molasses for her real medicine. No matter what she said, Flora soothed her. Everybody who came into the house had some story of that kind to tell. Flora said, "Where's my little girl, then? Where's my Ellie? This isn't my Ellie, this is some crosspatch got in here in place of her!"

In the winter evenings after she came in from helping Robert with the barn chores, Flora would wash and change her clothes and go next door to read Ellie to sleep. My mother might invite herself along, taking whatever sewing she was doing, on some item of her trousseau. Ellie's bed was set up in the big dining room, where there was a gas lamp over the table. My mother sat on one side of the table, sewing, and Flora sat on the other side, reading aloud. Sometimes Ellie said, "I can't hear you." Or if Flora paused for a little rest Ellie said, "I'm not asleep yet."

What did Flora read? Stories about Scottish life — not classics. Stories about urchins and comic grandmothers. The only title my mother could remember was "Wee MacGregor." She could not follow the stories very well, or laugh when Flora laughed and Ellie gave a whimper, because so much was in Scots dialect or read with that thick accent. She was surprised that Flora could do it — it wasn't the way Flora ordinarily talked, at all.

(But wouldn't it be the way Robert talked? Perhaps that is why my mother never reported anything that Robert said, never had him contributing to the scene. He must have been there, he must have been sitting there in the room. They would only heat the main room of the house. I see him black-haired, heavy-shouldered, with the strength of a plow horse, and the same kind of somber, shackled beauty.)

Then Flora would say, "That's all of that for tonight." She would pick up another book, an old book written by some preacher of their faith. There was in it such stuff as my mother had never heard. What stuff? She couldn't say. All the stuff that was in their monstrous old religion. That put Ellie to sleep, or made her pretend she was asleep, after a couple of pages.

All that configuration of the elect and the damned, my mother must have meant—all the arguments about the illusion and necessity of free will. Doom and slippery redemption. The torturing, defeating, but for some minds irresistible pileup of interlocking and contradictory notions. My mother could resist it. Her faith was easy, her spirits at that time robust. Ideas were not what she was curious about, ever.

But what sort of thing was that, she asked (silently), to read to a dying woman? This was the nearest she got to criticizing Flora.

The answer—that it was the only thing, if you believed it—never seemed to have occurred to her.

By spring a nurse had arrived. That was the way things were done then. People died at home, and a nurse came in to manage it.

The nurse's name was Audrey Atkinson. She was a stout woman with corsets as stiff as barrel hoops, marcelled hair the color of brass candlesticks, a mouth shaped by lipstick beyond its own stingy outlines. She drove a car into the yard—her own car, a dark-green coupe, shiny and smart. News of Audrey Atkinson and her car spread quickly. Questions were asked. Where did she get the money? Had some rich fool altered his will on her behalf? Had she exercised influence? Or simply helped herself to a stash of bills under the mattress? How was she to be trusted?

Hers was the first car ever to sit in the Grieveses' yard overnight.

Audrey Atkinson said that she had never been called out to tend a case in so primitive a house. It was beyond her, she said, how people could live in such a way.

"It's not that they're poor, even," she said to my mother. "It isn't, is it? That I could understand. Or it's not even their religion. So what is it? They do not care!"

She tried at first to cozy up to my mother, as if they would be natural allies in this benighted place. She spoke as if they were around the same age—both stylish, intelligent women who liked a good time and had modern ideas. She offered to teach my mother to drive the car. She offered her cigarettes. My mother was more tempted by the idea of learning to drive than she was by the cigarettes. But she said no, she would wait for her husband to teach her. Audrey Atkinson raised her pinkish-orange eyebrows at my mother behind Flora's back, and my mother was furious. She disliked the nurse far more than Flora did.

"I knew what she was like and Flora didn't," my mother said. She meant that she caught a whiff of a cheap life, maybe even of drinking establishments and unsavory men, of hard bargains, which Flora was too unworldly to notice.

Flora started into the great housecleaning again. She had the curtains spread out on stretchers, she beat the rugs on the line, she leapt up on the stepladder to attack the dust on the molding. But she was impeded all the time by Nurse Atkinson's complaining.

"I wondered if we could have a little less of the running and clattering," said Nurse Atkinson with offensive politeness. "I only ask for my patient's sake." She always spoke of Ellie as "my patient" and pretended that she was the only one to protect her and compel respect. But she was not so respectful of Ellie herself. "Allee-oop," she would say, dragging the poor creature up on her pillows. And she told Ellie she was not going to stand for fretting and whimpering. "You don't do yourself any good that way," she said. "And you certainly don't make me come any quicker. What you just as well might do is learn to control yourself." She exclaimed at Ellie's bedsores in a scolding way, as if they were a further disgrace of the house. She demanded lotions, ointments, expensive soap —most of them, no doubt, to protect her own skin, which she claimed suffered from the hard water. (How could it be hard? my mother asked her, sticking up for the household when nobody else would. How could it be hard when it came straight from the rain barrel?)

Nurse Atkinson wanted cream, too—she said that they should hold some back, not sell it all to the creamery. She wanted to make nourishing soups and puddings for her patient. She did make puddings, and jellies, from packaged mixes such as had never before entered this house. My mother was convinced that she ate them all herself.

Flora still read to Ellie, but now it was only short bits from the Bible. When she finished and stood up, Ellie tried to cling to her. Ellie wept; sometimes she made ridiculous complaints. She said there was a horned cow outside, trying to get into the room and kill her.

"They often get some kind of idea like that," Nurse Atkinson said. "You mustn't give in to her or she won't let you go day or night. That's what they're like, they only think about themselves. Now, when I'm here alone with her, she behaves herself quite nice. I don't have any trouble at all. But after you been in here I have trouble all over again, because she sees you and she gets upset. You don't want to make my job harder for me, do you? I mean, you brought me here to take charge, didn't you?"

"Ellie, now, Ellie dear, I must go," said Flora, and to the nurse she said, "I understand. I do understand that you have to be in charge and I admire you, I admire you for your work. In your work you have to have so much patience and kindness."

My mother wondered at this — was Flora really so blinded, or did she hope by this undeserved praise to exhort Nurse Atkinson to the patience and kindness that she didn't have? Nurse Atkinson was too thick-skinned and self-approving for any trick like that to work.

"It is a hard job, all right, and not many can do it," she said. "It's not like those nurses in the hospital, where they got everything laid out for them." She had no time for more conversation — she was trying to bring in "Make Believe Ballroom" on her battery radio.

My mother was busy with the final exams and the June exercises at the school. She was getting ready for her wedding, in July. Friends came in cars and whisked her off to the dressmaker's, to parties, to choose the invitations and order the cake. The lilacs came out, the evenings lengthened, the birds were back and nesting, my mother bloomed in everybody's attention, about to set out on the deliciously solemn adventure of marriage. Her dress was to be appliquéd with silk roses, her veil held by a cap of seed pearls. She belonged to the first generation of young women who saved their money and paid for their own weddings — far fancier than their parents could have afforded.

On her last evening, the friend from the post office came to drive her away, with her clothes and her books and the things she had made for her trousseau and the gifts her pupils and others had given her. There was great fuss and laughter about getting everything loaded into the car. Flora came out and helped. This getting married is even more of a nuisance than I thought, said Flora, laughing. She gave my mother a dresser scarf, which she had crocheted, in secret. Nurse Atkinson could not be shut out of an important occasion — she presented a spray bottle of cologne. Flora stood on the slope at the side of the house to wave goodbye. She had been invited to the wedding, but of course she had said she could not come, she could not "go out" at such a time. The last my mother ever saw of her was this solitary, energetically waving figure in her housecleaning apron and bandanna, on the green slope by the black-walled house, in the evening light.

"Well, maybe now she'll get what she should've got the first time round," the friend from the post office said. "Maybe now they'll be able to get married. Is she too old to start a family? How old is she, anyway?"

My mother thought that this was a crude way of talking about Flora and replied that she didn't know. But she had to admit to herself that she had been thinking the very same thing.

When she was married and settled in her own home, three hundred miles away, my mother got a letter from Flora. Ellie was dead. She had died firm in her faith, Flora said, and grateful for her release. Nurse Atkinson was staying on for a little while, until it was time for her to go off to her next case. This was late in the summer.

News of what happened next did not come from Flora. When she wrote at Christmas she seemed to take for granted that information would have gone ahead of her.

"You have in all probability heard," wrote Flora, "that Robert and Nurse Atkinson have been married. They are living on here, in Robert's part of the house. They are fixing it up to suit themselves. It is very impolite of me to call her Nurse Atkinson, as I see I have done. I ought to have called her Audrey."

Of course, the post-office friend had written, and so had others. It was a great shock and scandal and a matter that excited the district — the wedding as secret and surprising as Robert's first one had been (though surely not for the same reason), Nurse Atkinson permanently installed in the community, Flora losing out for the second time. Nobody had been aware of any courtship, and they asked how the woman could have enticed him. Did she promise children, lying about her age?

The surprises were not to stop with the wedding. The bride got down to business immediately with the "fixing up" that Flora mentioned. In came the electricity and then the telephone. Now Nurse Atkinson — she would always be called Nurse Atkinson — was heard on the party line lambasting painters and paperhangers and delivery services. She was having everything done over. She was buying an electric stove and putting in a bathroom, and who knew where the money was coming from? Was it all hers, got in her deathbed dealings, in shady bequests? Was it Robert's? Was he claiming his share — Ellie's share, left to him and Nurse Atkinson to enjoy themselves with, the shameless pair?

All these improvements took place on one side of the house only. Flora's side remained just as it was. No electric lights there, no fresh wallpaper or new venetian blinds. When the house was painted on the outside — cream with dark green trim — Flora's side was left bare. This strange open statement was greeted at first with pity and disapproval — poor Flora! — then with less sympathy, as a sign of Flora's stubbornness and eccentricity — she could buy her own paint and make it look decent — and finally as a joke. People drove out of their way to see it.

There was always a dance given in the schoolhouse for a newly married couple. A cash collection — called "a purse of money" — was presented to them. Nurse Atkinson sent out word that she would not mind seeing this custom followed, even though it happened that the family she had married into was opposed to dancing. Some people thought it would be a disgrace to gratify her, a slap in the face to Flora. Others were too curious to hold back. They wanted to see how the newlyweds would behave. Would Robert dance? What sort of outfit would the bride show up in? They delayed awhile, but finally the dance was held, and my mother got her report.

The bride wore the dress she had worn at her wedding, or so she said. But who would wear such a dress for a wedding at the manse? More than likely it was bought specially for her appearance at the dance. Pure white satin with a sweetheart neckline, idiotically youthful. The groom was got up in a new dark blue suit, and she had stuck a flower in his buttonhole. They were a sight. Her hair was freshly done to blind the eye with brassy reflections, and her face looked as if it would come off on a man's jacket, should she lay it against his shoulder in the dancing. Of course she did dance. She danced with every man except the groom, who sat scrunched into one of the school desks along the wall. She danced with every man present — they all claimed they had to do it, it was the custom — and then she dragged Robert out to receive the money and to thank everybody for their best wishes. To the ladies in the cloakroom she even hinted that she was feeling unwell, for the usual newlywed reason. Nobody believed her, and indeed nothing ever came of this hope, if she really had it. Some of the women thought that she was lying to them out of malice, insulting them, making them out to be so credulous. But nobody challenged her, nobody was rude to her — maybe because it was plain that she could summon a rudeness of her own to knock anybody flat.

Flora was not present at the dance.

"My sister-in-law is not a dancer," said Nurse Atkinson. "She is stuck in the olden times." She invited them to laugh at Flora, whom she always called her sister-in-law, though she had no right to do so.

My mother wrote a letter to Flora, after hearing about all these things. Being removed from the scene, and perhaps in a flurry of importance owing to her own newly married state, she may have lost sight of the kind of person she was writing to. She offered sympathy and showed outrage, and said blunt disparaging things about the woman who had — as my mother saw it — dealt Flora such a blow. Back came a letter from Flora saying that she did not know where my mother had been getting her information, but that it seemed she had misunderstood, or listened to malicious people, or jumped to unjustified conclusions. What happened in Flora's family was nobody else's business, and certainly nobody needed to feel sorry for her or angry on her behalf. Flora said that she was happy and satisfied in her life, as she always had been, and she did not interfere with what others did or wanted, because such things did not concern her. She wished my mother all happiness in her marriage and hoped that she would soon be too busy with her own responsibilities to worry about the lives of people that she used to know.

This well-written letter cut my mother, as she said, to the quick. She and Flora stopped corresponding. My mother did become busy with her own life and finally a prisoner in it.

But she thought about Flora. In later years, when she sometimes talked about the things she might have been, or done, she would say, "If I could have been a writer — I do think I could have been; I could have been a writer — then I would have written the story of Flora's life. And do you know what I would have called it? 'The Maiden Lady.'"

The Maiden Lady. She said these words in a solemn and sentimental tone of voice which I had no use for. I knew, or thought I knew, exactly the value she found in them. The stateliness and mystery. The hint of derision turning to reverence. I was fifteen or sixteen years old by that time, and I believed that I could see into my mother's mind. I could see what she would do with Flora, what she had already done. She would make her into a noble figure, one who accepts defection, treachery, who forgives and stands aside, not once but twice. Never a moment of complaint. Flora goes about her cheerful labors, she cleans the house and shovels out the cow byre, she removes some bloody mess from her sister's bed, and when at last the future seems to open up for her — Ellie will die and Robert will beg forgiveness and Flora will silence him with the proud gift of herself — it is time for Audrey Atkinson to drive into the yard and shut Flora out again, more inexplicably and thoroughly the second time than the first. She must endure the painting of the house, the electric lights, all the prosperous activity next door. "Make Believe Ballroom," "Amos 'n' Andy." No more Scottish or ancient sermons. She must see them drive off to the dance — her old lover and that cold-hearted, stupid, by no means beautiful woman in the white satin wedding dress. She is mocked. (And of course she has made over the farm to Ellie and Robert, of course he has inherited it, and now everything belongs to Audrey Atkinson.) The wicked flourish. But it is all right. It is all right — the elect are veiled in patience and humility and lighted by a certainty that events cannot disturb.

That was what I believed my mother would make of things. In her own plight her notions had turned mystical, and there was sometimes a hush, a solemn thrill in her voice that grated on me, alerted me to what seemed a personal danger. I felt a great fog of platitudes and pieties lurking, and incontestable crippled-mother power, which could capture and choke me. There would be no end to it. I had to keep myself sharp-tongued and cynical, arguing and deflating. Eventually I gave up even that recognition and opposed her in silence.

This is a fancy way of saying that I was no comfort and poor company to her, when she had almost nowhere else to turn.

I had my own ideas about Flora's story. I didn't think that I could have written a novel but that I would write one. I would take a different tack. I saw through my mother's story and put in what she left out. My Flora would be as wrong as hers was right. Rejoicing in the bad turns done to her and in her own forgiveness, spying on the shambles of her sister's life. A Presbyterian witch, reading out of her poisonous book. It takes a rival ruthlessness, the comparatively innocent brutality of the thick-skinned nurse, to drive her back, to flourish in her shade. But she *is* driven back, the power of sex and ordinary greed drive her back and shut her up in her own part of the house, with the coal-oil lamps. She shrinks, she caves in, her bones harden and her joints thicken and — Oh, this is it, this is it, I see the bare beauty of the ending I will contrive! — she becomes crippled herself, with arthritis, hardly able to move. Now Audrey Atkinson comes into her full power — she demands the whole house. She wants those partitions knocked out which Robert put up with Flora's help when he married Ellie. She will provide Flora with a room, she will take care of her. (Audrey Atkinson does not wish to be seen as a monster, and perhaps she really isn't one.) So one day Robert carries Flora — for the first and last time he carries her in his arms — to the room that his wife, Audrey, has prepared for her. And once Flora is settled in her well-lit, well-heated corner, Audrey Atkinson undertakes to clean out the newly vacated rooms — Flora's rooms. She carries a heap of old books out into the yard. It's spring again, housecleaning time, the season when Flora herself performed such feats, and now the pale face of Flora appears behind the new net curtains. She has dragged herself from her corner. She sees the light blue sky with its high skidding clouds over the watery fields, the contending crows, the flooded creeks, the reddening tree branches. She sees the smoke rise out of the incinerator in the yard, where her books are burning. Those smelly old books, as Audrey has called them. Words and pages, the ominous dark spines. The elect, the damned, the slim hopes, the mighty torments — up in smoke. There was the ending.

To me the really mysterious person in the story, as my mother told it, was Robert. He never has a word to say. He got engaged to Flora. He is walking beside her along the river when Ellie leaps out at them. He finds Ellie's thistles in his bed. He does the carpentry made necessary by his and Ellie's marriage. He listens or does not listen while Flora reads. Finally he sits scrunched up in the school desk while his flashy bride dances by with all the men.

So much for his public acts and appearances. But he was the one who started everything, in secret. He *did it to* Ellie. He did it to that skinny wild girl at a time when he was engaged to her sister, and he did it to her again and again when she was nothing but a poor botched body, a failed childbearer, lying in bed.

He must have done it to Audrey Atkinson, too, but with less disastrous results.

Those words, *did it to* — the words my mother, no more than Flora, would never bring herself to speak — were simply exciting to me. I didn't feel any decent revulsion or reasonable indignation. I refused the warning. Not even the fate of Ellie could put me off. Not when I thought of that first encounter — the desperation of it, the ripping and striving. I used to sneak longing looks at men, in those days. I admired their wrists and their necks and any bit of their chests a loose button let show, and even their ears and their feet in shoes. I expected nothing reasonable of them, only to be engulfed by their passion. I had similar thoughts about Robert.

What made Flora evil, in my story, was just what made her admirable, in my mother's — her turning away from sex. I fought against everything my mother wanted to tell me on this subject; I despised even the drop in her voice, the gloomy caution, with which she approached it. My mother had grown up in a time and in a place where sex was a dark undertaking for women. She knew that you could die of it. So she honored the decency, the prudery, the frigidity that might protect you. And I grew up in horror of that very protection, the dainty tyranny that seemed to me to extend to all areas of life, to enforce tea parties and white gloves and all other sorts of tinkling inanities. I favored bad words and a breakthrough, I teased myself with the thought of a man's recklessness and domination. The odd thing is that my mother's ideas were in line with some progressive notions of her times, and mine echoed the notions that were favored in my times. This in spite of the fact that we both believed ourselves independent, and lived in backwaters that did not register such changes. It's as if tendencies that seemed most deeply rooted in our minds, most private and singular, had come in as spores on the prevailing wind, looking for any likely place to land, any welcome.

Not long before she died, but when I was still at home, my mother got a letter from the real Flora. It came from that town near the farm, the town that Flora used to ride to, with Robert, in the cart, holding on to the sacks of wool or potatoes.

Flora wrote that she was no longer living on the farm.

"Robert and Audrey are still there," she wrote. "Robert has some trouble with his back but otherwise he is very well. Audrey has poor circulation and is often short of breath. The doctor says she must lose weight but none of the diets seem to work. The farm has been doing very well. They are out of sheep entirely and into dairy cattle. As you may have heard, the chief thing nowadays is to get your milk quota from the government and then you are set. The old stable is all fixed up with milking machines and the latest modern equipment, it is quite a marvel. When I go out there to visit I hardly know where I am."

She went on to say that she had been living in town for some years now, and that she had a job clerking in a store. She must have said what kind of store this was, but I cannot now remember. She said nothing, of course, about what had led her to this decision — whether she had in fact been put off her own farm, or had sold out her share, apparently not to much advantage. She stressed the fact of her friendliness with Robert and Audrey. She said her health was good.

"I hear that you have not been so lucky in that way," she wrote. "I ran into Cleta Barnes, who used to be Cleta Stapleton at the post office out at home, and she told me that there is some problem with your muscles and she said your speech is affected, too. This is sad to hear but they can do such wonderful things nowadays so I am hoping that the doctors may be able to help you."

An unsettling letter, leaving so many things out. Nothing in it about God's will or His role in our afflictions. No mention of whether Flora still went to that church. I don't think my mother ever answered. Her fine legible handwriting, her schoolteacher's writing, had deteriorated, and she had difficulty holding a pen. She was always beginning letters and not finishing them. I would find them lying around the house. *My dearest Mary,* they began. *My darling Ruth, My dear little Joanna (though I realize you are not little anymore), My dear old friend Cleta, My lovely Margaret.* These women were friends from her teaching days, her Normal School days, and from high school. A few were former pupils. I have friends all over the country, she would say, defiantly. I have dear, dear friends.

I remember seeing one letter that started out *Friend of my Youth.* I don't know whom it was to. They were all friends of her youth. I don't recall one that began with *My dear and most admired Flora.* I would always look at them, try to read the salutation and the few sentences she had written, and because I could not bear to feel sadness I would feel an impatience with the flowery language, the direct appeal for love and pity. She would get more of that, I thought (more from myself, I meant), if she could manage to withdraw, with dignity, instead of reaching out all the time to cast her stricken shadow.

I had lost interest in Flora by then. I was always thinking of stories, and by this time I probably had a new one on my mind.

But I have thought of her since. I have wondered what kind of store. A hardware store or a five-and-ten, where she has to wear a coverall, or a drugstore, where she is uniformed like a nurse, or a Ladies' Wear, where she is expected to be genteelly fashionable? She must have had to learn about food blenders or chain saws, negligees, cosmetics, even condoms. She would have to work all day under electric lights, and operate a cash register. Would she get a permanent, paint her nails, put on lipstick? And she must have found a place to live—a little apartment with a kitchenette, overlooking the main street, or a room in a boarding house. How could she go on being a Cameronian? How could she get to that out-of-the-way church, unless she managed to buy a car and learned to drive it? And if she did that she might drive not only to church but to other places. She might go on holidays. She might rent a cottage on a lake for a week, learn to swim, visit a city. She might eat meals in a restaurant, possibly in a restaurant where drinks were served. She might make friends with women who were divorced.

She might meet a man. A friend's widowed brother, perhaps. A man who did not know that she was a Cameronian or what Cameronians were. Who knew nothing of her story. A man who had never heard about the partial painting of the house or the two betrayals, or that it took all her dignity and innocence to keep her from being a joke. He might want to take her dancing, and she would have to explain that she could not go. He would be surprised but not put off—all that Cameronian business might seem quaint to him, almost charming. So it would to everybody. She was brought up in some weird religion, people would say. She lived a long time out on some godforsaken farm. She is a little bit strange but really quite nice. Nice-looking, too. Especially since she went and got her hair done.

I might go into a store and find her.

No, no. She would be dead a long time now.

But suppose I had gone into a store—perhaps a department store. I see a place with the brisk atmosphere, the straightforward displays, the old-fashioned modern look of the fifties. Suppose a tall, handsome woman, nicely turned out, had come to wait on me, and I had known, somehow, in spite of the sprayed and puffed hair and the pink or coral lips and fingernails—I had known that this was Flora. I would have wanted to tell her that I knew, I knew her story, though we had never met. I imagine myself trying to tell her. (This is a dream now, I understand it as a dream.) I imagine her listening, with a pleasant composure. But she shakes her head. She smiles at me, and in her smile there is a degree of mockery, a faint, self-assured malice. Weariness, as well. She is not surprised that I am telling her this, but she is weary of it, of me and my idea of her, my information, my notion that I can know anything about her.

Of course it's my mother I'm thinking of, my mother as she was in those dreams, saying, It's nothing, just this little tremor, saying with such astonishing lighthearted forgiveness, Oh, I knew you'd come someday. My mother surprising me, and doing it almost indifferently. Her mask, her fate, and most of her affliction, taken away. How relieved I was, and happy. But I now recall that I was disconcerted as well. I would have to say that I felt slightly cheated. Yes. Offended, tricked, cheated, by this welcome turnaround, this reprieve. My mother, moving rather carelessly out of her old prison, showing options and powers I never dreamed she had, changes more than herself. She changes the bitter lump of love I have carried all this time into a phantom — something useless and uncalled for, like a phantom pregnancy.

The Cameronians, I have discovered, are or were an uncompromising remnant of the Covenanters — those Scots who in the seventeenth century bound themselves, with God, to resist prayer books, bishops, any taint of popery or interference by the king. Their name comes from Richard Cameron, an outlawed or "field" preacher, soon cut down. The Cameronians went into battle singing the Seventy-fourth and the Seventy-eighth Psalms. They hacked the haughty archbishop of St. Andrews to death on the highway and rode their horses over his body. One of their ministers, in a mood of firm rejoicing at his own hanging, excommunicated all the other preachers in the world.

MARY GAITSKILL

THE GIRL ON THE PLANE

from *Mirabella*

MARY GAITSKILL was born in 1954 in Lexington, Kentucky, and grew up in the Detroit area. She left home at the age of sixteen and went to live in Canada, traveling from Montreal to Vancouver and back before settling in Toronto. At nineteen she decided she wanted to become a writer and returned to the United States to take a high school equivalency test and then attend community college. From there she went to the University of Michigan, where she took a BA. She moved to New York City in 1981.

Gaitskill published her first book, a story collection titled *Bad Behavior,* in 1988; the book was hailed by the *New York Times* as a work "of unusual importance at this time." She has since published two more collections of stories (*Because They Wanted To* and *Don't Cry*) and two novels (*Two Girls, Fat and Thin* and *Veronica*). She has taught writing at the graduate and undergraduate level since 1993.

Gaitskill became known for portraying sexuality in conflict with social norms; her work has more recently come to examine the social personality mystified by and in conflict with its own nature, or what critic Wyatt Mason called "that immutable question of how we manage to live in a seemingly inscrutable world."

Mary Gaitskill lives in Brooklyn, New York.

★

JOHN MORTON CAME down the aisle of the plane, banging his luggage into people's knees and sweating angrily under his suit. He had just run through the corridors of the airport, cursing and struggling with his luggage, slipping and flailing in front of the vapid brat at the seat assignment desk. Too winded to speak, he thrust his ticket at the boy and readjusted his luggage in his sticky hands. "You're a little late for a seat assignment," said the kid snottily. "I hope you can get on board before it pulls away."

He took his boarding pass and said, "Thanks, you little prick." The boy's discomfiture was heightened by his pretense of hauteur; it both soothed and fed John's anger.

At least he was able to stuff his bags into the compartment above the first seat he found. He sat down, grunting territorially, and his body slowly eased into a normal dull pulse and ebb. He looked at his watch; desk attendant to the contrary, the plane was sitting stupidly still, twenty minutes after takeoff time. He had the pleasing fantasy of punching the little bastard's face.

He was always just barely making his flight. His wife had read in one of her magazines that habitual lateness meant lack of interest in life, or depression or something. Well, who could blame him for lack of interest in the crap he was dealing with?

He glanced at the guy a seat away from him on the left, an alcoholic-looking old shark in an expensive suit, who sat staring fixedly at a magazine photograph of a grinning blonde in a white jumpsuit. The plane continued to sit there while stewardesses fiddled with compartments and women rolled up and down the aisles on trips to the bathroom. They were even boarding a passenger; a woman had just entered, flushed and vigorously banging along the aisle with her luggage. She was very pretty and he watched her, his body still feebly sending off alarm signals in response to its forced run.

"Hi," she said. "Can I sit here?"

"Of course." The force of his anger entered his magnanimity and swelled it hugely; he pinched his ankles together to let her by. She put her bag under the seat in front of her, sat down and rested her booted feet on its pale leather. The old shark next to her, with an appraising glance at her breasts through her open coat, made smile movements. The stewardess did her parody of a suffocating person reaching for an air mask, the pilot mumbled, the plane prepared to assert its unnatural presence in nature.

"They said I'd missed my flight by fifteen minutes," she said. "But I knew I'd make it. They're never on time." Her voice was unexpectedly small, with a rough, gravelly undertone that was seedy and schoolgirlish at once.

"It's bullshit," he said. "Well, what can you do?" She had large hazel eyes.

She smiled a tight, rueful smile that he associated with women who'd been fucked too many times, and which he found sexy. She cuddled more deeply into her seat, produced a *People* magazine and intently read it. He liked her profile — which was an interesting combination of soft (forehead, chin) and sharp (nose, cheekbones) — her shoulder-length, pale brown hair and her soft Mediterranean skin. He liked the coarse quality in the subtle downturn of her lips, and the heavy way her lids sat on her eyes. She was older than he'd originally thought, probably in her early thirties.

Who did she remind him of? A girl from a long time ago, an older version of some date or crush or screw. Or love, he thought gamely.

The pilot said they would be leaving the ground shortly. She was now reading something titled "AIDS Wedding — One Last Chance." He thought of his wife at home in Minneapolis, at the stove poking at something, in the living room reading, the fuzzy pink of her favorite sweater. The plane charged and tore a hole in the air.

The woman next to him was hurriedly flipping the pages of *People,* presumably looking for something as engrossing as "AIDS Wedding." When she didn't find it, she closed the magazine and turned to him in a way that invited conversation.

She said she'd lived in L.A. for eight years and that she liked it, even though it was "gross."

"I've never been to L.A.," he said. "I picture it being like *L.A. Law.* Is it like that?"

"I don't know. I've never seen *L.A. Law.* I don't watch TV. I don't own one."

He had never known a person who didn't own a TV, not even an old high school friend who lived in a slum and got food stamps. "You must read the newspapers a lot."

"No. I don't read them much at all."

He was incredulous. "How do you connect with the rest of the world? How do you know anything?"

"I'm part of the world. I know a lot of things."

He expelled a snort of laughter. "That's an awfully small perspective you've got there."

She shrugged and turned her head, and he was sorry he'd been rude. He glanced at her profile to read her expression and — of course; she reminded him of Patty LaForge, poor Patty.

He had met Patty at Meadow Community College in Coate, Minnesota. He was in his last semester; she had just entered. They worked in the student union cafeteria, preparing, serving and snacking on denatured food. She was a slim, curvy person with dark blond hair, hazel eyes and

remarkable legs and hips. Her beauty was spoiled by the aggressive res-
ignation that held her features in a fixed position and made all her expressions stiff. Her full mouth had a bitter downturn and her voice was
quick, low, self-deprecating and sarcastic. She presented her beautiful
body statically, as if it were a shield, and the effort of this presentation
seemed to be the source of her animation.

Most of the people he knew at Meadow were kids he'd gone to high
school and even junior high with. They still lived at home and still drove
their cars around together at night, drank in the small bars of Coate, ad-
ventured in Minneapolis and made love to each other. This late-adoles-
cent camaraderie gave their time at Meadow a fraught emotional quality that was like the shimmering fullness of a bead of water before it
falls. They were all about to scatter and become different from one another and this made them exult in their closeness and alikeness.

The woman on the plane was flying to Kentucky to visit her parents and
stopping over in Cincinnati.

"Did you grow up in Kentucky?" he asked. He imagined her as a big-
eyed child in a cotton shift playing in some dusty, sunny alley, some rural Kentucky-like place. Funny she had grown up to be this wan little
bun with too much makeup in black creases under her eyes.

"No, I was born there, but I grew up mostly in Minnesota near
Minneapolis."

He turned away, registered the little shock of coincidence and turned
back. The situation compounded: she had gone to Redford Community
College in Thorold, a suburb much like Coate. She had grown up in
Thorold, like Patty. The only reason Patty had gone to Meadow was that
Redford didn't exist yet.

He felt a surge of commonality. He imagined that she had experienced his adolescence and this made him experience it for a moment.
He had loved walking the small neat walkways of the campus through
the stiffly banked hedges of snow and harsh morning austerity, entering
the close food-smelling student union with the hard winter air popping
off his skin. He would see his friends standing in a conspiratorial huddle,
warming their hands on cheap cups of coffee; he always remembered
the face of a particular girl, Layla, turning to greet him, looking over
her frail sloped shoulder, her hair a bunched dark tangle, her round eyes
ringed with green pencil, her perfectly ordinary face compelling in its
configurations of girlish curiosity, maternal license, sexual knowledge,
forgiveness and femininity. A familiar mystery he had meant to explore

sometime and never did except when he grabbed her ass at a Halloween party and she smiled like a mother of four who worked as a porn model on the side. He loved driving with his friends to the Red Owl to buy alcohol and bagged salty snacks which they consumed as they drove around Coate playing the tape deck and yelling at each other, the beautiful ordinary landscape unpeeling before them, revealing the essential strangeness of its shadows and night movements. He loved driving with girls to the deserted housing development they called "the Spot," loved the blurred memories of the girls in the back seat with their naked legs curled up to their chests, their shirts bunched about their necks, their eyes wide with ardor and alcohol, beer and potato chips spilled on the floor of the car, the tape deck singing of love and triumph. He getting out of the car for a triumphant piss while the girl daintily replaced her pants. In the morning his mother would make him "cowboy eggs," eggs fried on top of bacon, and he would go through the cold to Meadow to sit in a fluorescent classroom and dream.

"Did you like growing up in that area?" she asked.

"Like it? It was the greatest time of my life." Some extremity in his voice made her look away, and as she did, he looked more fully at her profile. She didn't look that much like Patty, she wasn't even blond. But the small physical resemblance was augmented by a less tangible affinity, a telling similarity of speech and movement.

Patty belonged to a different crowd at Meadow. They were rougher than the Coate people, but the two groups were friendly. Patty was a strange, still presence within her group, with her hip thrust out and a cigarette always bleeding smoke from her hand. She was loose even by seventies standards, she had a dirty sense of humor and she wore pants so tight you could see the swollen outline of her genitals. She was also shy. When she talked she pawed the ground with her foot and pulled her hair over her mouth, she looked away from you and then snuck a look back to see what you thought of her. She was accepted by the Thorold people the way you accept what you've always known. The stiffness of her face and body contradicting her loose reputation, her coarse language expressed in her timid voice and shy manners, her beauty and her ordinariness all gave her a disconnected sexiness that was aggravating.

But he liked her. They were often a team at work and he enjoyed having her next to him, her golden-haired arms plunged in greasy black dishwater, or flecked with garbage as she plucked silverware from vile plates on their way to the dishwasher. She spooned out quivering red Jell-O or drew long bland snakes of soft ice cream from the stainless steel machine, she smoked, wiped her nose and muttered about a fight with her mother or a bad date. Her movements were resigned and bitter, yet her eyes and her nasty humor peeked impishly from under this weight. There was something pleasing in this combination, something congruent with her spoiled beauty.

It was a long time before he realized she had a crush on him. All her conversation was braided together with a fly strip of different boys she'd been with or was involved with, and she talked of all of them with the same tone of fondness and resentment. He thought nothing of it when she followed him outside to the field behind the union where they would walk along the narrow wet ditch, smoking pot and talking. It was early spring: dark, naked trees pressed intensely against the horizon, wet weeds clung to their jeans and her small voice bobbed assertively on the vibrant air. The cold wind gave her lips a swollen raw look and made her young skin grainy and bleached. "So why do you let him treat you like that?" "Ah, I get back at him. It's not really him, you know, I'm just fixated on him. I'm working out something through him. Besides, he's a great lay." He never noticed how often she came up behind him to walk him to class or sat on the edge of his chair as he lounged in the union. Then one day she missed work and a buddy of his said, "Hey, where's your little puppy dog today?" and he knew.

"Did you like Thorold?" he asked the girl next to him.

"No, I didn't." She turned toward him, her face a staccato burst of candor. "I didn't know what I was doing and I was a practicing alcoholic. I kept trying to fit in and I couldn't."

"That doesn't sound good." He smiled. How like Patty to answer a polite question from a stranger with this emotional nakedness, this urgent excess of information. She was always doing that, especially after the job at the cafeteria ended. He'd see her in a hallway, or the union lounge, where normal life was happening all around them, and she'd swoop into a compressed communication, intently twining her hair around her finger as she quickly muttered that she'd had the strangest dream about this guy David, in which a nuclear war was going on, and he, John, was in it too and —

"What did you do after Redford?" he asked the girl next to him.

"Screwed around, basically. I went to New York pretty soon after that and did the same things I was doing in Thorold. Except I was trying to be a singer."

"Yeah?" He felt buoyed by her ambition. He pictured her in a tight black dress, lips parted, eyes closed, bathed in cheap, sexy stagelight. "Didja ever do anything with it?"

"Not much." She abruptly changed expression, as though she'd just remembered not to put herself down. "Well, some stuff. I had a good band once, we played the club circuit in L.A. for a while six years ago." She paused. "But I'm mostly a paralegal now."

"Well, that's not bad either. Do you ever sing now?"

"I haven't for a long time. But I was thinking of trying again." Just like Patty she looked away and quickly looked back as if to check his reaction. "I've been auditioning. Even though — I don't know."

"It sounds great to me," he said. "At least you're trying. It sounds better than what I do." His self-deprecation annoyed him and he bulled his way through an explanation of what he did, making it sound more interesting than selling software.

A stewardess with a small pink face asked if they'd like anything to drink, and he ordered two little bottles of Jack Daniel's. Patty's shadow had a compressed can of orange juice and an unsavory packet of nuts; their silent companion by the window had vodka straight. He thought of asking her if she were married, but he bet the answer was no and he didn't want to make her admit her loneliness. Of course, not every single person was lonely, but he guessed that she was. She seemed in need of comfort and care, like a stray animal that gets fed by various kindly people but never held.

He thought of telling her that she reminded him of someone he'd known in Coate, but he didn't. He sat silently knocking back his whiskey and watching her roll a greasy peanut between her two fingers.

Out in the field they were sitting on a fallen branch, sharing a wet stub of pot. "I don't usually say stuff like this," said Patty. "I know you think I do because of the way I talk but I don't. But I'm really attracted to you, John." The wind blew a piece of hair across her cheek and its texture contrasted acutely with her cold-bleached skin.

"Yeah, I was beginning to notice."

"I guess it was kind of obvious, huh?" She looked down and drew her curtain of hair. "And I've been getting these mixed signals from you. I can't tell if you're attracted to me or not." She paused. "But I guess you're not, huh?"

Her humility embarrassed and touched him. "Well, I am attracted to you. Sort of. I mean, you're beautiful and everything. I'm just not attracted enough to do anything. Besides, there's Susan."

"Oh, I thought you didn't like her that much." She sniffed and dropped the roach on the raw grass; her lipstick had congealed into little chapped bumps on her lower lip. "Well, I'm really disappointed. I thought you liked me."

"I do like you, Patty."

"You know what I meant." Pause. "I'm more attracted to you than I've been to anybody for two years. Since Paul."

A flattered giggle escaped him.

"Well, I hope we can be friends," she said. "We can still talk and stuff, can't we?"

"Patty LaForge? I wouldn't touch her, man, the smell alone."

He was driving around with a carload of drunk boys who were filled with a tangle of goodwill and aggression.

"Ah, LaForge is okay."

He was indignant for Patty but he laughed anyway.

"Were you really an alcoholic when you lived in Thorold?" he asked.

"I still am, I just don't drink now. But then I did. Yeah."

He had stepped into a conversation that had looked nice and solid and his foot had gone through the floor and into the basement. But he couldn't stop. "I guess I drank too much then, too. But it wasn't a problem. We just had a lot of fun."

She smiled with tight terse mystery.

"How come you told me that about yourself? It seems kind of personal." He attached his gaze to hers as he said this; sometimes women said personal things to you as a way of coming on.

But instead of becoming soft and encouraging, her expression turned proper and institutional, like a kid about to recite. "It's part of the twelve-step program to admit it. If I'm going to admit it to other alcoholics in the program, I think I should talk about it in regular life too. It humbles you, sort of."

What a bunch of shit, he thought.

He was drinking with some guys at the Winner's Circle, a rough pick-up bar, when suddenly Patty walked up to him, really drunk.

"John," she gasped. "John, John, John." She lurched at him and attached her nail-bitten little claws to his jacket. "John, this guy over there really wants to fuck me, and I was going to go with him, but I don't want him, I want you, I want you." Her voice wrinkled into a squeak, her face looked like you could smear it with your hand.

"Patty," he mumbled, "you're drunk."

"That's not why, I always feel like this." Her nose and eyelashes and lips touched his cheek in an alcoholic caress. "Just let me kiss you. Just hold me."

He put his hands on her shoulders. "C'mon, stop it."

"It doesn't have to mean anything. You don't have to love me. I love you enough for both of us."

He felt the presence of his smirking friends. "Patty, these guys are laughing at you. I'll see you later." He tried to push her away.

"I don't care. I love you, John. I mean it." She pressed her taut body against his, one sweaty hand under his shirt, and arched her neck until he could see the small veins and bones. "Please. Just be with me. Please." Her hand stroked him, groped between his legs. He took her shoulders and shoved her harder than he meant to. She staggered back, fell against a table, knocked down a chair and almost fell again. She straightened and looked at him like she'd known him and hated him all her life.

He leaned back in his seat and closed his eyes, an overweight, prematurely balding salesman getting drunk on an airplane.

"Look at the clouds," said the girl next to him. "Aren't they beautiful?"

"What's your name?" he asked.

"Lorraine."

"I'm John." He extended his hand and she took it, her eyes unreadable, her hand exuding sweet feminine sweat.

"Why do you want to talk about your alcoholism publicly? I mean, if nobody asks or anything?"

Her eyes were steadfast, but her body was hesitant. "Well, I didn't have to just now. It's just the first thing I thought of when you asked me about Thorold. In general, it's to remind me. It's easy to bullshit yourself that you don't have a problem."

He thought of the rows and rows of people in swivel chairs on talk-show stages, admitting their problems. Wife beaters, child abusers, dominatrixes, porn stars. In the past it probably was a humbling experience to stand up and tell people you were an alcoholic. Now it was just something else to talk about. He remembered Patty tottering through a crowded party on smudged red high heels, bragging about what great blow jobs she gave. Some girl rolled her eyes and said, "Oh no, not again." Patty disappeared into a bedroom with a bottle of vodka and Jack Spannos.

He remembered a conversation with his wife before he married her, a conversation about his bachelor party. "It was no women allowed," he'd told her. "Unless they wanted to give blow jobs."

"Couldn't they just jump naked out of a cake?" she asked.

"Nope. Blow jobs for everybody."

They were at a festive restaurant drinking margaritas. Nervously, she touched her tiny straws. "Wouldn't that be embarrassing? In front of each other? I can't imagine Henry doing that in front of you all."

He smiled at the mention of his shy friend in this context. "Yeah," he said. "It probably would be embarrassing. Group sex is for teenagers."

Her face rose away from her glass in a kind of excited alarm, her lips parted. "You had group sex when you were a teenager?"

"Oh. Not really. Just a gangbang once."

She looked like an antelope testing the wind with its nose in the air, ready to fly. "It wasn't rape," she said.

"Oh, no, no." Her body relaxed and released a warm, sensual curiosity, like a cat against his leg. "The girl liked it."

"Are you sure?"

"Yeah. She liked having sex with a lot of guys. We all knew her, she knew us."

He felt her shiver inwardly, shocked and fascinated by this dangerous pack-animal aspect of his masculinity.

"What was it like?" she asked.

He shrugged. "It was a good time with the guys. It was a bunch of guys standing around in their socks and underwear."

Some kid he didn't know walked up and put his arm around him while he was talking to a girl named Chrissie. The kid's eyes were boyish and drunkenly enthusiastic, his face heavy and porous. He whispered something about Patty in John's ear and said, "C'mon."

The girl's expression subtly withdrew.

"What?" said John.

"Come on," said the kid.

"Bye bye," said Chrissie, with a gingerly wag of her fingers.

He followed the guy through the room, seizing glimpses of hips and tits sheathed in bright, cheap cloth, girls doing wiggly dances with guys who jogged helplessly from foot to foot, holding their chests proudly aloof from their lower bodies. The music made his organs want to leap in and out of his body in time. His friends were all around him.

A door opened and closed behind him, muffling the music. The kid who'd brought him in sat in an armchair, smiling. Patty lay on a bed with her skirt pulled up to her waist and a guy with his pants down straddling her face. Without knowing why, he laughed. Patty twisted her legs about and bucked slightly. For a moment he felt frightened that this was against her will—but no, she would have screamed. He recognized the boy on her as Pete Kopiekin, who was thrusting his flat hairy butt in the same dogged, earnest, woeful manner with which he played football.

Kopiekin got off her and the other guy got on; between them he saw her chin sticking up from her sprawled body, pivoting to and fro on her neck while she muttered and groped blindly up and down her body. Kopiekin opened the door to leave and a fist of music punched the room. His body jumped in shocked response and the door shut. The guy on top of Patty was talking to her; to John's amazement he seemed to be using love words. "You're so beautiful, baby." He saw Patty's hips moving. She wasn't being raped, he thought. When the guy finished he stood and poured the rest of his beer in her face.

"Hey," said John lamely, "hey."

"Oh man, don't tell me that, I've known her a long time."

When the guy left, he thought of wiping her face, but he didn't. His thoughts spiraled inward and he let them be chopped up by muffled guitar chords. He sat awhile, watching guys swarm over Patty and talking to the ones waiting. Music sliced in and out of the room. Then some guy wanted to pour maple syrup on her and he said, "No, I didn't go yet." He sat on the bed and, for the first time, looked at her, expecting to see the sheepish bitter look he knew. He didn't recognize her. Her rigid face was weirdly slack, her eyes fluttered open, rolled and closed, a strange mix of half-formed expressions flew across her face like swarming ghosts. "Patty," he said, "hey." He shook her shoulder. Her eyes opened, her gaze raked his face. He saw tenderness, he thought. He lay on her and tried to embrace her. Her body was leaden and floppy. She muttered and moved, but in ways he didn't understand. He massaged her breasts; they felt like they could come off and she wouldn't notice.

He lay there, supporting himself on his elbows, and felt the deep breath in her lower body meeting his own breath. Subtly, he felt her come to life. She lifted her head and said something; he heard his name.

He kissed her on the lips. Her tongue touched his, gently, her sleeping hands woke. He held her and stroked her pale, beautiful face.

He got up in such a good mood that he slapped the guy coming in with the maple syrup a high five, something he thought was stupid and usually never did.

The next time he saw Patty was at a Foreigner concert in Minneapolis; he saw her holding hands with Pete Kopiekin.

Well, now she could probably be on a talk show about date rape. It was a confusing thing. She may have wanted to kiss him or to give Jack Spannos a blow job, but she probably didn't want maple syrup poured on her. Really though, if you were going to get blind drunk and let everybody fuck you, you had to expect some nasty stuff. On the talk shows they always said it was low self-esteem that made them do it. His eyes rested on Lorraine's hands; she was wadding the empty nut package and stuffing it in her empty plastic cup.

"Hey," he said, "what did you mean when you said you kept trying to fit in and you couldn't? When you were in Thorold?"

"Oh you know." She seemed impatient. "Acting the part of the pretty, sexy girl."

"When in fact you were not a pretty, sexy girl?"

She started to smile, then gestured dismissively. "It was complicated."

It was seductive, the way she drew him in and then shut him out. She picked up her magazine again. Her slight arm movement released a tiny cloud of sweat and deodorant which evaporated as soon as he inhaled it. He breathed in deeply, hoping to smell her again. Sunlight pressed in with viral intensity and exaggerated the lovely contours of her face, the fine lines, the stray cosmetic flecks, the marvelous profusion of her pores. He thought of the stories he'd read in sex magazines about strangers on airplanes having sex in the bathroom or masturbating each other under blankets.

The stewardess made a sweep with a gaping white garbage bag and cleared their trays of bottles and cups.

She put down the magazine. "You've probably had the same experience yourself," she said. Her face was curiously determined, as if it were very important that she make herself understood.

"I mean doing stuff for other people's expectations or just to feel you have a social identity because you're so convinced who you are isn't right."

"You mean low self-esteem?"

"Well, yeah, but more than that." He sensed her inner tension and felt an empathic twitch.

"It's just that you get so many projections onto yourself of who and what you're supposed to be that if you don't have a strong support system it's hard to process it."

"Yeah," he said. "I know what you mean. I've had that experience. I don't know how you can't have it when you're young. There's so much crap in the world." He felt embarrassed, but he kept talking, wanting to tell her something about himself, to return her candor. "I've done lots of things I wish I hadn't done, I've made mistakes. But you can't let it rule your life."

She smiled again, with her mouth only. "Once, a few years ago, my father asked me what I believed to be the worst mistakes in my life. This is how he thinks, this is his favorite kind of question. Anyway, it was really hard to say because I don't know from this vantage point what would've happened if I'd done otherwise in most situations. Finally, I came up with two things, my relationship with this guy named Jerry and the time I turned down an offer to work with this really awful band that became famous. He was totally bewildered. He was expecting me to say 'dropping out of college.'"

"You didn't make a mistake dropping out of college." The vehemence in his voice almost made him blush; then nameless urgency swelled forth and quelled embarrassment. "That wasn't a mistake," he repeated.

"Well, yeah, I know."

"Excuse me." The silent business shark to their left rose in majestic self-containment and moved awkwardly past their knees, looking at John with pointed irony as he did so. Fuck you, thought John.

"And about that relationship," he went on. "That wasn't your loss. It was his." He had meant these words to sound light and playfully gallant, but they had the awful intensity of a maudlin personal confession. He reached out to gently pat her hand to reassure her that he wasn't a nut, but instead he grabbed it and held it. "If you want to talk about mistakes — shit, I raped somebody. Somebody I liked."

Their gaze met in a conflagration of reaction. She was so close he could smell her sweating, but at the speed of light she was falling away, deep into herself where he couldn't follow. She was struggling to free her hand.

"No," he said, "it wasn't a real rape, it was what you were talking about, it was complicated."

She wrenched free her hand and held it protectively close to her

chest. "Don't touch me again." She turned tautly forward. He imagined
her heart beating in alarm. His body felt so stiff he could barely feel his
own heart. Furiously, he wondered if the people around them had heard
any of this. Staring ahead of him he hissed, "Do you think I was dying
to hear about your alcoholism? You were the one who started this crazy
conversation."

He felt her consider this. "It's not the same thing," she hissed back.

"You don't understand," he said ineptly.

She was silent. He thought he dimly felt her body relax, emitting
some possibility of forgiveness. But he couldn't tell. He closed his eyes.
He thought of Patty's splayed body, her half-conscious kiss. He thought
of his wife, her compact scrappy body, her tough-looking flat nose and
chipped nail polish, her smile, her smell, her embrace which was both
soft and fierce. He imagined the hotel room he would sleep in tonight,
its stifling grid of rectangles, oblongs and windows that wouldn't open.
He dozed.

The pilot woke him with a command to fasten his seat belt. He sat
up and blinked. Nothing had changed. The girl at his side was sitting
slightly hunched with her hands resolutely clasped.

"God, I'll be glad when we're on the ground," he said.

She sniffed in reply.

They descended, ears popping. They landed with a flurry of baggage-
grabbing. He stood, bumped his head and tried to get into the aisle to
escape, but it was too crowded. He sat back down.

"Excuse me." She butted her way past him and into the aisle. He
watched a round vulnerable piece of her head move between the obstruction of shoulders and arms. She glanced backward, possibly to see
if he was going to try to follow her. The sideways movement of her hazel
iris prickled him. They burst from the plane and scattered, people picking up speed as they bore down on their destination. He caught up with
her as they entered the terminal. "I'm sorry," he said to the back of her
head. She moved farther away, into memory and beyond.

1995

JAMAICA KINCAID
XUELA

from *The New Yorker*

JAMAICA KINCAID was born in St. John's, Antigua, in 1949. Her mother, a homemaker, removed her from school to help support the family when her third and last brother was born because her stepfather, a carpenter, was ill and could not provide for them. Kincaid was sent to Scarsdale, New York, to work as an au pair. While there, she enrolled in evening classes at a community college, and later she attended Franconia College in New Hampshire on a full scholarship. However, she dropped out after a year and returned to New York, where she began writing, eventually becoming a staff writer for *The New Yorker*. She wrote for several magazines, and her stories appeared in *The Paris Review* and *The New Yorker*.

Kincaid often writes about colonialism as well as gender and sexuality. Many of her novels are loosely autobiographical, although she once said, "Everything I say is true, and everything I say is not true. You couldn't admit any of it to a court of law. It would not be good evidence."

The author of *At the Bottom of the River,* a collection of short stories, and the novels *Annie John, Lucy, The Autobiography of My Mother, Mr. Potter,* and *See Now Then,* Kincaid has received a Guggenheim Fellowship, a Lannan Literary Award, and the Prix Femina Étranger and is a member of the American Academy of Arts and Letters as well as the American Academy of Arts and Sciences. She lives in North Bennington, Vermont.

★

MY MOTHER DIED at the moment I was born, and so for my whole life there was nothing standing between me and eternity; at my back was always a bleak, black wind. I could not have known at the beginning of my life that this would be so; I only came to know this in the middle of my life, just at the time when I was no longer young and realized that I had less of some of the things I used to have in abundance and more of some of the things I had scarcely had at all. And this real-

ization of loss and gain made me look backward and forward: at my beginning was this woman whose face I had never seen, but at my end was
nothing, no one; there was nothing between me and the black room of
the world. I came to feel that for my whole life I had been standing on a
precipice, that my loss had made me vulnerable, that it had made me
hard and helpless; on knowing this, I became overwhelmed with sadness and shame and pity for myself.

When my mother died, leaving me a small child vulnerable to all
the world, my father took me and placed me in the care of the same
woman he paid to wash his clothes. It is possible that he emphasized to
her the difference between the two bundles; one was his child, perhaps
not the only child of his in the world but the only child he had had with
the only woman he had married so far, the other was his soiled clothes.
He would have handled one more gently than the other, he would have
given more careful instructions for the care of one than for the other, he
would have expected better care for one than the other — but which one
I do not know, because he was a vain man, his appearance was very important to him. That I was a burden to him then, I know; that his soiled
clothes were a burden to him then, I know; that he did not know how to
take care of me by himself, that he did not know how to clean his own
clothes himself then, I know.

He had lived in a very small house with my mother. He was poor, but
it was not because he was good; he had simply not done enough bad
things yet to get rich. The house was on a hill, and he had walked down
the hill balancing in one hand his child, in the other his clothes, and he
gave them, bundle and child, to this woman. She was not a relative of his
or of my mother's; her name was Eunice Paul, and she had six children
already, the last one still a baby. That was why she still had some milk
to give me, but in my mouth it tasted sour, and I would not drink it. She
lived in a house that was far from other houses, and from it there was a
broad view of the sea and the mountains, and when I was irritable and
unable to console myself she would prop me up on a pile of old clothes
and place me under a tree, and at the sight of that sea and those mountains, so unpitying, I would exhaust myself in tears.

Ma Eunice was not unkind: she treated me just the way she treated
her own children — but that is not to say that she was kind to her own
children. In a place like this, brutality is the only real inheritance and
cruelty is sometimes the only thing freely given. I did not like her, and
I missed the face I had never seen; I looked over my shoulder to see if
someone was coming, as if I were expecting someone to come, and Ma

Eunice would ask me what I was looking for, at first as a joke, but when, after a time, I did not stop doing it, she thought that it meant I could see spirits. I could not see spirits at all, I was just looking for that face, that face I would never see, even if I lived forever.

I never grew to love this woman my father left me with, this woman who was not unkind to me but who could not be kind because she did not know how — and perhaps I could not love her because I, too, did not know how. She fed me food forced through a sieve when I would not drink her milk and did not yet have teeth; when I grew teeth, the first thing I did was to sink them into her hand as she fed me. A small sound escaped her mouth then, more from surprise than from pain, and she knew this for what it was — my first act of ingratitude — and it put her on her guard against me for the rest of the time we knew each other.

Until I was four I did not speak. This did not cause anyone to lose a minute of happiness; there was no one who would have worried about it in any case. I knew I could speak, but I did not want to. I saw my father every fortnight, when he came to get his clean clothes. I never thought of him as coming to visit me; I thought of him as coming to pick up his clean clothes. When he came, I was brought to him, and he would ask me how I was, but it was a formality; he would never touch me or look into my eyes. What was there to see in my eyes then? Eunice washed, ironed, and folded his clothes; they were wrapped up like a gift in two pieces of clean nankeen cloth and placed on a table, the only table in the house, waiting for him to come and pick them up. His visits were quite steady, and so when one time he did not appear as he usually did I noticed it. I said, "Where is my father?"

I said it in English — not patois French or English but plain English — and that should have been the surprise; not that I spoke but that I spoke English, a language I had never heard anyone speak. Ma Eunice and her children spoke the language of Dominica, which is French patois, and my father, when he spoke to me, spoke that language also. But no one noticed; they only marveled at the fact that I had finally spoken. That the first words I said were in the language of a people I would never like or love is not now a mystery to me; almost everything in my life to which I am inextricably bound is a source of pain.

I was then four years old and saw the world as a series of sketches, soft strokes in charcoal; and so when my father would come and take his clothes away I saw only that he suddenly appeared on the small path that led from the main road to the door of the house in which I lived and then, after completing his mission, disappeared as he turned onto the road, where it met the path. I did not know what lay beyond the path; I did not know if after he passed from my sight he remained my father or dissolved into something altogether different and I would never see him again in the form of my father. I would have accepted it.

I did not talk and I would not talk.

One day, without meaning to, I broke a plate, the only bone-china plate that Eunice had ever owned, and the words "I am sorry" would not pass my lips. The sadness she expressed over this loss fascinated me; it was so intense, so overwhelming, so deep: she grabbed the thick pouch that was her stomach, she pulled at her hair, she pounded her bosom, large tears rolled out of her eyes and down her cheeks, and they came in such profusion that if they had become a new source of water, as in a myth or a fairy tale, my small self would not have been surprised. I had been warnèd repeatedly by her not to touch this plate, for she had seen me look at it with an obsessive curiosity. I would look at it and wonder about the picture painted on its surface, a picture of a wide-open field filled with grass and flowers in the most tender shades of yellow, pink, blue, and green; the sky had a sun in it that shone but did not burn bright; the clouds were thin and scattered about like a decoration, not thick and banked up, not harbingers of doom; it was nothing but a field full of grass and flowers on a sunny day, but it had an atmosphere of secret abundance, happiness, and tranquillity; underneath this picture, written in gold letters, was the word "Heaven." Of course it was not a picture of Heaven at all. It was a picture of the English countryside idealized, but I did not know that, I did not know that such a thing as the English countryside existed. And neither did Eunice; she thought that this picture was a picture of Heaven, offering as it did a promise of a life without worry or care or want.

When I broke the china plate on which this picture was painted, and caused Ma Eunice to cry so, I did not immediately feel sorry, I did not feel sorry shortly after; I only felt sorry long afterward, and by then it was too late to tell her so, she had died by then; perhaps she went to Heaven and it fulfilled what was promised on that plate. When I broke the plate, she cursed my dead mother, she cursed my father, she cursed me. The words she used were without meaning; I understood them, but they did not hurt me, for I did not love her. And she did not love me; she made me kneel down on her stone heap—which was situated in a spot that got direct sun all day long—with my hands raised high above my head and with a large stone in each hand. She meant to keep me in this

position until I said the words "I am sorry," but I would not say them, I
could not say them. It was beyond my own will; those words could not
pass my lips then. I stayed like that until she exhausted herself cursing
me and all whom I came from.

And should this punishment, redolent as it was in every way of the
relationship between captor and captive, master and slave, with its mo-
tif of the big and the small, the powerful and the powerless, the strong
and the weak, and against a background of earth, sea, and sky, and Eunice standing over me, metamorphosing into a succession of things furious and not human with each syllable that passed her lips; with her
dress of a thin, badly woven cotton, the bodice of a contrary color and
pattern that clashed with the skirt; her hair uncombed, unwashed for
many months, wrapped in a piece of old cloth that had been unwashed
for longer than her hair; the dress had once been new and clean, and
dirt had made it old but dirt had made it new again by giving it shadings
it did not have before, and dirt would finally cause it to disintegrate altogether, but she was not a dirty woman, she washed her feet every night;
the day was clear, it was not the rainy time, some men were on the sea
casting nets for fish, but they would not catch too many because it was a
clear day; and three of her children were eating bread and they rolled up
the inside of the bread into small pebblelike shapes and threw it at me
as I knelt there and they laughed at me; and the sky was without a cloud
and there was not a breeze, a fly flew back and forth across my face,
sometimes landing on a corner of my mouth; an overripe breadfruit fell
off its tree, and that sound was like a fist meeting the soft, fleshy part of a
body . . . All this, all this I can remember — should it have made a lasting
impression on me?

But as I was kneeling there I saw three land turtles crawling in and
out of the small space under the house, and I fell in love with them, I
wanted to have them near me, I wanted to speak only to them each day
for the rest of my life. Long after my ordeal was over — resolved in a way
that did not please Ma Eunice, for I did not say I was sorry — I took all
three turtles and placed them in an enclosed area where they could not
come and go as they pleased and where they were completely depen-
dent on me for food. I would bring to them the leaves of vegetables, and
water in seashells. I thought them beautiful, with their shells dark gray
with faint yellow circles, their long necks, their unjudging eyes, the slow
deliberateness of their crawl. But they would withdraw into their shells
when I did not want them to, and when I called them they would not
come out; to teach them a lesson, I took some mud from the riverbed

and covered up the small hole from which each neck would emerge, and I allowed it to dry; I covered over the place where they lived with stones, and for days afterward I forgot about them. When they came into my mind again, I went to take a look at them in the place where I had left them. They were by then all dead.

It was my father's wish that I be sent to school. It was an unusual request; girls did not attend school. I shall never know what made him do such a thing. I can only imagine that he desired such a thing for me without giving it too much thought, because in the end what could an education do for someone like me? I can only say what I did not have; I can only measure it against what I did have and find misery in the difference. And yet, and yet — it was for that reason that I came to see for the first time what lay beyond the path that led away from my house.

I can so well remember the feel of the cloth of my skirt and blouse — coarse because it was new — a green skirt and beige blouse, a uniform, its colors and style mimicking the colors and style of a school somewhere else, somewhere far away; and I had on a pair of brown canvas shoes and brown cotton socks which my father had got for me, I did not know from where. And to mention that I did not know where these things came from, to say that I wondered about them is really to say that this was the first time I had worn such things as shoes and socks, and they caused my feet to ache and swell and the skin to blister and break, but I was made to wear them until my feet got used to it. That morning was a morning like any other, so ordinary it was profound: it was sunny in some places and not in others, and the two (sunny, cloudy) occupied different parts of the sky quite comfortably; the green of the trees, the red burst of the flowers from the flamboyant trees, the sickly yellow fruit of the cashew, the smell of lime, the smell of almonds, the coffee on my breath, Eunice's skirt blowing in my face, and the stirring up of the smells that came from between her legs, which I shall never forget, and whenever I smell myself I am reminded of her; the river was low, so I did not hear the sound of the water rushing over stones; the breeze was soft, so the leaves did not rustle in the trees.

And I had these sensations of seeing, smelling, and hearing during my journey down the path that began at Eunice's door and ended where it met the road; and when I reached the road and placed my newly shod foot on it, that was the first time I had done so; I was aware of this. It was a road of small stones and dirt tightly packed together, and each step I took was awkward; the ground shifted, my feet slipped backward. The road stretched out ahead of me and then it vanished in a bend; we kept walking toward this bend and then we came to the bend and the bend gave way to more of the same road and then another bend. We came to my school long before the end of the last bend: it was a small building with one door and four windows; it had a wooden floor; there was a lizard crawling along a beam in the roof; there were three long desks lined up one behind the other; there was a large wooden table and a chair facing the three long desks; on the wall behind the wooden table and chair was a map; at the top of the map were the words "The British Empire." Those were the first words I learned to read.

In that room there were always boys; I did not sit in a schoolroom with other girls until I was older. I was not afraid in that new situation: I did not know how to be that then and do not know how to be that now. I was not afraid then, because my mother had already died, and that is the only thing a child is really afraid of; when I was born my mother was dead, and I had already lived all those years with Eunice, a woman who was not my mother and who could not love me, and I had lived without my father, never knowing when I would see him again, so I was not afraid for myself in this situation. (And if it is not really true that I was not afraid then, it was not the only time that I did not admit to myself my own vulnerability.)

At the time, each thing as it took place stood out in my mind with a sharpness that I now take for granted; it did not then have a meaning, it did not have a context, I did not yet know the history of events, I did not know their antecedents. My teacher was a woman who had been trained by Methodist missionaries; she was of the African people, that I could see, and she found in this a source of humiliation and self-loathing, and she wore despair like an article of clothing, like a mantle, or a staff on which she leaned constantly, a birthright which she would pass on to us without effort. She did not love us; we did not love her; we did not love one another, not then, not ever. There were seven boys and myself. The boys, too, were all of the African people. My teacher and these boys looked at me and looked at me: I had thick eyebrows; my hair was coarse, thick, and wavy; my eyes were set far apart from each other and they had the shape of almonds; my lips were wide and narrow in an unexpected way. I was of the African people, but not exclusively. My mother was a Carib woman, and when they looked at me this is what they saw; and it was my teacher who, at the end of the day, in bidding me good evening, called me Miss Boiled Fish — she thought me pale and weak.

I started to speak quite openly then — to myself frequently, to others only when it was absolutely necessary. We spoke English in school — proper English, not patois — and among ourselves we spoke French patois, a language that was not considered proper at all, a language that a person from France could not speak and could only with difficulty understand. I spoke to myself because I grew to like the sound of my own voice. It had a sweetness to me, it made my loneliness less, for I was lonely and wished to see people in whose faces I could see something of myself. Because who was I? My mother was dead; when I saw my father I could not tell what I meant to him.

I learned to read and write very quickly. My memory, my ability to retain information, to remember the tiniest detail, to recall who said what and when, was regarded as unusual, so unusual that my teacher, who was trained to think only of good and evil and whose judgment of such things was always mistaken, said I was evil, I was possessed — and to establish that there could be no doubt of this she pointed to the fact that my mother was a Carib woman.

My world, then — silent, soft, and vegetablelike in its vulnerability, subject to the powerful whims of others, diurnal, beginning with the pale opening of light on the horizon each morning and ending with a sudden onset of dark at the beginning of each night — was both a mystery to me and the source of much pleasure. I loved the face of a gray sky, porous, grainy, wet, following me to school for mornings on end, shooting down soft arrows of water on me; the face of that same sky when it was a hard, unsheltering blue, a backdrop for a cruel sun; the harsh heat that eventually became a part of me, like my blood; the massive trees, the stems of some of them the size of small trunks, that grew without restraint, as if beauty were only size, and which I could tell apart by closing my eyes and listening to the sound the leaves made when they rubbed together; and I loved that moment when the white flowers from the cedar tree started to fall to the ground with a silence that I could hear, their petals at first still fresh, a soft kiss of pink and white, then a day later crushed, wilted, and brown, a nuisance to the eye; and the river that had become a small lagoon when one day on its own it changed its course, on whose bank I would sit and watch families of birds, and frogs laying their eggs, and the sky turning from black to blue and blue to black, and rain falling on the sea beyond the lagoon but not on the mountain that was beyond the sea.

It was while sitting in this place that I first began to dream about my mother; I had fallen asleep on the stones that covered the ground around me, my small body sinking into this surface as if it were a bed of feathers. I saw my mother come down a ladder. She wore a long white gown, the hem of it falling just above her heels, and that was all of her that was exposed, just her heels; she came down and down, but no more of her was ever revealed. Only her heels, only the hem of the gown. At first I longed to see more, and then I became satisfied just to see her heels coming down toward me. When I awoke, I was not the same child I had been before I fell asleep. I longed to see my father and to be in his presence constantly.

On a day that began in no special way that I can remember, I was taught the principles involved in writing an ordinary letter. A letter has six parts: the address of the sender, the date, the address of the recipient, the salutation or greeting, the body of the letter, the closing of the letter. It was well known that a person in the position I was expected to oc-cupy — the position of a woman, and a poor one — would have no need whatsoever to write a letter, but the sense of satisfaction it gave every-one connected with teaching me this, writing a letter, must have been immense. I was beaten and harsh words were said to me when I made a mistake. The exercise of copying the letters of someone whose com-plaints or perceptions or joys were of no interest to me did not make me angry then; it only made me want to write my own letters, letters in which I would express my own feelings about my own life, as it ap-peared to me at seven years old. I started to write to my father. "My Dear Papa," I wrote, in a lovely, decorative penmanship, a penmanship born of beatings and harsh words. I would say to him that I was mistreated by Eunice in word and deed and that I missed him and loved him very much. I wrote the same thing over and over again. It was without de-tail; it was without color. It was nothing but the plaintive cry of a small, wounded animal: "My Dear Papa, you are the only person I have left in the world, no one loves me, only you can, I am beaten with words, I am beaten with sticks, I am beaten with stones, I love you more than any-thing, only you can save me." These words were not meant for my fa-ther at all, but the person for whom they were meant — I could see only her heel. Night after night I saw her heels, only her heels coming down to meet me.

I wrote these letters without any intention of sending them to my fa-ther; I did not know how to do that, to send them. I folded them up in such a way that if they were torn along the folds they would make eight small squares. There was no mysterious significance to this; I did it to make them fit more neatly under a large stone just outside the gate to my school. Each day, as I left, I would place a letter I had written to my father under it. I had, of course, written these letters in secret, during the small amount of time allotted to us as recess, or during some time when I was supposed to be doing other work but had finished before I was noticed. Pretending to be deeply involved in what I was supposed to be doing, I would write my father a letter.

This small cry for help did not bring me instant relief. I recognized my own misery, but that it could be alleviated—that my life could change, that my circumstances could change—did not occur to me.

My letters did not remain a secret. A boy named Roman had seen me putting them in their secret storage place and, behind my back, he removed them. He had no empathy or pity; any instinct to protect the weak had been destroyed in him. He took my letters to our teacher. In my letters to my father I had said, "Everyone hates me, only you love me," but I had not truly meant these letters to be sent to my father, and they were not really addressed to my father; if I had been asked then if I really felt that everyone hated me, that only my father loved me, I would not have known how to answer. But my teacher's reaction to my letters, those small scribblings, was fascinating to me—a tonic. She believed the "everybody" I referred to was herself, and only herself. She said that my words were calumny, a lie, libelous, that she was ashamed of me, that she was not afraid of me. My teacher said all this to me in front of the other pupils at my school. They thought I was humiliated, and they felt joy to see me brought so low. I did not feel humiliated at all. Her teeth were crooked and yellow, and I wondered then how they had got that way. Large half-moons of perspiration stained the underarms of her dress, and I wondered if when I became a woman I, too, would perspire so profusely and how it would smell. Behind her shoulder on the wall was a large female spider carrying its sac of eggs, and I wanted to reach out and crush it with the bare palm of my hand, because I wondered if it was the same kind of spider or a relative of the spider that had sucked saliva from the corner of my mouth the night before as I lay sleeping, leaving three small, painful bites. There was a drizzle of rain outside; I could hear the sound of it on the galvanized roof.

She sent my letters to my father, apparently to show me that she had a clear conscience. She said that I had mistaken her scoldings, which were administered out of love for me, as an expression of hatred and that this showed that I was guilty of the sin called pride. And she said that she hoped I would learn to tell the difference between the two, love and hate. And when she said this I did look in her face to see if I could tell whether it was true that she loved me and to see if her words, which so often seemed to be a series of harsh blows, were really an expression of love. Her face to me then did not appear loving, and perhaps I was mistaken—perhaps I was too young to judge, too young to know.

I did not immediately recognize what had happened, what I had done: however unconsciously, however without direction, I had, through the use of some words, changed my situation, I had perhaps even saved my life. To speak of my own situation, to myself or to others, is something I would always do thereafter. It is in that way that I came to be so extremely conscious of myself, so interested in my own needs, so interested in fulfilling them, aware of my grievances, aware of my pleasures. From this unfocused, childish expression of pain, my life was changed, and I took note of it.

My father came to fetch me wearing the uniform of a jailer. To him this had no meaning, it was without significance. He was returning to Roseau from the village of St. Joseph, where he had been carrying out his duties as a policeman. I was not told that he would arrive on that day, I had not expected him. I returned from school and saw him standing at the final bend in the road that led to the house in which I lived. I was surprised to see him, but I would only admit this to myself; I did not let anyone know.

The reason I had missed my father so—the reason he no longer came to the house in which I lived, bringing his dirty clothes and taking away clean ones—was that he had married again. I had been told about this, but it was a mystery to me what it might mean; it was not unlike when I had been told that the world was round and it was the first time I had heard such a thing. I thought, What could it mean, why should it be? My father had married again. He took my hand, he said something, he spoke in English, his mouth had begun to curl around the words he spoke, and it made him appear benign, attractive, even kind. I understood what he said: He had a home for me now, a good home; I would love his wife, my new mother; he loved me as much as he loved himself, perhaps even more, because I reminded him of someone he knew with certainty he had loved even more than he had loved himself. I would love my new home; I would love the sky above me and the earth below.

The word "love" was spoken with such frequency that it became a clue to my seven-year-old mind, a clue that the love being spoken of did not exist. My father's eyes grew small and then they grew big; he believed what he said, and that was a good thing, because I did not. But I would not have wanted to stop this progression, this going away from here; and though I did not believe him I did not have any reason not to, and I was not yet cynical, I did not yet think that behind everything I heard lay another story altogether.

I thanked Eunice for taking care of me. I did not mean it, I could not mean it, but I would mean it if I said it now. I did not say goodbye. All my belongings were in a muslin knapsack, and my father placed it in a bag that was strapped on the donkey he had been riding. He placed me on the donkey, and then he sat behind me. And this was how we looked as my back was turned on the small house in which I spent the first seven years of my life: a man and his small daughter on the back of a donkey at the end of an ordinary day, a day that had no meaning if you were less than a smudge on a page covered with print. I could hear my father's breath, it was not the breath of my life; the back of my head touched his chest from time to time; I could hear the sound of his heart beating through the shirt of his uniform, a uniform that made people afraid when they saw him coming toward them. His presence in my life then was a good thing, and it was too bad that he had not thought of changing his clothes. It was too bad that I noticed he had not done so; it was too bad that such a thing would matter to me.

This new experience of leaving the past behind — of going from one place to another and knowing that whatever had been would remain just as it had been — was something I immediately accepted, a gift. This simple movement, the turning of your back to leave something behind, is among the most difficult to make, but once it has been made you cannot imagine that it was at all hard to accomplish. I had not been able to do it all by myself, but I could see that I had set in motion the events that would make it possible. If I were ever to find myself sitting in that schoolroom again, or sitting in Eunice's yard again, sleeping in her bed, eating with her children, none of it would have the same power it had once had over me — the power to make me feel helpless and ashamed of my own helplessness.

I could not see the look on my father's face as we rode, I did not know what he was thinking, I did not know him well enough to guess. He set off down the road in the opposite direction from the schoolhouse. This stretch of road was new to me, and yet it had a familiarity that made me sad. Around each bend was the familiar dark green of the trees that grew with a ferociousness that no hand had yet attempted to restrain, green unrelenting and complete; nothing could be added to it and nothing could be taken away from it. Each precipice along the road was steep and dangerous, and a fall down one of them would result in death or a lasting injury. And each climb up was followed by a slope down, at the bottom of which clustered, along the road, a choke of flowering plants, each plant with a purpose not yet known to me. And each curve that ran left would soon give way to a curve that ran right.

The day then began to have the colors of an ending, the colors of a funeral, gray and mauve, and my sadness became manifest to me. I was a part of a procession of sadness, which was moving away from my old life, a life I had lived then for only seven years. I did not become overwhelmed, though. The dark of night came on with its usual suddenness. My father placed an arm around me then, as if to ward off something — a danger I could not see in the cool air, an evil spirit, a fall. His clasp was at first gentle; then it grew tighter; it had the strength of an iron band. I did not become overwhelmed.

We entered the village in the dark. There were no lights anywhere, no dog barked, we did not pass anyone. We entered the house in which my father lived, and there was a light coming from a beautiful glass lamp, something I had never seen before; the light was fueled by a clear liquid that I could see through the base of the lamp, which was embossed with the heads of animals unfamiliar to me. The lamp was on a shelf, and the shelf was made of mahogany, its brackets curling in the shape of two tightly closed paws. The room was crowded, containing a chair on which two people could sit at once, two other chairs on which only one person could sit, and a small, low table draped with a piece of white linen. The walls of the house and the partition that separated this first room from the other rooms of the house were covered with a kind of paper, and the paper was decorated with small pink roses. I had never seen anything like this before, except once, while looking through a book at my school — but the picture I had seen then was a drawing, illustrating a story about the domestic life of a small mammal who lived in a field with his family. In their burrow, the walls had been covered with similar paper. I had understood that story about the small mammal to be a pretense, something to amuse a child, but this was my father's very real house, a house with a bright lamp in a room, and a room that seemed to exist only for an occasional purpose.

At that moment I realized that there were so many things I did not know, not including the very big thing I did not know — my mother. I did not know my father; I did not know where he was from or whom and what he liked; I did not know the land whose surface I had just crossed on an animal's back; I did not know who I was or why I was standing there in that room of occasional purpose with the lamp. A great sea of what I did not know opened up before me, and its treacherous currents pulsed over my head repeatedly until I was sure I was dead. I had only fainted. I opened my eyes soon after that to see the face of my father's wife not too far above mine. She had the face of evil. I had no other face to compare it with; I only knew that this was the face of evil as far as I could tell. She did not like me. I could see that. She did not love me. I could see that. I could not see the rest of her right away — only her face. She was of the African people and the French people. It was nighttime and she was in her own house, so her hair was exposed; it was smooth and yet tightly curled, and she wore it parted in the middle and plaited in two braids that were pinned up in the back. Her lips were shaped like those of people from a cold climate: thin and ungenerous. Her eyes were black, and not with beauty but with deceit. Her nose was long and sharp, like an arrow; her cheekbones were also sharp.

She did not like me. She did not love me. I could see it in her face. My spirit rose to meet this obstacle. No love. I could live in a place like this. I knew this atmosphere all too well. Love would have defeated me. Love would always defeat me. In an atmosphere of no love I could live well; in this atmosphere of no love I could make a life for myself. She held a cup to my mouth; one of her hands brushed against my face, and it felt cold; she was feeding me a tea, something to revive me, but it tasted bitter, like a bad potion. My small tongue allowed no more than a drop of it to come into my mouth, but the bad and bitter taste of it warmed my young heart. I sat up. Our eyes did not meet and lock; I was too young to throw out such a challenge. I could then act only on instinct.

I was led down a short hallway to a room. It was to be my own room. My father lived in a house in which there were so many rooms that I could occupy my own. This small event immediately became central to my life: I adjusted to this evidence of privacy without question. My room was lit by a small lamp, the size of my fist, and I could see my bed: small, of wood, a white sheet on its copra-filled mattress, a square, flat pillow. I had a washstand, on which stood a basin and an urn that had water in it. I did not see a towel. (I did not then know how to wash myself properly in any case, and the lesson I eventually got came with many words of abuse.) There was not a picture on the wall. The walls were not covered with paper; the bare wood — pine — was not painted. It was the plainest of plain rooms, but it had in it more luxury than I had ever imagined; it offered me something I did not even know I needed; it offered me solitude.

All of my little being, physical and spiritual, could find peace here, in this little place where I could sit and take stock.

I sat down on the bed. My heart was breaking; I wanted to cry, I felt so alone. I felt in danger, I felt threatened; I felt as each minute passed that someone wished me dead. My father's wife came to say goodnight, and she turned out the lamp. She spoke to me then in French patois; in his presence she had spoken to me in English. She would do this to me through all the time we knew each other, but that first time, in the sanctuary of my room, at seven years old, I recognized this as an attempt on her part to make an illegitimate of me, to associate me with the made-up language of people regarded as not real — the shadow people, the forever humiliated, the forever low. Then she went to the part of the house where she and my father slept; it was far away; I could hear the sound of her footsteps fade; I could hear their voices as they spoke, the sounds swirling upward to the empty space beneath the ceiling; they had a conversation; I could not make out the words; the emotions seemed neutral, neither hot nor cold; there was some silence; there were short gasps and sighs; there was the sound of people sleeping, breath escaping through their mouths.

I lay down to sleep, to dream of my mother — for I knew I would do that, I knew I would make myself do that. She came down the ladder again and again, over and over, just her heels and the hem of her white dress visible; down, down, I watched her all night in my dream. I did not see her face. I was not disappointed. I would have loved to see her face, but I didn't long for it anymore. She sang a song, but it had no words; it was not a lullaby, it was not sentimental, not meant to calm me when my soul roiled at the harshness of life; it was only a song, but the sound of her voice was like treasure found in an abandoned chest, a treasure that inspires not astonishment but contentment and eternal pleasure.

All night I slept and in my sleep saw her feet come down the ladder, step after step, and I heard her voice singing that song, sometimes humming, sometimes through an open mouth. To this day she will appear in my dreams from time to time, but never again to sing or utter a sound of any kind — only as before, coming down a ladder, her heels visible and the white hem of her garment above them.

•   •   •

I came to my father's house in the blanket of voluptuous blackness that was the night; a morning naturally followed. I awoke to the same landscape that I had always known, each aspect of it beyond reproach, at once beautiful, ugly, humble, and proud; full of life, full of death, able to sustain the one, inevitably to claim the other.

My father's wife showed me how to wash myself. It was not done with kindness. My human form and odor were an opportunity to heap scorn on me. I responded in a fashion by now characteristic of me: whatever I was told to hate I loved. I loved the smell of the thin dirt behind my ears, the smell that comes from between my legs, the smell in the pits of my arms, the smell of my unwashed feet. Whatever about me caused offense, whatever was native to me, whatever I could not help and was not a moral failing — those things about me I loved with the fervor of the devoted. Her hands as they touched me were cold and caused me pain. In her was a despair rooted in a desire long thwarted; she had not yet been able to bear my father a child. She was afraid of me; she was afraid that because of me my father would think of my mother more often than he thought of her. On that first morning, she gave me some food, and it was old, moldy, as if she had saved it especially for me, in order to make me sick. I did not eat what she offered after that; I learned then how to prepare my own food and made this a trait by which others would know me: I was a girl who prepared her own food.

Parts of my life then, incidents in my life then, seem, when I remember them now, as if they were taking place in a very small, dark place, a place the size of a doll's house, and the doll's house is at the bottom of a cellar, and I am way up at the top of the stairs peering down into this little house trying to make out exactly what is happening down there. And sometimes when I look down at this scene certain things are not in the same place they were in the last time I looked; different things are in the shadows, different things are in the light.

Who was my father? Not just who was he to me, his child — but who was he? He was a policeman, but not an ordinary policeman; he inspired more than the expected amount of fear for someone in his position. He made appointments to see people, men, at his house, the place where he lived with his family — this entity of which I was now a sort of member — and he would make these people wait for hours or he wouldn't show up at all. They waited for him, sometimes sitting on a stone that was just inside the gate of the yard, sometimes pacing back and forth from inside the yard to outside the yard, causing the gate to creak, and this always made his wife cross, and she would complain to these people, speaking rudely to them, the rudeness way out of proportion to the annoyance of the creaky gate. They waited for him without complaint, sometimes falling asleep standing up, sometimes falling asleep as they sat on the ground. They waited, and when he did not show up they left and returned the next day, hoping to see him; sometimes they did, sometimes they did not. He suffered no consequences for his behavior; he just treated people in this way. He did not care, or so I thought at first — but of course he did care; it was well thought out, this way he had of causing suffering; he was part of a whole way of life on the island which perpetuated pain.

At the time I came to live with him, he had just mastered the mask that he wore for the remainder of his life: the skin taut, the eyes small and drawn back as though deep inside his head, so that it wasn't possible to get a clue to him from them, the lips parted in a smile. He seemed trustworthy. His clothes were always ironed, clean, spotless. He did not like people to know him very well; he tried never to eat food in the presence of strangers or in the presence of people who were afraid of him.

Who was he? I ask myself this all the time, to this day. Who was he? He was a tall man; his hair was red; his eyes were gray. He must have loved me then, he had told me so. I never heard him say words of love to anyone. He wanted me to continue going to school, but I did not know why. It was a great sacrifice that I should go to school, because, as his wife often pointed out, I would have been more useful at home. He gave me books to read. He gave me a life of John Wesley, and as I read it I wondered what the life of a man so full of spiritual tumult and piety had to do with me. My father had become a Methodist and attended church every Sunday; he taught Sunday school. The more money he had, the more he went to church. And the richer he became, the more fixed the mask of his face grew, so that now I no longer remember what he really looked like when I first knew him long ago, before I came to live with him. And so my mother and father then were a mystery to me: one through death, the other through the maze of living; one I had never seen, the other I saw constantly.

The world I came to know was full of treachery, but I did not remain afraid, I did not become cautious. I was not indifferent to the danger my father's wife posed to me, and I was not indifferent to the danger she thought my presence posed to her. So in my father's house, which was her home, I tried to cloak myself in an atmosphere of apology. I did not in fact feel sorry for anything at all, and I had not done anything, either deliberately or by accident, that warranted my begging for forgiveness, but my gait was a weapon — a way of deflecting her attention from me, of persuading her to think of me as someone who was pitiable, an ignorant child. I did not like her, I did not wish her dead, I only wanted her to leave me alone.

I would lie in my bed at night and turn my ear to the sounds that were inside and outside the house, identifying each noise, separating the real from the unreal: whether the screeches that crisscrossed the night, leaving the blackness to fall to the earth like so many ribbons, were the screeches of bats or of someone who had taken the shape of a bat; whether the sound of wings beating in that space so empty of light was a bird or someone who had taken the shape of a bird. The sound of the gate being opened was my father coming home long after the stillness of sleep had overtaken most of his household, his footsteps stealthy but sure, coming into the yard, up the steps, his hand opening the door to his house, closing the door behind him, turning the bar that made the door secure, walking to another part of the house; he never ate meals when he returned home late at night. The sound of the sea then, at night, could be heard clearly, sometimes as a soft swish, a lapping of waves against the shore of black stones, sometimes with the anger of water boiling in a cauldron resting unsteadily on a large fire. And sometimes, when the night was completely still and completely black, I could hear, outside, the long sigh of someone on the way to eternity; and this, of all things, would disturb the troubled peace of all that was real: the dogs asleep under houses, the chickens in the trees, the trees themselves moving about, not in a way that suggested an uprooting, just a moving about, as if they wished they could run away. And if I listened again I could hear the sound of those who crawled on their bellies, of those who carried poisonous lances, and those who carried a deadly poison in their saliva; I could hear the ones who were hunting, the ones who were hunted, the pitiful cry of the small ones who were about to be devoured, followed by the temporary satisfaction of the ones doing the devouring: all this I heard night after night. And it ended only after my hands had traveled up and down all over my own body in a loving caress, finally coming to the soft, moist spot between my legs, and a gasp of pleasure had escaped my lips which I would allow no one to hear.

1996

AKHIL SHARMA

IF YOU SING LIKE THAT FOR ME

from the *Atlantic Monthly*

AKHIL SHARMA was born in Delhi, India, in 1971 and moved to the United States when he was eight. He grew up in New Jersey and got his BA at Princeton University. Soon after, he won a Stegner Fellowship to the writing program at Stanford.

Sharma is the author of the novel *An Obedient Father*, winner of the 2001 PEN/Hemingway Award and the 2001 Whiting Writers' Award. He has published stories in *The Atlantic, Fiction, The Quarterly,* and *The New Yorker*.

Sharma's fiction explores Indian characters and immigrants struggling with family bonds and unexpected tragedy. The *New York Times* called his work "compassionate but unflinching."

Sharma's most recent book is the novel *Family Life*. He teaches at Rutgers University, Newark. This story received unsigned form rejections from *The New Yorker, Harper's, Esquire,* and *Playboy*.

★

L ATE ONE JUNE afternoon, seven months after my wedding, I woke from a short, deep sleep in love with my husband. I did not know then, lying in bed and looking out the window at the line of gray clouds, that my love would last only a few hours and that I would never again care for Rajinder with the same urgency—never again in the five homes we would share and through the two daughters and one son we would also share, though unevenly and with great bitterness. I did not know this then, suddenly awake and only twenty-six, with a husband not much older, nor did I know that the memory of the coming hours would periodically overwhelm me throughout my life.

We were living in a small flat on the roof of a three-story house in Defense Colony, in New Delhi. Rajinder had signed the lease a week before our wedding. Two days after we married, he took me to the flat. I had thought I would be frightened entering my new home for the first time, but I was not. I felt very still that morning, watching Rajinder in his gray sweater bend over and open the padlock. Although it was cold, I wore only a pink silk sari and blouse, because I knew that my thick eyebrows, broad nose, and thin lips made me homely, and to win his love I must try especially hard to be appealing, even though I did not want to be.

The sun filled the living room through a window that took up half a wall and looked out onto the concrete roof. Rajinder went in first, holding the heavy brass padlock in his right hand. In the center of the room was a low plywood table with a thistle broom on top, and in a corner three plastic folding chairs lay collapsed on the floor. I followed a few steps behind Rajinder. The room was a white rectangle. Looking at it, I felt nothing. I saw the table and broom, the window grille with its drooping iron flowers, the dust in which we left our footprints, and I thought I should be feeling something — some anxiety, or fear, or curiosity. Perhaps even joy.

"We can put the TV there," Rajinder said softly, standing before the window and pointing to the right corner of the living room. He was slightly overweight and wore sweaters that were a bit large for him. They made him appear humble, a small man aware of his smallness. The thick black frames of his glasses, his old-fashioned mustache, as thin as a scratch, and the fading hairline created an impression of thoughtfulness. "The sofa before the window." At that moment, and often that day, I would think of myself with his smallness forever, bearing his children, going where he went, having to open always to his touch, and whatever I was looking at would begin to waver, and I would want to run. Run down the curving dark stairs, fast, fast, through the colony's narrow streets, with my sandals loud and alone, until I got to the bus stand and the 52 came, and then at the ice factory I would change to the 10, and finally I would climb the wooden steps to my parents' flat and the door would be open and no one would have noticed that I had gone with some small man.

I followed Rajinder into the bedroom, and the terror was gone, an open door now shut, and again I felt nothing, as if I were marble inside. The two rooms were exactly alike, except the bedroom was empty. "And there, the bed," Rajinder said, placing it with a slight wave of his hand against the wall across from the window. He spoke slowly and firmly, as if he were describing what was already there. "The fridge we can put right there," at the foot of the bed. Both were part of my dowry. Whenever he looked at me, I either said yes or nodded my head in agreement.

We went outside and he showed me the kitchen and the bathroom, which were connected to the flat but could be entered only through doors opening onto the roof.

From the roof, a little after eleven, I watched Rajinder drive away on his scooter. He was going to my parents' flat in the Old Vegetable Market, where my dowry and our wedding gifts were stored. I had nothing to do while he was gone, so I wandered in and out of the flat and around the roof. Defense Colony was composed of rows of pale two- or three-story buildings. A small park, edged with eucalyptus trees, was behind our house.

Rajinder returned two hours later with his elder brother, Ashok, and a yellow van. It took three trips to bring the TV, the sofa, the fridge, the mixer, the steel plates, and my clothes. Each time they left, I wanted them never to return. Whenever they pulled up outside, Ashok pressed the horn, which played "Jingle Bells." I was frightened by Ashok, because, with his handlebar mustache and muscular forearms, he reminded me of my father's brothers, who, my mother claimed, beat their wives. Listening to his curses drift out of the stairwell each time he bumped against a wall while maneuvering the sofa, TV, and fridge up the stairs, I felt ashamed, as if he were cursing the dowry and, through it, me.

On the first trip they brought back two suitcases that my mother had packed with my clothes. I was cold, and when they left, I changed in the bedroom. My hands were trembling by then, and each time I swallowed, I felt a sharp pain in my throat that made my eyes water. Standing there in the room gray with dust, the light like cold, clear water, I felt sad and lonely and excited at being naked in an empty room in a place where no one knew me. I put on a sylvar kamij, but even completely covered by the big shirt and pants, I was cold. I added a sweater and socks, but the cold had slipped under my skin and lingered beneath my fingernails.

Rajinder did not appear to notice I had changed. I swept the rooms while the men were gone, and stacked the kitchen shelves with the steel plates, saucers, and spoons that had come as gifts. Rajinder and Ashok brought all the gifts except the bed, which was too big for them. It was raised to the roof by pulleys the next day. They were able to bring up the mattress, though, and the sight of it made me happy, for I knew I would fall asleep easily and that another eight hours would pass.

We did not eat lunch, but in the evening I made rotis and lentils on a kerosene stove. The kitchen had no light bulb, and I had only the stove's blue flame to see by. The icy wind swirled around my feet. Nearly thirty years later I can still remember that wind. I could eat only one roti, while Rajinder and Ashok had six each. We sat in the living room, and they spoke loudly of their family's farm, gasoline prices, politics in Haryana, and Indira Gandhi's government. I spoke once, saying that I liked Indira Gandhi, and Ashok said that was because I was a Delhi woman who wanted to see women in power. My throat hurt and I felt as if I were breathing steam.

Ashok left after dinner, and Rajinder and I were truly alone for the first time since our marriage. Our voices were so respectful, we might have been in mourning. He took me silently in the bedroom, on the mattress beneath the window with the full moon peering in. When it was over and Rajinder was sleeping, I lifted myself on an elbow to look at him. I felt somehow that I could look at him more easily while he was asleep. I would not be nervous, trying to hide my scrutiny, and if the panic came, I could just hold on until it passed. I thought that if I could see him properly just once, I would no longer be frightened; I would know what kind of a man he was and what the future held. But the narrow mouth and the stiff, straight way he slept, with his arms folded across his chest, said one thing, and the long, dark eyelashes denied it. I stared at him until he started flickering, and then I closed my eyes.

Three months earlier, when our parents introduced us, I did not think we would marry. The neutrality of Rajinder's features, across the restaurant table from me, reassured me that we would not meet after that dinner. It was not that I expected to marry someone particularly handsome. I was neither pretty nor talented, and my family was not rich. But I could not imagine spending my life with someone so anonymous. If asked, I would have been unable to tell what kind of man I wanted to marry, whether he should be handsome and funny. I was not even certain I wanted to marry, though at times I thought marriage would make me less lonely. What I wanted was to be with someone who could make me different, someone other than the person I was.

Rajinder did not appear to be such a man, and although the fact that we were meeting meant that our families approved of each other, I still felt safe. Twice before, my parents had sat on either side of me as I met men found through the matrimonial section of the Sunday *Times of India*. One received a job offer in Bombay, and Ma and Pitaji did not want to send me that far away with someone they could not be sure of. The other, who was very handsome and drove a motorcycle, had lied about his income. I was glad that he had lied, for what could such a handsome man find in me?

Those two introductions were also held in Vikrant, a two-story dosa restaurant across from the Amba cinema. I liked Vikrant, for I thought the place's obvious cheapness would be held against us. The evening that Rajinder and I met, Vikrant was crowded with people waiting for the six-to-nine show. We sat down and an adolescent waiter swept bits of sambhar and dosa from the table onto the floor. Footsteps upstairs caused flecks of blue paint to drift down.

As the dinner began, Rajinder's mother, a small, round woman with a pockmarked face, spoke of her sorrow that Rajinder's father had not lived to see his two sons reach manhood. Ashok, sitting on one side of Rajinder, nodded slowly and solemnly at this. Rajinder gave no indication of what he thought. After a moment of silence, Pitaji, obese and bald, tilted slightly forward and said, "It's all in the stars. What can a man do?" The waiter returned with five glasses of water, his fingers dipped to the second joint in the water. Rajinder and I were supposed to speak, but I was nervous, despite my certainty that we would not marry, and could think of nothing to say. We did not open our mouths until we ordered our dosas. Pitaji, worried that we would spend the meal in silence, asked Rajinder, "Other than work, how do you like to spend your time?" Then, to impress Rajinder with his sophistication, he added in English, "What hobbies you have?" The door to the kitchen, a few tables from us, was open, and I saw a cow standing near a skillet.

"I like to read the newspaper. In college I played badminton," Rajinder answered in English. His voice was respectful, and he smoothed each word with his tongue before letting go.

"Anita sometimes reads the newspapers," Ma said, and then became quiet at the absurdity of her words.

The food came and we ate quickly and mostly in silence, though all of us made sure to leave a bit on the plate to show how full we were.

Rajinder's mother talked the most during the meal. She told us that Rajinder had always been favored over his elder brother — a beautiful, hardworking boy who obeyed his mother like God Ram — and how Rajinder had paid her back by being the first in the family to leave the farm in Bursa to attend college, where he got a master's, and by becoming a bank officer. To get to work from Bursa he had to commute two and a half hours every day. This was very strenuous, she said, and Rajinder had long ago reached the age for marriage, so he wished to set up a household in the city. "We want a city girl," his mother said loudly, as if boasting of her modernity. "With an education but a strong respect for tradition."

"Asha, Anita's younger sister, is finishing her Ph.D. in molecular biology and might be going to America in a year, for further studies," Ma said slowly, almost accidentally. She was a short, dark woman, so thin that her skin hung loose. "Two of my brothers are doctors; so is one sister. And I have one brother who is an engineer. I wanted Anita to be a doctor, but she was lazy and did not study." My mother and I loved each other, but sometimes something inside her would slip, and she would attack me, and she was so clever and I loved her so much that all I could do was feel helpless.

Dinner ended and I still had not spoken. When Rajinder said he did not want any dessert, I asked, "Do you like movies?" It was the only question I could think of, and I had felt pressured by Pitaji's stares.

"A little," Rajinder said seriously. After a pause he asked, "And you, do you like movies?"

"Yes," I said, and then, to be daring and to assert my personality, I added, "very much."

Two days after that Pitaji asked me if I would mind marrying Rajinder, and because I could not think of any reason not to, I said all right. Still, I did not think we would marry. Something would come up. His family might decide that my B.A. and B.Ed. were not enough, or Rajinder might suddenly announce that he was in love with his typist.

The engagement occurred a month later, and although I was not allowed to attend the ceremony, Asha was, and she described everything. Rajinder sat cross-legged before the pandit and the holy fire. Pitaji's pants were too tight for him to fold his legs, and he had to keep a foot on either side of the fire. Ashok and his mother were on either side of Rajinder. The small pink room was crowded with Rajinder's aunts and uncles. The uncles, Asha said, were unshaven and smelled faintly of manure. The pandit chanted in Sanskrit and at certain points motioned for Pitaji to tie a red thread around Rajinder's right wrist and to place a packet of one hundred five-rupee bills in his lap.

Only then, as Asha, grinning, described the ceremony, did I realize that I would actually marry Rajinder. I was shocked. I seemed to be standing outside myself, a stranger, looking at two women, Anita and Asha, sitting on a brown sofa in a wide, bright room. We were two women, both of whom would cry if slapped, laugh if tickled. But one was doing her Ph.D. and possibly going to America, and the other, her elder sister, who was slow in school, was now going to marry and have children and grow old. Why will she go to America and I stay here? I wanted to demand of someone, anyone. Why, when Pitaji took us out of school, saying what good was education for girls, did Asha, then only in third grade, go and re-enroll herself, while I waited for Pitaji to change his mind? I felt so sad I could not even hate Asha for her thoughtfulness.

As the days until the wedding evaporated, I had difficulty sleeping, and sometimes everything was lost in a sudden brightness. Often I woke at night and thought the engagement was a dream. Ma and Pitaji mentioned the marriage only in connection with the shopping involved. Once, Asha asked what I was feeling about the marriage, and I said, "What do you care?"

When I placed the necklace of marigolds around Rajinder's neck to seal our marriage, I brushed my hand against his neck to confirm the reality of his presence. The pandit recited Sanskrit verses, occasionally pouring clarified butter into the holy fire, which we had just circled seven times. It is done, I thought. I am married now. I felt no different. I was wearing a bright red silk sari and could smell the sourness of new cloth. People were surrounding us, many people. Movie songs blared over the loudspeakers. On the ground was a red-and-black-striped carpet. The tent above us had the same stripes. Rajinder draped a garland around my neck, and everyone began cheering. Their voices smothered the rumble of the night's traffic passing on the road outside the alley.

Although the celebration lasted another six hours, ending at about one in the morning, I did not remember most of it until many years later. I did not remember the two red thrones on which we sat and received the congratulations of women in pretty silk saris and men wearing handsome pants and shirts. I know about the cold only because of the photos showing vapor coming from people's mouths as they spoke. I still do not remember what I thought as I sat there. For nearly eight years I did not remember Ashok and his mother, Ma, Pitaji, and Asha getting in the car with us to go to the temple hostel where the people from Rajinder's side were housed. Nor did I remember walking through the long halls, with moisture on the once white walls, and seeing in rooms, long and wide, people sleeping on cots, mattresses without frames, blankets folded twice before being laid down. I did not remember all this until one evening eight years later, while wandering through Kamla Nagar market searching for a dress for Asha's first daughter. I was standing on the sidewalk looking at a stall display of hairbands and thinking of Asha's husband, a tall, yellow-haired American with a soft, open face, who I felt had made Asha happier and gentler. And then I began crying. People brushed past, trying to ignore me. I was so alone. I was thirty-three years old and so alone that I wanted to sit down on the sidewalk until someone came and picked me up.

I did remember Rajinder opening the blue door to the room where we would spend our wedding night. Before we entered, we separated for a moment. Rajinder touched his mother's feet with his right hand and then touched his forehead with that hand. His mother embraced him. I did the same with each of my parents. As Ma held me, she whispered, "Earlier your father got drunk like the pig he is." Then Pitaji put his arms around me and said, "I love you," in English.

The English was what made me cry, even though everyone thought it was the grief of parting. The words reminded me of how Pitaji came home drunk after work once or twice a month and Ma, thin arms folded across her chest, stood in the doorway of his bedroom and watched him fumbling to undress. When I was young, he held me in his lap those nights, his arm tight around my waist, and spoke into my ear in English, as if to prove that he was sober. He would say, "No one loves me. You love me, don't you, my little sun-ripened mango? I try to be good. I work all day, but no one loves me." As he spoke, he rocked in place. He would be watching Ma to make sure she heard. Gradually his voice would become husky. He would cry slowly, gently, and when the tears began to come, he would let me go and continue rocking, lost gratefully in his own sadness. Sometimes he turned out the lights and cried silently in the dark for a half-hour or more. Then he locked the door to his room and slept.

Those nights Ma offered dinner without speaking. Later she told her own story. But she did not cry, and although Ma knew how to let her voice falter as if the pain were too much to speak of, and her face crumpled with sorrow, I was more impressed by Pitaji's tears. Ma's story included some beautiful lines. Lines like "In higher secondary a teacher said, In seven years all the cells in our body change. So when Baby died, I thought, It will be all right. In seven years none of me will have touched Baby." Other lines were as fine, but this was Asha's favorite. It might have been what first interested her in microbiology. Ma would not eat dinner, but she sat with us on the floor and, leaning forward, told us how she had loved Pitaji once, but after Baby got sick and she kept sending telegrams to Beri for Pitaji to come home and he did not, she did not send a telegram about Baby's death. "What could he do," she would say, looking at the floor, "although he always cries so handsomely?" I was dazzled by her words — calling his tears handsome — in comparison with which Pitaji's ramblings appeared inept. But the grief of the tears seemed irrefutable. And because Ma loved Asha more than she did me, I was less compassionate toward her. When Pitaji awoke and asked for water to dissolve the herbs and medicines that he took to make himself vomit, I obeyed readily. When Pitaji spoke of love on my wedding night, the soft, wet vowels of his vomiting were what I remembered.

Rajinder closed and bolted the door. A double bed was in the center of the room, and near it a small table with a jug of water and two glasses. The room had yellow walls and smelled faintly of mildew. I stopped crying and suddenly felt very calm. I stood in the center of the room, a fold of the sari covering my head and falling before my eyes. I thought, I will just say this has been a terrible mistake. Rajinder lifted the sari's fold and, looking into my eyes, said he was very pleased to marry me. He was wearing a white silk kurta with tiny flowers embroidered around the neck and gold studs for buttons. He led me to the bed with his hand on my elbow and with a light squeeze let me know he wanted me to sit. He took off the loose shirt and suddenly looked small. *No, wait. I must tell you,* I said. His stomach drooped. What an ugly man, I thought. *No. Wait,* I said. He did not hear or I did not say. Louder. *You are a very nice man, I am sure.* The hard bed with the white sheet dotted with rose petals. The hands that undid the blouse and were disappointed by my small breasts. The ceiling was so far away. The moisture between my legs like breath on glass. Rajinder put his kurta back on and poured himself some water and then thought to offer me some.

Sleep was there, cool and dark, as soon as I closed my eyes. But around eight in the morning, when Rajinder shook me awake, I was exhausted. The door to our room was open, and I saw one of Rajinder's cousins, a fat, hairy man with a towel around his waist, walk past to the bathroom. He looked in and smiled broadly, and I felt ashamed. I was glad I had gotten up at some point in the night and wrapped the sari on again. I had not felt cold, but I had wanted to be completely covered.

Rajinder, Ashok, their mother, and I had breakfast in our room. We sat around the small table and ate rice and yogurt. I wanted to sleep. I wanted to tell them to go away, to stop talking about who had come last night and brought what, and who had not but might still be expected to send a gift — tell them they were boring, foolish people. Ashok and his mother spoke while Rajinder just nodded. Their words were indistinct, as if coming from across a wide room, and I felt I was dreaming them.

I wanted to close my eyes and rest my head on the table. "You eat like a bird," Rajinder's mother said, looking at me and smiling.

After breakfast we visited a widowed aunt of Rajinder's who had been unable to attend the wedding because of arthritis. She lived in a two-room flat covered with posters of gods and smelling of mothballs and old sweat. As she spoke of how carpenters and cobblers were moving in from the villages and passing themselves off as upper-castes, she drooled from the corners of her mouth. I was silent, except for when she asked me about my education and what dishes I liked to cook. As we left, she said, "A thousand years. A thousand children," and pressed fifty-one rupees into Rajinder's hands.

Then there was the long bus ride to Bursa. The roads were so bad that I kept being jolted awake, and my sleep became so fractured that I dreamed of the bus ride and being awakened. And in the village I saw grimy hens peering into the well, and women for whom I posed demurely in the courtyard. They sat in a circle around me and murmured compliments. My head and eyes were covered as they had been the night before, and as I stared at the floor, I fell asleep. I woke an hour later to their praise of my modesty. That night, in the dark room at the rear of the house, I was awakened by Rajinder's digging between my legs, and although he tried to be gentle, I just wished it over. His face, flat and distorted, was above me, and his hands raised my nipples cruelly, resentful of being cheated, even though I never heard anger in Rajinder's voice. He was always polite. Even in bed he was formal. "Could you get on all fours, please?"

So heavy and still did I feel on the first night in our new rooftop home, watching Rajinder sleep on the moonlight-soaked mattress, that I wanted the earth and sky to stop turning and for it always to be night. I did not want dawn to come and the day's activities to start again. I did not want to have to think and react to the world. I fell asleep then, only to wake in panic an hour later at the thought of the obscure life I would lead with Rajinder. Think slowly, I told myself, looking at Rajinder asleep with an arm thrown over his eyes. Slowly. I remembered the year between my B.A. and my B.Ed., when, through influence, I got a job as a typist in a candle factory. For nearly a month, upon reaching home after work, I wanted to cry, for I was terrified at the idea of giving up eight hours a day, a third of my life, to typing letters concerning supplies of wax. And then one day I noticed that I no longer felt afraid. I had learned to stop thinking. I floated above the days.

In the morning I had a fever, and the stillness it brought with it spread into the coming days. It hardened around me, so that I did not feel as if I were the one making love or cooking dinner or going home to see Ma and Pitaji and behaving there as I always had. No one guessed it was not me. Nothing could break through the stillness, not even Rajinder's learning to caress me before parting my legs, or my growing to know all the turns of the colony's alleys and the shopkeepers calling me by name.

Winter turned into spring, and the trees in the park swelled green. Rajinder was thoughtful and generous. Traveling for conferences to Baroda, Madras, Jaipur, Bangalore, he always brought back saris or other gifts. The week I had malaria, he came home every lunch hour and cooked gruel for me. On my twenty-sixth birthday he took me to the Taj Mahal and arranged to have my family hidden in the flat when we returned in the evening. What a good man, I thought then, watching him standing proudly in a corner. What a good man, I thought, and was frightened, for that was not enough. I knew I needed something else, but I did not know what. Being his wife was not so bad. He did not make me do anything I did not want to, except make love, and even that was sometimes pleasant. I did not mind his being in the flat, and being alone is difficult. When he was away on his trips, I did not miss him, and he, I think, did not miss me, for he never mentioned it.

Summer came, and hot winds swept up from the Rajasthani deserts. The old cows that wander unattended on Delhi's streets began to die. The corpses lay untouched for a week sometimes; their tongues swelled and, cracking open the jaw, stuck out absurdly.

The heat was like a high-pitched buzzing that formed a film between flesh and bone, so that my skin felt thick and rubbery and I wished that I could just peel it off. I woke at four every morning to have an hour when breathing air would not be like inhaling liquid. By five the eastern edge of the sky was too bright to look at, even though the sun had yet to appear. I bathed both before and after breakfast and again after doing laundry but before lunch. As June progressed and the very air seemed to whine under the heat's stress, I stopped eating lunch. Around two, before taking my nap, I would pour a few mugs of water on my head. I liked to lie on the bed imagining that the monsoon had come. Sometimes this made me sad, for the smell of wet earth and the sound of the rain have always made me feel as if I have been waiting for someone all my life and that person has not yet come. I dreamed often of living near the sea, in a house with a sloping red roof and bright blue window frames, and woke happy, hearing water on sand.

And so the summer passed, slowly and vengefully, until the last week of June, when the *Times of India* began its countdown to the monsoon and I awoke one afternoon in love with my husband.

I had returned home that day after spending two weeks with my parents. Pitaji had had a mild heart attack, and I took turns with Ma and Asha being with him in Safdarjung Hospital. The heart attack was no surprise, for Pitaji had become so fat that even his largest shirts had to be worn unbuttoned. So when I opened the door late one night and saw Asha with her fist up, ready to start banging again, I did not have to be told that Pitaji had woken screaming that his heart was breaking.

While I hurried a sari and blouse into a plastic bag, Asha leaned against a wall of our bedroom, drinking water. It was three. Rajinder, in his undershirt and pajama pants, sat on the bed's edge and stared at the floor. I felt no fear, perhaps because Asha had said the heart attack was not so bad, or perhaps because I just did not care. The rushing and the banging on doors appeared to be the properly melodramatic behavior when one's father might be dying.

An auto-rickshaw was waiting for us downstairs, triangular, small, with plasticized cloth covering its frame. It seemed like a vehicle for desperate people. Before getting in, I looked up and saw Rajinder. He was leaning against the railing. The moon was yellow and uneven behind him. I waved and he waved back. Such formalities, I thought, and then we were off, racing through dark, abandoned streets.

"Ma's fine. He screamed so loud," Asha said. She is a few inches taller than I am, and although she too is not pretty, she uses makeup that gives angles to her round face. Asha sat slightly turned on the seat so that she could face me. "A thousand times we told him, Lose weight," she said, shaking her head impatiently. "When the doctor gave him that diet, he said, 'Is that before or after breakfast?'" She paused and added in a tight whisper, "He's laughing now."

I felt lonely sitting there while the city was silent and dark and we talked of our father without concern. "He wants to die," I said softly. I enjoyed saying such serious words. "He is so unhappy. I think our hopes are made when we are young, and we can never adjust them to the real world. He was nearly national champion in wrestling, and for the past thirty-seven years he has been examining government schools to see that they have the right PE equipment. He loves eating, and that is as fine a way to die as any."

"If he wants to die, wonderful; I don't like him. But why is he making it difficult for us?"

Her directness shocked me and made me feel that my sentimentality was dishonest. The night air was still bitter from the evening traffic. "He is a good man," I said unsteadily.

"The way he treated us all. Ma is like a slave."

"They are just not good together. It's no one's fault."

"How can it be no one's fault?"

"His father was an alcoholic."

"How long can you use your parents as an excuse?"

I did not respond at first, for I thought Asha might be saying this because I had always used Ma and Pitaji to explain away my failures. Then I said, "Look how good he is compared with his brothers. He must have had something good inside that let him be gentler than them. We should love him for that part alone."

"That's what he is relying on. It's a big world. A lot of people are worth loving. Why love someone mediocre?"

Broken glass was in the hallways of the hospital, and someone had urinated in the elevator. When we came into the yellow room that Pitaji shared with five other men, he was asleep. His face looked like a shiny brown stone. He was on the bed nearest the window. Ma sat at the foot of his bed, her back to us, looking out at the fading night.

"He will be all right," I said.

Turning toward us, Ma said, "When he goes, he wants to make sure we all hurt." She was crying. "I thought I did not love him, but you can't live this long with a person and not love just a bit. He knew that. When they were bringing him here, he said, 'See what you've done, demoness.'"

Asha took Ma away, still crying. I spent the rest of the night dozing in a chair next to his bed.

We fell into a pattern. Ma usually came in the morning, around eight, and I replaced her, hours later. Asha would take my place at three and stay until six, and then Ma's brother or his sons would stay until Ma returned.

I had thought I would be afraid of being in the hospital, but it was very peaceful. Pitaji slept most of the day and night because of the medicines, waking up every now and then to ask for water and quickly falling asleep again. A nice boy named Rajeeve, who also was staying with his father, told me funny stories about his family. At night Asha and I slept on adjacent cots on the roof. Before she went to bed, she read five pages of an English dictionary. She had been accepted into a postdoctoral program in America. She did not brag about it as I would have. Like Ma, Asha worked very hard, as if that were the only way to live and one needn't talk about it, and as if, like Ma, she assumed that we are all equally fortunate. But sometimes Asha would shout a word at me —"Alluvial!"—and then look at me as if she were waiting for a response. Once, Rajinder came to drop off some clothes, but I was away. I did not see him or talk with him for the two weeks.

Sometimes Pitaji could not sleep and he would tell me stories of his father, a schoolteacher, who would take Pitaji with him to the saloon, so that someone would be there to guide him home when he was drunk. Pitaji was eight or nine then. His mother beat him for accompanying Dadaji, but Pitaji, his breath sounding as if it were coming through a wet cloth, said that he was afraid Dadaji would be made fun of if he walked home alone. Pitaji told the story quietly, as if he were talking about someone else, and as soon as he finished, he changed the subject. I could not tell whether Pitaji was being modest or was manipulating me by pretending modesty.

He slept most of the day, and I sat beside him, listening to his little green transistor radio. The June sun filled half the sky, and the grounds-keeper walked around the courtyard of the hospital in wide circles with a water bag as large as a man's body slung over one shoulder. He was sprinkling water to keep the dust settled. Sometimes I hummed along to Lata Mangeshkar or Mohammed Rafi singing that grief is no letter to be passed around to whoever wants to read.

There were afternoons when Pitaji became restless and whispered conspiratorially that he had always loved me most. Watching his face, puffy from the drugs, his nose broad and covered with blackheads, as he said again that Ma did not talk to him or that Asha was indifferent to his suffering, I felt exhausted. When he complained to Asha, "Your mother doesn't talk to me," she answered, "Maybe you aren't interesting."

Once, four or five days before we took him home, as he was complaining, I got up from the chair and went to look out the window. Beyond the courtyard was a string of yellow-and-black auto-rickshaws waiting under eucalyptus trees. I wanted desperately for Asha to come, so that I could leave, and bathe, and lie down to dream of a house with a red-tiled roof near the sea. "You must forgive me," Pitaji said as I looked out the window. I was surprised, for I could not remember his ever apologizing. "I sometimes forget that I will die soon and so act like a man who has many years left." I felt frightened, for I suddenly wanted to love him but could not trust him enough.

From then until we went home, Pitaji spoke little. Once, I forgot to bring his lunch from home and he did not complain, whereas before he would have screamed and tried to make me feel guilty. A few times he began crying to himself for no reason, and when I asked why, he did not answer.

Around eleven the day Pitaji was released, an ambulance carried Ma, Pitaji, and me to the Old Vegetable Market. Two orderlies, muscular men in white uniforms, carried him on a stretcher up three flights of stairs into the flat. The flat had four rooms and was part of a circle of dilapidated buildings that shared a courtyard. Fourteen or fifteen people turned out to watch Pitaji's return. Some of the very old women, sitting on cots in the courtyard, asked who Pitaji was, although he had lived there for twenty years. A few children climbed into the ambulance and played with the horn until they were chased out.

The orderlies laid Pitaji on the cot in his bedroom and left. The room was small and dark, smelling faintly of the kerosene with which the bookshelves were treated every other week to prevent termites. Traveling had tired him, and he fell asleep quickly. He woke as I was about to leave. Ma and I were speaking in whispers outside his bedroom.

"I am used to his screaming," Ma said. "He won't get any greasy food here. But once he can walk . . ."

"He seems to have changed."

"Right now he's afraid. Give him a few days and he'll return to normal. People can't change, even if they want to."

"What are you saying about me?" Pitaji tried to call out, but his voice was like wind on dry grass.

"You want something?" Ma asked.

"Water."

As I started toward the fridge, Ma said, "Nothing cold." The clay pot held only enough for one glass. I knelt beside the cot and helped Pitaji rise to a forty-five-degree angle. His heaviness and the weakness of his body moved me. Like a baby holding a bottle, Pitaji held the glass with both hands and made sucking noises as he drank. I lowered him when his shoulder muscles slackened. His eyes were red, and they moved about the room slowly. I wondered whether I could safely love him if I did not reveal my feelings.

"More?" he asked.

"Only fridge water," I said. Ma was clattering in the kitchen. "I am going home."

"Rajinder is good?" He looked at the ceiling while speaking.

"Yes," I said. A handkerchief of light covered his face, and faint blue veins, like delicate, almost translucent roots, showed through the skin of his forehead. "The results for his exam came," I told him. "He will be promoted. He was second in Delhi." Pitaji closed his eyes. "Are you hurting?" I asked.

"I feel tired."

I too felt tired. I did not know what to do with my new love or whether it would last. "That will pass, the doctor said. Why don't you sleep?"

"I don't want to," he said loudly, and my love drew back.

"I must go," I said, but made no move to.

"Forgive me," he said, and again I was surprised. "I am not worried usually, but I get frightened sometimes. Sometimes I dream that the heaviness is dirt. What an awful thing to be a Muslim or a Christian." He spoke slowly, and I felt my love returning. "Once, I dreamed of Baby's ghost."

"Oh."

"He was eight or nine and did not recognize me. He did not look like me. I was surprised, because he was my son and I had always expected him to look like me."

I felt exhausted. Something about the story was both awkward and polished, which indicated deceit. But Pitaji never lied completely, and the tiring part was not knowing. "God will forgive you," I said. But why should he? I thought. Why do people always think hurting others is all right, as long as they hurt themselves as well?

"Your mother has not."

I placed my hand on his, knowing that I was already in the trap. "Shhh."

"At your birthday, when she sang, I said, 'If you sing like that for me every day, I will love you forever.'"

"She loves you. She worries about you."

"That's not the same. When I tell Asha this, she tells me I'm sentimental. Ratha loved me once. But she cannot forgive. What happened so long ago, she cannot forgive." He was blinking rapidly, preparing to

cry. "But that is a lie. She does not love me because," and he began crying without making a sound, "I did not love her for so long."

"Shhh. She loves you. She was just saying 'Oh, I love him so. I hope he
gets better, for I love him so.'"

"Ratha could have loved me a little. She could have loved me twenty
for my eleven." He was sobbing.

"Shhh. Shhh. Shhh." I wanted to run away, far away, and be someone
else.

The sleep that afternoon was like falling. I lay down, closed my eyes, and
plummeted. I woke as suddenly, without any half-memories of dreams,
into a silence that meant that the power was gone, and the ceiling fan
was still, and the fridge was slowly warming.

It was cool, I noticed, unsurprised by the monsoon's approach — for
I was in love. The window curtains stirred, revealing TV antennas and
distant gray clouds and a few sparrows wheeling in the air. The sheet lay
bunched at my feet. I felt gigantic. My legs stretched thousands of miles;
my head rested in the Himalayas and my breath brought the world rain.
If I stood up, I would scrape against the sky. But I was small and compact and distilled too. I am in love, I thought, and a raspy voice echoed
the words in my head, causing me to panic and lose my sense of om-
nipotence for a moment. I will love Rajinder slowly and carefully and
cunningly, I thought, and suddenly felt peaceful again, as if I were a lake
and the world could only form ripples on my surface, while the calm beneath continued in solitude. Time seemed endless, and I would surely
have the minutes and seconds needed to plan a method of preserving this love, like the feeling in your stomach when you are in a car going swiftly down a hill. Don't worry, I thought, and I no longer did. My
mind obeyed me limply, as if a terrible exhaustion had worn away all
rebellion.

I got up and swung my legs off the bed. I was surprised that my love
was not disturbed by my physical movements. I walked out onto the
roof. The wind ruffled the treetops, and small gray clouds slid across
the cool, pale sky. On the street eight or nine young boys played cricket.
The school year had just started, and the children played desperately, as
if they must run faster, leap higher, to recapture the hours spent indoors.

Tell me your stories, I would ask him. Pour them into me, so that I
know everything you have ever loved or been scared of or laughed at.
But thinking this, I became uneasy and feared that when I actually saw
him, my love would fade and I would find my tongue thick and unre-

sponsive. What should I say? I woke this afternoon in love with you. I love you too, he would answer. No, no, you see, I really love you. I love you so much that I think anything is possible, that I will live forever. Oh, he would say, and I would feel my love rush out of me.

I must say nothing at first, I decided. Slowly I will win his love. I will spoil him, and he will fall in love with me. And as long as he loves me, I will be able to love him. I will love him like a camera that closes at too much light and opens at too little, so his blemishes will never mar my love.

I watched the cricket game to the end. I felt very happy standing there, as if I had just discovered some profound secret. When the children dispersed, around five, I knew Rajinder would be home soon.

I bathed and changed into new clothes. I stood before the small mirror in the armoire as I dressed. Uneven brown aureoles, a flat stomach, the veins in my feet like pen marks. Will this be enough? I wondered. Once he loves me, I told myself. I lifted my arms and tried to smell the plantlike odor of my perspiration. I wore a bright red cotton sari. What will I say first? *Namastay*—how was your day? With the informal "you." How was your day? The words felt strange, for I had never before used the informal with him. I had, as a show of modesty, never even used his name, except on the night before my wedding, when I said it over and over to myself to see how it felt—like nothing. Now when I said "Rajinder," the three syllables had too many edges, and again I doubted that he would love me. "Rajinder, Rajinder," I said rapidly several times, until it no longer felt strange. He will love me because to do otherwise would be too lonely, because I will love him so. I heard a scooter stopping outside the building and knew that he had come home.

My stomach was small and hard as I walked onto the roof. The dark clouds made it appear as if it were seven instead of five-thirty. I saw him roll the scooter into the courtyard and I felt happy. He parked the scooter and took off his gray helmet. He combed his hair carefully to hide the growing bald spot. The deliberateness of the way he tucked the comb into his back pocket overwhelmed me with tenderness. We will love each other gently and carefully, I thought.

I waited for him to rise out of the stairwell. The wind made my petticoat, drying on the clothesline, go *clap, clap*. I was smiling rigidly. How was your day? How *was* your day? Was your day good? Don't be so afraid, I told myself. What does it matter how you say hello? Tomorrow will come, and the day after, and the day after that.

His steps sounded like a shuffle. Leather rubbing against stone. Something forlorn and steady in the sound made me feel as if I were twenty years older and this were a game I should stop or I might get hurt. Rajinder, Rajinder, Rajinder, how are you?

First the head: oval, high forehead, handsome eyebrows. Then the not so broad but not so narrow shoulders. The top two buttons of the cream shirt were opened, revealing an undershirt and some hair. The two weeks had not changed him, yet seeing him, I felt as if he were somehow different, denser.

"How was your day?" I asked him while he was still in the stairwell.

"All right," he said, stepping onto the balcony. He smiled, and I felt happy. His helmet was in his left hand and he had a plastic bag of mangoes in his right. "When did you get home?" The "you" was informal, and I felt a surge of relief. He will not resist, I thought.

"A little after three."

I followed him into the bedroom. He placed the helmet on the windowsill and the mangoes in the refrigerator. His careful way of folding the plastic bag before placing it in the basket on top of the refrigerator moved me. "Your father is fine?" I did not say anything.

Rajinder walked to the sink on the outside bathroom wall. I stood in the bedroom doorway and watched him wash his hands and face with soap. Before putting the chunk of soap down, he rinsed it of foam, and only then did he pour water on himself. He used a thin washcloth hanging on a nearby hook for drying.

"Yes," I said.

"What did the doctor say?" he asked, turning toward me. He is like a black diamond, I thought.

She said, I love you. "She said he must lose weight and watch what he eats. Nothing fattening. That he should rest at first and then start exercising. Walking would be best."

I watched Rajinder hang his shirt by the collar tips on the clothesline and suddenly felt sad at the rigorous attention to detail necessary to preserve love. Perhaps love is different in other countries, I thought, where the climate is cooler, where a woman can say her husband's name, where the power does not go out every day, where not every clerk demands a bribe. That must be a different type of love, I thought, where one can be careless.

"It will rain tonight," he said, looking at the sky.

The eucalyptus trees shook their heads from side to side. "The rain always makes me feel as if I am waiting for someone," I said, and then regretted saying it, for Rajinder was not paying attention, and perhaps it could have been said better. "Why don't you sit on the balcony, and I will make sherbet to drink?"

He took a chair and the newspaper with him. The fridge water was warm, and I felt sad again at the need for constant vigilance. I made the drink and gave him his glass. I placed mine on the floor and went to get a chair. A fruit seller passed by, calling out in a reedy voice, "Sweet, sweet mangoes. Sweeter than first love." On the roof directly across, a boy seven or eight years old was trying to fly a large purple kite. I sat down beside Rajinder and waited for him to look up so that I could interrupt his reading. When Rajinder looked away from the paper to take a sip of sherbet, I asked, "Did you fly kites?"

"A little," he answered, looking at the boy. "Ashok bought some with the money he earned, and he would let me fly them sometimes." The fact that his father had died when he was young made me hopeful, for I thought that one must suffer and be lonely before one can love.

"Do you like Ashok?"

"He is my brother," he answered, shrugging and looking at the newspaper. He took a sip of the sherbet. I felt hurt, as if he had reprimanded me.

I waited until seven for the power to return; then I gave up and started to prepare dinner in the dark. I sat beside Rajinder until then. I felt happy and excited and frightened being beside him. We spoke about Asha's going to America, though Rajinder did not want to talk about this. Rajinder had been the most educated member of his and my family and resented the idea that Asha would soon assume that position.

As I cooked in the kitchen, Rajinder sat on the balcony and listened to the radio. "This is Akashwani," the announcer said, and then music like horses racing played whenever a new program was about to start. It was very hot in the kitchen, and every now and then I stepped onto the roof to look at the curve of Rajinder's neck and confirm that the tenderness was still there.

We ate in the living room. Rajinder chewed slowly and was mostly silent. Once he complimented me on my cooking. "What are you thinking?" I asked. He appeared not to have heard. Tell me! Tell me! Tell me! I thought, and was shocked by the urgency I felt.

A candle on the television made pillars of shadows rise and collapse on the walls. I searched for something to start a conversation with. "Pitaji began crying when I left."

"You could have stayed a few more days," he said.

"I did not want to." I thought of adding, "I missed you," but that would have been a lie, and I would have felt embarrassed saying it, when he had not missed me.

Rajinder mixed black pepper with his yogurt. "Did you tell him you would visit soon?"

"No. I think he was crying because he was lonely."

"He should have more courage." Rajinder did not like Pitaji, thought him weak-willed, although Rajinder had never told me that. He knew Pitaji drank, but Rajinder never referred to this, for which I was grateful. "He is old and must remember that shadows creep into one's heart at his age." The shutter of a bedroom window began slamming, and I got up to latch it shut.

I washed the dishes while Rajinder bathed. When he came out, dressed in his white kurta pajamas, with his hair slicked back, I was standing near the railing at the roof's edge, looking out beyond the darkness of our neighborhood at a distant ribbon of light. I was tired from the nervousness I had been feeling all evening. Rajinder came up behind me and asked, "Won't you bathe?" I suddenly doubted my ability to guard my love. Bathe so we can have sex. His words were too deliberately full of the unsaid, and so felt vulgar. I wondered if I had the courage to say no and realized I didn't. What kind of love can we have? I thought.

I said, "In a little while. Comedy hour is about to start." We sat down on our chairs with the radio between us and listened to Maurya's whiny voice. This week he had gotten involved with criminals who wanted to go to jail to collect the reward on themselves. The canned laughter gusted from several flats. When the music of the racing horses marked the close of the show, I felt hopeful again, and thought Rajinder looked very handsome in his kurta pajamas.

I bathed carefully, pouring mug after mug of cold water over myself until my fingertips were wrinkled and my nipples erect. The candlelight made the bathroom orange and my skin copper. I washed my pubis carefully to make sure no smell remained from urinating. Rubbing myself dry, I became aroused. I wore the red sari again, with a new blouse, and no bra, so that my nipples would show.

I came and stood beside Rajinder, my arm brushing against his kurta sleeve. Every now and then a raindrop fell, and I wondered if I was imagining it. On balconies and roofs all around us I could see the dim figures of men, women, and children waiting for the first rain. "You look pretty," he said. Somewhere Lata Mangeshkar sang with a static-induced huskiness. The street was silent. Even the children were hushed. As the wind picked up, Rajinder said, "Let's close the windows."

The wind coursed along the floor, upsetting newspapers and climbing the walls to swing on curtains. A candle stood on the refrigerator. As I leaned over to pull a window shut, Rajinder pressed against me and cupped my right breast. I felt a shock of desire pass through me. As I walked around the rooms shutting windows, he touched my buttocks, pubis, stomach.

When the last window was closed, I waited for a moment before turning around, because I knew he wanted me to turn around quickly. He pulled me close, with his hands on my buttocks. I took his tongue in my mouth. We kissed like this for a long time.

The rain began falling, and we heard a roar from the people on the roofs nearby. "The clothes," Rajinder said, and pulled away.

We ran out. We could barely see each other. Lightning bursts would illuminate an eye, an arm, some teeth, and then darkness would come again. We jerked the clothes off and let the pins fall to the ground. We deliberately brushed roughly against each other. The raindrops were like thorns, and we began laughing. Rajinder's shirt had wrapped itself around and around the clothesline. Wiping his face, he knocked his glasses off. As I saw him crouch and fumble around helplessly for them, I felt such tenderness that I knew I would never love him as much as I did at that moment. "The wind in the trees," I cried out, "it sounds like the sea."

We slowly wandered back inside, kissing all the while. He entered me like a sigh. He suckled on me and moved back and forth and side to side, and I felt myself growing warm and loose. He sucked on my nipples and held my waist with both hands. We made love gently at first, but as we both neared climax, Rajinder began stabbing me with his penis and I came in waves so strong that I felt myself vanishing. When Rajinder sank on top of me, I kept saying, "I love you. I love you."

"I love you too," he answered. Outside, the rain came in sheets and the thunder was like explosions in caverns.

The candle had gone out while we made love, and Rajinder got up to light it. He drank some water and then lay down beside me. I wanted some water too, but did not want to say anything that would make him feel bad about his thoughtlessness. "I'll be getting promoted soon. Minaji loves me," Rajinder said. I rolled onto my side to look at him. He had his arms folded across his chest. "Yesterday he said, 'Come, Rajinderji, let us go write your confidential report.'" I put my hand on his stomach, and Rajinder said, "Don't," and pushed it away. "I said, 'Oh, I don't know whether that would be good, sir.' He laughed and patted me on the back. What a nincompoop. If it weren't for the quotas, he would never be manager." Rajinder chuckled. "I'll be the youngest bank manager in Delhi." I felt cold and tugged a sheet over our legs. "In college I had a schedule for where I wanted to be by the time I was thirty. By twenty-two I became an officer; soon I'll be a manager. I wanted a car, and we'll have that in a year. I wanted a wife, and I have that."

"You are so smart."

"Some people in college were smarter. But I knew exactly what I wanted. A life is like a house. One has to plan carefully where all the furniture will go."

"Did you plan me as your wife?" I asked, smiling.

"No. I had wanted at least an M.A., and someone who worked, but Mummy didn't approve of a daughter-in-law who worked. I was willing to change my requirements. Because I believe in moderation, I was successful. Everything in its place. And pay for everything. Other people got caught up in love and friendship. I've always felt that these things only became a big deal because of the movies."

"What do you mean? You love me and your mother, don't you?"

"There are so many people in the world that it is hard not to think that there are others you could love more."

Seeing the shock on my face, he quickly added, "Of course I love you. I just try not to be too emotional about it." The candle's shadows on the wall were like the wavery bands formed by light reflected off water. "We might even be able to get a foreign car."

The second time he took me that night, it was from behind. He pressed down heavily on my back and grabbed my breasts.

I woke at four or five. The rain scratched against the windows and a light like blue milk shone along the edges of the door. I was cold and tried to wrap myself in the sheet, but it was not large enough.

1997

JUNOT DÍAZ
FIESTA, 1980

from *Story*

JUNOT DÍAZ was born in the Dominican Republic in 1968. At the age of six he immigrated to New Jersey. He earned his BA from Rutgers College in 1992, working his way through by washing dishes, pumping gas, and delivering pool tables.

After graduation, Díaz worked at Rutgers University Press as an editorial assistant and created the quasi-autobiographical character Yunior, who appeared in a story he included as part of his application to the MFA program at Cornell University. The character became central to much of his later work, including the stories in *Drown*, his first collection, and *This Is How You Lose Her*. Díaz earned his MFA in 1995.

Díaz has described his writing as "a disobedient child of New Jersey and the Dominican Republic if that can be possibly imagined with way too much education."

He received the Pulitzer Prize for Fiction for his novel *The Brief Wondrous Life of Oscar Wao* in 2008 and was a 2012 MacArthur Fellow. Currently Díaz teaches creative writing at the Massachusetts Institute of Technology and is the fiction editor for *The Boston Review*.

★

MAMI'S YOUNGEST SISTER — my Tía Yrma — finally made it to the United States that year. She and Tío Miguel got themselves an apartment in the Bronx, off the Grand Concourse, and everybody decided that we should have a party. Actually, my dad decided, but everybody — meaning Mami, Tía Yrma, Tío Miguel, and their neighbors — thought it a dope idea. On the Friday of the party Papi got back from work around six. Right on time. We were all dressed by then, which was a smart move on our part. If Papi had walked in and caught us lounging around in our underwear, man, he would have kicked our asses something serious.

He didn't say nothing to nobody, not even to my moms. He just pushed past her, held up his hand when she tried to talk to him, and jumped into the shower. Rafa gave me the look and I gave it back to him; we both knew Papi had been out with the Puerto Rican woman he was seeing and wanted to wash off the evidence quick.

Mami looked really nice that day. The United States had finally put some meat on her; she was no longer the same flaca who had arrived here three years before. She had cut her hair short and was wearing tons of cheap-ass jewelry, which on her was kinda attractive. She smelled like herself, which meant she smelled good, like the wind through a tree. She always waited until the last possible minute to put on her perfume because she said it was a waste to spray it on early and then have to spray it on again once you got to the party.

We — meaning me, my brother, my little sister, and Mami — waited for Papi to finish his shower. Mami seemed anxious, in her usual dispassionate way. Her hands adjusted the buckle of her belt over and over again. That morning, when she had gotten us up for school, Mami told us that she wanted to have a good time at the party. I want to dance, she said, but now, with the sun sliding out of the sky like spit off a wall, she seemed ready to just get this over with.

Rafa didn't much want to go to no party either, and me, I never wanted to go anywhere with my family. There was a baseball game in the parking lot outside and we could hear our friends yelling, Hey, and, You suck, to one another. We heard the pop of a ball as it sailed over the cars, the clatter of an aluminum bat dropping to the concrete. Not that me or Rafa loved baseball; we just liked playing with the local kids, thrashing them at anything they were doing. By the sounds of the shouting, we both knew the game was close, either of us could have made a difference. Rafa frowned, and when I frowned back, he put up his fist. Don't you mirror me, he said.

Don't you mirror me, I said.

He punched me — I would have hit him back but right then Papi marched into the living room with his towel around his waist, looking a lot smaller than he did when he was dressed. He had a few strands of hair around his nipples and a surly closed-mouth expression, like maybe he had scalded his tongue or something.

Have they eaten? he asked Mami.

She nodded. I made you something.

You didn't let him eat, did you?

Dios mio, she said, letting her arms fall to her side.

Dios mio is right, Papi said.

I was never supposed to eat before our car trips, but earlier, when she had put out our dinner of rice, beans, and sweet platanos, guess who had been the first one to gobble his meal down? You couldn't blame Mami really, she had been busy — cooking, getting ready, dressing my sister Madai. I should have reminded her not to feed me but I hadn't been thinking. Even if I had, I doubt I would have told her.

Papi turned to me. Why did you eat?

Rafa had already inched away from me. I'd once told him I considered him a low-down chickenshit for moving out of the way every time Papi was going to smack me.

Collateral damage, he said. Ever heard of it?

No.

Look it up.

Chickenshit or not, right then I didn't dare glance at him. Papi was old-fashioned; he expected you to attend him, but not stare into his eyes, while you were getting your ass whupped. I studied Papi's belly-button, which was perfectly round and immaculate. Papi pulled me to my feet by my ear.

If you throw up —

I won't, I said, tears in my eyes, more out of reflex than pain.

It's not his fault, Mami said. I fed them before I reminded them about the party.

They've known about this party forever. How did they think we were going to get there? Fly?

He finally let go of my ear and I went back to my seat. Madai was too scared to open her eyes. Being around Papi all her life had turned her into a big-time wuss. Anytime Papi raised his voice her lip would start trembling, like it was some sort of specialized tuning fork. Rafa pretended that he had knuckles to crack, and when I shoved him, he gave me a *Don't start* look. But even that little bit of recognition made me feel better.

I was the one who was always in trouble with my dad. It was like my God-given role to piss him off, to do everything the way he hated. It didn't bother me too much, really. I still wanted him to love me, something that never seemed strange or contradictory until years later, when he was out of our lives.

Before I knew it Papi was dressed and Mami was crossing each one of us, solemnly, like we were heading off to war. We said, in turn, Bendición, Mami, and she poked us in our five cardinal spots while saying, Que Dios te bendiga.

This was how we began all our trips, the words that followed me every time I left the house.

None of us said anything else until we were in Papi's Volkswagen van. Brand new, lime green, bought to impress. Oh, we were impressed, considering we couldn't afford no VW van, used or new, but me, each time I got in that VW and Papi went above twenty miles an hour, I vomited. I'd never had trouble with cars before, and that van was like my curse. Mami suspected it was the upholstery. In her mind, American things — appliances, mouthwash, funny-looking upholstery — all seemed to have an intrinsic badness. Papi was careful about taking me anywhere in the VW, but when he did, like that night, I had to ride up front in Mami's usual seat so I could throw up out a window.

You okay? Mami asked over my shoulder as Papi got us onto the turnpike. She had her hand on the small of my neck. One thing about Mami, even when she was nervous, her palms never sweated.

I'm okay, I said, keeping my eyes straight ahead. I definitely didn't want to trade glances with Papi. He had this one look, furious and sharp, that always left me feeling bruised.

Toma. Mami handed me four mentas. She had thrown a few out her window at the beginning of our trip, an offering to Eshú; the rest were for me. Mami considered these candies a cure-all for any disorder.

I took one and sucked it slowly, my tongue knocking it up against my teeth. As always, it helped. We passed Newark Airport without any incident. If Madai had been awake she would have cried because the planes flew so close to the cars.

How's he feeling? Papi asked.

Fine, I said. I glanced back at Rafa and he pretended like he didn't see me. That was the way he was, both at school and at home. When I was in trouble, he didn't know me. Madai was solidly asleep, but even with her face all wrinkled up and drooling she looked cute.

I turned around and concentrated on the candy. Papi even started to joke that we might not have to scrub the van out tonight. He was beginning to loosen up, not checking his watch too much. Maybe he was thinking about that Puerto Rican woman or maybe he was just happy that we were all together. I could never tell. At the toll, he was feeling positive enough to actually get out of the van and search around under the basket for dropped coins. It was something he had once done to amuse Madai, but now it was habit. Cars behind us honked their horns and I slid down in my seat. Rafa didn't care; he just grinned back at the other cars. His actual job was to make sure no cops were coming. Mami shook Madai awake, and as soon as she saw Papi stooping for a couple of quarters she let out this screech of delight that almost took the top of my head off.

That was the end of the good times. Just outside the Washington Bridge, I started feeling woozy. The smell of the upholstery got all up inside my head and I found myself with a mouthful of saliva. Mami's hand tensed on my shoulder and when I caught Papi's eye, he was like, No way. Don't do it.

The first time I got sick in the van Papi was taking me to the library. Rafa was with us and he couldn't believe I threw up. I was famous for my steel-lined stomach. A third-world childhood could give you that. Papi was worried enough that just as quick as Rafa could drop the books off we were on our way home. Mami fixed me one of her honey-and-onion concoctions and that made my stomach feel better. A week later we tried the library again, and on this go-around I couldn't get the window open in time. When Papi got me home, he went and cleaned out the van himself, an expression of asco on his face. This was a big deal, since Papi almost never cleaned anything himself. He came back inside and found me sitting on the couch; I was feeling like hell.

It's the car, he said to Mami. It's making him sick.

This time the damage was pretty minimal, nothing Papi couldn't wash off the door with a blast of the hose. He was pissed, though; he jammed his finger into my cheek, a nice solid thrust. That was the way he was with his punishments: imaginative. Earlier that year I'd written an essay in school called "My Father the Torturer," but the teacher made me write a new one. She thought I was kidding.

We drove the rest of the way to the Bronx in silence. We only stopped once, so I could brush my teeth. Mami had brought along my toothbrush and a tube of toothpaste and while every car known to man sped by us she stood outside with me so I wouldn't feel alone.

Tío Miguel was about seven feet tall and had his hair combed up and out, into a demi-'fro. He gave me and Rafa big spleen-crushing hugs and then kissed Mami and finally ended up with Madai on his shoulder. The last time I'd seen Tío was at the airport, his first day in the United

States. I remembered how he hadn't seemed all that troubled to be in another country.

He looked down at me. Carajo, Yunior, you look horrible!

He threw up, my brother explained.

I pushed Rafa. Thanks a lot, ass-face.

Hey, he said. Tío asked.

Tío clapped a bricklayer's hand on my shoulder. Everybody gets sick sometimes, he said. You should have seen me on the plane over here. Dios mio! He rolled his small Asian-looking eyes for emphasis. I thought we were all going to die.

Everybody could tell he was lying. I smiled like he was making me feel better.

Do you want me to get you a drink? Tío asked. We got beer and rum.

Miguel, Mami said. He's young.

Young? Back in Santo Domingo, he'd be getting laid by now.

Mami thinned her lips, which took some doing.

Well, it's true, Tío said.

So, Mami, I said, when do I get to go visit the D.R.?

That's enough, Yunior.

It's the only pussy you'll ever get, Rafa said to me in English.

Not counting your girlfriend, of course.

Rafa smiled. He had to give me that one.

Papi came in from parking the van. He and Miguel gave each other the sort of handshakes that would have turned my fingers into Wonder bread.

Long time, compa'i, Tío said.

Compa'i, ¿como va todo?

Tía came out then, with an apron on and maybe the longest Lee Press-On Nails I've ever seen in my life. There was this one guru guy I'd seen in the *Guinness Book of World Records* who had longer nails, but I tell you, it was close. She gave everybody kisses, told me and Rafa how guapo we were — Rafa, of course, believed her — told Madai how bella she was, but when she got to Papi, she froze a little, like maybe she'd seen a wasp on the tip of his nose, but then she kissed him all the same. Just a peck really.

Look at that, Rafa whispered to me in English.

Mami told us to join the other kids in the living room. Tío said, Wait a minute, I want to show you the apartment. I was glad Tía said, Hold on, because from what I'd seen so far, the place had been furnished in Contemporary Dominican Tacky. The less I saw, the better. I mean, I liked plastic sofa covers but damn, Tío and Tía had taken it to another level. They had a disco ball hanging in the living room and the type of stucco ceilings that looked like stalactite heaven. The sofas all had golden tassels dangling from their edges. Tía came out of the kitchen with some people I didn't know and by the time she got done introducing everybody, only Papi and Mami were given the guided tour of the four-room, third-floor apartment. Me and Rafa joined the kids in the living room. Their parents wouldn't be over until late, but the kids had come over anyway. We were hungry, one of the girls explained, a pastelito in hand. The boy was about three years younger than me but the girl who'd spoken, Leti, was my age. She and another girl were on the sofa together and they were cute as hell.

Leti introduced them: the boy was her brother Wilquins and the other girl was her neighbor Mari. Leti had some serious tetas and I could tell that my brother was going to gun for her. His taste in girls was predictable. He sat down right between Leti and Mari, and by the way they were smiling at him I knew he'd do fine. Neither of the girls gave me more than a cursory one-two, which didn't bother me. Sure, I liked girls, but I was always too terrified to speak to them unless we were arguing or I was calling them stupidos, which was one of my favorite words that year. I turned to Wilquins and asked him what there was to do around here. Mari, who had the lowest voice I'd ever heard, said, He can't speak.

What does that mean?

He's mute.

I looked at Wilquins incredulously. He smiled and nodded, as if he'd won a prize or something.

Does he understand? I asked.

Of course he understands, Rafa said. He's not dumb.

I could tell Rafa had said that just to score points with the girls. Both of them nodded. Low-voice Mari said, He's the best student in his grade.

I thought, Not bad for a mute. I sat next to Wilquins. After about two seconds of TV, Wilquins whipped out a bag of dominoes and motioned to me. Did I want to play? Sure. Me and him played Rafa and Leti and we whupped their collective asses twice, which put Rafa in a real bad mood. Leti kept whispering into Rafa's ear, telling him it was okay.

In the kitchen I could hear my parents slipping into their usual modes. Papi's voice was loud and argumentative; you didn't have to be anywhere near him to catch his drift. And Mami, you had to strain your ears to hear her. I went into the kitchen a few times: once so the tíos could show off how much bullshit I'd been able to cram in my head the last few years, another time for a bucket-sized cup of soda. Mami and Tía were frying tostones and the last of the pastelitos. She appeared happier now, and the way her hands worked on our dinner you would think she had a life somewhere else making rare and precious things. She nudged Tía every now and then, shit they must have been doing all their lives. As soon as Mami saw me, though, she gave me the eye. Don't stay long, that eye said. Don't piss your old man off.

Papi was too busy arguing about Elvis to notice me. Then somebody mentioned Cubans and Papi had plenty to say about them, too.

Maybe I was used to him. His voice—louder than most adults'— didn't bother me none, though the other kids shifted uneasily in their seats. Wilquins got up to raise the volume on the TV, but Rafa said, I wouldn't do that. Muteboy had some balls. He did it anyway and then sat down. Wilquins's pop came into the living room a second later, a bottle of Presidente in hand. That dude must have had Spider-senses or something. Did you raise that? he asked Wilquins, and Wilquins nodded.

Is this your house? Pa Wilquins asked. He looked ready to kick Wilquins's ass but he lowered the volume instead.

See, Rafa said. You nearly got your ass *kicked*.

I met the Puerto Rican woman right after Papi had gotten the van. He was taking me on short trips, trying to cure me of my vomiting. It wasn't really working but I looked forward to our trips, even though at the end of each one I'd be sick. These were the only times me and Papi did anything together. When we were alone he treated me much better, like maybe I was his son or something.

Before each drive Mami always crossed me.

Bendición, Mami, I would say.

She would kiss my forehead. Que Dios te bendiga. And then she would give me a handful of mentas because she wanted me to be okay. Mami didn't think these excursions would cure me, but the one time she had brought it up to Papi, he had told her to shut up and what did she know about anything anyway?

Me and Papi didn't talk much. We just drove around our neighborhood. Occasionally he would ask, How is it?

And I would nod, no matter how I felt.

One day I got sick outside of Perth Amboy. Instead of taking me home like he usually did, he went the other way on Industrial Avenue,

stopping a few minutes later in front of a light blue house I didn't recognize. It reminded me of the Easter eggs we colored at school, the ones
we threw out the bus windows at other cars.

The Puerto Rican woman was there and she helped me clean up. She
had dry papery hands and when she rubbed the towel on my chest, she
did it hard, like I was a bumper she was waxing. She was very thin and
had a cloud of brown hair rising above her narrow face and the sharp-
est, blackest eyes you've ever seen.

He's cute, she said to Papi. What's your name? she asked me. Are you
Rafa?

I shook my head.

Then it's Yunior, right?

I nodded.

You're the smart one, she said, suddenly happy with herself. Maybe
you want to see my books?

They weren't hers. I recognized them as ones my father must have
left in her house. Papi was a voracious reader, couldn't even go cheating
without a paperback in his pocket.

Why don't you go watch TV? Papi suggested. He already had his hand
on her ass and didn't care that I was watching. He was looking at her like
she was the last piece of chicken on earth.

We got plenty of channels, she said. Use the remote if you want.

The two of them went upstairs and I was too scared of what was happening to poke around. I just sat there, ashamed, expecting something
big and fiery to crash down on all our heads. I watched a whole hour of
the news before Papi came downstairs and said, Let's go.

About two hours later the women laid out the food and like always nobody but the kids thanked them. It must have been some Dominican
tradition or something. There was everything I liked — chicharrónes,
fried chicken, tostones, sancocho, rice, fried cheese, yucca, avocado, potato salad, a meteor-sized hunk of pernil, even a tossed salad, which I
could do without — but when I joined the other kids around the serving table, Papi said, Oh, no you don't, and took the paper plate out of my
hand. His fingers weren't gentle.

What's wrong now? Tía asked, handing me another plate.

He ain't eating, Papi said. Mami pretended to help Rafa with the
pernil.

Why can't he eat?

Because I said so.

The adults who didn't know us made like they hadn't heard a thing and Tío just smiled sheepishly and told everybody to go ahead and eat. All the kids—about ten of them now—trooped back into the living room with their plates aheaping, and all the adults ducked into the kitchen and the dining room, where the radio was playing loud-ass bachatas. I was the only one without a plate. Papi stopped me before I could get away from him. He kept his voice nice and low so nobody else could hear him.

If you eat anything, I'm going to beat you. ¿Entiendes?

I nodded.

And if your brother gives you any food, I'll beat him, too. Right here in front of everybody. ¿Entiendes?

I nodded again. I wanted to kill him, and he must have sensed it because he gave my head a little shove.

All the kids watched me come in and sit down in front of the TV.

What's wrong with your dad? Leti asked.

He's a dick, I said.

Rafa shook his head. Don't say that shit in front of people.

Easy for you to be nice when you're eating, I said.

Hey, if I was a pukey little baby, I wouldn't get no food either.

I almost said something back but I concentrated on the TV. I wasn't going to start it. No fucking way. So I watched Bruce Lee beat Chuck Norris into the floor of the Coliseum and tried to pretend that there was no food anywhere in the house. It was Tía who finally saved me. She came into the living room and said, Since you ain't eating, Yunior, you can at least help me get some ice.

I didn't want to, but she mistook my reluctance for something else.

I already asked your father.

She held my hand while we walked; Tía didn't have any kids but I could tell she wanted them. She was the sort of relative who always remembered your birthday but who you only went to visit because you had to. We didn't get past the first-floor landing before she opened her pocketbook and handed me the first of three pastelitos she had smuggled out of the apartment.

Go ahead, she said. And as soon as you get inside, make sure you brush your teeth.

Thanks a lot, Tía, I said.

Those pastelitos didn't stand a chance.

She sat next to me on the stairs and smoked her cigarette. All the way down on the first floor we could hear the music and the adults and the television. Tía looked a ton like Mami; the two of them were both short and light-skinned. Tía smiled a lot and that was what set them the most apart.

How is it at home, Yunior?

What do you mean?

How's it going in the apartment? Are you kids okay?

I knew an interrogation when I heard one, no matter how sugar-coated or oblique it was. I didn't say anything. Don't get me wrong, I loved my tía, but something told me to keep my mouth shut. Maybe it was family loyalty, maybe I just wanted to protect Mami or I was afraid that Papi would find out — it could have been anything really.

Is your mom all right?

I shrugged.

Have there been lots of fights?

None, I said. Too many shrugs would have been just as bad as an answer. Papi's at work too much.

Work, Tía said, like it was somebody's name she didn't like.

Me and Rafa, we didn't talk much about the Puerto Rican woman. When we ate dinner at her house, the few times Papi had taken us over there, we still acted like nothing was out of the ordinary. Pass the ketchup, man. No sweat, bro. The affair was like a hole in our living room floor, one we'd gotten so used to circumnavigating that we sometimes forgot it was there.

By midnight all the adults were getting crazy on the dance floor. I was sitting outside Tía's bedroom, where Madai was sleeping, trying not to attract attention. Rafa had me guarding the door; he and Leti were in there, too, with some of the other kids, getting busy no doubt. Wilquins had gone across the hall to bed, so I had only the roaches to mess around with.

Whenever I peered into the main room I saw about twenty moms and dads dancing and drinking beers. Every now and then somebody yelled, Quisqueya! And then everybody else would yell and stomp their feet. From what I could see, my parents seemed to be enjoying themselves.

Mami and Tía spent a lot of time side by side, whispering, and I kept expecting something to come of this, a brawl maybe. I'd never once been out with my family when it hadn't turned to shit. We were a Doomsday on wheels. We weren't even theatrical or straight crazy like other families. We fought like sixth graders, without any real dignity. I guess the whole night I'd been waiting for a blowup, something between Papi and Mami. This was how I always figured Papi would be exposed, out in public, where everybody would know.

You're a cheater!

But everything was calmer than usual. And Mami didn't look like she was about to say anything to Papi. The two of them danced every now and then, but they never lasted more than a song before Mami rejoined Tía in whatever conversation they were having.

I tried to imagine Mami before Papi. Maybe I was tired, or just sad, thinking about the way my family was. Maybe I already knew how it would all end up in a few years, Mami without Papi, and that was why I did it. Picturing her alone wasn't easy. It seemed like Papi had always been with her, even when we were waiting in Santo Domingo for him to send for us.

The only photograph our family had of Mami as a young woman, before she married Papi, was the one that somebody took of her at an election party, which I found one day while rummaging for money to go to the arcade. Mami had it tucked into her immigration papers. In the photo, she's surrounded by laughing cousins I will never meet who are all shiny from dancing, whose clothes are rumpled and loose. You can tell it's night and hot and that the mosquitoes have been biting. She sits straight, and even in a crowd she stands out, smiling quietly like maybe she's the one everybody's celebrating. You can't see her hands but I imagined they're knotting a straw or a bit of thread. This was the woman my father met a year later on the Malecón, the woman Mami thought she'd always be.

Mami must have caught me studying her because she stopped what she was doing and gave me a smile, maybe her first one of the night. Suddenly I wanted to go over and hug her, for no other reason than I loved her, but there were about eleven fat jiggling bodies between us. So I sat down on the tiled floor and waited.

I must have fallen asleep, because the next thing I knew Rafa was kicking me and saying, Let's go. He looked like he'd been hitting off those girls; he was all smiles. I got to my feet in time to kiss Tía and Tío goodbye. Mami was holding the serving dish she had brought with her.

Where's Papi? I asked.

He's downstairs, bringing the van around. Mami leaned down to kiss me.

You were good today, she said.

And then Papi burst in and told us to get the hell downstairs before some pendejo cop gave him a ticket. More kisses, more handshakes, and then we were gone.

I don't remember being out of sorts after I met the Puerto Rican woman, but I must have been, because Mami only asked me questions when she thought something was wrong in my life. It took her about ten passes but finally she cornered me one afternoon when we were alone in the apartment. Our upstairs neighbors were beating the crap out of their kids, and me and her had been listening to it all afternoon. She put her hand on mine and said, Is everything okay, Yunior? Have you been fighting with your brother?

Me and Rafa had already talked. We'd been in the basement, where our parents couldn't hear us. He told me that yeah, he knew about her.

Papi's taken me there twice now.

Why didn't you tell me? I asked.

What the hell was I going to say?

I didn't say anything to Mami either. She watched me, very, very closely. Later I would think, maybe if I had told her, she would have confronted him, would have done something, but who can know these things? I said I'd been having trouble in school, and like that everything was back to normal between us. She put her hand on my shoulder and squeezed, and that was that.

We were on the turnpike, just past Exit 11, when I started feeling it again. I sat up from leaning against Rafa. His fingers smelled and he'd gone to sleep almost as soon as he got into the van. Madai was out, too, but at least she wasn't snoring. In the darkness, I saw that Papi had a hand on Mami's knee and that the two of them were quiet and still. They weren't slumped back or anything; they were both wide awake, buckled into their seats. I couldn't see either of their faces and no matter how hard I tried I could not imagine their expressions. Every now and then the van was filled with the bright rush of somebody else's headlights. Finally I said, Mami, and they both looked back, already knowing what was happening.

2000-2010

WITH THE EVENTS OF 9/11 CAME A SENSE THAT FICTION
and even literature was irrelevant. The irony so popular in the 1990s
suddenly seemed beside the point. New York, home to so many writers and publishers, was shaken to its core. In her foreword to the 2002
volume, series editor Katrina Kenison wrote, "Preoccupied with the
unfathomable changes in our world at large, it was almost impossible
to focus on the details of a smaller picture." In the 2003 volume, Nicole Krauss's story "Future Emergencies" indirectly addressed the attacks in New York. In 2004 Joyce Carol Oates and David Foster Wal-
lace published stories that featured, directly and indirectly, 9/11. Despite
the preponderance of flags raised and anthems sung across the country,
though, few stories romanticized patriotism or "denaturalized" (in series editor Edward O'Brien's words) the event.

Before long, short stories began to address, with both irony and outrage, the wars in Afghanistan and Iraq, Hurricane Katrina, and the 2008
economic collapse. Perhaps because of the Internet and its ability to
connect people instantaneously — or because of the location of the 9/11
attacks, closer to home than ever before — the grieving period necessary
for earlier generations to write effectively of war seemed to have shrunk.

Writers such as Jhumpa Lahiri, Edwidge Danticat, Daniel Alarcón,
and David Bezmozgis explored the immigrant experience in the United
States. Ha Jin, Mary Yukari Waters, and Aleksandar Hemon portrayed
current and historic postwar daily realities and cultural norms in other
countries.

The Great Recession brought about a sea change in magazine and
book publishing. The struggling economy coupled with the flood of
new e-readers that offered major discounts led to decreased circula-

tions in magazines as well as decreased book sales. Book publishers became less willing to take chances on story collections by new writers. Cuts were made at publishing houses. *The Atlantic* annexed its fiction to a separate fiction-only issue offered just once a year, and eventually stopped publishing this issue altogether in favor of occasionally featuring fiction in its monthly. Many magazines, such as *TriQuarterly*, opted to save production costs by moving entirely online.

There came a hunger for more entertaining short fiction. Genre-bending or -blending became popular. In 2005 guest editor Michael Chabon wrote:

> The original sense of the word *entertainment* is a lovely one of mutual support through intertwining . . . between reader and writer . . . We ought not to restrict ourselves to one type or category. Science fiction, fantasy, crime fiction — all these genres and others have rich traditions in the American short story, reaching straight back to Poe and Hawthorne . . . But the same process of commercialization and mass appeal that discredited entertainment, or the idea of literature as entertainment, also devastated our notion of the kinds of short stories that belong in college syllabi, prestigious magazines, or yearly anthologies of the best American short stories (another victory, in my view, for the enemies of pleasure, in their corporate or ivory towers).

After *Story* magazine folded, new magazines like *Tin House, McSweeney's,* and *Zoetrope: All-Story* became instrumental in discovering and publishing new talent.

In 2006 I was offered the role of series editor. At the time I was, like Ravenel and Kenison had been, an editor at Houghton Mifflin. I was raised in Concord, Massachusetts, attended McGill University in Montreal as an undergraduate, and got my MFA at Emerson College in Boston. I got a temp job as the receptionist at Houghton Mifflin, and before long I was hired as an assistant to an editor who published travel guides. When Houghton sold off this line of books, I was lucky to be hired as an assistant to a fiction editor, who went on to become publisher. I worked as an assistant and eventually an editor for nine years.

I suspect that my first year as series editor will be one of my most memorable. I published my first novel, gave birth to twins, and worked with Stephen King, who insisted on reading along with me to ensure that I gave close consideration to science fiction and horror. In my first foreword, I wrote, "I was drawn to stories that transcended something

... the stories I chose twisted and turned away from the familiar and ultimately took flight, demanding their own particular characters and structure and prose." I also mentioned my predilection for surprise, "[a story] that quietly taps the reader on the shoulder and then takes her breath away without revealing any of its secrets."

For the remainder of the decade I worked with Salman Rushdie, who was jarred by the number of stories about golf that Americans wrote; Alice Sebold, reluctant to have to name "the best" of anything; and Richard Russo, who, like Chabon, called in his introduction for stories to be entertaining as well as instructive.

My reading process is probably messier than my predecessors'. I mark up literary journals as I read, making comments beside the tables of contents about the stories that I like and why. I pull any story that I finish reading.

Long ago, Edward O'Brien wrote letters to notify authors that their story had been selected for inclusion in *The Best American Short Stories*. When I started as series editor, I e-mailed all the contributors. Occasionally I must reach them on Facebook. All my correspondence with authors and guest editors and magazine editors is now done online. Although I occasionally read online, I prefer that magazines print out digital stories and submit them to me via snailmail.

★　★　★

2000

JHUMPA LAHIRI
THE THIRD AND FINAL CONTINENT

from *The New Yorker*

JHUMPA LAHIRI was born in London in 1967 and raised in Rhode Island. She earned degrees in English, Creative Writing and Renaissance Studies from Barnard College and Boston University.

Lahiri's short story collection *Interpreter of Maladies* was published in 1999. The stories mostly explore the lives of recent immigrants and their children. Lahiri later wrote, "When I first started writing I was not conscious that my subject was the Indian-American experience. What drew me to my craft was the desire to force the two worlds I occupied to mingle on the page as I was not brave enough, or mature enough, to allow in life." Her story collection received the 2000 Pulitzer Prize for Fiction (rare for a story collection) as well as the PEN/Hemingway Award and *The New Yorker* Debut of the Year.

Lahiri's novel *The Namesake* was a finalist for the *Los Angeles Times* Book Prize. Lahiri is also the author of *Unaccustomed Earth,* which received the Frank O'Connor International Short Story Award, and *The Lowland,* a novel that was shortlisted for the Man Booker Prize and longlisted for the National Book Award, and won the DSC Prize for South Asian Literature. In the *New York Times*, Siddhartha Deb said that in Lahiri's work, "the political is always personal."

Lahiri is a member of the President's Committee on the Arts and Humanities, appointed by President Barack Obama. She was also appointed a member of the Committee on the Arts and Humanities. She is also a member of the American Academy of Arts and Letters.

Her first work written directly in Italian, "In Altre Parole," was published in 2015.

★

I LEFT INDIA IN 1964 with a certificate in commerce and the equivalent, in those days, of ten dollars to my name. For three weeks I sailed on the S.S. *Roma,* an Italian cargo vessel, in a cabin next to the ship's engine, across the Arabian Sea, the Red Sea, the Mediterranean, and finally to England. I lived in London, in Finsbury Park, in a house occupied entirely by penniless Bengali bachelors like myself, at least a dozen and sometimes more, all struggling to educate and establish ourselves abroad.

I attended lectures at LSE and worked at the university library to get by. We lived three or four to a room, shared a single, icy toilet, and took turns cooking pots of egg curry, which we ate with our hands on a table covered with newspapers. Apart from our jobs we had few responsibilities. On weekends we lounged barefoot in drawstring pajamas, drinking tea and smoking Rothmans, or set out to watch cricket at Lord's. Some weekends the house was crammed with still more Bengalis, to whom we had introduced ourselves at the greengrocer, or on the Tube, and we made yet more egg curry, and played Mukesh on a Grundig reel-to-reel, and soaked our dirty dishes in the bathtub. Every now and then someone in the house moved out, to live with a woman whom his family back in Calcutta had determined he was to wed. In 1969, when I was thirty-six years old, my own marriage was arranged. Around the same time, I was offered a full-time job in America, in the processing department of a library at MIT. The salary was generous enough to support a wife, and I was honored to be hired by a world-famous university, and so I obtained a green card, and prepared to travel farther still.

By then I had enough money to go by plane. I flew first to Calcutta, to attend my wedding, and a week later to Boston, to begin my new job. During the flight I read "The Student Guide to North America," for although I was no longer a student, I was on a budget all the same. I learned that Americans drove on the right side of the road, not the left, and that they called a lift an elevator and an engaged phone busy. "The pace of life in North America is different from Britain as you will soon discover," the guidebook informed me. "Everybody feels he must get to the top. Don't expect an English cup of tea." As the plane began its descent over Boston Harbor, the pilot announced the weather and time, and that President Nixon had declared a national holiday: two American men had landed on the moon. Several passengers cheered. "God bless America!" one of them hollered. Across the aisle, I saw a woman praying.

I spent my first night at the YMCA in Central Square, Cambridge, an inexpensive accommodation recommended by my guidebook which was within walking distance of MIT. The room contained a cot, a desk, and a small wooden cross on one wall. A sign on the door said that cooking was strictly forbidden. A bare window overlooked Massachusetts Avenue. Car horns, shrill and prolonged, blared one after another. Sirens and flashing lights heralded endless emergencies, and a succession of buses rumbled past, their doors opening and closing with a powerful hiss, throughout the night. The noise was constantly distracting, at times suffocating. I felt it deep in my ribs, just as I had felt the furious drone of the engine on the S.S. *Roma*. But there was no ship's deck to escape to, no glittering ocean to thrill my soul, no breeze to cool my face, no one to talk to. I was too tired to pace the gloomy corridors of the YMCA in my pajamas. Instead I sat at the desk and stared out the window. In the morning I reported to my job at the Dewey Library, a beige fortlike building by Memorial Drive. I also opened a bank account, rented a post office box, and bought a plastic bowl and a spoon. I went to a supermarket called Purity Supreme, wandering up and down the aisles, comparing prices with those in England. In the end I bought a carton of milk and a box of cornflakes. This was my first meal in America. Even the simple chore of buying milk was new to me; in London we'd had bottles delivered each morning to our door.

In a week I had adjusted, more or less. I ate cornflakes and milk morning and night, and bought some bananas for variety, slicing them into the bowl with the edge of my spoon. I left my carton of milk on the shaded part of the windowsill, as I had seen other residents at the YMCA do. To pass the time in the evenings I read the *Boston Globe* downstairs, in a spacious room with stained-glass windows. I read every article and advertisement, so that I would grow familiar with things, and when my eyes grew tired I slept. Only I did not sleep well. Each night I had to keep the window wide open; it was the only source of air in the stifling room, and the noise was intolerable. I would lie on the cot with my fingers pressed into my ears, but when I drifted off to sleep my hands fell away, and the noise of the traffic would wake me up again. Pigeon feathers drifted onto the windowsill, and one evening, when I poured milk over my cornflakes, I saw that it had soured. Nevertheless I resolved to stay at the YMCA for six weeks, until my wife's passport and green card were ready. Once she arrived I would have to rent a proper apartment, and from time to time I studied the classified section of the newspaper, or stopped in at the housing office at MIT during my lunch break to see what was available. It was in this manner that I discovered a room for immediate occupancy, in a house on a quiet street, the listing said, for

$8 per week. I dialed the number from a pay telephone, sorting through the coins, with which I was still unfamiliar, smaller and lighter than shillings, heavier and brighter than paisas.

"Who is speaking?" a woman demanded. Her voice was bold and clamorous.

"Yes, good afternoon, Madam. I am calling about the room for rent."

"Harvard or Tech?"

"I beg your pardon?"

"Are you from Harvard or Tech?"

Gathering that Tech referred to the Massachusetts Institute of Technology, I replied, "I work at Dewey Library," adding tentatively, "at Tech."

"I only rent rooms to boys from Harvard or Tech!"

"Yes, Madam."

I was given an address and an appointment for seven o'clock that evening. Thirty minutes before the hour I set out, my guidebook in my pocket, my breath fresh with Listerine. I turned down a street shaded with trees, perpendicular to Massachusetts Avenue. In spite of the heat I wore a coat and a tie, regarding the event as I would any other interview; I had never lived in the home of a person who was not Indian. The house, surrounded by a chain-link fence, was off-white with dark brown trim, with a tangle of forsythia bushes plastered against its front and sides. When I pressed the bell, the woman with whom I had spoken on the phone hollered from what seemed to be just the other side of the door, "One minute, please!"

Several minutes later, the door was opened by a tiny, extremely old woman. A mass of snowy hair was arranged like a small sack on top of her head. As I stepped into the house she sat down on a wooden bench positioned at the bottom of a narrow carpeted staircase. Once she was settled on the bench, in a small pool of light, she peered up at me, giving me her undivided attention. She wore a long black skirt that spread like a stiff tent to the floor, and a starched white shirt edged with ruffles at the throat and cuffs. Her hands, folded together in her lap, had long pallid fingers, with swollen knuckles and tough yellow nails. Age had battered her features so that she almost resembled a man, with sharp, shrunken eyes and prominent creases on either side of her nose. Her lips, chapped and faded, had nearly disappeared, and her eyebrows were missing altogether. Nevertheless she looked fierce.

"Lock up!" she commanded. She shouted even though I stood only a few feet away. "Fasten the chain and firmly press that button on the knob! This is the first thing you shall do when you enter, is that clear?"

I locked the door as directed and examined the house. Next to the bench was a small round table, its legs fully concealed, much like the woman's, by a skirt of lace. The table held a lamp, a transistor radio, a leather change purse with a silver clasp, and a telephone. A thick wooden cane was propped against one side. There was a parlor to my right, lined with bookcases and filled with shabby claw-footed furniture. In the corner of the parlor I saw a grand piano with its top down, piled with papers. The piano's bench was missing; it seemed to be the one on which the woman was sitting. Somewhere in the house a clock chimed seven times.

"You're punctual!" the woman proclaimed. "I expect you shall be so with the rent!"

"I have a letter, Madam." In my jacket pocket was a letter from MIT confirming my employment, which I had brought along to prove that I was indeed from Tech.

She stared at the letter, then handed it back to me carefully, gripping it with her fingers as if it were a plate heaped with food. She did not wear glasses, and I wondered if she'd read a word of it. "The last boy was always late! Still owes me eight dollars! Harvard boys aren't what they used to be! Only Harvard and Tech in this house! How's Tech, boy?"

"It is very well."

"You checked the lock?"

"Yes, Madam."

She unclasped her fingers, slapped the space beside her on the bench with one hand, and told me to sit down. For a moment she was silent. Then she intoned, as if she alone possessed this knowledge:

"There is an American flag on the moon!"

"Yes, Madam." Until then I had not thought very much about the moon shot. It was in the newspaper, of course, article upon article. The astronauts had landed on the shores of the Sea of Tranquillity, I had read, traveling farther than anyone in the history of civilization. For a few hours they explored the moon's surface. They gathered rocks in their pockets, described their surroundings (a magnificent desolation, according to one astronaut), spoke by phone to the president, and planted a flag in lunar soil. The voyage was hailed as man's most awesome achievement.

The woman bellowed, "A flag on the moon, boy! I heard it on the radio! Isn't that splendid?"

"Yes, Madam."

But she was not satisfied with my reply. Instead she commanded, "Say 'Splendid!'"

I was both baffled and somewhat insulted by the request. It reminded me of the way I was taught multiplication tables as a child, repeating after the master, sitting cross-legged on the floor of my one-room Tollygunge school. It also reminded me of my wedding, when I had repeated endless Sanskrit verses after the priest, verses I barely understood, which joined me to my wife. I said nothing.

"Say 'Splendid!'" the woman bellowed once again.

"Splendid," I murmured. I had to repeat the word a second time at the top of my lungs, so she could hear. I was reluctant to raise my voice to an elderly woman, but she did not appear to be offended. If anything the reply pleased her, because her next command was:

"Go see the room!"

I rose from the bench and mounted the narrow carpeted staircase. There were five doors, two on either side of an equally narrow hallway, and one at the opposite end. Only one door was partly open. The room contained a twin bed under a sloping ceiling, a brown oval rug, a basin with an exposed pipe, and a chest of drawers. One door led to a closet, another to a toilet and a tub. The window was open; net curtains stirred in the breeze. I lifted them away and inspected the view: a small back yard, with a few fruit trees and an empty clothesline. I was satisfied.

When I returned to the foyer the woman picked up the leather change purse on the table, opened the clasp, fished about with her fingers, and produced a key on a thin wire hoop. She informed me that there was a kitchen at the back of the house, accessible through the parlor. I was welcome to use the stove as long as I left it as I found it. Sheets and towels were provided, but keeping them clean was my own responsibility. The rent was due Friday mornings on the ledge above the piano keys. "And no lady visitors!"

"I am a married man, Madam." It was the first time I had announced this fact to anyone.

But she had not heard. "No lady visitors!" she insisted. She introduced herself as Mrs. Croft.

My wife's name was Mala. The marriage had been arranged by my older brother and his wife. I regarded the proposition with neither objection nor enthusiasm. It was a duty expected of me, as it was expected of every man. She was the daughter of a schoolteacher in Beleghata. I was told that she could cook, knit, embroider, sketch landscapes, and recite poems by Tagore, but these talents could not make up for the fact that she did not possess a fair complexion, and so a string of men had rejected her to her face. She was twenty-seven, an age when her parents had begun to fear that she would never marry, and so they were willing to ship their only child halfway across the world in order to save her from spinsterhood.

For five nights we shared a bed. Each of those nights, after applying cold cream and braiding her hair, she turned from me and wept; she missed her parents. Although I would be leaving the country in a few days, custom dictated that she was now a part of my household, and for the next six weeks she was to live with my brother and his wife, cooking, cleaning, serving tea and sweets to guests. I did nothing to console her. I lay on my own side of the bed, reading my guidebook by flashlight. At times I thought of the tiny room on the other side of the wall which had belonged to my mother. Now the room was practically empty; the wooden pallet on which she'd once slept was piled with trunks and old bedding. Nearly six years ago, before leaving for London, I had watched her die on that bed, had found her playing with her excrement in her final days. Before we cremated her I had cleaned each of her fingernails with a hairpin, and then, because my brother could not bear it, I had assumed the role of eldest son, and had touched the flame to her temple, to release her tormented soul to heaven.

The next morning I moved into the room in Mrs. Croft's house. When I unlocked the door I saw that she was sitting on the piano bench, on the same side as the previous evening. She wore the same black skirt, the same starched white blouse, and had her hands folded together the same way in her lap. She looked so much the same that I wondered if she'd spent the whole night on the bench. I put my suitcase upstairs and then headed off to work. That evening when I came home from the university, she was still there.

"Sit down, boy!" She slapped the space beside her.

I perched on the bench. I had a bag of groceries with me — more milk, more cornflakes, and more bananas, for my inspection of the kitchen earlier in the day had revealed no spare pots or pans. There were only two saucepans in the refrigerator, both containing some orange broth, and a copper kettle on the stove.

"Good evening, Madam."

She asked me if I had checked the lock. I told her I had.

For a moment she was silent. Then suddenly she declared, with the equal measures of disbelief and delight as the night before, "There's an American flag on the moon, boy!"

"Yes, Madam."

"A flag on the moon! Isn't that splendid?"

I nodded, dreading what I knew was coming. "Yes, Madam."

"Say 'Splendid!' "

This time I paused, looking to either side in case anyone was there to overhear me, though I knew perfectly well that the house was empty. I felt like an idiot. But it was a small enough thing to ask. "Splendid!" I cried out.

Within days it became our routine. In the mornings when I left for the library Mrs. Croft was either hidden away in her bedroom, on the other side of the staircase, or sitting on the bench, oblivious of my presence, listening to the news or classical music on the radio. But each evening when I returned the same thing happened: she slapped the bench, ordered me to sit down, declared that there was a flag on the moon, and declared that it was splendid. I said it was splendid, too, and then we sat in silence. As awkward as it was, and as endless as it felt to me then, the nightly encounter lasted only about ten minutes; inevitably she would drift off to sleep, her head falling abruptly toward her chest, leaving me free to retire to my room. By then, of course, there was no flag standing on the moon. The astronauts, I had read in the paper, had seen it fall before they flew back to Earth. But I did not have the heart to tell her.

Friday morning, when my first week's rent was due, I went to the piano in the parlor to place my money on the ledge. The piano keys were dull and discolored. When I pressed one, it made no sound at all. I had put eight dollar bills in an envelope and written Mrs. Croft's name on the front of it. I was not in the habit of leaving money unmarked and unattended. From where I stood I could see the profile of her tent-shaped skirt in the hall. It seemed unnecessary to make her get up and walk all the way to the piano. I never saw her walking about, and assumed, from the cane always propped against the round table, that she did so with difficulty. When I approached the bench she peered up at me and demanded:

"What is your business?"

"The rent, Madam."

"On the ledge above the piano keys!"

"I have it here." I extended the envelope toward her, but her fingers, folded together in her lap, did not budge. I bowed slightly and lowered the envelope, so that it hovered just above her hands. After a moment she accepted it, and nodded her head.

That night when I came home, she did not slap the bench, but out of habit I sat beside her as usual. She asked me if I had checked the lock, but she mentioned nothing about the flag on the moon. Instead she said:

"It was very kind of you!"

"I beg your pardon, Madam?"

"Very kind of you!"

She was still holding the envelope in her hands.

On Sunday there was a knock on my door. An elderly woman introduced herself: she was Mrs. Croft's daughter, Helen. She walked into the room and looked at each of the walls as if for signs of change, glancing at the shirts that hung in the closet, the neckties draped over the doorknob, the box of cornflakes on the chest of drawers, the dirty bowl and spoon in the basin. She was short and thick-waisted, with cropped silver hair and bright pink lipstick. She wore a sleeveless summer dress, a row of white plastic beads, and spectacles on a chain that hung like a swing against her chest. The backs of her legs were mapped with dark blue veins, and her upper arms sagged like the flesh of a roasted eggplant. She told me she lived in Arlington, a town farther up Massachusetts Avenue. "I come once a week to bring Mother groceries. Has she sent you packing yet?"

"It is very well, Madam."

"Some of the boys run screaming. But I think she likes you. You're the first boarder she's ever referred to as a gentleman."

She looked at me, noticing my bare feet (I still felt strange wearing shoes indoors, and always removed them before entering my room). "Are you new to Boston?"

"New to America, Madam."

"From?" She raised her eyebrows.

"I am from Calcutta, India."

"Is that right? We had a Brazilian fellow, about a year ago. You'll find Cambridge a very international city."

I nodded, and began to wonder how long our conversation would last. But at that moment we heard Mrs. Croft's electrifying voice rising up the stairs.

"You are to come downstairs immediately!"

"What is it?" Helen cried back.

"Immediately!"

I put on my shoes. Helen sighed.

I followed Helen down the staircase. She seemed to be in no hurry, and complained at one point that she had a bad knee. "Have you been walking without your cane?" Helen called out. "You know you're not supposed to walk without that cane." She paused, resting her hand on the banister, and looked back at me. "She slips sometimes."

For the first time Mrs. Croft seemed vulnerable. I pictured her on the floor in front of the bench, flat on her back, staring at the ceiling, her feet pointing in opposite directions. But when we reached the bottom of the staircase she was sitting there as usual, her hands folded together in her lap. Two grocery bags were at her feet. She did not slap the bench, or ask us to sit down. She glared.

"What is it, Mother?"

"It's improper!"

"What's improper?"

"It is improper for a lady and gentleman who are not married to one another to hold a private conversation without a chaperone!"

Helen said she was sixty-eight years old, old enough to be my mother, but Mrs. Croft insisted that Helen and I speak to each other downstairs, in the parlor. She added that it was also improper for a lady of Helen's station to reveal her age, and to wear a dress so high above the ankle.

"For your information, Mother, it's 1969. What would you do if you actually left the house one day and saw a girl in a miniskirt?"

Mrs. Croft sniffed. "I'd have her arrested."

Helen shook her head and picked up one of the grocery bags. I picked up the other one, and followed her through the parlor and into the kitchen. The bags were filled with cans of soup, which Helen opened up one by one with a few cranks of a can opener. She tossed the old soup in the saucepans into the sink, rinsed the pans under the tap, filled them with soup from the newly opened cans, and put them back in the refrigerator. "A few years ago she could still open the cans herself," Helen said. "She hates that I do it for her now. But the piano killed her hands." She put on her spectacles, glanced at the cupboards, and spotted my tea bags. "Shall we have a cup?"

I filled the kettle on the stove. "I beg your pardon, Madam. The piano?"

"She used to give lessons. For forty years. It was how she raised us after my father died." Helen put her hands on her hips, staring at the open refrigerator. She reached into the back, pulled out a wrapped stick of butter, frowned, and tossed it into the garbage. "That ought to do it," she said, and put the unopened cans of soup in the cupboard. I sat at the table and watched as Helen washed the dirty dishes, tied up the garbage bag, and poured boiling water into two cups. She handed one to me without milk, and sat down at the table.

"Excuse me, Madam, but is it enough?"

Helen took a sip of her tea. Her lipstick left a smiling pink stain on the rim of the cup. "Is what enough?"

"The soup in the pans. Is it enough food for Mrs. Croft?"

"She won't eat anything else. She stopped eating solids after she turned one hundred. That was, let's see, three years ago."

I was mortified. I had assumed Mrs. Croft was in her eighties, perhaps as old as ninety. I had never known a person who had lived for over a century. That this person was a widow who lived alone mortified me further still. Widowhood had driven my own mother insane. My father, who worked as a clerk at the General Post Office of Calcutta, died of encephalitis when I was sixteen. My mother refused to adjust to life without him; instead she sank deeper into a world of darkness from which neither I, nor my brother, nor concerned relatives, nor psychiatric clinics on Rash Behari Avenue could save her. What pained me most was to see her so unguarded, to hear her burp after meals or expel gas in front of company without the slightest embarrassment. After my father's death, my brother abandoned his schooling and began to work in the jute mill he would eventually manage, in order to keep the household running. And so it was my job to sit by my mother's feet and study for my exams as she counted and recounted the bracelets on her arm as if they were the beads of an abacus. We tried to keep an eye on her. Once she had wandered half-naked to the tram depot before we were able to bring her inside again.

"I am happy to warm Mrs. Croft's soup in the evenings," I suggested. "It is no trouble."

Helen looked at her watch, stood up, and poured the rest of her tea into the sink. "I wouldn't if I were you. That's the sort of thing that would kill her altogether."

That evening, when Helen had gone back to Arlington and Mrs. Croft and I were alone again, I began to worry. Now that I knew how very old she was, I worried that something would happen to her in the middle of the night, or when I was out during the day. As vigorous as her voice was, and as imperious as she seemed, I knew that even a scratch or a cough could kill a person that old; each day she lived, I knew, was something of a miracle. Helen didn't seem concerned. She came and went, bringing soup for Mrs. Croft, one Sunday after the next.

In this manner the six weeks of that summer passed. I came home each evening, after my hours at the library, and spent a few minutes on the piano bench with Mrs. Croft. Some evenings I sat beside her long after she had drifted off to sleep, still in awe of how many years she had spent on this earth. At times I tried to picture the world she had been born into, in 1866 — a world, I imagined, filled with women in long black skirts, and chaste conversations in the parlor. Now, when I looked at her hands with their swollen knuckles folded together in her lap, I imagined them smooth and slim, striking the piano keys. At times I came downstairs before going to sleep, to make sure she was sitting upright on the bench, or was safe in her bedroom. On Fridays I put the rent in her hands. There was nothing I could do for her beyond these simple gestures. I was not her son, and apart from those eight dollars, I owed her nothing.

At the end of August, Mala's passport and green card were ready. I received a telegram with her flight information; my brother's house in Calcutta had no telephone. Around that time I also received a letter from her, written only a few days after we had parted. There was no salutation; addressing me by name would have assumed an intimacy we had not yet discovered. It contained only a few lines. "I write in English in preparation for the journey. Here I am very much lonely. Is it very cold there. Is there snow. Yours, Mala."

I was not touched by her words. We had spent only a handful of days in each other's company. And yet we were bound together; for six weeks she had worn an iron bangle on her wrist, and applied vermilion powder to the part in her hair, to signify to the world that she was a bride. In those six weeks I regarded her arrival as I would the arrival of a coming month, or season — something inevitable, but meaningless at the time. So little did I know her that, while details of her face sometimes rose to my memory, I could not conjure up the whole of it.

A few days after receiving the letter, as I was walking to work in the morning, I saw an Indian woman on the other side of Massachusetts Avenue, wearing a sari with its free end nearly dragging on the footpath, and pushing a child in a stroller. An American woman with a small black dog on a leash was walking to one side of her. Suddenly the dog began barking. I watched as the Indian woman, startled, stopped in her path, at which point the dog leaped up and seized the end of the sari between its teeth. The American woman scolded the dog, appeared to apologize, and walked quickly away, leaving the Indian woman to fix her sari, and quiet her crying child. She did not see me standing there, and eventually she continued on her way. Such a mishap, I realized that morning, would soon be my concern. It was my duty to take care of Mala, to welcome her and protect her. I would have to buy her her first pair of snow boots, her first winter coat. I would have to tell her which streets to avoid, which way the traffic came, tell her to wear her sari so that the free end did not drag on the footpath. A five-mile separation from her parents, I recalled with some irritation, had caused her to weep.

Unlike Mala, I was used to it all by then: used to cornflakes and milk, used to Helen's visits, used to sitting on the bench with Mrs. Croft. The only thing I was not used to was Mala. Nevertheless, I did what I had to do. I went to the housing office at MIT and found a furnished apartment a few blocks away, with a double bed and a private kitchen and bath, for $40 a week. One last Friday I handed Mrs. Croft eight dollar bills in an envelope, brought my suitcase downstairs, and informed her that I was moving. She put my key into her change purse. The last thing she asked me to do was hand her the cane propped against the table, so that she could walk to the door and lock it behind me. "Good-bye, then," she said, and retreated back into the house. I did not expect any display of emotion, but I was disappointed all the same. I was only a boarder, a man who paid her a bit of money and passed in and out of her home for six weeks. Compared to a century, it was no time at all.

At the airport I recognized Mala immediately. The free end of her sari did not drag on the floor, but was draped in a sign of bridal modesty over her head, just as it had draped my mother until the day my father died. Her thin brown arms were stacked with gold bracelets, a small red circle was painted on her forehead, and the edges of her feet were tinted with a decorative red dye. I did not embrace her, or kiss her, or take her hand. Instead I asked her, speaking Bengali for the first time in America, if she was hungry.

She hesitated, then nodded yes.

I told her I had prepared some egg curry at home. "What did they give you to eat on the plane?"

"I didn't eat."

"All the way from Calcutta?"

"The menu said oxtail soup."

"But surely there were other items."

"The thought of eating an ox's tail made me lose my appetite."

When we arrived home, Mala opened up one of her suitcases, and presented me with two pullover sweaters, both made with bright blue wool, which she had knitted in the course of our separation, one with a V-neck, the other covered with cables. I tried them on; both were tight under the arms. She had also brought me two new pairs of drawstring pajamas, a letter from my brother, and a packet of loose Darjeeling tea. I had no present for her apart from the egg curry. We sat at a bare table, staring at our plates. We ate with our hands, another thing I had not yet done in America.

"The house is nice," she said. "Also the egg curry." With her left hand she held the end of her sari to her chest, so it would not slip off her head.

"I don't know many recipes."

She nodded, peeling the skin off each of her potatoes before eating them. At one point the sari slipped to her shoulders. She readjusted it at once.

"There is no need to cover your head," I said. "I don't mind. It doesn't matter here."

She kept it covered anyway.

I waited to get used to her, to her presence at my side, at my table and in my bed, but a week later we were still strangers. I still was not used to coming home to an apartment that smelled of steamed rice, and finding that the basin in the bathroom was always wiped clean, our two toothbrushes lying side by side, a cake of Pears soap resting in the soap dish. I was not used to the fragrance of the coconut oil she rubbed every other night into her scalp, or the delicate sound her bracelets made as she moved about the apartment. In the mornings she was always awake before I was. The first morning when I came into the kitchen she had heated up the leftovers and set a plate with a spoonful of salt on its edge on the table, assuming I would eat rice for breakfast, as most Bengali husbands did. I told her cereal would do, and the next morning when I came into the kitchen she had already poured the cornflakes into my bowl. One morning she walked with me down Massachusetts Avenue to MIT, where I gave her a short tour of the campus. The next morning before I left for work she asked me for a few dollars. I parted with them reluctantly, but I knew that this, too, was now normal. When I came home from work there was a potato peeler in the kitchen drawer, and a tablecloth on the table, and chicken curry made with fresh garlic and ginger on the stove. After dinner I read the newspaper, while Mala sat at the kitchen table, working on a cardigan for herself with more of the bright blue wool, or writing letters home.

On Friday, I suggested going out. Mala set down her knitting and disappeared into the bathroom. When she emerged I regretted the suggestion; she had put on a silk sari and extra bracelets, and coiled her hair with a flattering side part on top of her head. She was prepared as if for a party, or at the very least for the cinema, but I had no such destination in mind. The evening air was balmy. We walked several blocks down Massachusetts Avenue, looking into the windows of restaurants and shops. Then, without thinking, I led her down the quiet street where for so many nights I had walked alone.

"This is where I lived before you came," I said, stopping at Mrs. Croft's chain-link fence.

"In such a big house?"

"I had a small room upstairs. At the back."

"Who else lives there?"

"A very old woman."

"With her family?"

"Alone."

"But who takes care of her?"

I opened the gate. "For the most part she takes care of herself."

I wondered if Mrs. Croft would remember me; I wondered if she had a new boarder to sit with her on the bench each evening. When I pressed the bell I expected the same long wait as that day of our first meeting, when I did not have a key. But this time the door was opened almost immediately, by Helen. Mrs. Croft was not sitting on the bench. The bench was gone.

"Hello there," Helen said, smiling with her bright pink lips at Mala. "Mother's in the parlor. Will you be visiting awhile?"

"As you wish, Madam."

"Then I think I'll run to the store, if you don't mind. She had a little accident. We can't leave her alone these days, not even for a minute."

I locked the door after Helen and walked into the parlor. Mrs. Croft was lying flat on her back, her head on a peach-colored cushion, a thin white quilt spread over her body. Her hands were folded together on top of her chest. When she saw me she pointed at the sofa, and told me to sit down. I took my place as directed, but Mala wandered over to the piano and sat on the bench, which was now positioned where it belonged.

"I broke my hip!" Mrs. Croft announced, as if no time had passed.

"Oh dear, Madam."

"I fell off the bench!"

"I am so sorry, Madam."

"It was the middle of the night! Do you know what I did, boy?"

I shook my head.

"I called the police!"

She stared up at the ceiling and grinned sedately, exposing a crowded row of long gray teeth. "What do you say to that, boy?"

As stunned as I was, I knew what I had to say. With no hesitation at all, I cried out, "Splendid!"

Mala laughed then. Her voice was full of kindness, her eyes bright with amusement. I had never heard her laugh before, and it was loud enough so that Mrs. Croft had heard, too. She turned to Mala and glared.

"Who is she, boy?"

"She is my wife, Madam."

Mrs. Croft pressed her head at an angle against the cushion to get a better look. "Can you play the piano?"

"No, Madam," Mala replied.

"Then stand up!"

Mala rose to her feet, adjusting the end of her sari over her head and holding it to her chest, and, for the first time since her arrival, I felt sympathy. I remembered my first days in London, learning how to take the Tube to Russell Square, riding an escalator for the first time, unable to understand that when the man cried "piper" it meant "paper," unable to decipher, for a whole year, that the conductor said "Mind the gap" as the train entered each station. Like me, Mala had traveled far from home, not knowing where she was going, or what she would find, for no reason other than to be my wife. As strange as it seemed, I knew in my heart that one day her death would affect me, and stranger still, that mine would affect her. I wanted somehow to explain this to Mrs. Croft, who was still scrutinizing Mala from top to toe with what seemed to be placid disdain. I wondered if Mrs. Croft had ever seen a woman in a sari, with a dot painted on her forehead and bracelets stacked on her wrists. I wondered what she would object to. I wondered if she could see the red dye still vivid on Mala's feet, all but obscured by the bottom edge of her sari. At last Mrs. Croft declared, with the equal measures of disbelief and delight I knew well:

"She is a perfect lady!"

Now it was I who laughed. I did so quietly, and Mrs. Croft did not hear me. But Mala had heard, and, for the first time, we looked at each other and smiled.

I like to think of that moment in Mrs. Croft's parlor as the moment when the distance between Mala and me began to lessen. Although we were not yet fully in love, I like to think of the months that followed as a honeymoon of sorts. Together we explored the city and met other Bengalis, some of whom are still friends today. We discovered that a man named Bill sold fresh fish on Prospect Street, and that a shop in Harvard Square called Cardullo's sold bay leaves and cloves. In the evenings we walked to the Charles River to watch sailboats drift across the water, or had ice cream cones in Harvard Yard. We bought a camera with which to document our life together, and I took pictures of her posing in front of the Prudential building, so that she could send them to her parents. At night we kissed, shy at first but quickly bold, and discovered pleasure and solace in each other's arms. I told her about my voyage on the S.S. *Roma,* and about Finsbury Park and the YMCA, and my evenings on the bench with Mrs. Croft. When I told her stories about my mother, she wept. It was Mala who consoled me when, reading the *Globe* one evening, I came across Mrs. Croft's obituary. I had not thought of her in several months—by then those six weeks of the summer were already a remote interlude in my past—but when I learned of her death I was stricken, so much so that when Mala looked up from her knitting she found me staring at the wall, unable to speak. Mrs. Croft's was the first death I mourned in America, for hers was the first life I had admired; she had left this world at last, ancient and alone, never to return.

As for me, I have not strayed much farther. Mala and I live in a town about twenty miles from Boston, on a tree-lined street much like Mrs. Croft's, in a house we own, with a garden that saves us from buying tomatoes in summer. We are American citizens now, so that we can collect Social Security when it is time. Though we visit Calcutta every few years, we have decided to grow old here. I work in a small college library. We have a son who attends Harvard University. Mala no longer drapes the end of her sari over her head, or weeps at night for her parents, but occasionally she weeps for our son. So we drive to Cambridge to visit him, or bring him home for a weekend, so that he can eat rice with us with his hands, and speak in Bengali, things we sometimes worry he will no longer do after we die.

Whenever we make that drive, I always take Massachusetts Avenue, in spite of the traffic. I barely recognize the buildings now, but each time

I am there I return instantly to those six weeks as if they were only the other day, and I slow down and point to Mrs. Croft's street, saying to my son, Here was my first home in America, where I lived with a woman who was 103. "Remember?" Mala says, and smiles, amazed, as I am, that there was ever a time that we were strangers. My son always expresses his astonishment, not at Mrs. Croft's age but at how little I paid in rent, a fact nearly as inconceivable to him as a flag on the moon was to a woman born in 1866. In my son's eyes I see the ambition that had first hurled me across the world. In a few years he will graduate and pave his way, alone and unprotected. But I remind myself that he has a father who is still living, a mother who is happy and strong. Whenever he is discouraged, I tell him that if I can survive on three continents, then there is no obstacle he cannot conquer. While the astronauts, heroes forever, spent mere hours on the moon, I have remained in this new world for nearly thirty years. I know that my achievement is quite ordinary. I am not the only man to seek his fortune far from home, and certainly I am not the first. Still, there are times I am bewildered by each mile I have traveled, each meal I have eaten, each person I have known, each room in which I have slept. As ordinary as it all appears, there are times when it is beyond my imagination.

2000

ZZ PACKER
BROWNIES

from *Harper's Magazine*

ZZ PACKER was born in Chicago in 1973 and grew up in Atlanta and Louisville. She first published in *Seventeen* when she was nineteen years old. Packer attended Yale University and went on to study at Johns Hopkins University and the Iowa Writers' Workshop at the University of Iowa. She was then named a Stegner Fellow in fiction at Stanford University.

Her short story collection, *Drinking Coffee Elsewhere*, was published in 2003. The book was a finalist for the PEN/Faulkner Award, chosen as a *New York Times* Notable Book, and selected by John Updike for the *Today* show Book Club.

Packer said, "I think a lot of my characters wish race didn't matter as much as it does, but it does. When you are either in the minority as is the case for blacks in the U.S. or the oppressed majority as was formerly the case in South Africa, you don't have the luxury of being able to decide whether or not to pay attention to race, because if you don't, someone else will, and the surprise repercussions are far worse than preparing for the worst and being pleasantly surprised if the worst never occurs."

Packer won a Guggenheim Fellowship and was named one of America's Best Young Novelists by *Granta*, one of *The New Yorker*'s 20 Under 40, as well as one of *Smithsonian* magazine's Young Innovators in October 2007. She lives in San Francisco.

★

B Y THE END of our first day at Camp Crescendo, the girls in my Brownie troop had decided to kick the asses of each and every girl in Brownie Troop 909. Troop 909 was doomed from the first day of camp; they were white girls, their complexions like a blend of ice cream: strawberry, vanilla. They turtled out from their bus in pairs, their rolled-up sleeping bags chromatized with Disney characters — Sleeping Beauty, Snow White, Mickey Mouse — or the generic ones cheap parents bought

— washed-out rainbows, unicorns, curly-eyelashed frogs. Some clutched Igloo coolers and still others held on to stuffed toys like pacifiers, looking all around them like tourists determined to be dazzled.

Our troop wended its way past their bus, past the ranger station, past the colorful trail guide drawn like a treasure map, locked behind glass.

"Man, did you smell them?" Arnetta said, giving the girls a slow once-over. "They smell like Chihuahuas. *Wet* Chihuahuas." Although we had passed their troop by yards, Arnetta raised her nose in the air and grimaced.

Arnetta said this from the very rear of the line, far away from Mrs. Margolin, who strung our troop behind her like a brood of obedient ducklings. Mrs. Margolin even looked like a mother duck — she had hair cropped close to a small ball of a head, almost no neck, and huge, miraculous breasts. She wore enormous belts that looked like the kind weight lifters wear, except hers were cheap metallic gold or rabbit fur or covered with gigantic fake sunflowers. Often these belts would become nature lessons in and of themselves. "See," Mrs. Margolin once said to us, pointing to her belt. "This one's made entirely from the feathers of baby pigeons."

The belt layered with feathers was uncanny enough, but I was more disturbed by the realization that I had never actually *seen* a baby pigeon. I searched for weeks for one, in vain — scampering after pigeons whenever I was downtown with my father.

But nature lessons were not Mrs. Margolin's top priority. She saw the position of troop leader as an evangelical post. Back at the A.M.E. church where our Brownie meetings were held, she was especially fond of imparting religious aphorisms by means of acrostics — Satan was the "Serpent Always Tempting And Noisome"; she'd refer to the Bible as "Basic Instructions Before Leaving Earth." Whenever she occasionally quizzed us on these at the beginning of the Brownie meeting, expecting to hear the acrostics parroted back to her, only Arnetta's correct replies soared over our vague mumblings. "Jesus?" Mrs. Margolin might ask expectantly, and Arnetta alone would dutifully answer, "Jehovah's Example, Saving Us Sinners."

Arnetta made a point of listening to Mrs. Margolin's religious talk and giving her what she wanted to hear. Because of this, Arnetta could have blared through a megaphone that the white girls of Troop 909 were "wet Chihuahuas" without arousing so much as a blink from Mrs. Margolin. Once Arnetta killed the troop goldfish by feeding it a French fry covered in ketchup, and when Mrs. Margolin demanded an explanation, Arnetta claimed that the goldfish had been eyeing her meal for *hours,* until — giving in to temptation — it had leapt up and snatched the whole golden fry from her fingertips.

"*Serious* Chihuahua," Octavia added — though neither Arnetta nor Octavia could *spell* "Chihuahua" or had ever *seen* a Chihuahua. Trisyllabic words had gained a sort of exoticism within our fourth-grade set at Woodrow Wilson Elementary. Arnetta and Octavia, compelled to outdo each other, would flip through the dictionary, determined to work the vulgar-sounding ones like "Djibouti" and "asinine" into conversation.

"*Caucasian* Chihuahuas," Arnetta said.

That did it. Drema and Elise doubled up on each other like inextricably entwined kites; Octavia slapped the skin of her belly; Janice jumped straight up in the air, then did it again, just as hard, as if to slam-dunk her own head. No one had laughed so hard since a boy named Martez had stuck his pencil in the electric socket and spent the whole day with a strange grin on his face.

"Girls, girls," said our parent helper, Mrs. Hedy. Mrs. Hedy was Octavia's mother. She wagged her index finger perfunctorily, like a windshield wiper. "Stop it now. Be good." She said this loudly enough to be heard, but lazily, nasally, bereft of any feeling or indication that she meant to be obeyed, as though she would say these words again at the exact same pitch if a button somewhere on her were pressed.

But the girls didn't stop laughing; they only laughed louder. It was the word "Caucasian" that had got them all going. One day at school, about a month before the Brownie camping trip, Arnetta had turned to a boy wearing impossibly high-ankled floodwater jeans, and said, "What are *you? Caucasian?*" The word took off from there, and soon everything was Caucasian. If you ate too fast, you ate like a Caucasian; if you ate too slow, you ate like a Caucasian. The biggest feat anyone at Woodrow Wilson could do was to jump off the swing in midair, at the highest point in its arc, and if you fell (like I had, more than once) instead of landing on your feet, knees bent Olympic-gymnast-style, Arnetta and Octavia were prepared to comment. They'd look at each other with the silence of passengers who'd narrowly escaped an accident, then nod their heads, and whisper with solemn horror and haughtiness, "*Caucasian.*"

Even the only white kid in our school, Dennis, got in on the Caucasian act. That time when Martez stuck the pencil in the socket, Dennis had pointed, and yelled, "That was *so* Caucasian!"

· · ·

Living in the south suburbs of Atlanta, it was easy to forget about whites. Whites were like those baby pigeons: real and existing, but rarely thought about. Everyone had been to Rich's to go clothes shopping, everyone had seen white girls and their mothers coo-cooing over dresses; everyone had gone to the downtown library and seen white businessmen swish by importantly, wrists flexed in front of them to check the time on their watches as though they would change from Clark Kent into Superman any second. But those images were as fleeting as cards shuffled in a deck, whereas the ten white girls behind us — *invaders,* Arnetta would later call them — were instantly real and memorable, with their long shampoo-commercial hair, as straight as spaghetti from the box. This alone was reason for envy and hatred. The only black girl most of us had ever seen with hair that long was Octavia, whose hair hung past her butt like a Hawaiian hula dancer's. The sight of Octavia's mane prompted other girls to listen to her reverentially, as though whatever she had to say would somehow activate their own follicles. For example, when, on the first day of camp, Octavia made as if to speak, a silence began. "Nobody," Octavia said, "calls us niggers."

At the end of that first day, when half of our troop made its way back to the cabin after tag-team restroom visits, Arnetta said she'd heard one of the girls in Troop 909 call Daphne a nigger. The other half of the girls and I were helping Mrs. Margolin clean up the pots and pans from the ravioli dinner. When we made our way to the restrooms to wash up and brush our teeth, we met up with Arnetta midway.

"Man, I completely heard the girl," Arnetta reported. "Right, Daphne?"

Daphne hardly ever spoke, but when she did her voice was petite and tinkly, the voice one might expect from a shiny new earring. She'd written a poem once, for Langston Hughes Day, a poem brimming with all the teacher-winning ingredients — trees and oceans, sunsets and moons — but what cinched the poem for the grown-ups, snatching the win from Octavia's musical ode to Grandmaster Flash and the Furious Five, were Daphne's last lines:

> You are my father, the veteran
> When you cry in the dark
> It rains and rains and rains in my heart

She'd worn clean, though faded, jumpers and dresses when Chic jeans were the fashion, but when she went up to the dais to receive her prize journal, pages trimmed in gold, she wore a new dress with a velveteen bodice and a taffeta skirt as wide as an umbrella. All the kids clapped, though none of them understood the poem. I'd read encyclopedias the way others read comics, and I didn't get it. But those last lines pricked me, they were so eerie, and as my father and I ate cereal, I'd whisper over my Froot Loops, like a mantra, *"You are my father, the veteran. You are my father, the veteran, the veteran, the veteran,"* until my father, who acted in plays as Caliban and Othello and was not a veteran, marched me up to my teacher one morning, and said, "Can you tell me what the hell's wrong with this kid?"

I had thought Daphne and I might become friends, but she seemed to grow spooked by me whispering those lines to her, begging her to tell me what they meant, and I had soon understood that two quiet people like us were better off quiet alone.

"Daphne? Didn't you hear them call you a nigger?" Arnetta asked, giving Daphne a nudge.

The sun was setting through the trees, and their leafy tops formed a canopy of black lace for the flame of the sun to pass through. Daphne shrugged her shoulders at first, then slowly nodded her head when Arnetta gave her a hard look.

Twenty minutes later, when my restroom group returned to the cabin, Arnetta was still talking about Troop 909. My restroom group had passed by some of the 909 girls. For the most part, they had deferred to us, waving us into the restrooms, letting us go even though they'd gotten there first.

We'd seen them, but from afar, never within their orbit enough to see whether their faces were the way all white girls appeared on TV — ponytailed and full of energy, bubbling over with love and money. All I could see was that some rapidly fanned their faces with their hands, though the heat of the day had long passed. A few seemed to be lolling their heads in slow circles, half-purposefully, as if exercising the muscles of their necks, half-ecstatically, rolling their heads about like Stevie Wonder.

"We can't let them get away with that," Arnetta said, dropping her voice to a laryngitic whisper. "We can't let them get away with calling us niggers. I say we teach them a lesson." She sat down cross-legged on a sleeping bag, an embittered Buddha, eyes glimmering acrylic black. "We can't go telling Mrs. Margolin, either. Mrs. Margolin'll say something about doing unto others and the path of righteousness and all. Forget that shit." She let her eyes flutter irreverently till they half closed, as though ignoring an insult not worth returning. We could all hear Mrs. Margolin outside, gathering the last of the metal campware.

Nobody said anything for a while. Arnetta's tone had an upholstered confidence that was somehow both regal and vulgar at once. It demanded a few moments of silence in its wake, like the ringing of a church bell or the playing of taps. Sometimes Octavia would ditto or dissent whatever Arnetta had said, and this was the signal that others could speak. But this time Octavia just swirled a long cord of hair into pretzel shapes.

"*Well?*" Arnetta said. She looked as if she had discerned the hidden severity of the situation and was waiting for the rest of us to catch up. Everyone looked from Arnetta to Daphne. It was, after all, Daphne who had supposedly been called the name, but Daphne sat on the bare cabin floor, flipping through the pages of the Girl Scout handbook, eyebrows arched in mock wonder, as if the handbook were a catalogue full of bright and startling foreign costumes. Janice broke the silence. She clapped her hands to broach her idea of a plan.

"They gone be sleeping," she whispered conspiratorially, "then we gone sneak into they cabin, then we gone put daddy longlegs in they sleeping bags. Then they'll wake up. Then we gone beat 'em up till they flat as frying pans!" She jammed her fist into the palm of her hand, then made a sizzling sound.

Janice's country accent was laughable, her looks homely, her jumpy acrobatics embarrassing to behold. Arnetta and Octavia volleyed amused, arrogant smiles whenever Janice opened her mouth, but Janice never caught the hint, spoke whenever she wanted, fluttered around Arnetta and Octavia futilely offering her opinions to their departing backs. Whenever Arnetta and Octavia shooed her away, Janice loitered until the two would finally sigh, "What *is* it, Miss Caucasoid? What do you want?"

"Oh shut up, Janice," Octavia said, letting a fingered loop of hair fall to her waist as though just the sound of Janice's voice had ruined the fun of her hair twisting.

"All right," Arnetta said, standing up. "We're going to have a secret meeting and talk about what we're going to do."

The word "secret" had a built-in importance. Everyone gravely nodded her head. The modifier form of the word had more clout than the noun. A secret meant nothing; it was like gossip: just a bit of unpleasant knowledge about someone who happened to be someone other than yourself. A secret *meeting*, or a secret *club*, was entirely different.

That was when Arnetta turned to me, as though she knew doing so was both a compliment and a charity.

"Snot, you're not going to be a bitch and tell Mrs. Margolin, are you?"

I had been called "Snot" ever since first grade, when I'd sneezed in class and two long ropes of mucus had splattered a nearby girl.

"Hey," I said. "Maybe you didn't hear them right — I mean —"

"Are you gonna tell on us or not?" was all Arnetta wanted to know, and by the time the question was asked, the rest of our Brownie troop looked at me as though they'd already decided their course of action, me being the only impediment. As though it were all a simple matter of patriotism.

Camp Crescendo used to double as a high school band and field hockey camp until an arching field hockey ball landed on the clasp of a girl's metal barrette, knifing a skull nerve, paralyzing the right side of her body. The camp closed down for a few years, and the girl's teammates built a memorial, filling the spot on which the girl fell with hockey balls, upon which they had painted — all in nail polish — get-well tidings, flowers, and hearts. The balls were still stacked there, like a shrine of ostrich eggs embedded in the ground.

On the second day of camp, Troop 909 was dancing around the mound of nail polish–decorated hockey balls, their limbs jangling awkwardly, their cries like the constant summer squeal of an amusement park. There was a stream that bordered the field hockey lawn, and the girls from my troop settled next to it, scarfing down the last of lunch: sandwiches made from salami and slices of tomato that had gotten waterlogged from the melting ice in the cooler. From the stream bank, Arnetta eyed the Troop 909 girls, scrutinizing their movements to glean inspiration for battle.

"Man," Arnetta said, "we could bum-rush them right now if that damn lady would *leave*."

The 909 troop leader was a white woman with the severe pageboy hairdo of an ancient Egyptian. She lay sprawled on a picnic blanket, Sphinxlike, eating a banana, sometimes holding it out in front of her like a microphone. Beside her sat a girl slowly flapping one hand like a bird with a broken wing. Occasionally, the leader would call out the names of girls who'd attempted leapfrogs and flips, or of girls who yelled too loudly or strayed far from the circle.

"I'm just glad Big Fat Mama's not following us here," Octavia said. "At least we don't have to worry about her." Mrs. Margolin, Octavia assured us, was having her Afternoon Devotional, shrouded in mosquito netting, in a clearing she'd found. Mrs. Hedy was cleaning mud from her espadrilles in the cabin.

"I handled them." Arnetta sucked on her teeth and proudly grinned. "I told her we was going to gather leaves."

"Gather leaves," Octavia said, nodding respectfully. "That's a good one. They're so mad-crazy about this camping thing." She looked from ground to sky, sky to ground. Her hair hung down her back in two braids like a squaw's. "I mean, I really don't know why it's even called *camping* — all we ever do with Nature is find some twigs and say something like, 'Wow, this fell from a tree.'" She then studied her sandwich. With two disdainful fingers, she picked out a slice of dripping tomato, the sections congealed with red slime. She pitched it into the stream embrowned with dead leaves and the murky effigies of other dead things, but in the opaque water a group of small silver-brown fish appeared. They surrounded the tomato and nibbled.

"Look!" Janice cried. "Fishes! Fishes!" As she scrambled to the edge of the stream to watch, a covey of insects threw up tantrums from the wheatgrass and nettle, a throng of tiny electric machines, all going at once. Octavia snuck up behind Janice as if to push her in. Daphne and I exchanged terrified looks. It seemed as though only we knew that Octavia was close enough — and bold enough — to actually push Janice into the stream. Janice turned around quickly, but Octavia was already staring serenely into the still water as though she were gathering some sort of courage from it. "What's so funny?" Janice said, eyeing them all suspiciously.

Elise began humming the tune to "Karma Chameleon," all the girls joining in, their hums light and facile. Janice began to hum, against everyone else, the high-octane opening chords of "Beat It."

"I love me some Michael Jackson," Janice said when she'd finished humming, smacking her lips as though Michael Jackson were a favorite meal. "I will marry Michael Jackson."

Before anyone had a chance to impress upon Janice the impossibility of this, Arnetta suddenly rose, made a sun visor of her hand, and watched Troop 909 leave the field hockey lawn.

"Dammit!" she said. "We've got to get them *alone*."

"They won't ever be alone," I said. All the rest of the girls looked at me. If I spoke even a word, I could count on someone calling me Snot, but everyone seemed to think that we could beat up these girls; no one entertained the thought that they might fight *back*. "The only time they'll be unsupervised is in the bathroom."

"Oh shut up, Snot," Octavia said.

But Arnetta slowly nodded her head. "The bathroom," she said. "The bathroom," she said, again and again. "The bathroom! The bathroom!" She cheered so blissfully that I thought for a moment she was joking.

According to Octavia's watch, it took us five minutes to hike to the restrooms, which were midway between our cabin and Troop 909's. Inside, the mirrors above the sinks returned only the vaguest of reflections, as though someone had taken a scouring pad to their surfaces to obscure the shine. Pine needles, leaves, and dirty flattened wads of chewing gum covered the floor like a mosaic. Webs of hair matted the drain in the middle of the floor. Above the sinks and below the mirrors, stacks of folded white paper towels lay on a long metal counter. Shaggy white balls of paper towels sat on the sink tops in a line like corsages on display. A thread of floss snaked from a wad of tissues dotted with the faint red-pink of blood. One of those white girls, I thought, had just lost a tooth.

The restroom looked almost the same as it had the night before, but it somehow seemed stranger now. We had never noticed the wooden rafters before, coming together in great V's. We were, it seemed, inside a whale, viewing the ribs of the roof of its mouth.

"Wow. It's a mess," Elise said.

"You can say that again."

Arnetta leaned against the doorjamb of a restroom stall. "This is where they'll be again," she said. Just seeing the place, just having a plan, seemed to satisfy her. "We'll go in and talk to them. You know, 'How you doing? How long will you be here?,' that sort of thing. Then Octavia and I are gonna tell them what happens when they call any one of us a nigger."

"I'm going to say something, too," Janice said.

Arnetta considered this. "Sure," she said. "Of course. Whatever you want."

Janice pointed her finger like a gun at Octavia and rehearsed the line she'd thought up, " 'We're gonna teach you a *lesson*.' That's what I'm going to say." She narrowed her eyes like a TV mobster. " 'We're gonna teach you little girls a lesson!' "

With the back of her hand, Octavia brushed Janice's finger away. "You couldn't teach me to shit in a toilet."

"But," I said, "what if they say, 'We didn't say that. We didn't call anyone a N-I-G-G-E-R'?"

"Snot," Arnetta sighed. "Don't think. Just fight. If you even know how."

Everyone laughed while Daphne stood there. Arnetta gently laid her hand on Daphne's shoulder. "Daphne. You don't have to fight. We're doing this for you."

Daphne walked to the counter, took a clean paper towel, and carefully unfolded it like a map. With this, she began to pick up the trash all around. Everyone watched.

"C'mon," Arnetta said to everyone. "Let's beat it." We all ambled toward the restroom doorway, where the sunshine made one large white rectangle of light. We were immediately blinded and shielded our eyes with our hands, our forearms.

"Daphne?" Arnetta asked. "Are you coming?"

We all looked back at the girl, who was bending, the thin of her back hunched like a maid caught in stage limelight. Stray strands of her hair were lit nearly transparent, thin fiber-optic threads. She did not nod yes to the question, nor did she shake her head no. She abided, bent. Then she began again, picking up leaves, wads of paper, the cotton fluff innards from a torn stuffed toy. She did it so methodically, so exquisitely, so humbly, she must have been trained. I thought of those dresses she wore, faded and old, yet so pressed and clean; I then saw the poverty in them, I then could imagine her mother, cleaning the houses of others, returning home, weary.

"I guess she's not coming."

We left her, heading back to our cabin, over pine needles and leaves, taking the path full of shade.

"What about our secret meeting?" Elise asked.

Arnetta enunciated in a way that defied contradiction: "We just had it."

Just as we caught sight of our cabin, Arnetta violently swerved away from Octavia. "You farted," she said.

Octavia began to sashay, as if on a catwalk, then proclaimed, in a Hollywood-starlet voice, "My farts smell like perfume."

It was nearing our bedtime, but in the lengthening days of spring, the sun had not yet set.

"Hey, your mama's coming," Arnetta said to Octavia when she saw Mrs. Hedy walk toward the cabin, sniffling. When Octavia's mother wasn't giving bored, parochial orders, she sniffled continuously, mourning an imminent divorce from her husband. She might begin a sentence, "I don't know what Robert will do when Octavia and I are gone. Who'll buy him cigarettes?" and Octavia would hotly whisper *"Mama"* in a way that meant: Please don't talk about our problems in front of everyone. Please shut up.

But when Mrs. Hedy began talking about her husband, thinking about her husband, seeing clouds shaped like the head of her husband, she couldn't be quiet, and no one could ever dislodge her from the comfort of her own woe. Only one thing could perk her up — Brownie songs. If the rest of the girls were quiet, and Mrs. Hedy was in her dopey sorrowful mood, she would say, "Y'all know I like those songs, girls. Why don't you sing one?" Everyone would groan except me and Daphne. I, for one, liked some of the songs.

"C'mon, everybody," Octavia said drearily. "She likes 'The Brownie Song' best."

We sang, loud enough to reach Mrs. Hedy:

> I've something in my pocket;
> It belongs across my face.
> And I keep it very close at hand in a most convenient place.
> I'm sure you couldn't guess it
> If you guessed a long, long while.
> So I'll take it out and put it on —
> It's a great big Brownie Smile!

"The Brownie Song" was supposed to be sung as though we were elves in a workshop, singing as we merrily cobbled shoes, but everyone except me hated the song and sang it like a maudlin record, played at the most sluggish of rpms.

"That was good," Mrs. Hedy said, closing the cabin door behind her. "Wasn't that nice, Linda?"

"Praise God," Mrs. Margolin answered without raising her head from the chore of counting out Popsicle sticks for the next day's session of crafts.

"Sing another one," Mrs. Hedy said, with a sort of joyful aggression, like a drunk I'd once seen who'd refused to leave a Korean grocery.

"God, Mama, get over it," Octavia whispered in a voice meant only for Arnetta, but Mrs. Hedy heard it and started to leave the cabin.

"Don't go," Arnetta said. She ran after Mrs. Hedy and held her by the arm. "We haven't finished singing." She nudged us with a single look. "Let's sing 'The Friends Song.' For Mrs. Hedy."

Although I liked some of the songs, I hated this one:

> Make new friends
> But keep the o-old,
> One is silver
> And the other gold.

If most of the girls in my troop could be any type of metal, they'd be bunched-up wads of tinfoil maybe, or rusty iron nails you had to get tetanus shots for.

"No, no, no," Mrs. Margolin said before anyone could start in on "The Friends Song." "An uplifting song. Something to lift her up and take her mind off all these earthly burdens."

Arnetta and Octavia rolled their eyes. Everyone knew what song Mrs. Margolin was talking about, and no one, no one, wanted to sing it.

"Please, no," a voice called out. "Not 'The Doughnut Song.'"

"Please not 'The Doughnut Song,'" Octavia pleaded.

"I'll brush my teeth twice if I don't have to sing 'The Doughnut—'"

"Sing!" Mrs. Margolin demanded.

We sang:

> Life without Jesus is like a do-ough-nut!
> Like a do-ooough-nut!
> Like a do-ooough-nut!
> Life without Jesus is like a do-ough-nut!
> There's a hole in the middle of my soul!

There were other verses, involving other pastries, but we stopped after the first one and cast glances toward Mrs. Margolin to see if we could gain a reprieve. Mrs. Margolin's eyes fluttered blissfully, half-asleep.

"Awww," Mrs. Hedy said, as though giant Mrs. Margolin were a cute baby. "Mrs. Margolin's had a long day."

"Yes indeed," Mrs. Margolin answered. "If you don't mind, I might just go to the lodge where the beds are. I haven't been the same since the operation."

I had not heard of this operation, or when it had occurred, since Mrs. Margolin had never missed the once-a-week Brownie meetings, but I could see from Daphne's face that she was concerned, and I could see that the other girls had decided that Mrs. Margolin's operation must have happened long ago in some remote time unconnected to our own. Nevertheless, they put on sad faces. We had all been taught that adulthood was full of sorrow and pain, taxes and bills, dreaded work and dealings with whites, sickness, and death.

"Go right ahead, Linda," Mrs. Hedy said. "I'll watch the girls." Mrs. Hedy seemed to forget about divorce for a moment; she looked at us with dewy eyes, as if we were mysterious, furry creatures. Meanwhile, Mrs. Margolin walked through the maze of sleeping bags until she found her own. She gathered a neat stack of clothes and pajamas slowly, as though doing so were almost painful. She took her toothbrush, her toothpaste, her pillow. "All right!" Mrs. Margolin said, addressing us all from the threshold of the cabin. "Be in bed by nine." She said it with a twinkle in her voice, as though she were letting us know she was allowing us to be naughty and stay up till nine-fifteen.

"C'mon, everybody," Arnetta said after Mrs. Margolin left. "Time for us to wash up."

Everyone watched Mrs. Hedy closely, wondering whether she would insist on coming with us since it was night, making a fight with Troop 909 nearly impossible. Troop 909 would soon be in the bathroom, washing their faces, brushing their teeth — completely unsuspecting of our ambush.

"We won't be long," Arnetta said. "We're old enough to go to the restroom by ourselves."

Mrs. Hedy pursed her lips at this dilemma. "Well, I guess you Brownies are almost Girl Scouts, right?"

"Right!"

"Just one more badge," Drema said.

"And about," Octavia droned, "a million more cookies to sell." Octavia looked at all of us. *Now's our chance,* her face seemed to say, but our chance to do *what* I didn't exactly know.

Finally, Mrs. Hedy walked to the doorway where Octavia stood, dutifully waiting to say good-bye and looking bored doing it. Mrs. Hedy held Octavia's chin. "You'll be good?"

"Yes, Mama."

"And remember to pray for me and your father? If I'm asleep when you get back?"

"Yes, Mama."

• • •

When the other girls had finished getting their toothbrushes and wash-cloths and flashlights for the group restroom trip, I was drawing pictures of tiny birds with too many feathers. Daphne was sitting on her sleeping bag, reading.

"You're not going to come?" Octavia asked.

Daphne shook her head.

"I'm also gonna stay, too," I said. "I'll go to the restroom when Daphne and Mrs. Hedy go."

Arnetta leaned down toward me and whispered so that Mrs. Hedy, who had taken over Mrs. Margolin's task of counting Popsicle sticks, couldn't hear. "No, Snot. If we get in trouble, you're going to get in trouble with the rest of us."

We made our way through the darkness by flashlight. The tree branches that had shaded us just hours earlier, along the same path, now looked like arms sprouting menacing hands. The stars sprinkled the sky like spilled salt. They seemed fastened to the darkness, high up and holy, their places fixed and definite as we stirred beneath them.

Some, like me, were quiet because we were afraid of the dark; others were talking like crazy for the same reason.

"Wow," Drema said, looking up. "Why are all the stars out here? I never see stars back on Oneida Street."

"It's a camping trip, that's why," Octavia said. "You're supposed to see stars on camping trips."

Janice said, "This place smells like the air freshener my mother uses."

"These woods are *pine*," Elise said. "Your mother probably uses pine air freshener."

Janice mouthed an exaggerated "Oh," nodding her head as though she just then understood one of the world's great secrets.

No one talked about fighting. Everyone was afraid enough just walking through the infinite deep of the woods. Even without seeing anyone's face, I could tell this wasn't about Daphne being called a nigger. The word that had started it all seemed melted now into some deeper, unnameable feeling. Even though I didn't want to fight, was afraid of fighting, I felt as though I were part of the rest of the troop, as though I were defending something. We trudged against the slight incline of the path, Arnetta leading the way. I wondered, looking at her back, what she could be thinking.

"You know," I said, "their leader will be there. Or they won't even be there. It's dark already. Last night the sun was still in the sky. I'm sure they're already finished."

"Whose flashlight is this?" Arnetta said, shaking the weakening beam of the light she was holding. "It's out of batteries."

Octavia handed Arnetta her flashlight. And that's when I saw it. The bathroom was just ahead.

But the girls were there. We could hear them before we could see them.

"Octavia and I will go in first so they'll think there's just two of us. Then wait till I say, 'We're gonna teach you a lesson,'" Arnetta said. "Then bust in. That'll surprise them."

"That's what I was supposed to say," Janice said.

Arnetta went inside, Octavia next to her. Janice followed, and the rest of us waited outside.

They were in there for what seemed like whole minutes, but something was wrong. Arnetta hadn't given the signal yet. I was with the girls outside when I heard one of the Troop 909 girls say, "NO. That did NOT happen!"

That was to be expected, that they'd deny the whole thing. What I hadn't expected was *the voice* in which the denial was said. The girl sounded as though her tongue were caught in her mouth. "That's a BAD word!" the girl continued. "We don't say BAD words!"

"Let's go in," Elise said.

"No," Drema said. "I don't want to. What if we get beat up?"

"Snot?" Elise turned to me, her flashlight blinding. It was the first time anyone had asked my opinion, though I knew they were just asking because they were afraid.

"I say we go inside, just to see what's going on."

"But Arnetta didn't give us the signal," Drema said. "She's supposed to say, 'We're going to teach you a lesson,' and I didn't hear her say it."

"C'mon," I said. "Let's just go in."

We went inside. There we found the white girls, but about five girls were huddled up next to one big girl. I instantly knew she was the owner of the voice we'd heard. Arnetta and Octavia inched toward us as soon as we entered.

"Where's Janice?" Elise asked, then we heard a flush. "Oh."

"I think," Octavia said, whispering to Elise, "they're retarded."

"We ARE NOT retarded!" the big girl said, though it was obvious that she was. That they all were. The girls around her began to whimper.

"They're just pretending," Arnetta said, trying to convince herself. "I know they are."

Octavia turned to Arnetta. "Arnetta. Let's just leave."

Janice came out of a stall, happy and relieved, then she suddenly remembered her line, pointed to the big girl, and said, "We're gonna teach you a lesson."

"Shut up, Janice," Octavia said, but her heart was not in it. Arnetta's face was set in a lost, deep scowl. Octavia turned to the big girl, and said loudly, slowly, as if they were all deaf, "We're going to leave. It was nice meeting you, okay? You don't have to tell anyone that we were here. Okay?"

"Why not?" said the big girl, like a taunt. When she spoke, her lips did not meet, her mouth did not close. Her tongue grazed the roof of her mouth, like a little pink fish. "You'll get in trouble. I know. I know."

Arnetta got back her old cunning. "If you said anything, then you'd be a tattletale."

The girl looked sad for a moment, then perked up quickly. A flash of genius crossed her face: "I *like* tattletale."

"It's all right, girls. It's gonna be all right!" the 909 troop leader said. It was as though someone had instructed all of Troop 909 to cry at once. The troop leader had girls under her arm, and all the rest of the girls crowded about her. It reminded me of a hog I'd seen on a field trip, where all the little hogs would gather about the mother at feeding time, latching on to her teats. The 909 troop leader had come into the bathroom shortly after the big girl threatened to tell. Then the ranger came, then, once the ranger had radioed the station, Mrs. Margolin arrived with Daphne in tow.

The ranger had left the restroom area, but everyone else was huddled just outside, swatting mosquitoes.

"Oh. They *will* apologize," Mrs. Margolin said to the 909 troop leader, but Mrs. Margolin said this so angrily, I knew she was speaking more to us than to the other troop leader. "When their parents find out, every one a them will be on punishment."

"It's all right. It's all right," the 909 troop leader reassured Mrs. Margolin. Her voice lilted in the same way it had when addressing the girls. She smiled the whole time she talked. She was like one of those TV cooking show women who talk and dice onions and smile all at the same time.

"See. It could have happened. I'm not calling your girls fibbers or any-thing." She shook her head ferociously from side to side, her Egyptian-style pageboy flapping against her cheeks like heavy drapes. "It *could* have happened, see. Our girls are *not* retarded. They are *delayed* learn-ers." She said this in a syrupy instructional voice, as though our troop might be delayed learners as well. "We're from the Decatur Children's Academy. Many of them just have special needs."

"Now we won't be able to walk to the bathroom by ourselves!" the big girl said.

"Yes you will," the troop leader said, "but maybe we'll wait till we get back to Decatur—"

"I don't want to wait!" the girl said. "I want my Independence patch!"

The girls in my troop were entirely speechless. Arnetta looked as though she were soon to be tortured but was determined not to appear weak. Mrs. Margolin pursed her lips solemnly and said, "Bless them, Lord. Bless them."

In contrast, the Troop 909 leader was full of words and energy. "Some of our girls are echolalic—" She smiled and happily presented one of the girls hanging on to her, but the girl widened her eyes in horror and violently withdrew herself from the center of attention, as though she sensed she were being sacrificed for the village sins. "Echolalic," the troop leader continued. "That means they will say whatever they hear, like an echo—that's where the word comes from. It comes from 'echo.'" She ducked her head apologetically. "I mean, not all of them have the most *progressive* of parents, so if they heard a bad word they might have repeated it. But I guarantee it would not have been *intentional.*"

Arnetta spoke. "I saw her say the word. I heard her." She pointed to a small girl, smaller than any of us, wearing an oversized T-shirt that read: EAT BERTHA'S MUSSELS.

The troop leader shook her head and smiled. "That's impossible. She doesn't speak. She can, but she doesn't."

Arnetta furrowed her brow. "No. It wasn't her. That's right. It was *her.*"

The girl Arnetta pointed to grinned as though she'd been paid a com-pliment. She was the only one from either troop actually wearing a full uniform: the mocha-colored A-line shift, the orange ascot, the sash cov-ered with patches, though all the same one—the Try-It patch. She took a few steps toward Arnetta and made a grand sweeping gesture toward the sash. "See," she said, full of self-importance, "I'm a Brownie." I had a hard time imagining this girl calling anyone a "nigger"; the girl looked perpetually delighted, as though she would have cuddled up with a grizzly if someone had let her.

On the fourth morning, we boarded the bus to go home.

The previous day had been spent building miniature churches from Popsicle sticks. We hardly left the cabin. Mrs. Margolin and Mrs. Hedy guarded us so closely, almost no one talked for the entire day.

Even on the day of departure from Camp Crescendo, all was serious and silent. The bus ride began quietly enough. Arnetta had to sit beside Mrs. Margolin, Octavia had to sit beside her mother. I sat beside Daphne, who gave me her prize journal without a word of explanation.

"You don't want it?"

She shook her head no. It was empty.

Then Mrs. Hedy began to weep. "Octavia," Mrs. Hedy said to her daughter without looking at her, "I'm going to sit with Mrs. Margolin. All right?"

Arnetta exchanged seats with Mrs. Hedy. With the two women up front, Elise felt it safe to speak. "Hey," she said, then she set her face into a placid vacant stare, trying to imitate that of a Troop 909 girl. Emboldened, Arnetta made a gesture of mock pride toward an imaginary sash, the way the girl in full uniform had done. Then they all made a game of it, trying to do the most exaggerated imitations of the Troop 909 girls, all without speaking, all without laughing loud enough to catch the women's attention.

Daphne looked at her shoes, white with sneaker polish. I opened the journal she'd given me. I looked out the window, trying to decide what to write, searching for lines, but nothing could compare with the lines Daphne had written, *"My father, the veteran,"* my favorite line of all time. The line replayed itself in my head, and I gave up trying to write.

By then, it seemed as though the rest of the troop had given up making fun of the 909 girls. They were now quietly gossiping about who had passed notes to whom in school. For a moment the gossiping fell off, and all I heard was the hum of the bus as we sped down the road and the muffled sounds of Mrs. Hedy and Mrs. Margolin talking about serious things.

"You know," Octavia whispered, "why did *we* have to be stuck at a camp with retarded girls? You know?"

"*You* know why," Arnetta answered. She narrowed her eyes like a cat.

"My mama and I were in the mall in Buckhead, and this white lady just kept looking at us. I mean, like we were foreign or something. Like we were from China."

"What did the woman say?" Elise asked.

"Nothing," Arnetta said. "She didn't say nothing."

A few girls quietly nodded their heads.

"There was this time," I said, "when my father and I were in the mall and—"

"Oh, shut up, Snot," Octavia said.

I stared at Octavia, then rolled my eyes from her to the window. As I watched the trees blur, I wanted nothing more than to be through with it all: the bus ride, the troop, school—all of it. But we were going home. I'd see the same girls in school the next day. We were on a bus, and there was nowhere else to go.

"Go on, Laurel," Daphne said to me. It was the first time she'd spoken the whole trip, and she'd said my name. I turned to her and smiled weakly so as not to cry, hoping she'd remember when I'd tried to be her friend, thinking maybe that her gift of the journal was an invitation of friendship. But she didn't smile back. All she said was, "What happened?"

I studied the girls, waiting for Octavia to tell me to "shut up" again before I even had a chance to utter another word, but everyone was amazed that Daphne had spoken. I gathered my voice. "Well," I said. "My father and I were in this mall, but *I* was the one doing the staring." I stopped and glanced from face to face. I continued. "There were these white people dressed like Puritans or something, but they weren't Puritans. They were Mennonites. They're these people who, if you ask them to do a favor, like paint your porch or something, they have to do it. It's in their rules."

"That sucks," someone said.

"C'mon," Arnetta said. "You're lying."

"I am not."

"How do you know that's not just some story someone made up?" Elise asked, her head cocked, full of daring. "I mean, who's gonna do whatever you ask?"

"It's not made up. I know because when I was looking at them, my father said, 'See those people. If you ask them to do something, they'll do it. Anything you want.'"

No one would call anyone's father a liar. Then they'd have to fight the person, but Drema parsed her words carefully. "How does your *father* know that's not just some story? Huh?"

"Because," I said, "he went up to the man and asked him would he paint our porch, and the man said, 'Yes.' It's their religion."

"Man, I'm glad I'm a Baptist," Elise said, shaking her head in sympathy for the Mennonites.

"So did the guy do it?" Drema asked, scooting closer to hear if the story got juicy.

"Yeah," I said. "His whole family was with him. My dad drove them to our house. They all painted our porch. The woman and girl were in bonnets and long, long skirts with buttons up to their necks. The guy wore this weird hat and these huge suspenders."

"Why," Arnetta asked archly, as though she didn't believe a word, "would someone pick a *porch*? If they'll do anything, why not make them paint the whole *house*? Why not ask for a hundred bucks?"

I thought about it, and I remembered the words my father had said about them painting our porch, though I had never seemed to think about his words after he'd said them.

"He said," I began, only then understanding the words as they uncoiled from my mouth, "it was the only time he'd have a white man on his knees doing something for a black man for free."

I remembered the Mennonites bending like Daphne had bent, cleaning the restroom. I remembered the dark blue of their bonnets, the black of their shoes. They painted the porch as though scrubbing a floor. I was already trembling before Daphne asked quietly, "Did he thank them?"

I looked out the window. I could not tell which were the thoughts and which were the trees. "No," I said, and suddenly knew there was something mean in the world that I could not stop.

Arnetta laughed. "If I asked them to take off their long skirts and bonnets and put on some jeans, they would do it?"

And Daphne's voice—quiet, steady: "Maybe they would. Just to be nice."

2004

SHERMAN ALEXIE
WHAT YOU PAWN I
WILL REDEEM

from *The New Yorker*

A Spokane/Coeur d'Alene Indian, SHERMAN ALEXIE (b. 1966) was raised in Washington on the Spokane Indian Reservation. He said, "My mom and dad met when he moved to the rez, when he was five and she was fourteen. And she helped him get a drink at a water fountain. My mom was born in the house where her mom was born. So we were as isolated in the sense of Native Americans as anybody else. So, you know, I realized later on that when I left the rez to go to the White high school on the border of the rez I was a first-generation immigrant, you know? I'm an indigenous immigrant."

Alexie has published twenty-four books, including *The Lone Ranger and Tonto Fistfight in Heaven, Blasphemy, New and Selected Stories,* and *The Absolutely True Diary of a Part-Time Indian,* a novel for children. He has received the PEN/Faulkner Award for Fiction, the PEN/Malamud Award for Short Fiction, a PEN/Hemingway Citation for Best First Fiction, and the National Book Award for Young People's Literature.

Alexie's work tells of reservation life and American pop culture and combines irony with moments of surrealism. He is also known for his humor: "Humor in the face of incredible epic pain. I mean, Jewish folks invented American comedy . . . They have this incredible cultural power. And in a way, I wish that was us. In a way, that could have easily been us. You know? Indians with our storytelling and artistic ability could have created Hollywood. We could have created American comedy. So in some ways, we're the yin and yang of the American genocidal coin."

★

NOON

One day you have a home and the next you don't, but I'm not going to tell you my particular reasons for being homeless, because it's my secret story, and Indians have to work hard to keep secrets from hungry white folks.

I'm a Spokane Indian boy, an Interior Salish, and my people have lived within a hundred-mile radius of Spokane, Washington, for at least ten thousand years. I grew up in Spokane, moved to Seattle twenty-three years ago for college, flunked out after two semesters, worked various blue- and bluer-collar jobs, married two or three times, fathered two or three kids, and then went crazy. Of course, crazy is not the official definition of my mental problem, but I don't think asocial disorder fits it, either, because that makes me sound like I'm a serial killer or something. I've never hurt another human being, or, at least, not physically. I've broken a few hearts in my time, but we've all done that, so I'm nothing special in that regard. I'm a boring heartbreaker, too. I never dated or married more than one woman at a time. I didn't break hearts into pieces overnight. I broke them slowly and carefully. And I didn't set any land-speed records running out the door. Piece by piece, I disappeared. I've been disappearing ever since.

I've been homeless for six years now. If there's such a thing as an effective homeless man, then I suppose I'm effective. Being homeless is probably the only thing I've ever been good at. I know where to get the best free food. I've made friends with restaurant and convenience store managers who let me use their bathrooms. And I don't mean the public bathrooms, either. I mean the employees' bathrooms, the clean ones hidden behind the kitchen or the pantry or the cooler. I know it sounds strange to be proud of this, but it means a lot to me, being trustworthy enough to piss in somebody else's clean bathroom. Maybe you don't understand the value of a clean bathroom, but I do.

Probably none of this interests you. Homeless Indians are everywhere in Seattle. We're common and boring, and you walk right on by us, with maybe a look of anger or disgust or even sadness at the terrible fate of the noble savage. But we have dreams and families. I'm friends with a homeless Plains Indian man whose son is the editor of a big-time newspaper back east. Of course, that's his story, but we Indians are great storytellers and liars and mythmakers, so maybe that Plains Indian hobo is just a plain old everyday Indian. I'm kind of suspicious of him, because he identifies himself only as Plains Indian, a generic term, and not by a specific tribe. When I asked him why he wouldn't tell me exactly what he is, he said, "Do any of us know exactly what we are?" Yeah, great, a philosophizing Indian. "Hey," I said, "you got to have a home to be that homely." He just laughed and flipped me the eagle and walked away.

I wander the streets with a regular crew—my teammates, my defenders, my posse. It's Rose of Sharon, Junior, and me. We matter to one another if we don't matter to anybody else. Rose of Sharon is a big woman, about seven feet tall if you're measuring overall effect and about five feet tall if you're only talking about the physical. She's a Yakama Indian of the Wishram variety. Junior is a Colville, but there are about 199 tribes that make up the Colville, so he could be anything. He's good-looking, though, like he just stepped out of some "Don't Litter the Earth" public service advertisement. He's got those great big cheekbones that are like planets, you know, with little moons orbiting them. He gets me jealous, jealous, and jealous. If you put Junior and me next to each other, he's the Before Columbus Arrived Indian and I'm the After Columbus Arrived Indian. I am living proof of the horrible damage that colonialism has done to us Skins. But I'm not going to let you know how scared I sometimes get of history and its ways. I'm a strong man, and I know that silence is the best method of dealing with white folks.

This whole story really started at lunchtime, when Rose of Sharon, Junior, and I were panning the handle down at Pike Place Market. After about two hours of negotiating, we earned five dollars—good enough for a bottle of fortified courage from the most beautiful 7-Eleven in the world. So we headed over that way, feeling like warrior drunks, and we walked past this pawnshop I'd never noticed before. And that was strange, because we Indians have built-in pawnshop radar. But the strangest thing of all was the old powwow-dance regalia I saw hanging in the window.

"That's my grandmother's regalia," I said to Rose of Sharon and Junior.

"How you know for sure?" Junior asked.

I didn't know for sure, because I hadn't seen that regalia in person ever. I'd only seen photographs of my grandmother dancing in it. And those were taken before somebody stole it from her, fifty years ago. But it sure looked like my memory of it, and it had all the same color feathers and beads that my family sewed into our powwow regalia.

"There's only one way to know for sure," I said.

So Rose of Sharon, Junior, and I walked into the pawnshop and greeted the old white man working behind the counter.

"How can I help you?" he asked.

"That's my grandmother's powwow regalia in your window," I said.

"Somebody stole it from her fifty years ago, and my family has been searching for it ever since."

The pawnbroker looked at me like I was a liar. I understood. Pawnshops are filled with liars.

"I'm not lying," I said. "Ask my friends here. They'll tell you."

"He's the most honest Indian I know," Rose of Sharon said.

"All right, honest Indian," the pawnbroker said. "I'll give you the benefit of the doubt. Can you prove it's your grandmother's regalia?"

Because they don't want to be perfect, because only God is perfect, Indian people sew flaws into their powwow regalia. My family always sewed one yellow bead somewhere on our regalia. But we always hid it so that you had to search really hard to find it.

"If it really is my grandmother's," I said, "there will be one yellow bead hidden somewhere on it."

"All right, then," the pawnbroker said. "Let's take a look."

He pulled the regalia out of the window, laid it down on the glass counter, and we searched for that yellow bead and found it hidden beneath the armpit.

"There it is," the pawnbroker said. He didn't sound surprised. "You were right. This is your grandmother's regalia."

"It's been missing for fifty years," Junior said.

"Hey, Junior," I said. "It's my family's story. Let me tell it."

"All right," he said. "I apologize. You go ahead."

"It's been missing for fifty years," I said.

"That's his family's sad story," Rose of Sharon said. "Are you going to give it back to him?"

"That would be the right thing to do," the pawnbroker said. "But I can't afford to do the right thing. I paid a thousand dollars for this. I can't just give away a thousand dollars."

"We could go to the cops and tell them it was stolen," Rose of Sharon said.

"Hey," I said to her. "Don't go threatening people."

The pawnbroker sighed. He was thinking about the possibilities.

"Well, I suppose you could go to the cops," he said. "But I don't think they'd believe a word you said."

He sounded sad about that. As if he was sorry for taking advantage of our disadvantages.

"What's your name?" the pawnbroker asked me.

"Jackson," I said.

"Is that first or last?"

"Both," I said.

"Are you serious?"

"Yes, it's true. My mother and father named me Jackson Jackson. My family nickname is Jackson Squared. My family is funny."

"All right, Jackson Jackson," the pawnbroker said. "You wouldn't happen to have a thousand dollars, would you?"

"We've got five dollars total," I said.

"That's too bad," he said, and thought hard about the possibilities. "I'd sell it to you for a thousand dollars if you had it. Heck, to make it fair, I'd sell it to you for nine hundred and ninety-nine dollars. I'd lose a dollar. That would be the moral thing to do in this case. To lose a dollar would be the right thing."

"We've got five dollars total," I said again.

"That's too bad," he said once more, and thought harder about the possibilities. "How about this? I'll give you twenty-four hours to come up with nine hundred and ninety-nine dollars. You come back here at lunchtime tomorrow with the money and I'll sell it back to you. How does that sound?"

"It sounds all right," I said.

"All right, then," he said. "We have a deal. And I'll get you started. Here's twenty bucks."

He opened up his wallet and pulled out a crisp twenty-dollar bill and gave it to me. And Rose of Sharon, Junior, and I walked out into the daylight to search for nine hundred and seventy-four more dollars.

1 P.M.

Rose of Sharon, Junior, and I carried our twenty-dollar bill and our five dollars in loose change over to the 7-Eleven and bought three bottles of imagination. We needed to figure out how to raise all that money in only one day. Thinking hard, we huddled in an alley beneath the Alaska Way Viaduct and finished off those bottles — one, two, and three.

2 P.M.

Rose of Sharon was gone when I woke up. I heard later that she had hitchhiked back to Toppenish and was living with her sister on the reservation.

Junior had passed out beside me and was covered in his own vomit, or maybe somebody else's vomit, and my head hurt from thinking, so I left him alone and walked down to the water. I love the smell of ocean water. Salt always smells like memory.

When I got to the wharf, I ran into three Aleut cousins, who sat on a wooden bench and stared out at the bay and cried. Most of the homeless Indians in Seattle come from Alaska. One by one, each of them hopped a big working boat in Anchorage or Barrow or Juneau, fished his way south to Seattle, jumped off the boat with a pocketful of cash to party hard at one of the highly sacred and traditional Indian bars, went broke and broker, and has been trying to find his way back to the boat and the frozen north ever since.

These Aleuts smelled like salmon, I thought, and they told me they were going to sit on that wooden bench until their boat came back.

"How long has your boat been gone?" I asked.

"Eleven years," the elder Aleut said.

I cried with them for a while.

"Hey," I said. "Do you guys have any money I can borrow?"

They didn't.

3 P.M.

I walked back to Junior. He was still out cold. I put my face down near his mouth to make sure he was breathing. He was alive, so I dug around in his blue jeans pockets and found half a cigarette. I smoked it all the way down and thought about my grandmother.

Her name was Agnes, and she died of breast cancer when I was fourteen. My father always thought Agnes caught her tumors from the uranium mine on the reservation. But my mother said the disease started when Agnes was walking back from a powwow one night and got run over by a motorcycle. She broke three ribs, and my mother always said those ribs never healed right, and tumors take over when you don't heal right.

Sitting beside Junior, smelling the smoke and the salt and the vomit, I wondered if my grandmother's cancer started when somebody stole her powwow regalia. Maybe the cancer started in her broken heart and then leaked out into her breasts. I know it's crazy, but I wondered whether I could bring my grandmother back to life if I bought back her regalia.

I needed money, big money, so I left Junior and walked over to the Real Change office.

4 P.M.

Real Change is a multifaceted organization that publishes a newspaper, supports cultural projects that empower the poor and the homeless, and mobilizes the public around poverty issues. Real Change's mission is to organize, educate, and build alliances to create solutions to homelessness and poverty. It exists to provide a voice for poor people in our community.

I memorized Real Change's mission statement because I sometimes sell the newspaper on the streets. But you have to stay sober to sell it, and I'm not always good at staying sober. Anybody can sell the paper. You buy each copy for thirty cents and sell it for a dollar, and you keep the profit.

"I need one thousand four hundred and thirty papers," I said to the Big Boss.

"That's a strange number," he said. "And that's a lot of papers."

"I need them."

The Big Boss pulled out his calculator and did the math.

"It will cost you four hundred and twenty-nine dollars for that many," he said.

"If I had that kind of money, I wouldn't need to sell the papers."

"What's going on, Jackson-to-the-Second-Power?" he asked. He is the only person who calls me that. He's a funny and kind man.

I told him about my grandmother's powwow regalia and how much money I needed in order to buy it back.

"We should call the police," he said.

"I don't want to do that," I said. "It's a quest now. I need to win it back by myself."

"I understand," he said. "And, to be honest, I'd give you the papers to sell if I thought it would work. But the record for the most papers sold in one day by one vender is only three hundred and two."

"That would net me about two hundred bucks," I said.

The Big Boss used his calculator. "Two hundred and eleven dollars and forty cents," he said.

"That's not enough," I said.

"And the most money anybody has made in one day is five hundred and twenty-five. And that's because somebody gave Old Blue five hundred-dollar bills for some dang reason. The average daily net is about thirty dollars."

"This isn't going to work."

"No."

"Can you lend me some money?"

"I can't do that," he said. "If I lend you money, I have to lend money to everybody."

"What can you do?"

"I'll give you fifty papers for free. But don't tell anybody I did it."

"O.K.," I said.

He gathered up the newspapers and handed them to me. I held them to my chest. He hugged me. I carried the newspapers back toward the water.

5 P.M.

Back on the wharf, I stood near the Bainbridge Island Terminal and tried to sell papers to business commuters boarding the ferry.

I sold five in one hour, dumped the other forty-five in a garbage can, and walked into McDonald's, ordered four cheeseburgers for a dollar each, and slowly ate them.

After eating, I walked outside and vomited on the sidewalk. I hated to lose my food so soon after eating it. As an alcoholic Indian with a busted stomach, I always hope I can keep enough food in me to stay alive.

6 P.M.

With one dollar in my pocket, I walked back to Junior. He was still passed out, and I put my ear to his chest and listened for his heartbeat. He was alive, so I took off his shoes and socks and found one dollar in his left sock and fifty cents in his right sock.

With two dollars and fifty cents in my hand, I sat beside Junior and thought about my grandmother and her stories.

When I was thirteen, my grandmother told me a story about the Second World War. She was a nurse at a military hospital in Sydney, Australia. For two years, she healed and comforted American and Australian soldiers.

One day, she tended to a wounded Maori soldier, who had lost his legs to an artillery attack. He was very dark-skinned. His hair was black and curly and his eyes were black and warm. His face was covered with bright tattoos.

"Are you Maori?" he asked my grandmother.

"No," she said. "I'm Spokane Indian. From the United States."

"Ah, yes," he said. "I have heard of your tribes. But you are the first American Indian I have ever met."

"There's a lot of Indian soldiers fighting for the United States," she said. "I have a brother fighting in Germany, and I lost another brother on Okinawa."

"I am sorry," he said. "I was on Okinawa as well. It was terrible."

"I am sorry about your legs," my grandmother said.

"It's funny, isn't it?" he said.

"What's funny?"

"How we brown people are killing other brown people so white people will remain free."

"I hadn't thought of it that way."

"Well, sometimes I think of it that way. And other times I think of it the way they want me to think of it. I get confused."

She fed him morphine.

"Do you believe in heaven?" he asked.

"Which heaven?" she asked.

"I'm talking about the heaven where my legs are waiting for me."

They laughed.

"Of course," he said, "my legs will probably run away from me when I get to heaven. And how will I ever catch them?"

"You have to get your arms strong," my grandmother said. "So you can run on your hands."

They laughed again.

Sitting beside Junior, I laughed at the memory of my grandmother's story. I put my hand close to Junior's mouth to make sure he was still breathing. Yes, Junior was alive, so I took my two dollars and fifty cents and walked to the Korean grocery store in Pioneer Square.

7 P.M.

At the Korean grocery store, I bought a fifty-cent cigar and two scratch lottery tickets for a dollar each. The maximum cash prize was five hundred dollars a ticket. If I won both, I would have enough money to buy back the regalia.

I loved Mary, the young Korean woman who worked the register. She was the daughter of the owners, and she sang all day.

"I love you," I said when I handed her the money.

"You always say you love me," she said.

"That's because I will always love you."

"You are a sentimental fool."

"I'm a romantic old man."

"Too old for me."

"I know I'm too old for you, but I can dream."

"O.K.," she said. "I agree to be a part of your dreams, but I will only hold your hand in your dreams. No kissing and no sex. Not even in your dreams."

"O.K.," I said. "No sex. Just romance."

"Goodbye, Jackson Jackson, my love. I will see you soon."

I left the store, walked over to Occidental Park, sat on a bench, and smoked my cigar all the way down.

Ten minutes after I finished the cigar, I scratched my first lottery ticket and won nothing. I could win only five hundred dollars now, and that would be only half of what I needed.

Ten minutes after I lost, I scratched the other ticket and won a free ticket — a small consolation and one more chance to win some money.

I walked back to Mary.

"Jackson Jackson," she said. "Have you come back to claim my heart?"

"I won a free ticket," I said.

"Just like a man," she said. "You love money and power more than you love me."

"It's true," I said. "And I'm sorry it's true."

She gave me another scratch ticket, and I took it outside. I like to scratch my tickets in private. Hopeful and sad, I scratched that third ticket and won real money. I carried it back inside to Mary.

"I won a hundred dollars," I said.

She examined the ticket and laughed.

"That's a fortune," she said, and counted out five twenties. Our fingertips touched as she handed me the money. I felt electric and constant.

"Thank you," I said, and gave her one of the bills.

"I can't take that," she said. "It's your money."

"No, it's tribal. It's an Indian thing. When you win, you're supposed to share with your family."

"I'm not your family."

"Yes, you are."

She smiled. She kept the money. With eighty dollars in my pocket, I said goodbye to my dear Mary and walked out into the cold night air.

8 P.M.

I wanted to share the good news with Junior. I walked back to him, but he was gone. I heard later that he had hitchhiked down to Portland, Oregon, and died of exposure in an alley behind the Hilton Hotel.

9 P.M.

Lonesome for Indians, I carried my eighty dollars over to Big Heart's in South Downtown. Big Heart's is an all-Indian bar. Nobody knows how or why Indians migrate to one bar and turn it into an official Indian bar. But Big Heart's has been an Indian bar for twenty-three years. It used to be way up on Aurora Avenue, but a crazy Lummi Indian burned that one down, and the owners moved to the new location, a few blocks south of Safeco Field.

I walked into Big Heart's and counted fifteen Indians — eight men and seven women. I didn't know any of them, but Indians like to belong, so we all pretended to be cousins.

"How much for whiskey shots?" I asked the bartender, a fat white guy.

"You want the bad stuff or the badder stuff?"

"As bad as you got."

"One dollar a shot."

I laid my eighty dollars on the bar top.

"All right," I said. "Me and all my cousins here are going to be drinking eighty shots. How many is that apiece?"

"Counting you," a woman shouted from behind me, "that's five shots for everybody."

I turned to look at her. She was a chubby and pale Indian woman, sitting with a tall and skinny Indian man.

"All right, math genius," I said to her, and then shouted for the whole bar to hear. "Five drinks for everybody!"

All the other Indians rushed the bar, but I sat with the mathematician and her skinny friend. We took our time with our whiskey shots.

"What's your tribe?" I asked.

"I'm Duwamish," she said. "And he's Crow."

"You're a long way from Montana," I said to him.

"I'm Crow," he said. "I flew here."

"What's your name?" I asked them.

"I'm Irene Muse," she said. "And this is Honey Boy."

She shook my hand hard, but he offered his hand as if I was supposed to kiss it. So I did. He giggled and blushed, as much as a dark-skinned Crow can blush.

"You're one of them two-spirits, aren't you?" I asked him.

"I love women," he said. "And I love men."

"Sometimes both at the same time," Irene said.

We laughed.

"Man," I said to Honey Boy. "So you must have about eight or nine spirits going on inside you, enit?"

"Sweetie," he said. "I'll be whatever you want me to be."

"Oh, no," Irene said. "Honey Boy is falling in love."

"It has nothing to do with love," he said.

We laughed.

"Wow," I said. "I'm flattered, Honey Boy, but I don't play on your team."

"Never say never," he said.

"You better be careful," Irene said. "Honey Boy knows all sorts of magic."

"Honey Boy," I said, "you can try to seduce me, but my heart belongs to a woman named Mary."

"Is your Mary a virgin?" Honey Boy asked.

We laughed.

And we drank our whiskey shots until they were gone. But the other Indians bought me more whiskey shots, because I'd been so generous with my money. And Honey Boy pulled out his credit card, and I drank and sailed on that plastic boat.

After a dozen shots, I asked Irene to dance. She refused. But Honey Boy shuffled over to the jukebox, dropped in a quarter, and selected Willie Nelson's "Help Me Make It Through the Night." As Irene and I sat at the table and laughed and drank more whiskey, Honey Boy danced a slow circle around us and sang along with Willie.

"Are you serenading me?" I asked him.

He kept singing and dancing.

"Are you serenading me?" I asked him again.

"He's going to put a spell on you," Irene said.

I leaned over the table, spilling a few drinks, and kissed Irene hard. She kissed me back.

10 P.M.

Irene pushed me into the women's bathroom, into a stall, shut the door behind us, and shoved her hand down my pants. She was short, so I had to lean over to kiss her. I grabbed and squeezed her everywhere I could reach, and she was wonderfully fat, and every part of her body felt like a large, warm, soft breast.

MIDNIGHT

Nearly blind with alcohol, I stood alone at the bar and swore I had been standing in the bathroom with Irene only a minute ago.

"One more shot!" I yelled at the bartender.

"You've got no more money!" he yelled back.

"Somebody buy me a drink!" I shouted.

"They've got no more money!"

"Where are Irene and Honey Boy?"

"Long gone!"

2 A.M.

"Closing time!" the bartender shouted at the three or four Indians who were still drinking hard after a long, hard day of drinking. Indian alcoholics are either sprinters or marathoners.

"Where are Irene and Honey Boy?" I asked.

"They've been gone for hours," the bartender said.

"Where'd they go?"

"I told you a hundred times, I don't know."

"What am I supposed to do?"

"It's closing time. I don't care where you go, but you're not staying here."

"You are an ungrateful bastard. I've been good to you."

"You don't leave right now, I'm going to kick your ass."

"Come on, I know how to fight."

He came at me. I don't remember what happened after that.

4 A.M.

I emerged from the blackness and discovered myself walking behind a big warehouse. I didn't know where I was. My face hurt. I felt my nose and decided that it might be broken. Exhausted and cold, I pulled a plastic tarp from a truck bed, wrapped it around me like a faithful lover, and fell asleep in the dirt.

6 A.M.

Somebody kicked me in the ribs. I opened my eyes and looked up at a white cop.

"Jackson," the cop said. "Is that you?"

"Officer Williams," I said. He was a good cop with a sweet tooth. He'd given me hundreds of candy bars over the years. I wonder if he knew I was diabetic.

"What the hell are you doing here?" he asked.

"I was cold and sleepy," I said. "So I lay down."

"You dumb-ass, you passed out on the railroad tracks."

I sat up and looked around. I was lying on the railroad tracks. Dock-workers stared at me. I should have been a railroad-track pizza, a double Indian pepperoni with extra cheese. Sick and scared, I leaned over and puked whiskey.

"What the hell's wrong with you?" Officer Williams asked. "You've never been this stupid."

"It's my grandmother," I said. "She died."

"I'm sorry, man. When did she die?"

"Nineteen seventy-two."

"And you're killing yourself now?"

"I've been killing myself ever since she died."

He shook his head. He was sad for me. Like I said, he was a good cop.

"And somebody beat the hell out of you," he said. "You remember who?"

"Mr. Grief and I went a few rounds."

"It looks like Mr. Grief knocked you out."

"Mr. Grief always wins."

"Come on," he said. "Let's get you out of here."

He helped me up and led me over to his squad car. He put me in the back. "You throw up in there and you're cleaning it up," he said.

"That's fair."

He walked around the car and sat in the driver's seat. "I'm taking you over to detox," he said.

"No, man, that place is awful," I said. "It's full of drunk Indians."

We laughed. He drove away from the docks.

"I don't know how you guys do it," he said.

"What guys?" I asked.

"You Indians. How the hell do you laugh so much? I just picked your ass off the railroad tracks, and you're making jokes. Why the hell do you do that?"

"The two funniest tribes I've ever been around are Indians and Jews, so I guess that says something about the inherent humor of genocide."

We laughed.

"Listen to you, Jackson. You're so smart. Why the hell are you on the street?"

"Give me a thousand dollars and I'll tell you."

"You bet I'd give you a thousand dollars if I knew you'd straighten up your life."

He meant it. He was the second-best cop I'd ever known.

"You're a good cop," I said.

"Come on, Jackson," he said. "Don't blow smoke up my ass."

"No, really, you remind me of my grandfather."

"Yeah, that's what you Indians always tell me."

"No, man, my grandfather was a tribal cop. He was a good cop. He never arrested people. He took care of them. Just like you."

"I've arrested hundreds of scumbags, Jackson. And I've shot a couple in the ass."

"It don't matter. You're not a killer."

"I didn't kill them. I killed their asses. I'm an ass-killer."

We drove through downtown. The missions and shelters had already released their overnighters. Sleepy homeless men and women stood on street corners and stared up at a gray sky. It was the morning after the night of the living dead.

"Do you ever get scared?" I asked Officer Williams.

"What do you mean?"

"I mean, being a cop, is it scary?"

He thought about that for a while. He contemplated it. I liked that about him.

"I guess I try not to think too much about being afraid," he said. "If you think about fear, then you'll be afraid. The job is boring most of the time. Just driving and looking into dark corners, you know, and see-ing nothing. But then things get heavy. You're chasing somebody, or fighting them or walking around a dark house, and you just know some crazy guy is hiding around a corner, and hell, yes, it's scary."

"My grandfather was killed in the line of duty," I said.

"I'm sorry. How'd it happen?"

I knew he'd listen closely to my story.

"He worked on the reservation. Everybody knew everybody. It was safe. We aren't like those crazy Sioux or Apache or any of those other warrior tribes. There've only been three murders on my reservation in the last hundred years."

"That is safe."

"Yeah, we Spokane, we're passive, you know. We're mean with words. And we'll cuss out anybody. But we don't shoot people. Or stab them. Not much, anyway."

"So what happened to your grandfather?"

"This man and his girlfriend were fighting down by Little Falls."

"Domestic dispute. Those are the worst."

"Yeah, but this guy was my grandfather's brother. My great-uncle."

"Oh, no."

"Yeah, it was awful. My grandfather just strolled into the house. He'd been there a thousand times. And his brother and his girlfriend were drunk and beating on each other. And my grandfather stepped between them, just as he'd done a hundred times before. And the girlfriend tripped or something. She fell down and hit her head and started crying. And my grandfather kneeled down beside her to make sure she was all right. And for some reason my great-uncle reached down, pulled my grandfather's pistol out of the holster, and shot him in the head."

"That's terrible. I'm sorry."

"Yeah, my great-uncle could never figure out why he did it. He went to prison forever, you know, and he always wrote these long letters. Like fifty pages of tiny little handwriting. And he was always trying to figure out why he did it. He'd write and write and write and try to figure it out. He never did. It's a great big mystery."

"Do you remember your grandfather?"

"A little bit. I remember the funeral. My grandmother wouldn't let them bury him. My father had to drag her away from the grave."

"I don't know what to say."

"I don't, either."

We stopped in front of the detox center.

"We're here," Officer Williams said.

"I can't go in there," I said.

"You have to."

"Please, no. They'll keep me for twenty-four hours. And then it will be too late."

"Too late for what?"

I told him about my grandmother's regalia and the deadline for buying it back.

"If it was stolen, you need to file a report," he said. "I'll investigate it myself. If that thing is really your grandmother's, I'll get it back for you. Legally."

"No," I said. "That's not fair. The pawnbroker didn't know it was stolen. And, besides, I'm on a mission here. I want to be a hero, you know? I want to win it back, like a knight."

"That's romantic crap."

"That may be. But I care about it. It's been a long time since I really cared about something."

Officer Williams turned around in his seat and stared at me. He studied me.

"I'll give you some money," he said. "I don't have much. Only thirty bucks. I'm short until payday. And it's not enough to get back the regalia. But it's something."

"I'll take it," I said.

"I'm giving it to you because I believe in what you believe. I'm hoping, and I don't know why I'm hoping it, but I hope you can turn thirty bucks into a thousand somehow."

"I believe in magic."

"I believe you'll take my money and get drunk on it."

"Then why are you giving it to me?"

"There ain't no such thing as an atheist cop."

"Sure, there is."

"Yeah, well, I'm not an atheist cop."

He let me out of the car, handed me two fivers and a twenty, and shook my hand.

"Take care of yourself, Jackson," he said. "Stay off the railroad tracks."

"I'll try," I said.

He drove away. Carrying my money, I headed back toward the water.

8 A.M.

On the wharf, those three Aleuts still waited on the wooden bench.

"Have you seen your ship?" I asked.

"Seen a lot of ships," the elder Aleut said. "But not our ship."

I sat on the bench with them. We sat in silence for a long time. I wondered if we would fossilize if we sat there long enough.

I thought about my grandmother. I'd never seen her dance in her regalia. And, more than anything, I wished I'd seen her dance at a powwow.

"Do you guys know any songs?" I asked the Aleuts.

"I know all of Hank Williams," the elder Aleut said.

"How about Indian songs?"

"Hank Williams is Indian."

"How about sacred songs?"

"Hank Williams is sacred."

"I'm talking about ceremonial songs. You know, religious ones. The songs you sing back home when you're wishing and hoping."

"What are you wishing and hoping for?"

"I'm wishing my grandmother was still alive."

"Every song I know is about that."

"Well, sing me as many as you can."

The Aleuts sang their strange and beautiful songs. I listened. They sang about my grandmother and about their grandmothers. They were lonesome for the cold and the snow. I was lonesome for everything.

10 A.M.

After the Aleuts finished their last song, we sat in silence for a while. Indians are good at silence.

"Was that the last song?" I asked.

"We sang all the ones we could," the elder Aleut said. "The others are just for our people."

I understood. We Indians have to keep our secrets. And these Aleuts were so secretive they didn't refer to themselves as Indians.

"Are you guys hungry?" I asked.

They looked at one another and communicated without talking.

"We could eat," the elder Aleut said.

11 A.M.

The Aleuts and I walked over to the Big Kitchen, a greasy diner in the International District. I knew they served homeless Indians who'd lucked into money.

"Four for breakfast?" the waitress asked when we stepped inside.

"Yes, we're very hungry," the elder Aleut said.

She took us to a booth near the kitchen. I could smell the food cooking. My stomach growled.

"You guys want separate checks?" the waitress asked.

"No, I'm paying," I said.

"Aren't you the generous one," she said.

"Don't do that," I said.

"Do what?" she asked.

"Don't ask me rhetorical questions. They scare me."

She looked puzzled, and then she laughed.

"O.K., professor," she said. "I'll only ask you real questions from now on."

"Thank you."

"What do you guys want to eat?"

"That's the best question anybody can ask anybody," I said. "What have you got?"

"How much money you got?" she asked.

"Another good question," I said. "I've got twenty-five dollars I can spend. Bring us all the breakfast you can, plus your tip."

She knew the math.

"All right, that's four specials and four coffees and fifteen percent for me."

The Aleuts and I waited in silence. Soon enough, the waitress returned and poured us four coffees, and we sipped at them until she returned again, with four plates of food. Eggs, bacon, toast, hash brown potatoes. It's amazing how much food you can buy for so little money.

Grateful, we feasted.

NOON

I said farewell to the Aleuts and walked toward the pawnshop. I heard later that the Aleuts had waded into the saltwater near Dock 47 and disappeared. Some Indians swore they had walked on the water and headed north. Other Indians saw the Aleuts drown. I don't know what happened to them.

I looked for the pawnshop and couldn't find it. I swear it wasn't in the place where it had been before. I walked twenty or thirty blocks looking for the pawnshop, turned corners and bisected intersections, and looked up its name in the phone books and asked people walking past me if they'd ever heard of it. But that pawnshop seemed to have sailed away like a ghost ship. I wanted to cry. And just when I'd given up, when I turned one last corner and thought I might die if I didn't find that pawnshop, there it was, in a space I swear it hadn't occupied a few minutes ago.

I walked inside and greeted the pawnbroker, who looked a little younger than he had before.

"It's you," he said.

"Yes, it's me," I said.

"Jackson Jackson."

"That is my name."

"Where are your friends?"

"They went traveling. But it's O.K. Indians are everywhere."

"Do you have the money?"

"How much do you need again?" I asked, and hoped the price had changed.

"Nine hundred and ninety-nine dollars."

It was still the same price. Of course, it was the same price. Why would it change?

"I don't have that," I said.

"What do you have?"

"Five dollars."

I set the crumpled Lincoln on the countertop. The pawnbroker studied it.

"Is that the same five dollars from yesterday?"

"No, it's different."

He thought about the possibilities.

"Did you work hard for this money?" he asked.

"Yes," I said.

He closed his eyes and thought harder about the possibilities. Then he stepped into the back room and returned with my grandmother's regalia.

"Take it," he said, and held it out to me.

"I don't have the money."

"I don't want your money."

"But I wanted to win it."

"You did win it. Now take it before I change my mind."

Do you know how many good men live in this world? Too many to count!

I took my grandmother's regalia and walked outside. I knew that solitary yellow bead was part of me. I knew I was that yellow bead in part. Outside, I wrapped myself in my grandmother's regalia and breathed her in. I stepped off the sidewalk and into the intersection. Pedestrians stopped. Cars stopped. The city stopped. They all watched me dance with my grandmother. I was my grandmother, dancing.

2005

EDWARD P. JONES

OLD BOYS, OLD GIRLS

from *The New Yorker*

EDWARD P. JONES was born in Washington, D.C. His mother had come north from Virginia and North Carolina. Jones says, "She did what they called 'days work,' taking care of a white child and cooking and cleaning. Then somehow she met my father . . . He was a drinker, so things started going bad pretty early on. Within a few years she was on her own, working full-time, with three kids . . . We lived in eighteen different places by the time I was eighteen."

Jones won a scholarship to Holy Cross College and later earned his MFA at the University of Virginia. He began working for a tax newsletter, first as a proofreader and later as a columnist, a job he kept for more than ten years, all the while writing fiction. His first short story was published in *Essence* in 1976. Jones's first book of short stories, *Lost in the City,* was published in 1992 and won the PEN/Hemingway Award, was shortlisted for the National Book Award, and was the recipient of a Lannan Foundation Award. His first novel, *The Known World,* received the 2004 Pulitzer Prize for fiction. Of the book, critic Janet Maslin wrote, "Mr. Jones explores the unsettling, contradiction-prone world of a Virginia slaveholder who happens to be black." Jones was named a MacArthur Fellow for 2004. *All Aunt Hagar's Children,* his most recent collection of short stories, was published in 2006.

Jones's writing largely explores race in Washington, D.C., where he currently lives.

★

THEY CAUGHT HIM after he had killed the second man. The law would never connect him to the first murder. So the victim — a stocky fellow Caesar Matthews shot in a Northeast alley only two blocks from the home of the guy's parents, a man who died over a woman who was actually in love with a third man — was destined to lie in his grave without anyone officially paying for what had happened to him. It was almost as if, at least on the books the law kept, Caesar had got away with a free killing.

Seven months after he stabbed the second man — a twenty-two-year-old with prematurely gray hair who had ventured out of Southeast for only the sixth time in his life — Caesar was tried for murder in the second degree. During much of the trial, he remembered the name only of the first dead man — Percy, or "Golden Boy," Weymouth — and not the second, Antwoine Stoddard, to whom everyone kept referring during the proceedings. The world had done things to Caesar since he'd left his father's house for good at sixteen, nearly fourteen years ago, but he had done far more to himself.

So at trial, with the weight of all the harm done to him and because he had hidden for months in one shit hole after another, he was not always himself and thought many times that he was actually there for killing Golden Boy, the first dead man. He was not insane, but he was three doors from it, which was how an old girlfriend, Yvonne Miller, would now and again playfully refer to his behavior. Who the fuck is this Antwoine bitch? Caesar sometimes thought during the trial. And where is Percy? It was only when the judge sentenced him to seven years in Lorton, D.C.'s prison in Virginia, that matters became somewhat clear again, and in those last moments before they took him away he saw Antwoine spread out on the ground outside the Prime Property nightclub, blood spurting out of his chest like oil from a bountiful well. Caesar remembered it all: sitting on the sidewalk, the liquor spinning his brain, his friends begging him to run, the club's music flooding out of the open door and going *thumpety-thump-thump* against his head. He sat a few feet from Antwoine and would have killed again for a cigarette. "That's you, baby, so very near insanity it can touch you," said Yvonne, who believed in unhappiness and who thought happiness was the greatest trick God had invented. Yvonne Miller would be waiting for Caesar at the end of the line.

He came to Lorton with a ready-made reputation, since Multrey Wilson and Tony Cathedral — first-degree murderers both, and destined to die there — knew him from his Northwest and Northeast days. They were about as big as you could get in Lorton at that time (the guards called Lorton the House of Multrey and Cathedral), and they let everyone know that Caesar was good people, "a protected body," with no danger of having his biscuits or his butt taken.

A little less than a week after Caesar arrived, Cathedral asked him how he liked his cellmate. Caesar had never been to prison but had spent five days in the D.C. jail, not counting the time there before and during the trial. They were side by side at dinner, and neither man looked at the other. Multrey sat across from them. Cathedral was done eating in three minutes, but Caesar always took a long time to eat. His mother had raised him to chew his food thoroughly. "You wanna be a old man livin on oatmeal?" "I love oatmeal, Mama." "Tell me that when you have to eat it every day till you die."

"He all right, I guess," Caesar said of his cellmate, with whom he had shared fewer than a thousand words. Caesar's mother had died before she saw what her son became.

"You got the bunk you want, the right bed?" Multrey said. He was sitting beside one of his two "women," the one he had turned out most recently. "She" was picking at her food, something Multrey had already warned her about. The woman had a family — a wife and three children — but they would not visit. Caesar would never have visitors, either.

"It's all right." Caesar had taken the top bunk, as the cellmate had already made the bottom his home. A miniature plastic panda from his youngest child dangled on a string hung from one of the metal bedposts. "Bottom, top, it's all the same ship."

Cathedral leaned into him, picking chicken out of his teeth with an inch-long fingernail sharpened to a point. "Listen, man, even if you like the top bunk, you fuck him up for the bottom just cause you gotta let him know who rules. You let him know that you will stab him through his motherfuckin heart and then turn around and eat your supper, cludin the dessert." Cathedral straightened up. "Caes, you gon be here a few days, so you can't let nobody fuck with your humanity."

He went back to the cell and told Pancho Morrison that he wanted the bottom bunk, couldn't sleep well at the top.

"Too bad," Pancho said. He was lying down, reading a book published by the Jehovah's Witnesses. He wasn't a Witness, but he was curious.

Caesar grabbed the book and flung it at the bars, and the bulk of it slid through an inch or so and dropped to the floor. He kicked Pancho in the side, and before he could pull his leg back for a second kick Pancho took the foot in both hands, twisted it, and threw him against the wall. Then Pancho was up, and they fought for nearly an hour before two guards, who had been watching the whole time, came in and beat them about the head. "Show's over! Show's over!" one kept saying.

They attended to themselves in silence in the cell, and with the same silence they flung themselves at each other the next day after dinner.

They were virtually the same size, and though Caesar came to battle with more muscle, Pancho had more heart. Cathedral had told Caesar that morning that Pancho had lived on practically nothing but heroin for the three years before Lorton, so whatever fighting dog was in him could be pounded out in little or no time. It took three days. Pancho was the father of five children, and each time he swung he did so with the memory of all five and what he had done to them over those three addicted years. He wanted to return to them and try to make amends, and he realized on the morning of the third day that he would not be able to do that if Caesar killed him. So fourteen minutes into the fight he sank to the floor after Caesar hammered him in the gut. And though he could have got up he stayed there, silent and still. The two guards laughed. The daughter who had given Pancho the panda was nine years old and had been raised by her mother as a Catholic.

That night, before the place went dark, Caesar lay on the bottom bunk and looked over at pictures of Pancho's children, which Pancho had taped on the opposite wall. He knew he would have to decide if he wanted Pancho just to move the photographs or to put them away altogether. All the children had toothy smiles. The two youngest stood, in separate pictures, outdoors in their First Communion clothes. Caesar himself had been a father for two years. A girl he had met at an F Street club in Northwest had told him he was the father of her son, and for a time he had believed her. Then the boy started growing big ears that Caesar thought didn't belong to anyone in his family, and so after he had slapped the girl a few times a week before the child's second birthday she confessed that the child belonged to "my first love." "Your first love is always with you," she said, sounding forever like a television addict who had never read a book. As Caesar prepared to leave, she asked him, "You want back all the toys and things you gave him?" The child, as if used to their fighting, had slept through this last encounter on the couch, part of a living-room suite that they were paying for on time. Caesar said nothing more and didn't think about his 18k.-gold cigarette lighter until he was eight blocks away. The girl pawned the thing and got enough to pay off the furniture bill.

Caesar and Pancho worked in the laundry, and Caesar could look across the noisy room with all the lint swirling about and see Pancho sorting dirty pieces into bins. Then he would push uniform bins to the left and everything else to the right. Pancho had been doing that for three years. The job he got after he left Lorton was as a gofer at construction sites. No laundry in the outside world wanted him. Over the next two weeks, as Caesar watched Pancho at his job, his back always to him, he considered what he should do next. He wasn't into fucking men, so that was out. He still had not decided what he wanted done about the photographs on the cell wall. One day at the end of those two weeks, Caesar saw the light above Pancho's head flickering and Pancho raised his head and looked for a long time at it, as if thinking that the answer to all his problems lay in fixing that one light. Caesar decided then to let the pictures remain on the wall.

Three years later, they let Pancho go. The two men had mostly stayed at a distance from each other, but toward the end they had been talking, sharing plans about a life beyond Lorton. The relationship had reached the point where Caesar was saddened to see the children's photographs come off the wall. Pancho pulled off the last taped picture and the wall was suddenly empty in a most forlorn way. Caesar knew the names of all the children.

Pancho gave him a rabbit's foot that one of his children had given him. It was the way among all those men that when a good-luck piece had run out of juice it was given away with the hope that new owner-ship would renew its strength. The rabbit's foot had lost its electricity months before Pancho's release. Caesar's only good-fortune piece was a key chain made in Peru; it had been sweet for a bank robber in the next cell for nearly two years until that man's daughter, walking home from third grade, was abducted and killed.

One day after Pancho left, they brought in a thief and three-time rap-ist of elderly women. He nodded to Caesar and told him that he was Watson Rainey and went about making a home for himself in the cell, finally plugging in a tiny lamp with a green shade, which he placed on the metal shelf jutting from the wall. Then he climbed onto the top bunk he had made up and lay down. His name was all the wordplay he had given Caesar, who had been smoking on the bottom bunk through-out Rainey's efforts to make a nest. Caesar waited ten minutes and then stood and pulled the lamp's cord out of the wall socket and grabbed Rainey with one hand and threw him to the floor. He crushed the lamp into Rainey's face. He choked him with the cord. "You come into my house and show me no respect!" Caesar shouted. The only sound Rainey could manage was a gurgling that bubbled up from his mangled mouth. There were no witnesses except for an old man across the way, who would occasionally glance over at the two when he wasn't reading his Bible. It was over and done with in four minutes. When Rainey came to, he found everything he owned piled in the corner, soggy with piss. And Caesar was again on the top bunk.

They would live in that cell together until Caesar was released, four years later. Rainey tried never to be in the house during waking hours; if he was there when Caesar came in, he would leave. Rainey's names spoken by him that first day were all the words that would ever pass between the two men.

A week or so after Rainey got there, Caesar bought from Multrey a calendar that was three years old. It was large and had no markings of any sort, as pristine as the day it was made. "You know this one ain't the year we in right now," Multrey said as one of his women took a quarter from Caesar and dropped it in her purse. Caesar said, "It'll do." Multrey prized the calendar for one thing: its top half had a photograph of a naked woman of indeterminate race sitting on a stool, her legs wide open, her pussy aimed dead at whoever was standing right in front of her. It had been Multrey's good-luck piece, but the luck was dead. Multrey remembered what the calendar had done for him, and he told his woman to give Caesar his money back, lest any new good-fortune piece turn sour on him.

The calendar's bottom half had the days of the year. That day, the first Monday in June, Caesar drew in the box that was January 1st a line that went from the upper left-hand corner down to the bottom right-hand corner. The next day, a June Tuesday, he made a line in the January 2nd box that also ran in the same direction. And so it went. When the calendar had all such lines in all the boxes, it was the next June. Then Caesar, in that January 1st box, made a line that formed an X with the first line. And so it was for another year. The third year saw horizontal marks that sliced the boxes in half. The fourth year had vertical lines down the centers of the boxes.

This was the only calendar Caesar had in Lorton. That very first Monday, he taped the calendar over the area where the pictures of Pancho's children had been. There was still a good deal of empty space left, but he didn't do anything about it, and Rainey knew he couldn't do anything, either.

The calendar did right by Caesar until near the end of his fifth year in Lorton, when he began to feel that its juice was drying up. But he kept it there to mark off the days and, too, the naked woman never closed her legs to him.

In that fifth year, someone murdered Multrey as he showered. The killers — it had to be more than one for a man like Multrey — were never found. The Multrey woman who picked at her food had felt herself caring for a recent arrival who was five years younger than her, a part-time deacon who had killed a Southwest bartender for calling the deacon's wife "a woman without one fuckin brain cell." The story of that killing — the bartender was dropped head first from the roof of a ten-story building — became legend, and in Lorton men referred to the dead bartender as "the Flat-Head Insulter" and the killer became known as "the Righteous Desulter." The Desulter, wanting Multrey's lady, had hired people to butcher him. It had always been the duty of the lady who hated food to watch out for Multrey as he showered, but she had stepped away that day, just as she had been instructed to by the Desulter.

In another time, Cathedral and Caesar would have had enough of everything — from muscle to influence — to demand that someone give up the killers, but the prison was filling up with younger men who did not care what those two had been once upon a time. Also, Cathedral had already had two visits from the man he had killed in Northwest. Each time, the man had first stood before the bars of Cathedral's cell. Then he held one of the bars and opened the door inward, like some wooden door on a person's house. The dead man standing there would have been sufficient to unwrap anyone, but matters were compounded when Cathedral saw a door that for years had slid sideways now open in an impossible fashion. The man stood silent before Cathedral, and when he left he shut the door gently, as if there were sleeping children in the cell. So Cathedral didn't have a full mind, and Multrey was never avenged.

There was an armed-robbery man in the place, a tattooer with homemade inks and needles. He made a good living painting on both muscled and frail bodies the names of children; the Devil in full regalia with a pitchfork dripping with blood; the words "Mother" or "Mother Forever" surrounded by red roses and angels who looked sad, because when it came to drawing happy angels the tattoo man had no skills. One pickpocket had had a picture of his father tattooed in the middle of his chest; above the father's head, in medieval lettering, were the words "Rotting in Hell," with the letter "H" done in fiery yellow and red. The tattoo guy had told Caesar that he had skin worthy of "a painter's best canvas," that he could give Caesar a tattoo "God would envy." Caesar had always told him no, but then he awoke one snowy night in March of his sixth year and realized that it was his mother's birthday. He did not know what day of the week it was, but the voice that talked to him had the authority of a million loving mothers. He had long ago forgotten his own birthday, had not even bothered to ask someone in prison records to look it up.

There had never been anyone or anything he wanted commemorated on his body. Maybe it would have been Carol, his first girlfriend twenty years ago, before the retarded girl entered their lives. He had played with the notion of having the name of the boy he thought was his put over his heart, but the lie had come to light before that could happen. And before the boy there had been Yvonne, with whom he had lived for an extraordinary time in Northeast. He would have put Yvonne's name over his heart, but she went off to work one day and never came back. He looked for her for three months, and then just assumed that she had been killed somewhere and dumped in a place only animals knew about. Yvonne was indeed dead, and she would be waiting for him at the end of the line, though she did not know that was what she was doing. "You can always trust unhappiness," Yvonne had once said, sitting in the dark on the couch, her cigarette burned down to the filter. "His face never changes. But happiness is slick, can't be trusted. It has a thousand faces, Caes, all of them just ready to re-form into unhappiness once it has you in its clutches."

So Caesar had the words "Mother Forever" tattooed on his left biceps. Knowing that more letters meant a higher payment of cigarettes or money or candy, the tattoo fellow had dissuaded him from having just plain "Mother." "How many hours you think she spent in labor?" he asked Caesar. "Just to give you life." The job took five hours over two days, during a snowstorm. Caesar said no to angels, knowing the man's ability with happy ones, and had the words done in blue letters encased in red roses. The man worked from the words printed on a piece of paper that Caesar had given him, because he was also a bad speller.

The snow stopped on the third day and, strangely, it took only another three days for the two feet of mess to melt, for with the end of the storm came a heat wave. The tattoo man, a good friend of the Righteous Desulter, would tell Caesar in late April that what happened to him was his own fault, that he had not taken care of himself as he had been instructed to do. "And the heat ain't helped you neither." On the night of March 31st, five days after the tattoo had been put on, Caesar woke in the night with a pounding in his left arm. He couldn't return to sleep so he sat on the edge of his bunk until morning, when he saw that the "e"s in "Mother Forever" had blistered, as if someone had taken a match to them.

He went to the tattoo man, who first told him not to worry, then patted the "e"s with peroxide that he warmed in a spoon with a match. Within two days, the "e"s seemed to just melt away, each dissolving into an ugly pile at the base of the tattoo. After a week, the diseased "e"s began spreading their work to the other letters, and Caesar couldn't move his arm without pain. He went to the infirmary. They gave him aspirin and Band-Aided the tattoo. He was back the next day, the day the doctor was there.

He spent four days in D.C. General Hospital, his first trip back to Washington since a court appearance more than three years before. His entire body was paralyzed for two days, and one nurse confided to him the day he left that he had been near death. In the end, after the infection had done its work, there was not much left of the tattoo except an "o" and an "r," which were so deformed they could never pass for English, and a few roses that looked more like red mud. When he returned to prison, the tattoo man offered to give back the cigarettes and the money, but Caesar never gave him an answer, leading the man to think that he should watch his back. What happened to Caesar's tattoo and to Caesar was bad advertising, and soon the fellow had no customers at all.

Something had died in the arm and the shoulder, and Caesar was never again able to raise the arm more than thirty-five degrees. He had no enemies, but still he told no one about his debilitation. For the next few months he tried to stay out of everyone's way, knowing that he was far more vulnerable than he had been before the tattoo. Alone in the cell, with no one watching across the way, he exercised the arm, but by November he knew at last he would not be the same again. He tried to bully Watson Rainey as much as he could to continue the façade that he was still who he had been. And he tried to spend more time with Cathedral.

But the man Cathedral had killed had become a far more constant visitor. The dead man, a young bachelor who had been Cathedral's next-door neighbor, never spoke. He just opened Cathedral's cell door inward and went about doing things as if the cell were a family home — straightening wall pictures that only Cathedral could see, turning down the gas on the stove, testing the shower water to make sure that it was not too hot, tucking children into bed. Cathedral watched silently.

Caesar went to Cathedral's cell one day in mid-December, six months before they freed him. He found his friend sitting on the bottom bunk, his hands clamped over his knees. He was still outside the cell when Cathedral said, "Caes, you tell me why God would be so stupid to create mosquitoes. I mean, what good are the damn things? What's their function?" Caesar laughed, thinking it was a joke, and he had started to offer something when Cathedral looked over at him with a devastatingly serious gaze and said, "What we need is a new God. Somebody who knows what the fuck he's doing." Cathedral was not smiling. He returned to staring at the wall across from him. "What's with creatin bats? I mean, yes, they eat insects, but why create those insects to begin with? You see what I mean? Creatin a problem and then havin to create somethin to take care of the problem. And then comin up with somethin for that second problem. Man oh man!" Caesar slowly began moving away from Cathedral's cell. He had seen this many times before. It could not be cured even by great love. It sometimes pulled down a loved one. "And roaches. Every human bein in the world would have the sense not to create roaches. What's their function, Caes? I tell you, we need a new God, and I'm ready to cast my vote right now. Roaches and rats and chinches. God was out of his fuckin mind that week. Six wasted days, cept for the human part and some of the animals. And then partyin on the seventh day like he done us a big favor. The nerve of that motherfucker. And all your pigeons and squirrels. Don't forget them. I mean really."

In late January, they took Cathedral somewhere and then brought him back after a week. He returned to his campaign for a new God in February. A ritual began that would continue until Caesar left: determine that Cathedral was a menace to himself, take him away, bring him back, then take him away when he started campaigning again for another God.

There was now nothing for Caesar to do except try to coast to the end on a reputation that was far less than it had been in his first years at Lorton. He could only hope that he had built up enough good will among men who had better reputations and arms that worked 100 percent.

In early April, he received a large manila envelope from his attorney. The lawyer's letter was brief. "I did not tell them where you are," he wrote. "They may have learned from someone that I was your attorney. Take care." There were two separate letters in sealed envelopes from his brother and sister, each addressed to "My Brother Caesar." Dead people come back alive, Caesar thought many times before he finally read the letters, after almost a week. He expected an announcement about the death of his father, but he was hardly mentioned. Caesar's younger brother went on for five pages with a history of what had happened to the family since Caesar had left their lives. He ended by saying, "Maybe I should have been a better brother." There were three pictures as well, one of his brother and his bride on their wedding day, and one showing Caesar's sister, her husband, and their two children, a girl of four or so and a boy of about two. The third picture had the girl sitting on a couch beside the boy, who was in Caesar's father's lap, looking with interest off to the left, as if whatever was there were more important than having his picture taken. Caesar looked at the image of his father — a man on the verge of becoming old. His sister's letter had even less in it than the lawyer's: "Write to me, or call me collect, whatever is best for you, dear one. Call even if you are on the other side of the world. For every step you take to get to me, I will walk a mile toward you."

He had an enormous yearning at first, but after two weeks he tore everything up and threw it all away. He would be glad he had done this as he stumbled, hurt and confused, out of his sister's car less than half a year later. The girl and the boy would be in the back seat, the girl wearing a red dress and black shoes, and the boy in blue pants and a T-shirt with a cartoon figure on the front. The boy would have fallen asleep, but the girl would say, "Nighty-night, Uncle," which she had been calling him all that evening.

An ex-offenders' group, the Light at the End of the Tunnel, helped him to get a room and a job washing dishes and busing tables at a restaurant on F Street. The room was in a three-story building in the middle of the 900 block of N Street, Northwest, a building that, in the days when white people lived there, had had two apartments of eight rooms or so on each floor. Now the first-floor apartments were uninhabitable and had been padlocked for years. On the two other floors, each large apartment had been divided into five rented rooms, which went for twenty to thirty dollars a week, depending on the size and the view. Caesar's was small, twenty dollars, and had half the space of his cell at Lorton. The word that came to him for the butchered, once luxurious apartments was "warren." The roomers in each of the cut-up apartments shared two bathrooms and one nice-sized kitchen, which was a pathetic place because of its dinginess and its fifty-watt bulb and because many of the appliances were old or undependable or both. Caesar's narrow room was at the front, facing N Street. On his side of the hall were two other rooms, the one next to his housing a mother and her two children. He would not know until his third week there that along the other hall was Yvonne Miller.

There was one main entry door for each of the complexes. In the big room to the left of the door into Caesar's complex lived a man of sixty or so, a pajama-clad man who was never out of bed in all the time Caesar lived there. He *could* walk, but Caesar never saw him do it. A woman, who told Caesar one day that she was "a home health-care aide," was always in the man's room, cooking, cleaning, or watching television with him. His was the only room with its own kitchen setup in a small alcove — a stove, icebox, and sink. His door was always open, and he never seemed to sleep. A green safe, three feet high, squatted beside the bed. "I am a moneylender," the man said the second day Caesar was there. He had come in and walked past the room, and the man had told the aide to have "that young lion" come back. "I am Simon and I lend money," the man said as Caesar stood in the doorway. "I will be your best friend, but not for free. Tell your friends."

He worked as many hours as they would allow him at the restaurant, Chowing Down. The remainder of the time, he went to movies until the shows closed and then sat in Franklin Park, at Fourteenth and K, in good weather and bad. He was there until sleep beckoned, sometimes as late as two in the morning. No one bothered him. He had killed two men, and the world, especially the bad part of it, sensed that and left him alone. He knew no one, and he wanted no one to know him. The friends he had had before Lorton seemed to have been swept off the face of the earth. On the penultimate day of his time at Lorton, he had awoken terrified and thought that if they gave him a choice he might well stay. He might find a life and a career at Lorton.

He had sex only with his right hand, and that was not very often. He began to believe, in his first days out of prison, that men and women were now speaking a new language and that he would never learn it. His lack of confidence extended even to whores, and this was a man who had been with more women than he had fingers and toes. He began to think that a whore had the power to crush a man's soul. "What kinda language you speakin, honey? Talk English if you want some." He was thirty-seven when he got free.

He came in from the park at two-forty-five one morning and went quickly by Simon's door, but the moneylender called him back. Caesar stood in the doorway. He had been in the warren for less than two months. The aide was cooking, standing with her back to Caesar in a

crisp green uniform and sensible black shoes. She was stirring first one
pot on the stove and then another. People on the color television were
laughing.

"Been out on the town, I see," Simon began. "Hope you got enough
poontang to last you till next time." "I gotta be goin," Caesar said. He
had begun to think that he might be able to kill the man and find a way
to get into the safe. The question was whether he should kill the aide as
well. "Don't blow off your friends that way," Simon said. Then, for some
reason, he started telling Caesar about their neighbors in that complex.
That was how Caesar first learned about an "Yvonny," whom he had yet
to see. He would not know that she was the Yvonne he had known long
ago until the second time he passed her in the hall. "Now, our sweet
Yvonny, she ain't nothin but an old girl." Old girls were whores, young
or old, who had been battered so much by the world that they had only
the faintest wisp of life left; not many of them had hearts of gold. "But
you could probably have her for free," Simon said, and he pointed to
Caesar's right, where Yvonne's room was. There was always a small
lump under the covers beside Simon in the bed, and Caesar suspected
that it was a gun. That was a problem, but he might be able to leap to
the bed and kill the man with one blow of a club before he could pull
it out. What would the aide do? "I've had her myself," Simon said, "so
I can only recommend it in a pinch." "Later, man," Caesar said, and he
stepped away. The usual way to his room was to the right as soon as he
entered the main door, but that morning he walked straight ahead and
within a few feet was passing Yvonne's door. It was slightly ajar, and he
heard music from a radio. The aide might even be willing to help him
rob the moneylender if he could talk to her alone beforehand. He might
not know the language men and women were speaking now, but the
language of money had not changed.

It was a cousin who told his brother where to find him. That cousin,
Nora Maywell, was the manager of a nearby bank, at Twelfth and F
Streets, and she first saw Caesar as he bused tables at Chowing Down,
where she had gone with colleagues for lunch. She came in day after day
to make certain that he was indeed Caesar, for she had not seen him
in more than twenty years. But there was no mistaking the man, who
looked like her uncle. Caesar was five years older than Nora. She had
gone through much of her childhood hoping that she would grow up to
marry him. Had he paid much attention to her in all those years before
he disappeared, he still would not have recognized her — she was older,

to be sure, but life had been extraordinarily kind to Nora and she was now a queen compared with the dirt-poor peasant she had once been.

Caesar's brother came in three weeks after Nora first saw him. The brother, Alonzo, ate alone, paid his bill, then went over to Caesar and smiled. "It's good to see you," he said. Caesar simply nodded and walked away with the tub of dirty dishes. The brother stood shaking for a few moments, then turned and made his unsteady way out the door. He was a corporate attorney, making nine times what his father, at fifty-seven, was making, and he came back for many days. On the eighth day, he went to Caesar, who was busing in a far corner of the restaurant. It was now early September and Caesar had been out of prison for three months and five days. "I will keep coming until you speak to me," the brother said. Caesar looked at him for a long time. The lunch hours were ending, so the manager would have no reason to shout at him. Only two days before, he had seen Yvonne in the hall for the second time. It had been afternoon and the dead light bulb in the hall had been replaced since the first time he had passed her. He recognized her, but everything in her eyes and body told him that she did not know him. That would never change. And, because he knew who she was, he nodded to his brother and within minutes they were out the door and around the corner to the alley. Caesar lit a cigarette right away. The brother's gray suit had cost $1,865.98. Caesar's apron was filthy. It was his seventh cigarette of the afternoon. When it wasn't in his mouth, the cigarette was at his side, and as he raised it up and down to his mouth, inhaled, and flicked ashes, his hand never shook.

"Do you know how much I want to put my arms around you?" Alonzo said.

"I think we should put an end to all this shit right now so we can get on with our lives," Caesar said. "I don't wanna see you or anyone else in your family from now until the day I die. You should understand that, Mister, so you can do somethin else with your time. You a customer, so I won't do what I would do to somebody who ain't a customer."

The brother said, "I'll admit to whatever I may have done to you. I will, Caesar. I will." In fact, his brother had never done anything to him, and neither had his sister. The war had always been between Caesar and their father, but Caesar, over time, had come to see his siblings as the father's allies. "But come to see me and Joanie, one time only, and if you don't want to see us again then we'll accept that. I'll never come into your restaurant again."

There was still more of the cigarette, but Caesar looked at it and then dropped it to the ground and stepped on it. He looked at his cheap watch. Men in prison would have killed for what was left of that smoke. "I gotta be goin, Mister."

"We are family, Caesar. If you don't want to see Joanie and me for your sake, for our sakes, then do it for Mama."

"My mama's dead, and she been dead for a lotta years." He walked toward the street.

"I know she's dead! I know she's dead! I just put flowers on her grave on Sunday. And on three Sundays before that. And five weeks before that. I know my mother's dead."

Caesar stopped. It was one thing for him to throw out a quick statement about a dead mother, as he had done many times over the years. A man could say the words so often that they became just another meaningless part of his makeup. The pain was no longer there as it had been those first times he had spoken them, when his mother was still new to her grave. The words were one thing, but a grave was a different matter, a different fact. The grave was out there, to be seen and touched, and a man, a son, could go to that spot of earth and remember all over again how much she had loved him, how she had stood in her apron in the doorway of a clean and beautiful home and welcomed him back from school. He could go to the grave and read her name and die a bit, because it would feel as if she had left him only last week.

Caesar turned around. "You and your people must leave me alone, Mister."

"Then we will," the brother said. "We will leave you alone. Come to one dinner. A Sunday dinner. Fried chicken. The works. Then we'll never bother you again. No one but Joanie and our families. No one else." Those last words were to assure Caesar that he would not have to see their father.

Caesar wanted another cigarette, but the meeting had already gone on long enough.

Yvonne had not said anything that second time, when he said, "Hello." She had simply nodded and walked around him in the hall. The third time they were also passing in the hall, and he spoke again, and she stepped to the side to pass and then turned and asked if he had any smokes she could borrow.

He said he had some in his room, and she told him to go get them and pointed to her room.

Her room was a third larger than his. It had an icebox, a bed, a dresser with a mirror over it, a small table next to the bed, a chair just beside the door, and not much else. The bed made a T with the one window, which faced the windowless wall of the apartment building next door. The beautiful blue and yellow curtains at the window should have been somewhere else, in a place that could appreciate them.

He had no expectations. He wanted nothing. It was just good to see a person from a special time in his life, and it was even better that he had loved her once and she had loved him. He stood in the doorway with the cigarettes.

Dressed in a faded purple robe, she was looking in the icebox when he returned. She closed the icebox door and looked at him. He walked over, and she took the unopened pack of cigarettes from his outstretched hand. He stood there.

"Well, sit the fuck down before you make the place look poor." He sat in the chair by the door, and she sat on the bed and lit the first cigarette. She was sideways to him. It was only after the fifth drag on the cigarette that she spoke. "If you think you gonna get some pussy, you are sorely mistaken. I ain't givin out shit. Free can kill you."

"I don't want nothin."

"'I don't want nothin. I don't want nothin.'" She dropped ashes into an empty tomato-soup can on the table by the bed. "Mister, we all want somethin, and the sooner people like you stand up and stop the bullshit, then the world can start bein a better place. It's the bullshitters who keep the world from bein a better place." Together, they had rented a little house in Northeast and had been planning to have a child once they had been there two years. The night he came home and found her sitting in the dark and talking about never trusting happiness, they had been there a year and a half. Two months later, she was gone. For the next three months, as he looked for her, he stayed there and continued to make it the kind of place that a woman would want to come home to. "My own mother was the first bullshitter I knew," she continued. "That's how I know it don't work. People should stand up and say, 'I wish you were dead,' or 'I want your pussy,' or 'I want all the money in your pocket.' When we stop lyin, the world will start bein heaven." He had been a thief and a robber and a drug pusher before he met her, and he went back to all that after the three months, not because he was heartbroken, though he was, but because it was such an easy thing to do. He was smart enough to know that he could not blame Yvonne, and he never did. The murders of Percy "Golden Boy" Weymouth and Antwoine Stoddard were still years away.

He stayed that day for more than an hour, until she told him that she had now paid for the cigarettes. Over the next two weeks, as he got closer to the dinner with his brother and sister, he would take her cigarettes and food and tell her from the start that they were free. He was never to know how she paid the rent. By the fourth day of bringing her things, she began to believe that he wanted nothing. He always sat in the chair by the door. Her words never changed, and it never mattered to him. The only thanks he got was the advice that the world should stop being a bullshitter.

On the day of the dinner, he found that the days of sitting with Yvonne had given him a strength he had not had when he had said yes to his brother. He had Alonzo pick him up in front of Chowing Down because he felt that if they knew where he lived, they would find a way to stay in his life.

At his sister's house, just off Sixteenth Street, Northwest, in an area of well-to-do black people some called the Gold Coast, they welcomed him, Joanie keeping her arms around him for more than a minute, crying. Then they offered him a glass of wine. He had not touched alcohol since before prison. They sat him on a dark-green couch in the living room, which was the size of ten prison cells. Before he had taken three sips of the wine, he felt good enough not to care that the girl and the boy, his sister's children, wanted to be in his lap. They were the first children he had been around in more than ten years. The girl had been calling him Uncle since he entered the house.

Throughout dinner, which was served by his sister's maid, and during the rest of the evening, he said as little as possible to the adults — his sister and brother and their spouses — but concentrated on the kids, because he thought he knew their hearts. The grownups did not pepper him with questions and were just grateful that he was there. Toward the end of the meal, he had a fourth glass of wine, and that was when he told his niece that she looked like his mother and the girl blushed, because she knew how beautiful her grandmother had been.

At the end, as Caesar stood in the doorway preparing to leave, his brother said that he had made this a wonderful year. His brother's eyes teared up and he wanted to hug Caesar, but Caesar, without smiling, simply extended his hand. The last thing his brother said to him was "Even if you go away not wanting to see us again, know that Daddy loves you. It is the one giant truth in the world. He's a different man, Caesar. I think he loves you more than us because he never knew what happened to you. That may be why he never remarried." The issue of what Caesar had been doing for twenty-one years never came up.

His sister, with her children in the back seat, drove him home. In front of his building, he and Joanie said goodbye and she kissed his cheek and, as an afterthought, he, a new uncle and with the wine saying, *Now, that wasn't so bad,* reached back to give a playful tug on the children's feet, but the sleeping boy was too far away and the girl, laughing, wiggled out of his reach. He said to his niece, "Good night, young lady," and she said no, that she was not a lady but a little girl. Again, he reached unsuccessfully for her feet. When he turned back, his sister had a look of such horror and disgust that he felt he had been stabbed. He knew right away what she was thinking, that he was out to cop a feel on a child. He managed a goodbye and got out of the car. "Call me," she said before he closed the car door, but the words lacked the feeling of all the previous ones of the evening. He said nothing. Had he spoken the wrong language, as well as done the wrong thing? Did child molesters call little girls "ladies"? He knew he would never call his sister. Yes, he had been right to tear up the pictures and letters when he was in Lorton.

He shut his eyes until the car was no more. He felt a pained rumbling throughout his system and, without thinking, he staggered away from his building toward Tenth Street. He could hear music coming from an apartment on his side of N Street. He had taught his sister how to ride a bike, how to get over her fear of falling and hurting herself. Now, in her eyes, he was no more than an animal capable of hurting a child. They killed men in prison for being that kind of monster. Whatever avuncular love for the children had begun growing in just those few hours now seeped away. He leaned over into the grass at the side of the apartment building and vomited. He wiped his mouth with the back of his hand. "I'll fall, Caesar," his sister had said in her first weeks of learning how to ride a bicycle. "Why would I let that happen?"

He ignored the aide when she told him that the moneylender wanted to talk to him. He went straight ahead, toward Yvonne's room, though he had no intention of seeing her. Her door was open enough for him to see a good part of the room, but he simply turned toward his own room. His shadow, cast by her light behind him, was thin and went along the floor and up the wall, and it was seeing the shadow that made him turn around. After noting that the bathroom next to her room was empty, he called softly to her from the doorway and then called three times more before he gave the door a gentle push with his finger. The door had not opened all the way when he saw her half on the bed and half off. Drunk, he thought. He went to her, intending to put her full on the bed. But death can twist the body in a way life never does, and that was what it had done to hers. He knew death. Her face was pressed into the bed, at a crooked angle that would have been uncomfortable for any living person. One leg was bunched under her, and the other was extended behind her, but both seemed not part of her body, awkwardly on their own, as if someone could just pick them up and walk away.

He whispered her name. He sat down beside her, ignoring the vomit that spilled out of her mouth and over the side of the bed. He moved her head so that it rested on one side. He thought at first that someone had done this to her, but he saw money on the dresser and felt the quiet throughout the room that signaled the end of it all, and he knew that the victim and the perpetrator were one and the same. He screwed the top on the empty whiskey bottle near her extended leg.

He placed her body on the bed and covered her with a sheet and a blanket. Someone would find her in the morning. He stood at the door, preparing to turn out the light and leave, thinking this was how the world would find her. He had once known her as a clean woman who would not steal so much as a needle. A woman with a well-kept house. She had been loved. But that was not what they would see in the morning.

He set about putting a few things back in place, hanging up clothes that were lying over the chair and on the bed, straightening the lampshade, picking up newspapers and everything else on the floor. But, when he was done, it did not seem enough.

He went to his room and tore up two shirts to make dust rags. He started in a corner at the foot of her bed, at a table where she kept her brush and comb and makeup and other lady things. When he had dusted the table and everything on it, he put an order to what was there, just as if she would be using them in the morning.

Then he began dusting and cleaning clockwise around the room, and by midnight he was not even half done and the shirts were dirty with all the work, and he went back to his room for two more. By three, he was cutting up his pants for rags. After he had cleaned and dusted the room, he put an order to it all, as he had done with the things on the table — the dishes and food in mouse-proof canisters on the table beside the icebox, the two framed posters of mountains on the wall that were tilting to the left, the five photographs of unknown children on the bureau. When

that work was done, he took a pail and a mop from her closet. Mice had
made a bed in the mop, and he had to brush them off and away. He filled
the pail with water from the bathroom and soap powder from under the
table beside the icebox. After the floor had been mopped, he stood in
the doorway as it dried and listened to the mice in the walls, listened to
them scurrying in the closet.

At about four, the room was done and Yvonne lay covered in her un-
made bed. He went to the door, ready to leave, and was once more unable to move. The whole world was silent except the mice in the walls.

He knelt at the bed and touched Yvonne's shoulder. On a Tuesday
morning, a school day, he had come upon his father kneeling at his bed,
Caesar's mother growing cold in that bed. His father was crying, and
when Caesar went to him his father crushed Caesar to him and took the
boy's breath away. It was Caesar's brother who had said they should call
someone, but their father said, "No, no, just one minute more, just one
more minute," as if in that next minute God would reconsider and send
his wife back. And Caesar had said, "Yes, just one minute more." *The
one giant truth* . . . , his brother had said.

Caesar changed the bed clothing and undressed Yvonne. He got one
of her large pots and filled it with warm water from the bathroom and
poured into the water cologne of his own that he never used and bath-
oil beads he found in a battered container in a corner beside her dresser.
The beads refused to dissolve, and he had to crush them in his hands.
He bathed her, cleaned out her mouth. He got a green dress from the
closet, and underwear and stockings from the dresser, put them on her,
and pinned a rusty cameo on the dress over her heart. He combed and
brushed her hair, put barrettes in it after he sweetened it with the rest of
the cologne, and laid her head in the center of the pillow now covered
with one of his clean cases. He gave her no shoes and he did not cover
her up, just left her on top of the made-up bed. The room with the dead
woman was as clean and as beautiful as Caesar could manage at that
time in his life. It was after six in the morning, and the world was lighting up and the birds had begun to chirp. Caesar shut off the ceiling light
and turned out the lamp, held on to the chain switch as he listened to
the beginnings of a new day.

He opened the window that he had cleaned hours before, and right
away a breeze came through. He put a hand to the wind, enjoying the
coolness, and one thing came to him: he was not a young man anymore.

•   •   •

He sat on his bed smoking one cigarette after another. Before finding Yvonne dead, he had thought he would go and live in Baltimore and hook up with a vicious crew he had known a long time ago. Wasn't that what child molesters did? Now, the only thing he knew about the rest of his life was that he did not want to wash dishes and bus tables anymore. At about nine-thirty, he put just about all he owned and the two bags of trash from Yvonne's room in the bin in the kitchen. He knocked at the door of the woman in the room next to his. Her son opened the door, and Caesar asked for his mother. He gave her the $147 he had found in Yvonne's room, along with his radio and tiny black-and-white television. He told her to look in on Yvonne before long and then said he would see her later, which was perhaps the softest lie of his adult life.

On his way out of the warren of rooms, Simon called to him. "You comin back soon, young lion?" he asked. Caesar nodded. "Well, why don't you bring me back a bottle of rum? Woke up with a taste for it this mornin." Caesar nodded. "Was that you in there with Yvonny last night?" Simon said as he got the money from atop the safe beside his bed. "Quite a party, huh?" Caesar said nothing. Simon gave the money to the aide, and she handed Caesar ten dollars and a quarter. "Right down to the penny," Simon said. "Give you a tip when you get back." "I won't be long," Caesar said. Simon must have realized that was a lie, because before Caesar went out the door he said, in as sweet a voice as he was capable of, "I'll be waitin."

He came out into the day. He did not know what he was going to do, aside from finding some legit way to pay for Yvonne's funeral. The D.C. government people would take her away, but he knew where he could find and claim her before they put her in potter's field. He put the bills in his pocket and looked down at the quarter in the palm of his hand. It was a rather old one, 1967, but shiny enough. Life had been kind to it. He went carefully down the steps in front of the building and stood on the sidewalk. The world was going about its business, and it came to him, as it might to a man who had been momentarily knocked senseless after a punch to the face, that he was of that world. To the left was Ninth Street and all the rest of N Street, Immaculate Conception Catholic Church at Eighth, the bank at the corner of Seventh. He flipped the coin. To his right was Tenth Street, and down Tenth were stores and the house where Abraham Lincoln had died and all the white people's precious monuments. Up Tenth and a block to Eleventh and Q Streets was once a High's store where, when Caesar was a boy, a pint of cherry-vanilla ice cream cost twenty-five cents, and farther down Tenth was French Street, with a two-story house with his mother's doilies and a foot-long porcelain black puppy just inside the front door. A puppy his mother had bought for his father in the third year of their marriage. A puppy that for thirty-five years had been patiently waiting each working day for Caesar's father to return from work. *The one giant truth . . . Just one minute more.* He caught the quarter and slapped it on the back of his hand. He had already decided that George Washington's profile would mean going toward Tenth Street, and that was what he did once he uncovered the coin.

At the corner of Tenth and N, he stopped and considered the quarter again. Down Tenth was Lincoln's death house. Up Tenth was the house where he had been a boy and where the puppy was waiting for his father. A girl at the corner was messing with her bicycle, putting playing cards in the spokes, checking the tires. She watched Caesar as he flipped the quarter. He missed it and the coin fell to the ground, and he decided that that one would not count. The girl had once seen her aunt juggle six coins, first warming up with the flip of a single one and advancing to the juggling of three before finishing with six. It had been quite a show. The aunt had shown the six pieces to the girl — they had all been old and heavy one-dollar silver coins, huge monster things, which nobody made anymore. The girl thought she might now see a reprise of that event. Caesar flipped the quarter. The girl's heart paused. The man's heart paused. The coin reached its apex and then it fell.

2006

BENJAMIN PERCY
REFRESH, REFRESH

from *The Paris Review*

BENJAMIN PERCY (b. 1979) was raised in the high desert of central Oregon, the setting of much of his fiction, including "Refresh, Refresh." This story was inspired by a newspaper article about a rust belt town that lost over a dozen men when their National Guard unit was ambushed in Iraq. Percy transposed the tragedy into his own back yard, writing about the battleground at home. The title refers not only to the longing the boys feel as they refresh their e-mail, hoping to hear from their fathers, but also to the generational refreshment of troops, the inheritance of violence.

Percy attended Brown University for his BA and Southern Illinois University for his MFA. He has taught at the Iowa Writers' Workshop and at the MFA program at Iowa State University and Pacific University. He is the author of three novels, *The Dead Lands, Red Moon,* and *The Wilding,* as well as two books of short stories, *Refresh, Refresh* and *The Language of Elk.* His fiction is often said to defy easy categorization, blending together elements of literary, detective, sci-fi, western, and horror fiction. He says he is "neither fish nor fowl, both a literary and a genre writer, occupying a borderlands in between." He has also written for film, television, and comics.

Percy's fiction and nonfiction have been read on National Public Radio, performed at Symphony Space, and published by *Esquire* (where he is a contributing editor), *GQ, Time, Outside, Men's Journal,* the *Wall Street Journal, Glimmer Train, Tin House,* and *Ploughshares.* Percy is the recipient of a fellowship from the National Endowment of the Arts, the Whiting Writers' Award, the Plimpton Prize, and two Pushcart Prizes.

He lives in Northfield, Minnesota.

★

W HEN SCHOOL LET out the two of us went to my backyard to fight. We were trying to make each other tougher. So in the grass, in the shade of the pines and junipers, Gordon and I slung off our backpacks and laid down a pale green garden hose, tip to tip, making a ring. Then we stripped off our shirts and put on our gold-colored boxing gloves and fought.

Every round went two minutes. If you stepped out of the ring, you lost. If you cried, you lost. If you got knocked out or if you yelled stop, you lost. Afterward we drank Coca-Colas and smoked Marlboros, our chests heaving, our faces all different shades of blacks and reds and yellows.

We began fighting after Seth Johnson—a no-neck linebacker with teeth like corn kernels and hands like T-bone steaks—beat Gordon until his face swelled and split open and purpled around the edges. Eventually he healed, the rough husks of scabs peeling away to reveal a different face from the one I remembered—older, squarer, fiercer, his left eyebrow separated by a gummy white scar. It was his idea that we should fight each other. He wanted to be ready. He wanted to hurt those who hurt him. And if he went down, he would go down swinging as he was sure his father would. This is what we all wanted: to please our fathers, to make them proud, even though they had left us.

This was in Crow, Oregon, a high desert town in the foothills of the Cascade Mountains. In Crow we have fifteen hundred people, a Dairy Queen, a BP gas station, a Food4Less, a meatpacking plant, a bright green football field irrigated by canal water, and your standard assortment of taverns and churches. Nothing distinguishes us from Bend or Redmond or La Pine or any of the other nowhere towns off Route 97, except for this: we are home to the Second Battalion, Thirty-fourth Marines.

The Marines live on a fifty-acre base in the hills just outside of town, a collection of one-story cinder-block buildings interrupted by cheatgrass and sagebrush. Throughout my childhood I could hear, if I cupped a hand to my ear, the lowing of bulls, the bleating of sheep, and the report of assault rifles shouting from the hilltops. It's said that conditions here in Oregon's ranch country closely match the mountainous terrain of Afghanistan and northern Iraq.

Our fathers—Gordon's and mine—were like the other fathers in Crow. All of them, just about, had enlisted as part-time soldiers, as reservists, for drill pay: several thousand a year for a private and several thousand more for a sergeant. Beer pay, they called it, and for two weeks every year plus one weekend a month, they trained. They threw on their cammies and filled their rucksacks and kissed us good-bye, and the gates of the Second Battalion drew closed behind them.

Our fathers would vanish into the pine-studded hills, returning to us Sunday night with their faces reddened from weather, their biceps trembling from fatigue, and their hands smelling of rifle grease. They would talk about ECPs and PRPs and MEUs and WMDs and they would do pushups in the middle of the living room and they would call six o'clock "eighteen hundred hours" and they would high-five and yell, "Semper fi." Then a few days would pass, and they would go back to the way they were, to the men we knew: Coors-drinking, baseball-throwing, crotch-scratching, Aqua Velva–smelling fathers.

No longer. In January the battalion was activated, and in March they shipped off for Iraq. Our fathers — our coaches, our teachers, our barbers, our cooks, our gas station attendants and UPS deliverymen and deputies and firemen and mechanics — our fathers, so many of them, climbed onto the olive green school buses and pressed their palms to the windows and gave us the bravest, most hopeful smiles you can imagine and vanished. Just like that.

Nights, I sometimes got on my Honda dirt bike and rode through the hills and canyons of Deschutes County. Beneath me the engine growled and shuddered, while all around me the wind, like something alive, bullied me, tried to drag me from my bike. A dark world slipped past as I downshifted, leaning into a turn, and accelerated on a straightaway — my speed seventy, then eighty — concentrating only on the twenty yards of road glowing ahead of me.

On this bike I could ride and ride and ride, away from here, up and over the Cascades, through the Willamette Valley, until I reached the ocean, where the broad black backs of whales regularly broke the surface of the water, and even farther — farther still — until I caught up with the horizon, where my father would be waiting. Inevitably, I ended up at Hole in the Ground.

A long time ago a meteor came screeching down from space and left behind a crater five thousand feet wide and three hundred feet deep. Hole in the Ground is frequented during the winter by the daredevil sledders among us and during the summer by bearded geologists interested in the metal fragments strewn across its bottom. I dangled my feet over the edge of the crater and leaned back on my elbows and took in the black sky — no moon, only stars — just a little lighter than a raven.

Every few minutes a star seemed to come unstuck, streaking through the night in a bright flash that burned into nothingness.

In the near distance Crow glowed grayish green against the darkness — a reminder of how close to oblivion we lived. A chunk of space ice or a solar wind could have jogged the meteor sideways and rather than landing here it could have landed there at the intersection of Main and Farwell. No Dairy Queen, no Crow High, no Second Battalion. It didn't take much imagination to realize how something can drop out of the sky and change everything.

This was in October, when Gordon and I circled each other in the backyard after school. We wore our golden boxing gloves, cracked with age and flaking when we pounded them together. Browned grass crunched beneath our sneakers, and dust rose in little puffs like distress signals. Gordon was thin to the point of being scrawny. His collarbone poked against his skin like a swallowed coat hanger. His head was too big for his body, and his eyes were too big for his head, and football players — Seth Johnson among them — regularly tossed him into garbage cans and called him E.T.

He had had a bad day. And I could tell from the look on his face — the watery eyes, the trembling lips that revealed in quick flashes his buckteeth — that he wanted, he *needed*, to hit me. So I let him. I raised my gloves to my face and pulled my elbows against my ribs and Gordon lunged forward, his arms snapping like rubber bands. I stood still, allowing his fists to work up and down my body, allowing him to throw the weight of his anger on me, until eventually he grew too tired to hit anymore and I opened up my stance and floored him with a right cross to the temple. He lay there, sprawled out in the grass with a small smile on his E.T. face. "Damn," he said in a dreamy voice. A drop of blood gathered along the corner of his eye and streaked down his temple into his hair.

My father wore steel-toed boots, Carhartt jeans, and a T-shirt advertising some place he had traveled to, maybe Yellowstone or Seattle. He looked like someone you might see shopping for motor oil at Bi-Mart. To hide his receding hairline he wore a John Deere cap that laid a shadow across his face. His brown eyes blinked above a considerable nose underlined by a gray mustache. Like me, my father was short and squat, a bulldog. His belly was a swollen bag and his shoulders were broad, good for carrying me during parades and at fairs when I was younger. He laughed a lot. He liked game shows. He drank too much beer and smoked too many cigarettes and spent too much time with his buddies, fishing, hunting, bullshitting, which probably had something to do with why my mother divorced him and moved to Boise with a hairdresser and triathlete named Chuck.

At first, after my father left, like all of the other fathers, he would e-mail whenever he could. He would tell me about the heat, the gallons of water he drank every day, the sand that got into everything, the baths he took with baby wipes. He would tell me how safe he was, how very safe. This was when he was stationed in Turkey. Then the reservists shipped for Kirkuk, where insurgents and sandstorms attacked almost daily. The e-mails came less frequently. Weeks of silence passed between them.

Sometimes, on the computer, I would hit refresh, refresh, *refresh*, hoping. In October I received an e-mail that read: "Hi, Josh. I'm O.K. Don't worry. Do your homework. Love, Dad." I printed it and hung it on my door with a piece of Scotch tape.

For twenty years my father worked at Nosier, Inc. — the bullet manufacturer based out of Bend — and the Marines trained him as an ammunition technician. Gordon liked to say his father was a gunnery sergeant, and he was, but we all knew he was also the battalion mess manager, a cook, which was how he made his living in Crow, tending the grill at Hamburger Patty's. We knew their titles, but we didn't know, not really, what their titles meant, what our fathers *did* over there. We imagined them doing heroic things: rescuing Iraqi babies from burning huts, sniping suicide bombers before they could detonate on a crowded city street. We drew on Hollywood and TV news to develop elaborate scenarios where maybe, at twilight, during a trek through the mountains of northern Iraq, bearded insurgents ambushed our fathers with rocket launchers. We imagined them silhouetted by a fiery explosion. We imagined them burrowing into the sand like lizards and firing their M-16s, their bullets streaking through the darkness like the meteorites I observed on sleepless nights.

When Gordon and I fought we painted our faces — black and green and brown — with the camo grease our fathers left behind. It made our eyes and teeth appear startlingly white. And it smeared away against our gloves just as the grass smeared away beneath our sneakers — and the ring became a circle of dirt, the dirt a reddish color that looked a lot like scabbed flesh. One time Gordon hammered my shoulder so hard I couldn't lift my arm for a week. Another time I elbowed one of his kidneys, and he peed blood. We struck each other with such force and frequency that the golden gloves crumbled and our knuckles showed through the sweat-soaked, blood-soaked foam like teeth through a busted lip. So we bought another set of gloves, and as the air grew steadily colder we fought with steam blasting from our mouths.

Our fathers had left us, but men remained in Crow. There were old men, like my grandfather, whom I lived with — men who had paid their dues, who had worked their jobs and fought their wars and now spent their days at the gas station, drinking bad coffee from Styrofoam cups, complaining about the weather, arguing about the best months to reap alfalfa. And there were incapable men. Men who rarely shaved and watched daytime television in their once white underpants. Men who lived in trailers and filled their shopping carts with Busch Light, summer sausage, Oreo cookies.

And then there were vulturous men like Dave Lightener — men who scavenged whatever our fathers had left behind. Dave Lightener worked as a recruitment officer. I'm guessing he was the only recruitment officer in world history who drove a Vespa scooter with a Support Our Troops ribbon magnet on its rear. We sometimes saw it parked outside the homes of young women whose husbands had gone to war. Dave had big ears and small eyes and wore his hair in your standard-issue high-and-tight buzz. He often spoke in a too loud voice about all the insurgents he gunned down when working a Fallujah patrol unit. He lived with his mother in Crow, but spent his days in Bend and Redmond trolling the parking lots of Best Buy, ShopKo, Kmart, Wal-Mart, Mountain View Mall. He was looking for people like us, people who were angry and dissatisfied and poor.

But Dave Lightener knew better than to bother us. On duty he stayed away from Crow entirely. Recruiting there would be too much like poaching the burned section of forest where deer, rib-slatted and wobbly legged, nosed through the ash, seeking something green.

We didn't fully understand the reason our fathers were fighting. We understood only that they *had* to fight. The necessity of it made the reason irrelevant. "It's all part of the game," my grandfather said. "It's just the way it is." We could only cross our fingers and wish on stars and hit refresh, *refresh*, hoping that they would return to us, praying that we would never find Dave Lightener on our porch uttering the words *I regret to inform you* . . .

One time, my grandfather dropped Gordon and me off at Mountain View Mall, and there, near the glass-doored entrance, stood Dave Lightener. He wore his creased khaki uniform and spoke with a group of

Mexican teenagers. They were laughing, shaking their heads and walking away from him as we approached. We had our hats pulled low, and he didn't recognize us.

"Question for you, gentlemen," he said in the voice of telemarketers and door-to-door Jehovah's Witnesses. "What do you plan on doing with your lives?"

Gordon pulled off his hat with a flourish, as if he were part of some *ta-da!* magic act and his face was the trick. "I plan on killing some crazy-ass Muslims," he said and forced a smile. "How about you, Josh?"

"Yeah," I said. "Kill some people, then get myself killed." I grimaced even as I played along. "That sounds like a good plan."

Dave Lightener's lips tightened into a thin line, his posture straightened, and he asked us what we thought our fathers would think, hearing us right now. "They're out there risking their lives, defending our freedom, and you're cracking sick jokes," he said. "I think that's sick."

We hated him for his soft hands and clean uniform. We hated him because he sent people like us off to die. Because at twenty-three he had attained a higher rank than our fathers. Because he slept with the lonely wives of soldiers. And now we hated him even more for making us feel ashamed. I wanted to say something sarcastic, but Gordon was quicker. His hand was out before him, his fingers gripping an imaginary bottle. "Here's your maple syrup," he said.

Dave said, "And what is that for?"

"To eat my ass with," Gordon said.

Right then a skateboarder type with green hair and a nose ring walked from the mall, a bagful of DVDs swinging from his fist, and Dave Lightener forgot us. "Hey, friend," he was saying. "Let me ask you something. Do you like war movies?"

In November we drove our dirt bikes deep into the woods to hunt. Sunlight fell through tall pines and birch clusters and lay in puddles along the logging roads that wound past the hillsides packed with huckleberries and on the moraines where coyotes scurried, trying to flee from us and slipping, causing tiny avalanches of loose rock. It hadn't rained in nearly a month, so the crabgrass and the cheatgrass and the pine needles had lost their color, as dry and blond as cornhusks, crackling beneath my boots when the road we followed petered out into nothing and I stepped off my bike. In this waterless stillness, it seemed you could hear every chipmunk within a square acre rustling for pine nuts, and when the breeze rose into a cold wind the forest became a giant whisper.

We dumped our tent and our sleeping bags near a basalt grotto with a spring bubbling from it, and Gordon said, "Let's go, troops," holding his rifle before his chest diagonally, as a soldier would. He dressed as a soldier would too, wearing his father's overlarge cammies rather than the mandatory blaze-orange gear. Fifty feet apart, we worked our way downhill through the forest, through a huckleberry thicket, through a clear-cut crowded with stumps, taking care not to make much noise or slip on the pine needles carpeting the ground. A chipmunk worrying at a pinecone screeched its astonishment when a peregrine falcon swooped down and seized it, carrying it off between the trees to some secret place. Its wings made no sound, and neither did the blaze-orange-clad hunter when he appeared in a clearing several hundred yards below us.

Gordon made some sort of SWAT-team gesture — meant, I think, to say, stay low — and I made my way carefully toward him. From behind a boulder we peered through our scopes, tracking the hunter, who looked, in his vest and earflapped hat, like a monstrous pumpkin. "That cocksucker," Gordon said in a harsh whisper. The hunter was Seth Johnson. His rifle was strapped to his back and his mouth was moving — he was talking to someone. At the corner of the meadow he joined four members of the varsity football squad, who sat on logs around a smoldering campfire, their arms bobbing like oil pump jacks as they brought their beers to their mouths.

I took my eye from my scope and noticed Gordon fingering the trigger of his 30.06. I told him to quit fooling around, and he pulled his hand suddenly away from the stock and smiled guiltily and said he just wanted to know what it felt like having that power over someone. Then his trigger finger rose up and touched the gummy white scar that split his eyebrow. "I say we fuck with them a little."

I shook my head no.

Gordon said, "Just a little — to scare them."

"They've got guns," I said, and he said, "So we'll come back tonight."

Later, after an early dinner of beef jerky and trail mix and Gatorade, I happened upon a four-point stag nibbling on some bear grass, and I rested my rifle on a stump and shot it, and it stumbled backwards and collapsed with a rose blooming from behind its shoulder where the heart was hidden. Gordon came running, and we stood around the deer and smoked a few cigarettes, watching the thick arterial blood run from its mouth. Then we took out our knives and got to work. I cut around the anus, cutting away the penis and testes, and then ran the knife along the belly, unzipping the hide to reveal the delicate pink flesh and green-ish vessels into which our hands disappeared.

The blood steamed in the cold mountain air, and when we finished — when we'd skinned the deer and hacked at its joints and cut out its back strap and boned out its shoulders and hips, its neck and ribs, making chops, roasts, steaks, quartering the meat so we could bundle it into our insulated saddlebags — Gordon picked up the deer head by the antlers and held it before his own. Blood from its neck made a pattering sound on the ground, and in the half-light of early evening Gordon began to do a little dance, bending his knees and stomping his feet.

"I think I've got an idea," he said, and he pretended to charge at me with the antlers. I pushed him away and he said, "Don't pussy out on me, Josh." I was exhausted and reeked of gore, but I could appreciate the need for revenge. "Just to scare them, right, Gordo?" I said.

"Right."

We lugged our meat back to camp, and Gordon brought the deer hide. He slit a hole in its middle and poked his head through so the hide hung off him loosely, a hairy sack, and I helped him smear mud and blood across his face. Then, with his Leatherman, he sawed off the ant-lers and held them in each hand and slashed at the air as if they were claws.

Night had come on, and the moon hung over the Cascades, grayly lighting our way as we crept through the forest imagining ourselves in enemy territory, with tripwires and guard towers and snarling dogs around every corner. From behind the boulder that overlooked their campsite, we observed our enemies as they swapped hunting stories and joked about Jessica Robertson's big-ass titties and passed around a bot-tle of whiskey and drank to excess and finally pissed on the fire to ex-tinguish it. When they retired to their tents we waited an hour before making our way down the hill with such care that it took us another hour before we were upon them. Somewhere an owl hooted, its noise barely noticeable over the chorus of snores that rose from their tents. Seth's Bronco was parked nearby — the license plate read SMAN — and all their rifles lay in its cab. I collected the guns, slinging them over my shoulder, then I eased my knife into each of Seth's tires.

I still had my knife out when we were standing beside Seth's tent, and when a cloud scudded over the moon and made the meadow fully dark I stabbed the nylon and in one quick jerk opened up a slit. Gordon rushed in, his antler-claws slashing. I could see nothing but shadows, but I could hear Seth scream the scream of a little girl as Gordon raked at him with the antlers and hissed and howled like some cave creature hungry for man-flesh. When the tents around us came alive with confused voices, Gordon reemerged with a horrible smile on his face, and I followed him up the hillside, crashing through the undergrowth, leaving Seth to make sense of the nightmare that had descended upon him without warning.

Winter came. Snow fell, and we threw on our coveralls and wrenched on our studded tires and drove our dirt bikes to Hole in the Ground, dragging our sleds behind us with towropes. Our engines filled the white silence of the afternoon. Our back tires kicked up plumes of powder and on sharp turns slipped out beneath us, and we lay there in the middle of the road bleeding, laughing, unafraid.

Earlier, for lunch, we had cooked a pound of bacon with a stick of butter. The grease, which hardened into a white waxy pool, we used as polish, buffing it into the bottoms of our sleds. Speed was what we wanted at Hole in the Ground. We descended the steepest section of the crater into its heart, three hundred feet below us. We followed each other in the same track, ironing down the snow to create a chute, blue-hued and frictionless, that would allow us to travel at a speed equivalent to free fall. Our eyeballs glazed with frost, our ears roared with wind, and our stomachs rose into our throats as we rocketed down and felt as if we were five again — and then we began the slow climb back the way we came and felt fifty.

We wore crampons and ascended in a zigzagging series of switchbacks. It took nearly an hour. The air had begun to go purple with evening when we stood again at the lip of the crater, sweating in our coveralls, taking in the view through the fog of our breath. Gordon packed a snowball. I said, "You better not hit me with that." He cocked his arm threateningly and smiled, then dropped to his knees to roll the snowball into something bigger. He rolled it until it grew to the size of a large man curled into the fetal position. From the back of his bike he took the piece of garden hose he used to siphon gas from fancy foreign cars and he worked it into his tank, sucking at its end until gas flowed.

He doused the giant snowball as if he hoped it would sprout. It didn't melt — he'd packed it tight enough — but it puckered slightly and appeared leaden, and when Gordon withdrew his Zippo, sparked it, and held it toward the ball, the fumes caught flame and the whole thing erupted with a gasping noise that sent me staggering back a few steps.

Gordon rushed forward and kicked the ball of fire, sending it rolling, tumbling down the crater, down our chute like a meteor, and the snow beneath it instantly melted only to freeze again a moment later, making a slick blue ribbon. When we sledded it, we went so fast our minds emptied and we felt a sensation at once like flying and falling.

On the news Iraqi insurgents fired their assault rifles. On the news a car bomb in Baghdad blew up seven American soldiers at a traffic checkpoint. On the news the president said he did not think it was wise to provide a time frame for troop withdrawal. I checked my e-mail before breakfast and found nothing but spam.

Gordon and I fought in the snow wearing snow boots. We fought so much our wounds never got a chance to heal, and our faces took on a permanent look of decay. Our wrists felt swollen, our knees ached, our joints felt full of tiny dry wasps. We fought until fighting hurt too much, and we took up drinking instead. Weekends, we drove our dirt bikes to Bend, twenty miles away, and bought beer and took it to Hole in the Ground and drank there until a bright line of sunlight appeared on the horizon and illuminated the snow-blanketed desert. Nobody asked for our IDs, and when we held up our empty bottles and stared at our reflections in the glass, warped and ghostly, we knew why. And we weren't alone. Black bags grew beneath the eyes of the sons and daughters and wives of Crow, their shoulders stooped, wrinkles enclosing their mouths like parentheses.

Our fathers haunted us. They were everywhere: in the grocery store when we spotted a thirty-pack of Coors on sale for ten bucks; on the highway when we passed a jacked-up Dodge with a dozen hay bales stacked in its bed; in the sky when a jet roared by, reminding us of faraway places. And now, as our bodies thickened with muscle, as we stopped shaving and grew patchy beards, we saw our fathers even in the mirror. We began to look like them. Our fathers, who had been taken from us, were everywhere, at every turn, imprisoning us.

Seth Johnson's father was a staff sergeant. Like his son, he was a big man but not big enough. Just before Christmas he stepped on a cluster bomb. A U.S. warplane dropped it and the sand camouflaged it and he stepped on it and it tore him into many meaty pieces. When Dave Lightener climbed up the front porch with a black armband and a somber expression, Mrs. Johnson, who was cooking a honeyed ham at the time, collapsed on the kitchen floor. Seth pushed his way out the door and punched Dave in the face, breaking his nose before he could utter the words *I regret to inform you . . .*

Hearing about this, we felt bad for all of ten seconds. Then we felt good because it was his father and not ours. And then we felt bad again, and on Christmas Eve we drove to Seth's house and laid down on his porch the rifles we had stolen, along with a six-pack of Coors, and then, just as we were about to leave, Gordon dug in his back pocket and removed his wallet and placed under the six-pack all the money he had — a few fives, some ones. "Fucking Christmas," he said.

We got braver and went to the bars — the Golden Nugget, the Weary Traveler, the Pine Tavern — where we square-danced with older women wearing purple eye shadow and sparkly dream-catcher earrings and push-up bras and clattery high heels. We told them we were Marines back from a six-month deployment, and they said, "Really?" and we said, "Yes, ma'am," and when they asked for our names we gave them the names of our fathers. Then we bought them drinks and they drank them in a gulping way and breathed hotly in our faces and we brought our mouths against theirs and they tasted like menthol cigarettes, like burnt detergent. And then we went home with them, to their trailers, to their waterbeds, where among their stuffed animals we fucked them.

Midafternoon and it was already full dark. On our way to the Weary Traveler we stopped by my house to bum some money off my grandfather, only to find Dave Lightener waiting for us. He must have just gotten there — he was halfway up the porch steps — when our headlights cast an anemic glow over him, and he turned to face us with a scrunched-up expression, as if trying to figure out who we were. He wore the black band around his arm and, over his nose, a white-bandaged splint. We did not turn off our engines. Instead we sat in the driveway, idling, the exhaust from our bikes and the breath from our mouths clouding the air. Above us a star hissed across the moonlit sky, vaguely bright like a light turned on in a day-lit room. Then Dave began down the steps and we leapt off our bikes to meet him. Before he could speak I brought my fist to his diaphragm, knocking the breath from his body. He looked like a gun-shot actor in a Western, clutching his belly with both hands, doubled over, his face making a nice target for Gordon's knee. A snap sound preceded Dave falling on his back with blood coming from his already broken nose.

He put up his hands, and we hit our way through them. I punched him once, twice, in the ribs while Gordon kicked him in the spine and stomach and then we stood around gulping air and allowed him to struggle to his feet. When he righted himself, he wiped his face with his hand, and blood dripped from his fingers. I moved in and round-housed with my right and then my left, my fists knocking his head loose on its hinges. Again he collapsed, a bloody bag of a man. His eyes walled and turned up, trying to see the animal bodies looming over him. He opened his mouth to speak, and I pointed a finger at him and said, with enough hatred in my voice to break a back, "*Don't* say a word. Don't you dare. Not one word."

He closed his mouth and tried to crawl away, and I brought a boot down on the back of his skull and left it there a moment, grinding his face into the ground so that when he lifted his head the snow held a red impression of his face. Gordon went inside and returned a moment later with a roll of duct tape, and we held Dave down and bound his wrists and ankles and threw him on a sled and taped him to it many times over and then tied the sled to the back of Gordon's bike and drove at a peril-ous speed to Hole in the Ground.

The moon shone down and the snow glowed with pale blue light as we smoked cigarettes, looking down into the crater, with Dave at our feet. There was something childish about the way our breath puffed from our mouths in tiny clouds. It was as if we were imitating choo-choo trains. And for a moment, just a moment, we were kids again. Just a couple of stupid kids. Gordon must have felt this, too, because he said, "My mom wouldn't even let me play with toy guns when I was little." And he sighed heavily as if he couldn't understand how he, how we, had ended up here.

Then, with a sudden lurch, Dave began struggling and yelling at us in a slurred voice and my face hardened with anger and I put my hands on him and pushed him slowly to the lip of the crater and he grew silent. For a moment I forgot myself, staring off into the dark oblivion. It was beautiful and horrifying. "I could shove you right now," I said. "And if I did, you'd be dead."

"Please don't," he said, his voice cracking. He began to cry. "Oh fuck. Don't. Please." Hearing his great shuddering sobs didn't bring me the satisfaction I had hoped for. If anything, I felt as I did that day, so long ago, when we taunted him in the Mountain View Mall parking lot— shameful, false.

"Ready?" I said. "One!" I inched him a little closer to the edge. "Two!" I moved him a little closer still, and as I did I felt unwieldy, at once wild and exhausted, my body seeming to take on another twenty, thirty, forty years. When I finally said "*Three,*" my voice was barely a whisper.

We left Dave there, sobbing at the brink of the crater. We got on our bikes and we drove to Bend and we drove so fast I imagined catching fire like a meteor, burning up in a flash, howling as my heat consumed me, as we made our way to the U.S. Marine Recruiting Office, where we would at last answer the fierce alarm of war and put our pens to paper and make our fathers proud.

2006

TOBIAS WOLFF
AWAITING ORDERS

from The New Yorker

TOBIAS WOLFF was born in Birmingham, Alabama, in 1945. After a peripa-
tetic childhood with his mother, he dropped out of high school to join the
army. During his four years of service he became a paratrooper and a member
of the special forces and was sent to Vietnam. Upon his discharge he earned a
BA in English from Oxford University.

Wolff's books include the memoirs *This Boy's Life* and *In Pharaoh's Army:
Memories of the Lost War;* the short novel *The Barracks Thief;* four collections
of short stories, *In the Garden of the North American Martyrs, Back in the
World, The Night in Question,* and *Our Story Begins: New and Selected Stories;*
and the novels *Ugly Rumours* and *Old School.*

Wolff writes of characters reckoning with issues of identity and loyalty, and
of the role of storytelling in our lives and our intimate relationships. His work
has received numerous awards, including the PEN/Faulkner Award, the PEN/
Malamud and Rea Awards for Excellence in the Short Story, the Story Prize, the
Los Angeles Times Book Award, and the Academy Award in Literature from the
American Academy of Arts and Letters. Wolff is a professor at Stanford University.

★

S ERGEANT MORSE WAS pulling night duty in the orderly room
when a woman called, asking for Billy Hart. He told her that Spe-
cialist Hart had shipped out for Iraq a week earlier. She said, "Billy Hart?
You sure? He never said a word about shipping out."
"I'm sure."
"Well. Sweet Jesus. That's some news."
"And you are . . . ? If you don't mind my asking."
"I'm his sister."
"I can give you his e-mail. Hang on, I'll find it for you."

"That's O.K. There's people waiting for the phone. People who don't know any better than to breathe down other people's neck."

"It won't take a minute."

"That's O.K. He's gone, right?"

"Feel free to call back. Maybe I can help."

"Hah," she said, and hung up.

Sergeant Morse returned to the paperwork he'd been doing, but the talk of Billy Hart had unsettled him. He got up and went to the water cooler and drew himself a glass. He drank it and filled the glass again and stood by the door. The night was sullenly hot and still: just past eleven, the barracks quiet, only a few windows glowing in the haze. A meaty gray moth kept thumping against the screen.

Morse didn't know Billy Hart well, but he'd had his eye on him. Hart was from the mountains near Asheville and liked to play the hick for the cover it gave him. He was always running a hustle, Hart, engaged elsewhere when there was work to be done but on hand to fleece the new guys at poker or sell rides to town in his Mustang convertible. He was said to be dealing but hadn't got caught at it. Thought everyone else was dumb — you could see him thinking it, that little smile. He would trip himself up someday, but he'd do fine for now. Plenty of easy pickings over there for the likes of Billy Hart.

A good-looking troop, though. Some Indian there, those high cheekbones, deep-set black eyes; beautiful, really, and with that slow, catlike way about him, cool, aloof, almost contemptuous in the languor and ease of his movements. Morse had felt the old pull despite himself, knowing Hart was trouble but always a little taut in his presence, fighting the stubborn drift of his gaze toward Hart's face, toward that look of secret knowledge playing on his lips. Hart was approachable, Morse felt sure of it, open to whatever might offer both interest and advantage. But Morse kept his distance. He didn't give advantage, and couldn't take the gamble of a foolish entanglement — not now, anyway.

Morse had spent twenty of his thirty-nine years in the army. He was not one of those who claimed to love it, but he belonged to it as to a tribe, bound to those around him by lines of unrefusable obligation, love being finally beside the point. He was a soldier, no longer able to imagine himself as a civilian — the formlessness of that life, the endless petty choices to be made.

Morse knew that he belonged where he was, yet he had often put himself in danger of scandal and discharge through risky attachments. Just before his tour in Iraq, there'd been the Cuban waiter he met in a restaurant downtown; the waiter turned out to be married, and a gambling addict, and, finally, when Morse broke it off, a blackmailer. Morse would not be blackmailed. He wrote down his commanding officer's name and telephone number. "Here," he said, "go on, call him"—and though he didn't think the man would actually do it, Morse spent the next few weeks inwardly hunched as if against a blow. Then he shipped out and soon came to life again, ready for the next excitement.

This turned out to be a young lieutenant who joined Morse's unit the week Morse arrived. They went through orientation together, and Morse saw that the lieutenant was drawn to him, though the lieutenant himself seemed unsure of his own disposition, even when he surrendered to it—with an urgency only heightened by the near impossibility of finding private time and space. In fact, he was just discovering himself, and in the process he suffered fits of self-loathing so cruel and dark that Morse feared he would do himself harm, or turn his rage outward, perhaps onto Morse himself, or bring them both to grief by bawling out a drunken confession to a fatherly colonel in some officers' bar.

It didn't come to that. The lieutenant had adopted a mangy one-eared cat while they were on patrol; the cat scratched his ankle and the scratch got infected, and instead of going for treatment he played the fool and tried to tough it out and damn near lost his foot. He was sent home on crutches five months into his tour. By then, Morse was so wrung out that he felt not the slightest stirrings of pity—only relief.

He had no cause for relief. Not long after returning stateside, he was called to battalion headquarters for an interview with two smooth, friendly men in civilian clothes who claimed to be congressional aides from the lieutenant's home district. They said that there was a sensitive matter before their congressman that required closer knowledge of the lieutenant's service in Iraq—his performance in the field, his dealings with other officers and with the troops who served under him. Their questions looped around conversationally, almost lazily, but returned again and again to the lieutenant's relations with Morse. Morse gave nothing away, even as he labored to appear open, unguarded. He figured these men for army narcs, whatever else they said. They let several weeks go by before calling him to another meeting, which they canceled at the last minute. Morse was still waiting for the next summons.

He had often wished that his desires served him better, but in this he supposed he was not unusual—that it was a lucky man indeed whose desires served him well. Yet he had hopes. Over the last few months Morse had become involved with a master sergeant in division intelligence — a calm, scholarly man five years older than he. Though Morse could not yet think of himself as anyone's "partner," he had gradually forsaken his room in the N.C.O. quarters to spend nights and weekends at Dixon's town house off post. The place was stuffed with ancient weapons and masks and chess sets that Dixon had collected during his tours overseas, and at first Morse had felt a sort of nervous awe, as if he were in a museum, but that had passed. Now he liked having these things around him. He was at home there.

But Dixon was due to rotate overseas before long, and Morse would soon receive new orders himself, and he knew it would get complicated then. They would have to make certain judgments about each other and about themselves. They would have to decide how much to promise. Where this would leave them, Morse didn't know. But all that was still to come.

Billy Hart's sister called again at midnight, just as Morse was turning over the orderly room to another sergeant. When he picked up and heard her voice, he pointed at the door and the other man smiled and stepped outside.

"Would you like the address, then?" Morse asked.

"I guess. For all the good it'll do."

Morse had already looked it up. He read it to her.

"Thanks," she said. "I don't have a computer, but Sal does."

"Sal?"

"Sally Cronin! My cousin."

"You could just go to an Internet café."

"Well, I suppose," she said skeptically. "Say — what'd you mean, maybe you could help?"

"I don't know, exactly," Morse said.

"You said it, though."

"Yes. And you laughed."

"That wasn't an actual laugh."

"Ah. Not a laugh."

"More like . . . I don't know."

Morse waited.

"Sorry," she said. "Look, I'm not asking for help, O.K.? But how come you said it? Just out of curiosity."

"No reason. I didn't think it out."

"Are you a friend of Billy's?"

"I like Billy."

"Well, it was nice. You know? A real nice thing to say."

After Morse signed out, he drove to the pancake house she'd been calling from. As agreed, she was waiting by the cash register, and when he
came through the door in his fatigues he saw her take him in with a
sharp measuring glance. She straightened up — a tall woman, nearly as
tall as Morse himself, with close-cut black hair and a long, tired-looking
face, darkly freckled under the eyes. Her eyes were black, but otherwise
she looked nothing like Hart, nothing at all, and Morse was thrown by
the sudden disappointment he felt and the impulse to escape.

She stepped toward him, head cocked to one side, as if making a
guess about him. Her eyebrows were dark and heavy. She wore a sleeveless red blouse and hugged her freckled arms against the chill of the air
conditioning. "So should I call you Sergeant?" she said.

"Owen."

"Sergeant Owen."

"Just Owen."

"Just Owen," she repeated. She offered him her hand. It was dry and
rough. "Julianne. We're over in the corner."

She led him to a booth by the big window looking out on the parking lot. A fat-faced boy, maybe seven or eight, sat drawing a picture on
the back of a place mat among the congealed remains of eggs and waf-
fles and sausages. Holding the crayon like a spike, he raised his head
as Morse slid onto the bench across from him. He had the same fierce
brows as the woman. He gave Morse a long, unblinking look, then he
sucked in his lower lip and returned to his work.

"Say hello, Charlie."

He went on coloring for a time. Then he said, "Howdy."

"Won't say hello, this one. Says howdy now. Don't know where he got
it."

"That's all right. Howdy back at you, Charlie."

"You look like a frog," the boy said. He dropped the crayon and
picked up another from the clutter on the table.

"Charlie!" she said. "Use your manners," she added mildly, beckon-
ing to a waitress pouring coffee at the neighboring table.

"It's O.K.," Morse said. He figured he had it coming. Not because
he looked like a frog — though he was all at once conscious of his wide
mouth — but because he'd sucked up to the boy. *Howdy back at you!*

"What is wrong with that woman?" Julianne said as the waitress gazed dully around the room. Then Julianne caught her eye, and she came slowly over to their table and refilled Julianne's cup. "That's some picture you're making," the waitress said. "What is it?" The boy ignored her. "You've got yourself quite the little artist there," she said to Morse, then moved dreamily away.

Julianne poured a long stream of sugar into her coffee.

"Charlie your son?"

She turned and looked speculatively at the boy. "No."

"You're not my mom," the boy murmured.

"Didn't I just say that?" She stroked his round cheek with the back of her hand. "Draw your picture, nosy. Kids?" she said to Morse.

"Not yet." Morse watched the boy smear blue lines across the place mat, wielding the crayon as if out of grim duty.

"You aren't missing anything."

"Oh, I think I probably am."

"Nothing but back talk and mess," she said. "Charlie's Billy's. Billy and Dina's."

Morse would never have guessed it, to look at the boy. "I didn't know Hart had a son," he said, and hoped she hadn't heard the note of complaint that was all too clear and strange to him.

"Neither does he, the way he acts. Him and Dina both." Dina, she said, was off doing another round of rehab in Raleigh — her second. Julianne and Bella (Julianne's mother, Morse gathered) had been looking after Charlie, but they didn't get along, and after the last blowup Bella had taken off for Florida with a boyfriend, putting Julianne in a bind. She drove a school bus during the year and worked summers cooking at a Girl Scout camp, but with Charlie on her hands and no money for child care she'd had to give up the camp job. So she'd driven down here to try and shake some help out of Billy, enough to get her through until school started, or Bella decided to come home and do her share, fat chance.

Morse nodded toward the boy. He didn't like his hearing all this, if anything could penetrate that concentration, but Julianne went on as if she hadn't noticed. Her voice was low, growly, but with a nasal catch in it, like the whine of a saw blade binding. She didn't have the lazy music that Hart could play so well, but she seemed more truly of the hollows and farms of their home; she spoke of the people there as if Morse must know them, too — as if she had no working conception of the reach of the world beyond.

At first, Morse was expecting her to put the bite on him, but she never did. He did not understand what she wanted from him, or why, un- prompted, he had offered to come here tonight.

"So he's gone," she said finally. "You're sure."

"Afraid so."

"Well. Good to know my luck's holding. Wouldn't want it to get worse." She leaned back and closed her eyes.

"Why didn't you call first?"

"What, and let on I was coming? You don't know our Billy."

Julianne seemed to fall into a trance then, and Morse soon followed, lulled by the clink of crockery and the voices all around, the soft scratch- ing of the crayon. He didn't know how long they sat like this. He was roused by the tapping of raindrops against the window, a few fat drops that left oily lines as they slid down the glass. The rain stopped. Then it came again in a rush, sizzling on the asphalt, glazing the cars in the parking lot, pleasant to watch after the long, heavy day.

"Rain," Morse said.

Julianne didn't bother to look. She might have been asleep but for the slight nod she gave him.

Morse recognized two men from his company at a table across the room. He watched them until they glanced his way, then he nodded and they nodded back. Money in the bank — confirmed sighting of Sergeant Morse with woman and child. Family. He hated thinking so bitter and cheap a thought, and resented whatever led him to think it. Still, how else could they be seen, the three of them, in a pancake house at this hour? And it wasn't just their resemblance to a family. No, there was the atmosphere of family here, in the very silence of the table: Julianne with her eyes closed, the boy working away on his picture, Morse himself looking on like any husband and father.

"You're tired," he said.

The tenderness of his own voice surprised him, and her eyes blinked open as if she, too, were surprised. She looked at him with gratitude; and it came to Morse that she had called him back that night just for the reason she gave, because he had spoken kindly to her.

"I am tired," she said. "I am that."

"Look. Julianne. What do you need to tide you over?"

"Nothing. Forget all that stuff. I was just blowing off steam."

"I'm not talking about charity, O.K.? Just a loan, that's all."

"We'll be fine."

"It's not like there's anyone waiting in line for it," he said, and this was true. Morse's father and older brother, finally catching on, had gone cold on him years ago. He'd remained close to his mother, but she died just after his return from Iraq. In his new will, Morse named as sole beneficiary the hospice where she'd spent her last weeks. To name Dixon seemed too sudden and meaningful and might draw unwelcome attention, and anyway Dixon had made some sharp investments and was well fixed.

"I just can't," Julianne said. "But that is so sweet."

"My dad's a soldier," the boy said, head still bent over the place mat.

"I know," Morse said. "He's a good soldier. You should be proud."

Julianne smiled at him, really smiled, for the first time that night. She had been squinting and holding her mouth in a tight line. Then she smiled and looked like someone else. Morse saw that she had beauty, and that her pleasure in him had allowed this beauty to show itself. He was embarrassed. He felt a sense of duplicity that he immediately, even indignantly, suppressed. "I can't force it on you," he said. "Suit yourself."

The smile vanished. "I will," she said, in the same tone he had used, harder than he'd intended. "But I thank you anyhow. Charlie," she said, "time to go. Get your stuff together."

"I'm not done."

"Finish it tomorrow."

Morse waited while she rolled up the place mat and helped the boy collect his crayons. He noticed the check pinned under the saltshaker and picked it up.

"I'll take that," she said, and held out her hand in a way that did not permit refusal.

Morse stood by awkwardly as Julianne paid at the register, then he walked outside with her and the boy. They stood together under the awning and watched the storm lash the parking lot. Glittering lines of rain fell aslant through the glare of the lights overhead. The surrounding trees tossed wildly, and the wind sent gleaming ripples across the asphalt. Julianne brushed a lock of hair back from the boy's forehead. "I'm ready. How about you?"

"No."

"Well, it ain't about to quit raining for Charles Drew Hart." She yawned widely and gave her head a shake. "Nice talking to you," she said to Morse.

"Where will you stay?"

"Pickup."

"A pickup? You're going to sleep in a truck?"

"Can't drive like this." And in the look she gave him, expectant and mocking, he could see that she knew he would offer her a motel room, and that she was already tasting the satisfaction of turning it down. But that didn't stop him from trying.

"Country-proud," Dixon said when Morse told him the story later that morning. "You should have invited them to stay here. People like that, mountain people, will accept hospitality when they won't take money. They're like Arabs. Hospitality has a sacred claim. You don't refuse to give it, and you don't refuse to take it."

"Never occurred to me," Morse said, but in truth he'd had the same intuition, standing outside the restaurant with the two of them, wallet in hand. Even as he tried to talk Julianne into taking the money for a room, invoking the seriousness of the storm and the need to get the boy into a safe dry place, he had the sense that if he simply invited her home with him she might indeed say yes. And then what? Dixon waking up and playing host, bearing fresh towels to the guest room, making coffee, teasing the boy—and looking at Morse in that way of his. Its meaning would be clear enough to Julianne. What might she do with such knowledge? Out of shock and disgust, perhaps even feeling herself betrayed, she could ruin them.

Morse thought of that but didn't really fear it. He liked her; he did not think she would act meanly. What he feared, what he could not allow, was for her to see how Dixon looked at him, and then to see that he could not give back what he received. That things between them were unequal, and himself unloving.

So that even while offering Julianne the gift of shelter he felt false, mealy-mouthed, as if he were trying to buy her off; and the unfairness of suffering guilt while pushing his money at her and having his money refused proved too much for Morse. Finally, he told her to sleep in the damned truck then if that was what she wanted.

"I don't want to sleep in the truck," the boy said.

"You'd be a sight happier if you did want to," Julianne said. "Now come on—ready or not."

"Just don't try to drive home," Morse said.

She put her hand on the boy's shoulder and led him out into the parking lot.

"You're too tired!" Morse called after her, but if she answered he couldn't hear it for the drumming of the rain on the metal awning. They walked on across the asphalt. The wind gusted, driving the rain so hard that Morse had to jump back a step. Julianne took it full in the face and never so much as turned her head. Nor did the boy. Charlie. He was getting something from her, ready or not, walking into the rain as if it weren't raining at all.

2010-2015

ECONOMIC PRESSURES AND THE DIGITAL REVOLUTION continue to affect the publishing of short fiction. Borders Books closed in 2011. In 2013 e-books accounted for nearly 20 percent of larger publishers' revenue. New questions about the foundations of publishing have arisen: What should e-books cost? What value does a publisher bring to a book, and is it preferable for authors to self-publish?

Both publishers and literary magazines have become creative in seeking new readers. The paperback original can make a first short story collection more affordable. Online publication can provide substantial savings in production costs. In 2013 *Ploughshares*, one of the country's finest magazines, launched its Solos program, publishing individual long stories digitally on Kindle and Nook. *DailyLit* offers readers a program where they receive short stories — as well as installments of novels — via e-mail and soon on mobile devices.

I've been pleased to see writers begin to take more risks in their stories, whether by blending genres or paying direct homage to other writers or experimenting with the structure of the stories themselves. I've read stories in the form of e-mail exchanges, stories published on Twitter, stories written as online personal ads. The computer, and the Internet by extension, has become a real part of our landscape, and our authors are reckoning with this fact.

I continue to read stories about the Iraq war. I read stories about the mentally ill, the homeless and/or unemployed. I read stories about genetics, our manipulation of the environment, the undeniable presence of global warming. Thankfully, I've begun reading more stories that directly address homosexuality and transgender characters, too long all but absent from the series.

In my relatively short tenure, I have noticed an easing of tone in many American short stories, a more conversational vernacular that can be traced to the stories of Sherwood Anderson but also, more recently, to the blogosphere and Internet, where even many news headlines seem to have shed a certain level of formality. Of course, some things never change. For the past hundred years people have wondered about the relevance of fiction, the state of publishing, and the death of print. People have grappled with the definition of a short story: How long should it be? What parameters dictate its format?

For the past several years I've read every volume of *The Best American Short Stories* in order to cull stories for this book while reading for the annual volumes. Sometimes it's been difficult not to compare the present and the past, to view certain stories objectively from the vantage of their own very different time. Worming my way through the history of a country via its short stories has been a strange, wonderful, and utterly singular experience. I've developed and discarded theory after theory of influence. One of my earliest was that transportation must have been the basis for decades of fictional trends. At the start of the series, so many stories were set on ships or in pubs peopled by sailors and captains. Bravery at sea was the thing—man against nature, as well as the trustworthiness of told tales themselves. With the rise of the railroad came a sense of the vastness of our own country—an opening of communication between family members previously kept apart, lovers previously out of contact. Characters desired freedom and were held back not by geographical distance but by family and historical norms. The most influential mode of transportation had to be the automobile and the building of interstates—and with them came a dramatic increase in time spent alone. Not until the 1940s did interiority of character really catch on in American short stories. As people grew more isolated but free, writers delved into the human consciousness for a new sort of conflict. Happy endings grew even less common. Of course I could not ignore the impact of war, the economy, and civil rights on short fiction. But I was surprisingly aware the entire time that I read of the fact that how we move—how we are able to come together—defines how we think and therefore express ourselves.

One other trend has been undeniable. There has been a slow but steady movement toward diversity in American short stories: diversity of the gender and race and class of authors published in the series, too late when one looks back over the past 100 years; diversity of voice and structure, of style and content; finally and fortunately, diversity of format and genre and content. The history of the series and, if one is to extrapolate and generalize, of the American short story is a history of opening and acceptance. We still have a ways to go. There is plenty of room for more writers of color, as well as writers of diverse sexual and socioeconomic orientations. I wish I read more deftly handled humor, more genre-bending and experimental stories. That said, one can assert that the goals of the founders of the series — to highlight exceptional literary fiction, to provide an alternative to formulaic, commercial fiction — have certainly been and will continue to be met.

I have relied on a number of sources in order to gather the many voices, anecdotes, and other material, not to mention the stories, that appear in this book. In addition to the 100 volumes of *The Best American Short Stories*, and *Fifty Best American Short Stories* and *200 Years of Great American Short Stories*, both edited by Martha Foley, as well as *The Best American Short Stories of the Century*, edited by John Updike and Katrina Kenison, I consulted Roy S. Simmonds's *Edward J. O'Brien and His Role in the Rise of the American Short Story in the 1920s and 1930s*; Martha Foley's memoir, *The Story of Story Magazine*; and the editorial files at the office of Houghton Mifflin Harcourt and the Houghton Mifflin Archives at Harvard University. The author interviews in *The Paris Review* were invaluable to me, as were the *New York Times* and the *Washington Post*. I consulted a wide variety of magazines, from *People* to *Writer's Digest* to *The Daily Beast*. Thank you to Edward O'Brien, Martha Foley, Shannon Ravenel, and Katrina Kenison for your invaluable work, and for paving the way for me. Thanks to the latter two for being candid and wise in speaking about your work. Thank you to Nicole Angeloro, my unfathomably capable editor at Houghton Mifflin Harcourt, and to Andrea Schulz, Liz Duvall, and Laura Brady.

Lorrie Moore met the challenge of this project with great enthusiasm and a deep knowledge of her subject. To select but a few dozen short stories that both signified and transcended their time was no small feat. Admittedly, we bumbled forward at times. We wanted this book to serve as a retrospective of a century, a march through time looking through the lens of the American short story. Moore was a serious, thoughtful guest editor, uncomfortable, as was I, with the number of landmark stories that had to fall away from the final list. No book can contain all the best stories of a century. Any attempt at such a thing has to reflect its

editors' tastes and biases. That said, I am proud of our efforts and hope
that this time capsule will provide future readers a guided tour through
a century. A last note: Lorrie Moore refused to include any of her own
stories in this book, despite my best efforts to convince her otherwise.
I had to settle for her involvement on only one level. She has my deep
gratitude for introducing and coediting this book.

H.P.

★ ★ ★

2012

NATHAN ENGLANDER
WHAT WE TALK ABOUT WHEN
WE TALK ABOUT ANNE FRANK

from *The New Yorker*

NATHAN ENGLANDER was born on Long Island, New York, in 1970. He says, "I grew up in an Orthodox home in New York, where I had a right-wing, xenophobic, anti-intellectual, fire-and-brimstone, free-thought free, shtetl-mentality, substandard education. And so I began to look elsewhere; I began to read literature. Simple as that." Englander graduated from the State University of New York at Binghamton and the Iowa Writers' Workshop at the University of Iowa.

His first book, a story collection titled *For the Relief of Unbearable Urges*, was published in 1999. He later published a novel, *The Ministry of Special Cases*, and another story collection, *What We Talk About When We Talk About Anne Frank*. He was the 2012 recipient of the Frank O'Connor International Short Story Award and a finalist for the 2013 Pulitzer Prize. Englander was selected as one of "20 Writers for the 21st Century" by *The New Yorker* and received a Guggenheim Fellowship, a PEN/Malamud Award, the Bard Fiction Prize, the Berlin Prize, and the Sue Kaufman Prize from the American Academy of Arts and Letters.

The *New York Times Book Review* said of Englander's work, "Echoes of the two Isaacs, Bashevis Singer and Babel, can be heard throughout his pages, though Gogol is somewhere in the neighborhood too."

Englander lives in Brooklyn, New York, where he is Distinguished Writer-in-Residence at New York University.

★

THEY'RE IN OUR house maybe ten minutes and already Mark's lecturing us on the Israeli occupation. Mark and Lauren live in Jerusalem, and people from there think it gives them the right. Mark is looking all stoic and nodding his head. "If we had what you have down here in South Florida," he says, and trails off. "Yup," he says, and he's nodding again. "We'd have no troubles at all."

"You do have what we have," I tell him. "All of it. Sun and palm trees. Old Jews and oranges and the worst drivers around. At this point, we've probably got more Israelis than you." Debbie, my wife, puts a hand on my arm — her signal that I'm either taking a tone, interrupting someone's story, sharing something private, or making an inappropriate joke. That's my cue, and I'm surprised, considering how often I get it, that she ever lets go of my arm.

"Yes, you've got everything now," Mark says. "Even terrorists."

I look at Lauren. She's the one my wife has the relationship with — the one who should take charge. But Lauren isn't going to give her husband any signal. She and Mark ran off to Israel twenty years ago and turned Hasidic, and neither of them will put a hand on the other in public. Not for this. Not to put out a fire.

"Wasn't Mohamed Atta living right here before 9/11?" Mark says, and now he pantomimes pointing out houses. "Goldberg, Goldberg, Goldberg — Atta. How'd you miss him in this place?"

"Other side of town," I say.

"That's what I'm talking about. That's what you have that we don't. Other sides of town. Wrong sides of the tracks. Space upon space." And now he's fingering the granite countertop in our kitchen, looking out into the living room and the dining room, staring through the kitchen windows at the pool. "All this house," he says, "and one son? Can you imagine?"

"No," Lauren says. And then she turns to us, backing him up. "You should see how we live with ten."

"Ten kids," I say. "We could get you a reality show with that here in the States. Help you get a bigger place."

The hand is back pulling at my sleeve. "Pictures," Debbie says. "I want to see the girls." We all follow Lauren into the den for her purse.

"Do you believe it?" Mark says. "Ten girls!" And the way it comes out of his mouth, it's the first time I like the guy. The first time I think about giving him a chance.

Facebook and Skype brought Deb and Lauren back together. They were glued at the hip growing up. Went all the way through school together. Yeshiva school. All girls. Out in Queens till high school and then riding the subway together to one called Central in Manhattan. They stayed best friends until I married Deb and turned her secular, and soon after that Lauren met Mark and they went off to the Holy Land and shifted from Orthodox to *ultra*-Orthodox, which to me sounds like a repackaged detergent — ORTHODOX ULTRA®, now with more deep-healing power. Because of that, we're supposed to call them Shoshana and Yerucham now. Deb's been doing it. I'm just not saying their names.

"You want some water?" I offer. "Coke in the can?"

" 'You' — which of us?" Mark says.

"You both," I say. "Or I've got whiskey. Whiskey's kosher too, right?"

"If it's not, I'll kosher it up real fast," he says, pretending to be easygoing. And right then he takes off that big black hat and plops down on the couch in the den.

Lauren's holding the verticals aside and looking out at the yard. "Two girls from Forest Hills," she says. "Who ever thought we'd be the mothers of grownups?"

"Trevor's sixteen," Deb says. "You may think he's a grownup, and he may think he's a grownup — but we are not convinced."

Right then is when Trev comes padding into the den, all six feet of him, plaid pajama bottoms dragging on the floor and T-shirt full of holes. He's just woken up, and you can tell he's not sure if he's still dreaming. We told him we had guests. But there's Trev, staring at this man in the black suit, a beard resting on his belly. And Lauren, I met her once before, right when Deb and I got married, but ten girls and a thousand Shabbos dinners later — well, she's a big woman, in a bad dress and a giant blond Marilyn Monroe wig. Seeing them at the door, I can't say I wasn't shocked myself.

"Hey," he says.

And then Deb's on him, preening and fixing his hair and hugging him. "Trevy, this is my best friend from childhood," she says. "This is Shoshana, and this is —"

"Mark," I say.

"Yerucham," Mark says, and sticks out a hand. Trev shakes it. Then Trev sticks out his hand, polite, to Lauren. She looks at it, just hanging there in the air.

"I don't shake," she says. "But I'm so happy to see you. Like meeting my own son. I mean it." And here she starts to cry, and then she and Deb are hugging. And the boys, we just stand there until Mark looks at his watch and gets himself a good manly grip on Trev's shoulder.

"Sleeping until three on a Sunday? Man, those were the days," Mark says. "A regular little Rumpleforeskin." Trev looks at me, and I want to shrug, but Mark's also looking, so I don't move. Trev just gives us both his best teenage glare and edges out of the room. As he does, he says, "Baseball practice," and takes my car keys off the hook by the door to the garage.

"There's gas," I say.

"They let them drive here at sixteen?" Mark says. "Insane."

"So what brings you here after all these years?" I say.

"My mother," Mark says. "She's failing, and my father's getting old — and they come to us for Sukkot every year. You know?"

"I know the holidays."

"They used to fly out to us. For Sukkot and Pesach, both. But they can't fly now, and I just wanted to get over while things are still good. We haven't been in America —"

"Oh, gosh," Lauren says. "I'm afraid to think how long it's been. More than ten years. Twelve," she says. "With the kids, it's just impossible until enough of them are big."

"How do you do it?" Deb says. "Ten kids? I really do want to hear."

That's when I remember. "I forgot your drink," I say to Mark.

"Yes, his drink. That's how," Lauren says. "That's how we cope."

And that's how the four of us end up back at the kitchen table with a bottle of vodka between us. I'm not one to get drunk on a Sunday afternoon, but, I tell you, when the plan is to spend the day with Mark I jump at the chance. Deb's drinking too, but not for the same reason. I think she and Lauren are reliving a little bit of the wild times. The very small window when they were together, barely grown up, two young women living in New York on the edge of two worlds.

Deb says, "This is really racy for us. I mean, *really* racy. We try not to drink much at all these days. We think it sets a bad example for Trevor. It's not good to drink in front of them right at this age when they're all transgressive. He's suddenly so interested in that kind of thing."

"I'm just happy when he's interested in something," I say.

Deb slaps at the air. "I just don't think it's good to make drinking look like it's fun with a teenager around."

Lauren smiles and straightens her wig. "Does anything we do look fun to our kids?"

I laugh at that. Honestly, I'm liking her more and more.

"It's the age limit that does it," Mark says. "It's the whole American puritanical thing, the twenty-one-year-old drinking age and all that. We don't make a big deal about it in Israel, and so the kids, they don't even notice alcohol. Except for the foreign workers on Fridays, you hardly see anyone drunk at all."

"The workers and the Russians," Lauren says.

"The Russian immigrants," he says, "that's a whole separate matter. Most of them, you know, not even Jews."

"What does that mean?" I say.

"It means matrilineal descent, is what it means," Mark says. "With the Ethiopians there were conversions."

But Deb wants to keep us away from politics, and the way we're arranged, me in between them and Deb opposite (it's a round table, our kitchen table), she practically has to throw herself across to grab hold of my arm. "Fix me another," she says.

And here she switches the subject to Mark's parents. "How's the visit been going?" she says, her face all somber. "How are your folks holding up?"

Deb is very interested in Mark's parents. They're Holocaust survivors. And Deb has what can only be called an unhealthy obsession with the idea of that generation being gone. Don't get me wrong. It's important to me too. All I'm saying is there's healthy and unhealthy, and my wife, she gives the subject a *lot* of time.

"What can I say?" Mark says. "My mother's a very sick woman. And my father, he tries to keep his spirits up. He's a tough guy."

"I'm sure," I say. Then I look down at my drink, all serious, and give a shake of my head. "They really are amazing."

"Who?" Mark says. "Fathers?"

I look back up and they're all staring at me. "Survivors," I say, realizing I jumped the gun.

"There's good and bad," Mark says. "Like anyone else."

Lauren says, "The whole of Carmel Lake Village, it's like a D.P. camp with a billiards room."

"One tells the other, and they follow," Mark says. "From Europe to New York, and now, for the end of their lives, again the same place."

"Tell them that crazy story, Yuri," Lauren says.

"Tell us," Deb says.

"So you can picture my father," Mark says. "In the old country, he went to *heder*, had the *peyes* and all that. But in America a classic *galusmonger*. He looks more like you than me. It's not from him that I get this," he says, pointing at his beard. "Shoshana and I —"

"We know," I say.

"So my father. They've got a nice nine-hole course, a driving range, some greens for the practice putting. And my dad's at the clubhouse. I go with him. He wants to work out in the gym, he says. Tells me I should come. Get some exercise. And he tells me"— and here Mark points at his feet, sliding a leg out from under the table so we can see his big black clodhoppers—"'You can't wear those Shabbos shoes on the treadmill. You need the sneakers. You know, sports shoes?' And I tell him, 'I know what sneakers are. I didn't forget my English any more than your Yiddish is gone.' So he says, '*Ah shaynem dank dir in pupik.*' Just to show me who's who."

"Tell them the point," Lauren says.

"He's sitting in the locker room, trying to pull a sock on, which is, at that age, basically the whole workout in itself. It's no quick business. And I see, while I'm waiting, and I can't believe it—I nearly pass out. The guy next to him, the number on his arm, it's three before my father's number. You know, in sequence."

"What do you mean?" Deb says.

"I mean the number tattooed. It's the same as my father's camp number, digit for digit, but my father's ends in an eight. And this guy's, it ends in a five. That's the only difference. I mean, they're separated by two people. So I say, 'Excuse me, sir.' And the guy just says, 'You with the Chabad? I don't want anything but to be left alone. I already got candles at home.' I tell him, 'No. I'm not. I'm here visiting my father.' And to my father I say, 'Do you know this gentleman? Have you two met? I'd really like to introduce you, if you haven't.' And they look each other over for what, I promise you, is minutes. Actual minutes. It is—with *kavod* I say this, with respect for my father—but it is like watching a pair of big beige manatees sitting on a bench, each with one sock on. They're just looking each other up and down, everything slow. And then my father says, 'I seen him. Seen him around.' The other guy, he says, 'Yes, I've seen.' 'You're both survivors,' I tell them. 'Look. The numbers.' And they look. 'They're the same,' I say. And they both hold out their arms to look at the little ashen tattoos. To my father I say, 'Do you get it? The same, except his—it's right ahead of yours. Look! Compare.' So they look. They compare." Mark's eyes are popping out of his head. "Think about it," he says. "Around the world, surviving the unsurvivable, these two old guys end up with enough money to retire to Carmel Lake and play golf every day. So I say to my dad, 'He's right ahead of you. Look, a five,' I say. 'And yours is an eight.' And my father says, 'All that means is he cut ahead of me in line. There same as here. This guy's a cutter. I just didn't want to say.' 'Blow it out your ear,' the other guy says. And that's it. Then they get back to putting on socks."

Deb looks crestfallen. She was expecting something empowering. Some story with which to educate Trevor, to reaffirm her belief in the humanity that, from inhumanity, forms.

But me, I love that kind of story. I'm starting to take a real shine to these two, and not just because I'm suddenly feeling sloshed.

"Good story, Yuri," I say, copying his wife. "Yerucham, that one's got zing."

Yerucham hoists himself up from the table, looking proud. He checks the label of our white bread on the counter, making sure it's kosher. He takes a slice, pulls off the crust, and rolls the white part against the countertop with the palm of his hand, making a little ball. He comes over and pours himself a shot and throws it back. Then he eats that crazy dough ball. Just tosses it in his mouth, as if it's the bottom of his own personal punctuation mark — you know, to underline his story.

"Is that good?" I say.

"Try it," he says. He goes to the counter and pitches me a slice of white bread, and says, "But first pour yourself a shot."

I reach for the bottle and find that Deb's got her hands around it, and her head's bowed down, like the bottle is anchoring her, keeping her from tipping back.

"Are you okay, Deb?" Lauren says.

"It's because it was funny," I say.

"Honey!" Deb says.

"She won't tell you, but she's a little obsessed with the Holocaust. That story — no offense, Mark — it's not what she had in mind."

I should leave it be, I know. But it's not like someone from Deb's high school is around every day offering insights.

"It's like she's a survivor's kid, my wife. It's crazy, that education they give them. Her grandparents were all born in the Bronx, and here we are twenty minutes from downtown Miami but it's like it's 1937 and we live on the edge of Berlin."

"That's not it!" Deb says, openly defensive, her voice super high up in the register. "I'm not upset about that. It's the alcohol. All this alcohol. It's that and seeing Lauren. Seeing Shoshana, after all this time."

"Oh, she was always like this in high school," Shoshana says. "Sneak one drink, and she started to cry. You want to know what used to get her going, what would make her truly happy?" Shoshana says. "It was getting high. That's what always did it. Smoking up. It would make her laugh for hours and hours."

And, I tell you, I didn't see it coming. I'm as blindsided as Deb was by that numbers story.

"Oh, my God," Deb says, and she's pointing at me. "Look at my big bad secular husband. He really can't handle it. He can't handle his wife's having any history of naughtiness at all — Mr. Liberal Open-Minded." To me she says, "How much more chaste a wife can you dream of than a modern-day yeshiva girl who stayed a virgin until twenty-one? Honestly. What did you think Shoshana was going to say was so much fun?"

"Honestly-honestly?" I say. "I don't want to. It's embarrassing."

"Say it!" Deb says, positively glowing.

"Honestly, I thought you were going to say it was something like competing in the Passover Nut Roll, or making sponge cake. Something like that." I hang my head. And Shoshana and Deb are laughing so hard they can't breathe. They're grabbing at each other so that I can't tell if they're holding each other up or pulling each other down.

"I can't believe you told him about the nut roll," Shoshana says.

"And I can't believe," Deb says, "you just told my husband of twenty-two years how much we used to get high. I haven't touched a joint since before we were married," she says. "Have we, honey? Have we smoked since we got married?"

"No," I say. "It's been a very long time."

"So come on, Shosh. When was it? When was the last time you smoked?"

Now, I know I mentioned the beard on Mark. But I don't know if I mentioned how hairy a guy he is. That thing grows right up to his eyeballs. Like having eyebrows on top and bottom both. So when Deb asks the question, the two of them, Shosh and Yuri, are basically giggling like children, and I can tell, in the little part that shows, in the bit of skin I can see, that Mark's eyelids and earlobes are in full blush.

"When Shoshana said we drink to get through the days," Mark says, "she was kidding about the drinking."

"We don't drink much," Shoshana says.

"It's smoking that she means," he says.

"We still get high," Shoshana says. "I mean, all the time."

"Hasidim!" Deb screams. "You're not allowed!"

"Everyone does in Israel. It's like the sixties there," Mark says. "It's the highest country in the world. Worse than Holland and India and Thailand put together. Worse than anywhere, even Argentina — though they may have us tied."

"Well, maybe that's why the kids aren't interested in alcohol," I say.

"Do you want to get high now?" Deb says. And we all three look at her. Me, with surprise. And those two with straight longing.

"We didn't bring," Shoshana says. "Though it's pretty rare anyone at customs peeks under the wig."

"Maybe you guys can find your way into the glaucoma underground over at Carmel Lake," I say. "I'm sure that place is rife with it."

"That's funny," Mark says.

"I'm funny," I say, now that we're all getting on.

"We've got pot," Deb says.

"We do?" I say. "I don't think we do."

Deb looks at me and bites at the cuticle on her pinkie.

"You're not secretly getting high all these years?" I say. I really don't feel well at all.

"Our son," Deb says. "He has pot."

"Our son?"

"Trevor," she says.

"Yes," I say. "I know which one."

It's a lot for one day, that kind of news. And it feels to me a lot like betrayal. Like my wife's old secret and my son's new secret are bound up together, and I've somehow been wronged. Also, I'm not one to recover quickly from any kind of slight from Deb — not when there are people around. I really need to talk stuff out. Some time alone, even five minutes, would fix it. But it's super apparent that Deb doesn't need any time alone with me. She doesn't seem troubled at all. What she seems is focused. She's busy at the counter, using a paper tampon wrapper to roll a joint.

"It's an emergency-preparedness method we came up with in high school," Shoshana says. "The things teenage girls will do when they're desperate."

"Do you remember that nice boy that we used to smoke in front of?" Deb says. "He'd just watch us. There'd be six or seven of us in a circle, girls and boys not touching — we were so religious. Isn't that crazy?" Deb is talking to me, as Shoshana and Mark don't think it's crazy at all. "The only place we touched was passing the joint, at the thumbs. And this boy, we had a nickname for him."

"Passover!" Shoshana yells.

"Yes," Deb says, "that's it. All we ever called him was Passover. Because every time the joint got to him he'd just pass it over to the next one of us. Passover Rand."

Shoshana takes the joint and lights it with a match, sucking deep. "It's a miracle when I remember anything these days," she says. "After my first was born, I forgot half of everything I knew. And then half again with each one after. Just last night, I woke up in a panic. I couldn't remember if there were fifty-two cards in a deck or fifty-two weeks in a year. The recall errors — I'm up all night worrying over them, just waiting for the Alzheimer's to kick in."

"It's not that bad," Mark tells her. "It's only everyone on one side of your family that has it."

"That's true," she says, passing her husband the joint. "The other side is blessed only with dementia. Anyway, which is it? Weeks or cards?"

"Same, same," Mark says, taking a hit.

When it's Deb's turn, she holds the joint and looks at me, like I'm supposed to nod or give her permission in some husbandly anxiety-absolving way. But instead of saying, "Go ahead," I pretty much bark at Deb. "When were you going to tell me about our son?"

At that, Deb takes a long hit, holding it deep, like an old pro.

"Really, Deb. How could you not tell me you knew?"

Deb walks over and hands me the joint. She blows the smoke in my face, not aggressive, just blowing.

"I've only known five days," she says. "I was going to tell you. I just wasn't sure how, or if I should talk to Trevy first, maybe give him a chance," she says.

"A chance to what?" I ask.

"To let him keep it as a secret between us. To let him know he could have my trust if he promised to stop."

"But he's the son," I say. "I'm the father. Even if it's a secret with him, it should be a double secret between me and you. I should always get to know — even if I pretend not to know — any secret with him."

"Do that double part again," Mark says. But I ignore him.

"That's how it's always been," I say to Deb. And, because I'm desperate and unsure, I follow it up with "Hasn't it?"

I mean, we really trust each other, Deb and I. And I can't remember feeling like so much has hung on one question in a long time. I'm trying to read her face, and something complex is going on, some formulation. And then she sits right there on the floor, at my feet.

"Oh, my God," she says. "I'm so fucking high. Like instantly. Like, like," and then she starts laughing. "Like, Mike," she says. "Like, kike," she says, turning completely serious. "Oh, my God, I'm really messed up."

"We should have warned you," Shoshana says.

As she says this, I'm holding my first hit in, and already trying to fight off the paranoia that comes rushing behind that statement.

"Warned us what?" I say, my voice high, and the smoke still sweet in my nose.

"This isn't your father's marijuana," Mark says. "The THC levels. One hit of this new hydroponic stuff, it's like if maybe you smoked a pound of the stuff we had when we were kids."

"I feel it," I say. And I do. I sit down with Deb on the floor and take her hands. I feel nice. Though I'm not sure if I thought that or said it, so I try it again, making sure it's out loud. "I feel nice," I say.

"I found the pot in the laundry hamper," Deb says. "Leave it to a teenage boy to think that's the best place to hide something. His clean clothes show up folded in his room, and it never occurs to him that someone empties that hamper. To him, it's the loneliest, most forgotten space in the world. Point is I found an Altoids tin at the bottom, stuffed full." Deb gives my hands a squeeze. "Are we good now?"

"We're good," I say. And it feels like we're a team again, like it's us against them. Because Deb says, "Are you sure you guys are allowed to smoke pot that comes out of a tin that held non-kosher candy? I really don't know if that's okay." And it's just exactly the kind of thing I'm thinking.

"First of all, we're not eating it. We're smoking it," Shoshana says. "And even so, it's cold contact, so it's probably all right either way."

"'Cold contact'?" I say.

"It's a thing," Shoshana says. "Just forget about it and get up off the floor. Chop-chop." And they each offer us a hand and get us standing. "Come, sit back at the table," Shoshana says.

"I'll tell you," Mark says. "That's got to be the number-one most annoying thing about being Hasidic in the outside world. Worse than the rude stuff that gets said is the constant policing by civilians. Everywhere we go, people are checking on us. Ready to make some sort of liturgical citizen's arrest."

"Strangers!" Shoshana says. "Just the other day, on the way in from the airport. Yuri pulled into a McDonald's to pee, and some guy in a trucker hat came up to him as he went in and said, 'You allowed to go in there, brother?' Just like that."

"Not true!" Deb says.

"It's not that I don't see the fun in that," Mark says. "The allure. You know, we've got Mormons in Jerusalem. They've got a base there. A seminary. The rule is—the deal with the government—they can have their place, but they can't do outreach. No proselytizing. Anyway, I do some business with one of their guys."

"From Utah?" Deb says.

"From Idaho. His name is Jebediah, for real—do you believe it?"

"No, Yerucham and Shoshana," I say. "Jebediah is a very strange name." Mark rolls his eyes at that, handing me what's left of the joint. Without even asking, he gets up and gets the tin and reaches into his wife's purse for another tampon. And I'm a little less comfortable with this than with the white bread, with a guest coming into the house and smoking up all our son's pot. Deb must be thinking something similar, as she says, "After this story, I'm going to text Trev and make sure he's not coming back anytime soon."

"So when Jeb's at our house," Mark says, "when he comes by to eat and pours himself a Coke, I do that same religious-police thing. I can't resist. I say, 'Hey, Jeb, you allowed to have that?' People don't mind breaking their own rules, but they're real strict about someone else's."

"So are they allowed to have Coke?" Deb says.

"I don't know," Mark says. "All Jeb ever says back is 'You're thinking of coffee, and mind your own business, either way.'"

And then my Deb. She just can't help herself. "You heard about the scandal? The Mormons going through the Holocaust list."

"Like in *Dead Souls*," I say, explaining. "Like in the Gogol book, but real."

"Do you think we read that?" Mark says. "As Hasidim, or before?"

"They took the records of the dead," Deb says, "and they started running through them. They took these people who died as Jews and started converting them into Mormons. Converting the six million against their will."

"And this is what keeps an American Jew up at night?" Mark says.

"What does that mean?" Deb says.

"It means—" Mark says.

But Shoshana interrupts him. "Don't tell them what it means, Yuri. Just leave it unmeant."

"We can handle it," I say. "We are interested, even, in handling it."

"Your son, he seems like a nice boy."

"Do not talk about their son," Shoshana says.

"Do not talk about our son," Deb says. This time I reach across and lay a hand on her elbow.

"Talk," I say.

"He does not," Mark says, "seem Jewish to me."

"How can you say that?" Deb says. "What is wrong with you?" But Deb's upset draws less attention than my response. I'm laughing so hard that everyone turns toward me.

"What?" Mark says.

"Jewish to you?" I say. "The hat, the beard, the blocky shoes. A lot of pressure, I'd venture, to look Jewish to you. Like, say, maybe Ozzy Osbourne, or the guys from Kiss, like them telling Paul Simon, 'You do not look like a musician to me.'"

"It is not about the outfit," Mark says. "It's about building life in a vacuum. Do you know what I saw on the drive over here? Supermarket, supermarket, adult bookstore, supermarket, supermarket, firing range."

"Floridians do like their guns and porn," I say. "And their supermarkets."

"What I'm trying to say, whether you want to take it seriously or not, is that you can't build Judaism only on the foundation of one terrible crime," Mark says. "It's about this obsession with the Holocaust as a necessary sign of identity. As your only educational tool. Because for the children there is no connection otherwise. Nothing Jewish that binds."

"Wow, that's offensive," Deb says. "And closed-minded. There is such a thing as Jewish culture. One can live a culturally rich life."

"Not if it's supposed to be a Jewish life. Judaism is a religion. And with religion comes ritual. Culture is nothing. Culture is some construction of the modern world. It is not fixed; it is ever changing, and a weak way to bind generations. It's like taking two pieces of metal, and instead of making a nice weld you hold them together with glue."

"What does that even mean?" Deb says. "Practically."

Mark raises a finger to make his point, to educate. "In Jerusalem we don't need to busy ourselves with symbolic efforts to keep our memories in place. Because we live exactly as our parents lived before the war. And this serves us in all things, in our relationships too, in our marriages and parenting."

"Are you saying your marriage is better than ours?" Deb says. "Really? Just because of the rules you live by?"

"I'm saying your husband would not have the long face, worried his wife is keeping secrets. And your son, he would not get into the business of smoking without first coming to you. Because the relationships, they are defined. They are clear."

"Because they are welded together," I say, "and not glued."

"Yes," he says. "And I bet Shoshana agrees." But Shoshana is distracted. She is working carefully with an apple and a knife. She is making a little apple pipe, all the tampons gone.

"Did your daughters?" Deb says. "If they tell you everything, did they come to you first, before they smoked?"

"Our daughters do not have the taint of the world we grew up in. They have no interest in such things."

"So you think," I say.

"So I know," he says. "Our concerns are different, our worries."

"Let's hear 'em," Deb says.

"Let's not," Shoshana says. "Honestly, we're drunk, we're high, we are having a lovely reunion."

"Every time you tell him not to talk," I say, "it makes me want to hear what he's got to say even more."

"Our concern," Mark says, "is not the past Holocaust. It is the current one. The one that takes more than fifty percent of the Jews of this generation. Our concern is intermarriage. It's the Holocaust that's happening now. You don't need to be worrying about some Mormons doing hocus-pocus on the murdered six million. You need to worry that your son marries a Jew."

"Oh, my God," Deb says. "Are you calling intermarriage a Holocaust?"

"You ask my feeling, that's my feeling. But this, no, it does not exactly apply to you, except in the example you set for the boy. Because you're Jewish, your son, he is as Jewish as me. No more, no less."

"I went to yeshiva too, Born-Again Harry! You don't need to explain the rules to me."

"Did you just call me 'Born-Again Harry'?" Mark asks.

"I did," Deb says. And she and he, they start to laugh at that. They think "Born-Again Harry" is the funniest thing they've heard in a while. And Shoshana laughs, and then I laugh, because laughter is infectious — and it is doubly so when you're high.

"You don't really think our family, my lovely, beautiful son, is headed for a Holocaust, do you?" Deb says. "Because that would really cast a pall on this beautiful day."

"No, I don't," Mark says. "It's a lovely house and a lovely family, a beautiful home that you've made for that strapping young man. You're a real *balabusta*," Mark says.

"That makes me happy," Deb says. And she tilts her head nearly ninety degrees to show her happy, sweet smile. "Can I hug you? I'd really like to give you a hug."

"No," Mark says, though he says it really politely. "But you can hug my wife. How about that?"

"That's a great idea," Deb says. Shoshana gets up and hands the loaded apple to me, and I smoke from the apple as the two women hug a tight, deep, dancing-back-and-forth hug, tilting this way and that, so, once again, I'm afraid they might fall.

"It is a beautiful day," I say.

"It is," Mark says. And both of us look out the window, and both of us watch the perfect clouds in a perfect sky, so that we're both staring out as the sky suddenly darkens. It is a change so abrupt that the ladies undo their hug to watch.

"It's like that here," Deb says. And the clouds open up and torrential tropical rain drops straight down, battering. It is loud against the roof, and loud against the windows, and the fronds of the palm trees bend, and the floaties in the pool jump as the water boils.

Shoshana goes to the window. And Mark passes Deb the apple and goes to the window. "Really, it's always like this here?" Shoshana says.

"Sure," I say. "Every day. Stops as quick as it starts."

And both of them have their hands pressed up against the window. And they stay like that for some time, and when Mark turns around, harsh guy, tough guy, we see that he is weeping.

"You do not know," he says. "I forget what it's like to live in a place rich with water. This is a blessing above all others."

"If you had what we had," I say.

"Yes," he says, wiping his eyes.

"Can we go out?" Shoshana says. "In the rain?"

"Of course," Deb says. Then Shoshana tells me to close my eyes. Only me. And I swear I think she's going to be stark naked when she calls, "Open up."

She's taken off her wig is all, and she's wearing one of Trev's baseball caps in its place.

"I've only got the one wig this trip," she says. "If Trev won't mind."

"He won't mind," Deb says. And this is how the four of us find ourselves in the back yard, on a searingly hot day, getting pounded by all this cool, cool rain. It's just about the best feeling in the world. And, I have to say, Shoshana looks twenty years younger in that hat.

We do not talk in the rain. We are too busy frolicking and laughing and jumping around. And that's how it happens that I'm holding Mark's hand and sort of dancing, and Deb is holding Shoshana's hand, and they're doing their own kind of jig. And when I take Deb's hand, though neither Mark nor Shoshana is touching the other, somehow we've formed a broken circle. We've started dancing our own kind of hora in the rain.

It is the silliest and freest and most glorious I can remember feeling in years. Who would think that's what I'd be saying with these strict, suffocatingly austere people visiting our house? And then my Deb, my love, once again she is thinking what I'm thinking, and she says, face up into the rain, all of us spinning, "Are you sure this is okay, Shoshana? That it's not mixed dancing? I don't want anyone feeling bad after."

"We'll be just fine," Shoshana says. "We will live with the consequences." The question slows us, and stops us, though no one has yet let go.

"It's like the old joke," I say. Without waiting for anyone to ask which one, I say, "Why don't Hasidim have sex standing up?"

"Why?" Shoshana says.

"Because it might lead to mixed dancing."

Deb and Shoshana pretend to be horrified as we let go of hands, as we recognize that the moment is over, the rain disappearing as quickly as it came. Mark stands there staring into the sky, lips pressed tight. "That joke is very, very old," he says. "And mixed dancing makes me think of mixed nuts, and mixed grill, and *insalata mista*. The sound of 'mixed dancing' has made me wildly hungry. And I'm going to panic if the only kosher thing in the house is that loaf of bleached American bread."

"You have the munchies," I say.

"Diagnosis correct," he says.

Deb starts clapping at that, tiny claps, her hands held to her chest in prayer. She says to him, absolutely beaming, "You will not even believe what riches await."

The four of us stand in the pantry, soaking wet, hunting through the shelves and dripping on the floor. "Have you ever seen such a pantry?" Shoshana says, reaching her arms out. "It's gigantic." It is indeed large, and it is indeed stocked, an enormous amount of food, and an enormous selection of sweets, befitting a home that is often host to a swarm of teenage boys.

"Are you expecting a nuclear winter?" Shoshana says.

"I'll tell you what she's expecting," I say. "You want to know how Holocaust-obsessed she really is? I mean, to what degree?"

"To no degree," Deb says. "We are done with the Holocaust."

"Tell us," Shoshana says.

"She's always plotting our secret hiding place," I say.

"No kidding," Shoshana says.

"Like, look at this. At the pantry, with a bathroom next to it, and the door to the garage. If you sealed it all up — like put drywall at the entrance to the den — you'd never suspect. If you covered that door inside the garage up good with, I don't know — if you hung your tools in front of it and hid hinges behind, maybe leaned the bikes and the mower against it, you'd have this closed area, with running water and a toilet and all this food. I mean, if someone sneaked into the garage to replenish things, you could rent out the house. Put in another family without their having any idea."

"Oh, my God," Shoshana says. "My short-term memory may be gone from having all those children —"

"And from the smoking," I say.

"And from that too. But I remember from when we were kids," Shoshana says, turning to Deb. "You were always getting me to play games like that. To pick out spaces. And even worse, even darker —"

"Don't," Deb says.

"I know what you're going to say," I tell her, and I'm honestly excited. "The game, yes? She played that crazy game with you?"

"No," Deb says. "Enough. Let it go."

And Mark — who is utterly absorbed in studying kosher certifications, who is tearing through hundred-calorie snack packs and eating handfuls of roasted peanuts, and who has said nothing since we entered the pantry except "What's a Fig Newman?" — he stops and says, "I want to play this game."

"It's not a game," Deb says.

And I'm happy to hear her say that, as it's just what I've been trying to get her to admit for years. That it's not a game. That it's dead serious, and a kind of preparation, and an active pathology that I prefer not to indulge.

"It's the Anne Frank game," Shoshana says. "Right?"

Seeing how upset my wife is, I do my best to defend her. I say, "No, it's not a game. It's just what we talk about when we talk about Anne Frank."

"How do we play this non-game?" Mark says. "What do we do?"

"It's the Righteous Gentile game," Shoshana says.

"It's Who Will Hide Me?" I say.

"In the event of a second Holocaust," Deb says, giving in. "It's a serious exploration, a thought experiment that we engage in."

"That you play," Shoshana says.

"That, in the event of an American Holocaust, we sometimes talk about which of our Christian friends would hide us."

"I don't get it," Mark says.

"Of course you do," Shoshana says. "It's like this. If there was a Shoah, if it happened again — say we were in Jerusalem, and it's 1941 and the Grand Mufti got his way, what would Jebediah do?"

"What could he do?" Mark says.

"He could hide us. He could risk his life and his family's and everyone's around him. That's what the game is: would he — for real — would he do that for you?"

"He'd be good for that, a Mormon," Mark says. "Forget this pantry. They have to keep a year of food stored in case of the Rapture, or something like that. Water too. A year of supplies. Or maybe it's that they have sex through a sheet. No, wait. I think that's supposed to be us."

"All right," Deb says. "Let's not play. Really, let's go back to the kitchen. I can order in from the glatt kosher place. We can eat outside, have a real dinner and not just junk."

"No, no," Mark says. "I'll play. I'll take it seriously."

"So would the guy hide you?" I say.

"The kids too?" Mark says. "I'm supposed to pretend that in Jerusalem he's got a hidden motel or something where he can put the twelve of us?"

"Yes," Shoshana says. "In their seminary or something. Sure."

Mark thinks about this for a long, long time. He eats Fig Newmans and considers, and you can tell that he's taking it seriously — serious to the extreme.

"Yes," Mark says, looking choked up. "Jeb would do that for us. He would risk it all."

Shoshana nods. "Now you go," she says to us. "You take a turn."

"But we don't know any of the same people anymore," Deb says. "We usually just talk about the neighbors."

"Our across-the-street neighbors," I tell them. "They're the perfect example. Because the husband, Mitch, he would hide us. I know it. He'd lay down his life for what's right. But that wife of his."

"Yes," Deb says. "Mitch would hide us, but Gloria, she'd buckle. When he was at work one day, she'd turn us in."

"You could play against yourselves," Shoshana says. "What if one of you wasn't Jewish? Would you hide the other?"

"I'll do it," I say. "I'll be the Gentile, because I could pass best. A grown woman with an ankle-length denim skirt in her closet—they'd catch you in a flash."

"Fine," Deb says. And I stand up straight, put my shoulders back, like maybe I'm in a lineup. I stand there with my chin raised so my wife can study me. So she can decide if her husband really has what it takes. Would I have the strength, would I care enough—and it is not a light question, not a throwaway question—to risk my life to save her and our son?

Deb stares, and Deb smiles, and gives me a little push to my chest. "Of course he would," Deb says. She takes the half stride that's between us and gives me a tight hug that she doesn't release. "Now you," Deb says. "You and Yuri go."

"How does that even make sense?" Mark says. "Even for imagining."

"Sh-h-h," Shoshana says. "Just stand over there and be a good Gentile while I look."

"But if I weren't Jewish I wouldn't be me."

"That's for sure," I say.

"He agrees," Mark says. "We wouldn't even be married. We wouldn't have kids."

"Of course you can imagine it," Shoshana says. "Look," she says, and goes over and closes the pantry door. "Here we are, caught in South Florida for the second Holocaust. You're not Jewish, and you've got the three of us hiding in your pantry."

"But look at me!" he says.

"I've got a fix," I say. "You're a background singer for ZZ Top. You know that band?"

Deb lets go of me so she can give my arm a slap.

"Really," Shoshana says. "Look at the three of us like it's your house and we're your charges, locked up in this room."

"And what're you going to do while I do that?" Mark says.

"I'm going to look at you looking at us. I'm going to imagine."

"Okay," he says. "*Nu*, get to it. I will stand, you imagine."

And that's what we do, the four of us. We stand there playing our roles, and we really get into it. I can see Deb seeing him, and him seeing us, and Shoshana just staring at her husband.

We stand there so long I can't tell how much time has passed, though the light changes ever so slightly—the sun outside again dimming—in the crack under the pantry door.

"So would I hide you?" he says. And for the first time that day he reaches out, as my Deb would, and puts his hand to his wife's hand. "Would I, Shoshi?"

And you can tell that Shoshana is thinking of her kids, though that's not part of the scenario. You can tell that she's changed part of the imagining. And she says, after a pause, yes, but she's not laughing. She says yes, but to him it sounds as it does to us, so that he is now asking and asking. But wouldn't I? Wouldn't I hide you? Even if it was life and death—if it would spare you, and they'd kill me alone for doing it? Wouldn't I?

Shoshana pulls back her hand.

She does not say it. And he does not say it. And of the four of us no one will say what cannot be said—that this wife believes her husband would not hide her. What to do? What will come of it? And so we stand like that, the four of us trapped in that pantry. Afraid to open the door and let out what we've locked inside.

2012

JULIE OTSUKA

DIEM PERDIDI

from *Granta*

JULIE OTSUKA was born in 1962 and raised in California. She studied art at Yale and began a career as a painter before writing fiction. She received her MFA from Columbia.

Her first novel, *When the Emperor Was Divine*, tells the story of the internment of a Japanese American family. She is also the author of *The Buddha in the Attic*.

Otsuka is a recipient of the PEN/Faulkner Award, the Asian American Literary Award, the American Library Association Alex Award, France's Prix Femina Étranger, an Arts and Letters Award in Literature from the American Academy of Arts and Letters, and a Guggenheim Fellowship. A critic in *Granta* likened her writing to "a kind of hypnosis or meditation" due to the rhythmic and repetitive sentence structure.

Julie Otsuka lives in New York City.

★

S HE REMEMBERS HER name. She remembers the name of the president. She remembers the name of the president's dog. She remembers what city she lives in. And on which street. And in which house. *The one with the big olive tree where the road takes a turn.* She remembers what year it is. She remembers the season. She remembers the day on which you were born. She remembers the daughter who was born before you — *She had your father's nose, that was the first thing I noticed about her* — but she does not remember that daughter's name. She remembers the name of the man she did not marry — Frank — and she keeps his letters in a drawer by her bed. She remembers that you once had a husband, but she refuses to remember your ex-husband's name. *That man,* she calls him.

• • •

She does not remember how she got the bruises on her arms or going for a walk with you earlier this morning. She does not remember bending over, during that walk, and plucking a flower from a neighbor's front yard and slipping it into her hair. *Maybe your father will kiss me now.* She does not remember what she ate for dinner last night, or when she last took her medicine. She does not remember to drink enough water. She does not remember to comb her hair.

She remembers the rows of dried persimmons that once hung from the eaves of her mother's house in Berkeley. *They were the most beautiful shade of orange.* She remembers that your father loves peaches. She remembers that every Sunday morning, at ten, he takes her for a drive down to the sea in the brown car. She remembers that every evening, right before the eight o'clock news, he sets out two fortune cookies on a paper plate and announces to her that they are having a party. She remembers that on Mondays he comes home from the college at four, and if he is even five minutes late she goes out to the gate and begins to wait for him. She remembers which bedroom is hers and which is his. She remembers that the bedroom that is now hers was once yours. She remembers that it wasn't always like this.

She remembers the first line of the song "How High the Moon." She remembers the Pledge of Allegiance. She remembers her Social Security number. She remembers her best friend Jean's telephone number even though Jean has been dead for six years. She remembers that Margaret is dead. She remembers that Betty is dead. She remembers that Grace has stopped calling. She remembers that her own mother died nine years ago, while spading the soil in her garden, and she misses her more and more every day. *It doesn't go away.* She remembers the number assigned to her family by the government right after the start of the war: *13611.* She remembers being sent away to the desert with her mother and brother during the fifth month of that war and taking her first ride on a train. She remembers the day they came home: *September 9, 1945.* She remembers the sound of the wind hissing through the sagebrush. She remembers the scorpions and red ants. She remembers the taste of dust.

Whenever you stop by to see her, she remembers to give you a big hug, and you are always surprised at her strength. She remembers to give you a kiss every time you leave. She remembers to tell you, at the end of every phone call, that the FBI will check up on you again soon. She remembers to ask you if you would like her to iron your blouse for you before you go out on a date. She remembers to smooth down your skirt. *Don't give it all away.* She remembers to brush aside a wayward strand of your hair. She does not remember eating lunch with you twenty minutes ago and suggests that you go out to Marie Callender's for sandwiches and pie. She does not remember that she herself once used to make the most beautiful pies, with perfectly fluted crusts. She does not remember how to iron your blouse for you or when she began to forget. *Something's changed.* She does not remember what she is supposed to do next.

She remembers that the daughter who was born before you lived for half an hour and then died. *She looked perfect from the outside.* She remembers her mother telling her, more than once, *Don't you ever let anyone see you cry.* She remembers giving you your first bath on your third day in the world. She remembers that you were a very fat baby. She remembers that your first word was *No.* She remembers picking apples in a field with Frank many years ago in the rain. *It was the best day of my life.* She remembers that the first time she met him she was so nervous, she forgot her own address. She remembers wearing too much lipstick. She remembers not sleeping for days.

When you drive past Hesse Park, she remembers being asked to leave her exercise class by her teacher after being in that class for more than ten years. *I shouldn't have talked so much.* She remembers touching her toes and doing windmills and jumping jacks on the freshly mown grass. She remembers being the highest kicker in her class. She does not remember how to use the "new" coffeemaker, which is now three years old, because it was bought after she began to forget. She does not remember asking your father, ten minutes ago, if today is Sunday, or if it is time to go for her ride. She does not remember where she last put her sweater or how long she has been sitting in her chair. She does not always remember how to get out of that chair, and so you gently push down on the footrest and offer her your hand, which she does not always remember to take. *Go away,* she sometimes says. Other times, she just says, *I'm stuck.* She does not remember saying to you, the other night, right after your father left the room, *He loves me more than I love him.* She does not remember saying to you, a moment later, *I can hardly wait until he comes back.*

·   ·   ·

She remembers that when your father was courting her he was always on time. She remembers thinking that he had a nice smile. *He still does.* She remembers that when they first met he was engaged to another woman. She remembers that that other woman was white. She remembers that that other woman's parents did not want their daughter to marry a man who looked like the gardener.

She remembers that the winters were colder back then, and that there were days on which you actually had to put on a coat and scarf. She remembers her mother bowing her head every morning at the altar and offering her ancestors a bowl of hot rice. She remembers the smell of incense and pickled cabbage in the kitchen. She remembers that her father always wore nice shoes. She remembers that the night the FBI came for him, he and her mother had just had another big fight. She remembers not seeing him again until after the end of the war.

She does not always remember to trim her toenails, and when you soak her feet in the bucket of warm water, she closes her eyes and leans back in her chair and reaches out for your hand. *Don't give up on me.* She does not remember how to tie her shoelaces or fasten the hooks on her bra. She does not remember that she has been wearing her favorite blue blouse for five days in a row. She does not remember your age. *Just wait till you have children of your own,* she says to you, even though you are now too old to do so.

She remembers that after the first girl was born and then died, she sat in the yard for days, just staring at the roses by the pond. *I didn't know what else to do.* She remembers that when you were born, you too had your father's long nose. *It was as if I'd given birth to the same girl twice.* She remembers that you are a Taurus. She remembers that your birthstone is green. She remembers to read you your horoscope from the newspaper whenever you come over to see her. *Someone you were once very close to may soon reappear in your life,* she tells you. She does not remember reading you that same horoscope five minutes ago or going to the doctor with you last week after you discovered a bump on the back of her head. *I think I fell.* She does not remember telling the doctor that you are no longer married or giving him your number and asking him to please call. She does not remember leaning over and whispering to you, the moment he stepped out of the room, *I think he'll do.*

• • •

She remembers another doctor asking her, fifty years ago, minutes after the first girl was born and then died, if she wanted to donate the baby's body to science. *He said she had a very unusual heart.* She remembers being in labor for thirty-two hours. She remembers being too tired to think. *So I told him yes.* She remembers driving home from the hospital in the sky-blue Chevy with your father and neither one of them saying a word. She remembers knowing she'd made a big mistake. She does not remember what happened to the baby's body and worries that it might be stuck in a jar. She does not remember why they didn't just bury her. *I wish she was under a tree.* She remembers wanting to bring her flowers every day.

She remembers that even as a young girl you said you did not want to have children. She remembers that you hated wearing dresses. She remembers that you never played with dolls. She remembers that the first time you bled, you were thirteen years old and wearing bright yellow pants. She remembers that your childhood dog was named Shiro. She remembers that you once had a cat named Gasoline. She remembers that you had two turtles named Turtle. She remembers that the first time she and your father took you to Japan to meet his family, you were eighteen months old and just beginning to speak. She remembers leaving you with his mother in the tiny silkworm village in the mountains while she and your father traveled across the island for ten days. *I worried about you the whole time.* She remembers that when they came back, you did not know who she was and that for many days afterward you would not speak to her; you would only whisper in her ear.

She remembers that the year you turned five you refused to leave the house without tapping the door frame three times. She remembers that you had a habit of clicking your teeth repeatedly, which drove her up the wall. She remembers that you could not stand it when different-colored foods were touching on the plate. *Everything had to be just so.* She remembers trying to teach you to read before you were ready. She remembers taking you to Newberry's to pick out patterns and fabric and teaching you how to sew. She remembers that every night, after dinner, you would sit down next to her at the kitchen table and hand her the bobby pins one by one as she set the curlers in her hair. She remembers that this was her favorite part of the day. *I wanted to be with you all the time.*

·   ·   ·

She remembers that you were conceived on the first try. She remembers that your brother was conceived on the first try. She remembers that your other brother was conceived on the second try. *We must not have been paying attention.* She remembers that a palm reader once told her that she would never be able to bear children because her uterus was tipped the wrong way. She remembers that a blind fortuneteller once told her that she had been a man in her past life and that Frank had been her sister. She remembers that everything she remembers is not necessarily true. She remembers the horse-drawn garbage carts on Ashby, her first pair of crepe-soled shoes, scattered flowers by the side of the road. She remembers that the sound of Frank's voice always made her feel calmer. She remembers that every time they parted, he turned around and watched her walk away. She remembers that the first time he asked her to marry him, she told him she wasn't ready. She remembers that the second time she said she wanted to wait until she was finished with school. She remembers walking along the water with him one warm summer evening on the boardwalk and being so happy, she could not remember her own name. She remembers not knowing that it wouldn't be like this with any of the others. She remembers thinking she had all the time in the world.

She does not remember the names of the flowers in the yard whose names she has known for years. *Roses? Daffodils? Immortelles?* She does not remember that today is Sunday, and she has already gone for her ride. She does not remember to call you, even though she always says that she will. She remembers how to play "Clair de Lune" on the piano. She remembers how to play "Chopsticks" and scales. She remembers not to talk to telemarketers when they call on the telephone. *We're not interested.* She remembers her grammar. *Just between you and me.* She remembers her manners. She remembers to say thank you and please. She remembers to wipe herself every time she uses the toilet. She remembers to flush. She remembers to turn her wedding ring around whenever she pulls on her silk stockings. She remembers to reapply her lipstick every time she leaves the house. She remembers to put on her anti-wrinkle cream every night before climbing into bed. *It works while you sleep.* In the morning, when she wakes, she remembers her dreams. *I was walking through a forest. I was swimming in a river. I was looking for Frank in a city I did not know and no one would tell me where he was.*

•   •   •

On Halloween day, she remembers to ask you if you are going out trick-or-treating. She remembers that your father hates pumpkin. *It's all he ate in Japan during the war.* She remembers listening to him pray, every night, when they first got married, that he would be the one to die first. She remembers playing marbles on a dirt floor in the desert with her brother and listening to the couple at night on the other side of the wall. *They were at it all the time.* She remembers the box of chocolates you brought back to her after your honeymoon in Paris. "But will it last?" you asked her. She remembers her own mother telling her, "The moment you fall in love with someone, you are lost."

She remembers that when her father came back after the war, he and her mother fought even more than they had before. She remembers that he would spend entire days shopping for shoes in San Francisco while her mother scrubbed other people's floors. She remembers that some nights he would walk around the block three times before coming into the house. She remembers that one night he did not come in at all. She remembers that when your own husband left you, five years ago, you broke out in hives all over your body for weeks. She remembers thinking he was trouble the moment she met him. *A mother knows.* She remembers keeping that thought to herself. *I had to let you make your own mistakes.*

She remembers that, of her three children, you were the most delightful to be with. She remembers that your younger brother was so quiet, she sometimes forgot he was there. *He was like a dream.* She remembers that her own brother refused to carry anything with him onto the train except for his rubber toy truck. *He wouldn't let me touch it.* She remembers her mother killing all the chickens in the yard the day before they left. She remembers her fifth-grade teacher, Mr. Martello, asking her to stand up in front of the class so everyone could tell her goodbye. She remembers being given a silver heart pendant by her next-door neighbor, Elaine Crowley, who promised to write but never did. She remembers losing that pendant on the train and being so angry she wanted to cry. *It was my first piece of jewelry.*

She remembers that one month after Frank joined the Air Force he suddenly stopped writing her letters. She remembers worrying that he'd been shot down over Korea or taken hostage by guerrillas in the jungle.

She remembers thinking about him every minute of the day. *I thought I was losing my mind.* She remembers learning from a friend one night that he had fallen in love with somebody else. She remembers asking your father the next day to marry her. *"Shall we go get the ring?" I said to him.* She remembers telling him, *It's time.*

When you take her to the supermarket she remembers that coffee is Aisle Two. She remembers that Aisle Three is milk. She remembers the name of the cashier in the express lane who always gives her a big hug. *Diane.* She remembers the name of the girl at the flower stand who always gives her a single broken-stemmed rose. She remembers that the man behind the meat counter is Big Lou. "Well, hello, gorgeous," he says to her. She does not remember where her purse is and begins to panic until you remind her that she has left it at home. *I don't feel like myself without it.* She does not remember asking the man in line behind her whether or not he was married. She does not remember him telling her, rudely, that he was not. She does not remember staring at the old woman in the wheelchair by the melons and whispering to you, *I hope I never end up like that.* She remembers that the huge mimosa tree that once stood next to the cart corral in the parking lot is no longer there. *Nothing stays the same.* She remembers that she was once a very good driver. She remembers failing her last driver's test three times in a row. *I couldn't remember any of the rules.* She remembers that the day after her father left them, her mother sprinkled little piles of salt in the corner of every room to purify the house. She remembers that they never spoke of him again.

She does not remember asking your father, when he comes home from the pharmacy, what took him so long, or who he talked to, or whether or not the pharmacist was pretty. She does not always remember his name. She remembers graduating from high school with high honors in Latin. She remembers how to say, "I came, I saw, I conquered." *Veni, vidi, vici.* She remembers how to say, "I have lost the day." *Diem perdidi.* She remembers the words for "I'm sorry" in Japanese, which you have not heard her utter in years. She remembers the words for "rice" and "toilet." She remembers the words for "Wait." *Chotto matte kudasai.* She remembers that a white-snake dream will bring you good luck. She remembers that it is bad luck to pick up a dropped comb. She remembers that you should never run to a funeral. She remembers that you shout the truth down into a well.

• • •

She remembers going to work, like her mother, for the rich white ladies up in the hills. She remembers Mrs. Tindall, who insisted on eating lunch with her every day in the kitchen instead of just leaving her alone. She remembers Mrs. Edward deVries, who fired her after one day. *"Who taught you how to iron?" she asked me.* She remembers that Mrs. Cavanaugh would not let her go home on Saturdays until she had baked an apple pie. She remembers Mrs. Cavanaugh's husband, Arthur, who liked to put his hand on her knee. She remembers that he sometimes gave her money. She remembers that she never refused. She remembers once stealing a silver candlestick from a cupboard, but she cannot remember whose it was. She remembers that they never missed it. She remembers using the same napkin for three days in a row. She remembers that today is Sunday, which six days out of seven is not true.

When you bring home the man you hope will become your next husband, she remembers to take his jacket. She remembers to offer him coffee. She remembers to offer him cake. She remembers to thank him for the roses. *So you like her?* she asks him. She remembers to ask him his name. *She's my firstborn, you know.* She remembers, five minutes later, that she has already forgotten his name, and asks him again what it is. *That's my brother's name,* she tells him. She does not remember talking to her brother on the phone earlier that morning — *He promised me he'd call* — or going for a walk with you in the park. She does not remember how to make coffee. She does not remember how to serve cake.

She remembers sitting next to her brother many years ago on a train to the desert and fighting about who got to lie down on the seat. She remembers hot white sand, the wind on the water, someone's voice telling her, *Hush, it's all right.* She remembers where she was the day the men landed on the moon. She remembers the day they learned that Japan had lost the war. *It was the only time I ever saw my mother cry.* She remembers the day she learned that Frank had married somebody else. *I read about it in the paper.* She remembers the letter she got from him not long after, asking if he could please see her. *He said he'd made a mistake.* She remembers writing him back, "It's too late." She remembers marrying your father on an unusually warm day in December. She remembers having their first fight, three months later, in March. *I threw a chair.* She remembers that he comes home from the college every Monday at four. She remembers that she is forgetting. She remembers less and less every day.

·   ·   ·

When you ask her your name, she does not remember what it is. *Ask your father. He'll know.* She does not remember the name of the president. She does not remember the name of the president's dog. She does not remember the season. She does not remember the day or the year. She remembers the little house on San Luis Avenue that she first lived in with your father. She remembers her mother leaning over the bed she once shared with her brother and kissing the two of them good night. She remembers that as soon as the first girl was born, she knew that something was wrong. *She didn't cry.* She remembers holding the baby in her arms and watching her go to sleep for the first and last time in her life. She remembers that they never buried her. She remembers that they did not give her a name. She remembers that the baby had perfect fingernails and a very unusual heart. She remembers that she had your father's long nose. She remembers knowing at once that she was his. She remembers beginning to bleed two days later when she came home from the hospital. She remembers your father catching her in the bathroom as she began to fall. She remembers a desert sky at sunset. *It was the most beautiful shade of orange.* She remembers scorpions and red ants. She remembers the taste of dust. She remembers once loving someone more than anyone else. She remembers giving birth to the same girl twice. She remembers that today is Sunday, and it is time to go for her ride, and so she picks up her purse and puts on her lipstick and goes out to wait for your father in the car.

2013

GEORGE SAUNDERS
THE SEMPLICA-GIRL DIARIES

from *The New Yorker*

GEORGE SAUNDERS was born in 1958 in Texas and raised in Chicago, and graduated with a degree in geophysics from the Colorado School of Mines. He says, "Any claim I might make to originality in my fiction is really just the result of this odd background: basically, just me working inefficiently, with flawed tools, in a mode I don't have sufficient background to really understand. Like if you put a welder to designing dresses." He earned an MA in creative writing from Syracuse University in 1988.

Saunders is the author of eight books, including *Tenth of December,* which won the inaugural Folio Prize in 2013 (for the best work of fiction in English) and the Story Prize (best short story collection) and was a finalist for the National Book Award. He has received the MacArthur Award, a Guggenheim Fellowship, and the PEN/Malamud Prize for excellence in the short story and was recently elected to the American Academy of Arts and Sciences. In 2013 he was named one of the world's 100 most influential people by *Time* magazine.

Critic Alan Cheuse said, "George Saunders is the real thing, the successor to such dark comedians of ordinary speech as Donald Barthelme and Grace Paley. He's a Vonnegutian in his soul and, paradoxically, a writer like no one but himself." Saunders's fiction often explores the impact of modern consumerism and technology.

George Saunders teaches at Syracuse University and lives in the Catskills.

★

SEPTEMBER 3RD

Having just turned forty, have resolved to embark on grand project of writing every day in this new black book just got at OfficeMax. Exciting to think how in one year, at rate of one page/day, will have written three hundred and sixty-five pages, and what a picture of life and times then available for kids & grandkids, even great-grandkids, whoever, all are welcome (!) to see how life really was/is now. Because what do we know of other times really? How clothes smelled and carriages sounded? Will future people know, for example, about sound of airplanes going over at night, since airplanes by that time passé? Will future people know sometimes cats fought in night? Because by that time some chemical invented to make cats not fight? Last night dreamed of two demons having sex and found it was only two cats fighting outside window. Will future people be aware of concept of "demons"? Will they find our belief in "demons" quaint? Will "windows" even exist? Interesting to future generations that even sophisticated college grad like me sometimes woke in cold sweat, thinking of demons, believing one possibly under bed? Anyway, what the heck, am not planning on writing encyclopedia, if any future person is reading this, if you want to know what a "demon" was, go look it up, in something called an encyclopedia, if you even still have those!

Am getting off track, due to tired, due to those fighting cats. Hereby resolve to write in this book at least twenty minutes a night, no matter how tired. (If discouraged, just think how much will have been recorded for posterity after one mere year!)

SEPTEMBER 5TH

Oops. Missed a day. Things hectic. Will summarize yesterday. Yesterday a bit rough. While picking kids up at school, bumper fell off Park Avenue. Note to future generations: Park Avenue = type of car. Ours not new. Ours oldish. Bit rusty. Kids got in, Eva (middle child) asked what was meaning of "junkorama." At that moment, bumper fell off. Mr. Renn, history teacher, quite helpful, retrieved bumper (note: write letter of commendation to principal), saying he too once had car whose bumper fell off, when poor, in college. Eva assured me it was all right bumper had fallen off. I replied of course it was all right, why wouldn't it be all right, it was just something that had happened, I certainly hadn't caused. Image that stays in mind is of three sweet kids in backseat, chastened expressions on little faces, timidly holding bumper across laps. One end of bumper had to hang out Eva's window and today she has sniffles, plus small cut on hand from place where bumper was sharp.

Lilly (oldest, nearly thirteen!), as always, put all in perspective, by saying, Who cares about stupid bumper, we're going to get a new car soon anyway, when rich, right?

Upon arriving home, put bumper in garage. In garage, found dead large mouse or small squirrel crawling with maggots. Used shovel to transfer majority of squirrel/mouse to Hefty bag. Smudge of squirrel/ mouse still on garage floor, like oil stain w/embedded fur tufts.

Stood looking up at house, sad. Thought: Why sad? Don't be sad. If sad, will make everyone sad. Went in happy, not mentioning bumper, squirrel/mouse smudge, maggots, then gave Eva extra ice cream, due to I had spoken harshly to her.

Have to do better! Be kinder. Start now. Soon they will be grown and how sad, if only memory of you is testy, stressed guy in bad car.

When will I have sufficient leisure/wealth to sit on hay bale watching moon rise, while in luxurious mansion family sleeps? At that time, will have chance to reflect deeply on meaning of life, etc., etc. Have a feeling and have always had a feeling that this and other good things will happen for us!

SEPTEMBER 6TH

Very depressing birthday party today at home of Lilly's friend Leslie Torrini.

House is mansion where Lafayette once stayed. Torrinis showed us Lafayette's room: now their "Fun Den." Plasma TV, pinball game, foot massager. Thirty acres, six garages (they call them "outbuildings"): one for Ferraris (three), one for Porsches (two, plus one he is rebuilding), one for historical merry-go-round they are restoring as family (!). Across trout-stocked stream, red Oriental bridge flown in from China. Showed us hoofmark from some dynasty. In front room, near Steinway, plaster cast of hoofmark from even earlier dynasty, in wood of different bridge. Picasso autograph, Disney autograph, dress Greta Garbo once wore, all displayed in massive mahogany cabinet.

Vegetable garden tended by guy named Karl.

Lilly: Wow, this garden is like ten times bigger than our whole yard.

Flower garden tended by separate guy, weirdly also named Karl.

Lilly: Wouldn't you love to live here?

Me: Lilly, ha-ha, don't ah . . .

Pam (my wife, very sweet, love of life!): What, what is she saying wrong? Wouldn't you? Wouldn't you love to live here? I know *I* would.

In front of house, on sweeping lawn, largest SG arrangement ever seen, all in white, white smocks blowing in breeze, and Lilly says, Can we go closer?

Leslie Torrini: We can but we don't, usually.

Leslie's mother, dressed in Indonesian sarong: We don't, as we already have, many times, dear, but you perhaps would like to? Perhaps this is all very new and exciting to you?

Lilly, shyly: It is, yes.

Leslie's mom: Please, go, enjoy.

Lilly races away.

Leslie's mom, to Eva: And you, dear?

Eva stands timidly against my leg, shakes head no.

Just then father (Emmett) appears, says time for dinner, hopes we like sailfish flown in fresh from Guatemala, prepared with a rare spice found only in one tiny region of Burma, which had to be bribed out.

The kids can eat later, in the tree house, Leslie's mom says.

She indicates the tree house, which is painted Victorian and has a gabled roof and a telescope sticking out and what looks like a small solar panel.

Thomas: Wow, that tree house is like twice the size of our actual house.

(Thomas, as usual, exaggerating: tree house is more like one-third size of our house. Still, yes: big tree house.)

Our gift not the very worst. Although possibly the least expensive — someone brought a mini DVD player; someone brought a lock of hair from an actual mummy (!) — it was, in my opinion, the most heartfelt. Because Leslie (who appeared disappointed by the lock of mummy hair, and said so, because she already had one (!)) was, it seemed to me, touched by the simplicity of our paper-doll set. And although we did not view it as kitsch at the time we bought it, when Leslie's mom said, Les, check it out, kitsch or what, don't you love it?, I thought, Yes, well, maybe it is kitsch, maybe we did intend. In any event, this eased the blow when the next gift was a ticket to the Preakness (!), as Leslie has recently become interested in horses, and has begun getting up early to feed their nine horses, whereas previously she had categorically refused to feed the six llamas.

Leslie's mom: So guess who ended up feeding the llamas?

Leslie, sharply: Mom, don't you remember back then I always had yoga?

Leslie's mom: Although actually, honestly? It was a blessing, a chance for me to rediscover what terrific animals they are, after school, on days on which Les had yoga.

Leslie: Like every day, yoga?

Leslie's mom: I guess you just have to trust your kids, trust that their innate interest in life will win out in the end, don't you think? Which is what is happening now, with Les and horses. God, she loves them.

Pam: Our kids, we can't even get them to pick up what Ferber does in the front yard.

Leslie's mom: And Ferber is?

Me: Dog.

Leslie's mom: Ha-ha, yes, well, everything poops, isn't that just *it*?

After dinner, strolled grounds with Emmett, who is surgeon, does something two days a week with brain inserts, small electronic devices? Or possibly biotronic? They are very small. Hundreds can fit on head of pin? Or dime? Did not totally follow. He asked about my work, I told. He said, Well, huh, amazing the strange, arcane things our culture requires some of us to do, degrading things, things that offer no tangible benefit to anyone, how do they expect people to continue to even hold their heads up?

Could not think of response. Note to self: Think of response, send on card, thus striking up friendship with Emmett?

Returned to Torrinis' house, sat on special star-watching platform as stars came out. Our kids sat watching stars, fascinated. What, I said, no stars in our neighborhood? No response. From anyone. Actually, stars there did seem brighter. On star platform, had too much to drink, and suddenly everything I thought of seemed stupid. So just went quiet, like in stupor.

Pam drove home. I sat sullen and drunk in passenger seat of Park Avenue. Kids babbling about what a great party it was, Lilly especially. Thomas spouting all these boring llama facts, per Emmett.

Lilly: I can't wait till my party. My party is in two weeks, right?

Pam: What do you want to do for your party, sweetie?

Long silence in car.

Lilly, finally, sadly: Oh, I don't know. Nothing, I guess.

Pulled up to house. Another silence as we regarded blank, empty yard. That is, mostly crabgrass and no red Oriental bridge w/ancient hoofprints and no outbuildings and not a single SG, but only Ferber, who we'd kind of forgotten about, and who, as usual, had circled round and round the tree until nearly strangling to death on his gradually shortening leash and was looking up at us with begging eyes in which desperation was combined with a sort of low-boiling anger.

Let him off leash, he shot me hostile look, took dump extremely close to porch.

Watched to see if kids would take initiative and pick up. But no. Kids only slumped past and stood exhausted by front door. Knew I should take initiative and pick up. But was tired and had to come in and write in this stupid book.

Do not really like rich people, as they make us poor people feel dopey and inadequate. Not that we are poor. I would say we are middle. We are very, very lucky. I know that. But still, it is not right that rich people make us middle people feel dopey and inadequate.

Am writing this still drunk and it is getting late and tomorrow is Monday, which means work.

Work, work, work. Stupid work. Am so tired of work.

Good night.

SEPTEMBER 7TH

Just reread that last entry and should clarify.

Am not tired of work. It is a privilege to work. I do not hate the rich. I aspire to be rich myself. And when we finally do get our own bridge, trout, tree house, SGs, etc., at least will know we really earned them, unlike, say, the Torrinis, who, I feel, must have family money.

Last night, after party, found Eva sad in her room. Asked why. She said no reason. But in sketch pad: crayon pic of row of sad SGs. Could tell were meant to be sad, due to frowns went down off faces like Fu Manchus and tears were dropping in arcs, flowers springing up where tears hit ground. Note to self: Talk to her, explain that it does not hurt, they are not sad but actually happy, given what their prior conditions were like: they chose, are glad, etc.

Very moving piece on NPR re Bangladeshi SG sending money home: hence her parents able to build small shack. (Note to self: Find online, download, play for Eva. First fix computer. Computer super slow. Possibly delete "CircusLoser"? Acrobats run all jerky, due to low memory + elephants do not hop = no fun.)

SEPTEMBER 12TH

Nine days to Lilly's b-day. Kind of dread this. Too much pressure. Do not want to have bad party.

Had asked Lilly for list of b-day gift ideas. Today came home to envelope labeled POSSIBLE GIFT LIST. Inside, clippings from some catalogue: *"Resting Fierceness." A pair of fierce porcelain jungle cats are tamed (at least for now!) on highly detailed ornamental pillows, but their wildness* *is not to be underestimated. Left-facing cheetah: $350. Right-facing tiger:* $325. Then, on Post-it: DAD, SECOND CHOICE. *"Girl Reading to Little Sister" figurine: This childhood study by Nevada artist Dani will recall in porcelain the joys of "story time" and the tender moments shared by all. Girl and little girl reading on polished rock: $280.*

Discouraging, I felt. Because (1) why does young girl of thirteen want such old-lady gift, and (2) where does girl of thirteen get idea that $300 = appropriate amount for b-day gift? When I was kid, it was one shirt, one shirt I didn't want, usually homemade.

However, do not want to break Lilly's heart or harshly remind her of our limitations. God knows, she is already reminded often enough. For "My Yard" project at school, Leslie Torrini brought in pics of Oriental bridge, plus background info on SGs (age, place of origin, etc.), as did "every other kid in class," whereas Lilly brought in nineteen-forties condom box found last year during aborted attempt to start vegetable garden. Perhaps was bad call re letting her bring condom box? Thought, being historical, it would be good, plus perhaps kids would not notice it was condom box. But teacher noticed, pointed out, kids had big hoot, teacher used opportunity to discuss safe sex, which was good for class but maybe not so good for Lilly.

As for party, Lilly said she would rather not have one. I asked, Why not, sweetie? She said, Oh, no reason. I said, Is it because of our yard, our house? Is it because you are afraid that, given our small house and bare yard, party might be boring or embarrassing?

At which she burst into tears and said, Oh, Daddy.

Actually, one figurine might not be excessive. Or, rather, might be excess worth indulging in, due to sad look on her face when she came in on "My Yard" day and dropped condom box on table with sigh.

Maybe "Girl Reading to Little Sister," as that is cheapest? Although maybe giving cheapest sends bad signal? Signals frugality even in midst of attempt to be generous? Maybe best to go big? Go for "Resting Fierceness"? Put cheetah on Visa, hope she is happily surprised?

SEPTEMBER 14TH

Observed Mel Redden at work today. He did fine. I did fine. He committed minor errors, I caught them all. He made one Recycling Error: threw Tab can in wrong bucket. When throwing Tab in wrong bucket, made Ergonomic Error, by throwing from far away, missing, having to get up and rethrow. Then made second Ergonomic Error: did not squat when picking up Tab to rethrow, but bent at waist, thereby increasing risk of back injury. Mel signed off on my Observations, then asked me to re-Observe. Very smart. During re-Observation, Mel made no errors. Threw no cans in bucket, just sat very still at desk. So was able to append that to his Record. Parted friends, etc., etc.

One week until L's birthday.

Note to self: Order cheetah.

However, not that simple. Some recent problems with Visa. Full. Past full. Found out at YourItalianKitchen, when Visa declined. Left Pam and kids there, walked rapidly out with big fake smile, drove to ATM. Then scary moment as ATM card also declined. Nearby wino said ATM was broken, directed me to different ATM. Thanked wino with friendly wave as I drove past. Wino gave me finger. Second ATM, thank God, not broken, did not decline. Arrived, winded, back at YourItalianKitchen to find Pam on third cup of coffee and kids falling off chairs and tapping aquarium with dimes, wait staff looking peeved. Paid cash, w/big apologetic tip. Considered collecting dimes from kids (!). Still, overall nice night. Really fun. Kids showed good manners, until aquarium bit.

But problem remains: Visa full. Also AmEx full and Discover nearly full. Called Discover: $200 avail. If we transfer $200 from checking (once paycheck comes in), would then have $400 avail. on Discover, could get cheetah. Although timing problematic. Currently, checking at zero. Paycheck must come, must put paycheck in checking pronto, hope paycheck clears quickly. And then, when doing bills, pick bills totaling $200 to not pay. To defer paying.

Stretched a bit thin these days.

Note to future generations: In our time are such things as credit cards. Company loans money, you pay back at high interest rate. Is nice for when you do not actually have money to do thing you want to do (for example, buy extravagant cheetah). You may say, safe in your future time, Wouldn't it be better to simply not do thing you can't afford to do? Easy for you to say! You are not here, in our world, with kids, kids you love, while other people are doing good things for their kids, such as a Heritage Journey to Nice, if you are the Mancinis, or three weeks wreck-diving off the Bahamas, if you are Gary Gold and his tan, sleek son, Byron.

There is so much I want to do and experience and give to kids. Time going by so quickly, kids growing up so fast. If not now, when? When will we give them largesse and sense of generosity? Have never been to

Hawaii or parasailed or eaten lunch at café by ocean, wearing floppy straw hats just purchased on whim. So I worry: Growing up in paucity, won't they become too cautious? Not that they are growing up in paucity. Still, there are things we want but cannot have. If kids raised too cautious, due to paucity, will not world chew them up and spit out?

Still, must fight good fight! Think of Dad. When Mom left Dad, Dad kept going to job. When laid off from job, got paper route. When laid off from paper route, got lesser paper route. In time, got better route back. By time Dad died, had job almost as good as original job. And had paid off most debt incurred after demotion to lesser route.

Note to self: Visit Dad's grave. Bring flowers. Have talk with Dad re certain things said by me at time of paper routes, due to, could not afford rental tux for prom but had to wear Dad's old tux, which did not fit. Still, no need to be rude. Was not Dad's fault he was good foot taller than me and therefore pant legs dragged, hiding Dad's borrowed shoes, which pinched, because Dad, though tall, had tiny feet.

SEPTEMBER 15TH

Damn it. Plan will not work. Cannot get check to Discover in time. Needs time to clear.

So no cheetah.

Must think of something else to give to Lilly at small family-only party in kitchen. Or may have to do what Mom sometimes did, which was, when thing not available, wrap picture of thing with note promising thing. However, note to self: Do not do other thing Mom did, which was, when child tries to redeem, roll eyes, act exasperated, ask if child thinks money grows on trees.

Note to self: Find ad with pic of cheetah, for I.O.U. coupon. Was on desk but not anymore. Possibly used to record phone message on? Possibly used to pick up little thing cat threw up?

Poor Lilly. Her sweet hopeful face when toddler, wearing Burger King crown, and now this? She did not know she was destined to be not princess but poor girl. Poorish girl. Girl not-the-richest.

No party, no present. Possibly no pic of cheetah in I.O.U. Could draw cheetah but Lilly might then think she was getting camel. Or not getting camel, rather. Am not best drawer. Ha-ha! Must keep spirits up. Laughter best medicine, etc., etc.

Someday, I'm sure, dreams will come true. But when? Why not now? Why not?

SEPTEMBER 20TH

Sorry for silence but wow!

Was too happy/busy to write!

Friday most incredible day ever! Do not need to even write down, as will never forget this awesome day! But will record for future generations. Nice for them to know that good luck and happiness real and possible! In America of my time, want them to know, anything possible!

Wow wow wow is all I can say! Remember how I always buy lunchtime Scratch-Off ticket? Have I said? Maybe did not say? Well, every Friday, to reward self for good week, I stop at store near home, treat self to Butterfinger, plus Scratch-Off ticket. Sometimes, if hard week, two Butterfingers. Sometimes, if very hard week, three Butterfingers. But, if three Butterfingers, no Scratch-Off. But Friday won TEN GRAND!! On Scratch-Off! Dropped both Butterfingers, stood there holding dime used to scratch, mouth hanging open. Kind of reeled into magazine rack. Guy at register took ticket, read ticket, said, Winner! Guy righted magazine rack, shook my hand.

Then said we would get check, check for TEN GRAND, within week.

Raced home on foot, forgetting car. Raced back for car. Halfway back, thought, What the heck, raced home on foot. Pam raced out, said, Where is car? Showed her Scratch-Off ticket. She stood stunned in yard.

Are we rich now? Thomas said, racing out, dragging Ferber by collar.

Not rich, Pam said.

Richer, I said.

Richer, Pam said. Damn.

All began dancing around yard, Ferber looking witless at sudden dancing, then doing dance of own, by chasing own tail.

Then, of course, had to decide how to use. That night in bed, Pam said, Partially pay off credit cards? My feeling was yes, okay, could. But did not seem exciting to me and also did not seem all that exciting to her.

Pam: It would be nice to do something special for Lilly's birthday.

Me: Me too, exactly, yes!

Pam: She could use something. She has really been down.

Me: You know what? Let's do it.

Because Lilly our oldest, we have soft spot for her, soft spot that is also like worry spot.

So we hatched up scheme, then did.

Which was: Went to Greenway Landscaping, had them do total new yard design, incl. ten rosebushes + cedar pathway + pond + small hot tub + four-SG arrangement! Big fun part was, how soon could it be done? Plus, could it be done in secret? Greenway said, for price, could do in one day, while kids at school. (Note to self: Write letter praising Melanie, Greenway gal — super facilitator.)

Step two was: send out secret invites to surprise party to be held on evening of day of yard completion, i.e., tomorrow, i.e., that is why so silent in terms of this book for last week. Sorry, sorry, have just been super busy!

Pam and I worked so well together, like in old days, so nice and close, total agreement. That night, when arrangements all made, went to bed early (!!) (masseuse scenario — do not ask!).

Sorry if corny.

Am just happy.

Note to future generations: Happiness possible. And happy so much better than opposite, i.e., sad. Hopefully you know! I knew, but forgot. Got used to being slightly sad! Slightly sad, due to stress, due to worry vis-à-vis limitations. But now, wow, no: happy!

SEPTEMBER 21ST! LILLY B-DAY(!)

There are days so perfect you feel: This is what life about. When old, will feel whole life worth it, because I got to experience this perfect day.

Today that kind of day.

In morning, kids go off to school per usual. Greenway comes at ten. Yard done by two (!). Roses in, fountain in, pathway in. SG truck arrives at three. SGs exit truck, stand shyly near fence while rack installed. Rack nice. Opted for "Lexington" (midrange in terms of price): bronze uprights w/ Colonial caps, EzyReleese levers.

SGs already in white smocks. Microline strung through. SGs holding microline slack in hands, like mountain climbers holding rope. Only no mountain (!). One squatting, others standing polite/nervous, one sniffing new roses. She gives timid wave. Other says something to her, like, Hey, not supposed to wave. But I wave back, like, In this household, is okay to wave.

Doctor monitors installation by law. So young! Looks like should be working at Wendy's. Says we can watch hoist or not. Gives me meaningful look, cuts eyes at Pam, as in, Wife squeamish? Pam somewhat squeamish. Sometimes does not like to handle raw chicken. I say, Let's go inside, put candles on cake.

Soon, knock on door: doctor says hoist all done.

Me: So can we have a look?

Him: Totally.

We step out. SGs up now, approx. three feet off ground, smiling, swaying in slight breeze. Order, left to right: Tami (Laos), Gwen (Moldova), Lisa (Somalia), Betty (Philippines). Effect amazing. Having so often seen similar configuration in yards of others more affluent makes own yard seem suddenly affluent, you feel different about self, as if at last in step with peers and time in which living.

Pond great. Roses great. Path, hot tub great.

Everything set.

Could not believe we had pulled this off.

Picked kids up at school. Lilly all hangdog because her b-day and no one said Happy B-day at breakfast, and no party and no gifts so far.

Meanwhile, at home: Pam scrambling to decorate. Food delivered (BBQ from Snakey's). Friends arrive. So when Lilly gets out of car what does she see but whole new yard full of friends from school sitting at new picnic table near new hot tub, and new line of four SGs, and Lilly literally bursts into tears of happiness!

Then more tears as shiny pink packages unwrapped, "Resting Fierceness" plus "Girl Reading to Little Sister" revealed. Lilly touched I remembered exact figurines. Plus "Summer Daze" (hobo-clown fishing ($380)), which she hadn't even requested (just to prove largesse). Several more waves of happy tears, hugs, right in front of friends, as if gratitude/affection for us greater than fear of rebuke from friends.

Party guests played usual games, Crack the Whip, etc., etc., in beautiful new yard. Kids joyful, thanked us for inviting. Several said they loved yard. Several parents lingered after, saying they loved yard.

And, my God, the look on Lilly's face as all left!

Know she will always remember today.

Only one slight negative: After party, during cleanup, Eva stomps away, picks up cat too roughly, the way she sometimes does when mad. Cat scratches her, runs over to Ferber, claws Ferber. Ferber dashes away, stumbles into table, roses bought for Lilly crash down on Ferber.

We find Eva in closet.

Pam: Sweetie, sweetie, what is it?

Eva: I don't like it. It's not nice.

Thomas (rushing over with cat to show he is master of cat): They want to, Eva. They like applied for it.

Pam: Where they're from, the opportunities are not so good.

Me: It helps them take care of the people they love.

Eva facing wall, lower lip out in her pre-crying way.

Then I get idea: Go to kitchen, page through Personal Statements. Yikes. Worse than I thought: Laotian (Tami) applied due to two sisters already in brothels. Moldovan (Gwen) has cousin who thought she was becoming window-washer in Germany, but no: sex slave in Kuwait (!). Somali (Lisa) watched father + little sister die of AIDS, same tiny thatch hut, same year. Filipina (Betty) has little brother "very skilled for computer," parents cannot afford high school, have lived in tiny lean-to with three other families since their own tiny lean-to slid down hillside in earthquake.

I opt for "Betty," go back to closet, read "Betty" aloud.

Me: Does that help? Do you understand now? Can you kind of imagine her little brother in a good school, because of her, because of us?

Eva: If we want to help them, why can't we just give them the money?

Me: Oh, sweetie.

Pam: Let's go look. Let's see do they look sad.

(Do not look sad. Are in fact quietly chatting in moonlight.)

At window, Eva quiet. Deep well. So sensitive. Even when tiny, Eva sensitive. Kindest kid. Biggest heart. Once, when little, found dead bird in yard and placed on swing-set slide, so it could "see him fambly." Cried when we threw out old rocking chair, claiming it told her it wanted to live out rest of life in basement.

But I worry, Pam worries: if kid too sensitive, kid goes out in world, world rips kid's guts out, i.e., some toughness req'd?

Lilly, on other hand, wrote all thank-you notes tonight in one sitting, mopped kitchen without being asked, then was out in yard w/flashlight, picking up Ferber area with new poop-scoop she apparently rode on bike to buy w/own money at Fas Mart (!).

SEPTEMBER 22ND

Happy period continues.

Everyone at work curious re Scratch-Off win. Brought pics of yard into work, posted in cubicle, folks came by, admired. Steve Z. asked could he drop by house sometime, see yard in person. This a first: Steve Z. has never previously given me time of day. Even asked my advice: where did I buy winning Scratch-Off, how many Scratch-Offs do I typically buy, Greenway = reputable company?

Embarrassed to admit how happy this made me.

At lunch, went to mall, bought four new shirts. Running joke in department vis-à-vis I have only two shirts. Not so. But have three similar blue shirts and two identical yellow shirts. Hence confusion. Do not generally buy new clothes for self. Have always felt it more important for kids to have new clothes, i.e., do not want other kids saying my kids have only two shirts, etc., etc. As for Pam, Pam very beautiful, raised w/ money. Do not want former wealthy beauty wearing same clothes over and over, feeling, When young, had so many clothes, but now, due to him (i.e., me), badly dressed.

Correction: Pam not raised wealthy. Pam's father = farmer in small town. Had biggest farm on edge of small town. So, relative to girls on smaller farms, Pam = rich girl. If same farm near bigger town, farm only average, but no: town so small, modest farm = estate.

Anyway, Pam deserves best.

Came home, took detour around side of house to peek at yard: fish hovering near lily pads, bees buzzing around roses, SGs in fresh white smocks, shaft of sun falling across lawn, dust motes rising up w/sleepy late-summer feeling, LifeStyleServices team (i.e., Greenway folks who come by 3x/day to give SGs meals/water, take SGs to SmallJon in back of van, deal with feminine issues, etc., etc.) hard at work.

Inside, found Leslie Torrini over (!). This = huge. Leslie never over solo before. Says she likes the way our SGs hang close to pond, are thus reflected in pond. Calls home, demands pond. Leslie's mother calls Leslie spoiled brat, says no pond. This = big score for Lilly. Not that we are glad when someone else not glad. But Leslie so often glad when Lilly not glad, maybe is okay if, just once, Leslie = little bit sad while Lilly = riding high?

Girls go into yard, stay in yard for long time. Pam and I peek out. Girls getting along? Girls have heads together in shade of trees, exchanging girlish intimacies, cementing Lilly's status as pal of Leslie?

Leslie's mother arrives (in BMW). Leslie, Leslie's mother bicker briefly re pond.

Leslie's mom: But, Les, love, you already have three streams.

Leslie (caustic): Is a stream a pond, *Maman*?

Lilly gives me grateful peck on cheek, runs upstairs singing happy tune.

Note to self: Try to extend positive feelings associated with Scratch-Off win into all areas of life. Be bigger presence at work. Race up ladder (joyfully, w/smile on face), get raise. Get in best shape of life, start dressing nicer. Learn guitar? Make point of noticing beauty of world? Why not educate self re birds, flowers, trees, constellations, become true citizen of natural world, walk around neighborhood w/kids, patiently teaching kids names of birds, flowers, etc., etc.? Why not take kids to Europe? Kids have never been. Have never, in Alps, had hot chocolate in mountain café, served by kindly white-haired innkeeper, who finds them so sophisticated/friendly relative to usual snotty/rich American kids (who always ignore his pretty but crippled daughter w/braids) that he shows them secret hiking path to incredible glade, kids frolic in glade, sit with crippled pretty girl on grass, later say it was most beautiful day of their lives, keep in touch with crippled girl via e-mail, we arrange surgery for her here, surgeon so touched he agrees to do for free, she is on front page of our paper, we are on front page of their paper in Alps?

Ha-ha.

(Actually have never been to Europe myself. Dad felt portions there too small. Then Dad lost job, got paper route, portion size = moot point.)

Have been sleepwalking through life, future reader. Can see that now. Scratch-Off win was like wake-up call. In rush to graduate college, win Pam, get job, make babies, move ahead in job, forgot former presentiment of special destiny I used to have when tiny, sitting in cedar-smelling bedroom closet, looking up at blowing trees through high windows, feeling I would someday do something great.

Hereby resolve to live life in new and more powerful way, starting THIS MOMENT (!).

SEPTEMBER 23RD

Eva being a pain.

As I may have mentioned above, Eva = sensitive. This = good, Pam and I feel. This = sign of intelligence. But Eva seems to have somehow gotten idea that sensitivity = effective way to get attention, i.e., has developed tendency to set herself apart from others, possibly as way of distinguishing self, i.e., casting self as better, more refined than others? Has, in past, refused to eat meat, sit on leather seats, use plastic forks made in China. Is endearing enough in little kid. But Eva getting older now, this tendency to object on principle starting to feel a bit precious + becoming fundamental to how she views self?

Family life in our time sometimes seems like game of Whac-A-Mole, future reader. Future generations still have? Plastic mole emerges, you whack with hammer, he dies, falls, another emerges, you whack, kill?

Sometimes seems that, as soon as one kid happy, another kid "pops up," i.e., registers complaint, requiring parent to "whack" kid, i.e., address complaint.

Today Eva's teacher, Ms. Ross, sent home note: Eva acting out. Eva grouchy. Eva stamped foot. Eva threw fish-food container at John M. when John M. said it was his turn to feed fish. This not like Eva, Ms. R. says: Eva sweetest kid in class.

Also, Eva's artwork has recently gone odd. Sample odd artwork enclosed:

Typical house. (Can tell is meant to be our house by mock-cherry tree = swirl of pink.) In yard, SGs frowning. One (Betty) having thought in cartoon balloon: "OUCH! THIS SURE HERTS." Second (Gwen), pointing long bony finger at house: "THANKS LODES." Third (Lisa), tears rolling down cheeks: "WHAT IF I AM YOUR DAUHTER?"

Pam: Well. This doesn't seem to be going away.

Me: No, it does not.

Took Eva for drive. Drove through Eastridge, Lemon Hills. Pointed out houses w/SGs. Had Eva keep count. In end, of approx. fifty houses, thirty-nine had.

Eva: So, just because everyone is doing it, that makes it right.

This cute. Eva parroting me, Pam.

Stopped at Fritz's Chillhouse, had banana split. Eva had Snow-Melt. We sat on big wooden crocodile, watched sun go down.

Eva: I don't even — I don't even get it how they're not dead.

Suddenly occurred to me, w/little gust of relief: Eva resisting in part because she does not understand basic science of thing. Asked Eva if she even knew what Semplica Pathway was. Did not. Drew human head on napkin, explained: Lawrence Semplica = doctor + smart cookie. Found way to route microline through brain that does no damage, causes no pain. Technique uses lasers to make pilot route. Microline then threaded through w/silk leader. Microline goes in here (touched Eva's temple), comes out here (touched other). Is very gentle, does not hurt, SGs asleep during whole deal.

Then decided to level w/Eva.

Explained: Lilly at critical juncture. Next year, Lilly will start high school. Mommy and Daddy want Lilly to enter high school as confident young woman, feeling her family as good/affluent as any other family, her yard approx. in ballpark of yards of peers, i.e., not overt source of embarrassment.

This too much to ask?

Eva quiet.

Could see wheels turning.

Eva wild about Lilly, would walk in front of train for Lilly.

Then shared story w/Eva re summer job I had in high school, at Señor Tasty's (taco place). Was hot, was greasy, boss mean, boss always goosing us with tongs. By time I went home, hair + shirt always stank of grease. No way I could do that job now. But back then? Actually enjoyed: flirted with countergirls, participated in pranks with other employees (hid tongs of mean boss, slipped magazine down own pants so that, when mean boss tong-goosed me, did not hurt, mean boss = baffled).

Point is, I said, everything relative. SGs have lived very different lives from us. Their lives brutal, harsh, unpromising. What looks scary/unpleasant to us may not be so scary/unpleasant to them, i.e., they have seen worse.

Eva: You flirted with girls?

Me: I did. Don't tell Mom.

That got little smile.

Believe I somewhat broke through with Eva. Hope so.

Discussed situation w/Pam tonight. Pam, as usual, offered sound counsel: Go slow, be patient, Eva bright, savvy. In another month, Eva will have adjusted, forgotten, will once again be usual happy self.

Love Pam.

Pam my rock.

SEPTEMBER 25TH

Shit.

Fuck.

Family hit by absolute thunderclap, future reader.

Will explain.

This morning, kids sitting sleepily at table, Pam making eggs, Ferber under her feet, hoping scrap of food will drop. Thomas, eating bagel, drifts to window.

Thomas: Wow. What the heck. Dad? You better get over here.

Go to window.

SGs gone.

Totally gone (!).

Race out. Rack empty. Microline gone. Gate open. Take somewhat frantic run up block, to see if any sign of them.

Is not.

Race back inside. Call Greenway, call police. Cops arrive, scour yard. Cop shows me microline drag mark in mud near gate. Says this actually good news: with microline still in, will be easier to locate SGs, as microline limits how fast they can walk, since, fleeing in group, they are forced to take baby steps, so one does not get too far behind/ahead of others, hence causing yank on microline, yank that could damage brain of one yanked.

Other cop says yes, that would be case if SGs on foot. But come on, he says, SGs not on foot, SGs off in activist van somewhere, laughing butts off.

Me: Activists.

First cop: Yeah, you know: Women4Women, Citizens for Economic Parity, Semplica Rots in Hell.

Second cop: Fourth incident this month.

First cop: Those gals didn't get down by themselves.

Me: Why would they do that? They chose to be here. Why would they go off with some total—

Cops laugh.

First cop: Smelling that American dream, baby.

Kids beyond freaked. Kids huddled near fence.

School bus comes and goes.

Greenway field rep (Rob) arrives. Rob = tall, thin, bent. Looks like archery bow, if archery bow had pierced ear + long hair like pirate, was wearing short leather vest.

Rob immediately drops bombshell: says he is sorry to have to be more or less a hardass in our time of trial, but is legally obligated to inform us that, per our agreement w/Greenway, if SGs not located within three weeks, we will, at that time, become responsible for full payment of the required Replacement Debit.

Pam: Wait, the what?

Per Rob, Replacement Debit = $100/month, per individual, per each month still remaining on their Greenway contracts at time of loss (!). Betty (21 months remaining) = $2,100; Tami (13 months) = $1,300; Gwen (18 months) = $1,800; Lisa (34 months (!)) = $3,400.

Total: $2,100 + $1,300 + $1,800 + $3,400 = $8,600.

Pam: Fucksake.

Rob: Believe me, I know, that's a lot of money, right? But our take on it is—or, you know, their take on it, Greenway's take—is that we—or they—made an initial investment, and, I mean, obviously, that was not cheap, just in terms of like visas and airfares and all?

Pam: No one said anything to us about this.

Me: At all.

Rob: Huh. Who was on your account again?

Me: Melanie?

Rob: Right, yeah, I had a feeling. With Melanie, Melanie was some-times rushing through things to close the deal. Especially with Package A folks, who were going chintzy in the first place? No offense. Anyway, which is why she's gone. If you want to yell at her, go to Home Depot. She's second in charge of Paint, probably lying her butt off about which color is which.

Feel angry, violated: someone came into our yard in dark of night, while kids sleeping nearby, stole? Stole from us? Stole $8,600, plus ini-tial cost of SGs (approx. $7,400)?

Pam (to cop): How often do you find them?

First cop: Honestly? I'd have to say rarely.

Second cop: More like never.

First cop: Well, never yet.

Second cop: Right. There's always a first time.

Cops leave.

Pam (to Rob): So what happens if we don't pay?

Me: Can't pay.

Rob (uncomfortable, blushing): Well, that would be more of an issue for Legal.

Pam: You'd sue us?

Rob: I wouldn't. They would. I mean, that's what they do. They — what's that word? They garner your —

Pam (harshly): Garnish.

Rob: Sorry. Sorry about all this. Melanie, wow, I am going to snap your head back using that stupid braid of yours. Just kidding! I never even talk to her. But the thing is: all this is in your contract. You guys read your contract, right?

Silence.

Me: Well, we were kind of in a hurry. We were throwing a party.

Rob: Oh, sure, I remember that party. That was some party. We were all discussing that.

Rob leaves.

Pam (livid): You know what? Fuck 'em. Let 'em sue. I'm not paying. That's obscene. They can have the stupid house.

Lilly: Are we losing the house?

Me: We're not losing the —

Pam: You don't think? What do you think happens if you owe someone nine grand and can't pay?

Me: Look, let's calm down, no need to get all —

Eva's lower lip out in pre-crying way. Think, Oh, great, nice parenting, arguing + swearing + raising specter of loss of house in front of
tightly wound kid already upset by troubling events of day.

Then Eva bursts into tears, starts mumbling, Sorry sorry sorry.

Pam: Oh, sweetie, I was just being silly. We're not going to lose the
house. Mommy and Daddy would never let that —

Light goes on in my head.

Me: Eva. You didn't.

Look in Eva's eyes says, I did.

Pam: Did what?

Thomas: Eva did it?

Lilly: How could Eva do it? She's only eight. I couldn't even —

Eva leads us outside, shows us how she did: Dragged out stepladder,
stood on stepladder at end of microline, released left-hand EzyReleese
lever, then dragged stepladder to other end, released right-hand
EzyReleese. At that point, microline completely loose, SGs standing on
ground.

SGs briefly confer.

And off they go.

Am so mad. Eva has made huge mess here. Huge mess for us, yes, but
also for SGs. Where are SGs now? In good place? Is it good when illegal
fugitives in strange land have no money, no food, no water, are forced to
hide in woods, swamp, etc., connected via microline, like chain gang?

Note to future generations: Sometimes, in our time, families get into
dark place. Family feels: we are losers, everything we do is wrong. Parents fight at high volume, blaming each other for disastrous situation.
Father kicks wall, puts hole in wall near fridge. Family skips lunch. Tension too high for all to sit at same table. This unbearable. This makes
person (Father) doubt value of whole enterprise, i.e., makes Father (me)
wonder if humans would not be better off living alone, individually, in
woods, minding own beeswax, not loving anyone.

Today like that for us.

Stormed out to garage. Stupid squirrel/mouse stain still there after all
these weeks. Used bleach + hose to eradicate. In resulting calm, sat on
wheelbarrow, had to laugh at situation. Won Scratch-Off, greatest luck
of life, quickly converted greatest luck of life into greatest fiasco of life.

Laughter turned to tears.

Pam came out, asked had I been crying? I said no, just got dust in eyes from cleaning garage. Pam not buying. Pam gave me little side hug + hip nudge, to say, You were crying, is okay, is difficult time, I know.

Pam: Come on inside. Let's get things back to normal. We'll get through this. The kids are dying in there, they feel so bad.

Went inside.

Kids at kitchen table.

Opened arms. Thomas and Lilly rushed over.

Eva stayed sitting.

When Eva tiny, had big head of black curls. Would stand on couch, eating cereal from coffee mug, dancing to song in head, flicking around cord from window blinds.

Now this: Eva sitting w/head in hands like heartbroken old lady mourning loss of vigorous flower of youth, etc., etc.

Went over, scooped Eva up.

Poor thing shaking in my arms.

Eva (in whisper): I didn't know we would lose the house.

Me: We're not — we're not going to lose the house. Mommy and I are going to figure this out.

Sent kids off to watch TV.

Pam: So. You want me to call Dad?

Did not want Pam calling Pam's dad.

Pam's dad's first name = Rich. Actually calls self "Farmer Rich." Is funny because he is rich farmer. In terms of me, does not like me. Has said at various times that I (1) am not hard worker, and (2) had better watch self in terms of weight, and (3) had better watch self in terms of credit cards.

Farmer Rich in very good shape, with no credit cards.

Farmer Rich not fan of SGs. Feels having SGs = "showoffy move." Thinks anything fun = showoffy move. Even going to movie = showoffy move. Going to car wash, i.e., not doing self, in driveway = showoffy move. Once, when visiting, looked dubiously at me when I said I had to get root canal. What, I was thinking, root canal = showoffy move? But no: just disapproved of dentist I had chosen, due to he had seen dentist's TV ad, felt dentist having TV ad = showoffy move.

So did not want Pam calling Farmer Rich.

Told Pam we must try our best to handle this ourselves.

Got out bills, did mock payment exercise: If we pay mortgage, heat bill, AmEx, plus $200 in bills we deferred last time, would be down near zero ($12.78 remaining). If we defer AmEx + Visa, that would free up

$880. If, in addition, we skip mortgage payment, heat bill, life-insurance premium, that would still only free up measly total of $3,100.

Me: Shit.

Pam: Maybe I'll e-mail him. You know. Just see what he says.

Pam upstairs e-mailing Farmer Rich as I write.

SEPTEMBER 26TH

When I got home, Pam standing in doorway w/e-mail from Farmer Rich.

Farmer Rich = bastard.

Will quote in part:

Let us now speak of what you intend to do with the requested money. Will you be putting it aside for a college fund? You will not. Investing in real estate? No. Given a chance to plant some seeds, you flushed those valuable seeds (dollars) away. And for what? A display some find pretty. Well, I do not find it pretty. Since when are people on display a desirable sight? Do-gooders in our church cite conditions of poverty. Okay, that is fine. But it appears you will soon have a situation of poverty within your own walls. And physician heal thyself is a motto I have oft remembered when tempted to put my oar in relative to some social cause or another. So am going to say no. You people have walked yourselves into some deep water and must now walk yourselves out, teaching your kids (and selves) a valuable lesson from which, in the long term, you and yours will benefit.

Long silence.

Pam: Jesus. Isn't this just like us?

Do not know what she means. Or, rather, do know but do not agree. Or, rather, agree but wish she would not say. Why say? Saying is negative, makes us feel bad about selves.

I say maybe we should just confess what Eva did, hope for mercy from Greenway.

Pam says no, no: Went online today. Releasing SGs = felony (!). Does not feel they would prosecute eight-year-old, but still. If we confess, this goes on Eva's record? Eva required to get counseling? Eva feels: I am bad kid? Starts erring on side of bad, hanging out with rough crowd, looking askance at whole notion of achievement? Fails to live up to full potential, all because of one mistake she made when little girl?

No.

Cannot take chance.

When kids born, Pam and I dropped everything (youthful dreams of travel, adventure, etc.) to be good parents. Has not been exciting life. Has been much drudgery. Many nights, tasks undone, have stayed up late, exhausted, doing tasks. On many occasions, disheveled + tired, baby poop and/or vomit on our shirt or blouse, one of us has stood smiling wearily/angrily at camera being held by other, hair shaggy because haircuts expensive, unfashionable glasses slipping down noses because never was time to get glasses tightened.

And now, after all that, our youngest to start out life w/potential black mark on record?

That not happening.

Pam and I discuss, agree: must be like sin-eaters who, in ancient times, ate sin. Or bodies of sinners? Ate meals off bodies of sinners who had died? Cannot exactly recall what sin-eaters did. But Pam and I agree: are going to be like sin-eaters in sense of, will err on side of protecting Eva, keep cops in dark at all cost, break law as req'd (!).

Just now went down hall to check on kids. Thomas sleeping w/Ferber. This not allowed. Eva in bed w/Lilly. This not allowed. Eva, source of all mayhem, sleeping like baby.

Felt like waking Eva, giving Eva hug, telling Eva that, though we do not approve of what she did, she will always be our girl, will always be apple of our eye(s).

Did not do.

Eva needs rest.

On Lilly's desk: poster Lilly was working on for "Favorite Things Day" at school. Poster = photo of each SG, plus map of home country, plus stories Lilly apparently got during interview (!) with each. Gwen (Moldova) = very tough, due to Moldovan youth: used bloody sheets found in trash + duct tape to make soccer ball, then, after much practice with bloody-sheet ball, nearly made Olympic team (!). Betty (Philippines) has daughter, who, when swimming, will sometimes hitch ride on shell of sea turtle. Lisa (Somalia) once saw lion on roof of her uncle's "minilorry." Tami (Laos) had pet water buffalo, water buffalo stepped on her foot, now Tami must wear special shoe. "Fun Fact": their names (Betty, Tami, et al.) not their real names. These = SG names, given by Greenway at time of arrival. "Tami" = Januka = "happy ray of sun." "Betty" = Nenita = "blessed-beloved." "Gwen" = Evgenia. (Does not know what her name means.) "Lisa" = Ayan = "happy traveler."

SGs very much on my mind tonight, future reader.

Where are they now? Why did they leave?

Just do not get.

Letter comes, family celebrates, girl sheds tears, stoically packs bag, thinks, Must go, am family's only hope. Puts on brave face, promises she will return as soon as contract complete. Her mother feels, father feels: We cannot let her go. But they do. They must.

Whole town walks girl to train station/bus station/ferry stop? More tears, more vows. As train/bus/ferry pulls away, she takes last fond look at surrounding hills/river/quarry/shacks, whatever, i.e., all she has ever known of world, saying to self, Be not afraid, you will return, + return in victory, w/big bag of gifts, etc., etc.

And now?

No money, no papers. Who will remove microline? Who will give her job? When going for job, must fix hair so as to hide scars at Insertion Points. When will she ever see her home + family again? Why would she do this? Why would she ruin all, leave our yard? Could have had nice long run w/us. What in the world was she seeking? What could she want so much that would make her pull such desperate stunt?

Just now went to window.

Empty rack in yard, looking strange in moonlight.

Note to self: Call Greenway, have them take ugly thing away.

2014

LAUREN GROFF
AT THE ROUND EARTH'S
IMAGINED CORNERS

from Five Points

LAUREN GROFF was born in Cooperstown, New York, in 1978. She has a BA from Amherst College and an MFA from the University of Wisconsin-Madison, and was the Axton Fellow in Fiction at the University of Louisville.

Groff is the author of *The Monsters of Templeton*, a finalist for the Orange Prize for New Writers; the story collection *Delicate Edible Birds; Arcadia*, a finalist for the *Los Angeles Times* Book Prize for Fiction and a *New York Times* Notable Book of 2012; and a forthcoming novel, *Fates and Furies*. Her fiction has been published in *The New Yorker, The Atlantic*, and *Tin House* and anthologized in *The Pushcart Prize, PEN/O. Henry Prize Stories*, and three editions of *The Best American Short Stories*.

Groff writes with rich, evocative language about the intersection of mythology and desire. The *New York Times* called her work "timeless and vast."

She has lived in Gainesville, Florida, for nine years and has just begun to write about the state. This story is indebted to stories her father-in-law has told of his Florida childhood.

★

J UDE WAS BORN in a cracker-style house at the edge of a swamp that boiled with unnamed species of reptiles.

Few people lived in the center of Florida then. Air conditioning was for the rich, and the rest compensated with high ceilings, sleeping porches, attic fans. Jude's father was a herpetologist at the university, and if snakes hadn't slipped their way into their hot house, his father would have filled it with them anyway. Coils of rattlers sat in formaldehyde on the windowsills. Writhing knots of reptiles lived in the coops out back where his mother had once tried to raise chickens.

At an early age, Jude learned to keep a calm heart when touching fanged things. He was barely walking when his mother came into the kitchen to find a coral snake chasing its red and yellow tail around his wrist. His father was watching from across the room, laughing.

His mother was a Yankee, a Presbyterian. She was always weary; she battled the house's mold and humidity and devilish reek of snakes without help. His father wouldn't allow a black person through his doors, and they didn't have the money to hire a white woman. Jude's mother was afraid of scaly creatures and sang hymns in the attempt to keep them out. When she was pregnant with his sister one August night, she came into the bathroom to take a cool bath and, without her glasses, missed the three-foot albino alligator her husband had stored in the bathtub. The next morning, she was gone. She returned a week later. And after Jude's sister was born dead, a perfect petal of a baby, his mother never stopped singing under her breath.

Noise of the war grew louder. At last, it became impossible to ignore. Jude was two. His mother pressed his father's new khaki suit and then Jude's father's absence filled the house with a kind of cool breeze. He was flying cargo planes in France. Jude thought of scaly creatures flapping great wings midair, his father angrily riding.

While Jude napped the first day they were alone in the house, his mother tossed all of the jars of dead snakes into the swamp and neatly beheaded the living ones with a hoe. She bobbed her hair with gardening shears. Within a week, she had moved them ninety miles to the beach. When she thought he was asleep on the first night in the new house, she went down to the water's edge in the moonlight and screwed her feet into the sand. It seemed that the glossed edge of the ocean was chewing her up to her knees. Jude held his breath, anguished. One big wave rolled past her shoulders, and when it receded, she was whole again.

This was a new world, full of dolphins that slid up the coastline in shining arcs. Jude loved the wedges of pelicans ghosting overhead, the mad dig after periwinkles that disappeared deeper into the wet sand. He kept count in his head when they hunted for them, and when they came home, he told his mother that they had dug up 461. She looked at him unblinking behind her glasses and counted the creatures aloud.

When she finished, she washed her hands for a long time at the sink. "You like numbers," she said at last, turning around.

"Yes," he said. And she smiled and a kind of gentle shine came from her that startled him. He felt it seep into him, settle in his bones. She kissed him on the crown and put him to bed, and when he woke in the middle of the night to find her next to him, he tucked his hand under her chin where it stayed until morning.

He began to sense that the world worked in ways beyond him, that he was only grasping at threads of a far greater fabric. Jude's mother started a bookstore. Because women couldn't buy land in Florida for themselves, his uncle, a roly-poly little man who looked nothing like Jude's father, bought the store with her money and signed the place over to her. His mother began wearing suits that showed her décolletage and taking her glasses off before boarding the streetcars, so that the eyes she turned to the public were soft and somewhat misty. Instead of singing Jude to sleep as she had in the snake house, she read to him. She read Shakespeare, Hopkins, Donne, Rilke, and he fell asleep with their cadences and the sea's slow rhythm entwined in his head.

Jude loved the bookstore; it was a bright place that smelled of new paper. Lonely war brides came with their prams and left with an armful of Modern Library classics, sailors on leave wandered in only to exit, charmed, with sacks of books pressed to their chest. After hours, his mother would turn off the lights and open the back door to the black folks who waited patiently there, the dignified man in his watch cap who loved Galsworthy, the fat woman who worked as a maid and read a novel every day. "Your father would squeal. Well, foo on him," his mother said to Jude, looking so fierce she erased the last traces in his mind of the tremulous woman she'd been.

One morning just before dawn, he was alone on the beach when he saw a vast metallic breaching a hundred yards offshore. The submarine looked at him with its single periscope eye and slipped silently under again. Jude told nobody. He kept this dangerous knowledge inside him where it tightened and squeezed, but where it couldn't menace the greater world.

Jude's mother brought in a black woman named Sandy to help her with housework and to watch Jude while she was at the store. Sandy and his mother became friends, and some nights he would awaken to laughter from the veranda and come out to find his mother and Sandy in the night breeze off the ocean. They drank sloe gin fizzes and ate lemon cake, which Sandy was careful to keep on hand, even though by then sugar was getting scarce. They let him have a slice, and he'd fall asleep on Sandy's broad lap, sweetness souring on his tongue and in his ears the exhalation of the ocean, the sound of women's voices.

At six, he discovered multiplication all by himself, crouched over an anthill in the hot sun. If twelve ants left the anthill per minute, he thought, that meant 720 departures per hour, an immensity of leaving, of return. He ran into the bookstore, wordless with happiness. When he buried his head in his mother's lap, the women chatting with her at the counter mistook his sobbing for sadness. "I'm sure the boy misses his father," one lady said, intending to be kind.

"No," his mother said. She alone understood his bursting heart and scratched his scalp gently. But something shifted in Jude; and he thought with wonder of his father, of whom his mother had spoken so rarely in all these years that the man himself had faded. Jude could barely recall the rasp of scale on scale and the darkness of the cracker house in the swamp, curtains closed to keep out the hot, stinking sun.

But it was as if the well-meaning lady had summoned him, and Jude's father came home. He sat, immense and rough-cheeked, in the middle of the sunroom. Jude's mother sat nervously opposite him on the divan, angling her knees away from his. The boy played quietly with his wooden train on the floor. Sandy came in with fresh cookies, and when she went back into the kitchen, his father said something so softly Jude couldn't catch it. His mother stared at his father for a long time, then got up and went to the kitchen, and the screen door slapped, and the boy never saw Sandy again.

While his mother was gone, Jude's father said, "We're going home."

Jude couldn't look at his father. The space in the air where he existed was too heavy and dark. He pushed his train around the ankle of a chair. "Come here," his father said, and slowly the boy stood and went to his father's knee.

A big hand flicked out, and Jude's face burned from ear to mouth. He fell down but didn't cry out. He sucked in blood from his nose and felt it pool behind his throat.

His mother ran in and picked him up. "What happened?" she shouted, and his father said in his cold voice, "Boy's timid. Something's wrong with him."

"He keeps things in. He's shy," said his mother, and carried Jude away. He could feel her trembling as she washed the blood from his face. His father came into the bathroom and she said through her teeth, "Don't you ever touch him again."

He said, "I won't have to."

His mother lay beside Jude until he fell asleep, but he woke to the moon through the automobile's windshield and his parents' jagged profiles staring ahead into the tunnel of the dark road.

The house by the swamp filled with snakes again. The uncle who had helped his mother with the bookstore was no longer welcome, although he was the only family his father had. Jude's mother cooked a steak and potatoes every night but wouldn't eat. She became a bone, a blade. She sat in her housedress on the porch rocker, her hair slick with sweat. He stood near her and spoke the old sonnets into her ear. She pulled him to her side and put her face between his shoulder and neck and when she blinked, her wet eyelashes tickled him, and he knew not to move away.

His father had begun, on the side, selling snakes to zoos and universities. He vanished for two, three nights in a row, and returned with clothes full of smoke and sacks of rattlers and blacksnakes. He'd been gone for two nights when his mother packed her blue cardboard suitcase with Jude's things on one side and hers on the other. She said nothing, but gave herself away with humming. They walked together over the dark roads and sat waiting for the train for a long time. The platform was empty; theirs was the last train before the weekend. She handed him caramels to suck, and he felt her whole body tremble through the thigh he pressed hard against hers.

So much had built up in him while they waited that it was almost a relief when the train came sighing into the station. His mother stood and reached for Jude, and he smiled into her soft answering smile. Then Jude's father stepped into the lights and scooped him up. His body under Jude's was taut.

His mother did not look at her husband or her son. She seemed a statue, thin and pale. At last, when the conductor said "All aboard!" she gave an awful strangled sound and rushed through the train's door. The train hooted and slowly moved off. Though Jude shouted, it vanished his mother into the darkness without stopping.

Then they were alone, Jude's father and he, in the house by the swamp.

Language wilted between them. Jude was the one who took up the sweeping and scrubbing, who made their sandwiches for supper. When his father was gone, he'd open the windows to let out some of the reptile rot. His father ripped up his mother's lilies and roses and planted mandarins and blueberries, saying that fruit brought birds and birds brought snakes. The boy walked three miles to school where he told nobody he already knew numbers better than the teachers. He was small, but nobody messed with him. On his first day, when a big ten-year-old tried to sneer at his clothes, he leapt at him with a viciousness he'd learned from watching rattlesnakes and made the big boy's head bleed. The others avoided him. He was an in-between creature, motherless but not fatherless, stunted and ratty-clothed like a poor boy but a professor's son, always correct with answers when the teachers called on him, but never offering a word on his own. The others kept their distance. Jude played by himself, or with one of the succession of puppies that his father brought home. Inevitably, the dogs would run down to the edge of the swamp, and one of the fourteen- or fifteen-foot alligators would get them.

Jude's loneliness grew, became a living creature that shadowed him and wandered off only when he was in the company of his numbers. More than marbles or tin soldiers, they were his playthings. More than sticks of candy or plums, they made his mouth water. As messy as the world was, the numbers, predictable and polite, brought order.

When he was ten, a short, round man that the boy found vaguely familiar stopped him on the street and pushed a brown-paper package into his arms. The man pressed a finger to his lips, minced away. At home in his room at night, Jude unwrapped the books. One was a collection of Frost's poems. The other was a book of geometry, the world whittled down until it became a series of lines and angles.

He looked up and morning was sunshot through the laurel oaks. More than the feeling that the book had taught him geometry was the feeling that it had showed the boy something that had been living inside him, undetected until now.

There was also a letter. It was addressed to him in his mother's round hand. When he sat in school dividing the hours until he could be free, when he made the supper of tuna sandwiches, when he ate with his father who conducted to Benny Goodman on the radio, when he brushed his teeth and put on pajamas far too small for him, the four perfect right angles of the letter called to him. He put it under his pillow, unopened. For a week, the letter burned under everything, the way the sun on a hot, overcast day was hidden but always present.

At last, having squeezed everything to know out of the geometry book, he put the still-sealed envelope inside and taped up the covers and hid it between his mattress and box springs. He checked it every night after saying his prayers and was comforted into sleep. When, one night, he saw the book was untaped and the letter gone, he knew his father had found it and nothing could be done.

The next time he saw the little round man on the street, he stopped him. "Who are you?" he asked, and the man blinked and said, "Your uncle." When Jude said nothing, the man threw his arms up and said, "Oh, honey!" and made as if to hug him, but Jude had already turned away.

Inexorably, the university grew. It swelled and expanded under a steady supply of air conditioning, swallowing the land between it and the swamp until the university's roads were built snug against his father's land. Dinners, now, were full of his father's invective: did the university not know that his snakes needed a home, that this expanse of sandy acres was one of the richest reptile havens in North America? He would never sell, never. He would kill to keep it. Safe and whole.

While his father spoke, the traitor in Jude dreamed of the sums his father had been offered. So simple, it seemed, to make the money grow. Unlike other kinds of numbers, money was already self-fertilized; it would double and double again until at last it made a roiling mass. If you had enough of it, Jude knew, nobody would ever have to worry again.

When Jude was thirteen, he discovered the university library. One summer day, he looked up from the pile of books where he'd been contentedly digging — trigonometry, statistics, calculus, whatever he could find — to see his father opposite him. Jude didn't know how long he'd been there. It was a humid morning, and even in the library the air was stifling, but his father looked leathered, cool in his sunbeaten shirt and red neckerchief.

"Come on, then," he said. Jude followed, feeling ill. They rode in the pickup for two hours before Jude understood that they were going snaking together. This was his first time. When he was smaller, he'd begged to go, but every time, his father had said no, it was too dangerous, and Jude never argued that letting a boy live for a week alone in a house full of venom and guns and questionable wiring was equally unsafe.

His father pitched the tent and they ate beans from a can in the darkness. They lay side by side in their sleeping bags until his father said, "You're good at math."

Jude said, "I am," though with such understatement that it felt like a lie. Something shifted between them, and they fell asleep to a silence that was softer at its edges.

His father woke Jude before dawn and he stumbled out of the tent to grainy coffee with condensed milk and hot hush puppies. His father was after moccasins, and he gave Jude his waders and himself trudged through the swamp, protected only by jeans and boots. He'd been bitten so often, he said, he no longer brought antivenom. He didn't need it. When he handed his son the stick and gestured at a black slash sunning on a rock, the boy had to imagine the snake as a line in space, only connecting point to point, to be able to grasp it. The snake spun from the number one to the number eight to a defeated three and he deposited it in the sack.

They worked in silence all day, and when Jude climbed back up into the truck at the end of the day, his legs shook from the effort it took him to be brave. "So now you know," his father said in a strange holy voice, and Jude was too tired to take the steps necessary, then, and ever afterward until he was his father's own age, to understand.

His father began storing the fodder mice in Jude's closet, and to avoid the doomed squeaks, Jude joined the high school track team. He found his talent in the two-hundred-meter hurdles. When he came home with a trophy from the State Games, his father held the trophy for a moment, then put it down.

"Different if Negroes were allowed to run," he said.

Jude said nothing, and his father said, "Lord knows I'm no lover of the race, but your average Negro could outrun any white boy I know."

Jude again said nothing but avoided his father and didn't make him an extra steak when he cooked himself dinner. He still wasn't talking to him when his father went on an overnight trip and didn't come back for a week. Jude was used to it and didn't get alarmed until the money ran out and his father still didn't come home.

He alerted the secretary at the university who sent out a group of graduate students to where Jude's father had been seen. They found the old man in his tent, bloated, his tongue protruding from a face turned black; and Jude understood then how even the things you loved most could kill you.

· · ·

At the funeral, out of a twisted loyalty for his father, he avoided his uncle. He didn't know if his mother knew she'd been widowed; he thought probably not. He told nobody at school that his father had died. He thought of himself as an island in the middle of the ocean, with no hope of seeing another island in the distance, or even a ship passing by.

He lived alone in the house. He let the mice die, then tossed the snakes in high twisting parabolas into the swamp. He scrubbed the house until it gleamed and the stench of reptiles was gone, then applied beeswax, paint, polish until it was a house fit for his mother. He waited. She didn't come.

The day he graduated from high school, he packed his clothes and sealed up the house and took the train to Boston. He'd heard from his uncle that his mother lived there and so he'd applied and been accepted to college in the city. She owned a bookstore on a small, dark street. It took Jude a month of slow passing to gather the courage to go in. She was either in the back, or shelving books, or smiling in conversation with somebody, and he'd have a swim of darkness in his gut and know that it was fate telling him that today was not the day. When he went in, it was only because she was alone at the register, and her face — pouchy, waxy — was so sad in repose that the sight of it washed all thought from his head.

She rose with a wordless cry and flew to him. He held her stoically. She smelled like cats, and her clothes flopped on her as if she'd lost a lot of weight quickly. He told her about his father dying and she nodded and said, "I know. I dreamed it."

She wouldn't let him leave her. She dragged him home with her and made him spaghetti carbonara and put clean sheets on the couch for him. Her three cats yowled under the door to her bedroom until she came in with them. In the middle of the night, he woke to find her in her easy chair, clutching her hands, staring at him with glittering eyes. He closed his own and lay stiffly, almost shouting with the agony of being watched so.

He went to see her once a week but refused all dinner invitations. He couldn't bear the density or lateness of her love. He was in his junior year when her long-percolating illness overcame her and she too left him. Now he was alone.

There was nothing but numbers, then.

Later, there were numbers, the great ravishing machine in the laboratory into which he fed punched slips of paper, the motorcycle Jude rode because it roared like murder. He had been given a class to teach, but it was taken away after a month and he was told that he was better suited for research. In his late twenties, there were drunk and silly girls he could seduce without saying a word, because they felt a kind of danger coiled in him.

He rode his motorcycle too fast over icy roads. He swam at night in bays where great whites had been spotted. He bombed down ski slopes with only a hazy idea of the mechanics of snow. He drank so many beers he woke one morning to discover he'd developed a paunch as big as a pregnant woman's belly. He laughed to shake it, liked its wobble. It felt comforting, a child's pillow clutched to his midsection all day long.

By the time he was thirty, Jude was weary. He became drawn to bridges, their tensile strength, the cold river flowing underneath. A resolution was forming under his thoughts, like a contusion hardening under the skin.

And then he was crossing a road, and he hadn't looked first, and a bread truck, filled with soft dinner rolls so yeasty and warm that they were still expanding in their trays, hit him. He woke with a leg twisted beyond recognition, a mouth absent of teeth on one side, and his head in the lap of a woman who was crying for him, though she was a stranger, and he was bleeding all over her skirt, and there were warm mounds of bread scattered around them. It was the bread that made the pain return to his body, the deep warmth and good smell. He bit the hem of the woman's skirt to keep from screaming.

She rode with him to the hospital and stayed all night to keep him from falling asleep and possibly going into a coma. She was homely, three years older than he, a thick-legged antiques dealer who described her shop down a street so tiny the sun never touched her windows. He thought of her in the silent murky shop, swimming from credenza to credenza like a fish in an aquarium. She fed him rice pudding when she came to visit him in the hospital and carefully brushed his wild hair until it was flat on his crown.

He woke one night with a jerk: the stars were angrily bright in the hospital window and someone in the room was breathing. There was a weight on his chest, and when he looked down, he found the girl's sleeping head. For a moment, he didn't know who she was. By the time he identified her, the feeling of unknowing had burrowed in. He would never know her; knowledge of another person was ungraspable, a cloud. He would never begin to hold another in his mind like an equation, pure and entire. He focused at the part of her thin hair, which in the darkness and closeness looked like inept black stitches in white wax. He stared at the part until the horror faded, until her smell, the bitterness of unwashed hair, the lavender soap she used on her face, rose to him and he put his nose against her warmth and inhaled her.

At dawn, she woke. Her cheek was creased from the folds in his gown. She looked at him wildly and he laughed, and she rubbed the drool from the corner of her mouth and turned away as if disappointed. He married her because, during the night, to not marry her had ceased to be an option.

While he was learning how to walk again, he had a letter from the university down in Florida, making a tremendous offer for his father's land.

And so, instead of the honeymoon trip to the Thousand Islands, pines and cold water and his wife's bikini pressing into the dough of her flesh, they took a sleeping train down to Florida and walked in the heat to the edge of the university campus. Where he remembered vast oak hammocks, there were rectilinear brick buildings. Mossy pools were now parking lots.

Only his father's property, one hundred acres, was overgrown with palmettos and vines. He brushed the redbugs off his wife's sensible travel pants and carried her into his father's house. Termites had chiseled long gouges in the floorboards, but the sturdy cracker house had kept out most of the wilderness. His wife touched the mantel made of heart pine and turned to him gladly. Later, after he came home with a box of groceries and found the kitchen scrubbed clean, he heard three thumps upstairs and ran up to find that she had killed a blacksnake in the bathtub with her bare heel and was laughing at herself in amazement.

How magnificent he found her, a Valkyrie, half-naked and warlike with that dead snake at her feet. In her body, the culmination of all things. He didn't say it, of course; he couldn't. He only reached and put his hands upon her.

In the night, she rolled toward him and took his ankles between her own. "All right," she said. "We can stay."

"I didn't say anything," he said.

And she smiled a little bitterly and said, "Well. You don't."

They moved their things into the house where he was born. They put in air conditioning, renovated the structure, put on large additions. His wife opened a shop on the ground floor of the one building in town over four stories tall, though she had to drive to Miami and Atlanta to stock it with antiques. He sold his father's land, but slowly, in small pieces, at prices that rose dizzyingly with each sale. The numbers lived in him, warmed him, brought him a buzzing kind of joy. Jude made investments so shrewd that when he and his wife were in their mid-thirties, he opened a bottle of wine and announced that neither of them would ever have to work again. His wife laughed and drank but kept up with the store. When she was almost too old, they had a daughter and named her after his mother.

When he held the baby at home for the first time, he understood he had never been so terrified of anything as he was of this mottled lump of flesh. How easily he could break her without meaning to, she could slip from his hands and crack open on the floor, she could catch pneumonia when he bathed her, he could say a terrible thing in anger and she would shrivel. All the mistakes he could make telescoped before him. His wife saw him turn pale and plucked the baby from his hands just before he crashed down. When he came to, she was livid but calm. He protested, but she put the baby in his hands.

"Try again," she said.

His daughter grew, sturdy and blond like his wife, with no flash of Jude's genius for numbers. They were dry as biscuits in her mouth; she preferred music and English. For this, he was glad. She would love more moderately, more externally. If he didn't cuddle with her the way her mother did, he still thought he was a good father: he never hit her, he never left her alone in the house, he told her how much he loved her by providing her with everything he could imagine she'd like. He was a quiet parent, but he was sure she knew the scope of his heart.

And yet his daughter never grew out of wearing a singularly irritating expression, one taut with competition, which he first saw on her face when she was a very little girl at an Easter egg hunt. She could barely walk in her grass-stained bloomers, but even when the other children rested out of the Florida sunshine in the shade, eating their booty of chocolate, Jude's little girl kept returning with eggs too cunningly hidden in the sago palms to have been found in the first frenzy. She heaped them on his lap until they overflowed and shrieked when he told her firmly that enough was enough.

His fat old uncle came over for dinner once, then once a week, then became a friend. When the uncle died of an aneurysm while feeding his canary, he left Jude his estate of moth-eaten smoking jackets and family photos in ornate frames.

The university grew around Jude's last ten-acre parcel, a protective cushion between the old house and the rest of the world. The more construction around their plot of land, the fewer snakes Jude saw, until he felt no qualms about walking barefoot in the St. Augustine grass to take the garbage to the edge of the drive. He built a fence around his land and laughed at the university's offers, sensing desperation in their inflating numbers. He thought of himself as the virus in the busy cell, latent, patient. The swamp's streams were blocked by the university's construction, and it became a small lake, in which he installed some bubblers to keep the mosquitoes away. There were alligators, sometimes large ones, but he put in an invisible fence and it kept his family's dogs from coming too close to the water's edge and being gobbled up, and the gators only eyed them from the banks.

And then, one day, Jude woke with the feeling that a bell jar had descended over him. He showered with a sense of unease, sat at the edge of the bed for a while. When his wife came in to tell him something, he watched in confusion at the way her mouth opened and closed fishily, without sound.

"I think I've gone deaf," he said, and he didn't so much hear his words as feel them vibrating in the bones of his skull.

At the doctors', he submitted to test after test, but nobody understood what had gone wrong in his brain or in his ears. They gave him a hearing aid that turned conversation into an underwater burble. Mostly he kept it off.

At night, he'd come out into the dark kitchen, longing for curried chicken, raw onion, preserved peaches, tastes sharp and simple to remind himself that he was still there. He'd find his daughter at the island, her lovely mean face lit up by her screen. She'd frown at him and turn the screen to show him what she'd discovered: cochlear implants, audiologic rehabilitation, miracles.

But there was nothing for him. He was condemned. He ate Thanksgiving dinner, wanting to weep into his sweet potatoes. His family was gathered around him, his wife and daughter and their closest friends and their children, and he could see them laughing, but he couldn't hear the jokes. He longed for someone to look up, to see him at the end of the table, to reach out a hand and pat his. But they were too happy. They slotted laden forks into their mouths and brought the tines out clean. They picked the flesh off the turkey, they scooped the pecans out of the pie. After the supper, his arms prickling with hot water from the dishes, they sat together, watching football, and he sat in his chair with his feet propped up, and everyone fell asleep around him and he alone sat in vigil over them, watching them sleep.

The day his daughter went to college in Boston, his wife went with her.

She mouthed very carefully to him, "You'll be all right for four days? You can take care of yourself?"

And he said, "Yes, of course. I am an *adult*, sweetheart," but the way she winced, he knew he'd said it too loudly. He loaded their bags into the car, and his daughter cried in his arms, and he kissed her over and over on the crown of the head. His wife looked at him worriedly, but kissed him also and climbed inside. And then, silently as everything, the car moved off.

The house felt immense around him. He sat in the study, which had been his childhood bedroom, and seemed to see the place as it had been, spare and filled with snakes, layered atop the house as it was, with its marble and bright walls and track lights above his head.

That night, he waited, his hearing aid turned up so loud that it began to make sharp beeping sounds that hurt. He wanted the pain. He fell asleep watching a sitcom that, without sound, was just strange-looking people making huge expressions with their faces and woke up and it was only eight o'clock at night, and he felt as if he'd been alone forever.

He hadn't known he'd miss his wife's heavy body in the bed next to his, the sandwiches she made (too much mayonnaise, but he never told her so), the smell of her body wash in the humid bathroom in the morning.

On the second night, he sat in the black density of the veranda, looking at the lake that used to be a swamp. He wondered what had happened to the reptiles out there; where they had gone. Alone in the darkness, Jude wished he could hear the university in its nighttime boil around them, the students shouting drunkenly, the bass thrumming, the noise of football games out at the stadium that used to make them groan with irritation. But he could have been anywhere, in the middle of hundreds of miles of wasteland, for as quiet as the night was for him. Even the mosquitoes had somehow been eradicated. As a child, he would have been a single itchy blister by now.

Unable to sleep, Jude climbed to the roof to straighten the gutter that had crimped in the middle from a falling oak branch. He crept on his hands and knees across the asbestos shingles, still hot from the day, to fix the flashing on the chimney. From up there, the university coiled around him, and in the streetlights, a file of pledging sorority girls in tight, bright dresses and high heels slowly crawled up the hill like ants.

He came down reluctantly at dawn and took a can of tuna and a cold jug of water down to the lake's edge, where he turned over the aluminum johnboat his wife had bought for him a few years earlier, hoping he'd take up fishing.

"Fishing?" he'd said. "I haven't fished since I was a boy." He thought of those childhood shad and gar and snook, how his father cooked them up with lemons from the tree beside the back door and ate them without a word of praise. He must have made a face because his wife had recoiled.

"I thought it'd be a hobby," she'd said. "If you don't like it, find another hobby. Or *something*."

He'd thanked her but had never had the time to use either the rod or the boat. It sat there, its bright belly dulling under layers of pollen. Now was the time. He was hungry for something indefinable, something he thought he'd left behind him so long ago. He thought he might find it in the lake, perhaps.

He pushed off and rowed out. There was no wind, and the sun was already searing. The water was hot and thick with algae. A heron stood one-legged among the cypress. Something big jumped and sent rings out toward the boat, rocking it slightly. Jude tried to get comfortable but was sweating, and now the mosquitoes smelled him and swarmed. The silence was eerie because he remembered it as a dense tapestry of sound, the click and whir of sandhill cranes, the cicadas, the owls, the mysterious subhuman cries too distant to identify. He had wanted to connect with something, something he had lost, but it wasn't here.

He gave up. But when he sat up to row himself back, both oars had slid loose from their locks and floated off. They lay ten feet away, caught in the duckweed.

The water thickly hid its danger, but he knew what was there. There were the alligators, their knobby eyes even now watching him. He'd seen one with his binoculars from the bedroom the other day that was at least fourteen feet long. He felt it somewhere nearby, now. And though this was no longer prairie, there were still a few snakes, cottonmouths, copperheads, pygmies under the leaf rot at the edge of the lake.

There was the water itself, superheated until host to flagellates that enter the nose and infect the brain, an infinity of the minuscule, eating away. There was the burning sun above and the mosquitoes feeding on his blood. There was the silence. He wouldn't swim in this terrifying mess. He stood, agitated, and felt the boat slide a few inches from under him, and sat down hard, clinging to the gunwales. He was a hundred feet off-shore on a breathless day. He would not be blown to shore. He would be stuck here forever; his wife would come home in two days to find his corpse floating in its johnboat. He drank some water to calm himself. When he decided to remember algorithms in his head, their savor had stolen away.

For now there were silent birds and sun and mosquitoes; below, a world of slinking predators. In the delicate cup of the johnboat, he was alone, floating. He closed his eyes and felt his heart beat in his ears.

He had never had the time to be seized by doubt. Now all he had was time. Hours dripped past. He sweated. He was ill. The sun only grew hotter and there was no respite, no shade.

Jude drifted off to sleep, and when he woke he knew that if he opened his eyes, he would see his father sitting in the bow, glowering. Terrible son, Jude was, to ruin what his father loved best. The ancient fear rose in him, and he swallowed it as well as he could with his dry throat. He would not open his eyes, he wouldn't give the old man the satisfaction.

"Go away," he said. "Leave me be." His voice inside his head was only a rumble.

"I'm not like you, Dad," Jude said later. "I don't prefer snakes to people."

Even later, he said, "You were a mean, unhappy man. And I always hated you."

But this seemed harsh and he said, "I didn't completely mean that."

He thought of this lake. He thought of how his father would see Jude's life. Such a delicate ecosystem, so precisely calibrated, in the end destroyed by Jude's careful parceling of love, of land. Greed; the university's gobble. Those scaled creatures, killed. The awe in his father's voice that day they went out gathering moccasins; the bright, sharp love inside Jude, long ago, when he had loved numbers. Jude's promise was unfulfilled, the choices made not the passionate ones. Jude had been safe.

And here he was. Not unlike his father when he died in that tent. Isolated. Sunbattered. Old.

He thought in despair of diving into the perilous water, and how he probably deserved being bitten. But then the wind picked up and began pushing him back across the lake, toward his house. When he opened his eyes, his father wasn't with him, but the house loomed over the bow, ramshackle, too huge, a crazy person's place. He averted his eyes, unable to bear it now. The sun snuffed itself out. Despite his pain, the skin on his legs and arms blistered with sunburn and great, itching mosquito welts, he later realized he must have fallen asleep because when he opened his eyes again, the stars were out and the johnboat was nosing up against the shore.

He stood, his bones aching, and wobbled to the shore.

And now something white and large was rushing at him, and because he'd sat all day with his father's ghost, he understood this was a ghost too, and looked up at it, calm and ready. The lights from the house shined at its back, and it had a golden glow around it. But the figure stopped just before him, and he saw, with a startle, that it was his wife, that the glow was her frizzy gray hair catching the light, and he knew then that she must have come back early, that she was reaching a hand out to him, putting her soft palm on his cheek, and she was saying something forever lost to him, but he knew by the way she was smiling that she was scolding him. He stepped closer to her and put his head in the crook of her neck. He breathed his inadequacy out there, breathed in her love and the grease of her travels and knew he had been lucky; that he had escaped the hungry darkness, once more.